THREE
LITTLE
BIRDS

THREE LITTLE BIRDS

SAM BLAKE

CORVUS

First published in Great Britain in 2024 by Corvus, an imprint of Atlantic Books Ltd.

10 9 8 7 6 5 4 3 2

A CIP catalogue record for this book is available from the British Library.

Trade Paperback ISBN: 978 1 80546 012 1
E-book ISBN: 978 1 80546 013 8

Printed by CPI Group (UK) Ltd, Croydon CR0 4YY

Corvus
An imprint of Atlantic Books Ltd
Ormond House
26–27 Boswell Street
London
WC1N 3JZ

www.atlantic-books.co.uk

For Simon Trewin, my amazing agent,
who made all of this possible

Chapter 1

CARLA STEELE ROLLED her chair closer to her desk, her concentration fixed on the screen in front of her – on the damaged eye socket of a human skull. The early morning June sunshine filled her office from the window behind her, dust motes dancing like fractured spirits in its beam. She adjusted the monitor to reduce the glare.

She knew this image like she knew the tattoo on the inside of her wrist: three birds in flight, their wings outspread, the line below it – WITH BRAVE WINGS SHE FLIES – written in script across her pale skin. Across her heart.

Since the week she'd arrived to set up the Forensic Anthropology and Computer Enhancement department, affectionately known as FACE, in Ireland's Garda Headquarters, her days had begun and ended with this image filling her screen – with this case; with the sharply circumscribed semicircular entry wound on the left side of the occipital bone. She moved the image of the 3-D render around with the haptic Phantom lever, VR software allowing her to feel the structure of the skull as if it was in front of her. There was an exit wound at the rear, the bone demonstrating characteristic bevelling created by the direction of a bullet's motion.

Whenever she opened this file, the questions crowded into her head. With only the skull as evidence, she couldn't conclude absolutely that a bullet had been the actual cause of death, or hypothesise that it had been inflicted by someone other than the victim. But given that the skull had been found wrapped in a pale blue crocheted blanket, in a wardrobe, in an abandoned house, it seemed likely that someone had wanted to conceal this death. Someone who knew where the rest of the body was hidden, and exactly what had happened.

From the size of the aperture, the data suggested a medium-calibre bullet, most likely a .32. To Carla's experienced eye, the point of entry suggested an execution.

Carla scowled and flicked to the next screen: the finished render of the girl's face. This had been the first cold case she'd tackled when she'd been invited to set up FACE two years earlier. But despite an extensive media campaign, and her reputation as the woman who had rebuilt a skull mislabelled in the basement of a small museum and given a face to Ireland's famous Pirate Queen, she was no closer to finding out who the victim was.

It nagged at her like the onset of a migraine.

When she'd rebuilt this girl's face, she'd scanned it as she had so many others, using the three-dimensional software to create a model that allowed her to change the girl's skin tone and hairstyle. This was the skull of a teenager of partially Asian descent – one who had had enough anxiety in her life to grind her teeth.

But who? And why? And when?

This girl belonged to someone; she'd had a life, had lived and loved and had died – whether by her own hand or someone else's – violently. Despite the various impressions of her face that had been put out to the media, no one had come forward to suggest a name, or even a history.

Carla twirled her ring, a birthday gift from her cousin Rachel. They'd only met up for the first time this spring, two halves of the family totally unknown to each other until a DNA search had thrown up some unexpected results. They'd connected immediately, had had so much to talk about that Carla was planning a trip to London to visit Rachel and her partner Hunter and stay on their houseboat, as soon as she could get a week off. The ring was the perfect gift – a heavy silver skull, its diamanté eyes flashing in the summer light; Rachel had one just like it. Carla rolled it around her finger, the movement soothing. Deep inside her, she could feel the tragedy of this girl's death as if it was a physical thing. Heavy, like her ring.

Every time she opened the image, anger and sadness and stress and failure blended together, turning her stomach. Because it wasn't just this girl who caused her pain.

She was someone who found answers – it was her job, for goodness' sake – and yet this was another case she couldn't solve.

Carla closed her eyes, an image of Lizzie, her best friend, appearing in her head; the last time she'd seen her, frozen in time like a movie still. Lizzie, turning to wave as she headed off across Dublin's iconic O'Connell Bridge into the night, her red cashmere scarf wrapped almost to her eyes, a pair of brown felt reindeer antlers holding back her crazy auburn hair, flashing with tiny red lights like a warning of what was to come.

It would be her birthday soon.

A knock rang out on her office door and Carla jolted in her chair. She checked the time on her screen. It wasn't even nine.

'Come in.'

The door opened and a man's head appeared around it, followed by the unmistakable form of a Garda detective in plain clothes, whose serious look and creased forehead reminded her of one of the doctors she followed on YouTube. But this guy's eyes were a piercing blue, his dark hair sticking up, as if he fought a daily battle with keeping it flat.

'I was looking for a Dr Carla Steele.'

Carla raised her eyebrows and looked him up and down. His navy sports jacket looked crisp, but the creases in his pale blue open-necked shirt and sand-coloured chinos suggested he'd been driving for a while. His jacket flapped open as he came through the door, revealing the holster on his belt.

'You found her.'

'Oh.' His eyes opened in surprise. He quickly corrected the expression, blushing hard, and opened his mouth – trying, Carla imagined, to find something to say to hide his mistake.

She was never sure whether it was her nose ring, or the streak of white that contrasted so starkly with her long, almost black, hair, that was unexpected. Or the fact that she wore a T-shirt and jeans with Doc Martens to work. It didn't matter; since she'd arrived at Garda Headquarters, she'd been getting all sorts of looks – few of them complimentary. Sometimes she was sure it was just because she was a woman under thirty who had *Doctor* in front of her name. Despite their best efforts, the national Irish police force, An Garda Síochána – the guardians of the peace – was only twenty-five per cent female, although Forensic Services Ireland, where she was based, was closer to fifty per cent. Still not enough, in her opinion.

Suddenly feeling sorry for her visitor, Carla cut in, rescuing him from trying to form a sentence that was clearly taking its time coming.

'How can I help?'

He came fully into her office, a large brown cardboard evidence box under his arm, and pushed the door closed behind him.

'DS Jack Maguire, from Coyne's Cross, Mayo. We wondered if you could help us with this. They catalogued it in reception, said to bring it straight up.'

He proffered the box and Carla could see a printed label had been stuck to one side. Date and case number, the start of the digital trail that would map every item of forensic evidence connected to the contents of the box. It had been stuck firmly shut with brown packing tape.

'Let's see what you've got.' Rolling her chair away, she pulled open her desk drawer and looked for her Swiss Army knife. 'Try this. And sit down. We don't want any accidental slash injuries. It's Friday, and it's the bank holiday weekend. The hospitals will be busy enough with the carnage on the roads.'

Jack Maguire hesitated for a moment at the irony in her tone, but rather than coming back with a smart reply, as she'd expect from some, he sat down and opened the knife, his forehead creased.

He was a serious one. She liked that.

'What's the background?'

Concentrating on the box, Jack answered as he sliced through the tape.

'A couple of divers found it in the middle of Lough Coyne

on Monday. It was really deep. They were looking for a marine video camera that got dropped off a dive boat, some problem with the insurance.'

'Have you got the rest of the body?'

'Not yet. A team's been looking all week, but the lough's tidal. The rest of it could be anywhere at this stage.' He closed the blade of the knife. 'The pathologist took dental casts. He's taken other samples but we're no closer to identification. He thought you might be a better bet.'

Carla slid her chair closer to the desk. 'Extracting and amplifying DNA from bone is tricky on a good day, even assuming you have something to match it to – the environmental conditions can alter its integrity dramatically.'

Jack stood up again and flipped open the lid. Inside was a large brown paper evidence bag marked with the same file numbers as the outer covering. Lifting it carefully onto the desk, he unrolled the neck of the bag and gingerly lifted out its contents. Carla gave him a mental tick; the gentle way he was handling it showed respect for the victim. She'd seen so many who treated skeletal remains like the leftovers from last week's dinner.

Leaning forwards to look properly, Carla tucked a loose strand of white hair behind her ear.

'Did they find anything with it at all?'

'Like clothing, you mean?'

Looking across the skull at him, she nodded.

'Nothing. It was too deep for them to stay down long enough at the time, but they've been over the same area doing a proper search all week.' He hesitated. 'The thing is, we've had a spate of suicides. We were wondering if it was one of them.'

'Your suicides are predominantly male?'

It was Jack's turn to nod. 'They call it Suicide Point, the cliff path. God knows …' He trailed off as Carla reached for the skull.

Picking it up, she turned it gently, inspecting the yellowed cranium, fracture lines radiating across the right side. The mandible was intact, although some of the teeth were missing. She turned it again, looking at the orbital ridges, the same feeling building inside her that she'd had looking at the skull on the screen.

She could hear Lizzie's laughter around her, dancing like the high notes on a violin, infectious, melodious, as if she was standing in the corner of the room. She was always here, but at times like this her presence seemed stronger. Sometimes Carla felt that if she spun around fast enough, she'd see her. She'd tried so many times. Had, she'd thought, occasionally caught a glimpse of movement out of the corner of her eye. But never long enough to speak to her, to ask her where she was, what had happened that night. The night that had changed the course of all their lives.

Carla cleared her throat.

'Come up to the lab, we need to have a proper look.'

Chapter 2

DANIELLE BRENNAN FOUND herself wiping the counter again as she looked across the almost empty cafe and out of the windows filling the wall facing the lough. The search team was a good way out, and she had to strain her eyes to see the rescue RIB, its orange sides bright against the merging inky blues of the water. She had binoculars behind the coffee machine, but there was a bunch of photographers gathered outside and she didn't want to look as if she was taking too much interest in the activity on the water.

She shivered. It was roasting in here, with this crazy early summer heatwave, the sunshine beating in, but she knew it was cold out on the lough and at their deepest, the tidal waters were arctic.

Ruairi would tell her exactly what had gone on when they were on their own at home, just as he'd told her in excruciating detail how Kyle had spotted the skull and brought it up to the waiting boat. They'd been almost out of air, the team waiting on the surface anxiously peering down, trying to see if they'd located the lost equipment. She wasn't sure who had been more shocked – Ruairi and his dive team from the Adventure Centre, or herself as she'd heard the tale unfurl.

Danielle glanced over to the corner table, to the mother hunched over her coffee, the father twisted so he could see what was happening outside, his bald spot catching the light from the windows, the white hair around it still mussed as if he'd rushed out of the B & B they were staying in without smoothing it down. They'd been here every day since the story had broken.

Their lad had gone missing last autumn.

Danielle had found his car abandoned in the car park beside the coffee shop when she'd come to open up. It had been October, a chill wind whipping across the open water of the lough, the trees at the water's edge shedding their leaves like tears. He'd left a note, his mobile phone laid beside it on the worn seat of the battered red Toyota. Her heart had almost stopped as she'd realised. She'd fumbled with her mobile, walking around looking for a signal, calling Ruairi first, then summoning the Gardaí. The search and rescue crew had scrambled as Seamus, the local sergeant, had arrived, their two rescue RIBs combing the shore for signs.

But it had been too late.

They'd found his hi-tops a fortnight later, lying neatly beside the path at the highest point of the cliff.

Suicide Point.

Had he been walking away from her along the path, on his way up there as she'd arrived? When she'd realised, she'd been physically sick, hadn't been able to get the idea out of her head that she could have stopped him. Saved his parents the pain.

What if it had been her Ben? He was only thirteen, but didn't these problems start then, with boys in their early teens? He was quiet, an only child who spent too much time online. *Was that how it started?* Danielle couldn't bear the thought.

The guards had checked his dental records and assured the parents that the skull wasn't their son's, but they'd still come down from Dublin as soon as they'd heard. They intended to wait until the search was called off, still hopeful that there had been a mistake, or that more remains would be found.

Realising she was still wiping the counter, Danielle turned, rolling the cloth up, dropping it in the stainless steel sink, rubbing her damp hands unconsciously down the purple denim apron covering her faded cut-off jeans. The early morning sun was bouncing off the polished pine tables. She was only wearing a cotton vest top, but she could feel the sweat starting to slide down her back. She needed to open more windows before the place turned into an oven. All this glass was great for the views, for tourists visiting Lough Coyne, but it was a constant battle to keep the cafe a comfortable temperature.

Would they keep looking after this weekend? Would they find the rest of the body? She winced inside at the thought.

Pushing her bubbly strawberry blond curls behind her ear, Danielle turned her back on the outside world and leaned on the sink behind the counter, feeling the relief of the cool steel on her hands. She wasn't sure if it was the rising heat or the ongoing drama outside, but she could feel a pain beginning to form behind her eyes. She glanced over her shoulder again, trying to see if the boat was coming in.

This was day five, and they'd been out there for hours. It was well past nine now, and Ruairi had been at the water's edge every morning at first light with the Garda team, organising his staff at the Adventure Centre and the volunteers. Head of Lough Coyne's volunteer search and rescue crew, he loved all of this: the attention, the action; the journalists and the cameramen. Her stomach flipped at the thought. If there wasn't more news soon, stories would be dragged up; there'd be questions and more questions.

Picking up a couple of mugs from the stack still hot from the dishwasher, she put them under the spout of the coffee machine and hit the cappuccino button. The parents had been waiting in their car when she'd come to open up this morning, parked in almost the exact spot their son's red Toyota had been. Danielle had let them in as she got ready for the day. They'd looked pale and drawn, as if they hadn't slept. Looked like she felt.

The froth-filled mugs in her hand, Danielle heard the cafe door opening, the bell above it tinkling. Several of the journalists at the window turned to look as an attractive blonde came through, her long hair loose, skin-tight jeans topped off with a wide gold belt the same metallic shade as her roman sandals. Her cousin Melissa. Danielle headed over to the table the boy's parents were sitting at, slipping the mugs in front of them.

'Can I get you another croissant? You need to keep up your strength.'

The mother shook her head. Danielle patted her on the shoulder.

'I'm sure it won't be much longer.'

The older woman smiled weakly.

On her way to the counter, she could see Melissa hovering beside the till, taking off her sunglasses and sticking them on her head as she surreptitiously glanced at the couple in the corner. As Danielle reached her, she lowered her voice.

'How are you doing? Jules told me.' Without waiting for the answer, Melissa continued. 'You'd have thought the parents would have gone. I mean, why wait when they know it's not him?' She stopped speaking for a nanosecond, then continued. 'I wouldn't, I mean, not with all this press. Have you got any scones? The cottages are all booked for the bank holiday and the bakery's aren't ready yet. I've got people arriving today and I need to do the welcome baskets.'

'I'm grand, thanks. Body turning up in the lough was the perfect start to my week.' Danielle kept her own voice low, fighting to hide her irritation. The one thing you could rely on with Melissa was her focus being entirely on herself and her own problems. 'I've got scones – do you want fruit or plain?'

'Fruit. So what's the news? Does Ruairi think they'll find anything?'

Before Danielle could answer, Melissa's phone began to ring loudly. She raised her eyes and pulled it out of the designer shopper slung over her shoulder.

As Danielle reached into the display for the scones, dropping them into a brown paper bag, she could half hear Melissa's hurried conversation with her sister Julia. For once, she was keeping her voice down.

Across the cafe, two young mothers were looking at Melissa, their babies asleep in pushchairs beside them. Danielle knew them from the village; they were little older than she'd been when she'd had Ben, but had none of her naivety. They were here often enough – she'd seen the way they'd looked at Ruairi when he came in to pick up his lunch, how they flicked their long hair when they thought he was looking. She wasn't sure if he was the main draw, or if they came here because they could gossip with less chance of being overheard by the rest of Coyne's Cross – her customers were mainly tourists, school parties using the Adventure Centre. She was just far enough out of town not to be a regular haunt for the locals, which suited her fine. There had been enough talk the summer she got pregnant to last her a lifetime.

Danielle heard Melissa finish her call and, without drawing breath, she continued.

'Sean said they're wasting their time, they'll never find the rest of the body, the currents ...'

The cake tongs in her hand, Danielle looked at her sharply.

'Sean's suddenly an expert on currents now, is he?'

Melissa's husband had an opinion on everything – one that was always right, too. He'd made his money selling insurance, buying out the firm he'd worked for before he was thirty. Risk had always been his thing.

Danielle put the tongs down and slid the brown bag across the counter to Melissa.

'The guards said they're giving it till tonight, and then they're going to have to stop, at least until after the bank holiday. I don't know what happens then.'

Chapter 3

THE CORRIDORS OF Forensic Science Ireland were beginning to get busy as Carla led Jack Maguire to the lab. Techs in white coats, manila files in their hands, passed one another, their heads down, their brows furrowed. The exhibits were checked in downstairs: queues of Gardaí from all over the country brought in bags of forensic evidence, which were carefully catalogued and then sent for analysis. There was never a lull; crime was a growth industry.

Carla pushed open the door of the FACE lab, a series of interconnected rooms and offices, all painted regulation cream, computer terminals blinking along the counter on the far wall. In the middle of the room, two broad benches ran parallel to each other, at right angles to the door. Stainless steel sinks were sunk into them at intervals.

'Morning, guys. How's the head, Raph?' Carla grinned to a tall black man in a white lab coat, his top pocket packed with biros, who was examining a thick file. He turned, looked up at her over his glasses and winced. His close-cropped hair was beginning to grey at the temples, his face creased into laughter lines. Beside him, a woman in her twenties, her face pitted by acne, had one of the pages they had obviously been discussing in her hand. Her wavy straw-coloured hair was pulled up in a practical ponytail. Acknowledging Carla with a grin, she put her finger to her lips.

'Don't mention the war.'

Carla turned to Jack.

'It was Raphael's daughter's birthday party last night. She's an engineer with a star-filled future. This is Tina – soon to be Dr Antonia Marsh.'

The box under her arm, Carla ushered Jack into the lab.

'This is DS Jack Maguire from Coyne's Cross.'

Raph put his hand out, his mid-Atlantic accent strong.

'Raphael Montgomery. Nice to meet you. I read about your find in the paper.'

Jack shook Raph's hand.

'He's hoping we can help.' Carla glanced at the paperwork on the counter top. 'How are you getting on with the others?'

Tina put down the page she'd been looking at. 'The 3-D renders are all done, they're ready to get out to the media. I've notified the detectives in charge.'

Carla smiled appreciatively. 'Let's hope they land some sort of response. Your timing is good, DS Maguire, we can get started straight away.'

'How long will it take?' Jack came to stand beside her as she put the box down on the bench. Its white melamine top was spotless, reflecting the harsh overhead lights. 'To build the face, I mean?'

Carla pulled up the top flap of the box. 'Usually it takes a day to make the cast, and then about two days for us to build the face. Overall, about a week to do a single reconstruction in clay. We gather as much data as we can from the scene, from the rest of the body, to create several different renders. That's the artistic bit. The work we do isn't an identification, it's a tool in the identification process, predicting the facial features from all the evidence we have.'

'And if you don't have anything else, any other information, like this, how do you do it then?'

Carla lifted out the skull as Tina bent down and, opening a cupboard below the bench, pulled out a piece of steel pipe welded to a flat plate.

'What on earth's that?' Puzzled, Jack looked thoughtfully at what resembled an entry-level plumbing project, or a grotesque instrument of torture.

'A stand.'

Tina screwed another curved plate onto the top of it – one which had grippers on either side. She pushed it towards Carla, who took a moment to settle the skull onto the top plate, resting the jaw on the slanted shelf that connected it to the upright. She glanced at Jack.

'The stand ensures the model we build is at the right angle. It'll need adjusting before we start, but this will work for now.'

Carla crossed her arms and took a long look at the skull. The fracture lines were clear. Whatever had happened to this victim had involved a perimortem blow to the head – there was no sign that the fractures had had time to heal.

She turned to Jack. 'We can tell a lot about the victim from the bones themselves, if they can be found. You said you suspected this was a suicide?'

Jack shrugged, his blue eyes serious. 'Nothing's certain until we have an ID. The most recent disappearance was last October, but we've ruled him out from his dental records. Before him, there was one the previous February – a lad in his twenties, but he'd never been to the dentist, unfortunately.'

As he was speaking, Carla began shaking her head. Wrinkling her nose, she sighed.

'It's not him.'

'How can you tell?'

Before she could answer, Raph leaned over to take a closer look, his voice practical as he replied.

'First off, if your guy went in in February, this definitely isn't him. The bottom of a lough is very cold, whatever the ambient temperature. It slows decomposition. If your guy's in there, he'll probably still be intact. This is likely to have been in the water for a number of years.'

19

Carla pursed her lips, looking hard at the skull. There was that feeling again: the black hole in her gut. Sometimes it felt as if she was poised at the mouth of a tunnel – at least, that's how it manifested in her dreams. A tunnel where there was no light, and water dripped from the ceiling. She always felt as if it was pulling her in, but she never got more than a few steps before she woke up, sweating, a cry dying on her lips. That was the worst of it. She was sure the tunnel held the answers she needed, but it was terrifying, or something in it was terrifying. Sensing a movement in the corner of the lab, Carla glanced over her shoulder quickly, but of course there was nothing there. Again. And nobody else seemed to have noticed.

She cleared her throat. 'I think the guys will agree with me – this is a teenager. And as Raph says, they didn't go into the water recently. We'll have a clearer idea of age when we do some tests. But I don't think it's a him, I'm pretty sure it's a her.'

'Christ …' Jack trailed off, running his hand through his dark hair, more spikes springing up as if they'd been waiting for their moment. 'I better let them know at the station. You definite? How can you tell?'

Carla glanced sideways at him, but he seemed genuinely surprised – it wasn't as if he didn't believe her. Despite four years of anatomical science, a year of life drawing and sculpture, a PhD in facial reconstruction *and* an international reputation, Carla was regularly challenged on her findings. Not least in court.

'Every individual is unique, but we work off aggregated data, and experience. You see here – the supraorbital ridge? Female skulls have a rounded forehead. This ridge along the brow is much more prominent in males. And the jawline is quite different. In females, as you can see here, the edge of the jaw slopes gently towards the ear.' She pointed to show him. 'And if you look, there are no wisdom teeth. So, my first thoughts are that this is a skull that hasn't fully developed. And ...' She bit her lip. 'Typically, male skulls are heavier than female, the bone is thicker, and the areas of muscle attachment are more defined.' She picked up a biro and pointed. 'Women tend to have round eye sockets with sharp edges to the upper borders, whereas a male has squarer orbits with blunter upper eye margins. See here.' She pointed to the side of the skull, now at eye level on its stand. 'This could be a young, feminine-looking male, but I'm thinking female.'

'And you think it's been in the water for years?'

'Definitely. You'll need to go through the files for disappearances much further back than February last year.'

Before Carla could continue, there was a sharp knock on the lab door. They all turned as a heavily built redhead in a smart black trouser suit put her head around it, her curly hair drawn into a neat twist.

21

'I want a word with you, Steele. Nigel puked in my shoes.'

Carla winced. 'Crap, sorry. Did he …? I'll—' She stopped herself, one eyebrow raised. She knew the answer before she said it. 'The good ones?'

'Of course, I don't own cheap shoes.' Her voice was clipped, her anger rolling off her in waves that Carla was sure they could all feel. Before Carla could say more, she continued, 'Aren't you going to introduce us? Who's this?'

'Oh, sorry – DS Jack Maguire from Coyne's Cross. This is his.' Carla pointed to the skull.

'Grace Franciosi – Doctor … Coyne's Cross?' She stopped speaking for a moment as if she was thinking. 'I've always wanted to go there. Glacial lough and monastic settlement? You've a round tower and—'

Jack cut in. 'A Celtic cross. Yep, that's us.'

'Nice.'

Grace looked at Jack a moment too long, an approving smile on her face, all thoughts of Nigel and her shoes obviously forgotten.

Carla looked at the skull critically. 'I'm going to need to see the recovery site. Connecting the remains to where they're found helps me build a picture of who and why.'

She'd barely finished the sentence when Grace jumped in.

'Why don't we go down tomorrow for a long weekend? You're not climbing mountains, and it's a bank holiday – and the view is great.'

Carla cringed inside. Had Grace really said that? Had she no shame? Maguire was very nice to look at, but Carla was quite sure he was the type of guy who needed a gentler approach. And Grace could be an awful tease where men were concerned; it was more that she liked pretty things than was actually interested in a relationship, although she'd dated boys in college. Grace was Carla's polar opposite in every way: she described herself as 'big boned' where Carla was slight; she was forthright, where Carla opted for tact. They'd first met at Trinity College, what felt like a hundred years ago, and Grace hadn't changed one jot. She'd been pushy and focused in those days, and hadn't let anything get in her way. Now she was an absolute perfectionist in everything, from her first-class degree to her ground-breaking PhD in forensic psychology, her designer suits to her manicures. Despite Grace's pushiness, Carla was completely in love with her, but then she knew what was under the flawless veneer.

Jack looked as if he needed rescuing again.

Time to change the subject.

'Suit's good. Going somewhere nice?'

Grace pulled a face. 'UCD. I've ninety detectives and another hundred and fifty tuning in on Zoom to find out how to interview sex offenders. Building a rapport is top of the list.'

'I can see that going well.'

'Indeed. I'll call when I'm done and we can plan our adventure. Grab the moment while you've a gap.'

With the renders of the two skulls they'd just finished working on going out to their investigative teams, Carla knew they had a few days before they'd be ready to call any press conferences.

'Sounds like a plan. I'll sort out Nigel and the shoes, promise.'

'I left them in the laundry room sink.'

Grace closed the door, leaving as quickly as she had appeared, the ringing sound of her heels on the tiled floor receding as she headed for the lift.

Jack turned to Carla, his eyebrows raised.

'I've just worked it out. She's *the* Dr Franciosi – she fronted that cold case series on TV?'

'Yep. The one and only. Whatever they claim, she eats serial killers for breakfast.'

He winced. 'Shoes don't sound good.'

'I'm going to have to take him to the vet.' For a split second, Jack looked utterly confused. Carla almost laughed. 'Nigel's my cat, not my boyfriend. They hate each other. Have done since she moved in. I think he finds her a bit much.'

Jack raised his eyebrows as if he could relate, but said instead, 'So what happens next?' He indicated the skull.

'Next we use something called alginate to create a mould from your skull. Then a resin reproduction, to work on. We usually make two casts. That's where these guys come in. Can you find out if there have been any teenagers reported missing in the area?'

He nodded. 'Will do, but they could be from anywhere. Are you serious about coming down?'

'I find it invaluable to see where the victim was found, it helps me build a picture of who they were. I try and get to all locations if I can. Bonus, if it's the middle of the summer and the location is as beautiful as Coyne's Cross.'

'Grand. So do you need me here for anything now?'

She shook her head. 'Just a few forms. The cast will need to set – it takes a couple of days, so we'll be ready to start reconstruction work on Tuesday. We should have a face for you by the end of next week.'

Jack nodded again. 'I'm staying with my brother here in Dublin tonight. Babysitting his three kids. His wife has MS, and they need a night out. But I can head back to Mayo in the morning, and show you the location? I can be there for lunchtime.'

'Are you sure? Sounds like you had family plans for the weekend?'

'My brother's a barrister, he'll understand. I'm up a lot since his wife came out of remission.'

'If you're sure, give me your card and I'll text you when we get there. Grace will book somewhere.'

'She'll have problems finding a five-star hotel in Coyne's Cross.'

Carla almost smiled. There was a reason why he was a detective; he'd summed Grace up in one line.

'Don't worry, we'll manage. I'll see you in the morning, so?'

Chapter 4

NIGEL WAS SITTING on the doorstep, waiting for Carla when she got home, the wheels of her Fiat 500X crunching on the gravel lane leading to their slate-grey Georgian front door. Grace's silver Mercedes sport was already tucked in beside the high laurel bush bordering the garden. Carla pulled in behind her.

The one disadvantage of this house was the parking. Nobody wanted to pay almost two million euros for a house that had a pedestrian right of way that passed the front door, and no off-street space for the sort of cars you owned if you could afford a property like this.

But it suited Carla fine.

As long as Lizzie's property developer father Eoin couldn't – or didn't want to – sell it, she had it essentially rent-free. And on the tough days, when she was feeling down, she'd walk the five minutes to Sandymount Strand, the flat three-kilometre beach nature reserve that stretched out around Dublin Bay like a hug. It was the place she and Lizzie had always gone to blow away a late Saturday night, to dissect their latest relationship crises, to do star jumps and sprint starts when their jeans got a bit tight.

The house and the location made her feel close to Lizzie.

They'd moved in here halfway through their first year at Trinity, the five-bedroom house shared with friends, their housemates changing as each term progressed ... until they'd reached their third year, and the Christmas Lizzie had disappeared. Carla had stayed here then, ensuring there was always someone in, just in case Lizzie came home, obsessively checking the house phone for missed calls.

And then, when she'd needed to get away, to leave Dublin, Eoin had been mysteriously unable to sell the property. It had lain empty until Carla came home, her PhD in her hand and a new direction in her life. 'Bringing the missing home' had been the headline in the *Irish Times* profile when she'd set up FACE. It had made her tear up.

There was one person Carla needed to bring home, but she had to find her first.

Nigel curled around her legs as Carla got out of the car, her arms full of files, the smell of the receding tide blending with a barbecue in one of her neighbour's gardens. It was after six, but the heat hadn't abated much, even with the gentle sea breeze, the sun reflecting relentlessly off the car's metallic paprika paintwork. At least it was cooler here than in the middle of Dublin city. The air seemed to hang in dense pockets around the nineteenth-century Garda HQ located in the middle of the huge Phoenix Park. The Liffey river was that bit too far away to funnel in any fresh air.

She closed the car door with her bum.

'Why Grace's shoes, Nige? You've got the whole garden to puke in, you know. What did she do to you?'

Nigel opened his beryl-green eyes wide and yowled as if he was replying, then jumped up, putting his dusty front paws on her jeans.

'I can't pick you up.' Carla proffered her pile of paperwork as the reason why, and clicked the central locking on her key fob. 'Let's get inside and see if she's forgiven you, will we?'

Juggling with the files, Carla headed for the front door, stooping to get her key in the lock as Nigel jumped up again and tried to push it open himself. The rich colour of marmalade, his coat was thick and long, the ginger tones catching the evening sunshine. He had to be boiling. Carla definitely was. Despite the air conditioning in the car, she could already feel herself heating up as the sun beat down on the back of her black T-shirt.

Suddenly the door swung open and Nigel darted inside. The cool of the hall met Carla like a caress. Inside, pushing the door closed behind her, she smiled. In typical Grace style, there were two overnight bags packed and positioned neatly beside the hall table. Carla's black nylon climbing bag, with a metal carabiner still clipped to the handle from her last trip, sat beside a distinctly more stylish, distressed leather holdall with a dangly designer logo hanging from the zip. Carla didn't even want to know what it might have cost.

As Carla headed through to the white-painted kitchen, she spotted a knife and the ends of a lemon and an orange sitting on a wooden chopping board on the granite counter. The stalks from a generous sprig of mint were a clear indication that Grace had mixed a large jug of Pimm's and, Carla guessed, would now be sitting out on the patio under the parasol, her earbuds in as she listened to an audiobook.

Heading to the glazed end of the kitchen, Carla dumped her files on the scrubbed pine farmhouse table and stuck her head out of the open patio doors. Grace had changed into a pair of exceedingly unflattering garden-use-only shorts and a sun top, and installed herself on a reclining chair, exactly as Carla had expected, her hair now loose and curling around her shoulders, sunglasses on the table beside her, her earbuds connected to her phone.

She looked as if she was asleep, but Carla knew she only had her eyes closed. Grace was a terrible sleeper, had the nervous energy of a ten-year-old. But this was her Zen time. She'd learned she could switch off once one part of her brain was kept busy, and audiobooks were her answer. She'd been working her way through the complete works of Agatha Christie since the start of this hot spell. Beside her, too, was a pair of tall glasses and the jug of Pimm's, ice cubes still floating at the top. Grace had obviously only just got home ahead of her.

Right now, Pimm's was exactly what Carla needed, but first she wanted to kick off her boots, peel off her jeans, and change into something cooler, and she knew Grace had had a busy day, she'd let her rest for a few more minutes.

Nigel, however, had other ideas. Before Carla could stop him, he'd materialised beside the lounger and launched himself to land neatly on Grace's broad stomach, with, from her reaction, his claws extended.

'Holy fucking God!'

Carla was quite sure all the neighbours could hear Grace's screech as she shot upright and walloped Nigel off. He let out a loud hiss as he landed on the patio slabs and shot into the kitchen. Grace caught sight of Carla and scowled. She didn't need to say anything.

'He loves you, you know, it's just his way of showing it.' Grace's scowl deepened as Carla stepped out onto the patio to give her a kiss. 'He does, honestly.' Before Grace could reply, Carla continued. 'Did you find a hotel for the weekend?'

Grace's expression changed, her face, still heavy with the day's make-up, lighting up.

'I've booked a cottage. Thatched. Right beside the lough. It just been renovated, it's very expensive and it looks *glorious*. The fridge will be full, the wine's being delivered in the morning. All we have to do is turn up.' She couldn't resist a smug smile. 'Everything's organised, it's going to be gorgeous.' She blew Carla a kiss.

Carla shook her head to herself. Grace loved having a project to work on – and being in control. She wasn't even a recovering perfectionist. But she'd obviously forgotten that the reason they were going to Coyne's Cross was to look at what could well turn out to be a murder scene.

Chapter 5

'WHAT SORT OF time do you call this?'

Jack Maguire's sister-in-law Orla raised one eyebrow, and reversed her wheelchair into the wooden-floored hall to let him in through the front door. Light flooded the space from the glazed porch behind him and from the open patio doors in the kitchen. When they'd remodelled the house to allow wheelchair access, Brian and Orla had painted everything white. It never ceased to amaze Jack that the 1950s four-bedroom semi still looked like a show house – but then Orla was an accountant and liked things to be precise. And having a cleaner definitely helped.

Grinning, Jack opened his mouth to answer, but was cut off by a war cry coming from the kitchen.

'Uncle Jack!'

Their voices set on 'loud', three children of varying sizes and one large collie hurtled in from the back garden, straight through the kitchen and into the hallway. Scarlett, already tall for her nine years, her brother Ollie, two years younger, and Leo – at four, the baby of the family – wrapped their arms around him, almost knocking him over. Buster leaped up to try and lick his nose. Grinning, Jack steadied himself on the door frame.

'Sorry I'm so late. I had a swift half with one of the lads I was in Templemore with after work. So, what have you guys all been doing?'

The words *garden*, *trampoline* and *water* merged as they all shouted at once.

'Kids, give him a bit of peace. He's had a long day and you've got him all evening. Scarlett, take the boys back outside now before we think about dinner.'

'Pizza from Domino's?' Ollie's freckled face was hopeful, prompting his little brother to start bouncing like a pogo stick, his long blond curls flopping into his face. Using a grubby palm to push his hair out of his eyes, Leo suddenly froze, bent in the middle as if ready to spring, his eyes locked on Jack's.

'I want twisted dough balls.'

It was as if the pause in jumping was the calm before the storm.

'Chicken wings!'

'I want Chinese actually, Mum, we haven't had that for aaaages.'

The cacophony started again.

'Out!' Orla gestured with her thumb and, as if propelled by the promise of takeaway, the three hurtled outside again, followed by the dog, picking up their game where they had left off, accompanied by excited barks.

'Thanks for this, Jack, it's a real treat for them. They get sick of Brian working, and me … Well, I'm pretty useless these days.'

'Don't be daft.'

Jack leaned down to give her a hug, her shoulder blade sharp against the thin cotton of her pink T-shirt. He pretended he hadn't noticed. With her dark hair cropped in a pixie cut, she was looking paler since he'd last seen her, the circles under her eyes a delicate plum.

He looked at her reproachfully. 'They love having you at home. Isn't being here better than being in an office on the other side of the city and having them brought up by minders?'

Orla threw him a half-smile and, spinning her wheelchair around, headed into the kitchen.

'Put that thing in the safe. Brian will be down in a minute. He's looking forward to seeing you.'

Jack dipped into the modern living room, moving the books concealing their home safe from prying eyes. Swinging the door open, unbuckling his belt, he slid the holster off it and put it inside, fishing the cartridge out of his pocket and putting that in, too. He closed the door and checked it to make sure it had locked. A few minutes later he was in the kitchen again, where Orla was looking out of the open French windows, watching the children play.

Hearing him behind her, she looked over her shoulder with a grin.

'Here, pour me a gin and tell me what you've been up to in the Park.'

'At your service.'

Jack glanced outside to see what the children were doing and opened the fridge. The contents always made him smile. His own fridge in Coyne's Cross was basically bacon, eggs, sausages, milk, bread and cheese. Not that he often ate at home. Here, Frubes were tumbled on top of Actimels; a cling-filmed plate of what looked like an omelette balanced precariously on top of a carton of coleslaw.

He'd learned early on in his career that you could tell a lot about a person from the contents of their fridge.

For a fleeting moment, he wondered what Carla Steele had in her fridge. Leftover Chinese takeaway, he'd bet; she didn't strike him as the type of woman who fussed over a stove. But Grace? She gave off the aura of someone who was good at everything; she was probably a brilliant cook, too, had a shelf for lemon grass and quails' eggs.

Closing the fridge door, Jack flipped open the cupboard beside his head and pulled down the tall glasses Orla loved. She had to keep them high out of reach of the kids, but that meant only he and Brian could reach them.

Now pulled in under the modern pine kitchen table, Orla put her elbows on it, waiting for him to cut a lemon into slices.

'So, what brings you up? That skull? I saw it on the news.'

'You and half the world. Yes, there's a forensic facial reconstruction specialist based at headquarters. She's going to give it a go.'

'Carla Steele?' Jack turned as his brother walked into the kitchen behind him. 'I'd be very interested to hear more about her. Don't keep all that lemon to yourself.'

Jack turned to give him a hug. Brian was only two years older than him, but already losing his hair and spreading around his middle, the navy polo shirt he was wearing less than flattering. He looked about ten years older than Jack, but then he had enough worry for both of them.

Pulling out of the hug, Jack looked at him, one eyebrow raised.

'Aren't you driving? Where are you two off to tonight?'

'Well, we were going to go to a play at the Gate, but someone ...' Orla looked at Brian pointedly, 'forgot to book the tickets.'

Brian winced. 'We thought we'd go out for a quick Italian instead. There's a lovely place around the corner – we can walk.'

'Your brother really knows how to treat a girl on her night off.'

Brian opened his mouth to reply, but Jack held up a warning finger and, opening another cupboard, pulled out a bottle of Bombay Sapphire.

'Before you perjure yourself, get the lady some ice.'

Brian picked up the glasses and filled each of them from the dispenser on the fridge door, passing them to Jack. A moment later, Orla had a glass in front of her.

Jack turned around to lean on the counter. The noise level hadn't changed outside, although the children had moved on from the trampoline to playing with the hosepipe. Beside him, Brian took a sip, closing his eyes as the gin hit the spot.

'Boy, I needed that. What a week.'

'New case?' Jack glanced across at him. Brian nodded slowly, taking another sip and savouring the drink. 'But you can't say anything?'

Brian shrugged. Ever since he'd qualified for the Bar and gone into criminal defence, they'd had to be careful what they discussed, even at home.

'So tell me about Carla Steele. Is she as terrifying as people say?'

Jack looked at him, puzzled. 'Who says she's terrifying? She seemed very nice to me. Bit alternative – she's got this nose ring – but she seems to be eminently capable.'

'My colleagues think she's a tiger. You're safe, you'll never have to cross-examine her. She's one clever lady. And she looks about fifteen with that streak in her hair and the tattoo. Perhaps she's got a picture of Dorian Gray in her attic.' Brian pouted sadly. 'I need to take notes.'

'That's really not a good look, darling.' Orla's teasing smile was half hidden by the glass.

Brian hastily straightened his face. 'Sorry. So, tell me what you were doing up here, apart from supplying invaluable babysitting services.'

Jack grinned. 'Dropping in the skull that was found in the lough on Monday. The work Carla does is fascinating. She looked at it and she could tell so much just from the bone structure.'

'She is the top skull woman in the country – I've heard, in Europe. So you would sort of expect that. Interesting to hear she didn't eat you, though. That's good.'

Jack grinned, pursing his lips playfully. 'Guess who else I met?'

Orla put her glass down, her eyes narrowed. 'Who? Spit it out. Bono?'

Ignoring her, Brian looked at the ceiling as if he was trying hard to guess. 'Do I get a prize? Free babysitting next week, too?'

Jack laughed. 'Maybe. I've got to get back down to Coyne's Cross in the morning, I'm afraid, so I'll owe you a night.'

'Stop messing. Who?' Orla glared at them both.

They said it in unison.

'Dr Grace Franciosi.'

Jack looked at his brother. 'How did you know that?'

'I know many things, little bro. Like the great doctor has an office in Forensic Science Ireland, as well as her very salubrious private office. And she's shacked up with Dr Steele.'

'What do you mean "shacked up with"?' Jack's eyebrows met.

Brian opened his eyes meaningfully. 'Like they're an item.'

'For goodness' sake, Bri, what sort of dinosaur are you?' Orla looked at her husband, appalled, as Jack did a double take.

'Really? I'm sure she was hitting on me earlier.'

Orla laughed. 'It's those blue eyes, Jack, I keep telling you they'll get you into trouble.'

Chapter 6

'HOW DID YOU even find this place?'

Carla reached into the footwell of Grace's car for her black nylon backpack as they pulled into a narrow lane, the hedges on either side a riot of summer flowers.

Grace glanced across at Carla as she answered, 'Google, obviously.'

Carla almost laughed. It *was* a stupid question. The night before, Grace had said she'd found a cottage, but had only raised her eyebrows mysteriously when Carla had probed for more details.

If she hadn't needed to see the recovery site, Carla would have happily spent the weekend working on the pile of academic research papers she'd compiled for the lectures she was due to give to the New York Police Department, and walking on the beach, trying to catch the cool sea breeze. But seeing the victim's last resting place was crucial to the bigger picture. There was always a reason – no matter how seemingly random – they had ended up in a particular place.

It often led to their identification – and ultimately, how they had got there … and why.

And she wanted to start working on the Coyne's Cross face as soon as the casts were ready.

Her department was usually the last stop in the investigative process, after everyone else had already drawn a blank. Once a skull was entrusted to her, she felt personally responsible for finding the answers.

So far, apart from Girl X, they'd had a remarkable success rate. Sometimes things didn't move as quickly as she'd like, but the cases were rarely recent and often needed several elements to come together for the public's mind to be jogged – for someone to realise they knew the victim, or had seen them in their last hours. Sometimes it was the pattern on a piece of curtain, or a missing tooth, that gave them the break, but whatever the extra element was, it was always coupled with the victim's likeness.

The sun was already hot when they'd left home this morning, although it was early, and they'd enjoyed the opportunity to take the top down on the car. Coyne's Cross was literally on the other side of the island of Ireland, and as they'd left the main roads behind them, heading across the countryside, it felt as if they were entering a different world.

They'd just passed a set of grand eagle-topped gates marked COYNE HOUSE when Carla spotted a smart painted sign for *Lake View Cottage*, pointing to the next turn on the right. Swinging through a smaller set of open wrought-iron gates, Grace had slowed, taking her precious Mercedes gently over the uneven road surface. It must have been tarmacked once, but it looked as if that could have been a lifetime ago.

Carla had googled Coyne's Cross herself when Jack had left the previous day. It was one of Ireland's famous monastic sites, the sort of place you went to on school trips, although she'd never been. As she'd flicked through the images on her phone, she could see why the monks had settled there: it was a stunning location.

As they passed through the small town on the way, glowing in the June sunshine, the broad straight main street had already been busy with Saturday shoppers. Coyne's Cross had everything you'd need – a post office, pharmacy, bakery, several boutiques, a general store and the essential fast food takeaway. The brightly coloured shops were punctuated by a large pub in the middle of the main street, and beside it, a small hotel.

As they'd crawled along behind a tractor that had swung out rather unexpectedly into their path from beside the staunch granite church, Carla could see what Jack Maguire had meant about five star hotels being in short supply. The Coyne Lodge looked comfortable and cosy, but the bright yellow paintwork and dark green shutters would have offended Grace's sense of design before they'd even walked through the door. It was the perfect spot for tourists – no doubt it was all dark wood, with a statue of the Child of Prague on the stairs – but it didn't quite meet Grace's expectations in relation to the perfect weekend getaway.

Carla had stayed in a lot worse on climbing or caving trips, but Grace didn't do the sort of exercise that could get you killed, so hadn't enjoyed the delights of rural Irish hospitality to quite the same extent. She much preferred the sleek designer luxury of hotels like Dublin's 1796, or New York's opulent Frederick Hotel overlooking Central Park.

'Here we are.'

Swinging in through another set of wide stone gateposts, Grace pulled up in front of a white pebble-dashed picture-postcard cottage with bright red shutters and a deep thatch cut in an intricate design. It was surrounded by wild borders overgrown with brambles, knotted with convolvulus, and splashed with pink and sunshine-yellow flowers, and behind the building, the lough stretched as far as Carla could see. The water glistened in the sunshine, mountains rising purple and brooding in the background.

There was a dark blue BMW X2 4 × 4 parked outside the cottage, and as Grace pushed up her sunglasses and opened her car door, a blonde woman jumped out of the driver's side and came around the back, her hand out. She was wearing a red halter-neck sundress and matching wedge-heeled espadrilles, and looked more as if she was organising a fashion shoot than letting a cottage.

'Hi, I'm Melissa. You found us. Dublin's closer than you think with the new road.'

Climbing out of the car, her legs stiff, Carla swung her backpack on her shoulder, pushing her dark hair away from her face with her sunglasses.

'It is. This place is lovely. I'm amazed it wasn't booked for the bank holiday.'

'It's a bit out on its own, people tend to be herd animals and want to be a bit closer to the town. You came in through the west gate, but around the main house we've developed a complex in the barns and stables. On the lough like this, but a bit closer to civilisation and the pub. Those properties have a waiting list.' She smiled. 'We decided to go for five star everything in this cottage, but some people just can't live without Wi-Fi, particularly when the phone reception's a bit limited.'

Carla looked at Melissa for a long moment and then back at Grace.

'No Wi-Fi?'

'No Wi-Fi, no distractions. You can't enjoy the scenery if you're glued to your phone.' Grace opened her eyes wide to emphasise her point.

'And, erm …' Melissa looked uncomfortably from Grace to Carla. 'There's only one bedroom …'

Carla almost laughed as Grace turned her full charm on Melissa.

'It has a king-size bed. That's all we need.'

Inside, the cottage was just as pretty as it was outside, polished wooden floors giving way to flagstones in the kitchen, low beams spanning a cosy sitting room, a log-burning stove the focal point at one end, a forest green Aga in the kitchen area at the other. It was gloriously cool inside, tiny windows keeping the heat out. Perfect for now, but, Carla could imagine, perishing in winter. As if Melissa had read her mind, she pointed to a thermostat on the wall.

'We've installed a Nest heating system, it's all underfloor and there's always loads of hot water. This room is obviously the kitchen living area, the spiral staircase takes you up to the bedroom, and out here is the deck.'

Crossing the wooden floor, she pushed open double glass-paned doors to reveal wooden decking overlooking the lough. A balustrade ran around it, enclosing a beautiful table with a brightly patterned mosaic top in the middle of the space and a barbecue in one corner. Carla stepped outside, walking over to the edge of the deck. Behind her, she heard Melissa showing Grace how to adjust the wine cooler.

'If you've any problems, Terry Walsh is our maintenance man. His number is in the file on the coffee table. He's very reliable, looks after all the properties. Just give him a call and he'll be straight over. He put away your deliveries earlier, so he knows you're expected.'

Leaning on the smooth wooden balustrade, Carla looked out across the water, ripples forming as fish moved with the currents. She could hear them surfacing to catch flies, flopping back into the water.

There was no beach here; instead, steep scrub led down to the water's edge. As she leaned forwards, Carla could see a little jetty reaching out like a finger, steep steps cut into the rock leading down to it. In the shade of the overhanging trees – willow and alder – the water was inky black. Cold and deep. Carla shivered.

How had the remains ended up here?

Before she could form the thought fully, her phone pipped with a text.

Jack Maguire.

She turned to go inside, a movement out on the water catching her eye. Another fish? She wasn't sure.

She called through to Grace, who was still in the kitchen.

'Jack Maguire's just texted. He wants to meet us later at a place called the Coffee Dock, beside the Adventure Centre. I think we passed a sign for it just after the town, before Coyne House?'

Melissa appeared at the double doors. 'That's my cousin's place – Danielle Brennan. Her husband runs the Adventure

Centre, he's head of the search and rescue team.' She hesitated, the curiosity obviously killing her. 'You're friends of Jack's?'

Chapter 7

A S MELISSA PULLED up in front of Coyne House, parking behind her husband Sean's colour co-ordinated blue BMW 5 series estate, he was coming down the broad granite steps dressed for a meeting, his usual black jeans and T-shirt replaced by a lightweight navy linen suit and crisp white shirt, his jacket slung over his shoulder. He looked delicious whatever he was up to.

Slipping out of her X2, Melissa came around to the front and put her hands on her hips, her head cocked questioningly to one side.

'And where are you off to on a Saturday looking so slick?'

Sean grinned and raised his eyebrows mischievously. 'Some good news at last. The Ferryman deal has just landed. Cressida Howard's flying to Italy tomorrow and wants to see me to sign today.' He wiggled his shoulders as if he was dancing and grinned at her.

Melissa narrowed her eyes and fought a smile herself. She could hardly get annoyed with him for working on a

Saturday when he was going to a meeting as important as this. As he'd said more than once, it would really put Elite Insurance on the map. And they needed something good to happen. She'd barely slept this week.

'I'll put the Bolly on ice.' Melissa pulled her long blond hair into a knot to allow what little breeze there was to cool her neck. Despite wearing one of the lightest dresses she owned, she was already boiling, and she had loads to do today to make sure the new guests were settled into the cottages. But right now, Sean's meeting was much more interesting. 'Any chance you can get us an invitation to one of Cressida's parties?'

'That comes next. Let me sign her first.'

Melissa laughed as she came across to lean on the boot of his car, the metallic paint hot, and put her hands into the pockets of her sundress. 'How long are you going to be?'

Sean clicked the central locking and, opening the rear door, reached in to hang up his jacket. 'I don't have to go all the way to Dublin, thank God. She's meeting someone for lunch in that restaurant with the Michelin star in Athlone. I don't know how long I'll be with her. I suppose it depends what time she finishes lunch, but I should be back early evening, I'd guess.'

'Perfect. We can eat outside. I want Terry to put another coat of varnish on the garden table, though, before this weather breaks, so we might have to eat on our knees.'

'I can manage that. Isn't he up at the church today, though?'

Melissa scowled. 'Damn, yes. I should have got him to do it yesterday. Honestly, I've so much on this weekend I don't know if I'm coming or going. I just met the couple who've taken Lake View for the weekend.' She raised her eyebrows and pulled a face.

Sean laughed. 'What's wrong with them?'

'It's two women. Together.'

'Jesus, Mel, you're the worst. What's wrong with that?' He shook his head, grinning. 'Sounds like fun to me.'

Melissa slapped him playfully, relief surging through her that he'd come out of the black mood that had hovered over him for the last few days. 'Don't be so bold.'

'I know, I can't help it. Don't tell Terry, though, in case they need something fixing. He's odd enough with strangers.'

'He's fine, he's just been living on his own for too long, I think. And he already knows they're there. They ordered a load of wine and cheese that was delivered this morning. He sorted it all out.' She looked at him reproachfully. 'He's a good worker, I don't know what I'd do without him – and he does such a lovely job up at the church. That graveyard hasn't looked so good in years.' Melissa drew in a sharp breath, suddenly realising what she'd said.

Avoiding her eye, Sean closed the car door.

Melissa kept her voice low – not that there was anyone within half a mile who could hear them. 'Has Seamus said anything? About the skull, I mean? What's happening with it?'

Sean's uncle Seamus had made it his business to know what was going on in Coyne's Cross since he'd managed to swing a transfer from Cork twenty years before. Nobody in the family had ever found out how he'd managed it – Gardaí were rarely stationed in their home towns – but they hadn't complained.

Sean shook his head. 'Jack Maguire took it up to Dublin for forensics or something yesterday. Sheamy thinks it's all nonsense. He said there's been someone jumping into the lough to try and top themselves at least once a year for as long as he can remember. He reckoned it has to be one of them.'

Melissa's eyebrows knitted for a moment, then she changed the subject abruptly.

'Will I ask Jules over tonight to celebrate this deal? She could drop over before the evening shift. She hasn't been over for ages.'

'She might prefer a night to herself. I don't think she's working this weekend.'

'Isn't she? Bank holiday weekend? That's not like her. How do you know?'

Sean shrugged. 'I think Ruairi mentioned it. Someone must have done. Can't remember who.'

Ruairi? How would he know?

Melissa couldn't quite work that one out, but she had too much on her mind to wonder.

'Maybe that's why she's not answering her phone. I bet she's gone to the bloody spa and not told me. She had their new brochure the last time I saw her.'

'You don't have to do everything together, you know. Give her some space.'

Melissa glared at him. 'She's my sister. And I've hardly seen her in the last six months. God knows what she's been doing. She's either working or too tired to meet up. I'm starting to think she's avoiding me.' Melissa pushed a stray hair out of her face. 'Why don't you ask Ruairi and Dani over tonight as well? I'll text Jules. It's a gorgeous day, and getting Ferryman on board is definitely something to celebrate.' She grinned her Cheshire cat grin and held out her tanned hand, as if she was inspecting the back of it, several large diamonds flashing in the sunshine. 'I can feel a new ring coming on.'

'Some chance. We've got to get the boathouse renovated first, and the cottages could do with a lick of paint.' He leaned forwards to kiss her. 'Let's not have Ruairi and Dani. Invite Jules if you have to, but it would be nice to be on our own.'

'Have you fallen out with Ruairi or something? I thought you two were as thick as thieves. He's always here for some reason or another.'

'That's business, and of course we haven't fallen out. Him and Dani would be great on their own. I don't want Jules to feel like a gooseberry.'

Melissa rolled her eyes. 'As if. It's not like she hasn't known them forever. Leave it with me, I'll sort it *all* out.'

Chapter 8

THE COFFEE DOCK, where Carla and Grace were due to meet Jack Maguire, was busy when they got there, the huge car park almost full. On their third tour, Carla spotted a space.

'Look, can you get in there, on the end?'

Braking, Grace looked across at Carla, scowling. 'I'm not sure that's actually a space.'

Grace was paranoid about someone damaging her car; she hated tight spaces where the Mercedes might get clipped by someone's door as they got into their own vehicle. She had a point – it was beautiful, and incredibly comfortable for longer distances, but really, it was only a car.

'If I get out now, you can pull in on the end beside that Volvo. He'll be as worried about his paintwork as you are. And look – there's no one on the other side, you should be able to shimmy out up the verge.' Carla swung open the door, and looked at Grace questioningly.

'I'm not sure I'm shimmy-shaped, but let's try it. Do you need to stay long? I might move it up to the road.'

Carla shrugged. 'I've honestly no idea. We'll know when we meet Jack, and you can decide if you want to move it.'

The broad veranda that wrapped itself around the Coffee Dock's huge windows was full, every table occupied. Looking directly over the water, down the length of the lough, it offered a magnificent view, but Carla was pretty sure it wasn't the surrounding mountains that those occupying the tables were interested in.

Spotting Jack sitting at a table inside at the far end, Carla headed through the open doors. It was busy in here too, families in bank holiday mode trying to keep out of the afternoon sun. Jack stood up as they reached him, today in a moss-coloured lightweight jacket and chinos. He'd ditched the tie, his pale lemon shirt open at the neck.

'Ladies, grab a pew. How was your trip down?'

Carla pulled out a chair opposite Jack that was tucked into the window and, sitting down, pushed her backpack underneath it.

'Gorgeous, actually. Grace has a convertible. I think it's the first time I've been properly cool in weeks.'

Pulling out her own chair, Grace added, 'The traffic was heavy enough, but we left early. We did it in just over four hours, with a lovely long stopover for breakfast on the way.'

'You made good time. Where are you staying?'

Grace picked up the menu and scanned it as Carla answered.

'Grace found a house on the other side of the town, right on the edge of the lough – Lake View Cottage.'

'Melissa Hardiman's place? That's nice all right. I heard they spent thousands getting it done up. New thatch and underfloor heating.'

Grace turned back to him. 'I think we're the first people in. It's fabulous, all Farrow and Ball and Fired Earth.'

Carla smiled as Jack looked blank. 'Top-end paint finishes and tiles. It's very nice.' She almost added, 'And very expensive,' but thought better of it. She and Grace didn't get much chance to go away together anywhere unless it was work-related. Trying to get their holidays to coincide always seemed to get messed up by court dates and Carla's army survival training sessions. 'So, anything new at your end?'

Before Jack could reply, the waitress appeared beside them.

'What can I get you? Sorry for the delay.'

Carla smiled at her. Despite the cut-off jeans and sleeveless top under her purple apron, her face was flushed. She looked as if she was melting.

'You're busy today.'

'Manic. It's normally pretty hectic on a bank holiday, especially with the weather, but now the news seems to have brought every armchair sleuth out of the woodwork. It's honestly mental.'

Carla glanced over her shoulder. She'd noticed as she came in that there seemed to be a disproportionate number of attractive young people in their twenties and thirties who had stopped for lunch.

Seeing her looking at the tables outside, the waitress continued. 'They're all true crime YouTubers, apparently. There are more GoPros out there and selfies being taken than I've ever seen. They said there's a hashtag – #thebodyinthelake.' She shook her strawberry blond head despairingly. 'I'm Danielle, by the way.'

'Danielle and her husband Ruairi own the Adventure Centre and this place.' Jack gestured with his head to the building they could see through the windows beside them.

A paved boat-slip cut down to the water between the coffee shop and a gabled building that looked as if it had been converted from a stone-walled barn. At the front was a glazed porch that appeared to be a reception area, the doors pinned open to what little breeze was coming off the water. Groups of teenagers in swimming shorts hung around the front, some of them in life jackets, others sitting on the edge of the wall that dropped to the water's edge. Concrete stanchions linked by heavy iron chains ran along the edge to prevent people falling in.

'For our sins.' Danielle was looking across the slipway at the closest group of teens. 'Right, hit me up. What do you fancy?'

'Coffee definitely. Americano for me, latte for Steele.' Grace put the menu down as Danielle jotted their order on the pad in her hand.

'Another one for you, Jack?' He nodded. 'Anything to eat?'

'A Caesar salad with chicken would be amazing,' said Grace, 'and some sweet potato fries. For you, babes?'

Carla smiled; food took priority over everything, even the car, with Grace. Although she'd already had a big breakfast, Carla ordered her favourite. 'I'd love a superfood salad, if you've got it?'

Danielle nodded. 'Coming right up. I'll get yours now, too, Jack.'

Carla watched Danielle as she returned to the till area and passed the order over to the two young girls working behind the counter. They looked as if they were still in school.

A similar age, she was sure, to the victim whose face she was about to rebuild.

How had she ended up in the lake?

Cause of death wasn't her remit, but Carla knew the initial presumption that all water-related deaths were accidental drownings had messed up investigations in the past. Her job was to find out the *who*, so others could find out the *why*, although that hadn't stopped her becoming significantly involved in cases in the past.

There was always a moment before she started the reconstruction process when she felt a connection with the skull, as if the victim was waiting to show her their identity. Three-dimensional modelling had become so sophisticated that their software could produce an incredibly accurate likeness, but a computer image missed something that was captured in the clay reconstruction. She'd seen, over and over again, how a physical model could jog people's minds far better than a picture on a screen. And that connection often pulled her into finding out the *why*; she just couldn't help it. She had a scientist's enquiring mind, and over the years, she'd learned that things were rarely as they seemed on the outside.

'Sorry, I missed that.' Suddenly catching their conversation, Carla tuned back in to what Grace and Jack were talking about.

'Jack was just asking me about the offender profile.'

'Like "who would drop a body in a lough?"'

Grace nodded. 'But that's making the assumption that this wasn't an accident, or suicide.' She turned back to Jack. 'Carla mentioned you had a few of those.'

Conscious of where they were, Carla kept her voice low. 'We have to keep an open mind, but there is a comminuted fracture that can only have been caused by a blow to the head. Whether that was accidental or deliberate remains to be seen.'

Before she could say more, there was a commotion behind her as the woman in the red sundress they'd met earlier came hurriedly in through the open door and almost fell over a small child. Carla turned in her chair. Righting the child, the woman looked up and, spotting them, came straight over.

'Hi there. I see you found each other.' Jack started to reply, but she cut in. 'You haven't heard from Jules, have you Jack? I've been trying to get hold of her. I've just come in to see if Dani's seen her.'

Obviously annoyed, she turned towards the counter as Danielle appeared carrying their coffees.

'Why aren't you answering your phone? I've been ringing all morning. Sean's gone to meet a client and I've so much to do today. Have you seen Jules?'

Slipping their cups onto the table, Carla could see that Danielle was equally annoyed at being accosted in front of her customers.

'Food won't be a minute. Anything else, just holler. Do you want to come to the counter, Melissa? We've been flat out all morning, I haven't even looked at my phone. What's the problem?'

Chapter 9

AS CARLA FOLLOWED Jack along the water's edge, she was glad she'd worn her Converse and had slathered on the sunscreen. Despite inheriting sallow skin that tanned easily from her Spanish mother, she could feel the sun beating down on her exposed shoulders, the overhanging trees offering patchy shade as they followed the narrow path that seemed to circle the lake edge like a noose.

Grace's horrified face at the thought of trekking through woodland in this heat had made Carla smile. But she was ginger, and definitely not as athletic as Carla. Suddenly remembering she needed to move her car, Grace had decided to explore the waterside spa further around the lake and had left them to it.

Carla slapped a fly away. Grace had made the right decision – she would have hated every step of this expedition along the narrow, uneven path.

Stopping ahead of her, a line of sweat soaking the back of his short-sleeved shirt, Jack raised his arm, pointing out into the middle of the lake.

'This is where they found it – can you see the buoy?'

Squinting into the sun, Carla could see a red shape bobbing in the water. 'Long way out.'

'The lough has some very strange currents. Storms and heavy rain create surges where the water comes off the hills down the river. That hits the incoming tide and can create some really dangerous whirlpools. The channel between here and Monastery Island is called Dead Man's Gully locally, for good reason.'

Carla slapped away another fly. 'It would definitely be helpful to know if the body went in from the shore, or off a boat. Have there been any man overboard alerts where there's been no recovery?'

'We have them regularly, but they usually turn up. Danielle's husband Ruairi heads up the search and rescue team. He's lived here all his life, knows the lough well.' Jack paused. 'I called the station when I left you yesterday. They're looking back over missing persons' cases, should have something for us today. The PULSE system came into operation in 1999. Before then it's all physical files. I don't know how far we need to go back.'

'I can take a look at PULSE when I get to the office, there might be something that jumps out. It's impossible to give a time frame at this stage.' Carla looked out at the water, trying to get her bearings. 'Where are we in relation to our cottage?'

Jack indicated with his arm, swooshing away a bluebottle as he did so. 'Jaysus, the flies are bad today. You're a good bit further down on this shore. Melissa Hardiman's place is just beyond those trees, between here and you.'

'She mentioned a complex of holiday cottages?'

Jack swiped another fly away from his face. 'She's converted all the barns and outhouses around Coyne House. Her parents bought it years ago, as a holiday house, would you believe it? Her dad was an antiques dealer, I think. Her mother was some sort of interior designer.'

That explained how the cottage had ended up looking like something out of Country Homes *magazine.*

Jack continued. 'Never could understand why her and her sister Julia wanted to stay in Coyne's Cross. They're the sort who could have made it in London or New York.'

Carla put her hands on her hips, leaning back to let what little breeze there was circulate between her T-shirt and her backpack. 'That's Julia who isn't answering her phone?'

'Yep. Jules runs the Coyne Arms – the pub and the hotel. It's got a good restaurant, if you're looking for somewhere for dinner. She's quieter, has had her problems. She's not quite so …' He shrugged, searching for the word.

'Melissa's pretty full-on.'

'That's one way to describe her. I mean, she's doing very well. It's that pushiness that's made her so successful, but I'm glad I'm not married to her.'

Carla laughed. She was about to reply when Jack's phone rang. He pulled it out of his pocket, turning away from her to answer.

The distraction gave Carla a moment to properly absorb the location. The water was a stunning blue, mirroring the cloudless sky, the mountains that rose around the lough dark and brooding, majestic in their embrace.

Taking a step closer to the water's edge, she looked out, the image of the skull in her lab clear in her head.

What had happened here? How had the body ended up in such a deep part of the lake?

She could see from the waters swirling around the buoy that the current was strong, as Jack had suggested, but had it carried the body out to the middle, or had their victim been dropped into the water from a boat?

Beside her, Jack finished his call. 'Donna's made a list of missing persons. There's only two girls she can find reference to – a Gemma Langan, she disappeared in 2009, and Kellie Murphy in 2018. A guy called Peter Drew was convicted for Langan's murder, got twenty years, but they never found the body. She was seventeen.'

Jack looked out across the lough. 'I'll need to find out more about the Murphy girl.' He paused. 'But Donna says Seamus, the front office sergeant here, remembers the Langan case well. He said Peter Drew was what they called a bit simple back then.' He narrowed his eyes, as if he was trying to remember. 'I was brought up here, but we left years before then. I can remember my parents talking about the lad who looked after the church being in trouble – it must have been on the news. I was in university by then, but I've a vague memory of him liking the rabbits in the churchyard – I'm not sure why that's stuck. I probably only met him once or twice properly, but I saw him around the town. All the kids knew him, they took the piss a bit because he looked slow. You know how cruel kids can be.' Jack looked out over the water again. 'Seamus reckons Drew buried her up at the graveyard. He used to do the odd jobs up there, keep the place tidy. He doesn't think the skull can possibly be Gemma Langan's. He said Drew was terrified of water.'

Chapter 10

CARLA BATTED AWAY yet another fly and looked at Jack. 'How did they convict without a body?'

Jack slipped his phone into the pocket of his chinos. 'We'll need to look at the case files, but apparently her mobile phone was found in Drew's van.' He hesitated. 'Do you want to keep walking or head back? There's not much further we can go on this side of the water.'

'Let's go back. I'll text Grace – if she's going to be a while, it would be good to have a look at those missing person files and see if there are any other possibilities.'

'Good plan.' He turned around. 'Will we go through the woods instead of along the path? It's a bit longer, but we'll be out of the sun. I think my neck's been fried.'

'Lead the way. I'm surprised there aren't more people out walking.'

Jack stepped into the trees along a track that Carla would never have noticed if she'd been on her own. He held a long trailing bramble aside to let her pass.

'Very few people walk on this side. The other side of the lough has a proper marked walkers' route – it's part of the Coyne Way that takes you all the way to the round tower. There's a stretch of a beach and more to look at. The path on this side peters out when you get closer to Coyne House, and then disappears completely until you get to the other end of the estate.'

Carla nodded, remembering the steep descent to the little jetty below their cottage. There had been no sign of a path.

'Because there are fewer people, the deer are more active on this side,' Jack explained. 'Their trails criss-cross the rabbit tracks.'

Weaving between the trees, they suddenly came out onto a worn path.

'You can see where they've flattened the vegetation. The woods thin out closer to the avenue that runs down to Coyne House. There's lots of grazing for them.'

'I wonder how they cope with the flies?' said Carla. 'The air's thick with them. The heat must be bringing them out.'

'Something is. I haven't seen this many for a long time.'

There was something in his voice that made Carla look up from where she'd been carefully stepping through the bracken and leaf matter, the going uneven despite the deer having forged a way through. Ahead of her, Jack had stopped, his hands on his hips as he slowly scanned the woods around them.

'Can you hear them? The buzzing?'

Carla had been making so much noise going through the undergrowth, she hadn't noticed any sounds apart from her own breathing. Coming up to stand beside him, she caught her breath, brushing another fly out of her face.

'I can hear something. Do you think there's a deer carcass or something further up?'

'I'm not sure.'

Carla listened hard. To her left, through the trees, she could hear the water lapping gently on the shore, could see glimpses of blue. She turned around, her back to the water. The ground sloped upwards away from them.

'I think the sound's coming from up there.'

Jack hesitated for a moment. 'Do you mind if we go and look? There's been a rash of lamping recently. Poachers driving into the woods with incredibly bright lights. The deer get dazzled and freeze, but some of the poachers are lousy shots. They wing the deer instead of killing them, and then the deer run as far as they can before they collapse. It's pretty awful. It's a miracle they haven't shot any people, in all honesty.'

'Of course, lead the way. Is this common land?'

He set off along a narrow path up the incline, the layers of dead leaves crunching underfoot.

'No, it's part of the Coyne House estate. That's another reason the public right of way is on the other shore. Sean,

Melissa's husband, wants to create a nature reserve, so he encourages the deer and discourages the tourists. He was furious when he found out they're being targeted by poachers. We've had to have words about him patrolling the land at night. If he doesn't get himself shot, there's a danger he'll end up shooting someone else.'

Behind Jack, Carla kept her eyes on the ground in front of her as he continued.

'We're not that far from the avenue here. It links the house to the main road.'

Carla looked up to answer him and caught a flash of white through the trees. For a moment she thought it was a deer's white rump. 'There's something over there ...'

A few feet ahead of her on the path, Jack looked in the direction she was pointing. 'And the noise is getting louder. You OK?'

'No problem.' Carla hitched her backpack up higher and flicked her hair over her shoulder. 'We can cut across— Whoa ...' Carla had taken a step sideways, the movement enough to give her a clearer view through the trees. 'It's not a deer. I think you're going to need to call an ambulance.'

Chapter 11

IT WAS THE smell that hit Carla first as they got closer.
Jack already had his phone stuck to his ear, giving detailed
instructions to the 999 despatcher as she approached the
tree she'd seen from below. She held her hand firmly over
her mouth.

What little breeze there was seemed trapped by the trees.
The sweet smell of rotting meat, exacerbated by the heat,
hung like a mist. It was so strong Carla could almost see it.
She swatted away another fly. They were huge and seemed
to be coming from everywhere, their buzzing eager and
excited. Every now and then one flew past Carla that seemed
to be in a stupor, slower and dopey.

As she approached, Carla's suspicions were confirmed.
The body of a woman was hanging from a ragged length of
blue nylon rope that had been thrown over a stout branch
and looped around it twice to take her weight.

Approaching from behind, it took a moment for Carla
to realise why the sound of buzzing was so intense, but

as she rounded the trunk she gagged. The woman's long dark blond hair hung around her face in tangles, matted with leaves, her head forced unnaturally to one side by the tension of the rope. And her chest was a seething mass of bluebottles. Carla could see yellow clusters of eggs already laid between their moving iridescent bodies.

'Don't get too close, I need to secure the scene. Is there any sign of life?'

Carla shook her head. She wasn't a medical doctor, but she'd seen enough bodies in her career to know death when she saw it. She'd been inside a mortuary more times than she could remember.

Taking a step away, Carla tried to take in as much detail of the scene as she could, mentally noting the picture for her statement later. They were the first on the scene, and despite the attention to detail of the Scenes of Crime team, the photographers, and those who would eventually remove the body – all of whom would be arriving shortly – she knew how important that statement could be.

The woman's clothing was soaked in blood from what had to be a large gaping wound – one that was attracting the flies. Carla couldn't see how big it was, but it appeared to be in the centre of her chest, and from the direction of the blood flow, it looked as if it had been inflicted after she'd been hoisted into the tree, or, at least, she'd been still bleeding when she'd been strung up.

There was no way in Carla's mind that this could be a suicide. She'd heard of some strange deaths, but if this woman had cut herself before she looped the noose around her neck, she wouldn't have had the strength to haul herself up – there was no sign of a tree stump or a rock she could have jumped from. And if she'd cut herself in the tree, the knife or whatever she had used would be lying at her feet.

This was murder.

And from the conversation she could hear behind her, Jack was thinking exactly the same thing.

The front of the woman's jeans was dark, the fabric stiff where the blood had dried. A lot of blood. As Carla had approached from behind, she'd seen the staining of defecation, too. It looked to Carla as if she'd died right here, her bowels loosening at the moment life passed.

'Holy God.' Jack came up beside her, his hand over his mouth and nose, his eyes wide.

Carla glanced at him. 'Very dead. But less than twelve hours, I'd say, or those eggs would have started to hatch. I can't see any signs of maggots.'

'Well, that's something we can be grateful for, I suppose.'

'Do you know who she is?'

Jack continued to stare at the woman, as if he hadn't heard Carla.

The woman's eyes were open. Carla wasn't close enough to see if there was evidence of petechiae, the spotting caused by the blood vessels in her eyes breaking, but it was one of the first things the pathologist would find if the woman had died by hanging.

Given her injuries, Carla wasn't so sure that was the case.

Had she been hung here and tortured, cut open to die of blood loss – or shock, more likely – before her body was allowed to swing?

Judging from the staining to her jeans, it looked as if she had bled profusely, which meant that her heart had still been pumping when she was cut open.

The woman's tongue was swollen and protruding from lips already turning black. As Carla looked at her, she realised that she had been wearing a white T-shirt with some sort of logo on the front, with her three-quarter length jeans. Her arms lay uselessly at her sides, a gold-coloured watch on her right wrist.

So theft wasn't the motive.

And her jeans were done up, tightly belted at her slim waist, the T-shirt tucked in neatly as if she'd done it herself.

So she hadn't been raped, unless she'd been attacked and redressed.

A pair of navy wedge-heeled shoes were positioned in a dark patch of leaf matter just in front of her – stained, Carla guessed, with blood and urine. Sitting neatly side by side, the shoes looked utterly incongruous. They obviously hadn't fallen from her feet like that.

'She's been displayed. Look at the way her shoes have been positioned. They were put there after she was killed.'

Jack glanced up the slight incline they were standing on. 'I think you're right. And she's facing the avenue. I don't think you'd see her if you were leaving, but you might if you were looking this way coming in. See – the trees get thinner as you get closer to the road. This is the last one big enough to take her weight.' Jack looked around, double-checking that he was right. 'And closer to the water the bushes are thicker.' In the distance they heard the approach of sirens. 'Thank God. I called in everyone.'

Carla let out a breath she suddenly realised she'd been holding. 'That rope's pretty worn.'

'Looks like marine rope. You know – that stuff they use on fishing boats for fenders? My dad used to use it for everything when he had a boat down here.'

The rope was taut, a noose feeding around the woman's neck, the knot to one side. A thin line of saliva ran from the corner of her mouth. Another sign in Carla's mind that she had been alive when she'd been roped up, rather than killed and then hoisted into the tree.

It really was as if the killer was making a statement.

She could almost hear Grace's voice in her head. Suddenly thinking of her, Carla swatted away another fly and pulled her hair off her face, tying it up with the elastic hair tie around her wrist. She could focus better when it was out of her way.

Reaching into her pocket, Carla pulled out her phone to text Grace. Whatever plans Grace had had for their evening looked as if they were going to be on hold, at least until she'd given her statement. And she really didn't much feel like eating a big meal after this.

The sirens they'd first heard had been joined by more, and were suddenly louder now. Then the first one stopped abruptly.

'Do you know who it is?' Carla asked again as she looked at the girl's face. Even with the disfigurement of death, the woman's skin bloated and discoloured, she felt a flicker of recognition dawning.

Before she could work it out, Carla heard doors slamming and voices coming through the woods.

'Over here!' Jack put up his arm and waved.

Moments later a pair of paramedics appeared, jogging towards them. Carla heard more vehicles pulling up behind them as the two men got closer, slowing as they got a clearer look at the body and realised the need for speed had passed. A moment later they were standing beside Jack.

'Not sure you needed us, mate. She doesn't look like she's going anywhere.'

Jack let out a sigh. 'That's for sure. I didn't know when I put the call in, though. We need to wait for the Technical Bureau before we remove her and preserve the scene. I think we can be pretty sure life's extinct.'

The paramedics weren't going to argue. Both in their fifties, one of them was shaking his bald head slowly.

'What the fuck happened?'

Jack shrugged. 'Let's hope we can find out.' He turned to Carla, pausing before he spoke. 'It's Julia Hardiman, Melissa's sister. I'd guess this is the reason why she wasn't answering her phone.'

Chapter 12

SITTING ON THE rear step of the ambulance, the doors open wide, Carla could see enough of the taped-off crime scene to know what was going on. The paramedics had pulled the vehicle up at right angles to the road, creating a roadblock. Now in the front seat with the radio on, they were having a sandwich and a cup of tea before they were required to move the body to the nearby hospital. Jack had said the state pathologist, normally based in Dublin, was in Limerick, and would call to the scene as soon as the team were finished. Then the body would be removed to Our Lady's Hospital in Kilkeel for the post-mortem. Carla knew the pathologist well; he was only a few years older than she was, and keen. He'd served his apprenticeship in inner London, had been delighted when he'd got the Irish job, bringing his wife and toddler home to Dublin.

Below her, blue and white crime scene tape had been slung around the trees, corralling the body, preventing anyone from inadvertently wandering over a piece of crucial evidence. A pathway of metal plates had been laid like stepping stones on the leaf matter surrounding the tree, enabling the crime scene investigation officers, the hoods of their white suits pulled up, to move safely around.

The area around the body would be divided into a grid and each section searched to ensure the killer hadn't dropped something crucial – like the knife he'd used to carve her open. Carla's stomach lurched slightly at the memory of the bluebottles excitedly laying their eggs on the perfect host. The flies themselves fed off nectar, but the maggots feasted on rotting meat.

She closed her eyes and let out a sigh, knowing this scene would be one that stayed with her. She wanted to rub away the heat and the dirt from her face, but until she washed her hands properly, that could wait. She'd used lashings of hand sanitiser, but it would take proper soap and water to shift the cloying feel of death.

Opening her eyes, Carla could see the photographer was still taking pictures, the flash popping as he moved around, taking shots from every conceivable angle. They would be vital later in court.

At least Carla hoped they would.

This was a brutal killing, completely at odds with what she'd seen of Coyne's Cross so far, the slightly sleepy lakeside town making the most of its natural assets to attract the tourists who came here in droves. Although sleepy towns hid all sorts of secrets. She knew that better than anyone.

Girl X had been found on the outskirts of a town like this.

Carla's mind went back to the image trapped inside her computer screen.

Who left someone's head in a wardrobe?

Even Grace had problems working that one out.

Carla could feel her thoughts beginning to spiral – Lizzie's face starting to intrude. She'd had long hair. She'd been wearing jeans the last time Carla had seen her.

The sound of her phone ringing broke into Carla's thoughts. Grace.

Thank God.

She needed to hear her voice.

Despite seeing death close to as often as she did, Carla never got used to it. She'd tried not to, but she seemed to form an emotional attachment with every victim, the drive to discover their story just as strong as it had been with her first case. Maintaining a mental distance, like the two paramedics she could vaguely hear chatting behind her, was the only way police and forensics professionals managed to keep going into work, avoiding PTSD at every call. But Carla had always been different.

Putting her phone to her ear, Carla played with the end of her ponytail.

She felt filthy, sticky with sweat. Her voice caught in her throat as she spoke.

'How are you doing, hun?'

She heard Grace turn down a radio before she replied, the sound of children playing and laughing in the distance. She must be in the car.

'I'm back at the cafe. I've only just seen your text. What the feck?'

'I know. It's pretty horrific, G. She's been displayed, and—'

Grace interrupted her. 'Can I see the crime scene photos?'

'I don't know, it's not my case. Or yours, come to that. I'll ask Jack.'

'Did you take any photos yourself?'

Carla sighed inwardly. Grace had switched into work mode, her tone staccato, professional.

Why the heck would she have taken photos of a hanging body on her personal phone?

Carla kept her voice level. 'No, I didn't. I can describe it to you and draw diagrams if you need them, when I get back. I'll need a shower and a very large gin and tonic first, though.'

Grace's voice softened. 'Course, babes. Does Jack have any idea who it is?'

'Yes, but I'll tell you at home. It's just so weird, this place is so pretty and this killing is just so … ugly.'

'Murder's never pretty, you know that, babes. But it sounds to me like that location has been chosen for a reason.'

Carla took a ragged breath and let it out again. Grace's skill was thinking like a killer. A couple of years ahead of her and Lizzie in Trinity, Grace had made her mark with An Garda Síochána and the public with a landmark case before Carla had even finished her PhD.

'Jack said it was the strongest tree, that she'd be seen from the road. But maybe there's more to it than that?'

'Seems likely to me. It's a lot of bother kidnapping a woman and then dragging her off the main road to string her up in the woods. Surely it would have been easier to dump her in the lake?'

'Like our skull? Maybe he doesn't like water?'

Something Jack had said earlier tried to nudge into Carla's thoughts, but there wasn't room for it right now. Her head was full. She needed to decompress and sort everything out before the patterns would start to emerge and she'd see the links that connected the dots. Sometimes she felt as if the pieces of evidence she had were like constellations of stars, their grouping a meaning she couldn't see until she looked really hard. Unlike the lines in your palm, the stars never changed. Every item of evidence was a fixed point that added to the picture.

'There are some case notes at the station Jack was going to show me. They seem to have a good few missing persons' reports.'

'I think your cold case may just have been bumped off the top of the list, lovely – let's hope they already pulled the files this morning. Do you want me to meet you there? If he gives you the OK, we could go through them together at the cottage. I'm organising dinner.'

Carla hoped Grace wasn't planning on trying to order in. She was a city girl born and bred, but Carla had only noticed one takeaway in Coyne's Cross and she didn't think Grace would be impressed with fish and chips, even if it was delivered. She was about to reply when Jack appeared around the door of the ambulance.

'I've got to go. Call you later.'

Carla ended the call and put her phone down. Jack looked like she felt, his face strained and streaked with sweat.

He sighed as he spoke. 'You OK?'

'Better than she is.' Carla looked back through the trees.

'That wouldn't be difficult. I've got to get back and talk to Melissa. I need to get changed first.' He drew in a deep breath. 'I can't believe this, it's normally so peaceful here. One of the reasons we ended up moving back up to Dublin was because my mum couldn't deal with the quiet.'

Carla looked up at him, curiously. She'd half wondered about his links to the area when he'd mentioned it earlier, but the conversation had moved on before she'd had a chance to ask.

'How did you end up stationed here? I thought that didn't happen?'

He drew in a breath, his concentration on the activity below them.

'I've only been back a couple of years, but I've no family in the area any more, no close ties. And they had a gap here they couldn't fill, so it got approved. I was stationed in Limerick, I wanted to get out of the city.' He sighed, obviously not planning to elaborate. Carla felt as if the shutters had come down. Then he looked at her again. 'Sorry about this, but ...'

Carla smiled, shaking her head. 'I know, going through old files isn't exactly going to be a priority. Grace is going to meet me at the station. Can you release the files to me and we can go through them? We'll be out of everyone's way at the cottage.'

'No problem – we'll need to set up an incident room. District headquarters is in Kilkeel, but it'll be too far for a team to trek back and forth.' Jack was staring at the taped-off area of woodland as he spoke, half to himself. He turned his attention to Carla. 'We've got files going back to 1990 in the station archive. Do you think that's far enough?'

'Honestly, I've no idea. Your skull could be from the 1800s, but I'd guess it'll be a start. When I get to the lab and start rebuilding we'll have a much clearer idea, but it'll save a trip if I can have a look now.'

'Grand, I'll get one of the lads to drop us down. Donna's co-ordinating everything at the station. She'll take your statement.' He sighed, his eyes on the ground as he shook his head. 'I mean, what are the chances?' He looked up at her.

'Seriously, the worst we have here are tourists' cars getting broken into, the usual drunk and disorderly ... domestics. Then we find a skull and the whole world goes mad, and now ... this.'

Chapter 13

COYNE'S CROSS GARDA Station was humming when Carla and Jack got there. As they pulled up into the lane beside what had been an elegant double-fronted Victorian house before it became a Garda station, Carla could see the entrance hall was full.

News of something happening had clearly leaked out.

At the end of a black and red tiled path, double doors thickly overpainted in regulation navy blue were standing open to the summer evening air. Through them, Carla caught a glance of a grand entrance hall that had been sectioned off with a wooden partition and a glazed window. Several people were leaning on the internal walls; one guy was sitting on the broad curved step outside. The laptop bag beside him and the fact that he had his mobile glued to his ear suggested press.

Grace was already parked outside, the soft roof of her car up, the windows open. She glanced up as the patrol car swung past her, catching Carla's eye, nodding to indicate that she was happy to wait.

Nobody had said much on the way back from the woods. The uniformed driver of the patrol car had acknowledged Carla politely in the rear-view mirror as she'd climbed into the car, Jack hauling on his seatbelt in the front.

Earlier, as the various discussions had reached her on what little breeze had come off the lake, it was very clear that everyone knew Julia Hardiman. The level of shock was almost palpable.

Single, in her early thirties, Julia had lived in a cottage on the corner of what had been her parents' estate. When she'd learned that, Carla had heard Grace in her head again, speculating about why this location had been chosen – perhaps whoever had killed her hadn't had to bring her body far at all.

From the constant stream of chatter coming through the car radio, Carla knew that Julia's home had been cordoned off and her office in the hotel was about to be searched. Jack needed to get over to her sister Melissa, before the locals started putting two and two together and rumours reached her first.

In the concrete yard behind the station, the driver pulled up beside a row of civilian cars. To Carla's right, another long low building ran the width of the yard, the feet of the huge communications mast that was a feature of every station planted firmly in the corner. From behind, the house looked much more like a barracks, the white vertical blinds on every window prison-like, utilitarian; no sign of the roses and window boxes that made the front of the building almost welcoming. Despite the sunshine, the lights seemed to be switched on inside.

'I'll bring you in through the back. Donna won't be long.' Jack had his door open before the car had fully come to a stop.

Carla grabbed her backpack and swung her own door open. 'You go on, leave me, I'll be grand. You need to get moving.'

Jack threw her a smile of thanks, strode over to a narrow pale blue door set into the rear of the building and punched in an access code. He had disappeared before she'd closed the car door. Waiting for Carla, the driver indicated that she should follow, his face troubled.

Carla followed him to the door. 'You knew her?'

'Everyone did. Always smiling. Not a party girl, like, but solid. She'll be missed.'

'Was she seeing anyone?'

He shook his head. 'She dated, like. Not many from the town, she liked to be private, but she's been single recently. A good while, I think.'

Carla smiled sympathetically, but it sounded as if the locals had kept a close eye on Julia's love life. One of the problems of being in the public eye in a small town was also being on their lips – no doubt her every move had caused ripples of gossip. It didn't surprise Carla that Julia Hardiman had dated outside Coyne's Cross.

As the guard pushed the door open and led her down a cool, white-painted corridor, they passed a hatch that opened into the custody suite. Several more doors opened off the passage to her left. They were firmly shut now, but she guessed they were interview rooms. At the end was another code-locked door.

They emerged into what must have been the hallway of the original house, and her escort took her straight into a large office on the right. It ran from the front to the rear, the elaborate Victorian architrave and ceiling roses, together with two huge Cork marble fireplaces, a giveaway that this had once been an elegant home.

Now the walls were covered in cream-painted woodchip paper, peaked hats and body armour piled on top of a battalion of grey steel filing cabinets that ran along the wall to her left. On the opposite side of the room, broad desks littered with coffee cups sat at right angles to the wall. It had the tired air of a building used 24–7.

'Sit yourself down. There's hardly anyone here, with everyone out on this one. Donna will be in in a sec to take your statement.'

The words were hardly out of his mouth when a stocky sergeant, who looked to be in his late fifties, came into the office behind them. He was wearing the old-style blue serge uniform tunic, its gold buttons polished to a shine. His thinning hair was slicked over his head in a cow's lick; his eyebrows were raised as if Carla had personally affronted him somehow.

'Who's this we have here now, Garda Keane?'

Carla sat down in the nearest chair. Before the guard with Carla could reply, a woman in her early twenties, whom Carla guessed must be Donna, stuck her head around the door frame and raised her eyebrows behind the older man.

'This is Dr Steele from the Park, Seamus. She was with Jack when they found the body. I'm just about to take her statement.'

The older man turned to look at Donna. 'From headquarters, is it? It's a long time since I've been up to the Phoenix Park. Are you the lassie who does the skulls?' He didn't attempt to hide his curiosity. 'Seamus Twomey – Sergeant. I run the office, not much comes in here that I'm not involved with.'

Carla didn't quite know how to follow that. Fortunately she didn't have to. As if Garda Keane saw this as an opportune moment to escape, he turned to her.

'I'll leave you in Donna's capable hands. I'm away back to Coyne House, Seamus. I'll give you an update when I get there.'

It was obviously the right thing to say. Twomey nodded briskly. 'You do that. DI Rainsford's on his way over from Kilkeel, I'll be speaking to him shortly.'

Garda Keane dodged out of the door and around Donna before vanishing down the corridor. Carla heard the door slam.

Donna came properly into the office. Petite, with her dark hair in a ponytail, she was in plain clothes – smart navy linen trousers, low heels and a honey-coloured wrap top. 'Can I get you a cup of tea?'

Carla smiled gratefully. She didn't think she'd ever needed a cup of tea more.

Chapter 14

DANIELLE PULLED THE boot of her Nissan Pathfinder open and slid the plastic container of leftover salads and cakes, and the tureen of soup she'd brought from the Coffee Dock, towards her. One of the bonuses of running the cafe was that she rarely had to cook. Anything they couldn't use the next day had to be eaten by someone, and she couldn't bear waste.

Picking up the container, Danielle realised that Ruairi's own Pathfinder 4 × 4 wasn't in the drive, and put it down again. She'd look some eejit standing on the doorstep with her arms full, waiting for him to answer the bell when he wasn't even here. Not that there were any neighbours to see, thank God, only sheep in the fields that swept away towards the mountains.

Leaving the boot open, she went and unlocked the front door, disabling the house alarm before returning for the box. Juggling with it, Danielle banged the boot door shut with her bum.

A moment later the house alarm went off, its siren ear-splitting.

What the feck?

Hurrying inside, Danielle dumped her load on the hall table and went back to check the panel. She punched in the number as fast as she could to stop the noise and looked for her phone to call the alarm company.

She had no idea what had set the alarm off, but she could work that out in a minute. First she needed to stop anyone calling the guards, and text Ruairi super fast. He'd set up some fancy notification thing on his phone, so he got a text if the alarm was triggered. He was going to kill her. He was always on about how false alarms made the alarm company take their eye off the ball; how one day, when they really needed the Gardaí they'd be all day getting here.

Searching her jeans pockets for her phone, Danielle realised she'd left it in her bag in the jeep. Sprinting outside, she hauled the passenger door open and tipped her bag out, finding her phone and searching for the number. She got through after one ring, the alarm company operative concerned about her breathlessness.

'This is Danielle Brennan from Ard na Gréine. No, everything's fine, really. It was me, I must have put the wrong number in. Yes, all completely fine. And thanks so much.'

Ending the call, she texted Ruairi.

False alarm, all good with central station.

Danielle let out a breath and looked at the contents of her handbag tumbled on the seat of her car. She was almost too tired to pick it all up. Staring at it for a minute, gathering her thoughts, she scooped everything into her bag and slammed the door shut.

God, she was exhausted – her legs felt heavy and her lower back was aching. She must have walked a hundred miles between the deck outside and the servery; there hadn't been a minute's break all day. Even when they'd heard the sirens late in the afternoon nobody had moved, a rumour crossing the deck that someone had got caught in a current at Dead Man's Gully. Danielle doubted it. The rescue crew would have been straight out if there was a problem on the water. It was just as likely to be a car accident. Every bank holiday there seemed to be something awful happening on the roads.

But at least all the running around the cafe was one way to keep fit, and it meant she didn't have to worry about calories – or, more specifically, the generous wedge of New York cheesecake she'd brought home with her.

Right now, all she wanted to do was crash out with a nice cup of tea. And assuming she didn't fall asleep on the sofa, she had a half bottle of white wine waiting in the fridge for when Ruairi got home. She didn't think they'd sat out yet once this summer, and the weather was perfect this evening to watch the sun setting over the mountains. Then she'd get an early night.

Tomorrow was going to be just as busy.

Part of her was dearly missing Ben – she'd brought home his favourite raspberry scones to throw in the freezer for when he got home from his dad's – but part of her was also relieved she had the house to herself. Even in weather like this, he'd prefer to be at home than hanging out with his friends down by the Adventure Centre, which meant she'd be worrying about him and constantly trying to find ways to get him outside. And right now, the thought of sitting down and never moving again was overriding her maternal feelings.

Ben would be having a ball in Dublin with his dad. City kids loved getting out to the country, out on the water on hot summer weekends, but Ben didn't like crowds; he much preferred a museum or a hot cinema, topped off with Captain America's spicy wings and a hot fudge sundae.

Inside the house, Danielle left the front door open while she brought the box of food through to the kitchen. It looked as if Ruairi must have been home some time during the day. He'd left a roll of duct tape on the end of the counter, had moved the newspapers she'd stacked in front of the back door, ready for recycling, onto the table. Danielle shook her head, annoyed. The washing she'd brought in this morning was still in the basket on the chair – not that she'd imagine he'd ever think of bringing that upstairs. But damn him, he never cleared up after himself. As if she didn't have enough to do.

If he made a sandwich, he left the mayonnaise out on the board with the lid off and the lettuce wilting next to it.

Danielle started to load the food into the fridge. Sliding the plate containing her cheesecake and a strawberry tart for Ruairi onto the shelf, she closed the door and filled the kettle, popping it on while she went to close the front door and check the alarm panel.

It was still flashing, the digital readout showing the alarm event. Danielle looked at it, puzzled. She was sure she hadn't put the wrong number in. The house alarm code was the same number as the Coffee Dock – her birthday; she used it at least four times a day. But the panel was showing her that the trigger had been the front door.

Her hands on her hips, Danielle narrowed her eyes. How could that be right? Ruairi was fastidious about setting the alarm when he left, obsessive about God knew what gear he had in the garage. A few years ago, a spate of tiger kidnappings had made him change all their routines – their house was isolated, and they both ran businesses that took in a lot of cash. He'd never, ever have left the house without putting the alarm on.

So how had it gone off now, and be showing the front

door as the reason? When she came in, and put the number in, had she turned the alarm on, not off? And the open front door had triggered it? How was that possible?

Chapter 15

'HERE WE ARE.' Waiting for her at the bottom of the cottage's spiral staircase, Grace handed Carla a large glass of white wine. She didn't know how Grace had managed it, given the time and resources available, but a delicious smell was coming from the oven. Grace looked at her over the top of her tortoiseshell reading glasses. 'You sure you're OK?'

Carla accepted the wine gratefully and took a large sip. 'I am now.' She put one hand to her wet hair. 'I borrowed your brush, I think I left mine at home.'

Grace smiled, shaking her head, turning to pick up her own glass. 'A hairbrush is the least of your problems, babes.'

'I know.'

Carla sighed and pulled at the collar of the white fluffy robe she'd found behind the bathroom door. Her skin was still pink from a very long, very hot shower, and now she felt clean, but even in the cool of their stone living room she felt a bit suffocated. The warmth of the oven had brought the temperature up a few degrees that Carla was sure she'd appreciate in winter, but right now she was finding a little stifling.

'Let's sit outside, I need some air.'

Heading out through the double doors onto the deck, Carla could see Grace had already lit two lemon-scented candles, which were burning merrily on the mosaic table, keeping the midges away. Grace was allergic to insect bites, and doused herself in spray repellent at this time of year. One of the blood spatter team at work had told Carla it was something to do with how fast your blood coagulated – if it clotted quickly, the insects had to pump more of their blood thinner into you, which then produced the reaction. But right now Carla didn't have a lot of headspace for thoughts on insects and blood. She'd seen enough for one day.

Carla sat down gratefully, enjoying what little breeze there was coming off the water. The view was perfect, the sun low in the sky, the evening balmy. The lough stretched away from them, fish jumping for the flies that hung in clouds over water as still as silk. And framing it all, the dark shape of the mountains.

Pulling up the chair beside her, Grace sat down with a sigh.

'Hit me with it. All the details.'

It didn't take Carla long to bring Grace up to date. She sipped her wine as she listened.

'So you've got the files for twenty-four hours? We'll go through them after dinner.'

Grace lined the foot of her glass up with the random coloured shards of china that had been used to create the table top. Carla smiled to herself; Grace was the one who sought order in everything.

'I know it's not your case, but I've been thinking about the location – where you found her, and the proximity of what seems to be the kill site to the water.' Grace screwed up her face. 'If very few people walk on that side of the lough, and it's all private land, I think you found her a lot sooner than the killer had anticipated. I think he was expecting someone from the estate to find her – Melissa herself, or her husband perhaps, particularly if Jack's right about the husband patrolling for poachers. Which is interesting in itself.'

'Tell me what you're thinking.' Carla took another sip. The wine was hitting its mark.

'First thoughts – is the lough meaningful to either perp or victim? Let's assume it's a he, given the physical strength required to haul a woman into a tree. I think he knows the area, he knows this land. Does that mean he's left the body there so he can see what's happening? So he has easy, legitimate access to the periphery of an area that will be cordoned off?'

Carla glanced at Grace as she spoke. Her freckled face was creased in concentration. She'd pulled her red hair into a ponytail, was only wearing a slick of make-up, the blue of her eyes picked up by the cornflower linen dress she was wearing.

Unaware Carla was studying her, Grace continued. 'It could be that he had a relationship with the victim and wants to be able to revisit the dump site to relive it, either pre-murder, or in the act of the murder.' Carla winced. 'Or it could be that he has a reason to be near the lake so when the murder, or disappearance, or body is discovered, he'd be likely to overhear conversations among the locals, the gossip at the bar she worked in, or from customers at the coffee shop.'

'You mean he wants to be the centre of attention? That people talking about what he's done will stoke his ego?'

Grace picked up her wine. 'It's one possibility. That might give him a sense of power, a thrill, or it might simply soothe his need to know who knows what, and what the speculation is.'

'You make it sound like he enjoys killing.'

'It's a distinct possibility. You said that Jack said this tree was just about visible from the road if you're driving into the estate? While there's deliberation in that, there's also inherent danger in him being discovered in the act – he could have hidden it much more deeply in the woodland. But that chance of discovery could be part of the thrill. It'll be interesting to read the pathologist's report, and find out the order of events and how she actually died.'

'I hope to God she wasn't alive when he cut her. That level of blood loss could have happened soon after death.'

Grace put her hand on Carla's arm. 'Try not to think about that. You can't control what happened, or the outcome, and there's no point in worrying about it until you know what to worry about.'

Grace stood up before Carla could reply, then put her hand along her shoulder, bent down and kissed her. 'Really, you know what I say about worrying. It doesn't make anything better – it's an utterly pointless emotion that sabotages your ability to operate effectively. Let's eat, and try and park today's events until we have more information. There are other things to focus on that we *can* control, like finding out more about your skull. And I haven't even told you about the spa yet. You won't believe how soft my skin is.'

Grace threw her a cheeky wink and swirled into the house, leaving a trail of perfume behind her.

Chapter 16

'SO, CAN YOU tell me when you last spoke to Julia?'

Jack Maguire was sitting on the edge of Melissa Hardiman's turquoise velvet sofa, his notebook open on his knee. He'd changed quickly into the spare chinos and pale pink short-sleeved shirt he kept in his locker at the station before he'd come over to Coyne House. Someone had collected the detective unit car he'd left parked outside the Coffee Dock with his jacket in it, but despite the rest of his clothes still being crisp from the dry cleaners, he felt a mess. He wasn't sure if that was due to the elegance of the room, or the feeling of death clinging to him. It sort of seeped into your pores, and only a hot shower would shift it. He hadn't had time to shower at the station, but that was exactly what he was going to do the minute he got home to his two-bed terrace at the bottom of the main street. With everything that had happened today, right now, the thought of shutting his own bright red front door on the world and pouring himself a large whiskey had never felt more necessary.

He just wasn't too sure when that might happen.

Opposite him, Melissa took a shaky breath. 'I normally talk to her every few days. She's been really busy recently, though, I'm not sure why. Whenever I suggested lunch, she seemed to have something else on.' Melissa shook her head. 'I feel like I haven't spoken to her properly for ages. She left a message on my phone when she was leaving work on Friday night, just saying she'd call over the weekend. I was in the bath, I didn't hear it ring, and then we spoke really briefly yesterday. I was busy and I meant to call back.' She tried to fight the tears back. 'But now it's too late …'

Jack opened his mouth to speak, but changed his mind, giving Melissa a few more minutes. This was always the hardest part of any investigation – trying to get crucial information out of distraught relatives. Being told you'd lost a loved one to murder didn't do anything for anybody's recall.

But relatives' *reactions* could be surprisingly telling, too.

Sitting opposite Melissa and Sean in their grand drawing room, Jack watched them both carefully. They were each a picture of shock, eyes red and faces pale, but there was no getting away from the fact that the majority of victims of violence knew their killers, and information learned now could, as they said on every cop show that had ever been made, be crucial.

Beside him, the family liaison officer from Kilkeel was sitting quietly. Jack knew she was observing them, too, and they'd compare notes later. In her late forties, and as she herself liked to say, 'well padded', Ruth Stanley was someone who exuded calm control, from her tidy blond bun to her polished shoes. She was brilliant at her job.

But sitting here, even with Ruth and all her common sense next to him, Jack was starting to feel as if he'd walked into a soap opera.

From the cleverly positioned lighting shining up from the flower bed in the front of the house outside, to this TV-set of a drawing room with its polished surfaces, silver-framed photographs and grand piano, today was starting to feel utterly unreal. Sitting with their arms wrapped around each other, Melissa and Sean looked like reality TV stars, perfectly groomed, worked-out and tanned, their clothes so simple that they were clearly expensive. Everyone was always saying they were the perfect couple. Good-looking, well-off, with a thriving business, they appeared to have it all.

But appearances could be deceptive.

Ruth's radio, clipped to her soft blue marl uniform polo shirt, flashed to alert her to a call. She put her earpiece in, glancing at Jack, listening before she spoke.

'Are you expecting anyone, Sean? An SUV's heading this way. It just ran past the sentry on the avenue. It was going too fast for them to get the registration.'

Sean looked at her, puzzled. 'Only Dr Morris, but he'd have stopped.'

As if completely unaware of their exchange, Melissa put her hand to her face, the diamonds on her fingers catching the light. 'When she called yesterday I was getting scones at the cafe. She said she needed to get some bits done at the cottage. The back door lock kept sticking, and there was something about the shower – the head was dripping, I think. I wasn't really listening, to be honest. The bank holiday weekend is always so busy, I had a million other things to do at the rental cottages and Terry, who does our maintenance, had a list as long as your arm.'

'That's Terry Walsh who does the churchyard, too? He lives on the estate?'

Answering for Melissa, Sean nodded. 'In the lodge by the north gate. We were blessed when he showed up looking for work. I'm away a lot and Arthur, the old groundsman – he'd been on the estate all his life – just got slower and slower with his arthritis. Melissa really needed someone reliable to help her with the place. Terry's worth his weight in gold.'

Beside Jack, Ruth stood up, her hand pressed to her earpiece. 'Excuse me for a moment.'

Jack smiled at them both encouragingly. He wanted to get his questions over with before anyone landed on them. 'Had Julia mentioned the door before?'

Melissa shrugged. 'A few times. It's an old door, it needs replacing, but you know how you never quite get to these

106

things. It wasn't like she couldn't lock it – it was getting it open that was the problem.'

Sean pulled Melissa to him as she dissolved into silent sobs. She'd changed clothes since Jack had seen her earlier, was now wearing a white silk T-shirt and jeans, her blond hair bright against Sean's white shirt.

Sean looked at him, his irritation at the questioning clear. 'Is this really necessary now, Jack? Could you wait until the morning?'

Before Jack could answer, Melissa pulled her head away from his shoulder and shook her head. 'When did this happen? I keep thinking we could have driven past her today, I just never looked, I was too busy …'

Another sob ripped through her as they heard the sound of a car pulling up fast on the gravel outside, a door slamming. A moment later, there was a hammering on the front door.

Trying to unwind himself from Melissa, Sean started to stand to go and answer it.

'Don't worry, you stay there, I'll get it.' Ruth patted the air to indicate he should sit.

A moment later they heard a rattle as Ruth opened the front door, and then a man's voice.

'Christ! Is Mel here? And Sean? What happened? I've only just heard.'

Jack couldn't hear Ruth's reply clearly, only the comforting low tone of her voice. The caller wasn't so calm, though, and a second later Ruairi Brennan burst through the living room door, his face bleached white, eyes frantic.

'Is it true? About Jules? I was getting into the car and heard it on the radio, then on Facebook people were saying it was her ...' He looked at them in disbelief.

Having closed the door, Ruth appeared behind him.

'Why don't you sit down? I'm Ruth. You know DS Maguire?'

Chapter 17

DINNER WAS DELICIOUS. Carla had thought she may never eat again earlier that afternoon, as she'd sat at the edge of the crime scene watching the SOCOs at work, but Grace had procured an Italian chicken pasta dish from a deli recommended by the girls at the spa, and Carla had discovered she was actually starving.

In typical Grace fashion, she'd apparently left her credit card with the spa receptionist and had them phone ahead and book dinner for tonight, plus breads and cold meats for lunch tomorrow, collecting everything, beautifully presented in a chill bag, as she'd headed to the Garda station.

There was something about Grace that made people do things for her; Carla was never sure whether it was because she oozed the wealthy privilege that only came from a private school education, or if everyone just fell in love with her when they met her. She had a luminosity, a magnetism, that worked on men and woman alike. Getting an appointment at the spa at all was a perfect example.

Carla was sure it was crazy busy for the bank holiday, yet Grace must have just driven up and walked right in.

But as Carla curled up on the sofa beside her, the pile of missing person files on the driftwood coffee table in front of them, she wasn't worrying about 'the Grace effect', as she called it. Grace's life looked perfect from the outside, but Carla knew the truth of her neurotic, controlling mother and the bleakness of her teenage years. While Carla had been battling it out in the freezing mud of the hockey pitch at her mixed school, catching the bus for the twenty-minute ride there and back each day, Grace had been locked up with a bunch of nuns in a castle-like girls' school that sounded horrific. Carla's dad was a bricklayer, his job a long way from Grace's father's role as one of the country's leading heart surgeons, but it was very clear from what Grace had told her of her childhood, that money didn't buy you happiness.

With her feet tucked into the robe, her knees up on the sofa, Carla pulled another file off the pile onto her lap. Beside her, Grace had kicked off her shoes, her toenails now a coral pink to match her newly gelled fingernails, a file open on her knee. Grace took another sip of wine and put it down on the stone tiles beside the sofa, the foot of the glass making a comforting ringing sound. Grace had plugged her phone into the Bose speaker she travelled with, and found their favourite album. Adele's smoky voice was perfect to relax to.

Grace turned over a page. 'This one is a possibility. Just twenty, gay, thrown out of home when he came out to his parents aged sixteen. Was sleeping on the boyfriend's mum's couch for three years. Good God, how do people live like that? Then he discovered the boyfriend was cheating. He disappeared in 1998, was originally from Kilkeel, but used to hang out here a lot as a child – Sunday afternoon walks, and brought the boyfriend here a few times.'

Carla leaned over to read the page Grace had open. 'Emotional attachment to the lough, and obviously more than his fair share of emotional instability. Let me look at his description.'

Grace flipped the first page over again. A photograph had been pinned to the top of it, a teenager in a check shirt and jeans holding an ice cream, smiling cheekily at the camera. He was a good-looking lad. The picture had obviously been taken in the summer during happier times. Carla felt the bottle of sadness that she normally kept firmly stoppered inside her open a crack, emotion seeping out like ink.

'Five eight, slim build. Does he sound like he could be your skull? His face is quite feminine.'

'Christ. What a tragedy. I mean he could have been anyone, could have gone on to do something that made a difference in the world.' Carla sighed. 'But yes, he's a definite maybe. Jack said they'd checked the dental records where they could, but there are still a lot unaccounted for.'

'They could hardly check every missing person in Ireland.'

'Exactly. At times like this you wish there was a proper national database, that DNA and dental records and Garda activity was all sort of combined so the computer did the cross-checking.'

'Babes, this is Ireland. There was almost a strike when they introduced PULSE in the first place. I'll put him on the possible pile.'

Carla looked at the pile they were creating on the end of the coffee table. They were two thirds of the way through the original files, and had only come across three possibles so far: all young men in the correct age range, their information in buff-coloured files. The next two files were blue. She opened the first one.

'Ah, this is one of the girls Jack mentioned.' Carla ran her finger down the first page. 'Kellie Murphy, nineteen, from Stoney Pass, went missing in Kilkeel on the way home from a nightclub in November 2018, last seen waiting at a taxi rank. Five four, blonde, slim build.' Carla closed her eyes for a minute. 'I think I saw a signpost for Stoney Pass on the way down. That's close to here.'

'She doesn't sound like a suicide. More like an abduction. And if you needed to dispose of a body, the mountains or the lake would be solid options.'

'Exactly.'

Carla scanned the page. Another missing person, another

void in someone's life. It was not knowing that was the worst – not knowing what had happened, or why. Not knowing if they were alive or dead. Part of her kept hoping that one day Lizzie would just walk through the front door … She was sure Kellie Murphy's family felt the same.

She put the file on her 'possibles' pile and reached for the next one.

'This is the other girl. Gemma Langan, the one there was a prosecution for.' She looked down the page. 'Vanished after a party held at … Oh, this is interesting – Coyne House. She was seventeen.' Carla frowned as she flipped the page and read the printout of the original missing person's report. 'She was a pretty girl, too.' She lifted the photocopy of the photograph attached to the page.

'But that's not the whole file, if there was a prosecution?'

'No, only a hard copy of the original missing person's report, and…' she turned the page, 'someone's made a note of the key prosecution points. I'll check PULSE when I get back. There are probably a couple of hundred witness statements alone.'

'Is the judgement there?'

Carla flicked to the end of the file. 'Just a summary document.'

Before Carla could read any more, there was a sharp knock at the front door. She looked up, surprised.

'Who's that?'

Grace turned and gave her an amused look. 'I'm brilliant at many things, but seeing through walls isn't one of them.'

Struggling forwards on the sofa, she levered herself up and padded over to the front door.

Carla heard Jack's voice before she saw him. Craning her head over the back of the sofa, for a moment she wondered if Grace would remember that she wasn't dressed.

'Come on in, she's here.'

Grace stepped away from the door and Carla winced slightly inside. She didn't have anything on under the robe, and really, she wasn't sure she knew Jack Maguire well enough yet to meet him half-naked. Even with their afternoon of bonding over Julia Hardiman's body.

As Grace showed him in and he came around the end of the sofa, seeing she was in a robe, he was as embarrassed as she was, the blush hitting his face hard.

'Oh, God, I'm sorry, I should have called. The reception can be really bad down here, though, so I thought it would be better to drop in.'

'You're fine, sit down. I'll just nip up and put some clothes on. Grace will get you a glass of wine. Are you allowed one?'

Jack let out a breath. 'Probably not, but a small one would be very welcome. I've only just left Coyne House.'

Slipping off his linen jacket and throwing it over the back of the easy chair, Jack sat down and rubbed his hand across his face. 'Took a bit longer than I thought. The family liaison

114

officer from Kilkeel came with me. We needed to get their statements, but I left the doctor with Melissa in the end. She needed to be sedated. It's been one bloody laugh after another today.'

'Give me five to put some clothes on.' Carla stood up, putting the file she'd been reading onto the pile. 'I need to talk to you about these cases.'

Chapter 18

AS DANIELLE TURNED in through the gates of Coyne House, the trees on the avenue brooding in the dusk, she could see blue lights flashing ahead of her. Slowing for a second, she took a moment to breathe, focusing on inhaling and exhaling, counting away the panic she could feel building inside her. It was like a pressure cooker, all the emotion and worry of the past swirling inside with the horrific news about Julia, like some giant chemical reaction.

A chemical reaction that was making her feel physically sick.

Thank God she hadn't started on the wine when she'd got home from work. Once she'd sat down on the couch with her tea, she hadn't had the energy to move anywhere. Then the guards had called to the door: Donna Sullivan and a female Garda she didn't know. She'd thought it was Ruairi and he'd forgotten his key. Hauling herself up, the muscles in her bum and legs aching as if she'd done a workout, she'd nearly died when she'd opened the door, her mind immediately leaping to Ben.

Putting the Pathfinder into *Park*, Danielle closed her eyes, focusing on her breathing. The minute the two of them had left, she'd picked up her phone to see a string of missed calls from Sean.

What a night to leave it on silent.

She'd called him then, but he'd been barely able to speak on the phone, had said there was a roadblock on the avenue, but to tell them who she was and they'd let her through. Melissa was hysterical – he needed her to come as quickly as she could.

There was still no sign of Ruairi, so she'd texted him to say she was going over to Melissa's and to follow her if he got in before she got back.

Where the hell was he? He must have heard by now. Why hadn't he at least texted?

Opening her eyes, Danielle looked at the lights dancing ahead of her under the trees. It was even darker there, thank God. The guards had said Jules had been found near the avenue; she could see the shapes of vehicles pulled over, but not much more. If she kept her eyes dead ahead, she hoped that was all she'd see.

This all felt so unreal.

Since Melissa and Jules's parents had died, they'd been Melissa's family – Danielle and Ruairi and Ben. Mel couldn't stand Sean's mother and her gossipy country ways, saw her as little as possible.

Pushing her 4 × 4 into *Drive*, Danielle moved off slowly down the avenue. As she got closer to the concentration of vehicles, in her peripheral vision she became aware of arc lights in the trees, caught flashes of people in white suits up ahead. She pulled past two patrol cars and then realised there was a guard in a hi-vis vest, flagging her down. Stopping beside him, she buzzed down the window, about to explain, but the young lad who had stopped her was from Coyne's Cross – Matt, who coached the under-16's; she couldn't remember his surname.

Taking one look at Danielle, he gave her a respectful nod and waved her through, his face grim.

Continuing down the avenue, with sheep peacefully grazing in the field on her left, their eyes eerily illuminated by her headlights, Danielle could see rabbits bobbing about on the neatly trimmed grass verge at the side of the lane. It all looked so perfect, so well kept. As if nothing could possibly go wrong here.

Ahead of her, a second set of eagle-topped pillars marked the entrance to the house, ornate wrought-iron gates standing wide open.

She could see that the circular driveway was already filled with vehicles as she pulled in. Sean's BMW was parked at the bottom of the sweeping steps as if it had been driven in at speed and abandoned. Behind it, the doctor's car was more tidily parked, a smaller Garda car between them. Beyond them, Melissa's X2. Jules had joked about Ruairi and Sean both buying his and hers matching cars.

Pulling in on the opposite side of the fountain that acted as a roundabout in the middle of the drive, Danielle climbed out. She could already feel tears hot on her cheeks, hastily brushed them away. She needed to stay together for Melissa; this was so much worse for her.

Glancing quickly at her phone to see if Ruairi had texted, she could see it was already past nine o'clock. *Why hadn't he called?* She couldn't tell him this over the phone, needed to see him to break the news, if he hadn't already heard. *How could he not know?* This was Coyne's Cross – everyone knew everything. Almost.

Her runners crunching on the gravel, Danielle walked slowly towards the huge double front door. Her foot was on the bottom step when one side of the carved door opened and the doctor emerged, a golf jumper barely concealing his paunch, his jowly face florid. Seeing Danielle, he spoke quickly to whoever was behind him and came to meet her on the step.

'Dreadful thing to happen. I'm glad you're here, she needs someone until she falls asleep.' He kept his voice low. 'Your husband was here earlier. It's good for her to have friends and family around her. She's much calmer now, but you all need to keep an eye on her. I've left a prescription with Sean.'

Not meeting her eye, he patted her on the arm and headed for his car.

Ruairi had been here? Why hadn't he told her?

Watching the doctor go, Danielle turned to the door and saw Sean waiting for her. He opened it wider to let her into the grand hall, the huge chandelier sending prisms of light over the oak boards and dark wood panelling. His face strained, he hugged her.

'Thanks for coming. She's in the drawing room, come inside.'

Following him through another set of double doors, Danielle could see someone had lit the fire. Despite the heat outside, the room felt chill. Sitting on the end of a sofa, Melissa was huddled next to it. She'd pulled on one of Sean's jumpers over her T-shirt and jeans and had a throw wrapped around her shoulders, its soft teal and orange squares adding a splash of colour to the otherwise muted palette of the room. Danielle had always loved its proportions and plasterwork, the huge curved windows that looked over the lawns to one side and over the drive at the front of the house. But she wasn't looking at the room now.

Melissa's hands were clasped between her knees as if she was trying to stop them from shaking. Opposite her, on a matching sofa, a guard Danielle didn't recognise was sitting with a notebook open on her knee.

Hurrying over to sit down beside her, Danielle put her arms around Melissa, who turned into her embrace, burying her head in her shoulder. Danielle glanced quickly at Sean; he'd come in behind her, his hands in the pockets of his trousers as if he didn't really know where to put them.

He introduced Danielle, his voice strained. 'This is Danielle Brennan, Mel and Jules's cousin. She runs the Coffee Dock down at the Adventure Centre. She's Ruairi's wife.'

'Ruth Stanley. I'm from Kilkeel. I'm the family liaison officer. It's time I went, I think.'

Danielle flicked her a smile. 'Was Ruairi here? I've been trying to get hold of him.'

The guard nodded. 'He left about forty minutes ago.' Danielle could feel the guard looking at her. 'Melissa was just saying she felt Julia has been a bit secretive the last few months, that she hasn't dropped up to the house as much as she used to. She was wondering if she'd met someone on Tinder. Had she mentioned anything to you?'

Conscious of Melissa's head on her shoulder, Danielle shook her own head marginally. 'I've hardly seen her much either. I mean, around the town and stuff, but she hasn't called into the cafe for ages.'

'Anything you can tell us about her movements would be really useful. Will you call me if you think of anything?' Ruth stood up and handed Danielle her card. 'My mobile's on that. I'll be back in the morning, but call me any time.'

Danielle smiled an acknowledgement. Beside her, she could feel Melissa's shoulders starting to shake as she tried to hold in her sobs.

Ruth hovered for a movement, then bent to pick up her hat from sofa. 'I'll leave you to it.'

Sean showed her out and Danielle caught the word *counsellor* as they walked into the hall. Melissa pulled away from her, her face streaked with tears, her voice little more than a whisper.

'My God, Dani, what am I going to do? It's like the worst nightmare.'

Danielle pulled her into a hug. 'They'll catch whoever it was, there are guards everywhere. You just rest, you'll be utterly drained. Have you taken what the doctor gave you?'

Melissa's face creased. 'He gave me something to help me sleep. But I don't want to sleep. I just want Jules back.'

Chapter 19

SKIPPING UP THE wooden spiral staircase, Carla threw the bathrobe onto the bed and got dressed as quickly as she could. Grace had opened all the windows upstairs, but the huge bedroom and its en suite were still stuffy and hot under the thatch. Carla had no idea how she was going to sleep.

Rifling through her bag, she rooted out clean underwear and a sports bra, pulling them on, shaking out a T-shirt and the lightweight grey marl joggers she'd brought with her. Grace had unpacked as soon as they'd arrived, hanging her beautiful clothes on hangers, but Carla was so used to climbing trips where her gear was thrown into the corner of a hostel or tent, or caving, where changing fast from freezing, wet clothes didn't allow for a battle with a coat hanger, that she rarely unpacked when she travelled. As a rule, she never bought clothes that needed ironing either, so it wasn't a problem.

Downstairs, Jack was sitting in the easy chair, chatting to Grace as she pottered around the kitchen area. Hearing the creak of the stairs as Carla trotted down them, Grace handed her a wooden board heavy with cheese and cold meats.

'Here, take this. I'll bring plates and the bread over.' Grace turned to Jack. 'I'm guessing you haven't eaten?'

Jack shook his head, his eyes lighting up as he saw what was in Carla's hand. He lifted the bulky files from the table in front of him onto the floor.

'Thank you. You have no idea how much I need this.'

Coming to join them, Grace slipped knives and plates onto the table and went to the wine cooler to open another bottle of white. Carla was stuffed after dinner earlier, but Jack looked exhausted and famished in equal measures, his cheeks hollow in the light from the standard lamp. It was dusky outside, the sound of evening birdsong coming in through the open doors to the deck, but the tiny windows in the living area made the inside dark – they'd had to put on lamps when they'd come in to read the files.

Jack cut a chunk of the oozing Brie and pasted it onto the bread Carla had given him. 'This looks delicious.'

Grace smiled her agreement as she rejoined them, the chilled bottle in her hand. 'Jack was telling me he did law before he joined the guards.'

Carla felt her eyebrows shoot up. Studying law was intense and tough. And it paid a damn sight better than An Garda Síochaná. How had Grace managed to find that out in the two minutes she'd been upstairs?

'I hope Grace didn't give you the third degree?'

Jack smiled as Grace tried to look put out.

'I'm just interested in people.' She said it deliberately innocently, throwing Carla a teasing grin.

'You mentioned your brother. You never mentioned you'd studied law, too.'

Jack shrugged. 'I only did it to please my parents. I always wanted to join the job. It was a means to an end. It's useful, to be honest. Helps when we need to put a case together. I'm always focused on the evidence and how it stacks up.'

'How did you get on with Melissa? How is she?'

Jack grimaced and picked up his glass. It had ice in it, bubbles rising to the surface. Grace made a mean spritzer.

'Distraught. Utterly. I've actually never seen anyone take a death that badly before.'

'They *are* sisters.'

Jack nodded in response to Grace's point. 'And Irish twins. There's only ten months between them. Maybe that's why they look so alike – sorry, looked.' He sighed. 'We needed to find out when she'd last heard from Julia, but by the time her husband Sean got home, she was really worked up. He was down the country somewhere, meeting a client. Didn't get back until about seven. He ended up calling her GP. What time is it now?'

'It's only nine o'clock.' Grace picked up her phone to check.

'Feels like about midnight.' Carla could see from Jack's face that he agreed with her.

'I took a statement from Sean and tried to talk to Melissa again, but I wasn't getting anywhere so I left them to it. The family liaison said she'd stay a bit longer. We'll go back tomorrow when the dust has settled. It's a priority to work out where everyone was this afternoon.'

Carla bent forwards to smear some cheese onto the bread. It looked too good not to try. 'Did you tell Melissa what had happened?' She looked up at him as she spoke and Jack grimaced.

'Not all the details. I had to give her the basic facts.'

Grace sighed. 'Melissa said all her cottages were full this weekend – the ones in the main complex. Have you got a lot of people to interview?'

'Sure have. The town's flooded with holidaymakers. She's got eight cottages altogether, with varying levels of occupancy.'

'You think it could be someone from out of town?'

'It seems to be the most likely possibility at this stage. I just keep wondering – why now? What's happened that would make Julia a target on a bank holiday weekend? You saw how many people there were down at the Coffee Dock this morning. Every bed and breakfast is booked out. It's almost like the killer wants someone to see him, so he can get caught.'

Carla shrugged. 'Maybe it's the heat?'

Grace reached for her wine. 'That's not actually as mad as it sounds.' She turned to Jack. 'Carla said Julia was single. Could she have been using a dating app? Maybe someone came to see her specifically, and it wasn't a random thing. Almost everyone has the bank holiday off unless they work in the services or retail.'

'Melissa thought she could have been on Tinder. We'll check with them and get her phone records, see who she's been talking to and texting. She'd booked the weekend off – well, Saturday and Sunday, which is pretty unusual, given how busy it is over the bank holiday weekend, but her bar manager said she hadn't been sleeping well and needed a break. She rarely got to take two days off together, apparently, and that takes its toll. They are expecting to be hammered on Monday, too.'

Carla picked up her glass. 'Did you find her phone? I heard someone at the station say it wasn't with her body or in her house.'

Jack shook his head. 'It's missing. We've triangulated its location from when it was last switched on. It looks like it's nearby, but it's not in her car either. Melissa had her Apple ID and password – they bought their phones together and got them set up in the shop, so she wrote it in her diary, which is very handy. One of our tech guys might be able to get better data. It's possible she may have dropped it when she was attacked and it's in the undergrowth somewhere.'

Grace took a sip of her wine. 'Given what Carla's told me about the location of the body, I feel this had to be someone who knows their way around here, rather than someone from out of town she's met recently. Let's face it, very few murders are random acts of violence committed by strangers. That doesn't mean it's someone living here, but perhaps someone who was brought up here and has come back for the weekend, maybe. With those cottages full, I'd guess the avenue into the estate would be a busy place. It's a risky location when there are acres of woods he could have picked.' Grace twirled the stem of her glass. 'But you're right. I'm wondering if the bank holiday has any significance.'

'Did Carla tell you about the mutilation? I left that bit out when I was talking to Melissa. I think it's important we keep the key details of this to ourselves.'

Grace nodded. 'That's what makes the whole scene feel more deliberate. I mean, her shoes were laid just out of reach – was that to suggest that she couldn't run away, or are they some sort of fetish? I've so many questions. Carla said it didn't look like she was sexually assaulted.'

'I don't think we're going to know what the extent of Julia's injuries are until we have the pathologist's report.' He paused. 'Which I hope will be tomorrow.'

Chapter 20

'HERE YOU GO, babes.'

Carla surfaced groggily from sleep and slowly turned over to find Grace slipping a cup of tea onto her bedside table.

'What time is it?'

'Eight thirty. How's the head?'

Carla pulled her hair out of her face, the dark and white strands intertwined where they'd tangled in her sleep. Jack had left after he'd brought them up to date the night before, anxious to check in at the incident room. But they'd managed to polish off another bottle of wine between them.

'How much did we drink?'

'Don't ask. There was plenty of food, though. It's not like you were out partying on an empty stomach.'

'Tell my head that.' Carla pulled her hair back and blinked in the sunlight streaming into the room.

'I've got paracetamol. Come on, have your tea. You just need loads of liquids today. I'd say you got dehydrated after being out all day yesterday. That's making you feel worse.'

Carla pushed herself up in the bed and reached for her tea. 'That and finding a body covered in bloody flies. I've always hated flies.'

Grace pulled back the duvet and climbed in beside her. At the foot of the bed, on the opposite wall, the roof sloped right down to a window that looked directly out over the water. Carla pulled the pillow up behind her so she could see out properly.

'My God, this is bliss. We need to come here again when there are no bodies.'

'*That* is a *very* good idea.' Grace smirked at her and reached for her coffee.

'You lech. You just fancy DS Jack Maguire.'

Grace grinned into her tea. 'He's a very intelligent man. *And* he has a gun.'

Carla gave her a side eye. 'I'd imagine he's going to be pretty busy today.'

'I know, I thought that. Do you fancy a wander to the round tower later? Apparently you can see across to Monastery Island from the top of the lough. It's supposed to be a two-hour walk and there's a little coffee truck thing beside the tower. Then two hours back. And it's all flat. I don't do hills.'

Carla grinned. 'How do you know all that?'

'Guide book on the coffee table. I took a look at it while

I was waiting for the kettle. The ruin of St Columcille's Church is on the island. It's supposed to be haunted. Which honestly doesn't surprise me, given that the rapids there are known as Dead Man's Gully. There's a whole network of caves under the island as well, apparently.' Carla sipped her tea as Grace continued. 'The guide book's got loads of info in it about what you can do round here. Melissa Hardiman has thought of everything.'

'Christ, I wonder how she is this morning. What a nightmare.'

Grace sipped her tea. 'Didn't Jack say the woman who runs the Coffee Dock is her cousin? Given the circumstances, she might not be open today. We'd better take water from here just in case.'

Carla replaced her tea on the bedside table and snuggled in beside her. 'You're full of heart.'

Two hours later, Grace pulled in to one of the few empty spaces left in the car park beside the Coffee Dock. It was as busy as it had been the previous day, the deck overlooking the lough, packed.

'She *is* open.' Carla pulled a face, her eyes wide with exaggerated surprise. She'd been fully sure Danielle would have been closed today.

'Don't be so judgemental. Perhaps she's got one of the girls opening up for her. It is a bank holiday Sunday, remember.

After being closed for so long during the pandemic, she probably needs to stay open and take every penny she can. Come on, let's have a coffee before we get going. That cheesecake they had yesterday was to die for.'

Before Carla could comment, a patrol car pulled into the car park and stopped beside the broad steps leading to the cafe's outside area. The front passenger door swung open and Jack got out. The detective who had taken Carla's statement the previous day got out of the rear door and looked around her as she closed it. The car slid off to double-park behind a Range Rover, the driver pulling out the radio to report his location.

Carla glanced across at Grace. 'Let's give them a head start. Put the radio on there, we'll see what the news is saying.'

'Good plan. They need some space without you arriving on top of them, Dr Steele, Queen of Skulls.'

Carla threw her a withering look. 'Hopefully Jack can give us an update. I really want to know what's in that pathologist's report. I know it's not technically our case, but ...'

Grace raised her eyebrows. 'You can't get much more involved than finding the body, babes, and honestly, I'm sure Jack will appreciate the help.'

Chapter 21

BEHIND THE COUNTER in the Coffee Dock, Danielle wiped her palms down her jeans and deliberately tucked her bobbed curls behind her ears. Outside, she could see Niamh and Becky were busy clearing the tables and taking orders.

She didn't really know what the hell she was doing here today. There was a lull now, but everyone who had come inside seemed to look at her funny. Although that could have been in her head. The locals seemed to be steering clear of the place this morning.

Except Sergeant Twomey, who had come in for his morning scones as usual, as if it was a completely normal day, as if he didn't have anything else to be doing. She knew people had to take breaks, but with a murder investigation blowing up, she'd sort of expected him to be too busy to drive over here. He must have had his salary in scones from the Coffee Dock over the years. But then he was well known for it in the town. She'd dropped them into a paper bag without speaking.

Danielle closed her eyes for a second, trying to centre herself. Her thoughts were flying this morning, as if she'd had too much coffee or something.

Too much had happened.

Even Niamh and Becky had hardly said a word to her until first break, hadn't known where to look. When they'd caught up with the orders and had a few minutes' quiet, she'd taken them into the rear corridor beside the servery and assured them everything was fine. They'd heard about Jules, of course – not that she had any more details than they did – but she'd told them what she knew so at least they had the right information. Then Jack Maguire had phoned, saying he needed a chat and would she prefer to meet him at home.

Holy God.

Last night, when she'd got home, she'd found Ruairi passed out on the sofa, a bottle of whiskey beside him, and this morning he had had the hangover from hell. He'd barely spoken to her except to insist he dropped her to work in case the café was crawling with press. She hadn't had the energy to argue. You could cut the tension with a knife.

That was one of the reasons she'd decided to come in. Jules was *her* cousin, for Christ's sake.

One thing she was sure of was that she couldn't meet Jack at the house and risk a row when Ruairi found out. He hated strangers snooping about the place, and the Gardaí needing to talk to her would somehow end up being her fault.

Glancing at the till readout, Danielle checked the time. Jack would be here shortly, and she was still trying to decide if she should talk to him here in the cafe, or out in the staff kitchen. But it was stuffy and airless out the back, even with all the windows open, and she didn't think she could be shut up in the tiny room with him and one of his colleagues listening to what had happened. The very thought of it made her feel claustrophobic and want to scream. Danielle leaned on the chill steel of the counter and took a deep breath, trying to slow her heart.

Right now the inside tables were almost empty; everyone was out on the deck enjoying the weather. And she couldn't see anyone local out there yet – so nobody outside would know she was Jules's cousin, or what Jack had come to talk about. Or even, with a bit of luck, that Jack was in the guards.

Panic fluttered in her chest as she took another breath.

What the hell had happened? Who had done this?

A movement outside made her look up, and she spotted Jack Maguire walking across in front of the windows, followed by Donna Sullivan wearing a navy linen trouser suit, the collar of her pink linen shirt standing up. Neither of them looked in the slightest bit like tourists.

So much for no one guessing what they would be talking about.

* * *

'Are you sure you don't mind chatting out here? It feels a bit public?'

Jack kept his voice low as he spoke, glancing up at Becky with a grateful smile as she slipped a cappuccino in front of him. Donna was sitting beside him, and Danielle could feel her looking across the table at her.

'No, really, it's fine.' Danielle sighed, feeling she had to explain. 'I needed to come in to sort the girls out, and I thought I'd go mad at home.'

'You don't have a space out back that's more private?' Donna spoke this time, her dark eyebrows meeting in a frown. Danielle shook her head.

'The staff room is so tiny we'd barely fit. This is fine. Do you know … anything … yet?'

Jack shook his head. 'Early days. We need to find out where everyone was between when Julia spoke to Melissa on the phone on Friday morning and when we found her yesterday afternoon. We're talking to as many people as we can this morning.' He took a sip of his coffee.

'They always say on the TV, the first forty-eight hours are crucial?'

Danielle left the question hanging there.

'They are, and that's why we've got a big team assembled, detectives from Kilkeel as well as our own people, and the incident room is set up here. This is a small town, we'll find him.'

'You think it was a him?' Danielle hesitated. 'I mean, you're sure? Was there …?' She trailed off but she could see from Jack's face that he knew exactly what she meant.

'She wasn't sexually assaulted, no, but we've reason to believe whoever did this needed significant personal strength – that would suggest a man.'

He pulled a notebook out of the top pocket of his shirt. Danielle realised Donna had already taken hers out of her handbag.

'Can I ask you some questions now?'

'Of course, fire away. Whatever you need to know.'

'Where were you on Friday?'

Danielle smiled weakly. 'Here, all day and yesterday until about six thirty, when we finished clearing up. Sorry, six thirty both days. I told Donna and her colleague when they called over last night.'

Jack smiled encouragingly. 'Sorry if we're doubling up. Sometimes it takes a while for people to remember what they were doing. And in the evening on Friday?'

'Home. I was knackered, to be honest. This heat.'

'And Ruairi?'

'At the Adventure Centre all day and all evening – both days, too. It's really busy and he lost a lot of time on his paperwork last week when they found that skull. My God, it's unbelievable.' Danielle felt a tear roll down her cheek. She brushed it away. 'I'm sorry.'

'Don't be. If you need to stop, just say and we can find somewhere more private.'

'I'm fine, really. Well, as fine as I can be.'

His face was understanding. 'Tell me about the last time you saw Julia.'

Danielle bit her lip. 'Last week, I think. I was off on Wednesday – I went into town to do the supermarket shop. I had to go to the post office, too. I saw her across the street. Waved. She was going into the hotel.' Danielle shrugged. 'The last time I spoke to her was probably the week before. I'm not sure.'

Beside Jack, Donna leaned forwards. 'And do you know anything about who she might have been dating? If there was anyone serious in her life?'

Danielle sighed ruefully. 'She's not really had any long-term relationships, a couple that were for a few years, but nothing that looked like it had potential. She never really wanted to settle down and have kids. She loved her job and she had her own place. The hotel trade is tough, long hours. But she loved it.'

Danielle could feel Jack looking at her as he spoke. 'So no one recent?'

She shook her head. 'She'd had a few dates, but nothing serious. I was in the bar about a month ago, waiting for Ruairi. He'd got caught up at work, and she came and joined me for a chat. She seemed to be so happy. We were looking at her Tinder, laughing at these God-awful men who had photoshopped their profile pictures. One of them kept texting her, awful stuff, but she thought it was hilarious. She blocked him, but she said she was going to put up all his texts on her Facebook page.'

'Do you know his name?' Donna again.

Danielle shook her head. 'There must be some way to see who she was talking to on Tinder? To get into her account. They can tell you?'

Jack smiled reassuringly. 'We'll find out. Did she mention anything out of the ordinary happening recently? Maybe someone hanging about the bar?'

'No.' Danielle shook her head. 'I've barely seen her in the last six months, to be honest. I did wonder if she was dating someone from out of town. I've no idea, Melissa will know, though.'

Chapter 22

AS THEY SWITCHED on the radio news, Grace had spotted a car reversing out of a space overlooking the lough, and slipped into it. It was a perfect spot for people-watching, which seemed to be exactly what the guard in the patrol car was doing – keeping an eye on everyone. When Carla needed some thinking space, she often sat on a bench overlooking the beach at home, listening to the gulls and the sound of the water, watching people jog past, or walk their dogs.

From where they were sitting, on this side of the Coffee Dock, they could see a narrow strip of beach busy with people waiting to take out the colourful kayaks that were stacked up on racks. Small children in life jackets were running between the legs of teens and adults, even smaller children were parked beside buckets and spades. It was the perfect bank holiday picture.

When Carla and Grace finally walked into the cafe, they could see Jack and Donna sitting down with Danielle at the far end – at the same table where they'd met Jack the previous day. As if he knew they were there, he turned and glanced up as they entered, catching Carla's eye. He must have caught their reflection in the cooler on the opposite wall. Carla raised her eyebrows in acknowledgement.

'Come on, let's sit over here. We can see the water and ...' Grace looked at Carla. 'I was about to say there won't be any bugs inside.'

Carla pulled a face and followed her to a table in the corner, swinging her backpack onto the floor beside her chair. Unlike yesterday, it was quiet inside. The only other occupants were a young couple with two small children, all speaking in rapid French. They probably hadn't tuned in to the Irish news and were oblivious to the heavy air of expectation that seemed to hang in the corners of the cafe. Both the waitresses were outside, their order notepads in their hands, and as Carla watched them, she could see they were continually turning to look inside, checking to see what was going on. The sound of laughter and children playing rose from the beach, merging with the gentle burble of conversation coming from the deck area, the sounds washing in like the tide through the open double doors. As if life was completely normal. It was for some.

Grace picked up the tall, narrow menu, a pen-and-ink illustration of the lough and the round tower overlooking the island on the front, but Carla could see that she was only half concentrating on it. Her eyes flicked discreetly over to Jack's table, and Danielle's pale, tear-stained face. 'Everyone seems to be giving her a bit of space. That's nice.'

Carla grimaced. 'Not so sure about that. It's like the valley of the squinting windows out there. They're only hanging to find out what's happening inside.'

Grace lowered the menu and looked out of the huge picture window beside them. 'You're right.' She shook her head. 'Let's focus on fuelling up for this hike. I'm sure Jack'll be over when he gets a minute.'

'It's not exactly a hike, G.' Carla was only half concentrating as she spoke. She picked up a second menu sticking out of a wooden box containing napkins and cutlery, but was focusing entirely on trying to hear what was being said on the other side of the cafe.

She jumped as the waitress appeared from behind her.

'What can I get you?'

As she spoke, Carla heard the scraping of chair legs on the wooden floor. Danielle was standing up, leaning one hand on the table as she listened to Jack and his colleague, at the same time anxiously tucking her curly strawberry blond hair behind her ear. Carla handed Grace the menu.

'You order for me, sweetie. I can't decide.'

She could see Grace understood that she was trying to listen in. Carla didn't even register what Grace said to the waitress, but it was clear enough for the girl to nod and move off towards the counter as Jack stood up and followed Donna towards the main door. As he got level with their table, he said something to her and peeled off in their direction. Donna glanced over and, recognising Carla, nodded to her. Then, hooking her handbag over her shoulder, she headed out into the sunshine in the direction of the car park.

'Morning. How you doing?' Jack pulled out the chair beside Carla and sat down with a sigh.

From across the table, Grace looked at him. 'Better than you, by the looks of things. Did you get any sleep?'

'A few hours. I was in at six.' He lowered his voice, gesturing to the packed deck. 'Apparently I wasn't the only one out early. Word has spread already.'

Quickly glancing outside, Carla nodded and turned to look back into the room, checking where the waitress was. Busy at the coffee machine, the young girl kept turning around to speak to Danielle, who was leaning on the end of the counter as if all the air had been sucked out of her. Her shoulders hunched, she was staring at a spot on the floor, barely registering what the girl was saying. As Carla sat back, Jack glanced in the direction she'd been looking.

'She's still in shock. But she wanted to meet us here.' Turning his head away from the window, he almost whispered. Carla could see he thought Danielle should have stayed at home today. She tended to agree with him.

Grace leaned forwards, her voice just as low. 'People find comfort in routine. I know it might not be what you'd do, but in coming into work, she's displacing the emotion. In her mind, if everything is still standing and nothing has changed, then perhaps the awful thing didn't really happen.' Jack raised his eyebrows as if he was trying hard to believe her as she continued. 'Different people deal with trauma in different ways.'

Jack put his elbow on the table and pinched the bridge of his nose. 'Well, that's true.'

Carla gave him a nudge. 'Anything from the pathologist?'

'In a nutshell?' He glanced behind him to see where the waitresses had gone, and then outside again, as if someone might be listening. 'There's a puncture mark on her left shoulder – through her T-shirt, which suggests she may have been drugged. We won't have toxicology for a while, though. And …'

Grace raised her finger discreetly to hush him as the waitress headed across from the counter with their coffees and cake: cheesecake for Grace, a slice of chocolate fudge for Carla, served on heavy, hand-thrown earthenware plates.

'Thanks so much.' Grace smiled up at the waitress. 'Not so busy inside today?'

The young girl looked uncomfortable. 'Er … no.'

Grace smiled at her reassuringly. 'We'll shout if we need anything. We're all good here.'

The girl nodded gratefully and returned to the counter to pick up her cloth and notebook before heading outside again.

Carla looked at Grace reproachfully. 'Are you trying to get me fat?'

Smirking at her, Grace picked up her fork and speared the cheesecake. 'You're too skinny, I keep telling you. You'd only last twenty minutes in a zombie apocalypse.'

Jack's face broke into a grin and he shook his head as he looked across at Grace. 'That's a real possibility, Dr Franciosi?'

She answered with her mouth full. 'You never know what's around the corner, DS Maguire. Look at you yesterday.'

He sighed loudly. 'True.'

'So?' Carla looked at him expectantly, rolling her fork in the air to indicate she wanted to hear more.

'You sure you want this while you're eating?'

'You're fine, I work with dead people. Skulls are my thing, remember.'

Jack took in a slow breath. 'He tried to remove her heart.'

Carla's fork froze in mid-air. 'He what?'

'The damage to her chest was caused by a large, smooth steel blade. He broke her sternum and cut away a substantial part of her heart. Maybe he thought he'd got it all, but anyway, he didn't quite.'

Carla continued to stare at him. She didn't know why she was so surprised. She'd seen the blood. And the flies. But she hadn't expected that.

'And then he strung her up in the tree?'

'It's looking that way. The leaf matter in her hair and the blood on the ground indicate she was lying underneath the tree when most of the cutting was done. Then he lifted her to slip the noose over her head.'

Across the table, Grace chewed thoughtfully. 'She bled out?'

'Yep. The pathologist thinks the shock of open-heart surgery didn't exactly help.'

Grace took another forkful of cheesecake, then held it poised between her plate and her mouth, looking at him as if a lightbulb had lit in her head. 'Do you think he was purging her? Cutting her heart to remove tainted blood?'

Jack looked at Grace in surprise. 'I have no earthly idea. I'm still struggling with the flies. What makes you think that?'

Grace put the fork in her mouth, chewing as she thought. 'There's something about the method that's almost ritualistic. He could have just cut her throat and been done with it. He must have been covered in blood, especially if he lifted her afterwards. I don't think it's possible to do that and *not* get totally saturated.'

Carla screwed up her nose, thinking. 'Do you think he was wearing protective clothing – an overall of some sort?'

'Given that nobody's come forward to say they saw a guy wandering around looking like an extra from a horror movie, it seems likely.' Jack grimaced. 'So far forensics have found a size twelve footprint from a Dunlop boot, but they aren't completely sure if it's a hiking boot or a workman's boot. But that would suggest a man who is five foot nine to six foot two, and I'd be erring towards the taller end of the range. The lack of fibres and any other trace evidence would suggest a lot of planning went into this.' Jack looked her ruefully. 'I'm sorry, I have to go, but I think we need to talk properly. Can you both come into the incident room? Would you mind looking at the scene shots, Grace?'

Carla glanced over at Grace. 'We *were* going for a walk, but we can come over as soon as we've finished here. I need to talk to you about those cold cases, too.'

Grace nodded. 'I'd like to get the full picture. Why don't we go back to the cottage and get the files and meet you at the station?'

'Text me when you're ready, I'll make sure I'm there.'

Chapter 23

RUAIRI BRENNAN DUCKED into the rear of his 4 × 4 and slotted the metal plates into the base of the boot, flipping the carpet over them. Behind him, the water lapped and sucked under the old wooden landing stage, the boards ravaged by the weather, railings pitted. Reaching for his life jacket and the diesel can lying at his feet on the dirt road, he returned them to the boot, leaning in to pull his wetsuit and heavy weather jackets into place.

As he pushed the door closed, he started at a voice behind him.

'Afternoon. Another hot one.'

Ruairi turned around to find Terry Walsh, the Coyne estate maintenance man, standing at the bend in the overgrown lane, a toolbox in his hand. His wrinkled skin tanned, he was wearing a tatty pair of trousers that might have once been pink and a greying white polo shirt. To Ruairi, they looked a lot like Sean's old clothes. Sean always wore pink sailing trousers with his blazer whenever he went to the yacht club on the other side of the bay.

Ruairi leaned on the spare wheel mounted on the rear door and forced himself to relax. *How long had Walsh been there?*

'It is ...' Ruairi sighed deeply, slipping one hand casually into the front pocket of his jeans. 'I needed some space. A bit of air.' He indicated the water with his head. 'I was just looking for my binoculars – thought I saw a shag.'

'Cormorant. Bigger lads. There's a few of them now. Never seen more than three together, but they've been breeding here for years. They nest out on the island.' Terry indicated the rocky outcrop with a movement of his grey head.

Far enough away from the shore to need a boat to reach it, the ruins of an ancient church were just visible through the thick undergrowth and trees crowding to the edge of Monastery Island. Separated from land by the constantly churning waters of Dead Man's Gully, the island was a bird sanctuary now, the public prohibited from visiting. A small sandy beach, not visible from here, was the only place to land for the researchers and ornithologists who monitored the avian population.

Ruairi tried to look as if he was interested, and then gazed out across the water. Despite the heat of the sun on his face, he felt chill.

'They train them to fish for them in Japan. They can dive deep.'

'Really?'

One thing Ruairi definitely didn't want to talk about right now was anything diving into the waters of the lough. He stuck his other hand into his jeans and levered himself off the Pathfinder's spare wheel. Walking towards the edge of the landing stage, he glanced casually at the rough-hewn stone steps winding down beside it, and then looked out towards the horizon.

'Nice and quiet here.' Ruairi said it loudly.

'It is. Terrible business, that. Just terrible.'

Behind him, Ruairi heard Terry's toolbox rattle. He turned around. The older man hadn't moved, but had switched the box from one hand to the other.

What should he say?

He couldn't talk about Jules now without breaking down. Ruairi cleared his throat.

'Fixing something?'

'Wanted to check out the railings.' Terry indicated the rickety landing stage. 'Don't need any more tragedies around here.'

Chapter 24

CARLA WATCHED JACK weave through the tables outside the Coffee Dock and jog down the steps to the car park and the waiting patrol car. She could see a ripple pass through the diners outside as they realised who he was, perhaps recognising him from the TV news. His passage left a wake of inclined heads, and, she was sure, speculation.

Carla could understand locals wanting to know what was going on – whether they knew Julia, or had heard details of her killing – but these murder tourists made her feel distinctly uncomfortable.

Turning her attention to the table, she felt Grace's blue eyes on her. She had her hair clipped up in a twist today, was sipping her coffee, holding the mug cupped in two hands. 'What?'

Grace shook her head. 'Just admiring your bone structure.'

Carla threw her a withering look. She knew she spent a lot of time talking about bone structure, about the depths of muscle and the impact lifestyle could have on the faces of the skulls she reconstructed, but right now she could do without Grace winding her up.

'Are you sure you don't mind not going for that walk? That was the whole reason you wanted to come to Coyne's Cross – to see the round tower and the island.'

Grace shook her head and put her coffee down. 'That was before Coyne's Cross became murder central. You know me, I love a good crime scene.' Grace kept her voice low, but Carla still glanced anxiously over to where Danielle was now wiping an empty table, her face trance-like.

'Shush, will you. God, you've no tact.'

Grace arched her eyebrows, but before she could respond, they both became aware that Danielle was walking towards them. Carla opened her eyes wide. This wasn't going to be an easy conversation. Before Danielle was halfway across the room, Carla turned in her seat and, as if she'd just spotted her, smiled and stood up. She kept her voice low as Danielle reached her.

'I'm really so very sorry.'

Thrusting her hands into the front pocket of her apron, Danielle smiled weakly. 'I don't want to disturb you, but do you have a minute?' She swayed slightly as she spoke, grief etched on her face.

'Of course, but let's go into the corner, away from the window, will we?'

Carla glanced at Grace, whose nod that she should go

ahead alone was so fractional that Carla would have missed it if all her senses hadn't been on full alert. Scooping her backpack off the floor and putting it down where she had been sitting, Carla pushed the chair Jack had used firmly in under the table.

Danielle seemed to be somehow frozen in mid-thought, barely registering that Carla was beside her. Taking her arm, Carla guided her to the far end of the cafe, to the table she'd sat at with Jack. Carla pulled out a chair for her and Danielle sat down heavily, facing the door. About to sit down herself, Carla caught the eye of the girl who had served them earlier. She hurried over.

'Can we get a glass of iced water, and maybe a peppermint tea?' She paused. 'Have you eaten, Danielle?' Before she could answer, Carla turned to the girl again. 'And maybe a ciabatta sandwich with some of that lovely ham? Keep it simple?'

The girl nodded and Carla turned back to the polished pine table to sit down properly. 'I know this is an awful shock.'

Danielle looked at her as if she wasn't quite seeing her, eyes red-rimmed, her face startlingly pale even under her make-up and normally healthy outdoor glow. Blinking, she seemed to return from wherever her mind had been.

'Jack said you found her. That you were with him when ...' She faltered. 'He found her ...'

Carla reached across the table and took Danielle's hand. Danielle could only be a few years older than her, and although they had only chatted briefly yesterday, Carla felt a strong connection to her, as if she'd known her for a long time. Perhaps it was shared loss.

'Yes – yes, I was.'

'He said you're with the guards, too. That you're in a specialist unit?'

'That's right. I work for Forensic Science Ireland up at Garda Headquarters in the Phoenix Park.'

Danielle took it in as if she was trying to process the information. She closed her eyes for a moment, then opened them before continuing. 'I just needed to know. To know if I could talk to you. None of this makes any sense, it's like we've all been picked up like dice and shaken, and then flung back onto the ground. I keep asking myself why. Why her? Why like that? Why there?'

Carla leaned forwards so she could speak without being overheard. 'I know – I know how awful it is. I lost my best friend. It was a few years ago now, but the pain doesn't stop or go away, and I remember the first days like it was yesterday.' She stopped speaking for a moment, working on keeping her emotions in check, then continued, trying to keep her tone practical. 'At this stage of any investigation there are lots of questions, but please believe me, we will do our absolute best to get answers. There's a whole team at the station here in Coyne's Cross who are dedicated to this case.'

Danielle seemed to take this in, then looked Carla directly in the eye. 'Will they find him? I mean, it's so random. It could have been any of us.'

'This type of thing is very rare, whatever the tabloid headlines claim, but the guards here will be bringing in experts to help them. They want to know who did this as badly as you do.'

Danielle nodded slowly. She was so obviously in deep shock that Carla wanted to move around to the other side of the table and put her arm around her. At that moment, the waitress arrived beside them with a tray and slipped the tea and a glass with ice and slices of lemon in it onto the table, followed by a delicious-looking sandwich. Danielle seemed barely to notice. Carla smiled her thanks.

'Try and drink. It's very hot outside, you need to keep your strength up and it's very easy to get dehydrated. The tea will help calm you, too.'

Obediently, Danielle picked up the water and drank it down, then turned her attention to the tea. Carla hid her surprise. She'd expected Danielle to be defensive, or prickly at being told what to do. But even strong, capable women appreciated someone doing their thinking for them at times like this.

The mug of tea in one hand, Danielle sighed and closed her eyes for a moment. She rubbed her forehead and pushed a stray curl off her face.

'Thank you. You're right.'

'Do you have anyone who can sit with you, perhaps at home? It might be a bit more private than here?'

Danielle shook her head. 'Ruairi needed to come into the centre. It's so busy this weekend and he's already short-handed. Ben, my son, is with his dad in Dublin. I couldn't stay on my own.'

Carla smiled. 'How old is Ben?'

'Thirteen. He gets fed up down here in the summer when we're working. He really wants to go to school up in Dublin and live with his dad. He loves the water, but he's not in the slightest bit competitive. He and Ruairi don't really speak the same language.' Danielle fought a sad smile.

'Teenagers have lots of ideas about what they'd like, that aren't always practical. I bet he hasn't thought about how much he'd miss you.' Carla hesitated, silently grateful that at least one person in the middle of this family was away from what was happening. 'Have you spoken to Melissa?'

Danielle's face clouded and she picked up the sandwich, taking a bite, chewing slowly. Carla let her take her time as she continued.

'Are you close, as a family?'

Danielle shrugged, finishing her mouthful. 'We were when we were in school. Mel and Jules went to a private school up in Dublin, but they came down here for weekends and every holiday. I always felt like the country cousin a bit.

They seemed to bring a bit of Dublin glamour with them. They always had the latest phones and make-up, and tons of clothes.' She took another bite, as if she was conscious that Carla was expecting her to eat. Swallowing, she continued. 'We hung out all summer. Every summer. They sometimes went skiing at Christmas, but they were usually here for Easter and mid-term breaks.'

'And when they left school, they decided to settle here, instead of Dublin?'

Taking her time answering, Danielle took another bite, as if she was measuring her thoughts with each mouthful. 'Melissa was dating Sean. It was all a bit long-distance when she was in school, but down here they were the perfect couple everyone was talking about. She loved the romance of it, and being the only girl in her year with a real live boyfriend, and he loved the respect that came with dating the daughter of the big house, even if they didn't see each other very often.' She reached for her tea and took another sip, pausing before she continued. 'Then he went up to UCD, and she left school and worked for an events company up in Dublin. When he graduated, they came back here together. I think she kept her maiden name when they got married because of the house,' Danielle sighed. 'Mel and Jules's parents, my aunt and uncle, were killed in an accident in Greece the next summer and Melissa took over running the estate. She was the one who decided to let the cottages, to turn the place into a venue. Jules trained in hotel management, so she helped to start with, but then the job in the Coyne Arms came up. I think she needed some space from Melissa, to be honest. They are sisters, there's less than a year between them, but personality-wise they are very different.'

It felt like a long speech, but it filled in some of the gaps in what Jack had been able to tell her. He'd been a good few years behind them all in school – enough not to have been aware of them when he lived in Coyne's Cross. And then he'd left and his family had only come back for the odd holiday – his mother had far preferred Spain.

Carla had only met Melissa briefly, but she'd got the distinct impression that she enjoyed the status that living in the big house gave her, which concurred with everything she was hearing

Danielle put her sandwich down. 'I just keep thinking how terrified Jules must have been.'

Chapter 25

GRACE PULLED INTO the narrow lane at the rear of the Garda station and stopped at the barrier to press the intercom. Whoever was on the gate had spotted her arriving and buzzed her straight through. She eased into a space that must have just been vacated, directly under the communication tower. On the opposite side of the concrete yard, the patrol cars and personal vehicles belonging to those on duty were double-parked and squeezed in close together.

'Do you think it'll be OK here?' Grace looked anxiously in her rear-view mirror as she turned off the engine.

Carla looked across at her, one eyebrow raised. 'It's a Garda station.'

'Precisely my point. They might care about their personal cars, but have you seen how some of them drive?'

'It'll be fine.' Carla opened her door carefully, slithering out beside the steel leg of the communication tower, careful to avoid touching the hot metal as the afternoon sun hit her full force. She'd changed out of her shorts into a loose-fitting black sundress when they dropped in to the cottage to collect the files, but the sun was still intense. The stone in the yard seemed to have absorbed it, the heat reflecting off the walls and concrete. It was like an oven. And Carla didn't imagine inside would be much better. Air conditioning wasn't something that was needed in Ireland as a general rule, but perhaps they'd have ceiling fans. She sure hoped so.

'Come on, let's get inside before we melt.'

As she spoke, Jack appeared at the blue door she'd gone in through the previous day. Holding it open, he waited for them to join him.

Grace pipped the central locking, breathing in as she squeezed down between the cars. Carla smothered a smile. She wasn't about to comment on Grace's cheesecake consumption and risk her sulking for the rest of the day. Fortunately, Grace misunderstood her smirk.

'What? Don't look at me like that. You don't think I'm leaving the car unlocked, do you? You just said this is a Garda station – there are criminals?' She inclined the end of the sentence as if Carla was being ridiculous.

Reaching the rear of the sleek silver Mercedes, Grace clicked open the boot and picked up an armful of files. Pushing her sunglasses onto the top of her head to hold back her hair, Carla bent over to take the rest.

Jack waited for them at the door as they crossed the yard.

'Ladies, welcome. Come straight on upstairs. I'm only just in myself. The incident room is on the first floor.'

He stood aside to let them into the narrow passage, dark and – thankfully – cool, and taking Grace's pile of files in his arms, led the way through to the hallway behind the public office.

Yesterday Donna had taken her statement in one of the small white-painted interview rooms beside the custody suite, but Carla hadn't really been paying attention to the decor. The floor here was tiled with black and white marble, a sweeping mahogany stair rail curving around into the hallway. This place must have been beautiful before it became state property.

Jack's foot was hardly on the bottom stair when Seamus Twomey appeared from the front office. He opened his mouth to speak, but Jack cut him off.

'Afternoon, Seamus. You've met Dr Steele – this is Dr Franciosi. I'm just taking them up to the incident room.'

Before the sergeant could answer, Jack headed up the stairs, his feet ringing on the wooden treads.

Carla smiled and hurried up behind Jack, willing Grace to follow her.

'Excuse us, under pressure for time.' Grace managed to make it sound apologetic and conspiratorial at the same time. She'd obviously read Seamus Twomey precisely. Carla had no doubt that Twomey's inquisitive nature and local knowledge were ideal for the public office, but they could do without him holding them up.

At the top of the stairs, Carla looked over her shoulder and smirked as Grace raised her eyes to the ceiling. They'd both dealt with old-school Gardaí on many occasions. There were Seamus Twomeys all over the country; he had to be close to retirement.

'This place is lovely, Jack, it must have been an amazing house.'

Carla could see Grace taking in the landing area as she spoke. Many of the original features were still intact upstairs, too. Ornate architrave and coving made the plain cream painted landing look elegant, despite the lino that someone had laid and the row of grey steel filing cabinets lining the walls between the doorways.

As if he hadn't heard her, Jack called to them, 'In here. You can put the files down on the conference table and I'll get them sorted out later.'

The once elegant reception rooms on this side of the house had been knocked into one, as they had downstairs, but this time folding wooden doors enabled a semblance of privacy between them when it was needed. At the front of the house, a huge picture window with regulation vertical white blinds overlooked the street, light flooding in. A massive oval conference table dominated the space. At the other end, free-standing hessian boards had been set up against the internal walls, directly opposite a white marble fireplace, its mantel stained with coffee rings. Another huge window at the far end of the room let in even more light.

Taking a step inside, her Converse silent on the scratched wooden floor, Carla could see a huge map of the area dominating the far board. Beside it, covering the middle board, were the photos taken in the woods. Chairs had been laid out in rows in a semicircle facing the display, some slightly askew, as if the team had left quickly after their morning briefing. Grace skirted the chairs and, opening the flap of her handbag, slipped on her reading glasses, bending to look at the images pinned in the centre of the display. Carla followed her.

Carla indicated a townland halfway between Coyne's Cross and Kilkeel on the map.

'Stoney Pass. That's where one of your missing girls was from – Kellie Murphy. It's as close to here as it is to Kilkeel.'

Jack had deposited the bundle of files in his arms and now came to join them. 'It is. She disappeared in 2018, from a taxi rank after a night out. She was working in a car dealership in Kilkeel, dating one of the mechanics. I knew it sounded familiar – her case came up in a discovery request a while ago. Something to do with an insurance claim. It was before my time here, but Seamus would have been around then, if you want to talk to him.' Carla gave him a side eye. He smiled. 'Or not, as the case may be.'

Jack pointed at the board.

'This is, fairly obviously, a map of the lough. Here's the Coffee Dock and Adventure Centre. You can see the location where the skull was found marked here.' He tapped the map with his forefinger. 'We walked this way, Carla.' He ran a finger around the water's edge. 'Here's Melissa Hardiman's place, and on the other side of it, here's your cottage. That's Monastery Island a bit further on.'

'Coyne House is a big place.' Carla narrowed her eyes as she looked at the shapes of the buildings marked on the map. Between the main house and the lough was a series of long buildings. 'These are the rest of the holiday cottages?'

'Yep. That used to be a stone barn, and on this side were the staff cottages. And there's the jetty. This building is a boathouse.' Jack tapped the map again. 'This is the perimeter of the estate – it goes right from the edge of the Adventure Centre to the sea. And up here, on the opposite side of the avenue near the main entrance, is Julia's cottage. It used to be the old gamekeeper's house. It's very like yours, maybe a bit smaller, no thatch.'

'And no view.'

He shook his head.

Carla bit her lip. 'Have you got a time of death?'

'The heat is causing a few issues, but the pathologist agreed with you.' Jack looked pensive as he spoke. 'From the insect activity, it looks like she'd been dead for less than twelve hours when we found her. So we're probably looking at the early hours of Saturday morning, or perhaps late Friday night, if her body was kept somewhere away from flies.'

Without turning around, Grace said, 'I love how in cop dramas they always know to the minute.' Lowering her glasses, she turned to look at him. 'Don't you wish it was always like that in real life?'

Jack stuck his hand in his trouser pocket. 'It would make our job a lot easier. Dr Hussain has more tests to run, so we'll see if he can get closer.'

Grace went back to peering at the photographs.

Taking a step away to look at the photos, Carla pulled her hair off her neck, twirling it in a knot and holding it up to let some air circulate. She'd taken it down when she'd returned to the cottage and forgotten to bring the clip out with her. It was hot up here, even with the windows open, and she could feel the sweat sliding down her back despite her billowing A-line dress. 'Who do you think the last person to see her was?'

'At the moment, we think it was the bar manager at the Coyne Arms, when she left work at about eleven on Friday night. Basically, we've got a window from then to when we found her on Saturday at – what? Four o'clock? – unaccounted for. Tommy O'Shea, the bar manager, said she seemed in great form. He told her he'd cash and lock up. He knew she'd booked the next couple of days off, and suggested she left a bit early.'

'Do you think she went straight home? Could she have been meeting someone?' Grace crossed her arms as she looked at the photographs of Julia's body hanging in the tree. Beside it was a blow-up of her face in happier times. It was slightly blurred, but she was laughing. Her hair was pulled off her face, her blue eyes sparkling; it looked as if she was at a party, perhaps. Grace looked from the party shot, back to the body. 'She was an attractive lady. Not easy to recognise, though, given the state of her.'

'I know her pretty well. I was able to identify her.'

Carla glanced sideways at Jack as he spoke, detecting something in his tone that she couldn't quite put her finger on.

She let her hair go and crossed her arms. 'Do you think she was home all morning yesterday?'

'When the cottage was searched they found a plate in the sink, teacup on the draining board, so it looked like she'd had breakfast, but that could have been on Friday morning, of course. There was a bottle of sun cream on the kitchen counter and an empty wineglass. Bottle was in the fridge.'

Grace turned around to look at him over her glasses. 'Like she'd got home from work and had a drink?'

'Maybe.' Jack shrugged. 'Her car was parked outside. We're working our way around the town, picking up the

CCTV, checking to see if she went anywhere yesterday morning, but it doesn't look like she left the estate.' He stuck his hands in his pockets. 'The thing is, her back door lock was a bit dodgy. Apparently she'd been waiting for this guy Terry who does Melissa's odd jobs to fix it, but every time he arranged to drop in, something happened in one of the cottages and he had to cancel.'

Grace slipped her glasses onto her nose and moved over to look at the map. 'Melissa thinks someone may have got in that way?'

'It's a possibility. Unless Jules let them in.'

Carla put her head on one side, thinking. 'Any sign of a disturbance inside her cottage?'

'Not that the guys could see. SOCOs are still there.' Jack cleared his throat. 'She's got one of those magnetic knife blocks on the wall over the kitchen counter. The largest knife is missing.'

Chapter 26

DANIELLE'S THUMB HOVERED over the call button on her phone. Ruairi was always saying that she talked too much, but right now she didn't know what she was going to say. She needed to call Melissa, but what words did you use?

Danielle looked at the time. It was almost three. She should have called mid-morning, and now it was almost mid-afternoon. She stood in the middle of the kitchen floor, staring blindly out of the window. The woman with the streak in her hair – Carla, Danielle thought her name was – had dropped her home after their chat. Everything had suddenly felt as if it was closing in on top of her – first the skull, and now this.

She tapped the phone on her teeth; she couldn't put this off any longer.

It took Melissa a few seconds to answer, and when she did she sounded a bit groggy.

'Hey, Mel, it's me. How are you doing?'

There was a sigh at the other end. 'Oh shit, Dan, how can this be happening?'

'I know. Have you been asleep?'

'Yes, yes, I just woke up. Well, half an hour ago. Sean brought me a coffee, he's heading down to the town.'

'You're on your own?' Danielle's tone was sharper than she intended.

'Yes, but I'm fine, Dani. The guards were here all morning apparently. Sean's driving me mad, fussing. I just want to be on my own right now. I've sent him to the shop.'

'Jack Maguire's running everything. He's a good guy.'

'Yes, he was here last night. I just need my head to stop, Dan. I keep thinking about it, imagining … Sean said he wouldn't be long, but I think we both need a bit of space. I know he and Ruairi are joined at the hip, but he's got no real siblings, he doesn't know what it's like.'

Danielle sighed. 'Ruairi always says Sean understands him, as if I don't.' She caught herself; Melissa didn't want to hear her problems now. 'I came home from work, but it's too quiet here. Ben's still at his dad's and Ruairi's at the office. I thought going to work would keep my mind occupied, but it probably wasn't the most sensible thing I've ever done, under the circumstances.'

'I know, but the walls start to close in on you, don't they? I feel like that, too. I'm going to get some air before the guards come back. They've given us a family liaison officer.

169

She's lovely, but I can't have people in the house the whole time.' Melissa's voice wavered. 'I just keep asking myself why. Nothing makes any sense. Thank God Mum and Dad are gone.'

Danielle cleared her throat. 'Have you thought about a funeral yet?'

Melissa let out a breath. 'I don't know when we can get her body back. They have to do all sorts of tests. As if this isn't bad enough already. But it'll be in the church and she'll be next to Mum and Dad. I just hope it's soon. I can't bear this limbo. I feel like time has stopped, like it's frozen. That's why I had to get Sean out of here and get some peace for a few minutes, otherwise I thought I was going to literally scream. All the questions.'

'I know – me, too. But I'm here, OK. Just call. You know that – any time, night or day.'

'Thanks, Dani, I've always been able to rely on you. I think I'm going to walk down to the lake.'

'If you want me to come by, just say. I've got cheesecake.'

Danielle could almost hear a glimmer of a smile in Melissa's voice.

'Thanks, Dan.'

The call ended, and Danielle closed her eyes and leaned against the smooth wall.

Christ, what was worse – the silence here or the whispers at work?

170

She needed to get some space, too, so she could shut out the world.

'*I've always been able to rely on you.*' The words swirled around her head like torn pieces of paper caught on the breeze.

Chapter 27

IN COYNE'S CROSS Garda Station, Grace took a step away from the incident board and took her glasses off.

'Assuming he did, and you won't know until you find it, using a knife from her own kitchen sounds rather opportunist. This was well planned. Had to be.' Her eyes still fixed on the scene photos, Grace frowned. 'He's an organised killer. This isn't a crime of passion – there'd be more mess. It's methodical.'

Glancing at Jack, Carla turned around and, picking up one of the chairs, spun it so she could perch on the back. She'd had enough of standing; her lower back was starting to ache. 'Maybe he knew her. He'd been to the house before. He knew the knife would be there. Assuming that was the murder weapon, of course, which could be a bit of a leap if it's in the dishwasher.'

Grace waved at the map with her glasses. 'I don't think the SOCOs would miss that, do you? But I think you're right. Look how long the drive is and how isolated the cottage is. He'd have to have known the house was there. This isn't random.'

Carla glanced at her. 'He'd need a vehicle of some sort, though? Her cottage is a long way from the gate. And he has to have got blood on him doing all that butchering. He'd need to change his clothes.'

Grace nodded slowly. 'Like we said, I'd guess he brought overalls of some sort, which would indicate even more detailed planning – and, yes, he'd need to take them off and conceal them. A vehicle would certainly be the perfect solution.'

Jack looked at them, his eyebrows raised. 'Bloody hell, you two are some double act, aren't you? I think you need to come to the briefing meeting.'

Grace glanced at him and grinned. 'She brings out the best in me. But seriously, the timing still seems strange to me. You'd think he'd pick a quieter time – even Thursday night, when not so many people were about.'

Jack stuck his hands in the pockets of his chinos. 'Given that her body would have been easier to see if you were driving *into* the estate rather than on the way out, I reckon he expected her to be found as people came back in on Saturday afternoon.'

Carla shivered. 'I'm sure there are families with kids staying in those cottages. Like that French family we saw. Can you imagine if a child had seen her?'

Grace tapped the arm of her glasses on her teeth. 'He wanted her to be found. Timing is always going to be a problem in a public place, even one on private land.'

As she spoke, Jack's phone began to ring.

'Won't be a minute.' Putting the phone to his ear, he walked to the other end of the conference room, his footsteps ringing on the bare boards.

Carla caught Grace's eye. 'We'd better move. His people will be coming in soon and it's not our case. We don't want to rub anyone up the wrong way.'

Grace looked at her blankly. 'Why would we do that?'

Carla sighed. 'We're from the Park, G – Garda Headquarters. This is a country station. We need to be invited.'

'Hasn't Jack invited us?'

'Yes, but you know what I mean. Formally. We don't want anyone to get the hump about Dublin trying to run their investigation and then things go wrong. I need them to co-operate on the skull, and they're going to be under serious pressure now.'

'No problem. It's still early, we might get that walk to the round tower in after all?'

As she spoke, Jack finished his call and, coming into their half of the room, caught the end of what she was saying.

'If you're going to take an evening walk, be careful. We don't know if this guy will strike again.'

'That's what Danielle was worried about.' Carla sighed, getting ready to move. 'We persuaded her to go home, that she needed a bit of privacy. We dropped her off before we went back to the cottage, but she was getting anxious about the teenagers that hang around the lough at the weekends.'

'Well, it's just as well she's at home. Apparently the national TV news has turned up now. They've got a van in the car park next to the Coffee Dock and are interviewing anyone they can get their hands on.' Jack moved the chair Carla had been sitting on into line with the others. 'We'll move them on, but I'm glad you took Danielle home. How was she?'

'Catatonic. I mean, you'd expect it, but she is really shocked. She and Julia must have been close. I wasn't keen on leaving her on her own, but she said a friend would call over. I didn't really believe her, to be honest, but she's an adult. She tried her husband, but he wasn't answering his phone.'

'Ruairi went into work as well. Donna was meeting him there to take his statement. Perhaps he was talking to them when she rang?'

Carla shrugged. 'Seemed a bit odd to me. She tried him a few times.'

Grace folded up her glasses and replaced them in her bag decisively. 'We'd better get out of the way, this place will probably be heaving shortly.'

'DI Rainsford has a case conference arranged for six so we can see where we are. Do you want to talk about these cases, Carla?' Jack indicated the files still sitting on the conference table.

'I went through them again and narrowed it down to three possibles in that pile – I've taken photos for reference. But this investigation takes priority. I'm sure you've enough to do.' She stood up. 'We're heading back to Dublin at lunchtime tomorrow. I'll be starting work on the reconstruction on Tuesday, and I'll go through PULSE to check the details on these cases when I'm at the office.'

Chapter 28

HER ARMS TIGHTLY folded, Danielle rested her head on the cool glass of the bedroom window and looked out across the fields. It was nearing five o'clock, but this day felt as if it was going on forever – as if she'd lived a whole lifetime since Donna Sullivan had rung the doorbell and told her about Julia. She'd barely slept. Now it felt like the minutes had begun to stretch, time elastic, as if the day was never going to end.

And the heat was making it all the more claustrophobic, hard to breathe.

It had been so busy at the cafe the previous day, and she'd hardly sat down when the front doorbell had rung. Seeing the two female Gardaí on the step, her stomach had lurched as all sorts of scenarios jumped into her head.

But none of them the gut-crunching reality.

The moment they'd said that Ben was safe, she'd collapsed inside, like a balloon deflating. It had taken a few minutes to compute what they were saying about Jules.

Closing her eyes, Danielle felt a dark wave of fear wash over her again, making her sick to her stomach. She didn't know if it was the shock, or the lack of sleep, or what, but she didn't seem to be able to form cohesive thoughts – to find a way to focus on what she should do next. What *was* she supposed to do?

Outside a sheep called across the field, its cry plaintive and distant, and Danielle was glad once again that Ruairi had insisted on building this house so far from the town. So far away from the water. Isolated in the middle of the fields, it had its back to the mountains and was built low into the gentle roll of the hillside, with not another house in view of the dormer window she was looking out of now. Unlike in the town, here no one was watching, or trying to overhear their conversations.

Danielle pulled her phone out of the rear pocket of her jeans to check the time. Her text to Melissa was still unanswered. Had she even seen it? Questions swirled in Danielle's head.

What happened next?

And where the hell was Ruairi?

He'd dropped her off at the cafe this morning before swinging around to the Adventure Centre. She'd texted him to say that she wasn't feeling well and needed to go home. He hadn't answered, so the forensics woman had offered to give her a lift. She'd texted him again to say Becky would put the cash in the safe and she'd sort it out in the morning. He still hadn't replied.

Why was that even a surprise?

Should she try his pager?

He kept his phone with him wherever he was – in the office or on the water, in case search and rescue got a call – but the reception was patchy, and the pager was often more reliable. But perhaps he wasn't answering his phone because he could see it was her calling? If that was the case, he'd be the same when he saw her number dancing in red on the pager screen.

He always claimed he couldn't answer because he was busy, putting boats into the water or dealing with customers. But was that true, or did he just not want to speak to her? The questions gnawed at her. Normally she ignored them, focused on work, on Ben, tried to quell the nag. But how many times had he said he was at the Adventure Centre, that he had so much paperwork to do that he had to stay late?

The first few times she'd believed him, but gradually doubt had seeped in. Eventually she'd driven over there at night and seen his car outside and his office light on. So that much was true, but she couldn't tell from outside if he was on his own.

There had been so many lies. Like a giant sticky web with all of them caught in different corners, struggling to escape. Trapped by a big black spider in the middle.

There was so much he'd never told her, no matter how many times she asked. Like where the money for the house had come from. Or, for that matter, where the money to develop the Adventure Centre and the cafe had come from.

Danielle jumped as her phone began to ring in her hand. She looked at it, not registering what was happening. She was starting to feel as if everything was piling in on top of her, and now the mobile number flashing on the screen wasn't one she recognised.

'Hello? Danielle Brennan.' She answered tentatively, then cleared her throat. It was bound to be a business call – someone ordering cakes or wanting to book a table. 'How can I help?'

'Danielle, it's Jack Maguire. Dr Steele said she dropped you home.'

Danielle hesitated. 'Yes, it was very nice of her. I needed a rest. Is there a problem?'

There was a pause, as if Jack was going to say something but changed his mind.

'I'm ringing because we need all the CCTV from the cafe. Your system covers the car park and the Adventure Centre as well, right?'

CCTV? It took a moment for her to understand him.

'Oh, yes. Yes, it does—'

He interrupted her, relief clear in his voice. 'Great, that's great. It's just I dropped in earlier and Becky doesn't know how the system works, how to download the recordings. We're collecting everything we can find from the town out to Coyne House. I was wondering if you could—'

This time she interrupted him. 'It's all recorded digitally.' She paused; *she needed to get out of the house.* 'I can run over now and send the files over to you. I can cash up at the same time.'

'That would be great. I'll text you my email address.'

Chapter 29

THE LATE AFTERNOON air felt heavy and still as Carla and Grace returned to the car from the supermarket, carrying their shopping. They'd decided against a walk, opting to make use of the barbecue on the deck instead, but obviously the whole town had had the same idea and the car park was packed. Grace had finally found a spot on the far side, tucked in beside a red brick wall, part of which looked as if it had been used by the youth of Coyne's Cross as a visual message board.

Carla had always liked graffiti, as a form of communication as well as an art form. She'd only been vaguely aware of it when she'd got out of the car, but she looked at the wall with interest now. She could just make out the edges of letters daubed on the brick under the tags and cartoon-like images. Not graffiti; more like a proclamation. Some of the thick white paint had been scrubbed off, but she could see the end of an E and a W, and then a K and an I. It took her a moment, but then she realised what it said: DREW IS A KILLER.

Peter Drew, the churchyard odd-job man convicted of Gemma Langan's murder.

Jack's words about Drew being slow, and the cruelty of the local kids, came back to her. His memories had been from long before Gemma's death; Carla could imagine what had been said when Drew was arrested.

If Drew's arrest and conviction had fuelled local gossip, Julia's murder must be setting it on fire.

Interrupting Carla's thoughts, ahead of her, Grace clicked the central locking and the rear lights of her car flashed in response, the boot slowly opening. Just as she reached it, Carla's phone pipped with a text.

Grace lifted the insulated bags inside as Carla swung her backpack off her shoulder, retrieving her phone to look at the message.

'It's Raph.' Carla glanced at Grace. 'About those two reconstructions we did last week. He's just heard from Donegal – Train Ticket Man has been identified.' Forgetting the graffiti, Carla punched the air. Before she could reply, the phone pipped again. 'Whoa. And he says there are some good leads coming in on Welsh Woman, too – she was the other one we did.'

Grace laughed at her. 'Get in, it's baking standing out here. You're going to have to remind me of the details of these cases. I can't keep up with your nicknames, it's like you've got a club going for mispers.'

Her eyes still on the screen, Carla texted back, then opened the passenger door of the low-slung Mercedes, slinging her backpack into the footwell. As she slipped into the front seat, the phone rang and, glancing at Grace, she answered quickly.

It didn't take Raph long to fill her in.

Beside her, Grace put the key in the ignition and lowered the convertible roof.

'That's brilliant, Raph. Have you called Tina? Yes, perfect. I'll be back in Dublin tomorrow, I can do the interview tomorrow afternoon? I'll come into the office first.'

Grace looked across at her. 'What's happening now?'

Carla reached for her backpack to slip her phone inside, and pulled her sunglasses out from the front of her dress, where she'd hung them while they were in the supermarket. She put them on. '*Six One* news want to do a piece tomorrow.'

'On which case?' Reaching for her own sunglasses, Grace looked at her critically. 'You'll have to wash your hair.'

'Thanks a bunch. Train Ticket Man mainly, except he's got a name now.' Carla caught a puzzled expression on Grace's face. 'I told you about them both, you have to keep up. It's amazing, isn't it? You get no bite for ages and then they all come together.'

Grace looked over at her. 'Like buses?'

Carla threw her a withering look. 'We've literally just

finished these two and sent them to the teams investigating. They got them out to the media, and ... boom, look what happens.'

'So remind me?' Grace looked behind her to reverse out of the space.

'Train Ticket Man is the one who was found in that skip in Buncrana. Remember I went up there when you were at that conference in Paris? He was badly decomposed, but the lads found a train ticket in his pocket—'

Grace interrupted her. 'Carla ... The lads?'

Carla looked across at her impatiently as she paused at the junction to pull out of the supermarket car park. 'You know who I mean. I'm sure there were women involved, but it's a collective term.'

'Language sets a precedent, though, I keep saying it.'

Carla let out a sigh. One of Grace's pet subjects was how the use of language impacted society. She was dead right: while people continued to talk about 'violence against women', the woman would always be the object and somehow the cause – the persons perpetrating the violence were rarely mentioned. But Carla didn't want to start that debate now. It was her policy in life to focus on the things where she could make an impact. A global change in societal norms was Grace's area, not hers.

'Do you want to hear this or not?' Carla couldn't keep the satisfaction out of her tone. This case had been finally cracked entirely due to the facial reconstruction work she and her team had done, and it always felt good.

'Go on, tell me about Train Ticket Man. I can see I won't get any peace until you do. He's the guy who bought the ticket with cash at Connolly, and the CCTV camera had pigeon shit on it?'

'Precisely, that's him. One of the cameras across the station picked him up, but he was wearing a hoodie so it didn't help, and neither did the cash. But …' Carla grinned triumphantly. 'When we issued our image and photos of the finished reconstruction, one of the staff in Bray DART Station recognised him as a regular traveller. They tracked *their* CCTV and discovered he'd usually used a bank card to buy his ticket.'

'They sure it's the same guy? This was five years ago.' Grace didn't sound convinced.

'It looks like he disappeared the weekend of that soccer match, the one where the three guys got stabbed on the way home. The CCTV was saved at all the DART stations. It's pretty ropey, but the guy at Bray was sure it was this lad when he saw the information we put out. Personally, I'm maintaining the face was the clincher, but it needed the other details – what he was wearing, and the train ticket – to come together. And the fact that the station attendant's sister had just had a baby and wanted to call it Rocky.'

Grace's eyebrows shot up. 'Run that by me again.'

'Train Ticket Man was known as Rocky – he was an ex-meth-head – it was one of the reasons the attendant persuaded the sister it wasn't a good plan. The name stuck in his head.'

'I *am* glad. The poor child.'

'Anyway, when they had a name, he came up on PULSE – he disappeared from a hostel in 2015. Result.'

At the end of the main street, Grace indicated to turn right towards the cottage, green fields rolling away from the road on one side, woodland on the other. A low stone wall, the mica in the granite glistening in the sunshine, edged the road. Carla glanced over at the grazing sheep, one kneeling so it could crop the grass more efficiently.

'And what's the story with the Welsh one?' Grace's voice interrupted her thoughts.

'We don't know for sure she's Welsh, but she was found on a beach in South Wales. They thought she might be a suicide from here who had been picked up by a current and carried right across the Irish Sea. The police in Wales released the story on Friday, at the same time as Train Ticket Man went out to the Irish media.'

'Rocky,' Grace corrected her.

'Indeed, we'll have to rechristen him in the office. But it looks like she could be one of theirs. There are some names coming in.'

'Do they think it was suicide?'

Carla shook her head. 'Unlikely, Raph says. If the name that has been suggested confirms, the woman they are looking at had a history of domestic abuse.'

Grace winced. 'Not really grounds for celebration.'

'At least if we know who she is, we're one step closer to nailing the bastard who put her in the water.'

'This is very true. And without your department, neither of them would have been identified.' She reached over and patted Carla's knee, smiling. 'I'm very proud of you.'

'I'm very proud of me, too.' Carla smirked at her.

Chapter 30

A S RUAIRI BRENNAN pulled into the car park in Kilkeel, he glanced at the clock on his dash. It was just after six. He let out a deep breath. He didn't want to have this meeting – and he certainly didn't want to have it now – but he needed answers. And he needed to get rid of the contents of the Pathfinder.

It took him a minute to spot a free space. The car park was packed with shiny new 4 × 4 vehicles, lined up like soldiers waiting for battle.

Ruairi got out of the SUV and put on his sunglasses, reaching in for a jacket he kept on the rear seat. It was too hot for a jacket, even a lightweight one, but it made him feel smarter, more in control. Sean was always going on about dressing the part for work, and – sometimes – Ruairi had to admit that he was right.

The right gear was essential for every job.

He took a shaky breath and reached into the compartment in the door. A couple of pills would help steady his nerves. It had been an emotional day. Spilling some out onto his palm, he threw them into his mouth and put the canister back, taking a second to let them go down. Outside on the main road, even at this time on a bank holiday Sunday evening, the traffic was loud, Kilkeel still in full swing, reminding him yet again why he lived out of town and worked on the water.

The back door to the office corridor opened directly into the car park, sophisticated security cameras following his every move. He raised his hand to buzz at the intercom and heard the bolt in the door shoot backwards. He pulled the door open, the metal handle hot.

They were both sitting in the office when he got there: father and son.

Ken Cahill was behind his huge antique walnut desk, its extravagance emphasised by scrolled legs and carvings of fruit and flowers. Laurence Cahill looked as if he'd been poured into a leather wing chair, one half of a pair on the right of the office, his feet on an occasional table in front of it. His long hair needed a wash.

Ruairi hesitated for a minute at the glass door, summoning the swagger that had got him here in the first place.

Spotting Ruairi a fraction of a second before he opened the door, Ken stood up. 'Ruairi, mate, so good to see you.'

As Ruairi came into the office, Ken slipped around his huge desk, his hand out. Short and stocky, he was wearing a lemon polo shirt that deepened his tan; he looked as if he was between the golf course and the office. His navy chinos were pressed perfectly, dark brown woven Italian shoes polished to a mirrored shine. The shoes would be handmade, probably cost as much as a Nelo competition kayak. Ruairi took Ken's hand and the older man pulled him into a man hug.

'What the fuck's going on over in Coyne's Cross, mate? We heard on the news.'

Letting Ruairi go, Ken stepped away to sit casually on his desk, his trouser legs rising to reveal the tassels on his shoes.

'Say hello, Laurence, don't be a prick.' Ken said it without taking his eyes off Ruairi, his tone steel-edged.

Laurence removed his feet from the table, sat up and nodded sharply to Ruairi.

'Keys.' Again the fake smile; Ken's dark eyes were still locked on Ruairi. 'Is it all there?'

'Obviously not.'

Not taking his eyes off Ken, Ruairi stuck his arm out and held the keys out to Laurence, letting them dangle. Laurence got up begrudgingly and swiped them out of Ruairi's hand. His father looked at him.

'Take it into the garage and close the doors. Be careful now, don't leave a trace. And be quick, we don't want to keep this man from his work. Or his lovely wife.'

Without speaking, Laurence left the office. There was something about that lad that always made Ruairi want to punch him. Today more than ever.

'Have we got a problem, Ruairi boy?'

'You tell me, Ken. Jules was sound. Did she do something to piss you off?'

Pursing his lips, Ken shook his head. 'What makes you think I'm involved?'

'History. You've a bit of a track record.'

Ken shook his head as if it wasn't relevant. 'That was different. She had a big mouth, knew way too much about the operation. Gary thought he could keep her under control, but we don't employ him to think.' He paused. 'She started asking questions about the modifications to certain vehicles – yours specifically, as you well know. Got too clever for her own good.' Ken looked at him pointedly.

Ruairi ignored the jibe. 'The bastard cut Jules's heart out. He was sending someone a message.'

Ken wrinkled his face in distaste. 'Nasty. Nice girl … useful. She's a loss. I'm devastated.'

Ruairi didn't believe him for a second.

Chapter 31

'WHAT TIME DO you want to eat?'

Grace lay back in the chair on the deck and put her face to the sun. She'd already lit citronella candles and sprayed the whole area with insect repellent. Now it hung, cloying, in the air, but it meant she could enjoy the evening sunshine.

'Maybe seven?' Carla reached for an olive from the earthenware bowl on the table. 'Those steaks will cook super-fast and we've got everything else bought.'

'Perfect.' Her eyes still closed, Grace took a sip of her wine as Carla's phone pipped with another text. 'Can you turn that off, or are the messages vital?' Carla frowned, about to retort about Grace's own hours, as she continued. 'Why are you looking at me like that? It's a bank holiday Sunday evening, Dr Steele. You're entitled to a day off.'

'Crime doesn't take a day off, G, you know that. And that was RTE confirming the interview tomorrow. Just because we know who Rocky was doesn't mean we know who killed him, and how he wound up in a skip in the corner of a scrapyard in Donegal.'

'Fair point.'

Carla put her phone on the table and shifted in the chair, pulling her hair up onto the top of her head, letting the whisper of breeze cool her neck. 'Sometimes these things all fall into place. Once you have a face to add to the other shreds of evidence, it brings everything together in someone's mind. I just wish we knew more about Girl X. I'm not going to rest until I find out her story.'

Grace reached over and patted Carla's arm. 'I know. But you've done all you can getting her picture out there. Maybe as forensics improve, there might be more information they can get off that blanket that'll give you something to work with?'

Carla sighed. 'It's been checked for everything – pollen, washing powder, DNA and fibres, obviously. I've sent all the information we have to Interpol. I think you could be right that she was trafficked. There are definite traces of Asian heritage in her bone structure, and the strands of hair that were found.'

Carla recalled the abandoned house where the girl's skull had been hidden. The bunch of teenagers who had broken in, looking for somewhere warm and dry to get up to God only knew what, had got some shock.

It hadn't been quite as bleak as the oily quagmire of a

scrapyard Train Ticket Man had been found in, the wind almost cutting through Carla as she trudged to see Rocky's last resting place. At least they'd had his body, though – scraps of clothing to work from, and the crucial train ticket in his pocket. With Girl X, they had nothing more than a decomposed head in an abandoned house, and tattered wallpaper. The orange cabinets in the kitchen, their doors hanging off, had looked like smoker's teeth.

Carla suddenly realised Grace was looking at her. 'You'll find out who she was,' Grace said. 'You're like a terrier after a rat when you pick up a scent. That's why you're so good at what you do.'

Carla stared out at the lake, the part of her heart that had died when Lizzie had disappeared heavy in her chest. There was a very good reason she didn't let cases go, why she pursued them beyond what was logical.

'Let's get those steaks on and have an early night.' Grace looked out over the lough. 'We want to make the most of this place before we have to hit the road tomorrow. What time's this interview?'

'Half two at the office.'

Grace levered herself out of the chair. 'Just as well. I can see us getting hauled into the investigation here if we're not careful.'

Carla cocked one eyebrow at her. 'Why's that a problem, if we can help?'

Grace stood up. 'I'm not sure we can – not materially, at least. I think Jack thinks I'm a profiler, that I can tell him who his killer is, and we both know that's not what I do ...'

Carla looked at her reproachfully. 'You're pretty good at it.'

'Victimology – understanding and interpreting the way people kill – isn't the same as identifying who they might be. I've no idea how some of these profile conclusions are reached sometimes. "Uneducated white male in his forties."' Grace shrugged. 'You can tell a lot about a killer's intentions from his behaviour, but I think sometimes profiles can end up leading law enforcement up the garden path.'

'They are usually pretty accurate.'

'That's because they can be very vague. Geographical profiling and behavioural analysis is much sounder, in my opinion. But as you know, I'm keeping that to myself.'

Carla couldn't stop a grin cracking across her face. 'You don't keep anything to yourself, G. Who are you kidding?'

Grace glared at her playfully. 'More wine? Then let's get these steaks on. I'll waste away if I don't eat soon.'

Carla spluttered into her glass. It was as if Grace was able to read Carla's mind; she always found a way to lift her mood. She'd been Lizzie's friend, too.

'You cheeky wench. Watch it or—'

Grace didn't get any further with her threat as Carla's phone began to ring, Jack Maguire's name flashing on the screen.

'Pick that up and see if he wants to come over for some food.' Grace raised her eyebrows suggestively. 'He looks like he needs looking after.'

Chapter 32

SITTING AT HER desk in the Coffee Dock's tiny office, Danielle could hear Becky and Niamh chatting outside as they replenished the paper cups and filled the coffee machine ready for the morning trade.

She really had no idea how she was going to get through the following day. Or the next one. She felt a pang of guilt at leaving the girls alone this afternoon – they hadn't said a word when she'd left, but they couldn't run the place on their own; she needed to get on track. Bank holiday Mondays were always manic.

Switching on her computer, Danielle waited a second and punched in the password, clicking on the camera icon on the desktop to access the security footage that recorded to the hard drive. She'd forgotten to ask Jack Maguire what exactly he wanted – whether there was a specific day or time that he was interested in – and hadn't he said he wanted the Adventure Centre cameras, too? The data was all saved together on her computer.

She closed her eyes for a second, her breath catching painfully in her chest. At least coming here gave her something to do, something to focus on.

Danielle felt her heart clench. She'd thought the skull was her biggest problem, but now this ...

Would the CCTV show them anything? Ruairi was paranoid about anyone breaking into the Adventure Centre. He'd installed state-of-the-art video cameras covering the car park, cafe and deck areas, and even more on the slip covering the reception area. After a robbery at a cafe in Lough Derg, Danielle had asked about having them installed inside the cafe as well, but that had been too expensive, apparently. What could anyone steal? A handbag from a customer, a few cans of Coke? The alarm was enough.

But what could the guards be looking for that might be on their security video? Surely they didn't think the killer had been hanging around one of the car parks? Danielle felt herself shudder.

In all honesty, she didn't really want to know what Jack was looking for. If they thought the killer had been here – and with the number of visitors they'd had this weekend, between the sunshine and the skull, it was entirely possible – Danielle reckoned she'd have a full-on panic attack.

Perhaps that was the reason she couldn't face the thought of Monday. Was the killer one of the customers who would come in to nurse a coffee, listening to the talk, sating himself on the gossip?

Danielle shook the thought away. She'd spent years building the business, getting her head straight and focusing on making it work. She loved people, loved the chat, loved being busy. She couldn't let everything slip now.

Highlighting the last seven days, she clicked to upload all the videos in WeTransfer. One eye on the file's progress, she tipped out the cash bag onto her reconciliation book and began to sort out the notes and the Visa slips.

'Becky, can you do the Visa reconciliation?' Leaning back in her chair, Danielle called through the open door to the servery area. 'Just leave it in the machine and I'll come and get it.'

Before Becky could answer, Danielle heard banging and the rattle of the keys in the front door as the girls got ready to leave and Niamh's voice: 'My dad's here to collect us.'

Danielle stood up and went down the short corridor to the servery door, checking in the staff kitchen as she passed. The girls had tidied up after themselves, wiping down the table. They'd left the window open to try and get some air into the place; she made a mental note to remember to close it.

In the servery, Danielle could see the Visa machine was churning out its ribbon-like reconciliation. At the end of the counter, the girls were taking off their aprons and picking up their bags.

'Night, girls, I'll see you in the morning. No need to be here before ten. I'll make sure we're ready to go before we open the doors. Thanks for today, I know you were flat out.'

Both girls smiled and waved as they slipped out the front door, Niamh's dad waving, too, from outside. He hooshed the girls along as Danielle crossed the cafe and locked the doors behind them.

Reaching up to shoot the top bolt, then turning her keys in the door, Danielle paused for a moment, looking out over the lake. It was like a mirror, the trees on either bank reflected in the water, their shadows dark. She could already see flies dancing in clouds.

It had taken her a long time to come to terms with being this close to the water – to overcome her fear of it, of what it held. But there was something about the lough that kept drawing her back; she couldn't seem to escape it. When she'd broken up with Ben's dad, she'd felt the pull, and had come home from Dublin. She'd told everyone it was because she wanted Ben to grow up with fresh air and around his people, but it had been more than that.

She'd only been dating Ruairi a couple of months when he'd come up with the idea for the Adventure Centre, and she'd been caught up in the excitement of a huge project, working evenings and weekends to make it a reality.

She suddenly became aware of the silence, and headed to the counter, tearing off the Visa printout as she went past.

Everyone seemed to have gone home early this evening. The lights were on in the Adventure Centre reception, but there was no one hanging about. Ruairi would be at his desk, doing his own tot of the day's business. She'd call him again when she finished up.

Sitting down at her desk, she started at a noise coming from the staff kitchen. Freezing, she listened hard, but … nothing.

Was it her imagination? She shivered. *Perhaps she should come in early in the morning and do the day's prep then, rather than stay now?*

Feeling distinctly uneasy, Danielle rubbed her face, trying to massage away her lack of sleep, and the nip of fear that was making her head start to race.

Remembering the security video, Danielle woke the computer screen up. The files had uploaded, so she clicked on the transfer link to share it with Jack, then glanced over the reconciliation sheet. She only had to do the final tot, and then she'd call Ruairi.

Chapter 33

'I'LL CLEAR, YOU stay there.' Grace stood up and stretched. 'God, I've eaten too much again. I do wish you'd stop me.'

Carla looked at her reproachfully as Grace piled their plates haphazardly. 'As if you'd let me.'

Grace grinned. 'OK, maybe I'd be grossly insulted and never speak to you again. Blimey, though …' She adjusted the tie on her dress. 'Just as well I'm not wearing shapewear, I'd be cut in two.' She looked thoughtful. 'Maybe we need to develop some sort of safe word or code I can blithely ignore.'

Laughing, Carla shook her head. 'I'm not getting into policing your plate when you've had a few glasses of wine. I know what's good for me. Let me help clear?'

Grace held up both hands as if she was stopping traffic. 'Stay there and relax. I'm only going to load the dishwasher, it's not exactly strenuous. I downloaded that podcast about the murder your cousin was involved in at Hare's Landing when I was at the spa. I just want to listen to the last ten minutes. It's mad you didn't even know her then, with everything that happened.' Grace shook her head. 'The whole DNA-finding-your-family thing is bonkers. Will you be OK on your own?'

Carla smiled. 'I think so. If a knife-wielding killer appears out of the bushes, I'll be sure to scream.'

Grace picked up the plates and tutted, shaking her head in mock despair.

As Grace clattered around the kitchen, Carla poured herself another glass of wine. The air was still warm and the dusk seemed possessed of a stillness, as the evening slipped towards night, that made her feel as if she was somehow separated from the rest of the world. She loved the privacy of their garden at home, of walking on the beach early in the morning, but being so close to the city there was always that hum of life in the background, like white noise. Here, the only sounds were the timbers of the deck creaking as the wood cooled, and the calls of birds as they settled down for the evening.

Looking out over the water, listening to the gentle plop of fish, Carla's mind wandered to the skull in her office that had started its journey so close to here. Whoever it belonged to had been missing for a significant amount of time. And they must have people who missed them, who wondered where they were. Just like Lizzie.

Grace hadn't told her much about the podcast she was

listening to, but from what Rachel, her cousin, had said, Carla knew that it was about missing people, too. Suddenly she felt tears pricking at her eyes. She tried to catch them on her finger and wipe them away. She'd obviously had too much wine and too much drama for one weekend.

It was the not knowing that was the worst: not knowing what happened; not knowing if she could have stopped it; not knowing if she'd done something that day that had created a ripple effect, ending up with Lizzie being in the wrong place at the wrong time. Had she been abducted? Had an accident? There was no way, Carla was absolutely sure, that she would have disappeared voluntarily. Something had happened.

And the thing was, you couldn't just vanish – not completely.

Or, at least, it happened very rarely.

You could disappear, reinvent yourself as someone else, with a new life in a new place. That was one thing, but if you vanished and died as a result, your body would slowly decay, but something would always be left: a bone fragment, or – like here in Coyne's Cross, and with Girl X – a skull. Skulls survived for thousands of years, and they held a key to identity that was so much more powerful than something like DNA. They held the victim's likeness.

That's what had attracted Carla to facial reconstruction in the first place.

That, and needing to do something that might help Lizzie.

If Lizzie was dead, then there had to be some of her left somewhere, part of her that was waiting for Carla to find it. Carla looked at her wrist, at the birds tattooed across it. She'd gone over that night so many times in her head, waving Lizzie goodbye. The city was criss-crossed with CCTV; even then there had been traffic cameras and cameras on ATMs, on the building site close to the river. Lizzie had been captured on film crossing O'Connell Bridge and then turning down the Quays to walk to her bus stop. And then she'd disappeared.

She'd never got on the bus. The guards couldn't even be sure she'd got to the bus stop.

It had been a drizzly night coming up to Christmas, the streets always busy in the city centre, more so with crowds out at Christmas parties, every pub full. Over the following days, Carla and her friends had gone around to every cafe, every pub, with photographs; they'd put posters up everywhere; they'd set up a Find Lizzie Facebook page. One of their friends who was studying media had taken over as if it was a PR campaign: she'd arranged for them to blanket the radio stations, had sent releases to the regional press, scheduled posts on Twitter for every anniversary.

Everything – they'd tried everything.

Someone *must* have seen something and not realised. Someone else had to be involved. They all knew it only needed one thing to jog someone's memory.

Carla looked up suddenly, catching a movement out of the corner of her eye. A flash of auburn, the colour of Lizzie's hair. A tawny owl, maybe? Last night, sleeping fitfully, her head full of nightmarish images, she'd heard an owl hooting, the sound eerie and haunting. Did owls fly about this early in the evening?

Carla closed her eyes. Her imagination always played tricks on her when she got like this, although a tiny part of her felt so strongly that it really *was* Lizzie – that she was trying to guide her somehow.

Carla reached for her wine and took a sip. Every single face she rebuilt was a step on the path to finding Lizzie. Sometimes it felt like a great rope bridge, one of those huge ones that hung across a gorge, with wooden treads spaced out along its length.

Every time she identified someone who had been lost, like the Coyne's Cross skull and, eventually, Girl X, was another step towards finding Lizzie. Carla wasn't sure how such random cases could be connected, but she could feel it, like electricity in the air. It was as if the girls who were lost had somehow connected in another place and were out there in the ether, trying to help their people find them. Helping Carla.

One day she'd find Lizzie, and understand what had happened to her, and she was going to make sure that whoever had hurt her paid the price. Blinking away tears, Carla looked out across the silence of the lough. She wasn't going to stop until she'd found her.

Chapter 34

THE TEAM BRIEFING had been just as draining as Jack had known it would be. Now, trotting down the stairs to the basement, he let out an involuntary sigh.

The mood was grim, but there was also an underlying anger that anyone could have picked their town to do something like this – and to a popular, gregarious, bloody lovely woman whom they all knew well. They might be a young team, but they had the detective unit in from Kilkeel on this, too, and they were going to catch this killer. As Jack had outlined Grace Franciosi's thoughts to everyone earlier, he'd looked around and seen the cold determination in their eyes. Jules was one of their own; she'd lived here all her life, and they weren't having it.

Doubling around the end of the staircase in the hallway, Jack headed down the last flight of stairs to the basement. Matt Curran had buzzed him to say he had found something on the CCTV tapes he'd been going through.

Christ, he hoped this could be a break.

'Jaysus, how can you work in here?'

Jack took a step back to let the funk out, and let some fresh air in to the CCTV viewing room. The room was hot, and stank of a rich combination of takeaway food and Lynx deodorant.

In the middle of eating a ham salad roll the size of a half baguette, Matt turned and looked at Jack over the top of a pair of nerdy-looking glasses, his thick straw-coloured hair typically unruly, and threw him a cheeky grin. For a moment Jack wondered when he'd started wearing glasses, simultaneously realising they were the blue light glasses that Matt had mentioned in the rec room a few weeks ago – they reduced the screen glare.

There were times when Jack felt like a dinosaur in this station. Apart from Seamus, who was like part of the Victorian furniture, he was probably one of the oldest here. Not that he didn't enjoy the craic and appreciate the agility of a young team, but he was sure they thought he'd come in on the Ark sometimes.

'You sound like my mam.'

Jack almost smiled, shaking his head, all his suspicions confirmed.

'Does your bedroom stink, too?' He took a step inside and toyed with the idea of leaving the door propped open.

Seeing his hesitation, Matt indicated he should close it. 'Keeps "people" out.' He kept his voice low as the heavy door fell closed. 'Seamus would be in here every spare minute, wringing his hands and busybodying, checking out who was where, and when, if it was any more comfortable. There's method in everything, you know. He's a devil for the gossip, that man.'

Despite the wave of darkness he was feeling after updating the team, the briefing meeting definitely one of the most sombre he'd ever held, Jack couldn't resist a grin.

Matt couldn't be closer to the truth. Seamus made it his business to know everything about everyone.

Jack cleared his throat. 'I couldn't possibly comment.' He pulled out a chair and sat down beside Matt.

The room was the size of a small bedroom, the desk and walls supporting a raft of monitors that fed live CCTV pictures from the Garda traffic cameras spread across the town directly to the station. It was an impressive set-up; you just needed a special sort of brain to monitor them and not get a raging headache. It hadn't taken long for Seamus to realise that Matt's gaming abilities made him the de facto candidate.

'So, what have you got for me?'

'We've got Julia Hardiman leaving the Coyne Arms at eleven – 10.55, actually. I've got their CCTV here.'

Matt flicked a button and one of the screens changed into quarters, to show four blurry black and white images of the car park behind the hotel. It was full.

As Jack watched, in the bottom right, Julia emerged from the staff entrance at the rear of the building and walked across the car park, her phone to her ear. The camera top left picked her up from the front as she came into range.

'That's the call she made to Melissa.' Matt took another bite of his roll, nodding in the direction of the screen. 'According to her phone records, she left a message.'

Jack double-checked the time on the screen. He felt as if he had Jules's last movements tattooed into his brain. 'It is indeed.'

They watched as she crossed the car park, the floodlights elongating her shadow. She was wearing heels and a short, tight, dark-coloured dress, a jacket slung around her shoulders. Which meant she'd got home and changed before she'd been killed.

Although, of course, the fact that when Jack had found her she'd been wearing her jeans didn't mean she'd gone home on her own. One thing he'd made very clear to the team upstairs was that they needed to look at every single detail. There was no room for assumptions, or for taking what someone said at face value; everything needed to be checked.

'She doesn't look like she's in a hurry or worried about anything.' Jack peered at the images. 'Just stop it there.' He raised his hand quickly and Matt hit the *pause* button, finishing his mouthful at the same time.

Matt pointed at the screen. 'That's a cat. I thought the exact same thing when I saw the movement. I've slowed it all down and checked all the shadows. No one following her. Not from here, at least.'

Jack rolled his finger to indicate Matt should hit *play* again as he kept his eyes locked on the screen. The images were slightly fuzzy. They'd had issues with the poor quality of the hotel's security footage in the past – this was supposed to be the upgraded version. Jack tried to curb his rising impatience. The hotel's owner was based in Dublin, and had only replaced the system when there had been a big fight in the bar. His insurance had refused to pay out because the footage was so bad, no one involved was identifiable.

Jack could feel his heart rate increasing involuntarily as he watched Jules get into her car. He sat forwards in the hard plastic chair, the edge biting into his thighs. Watching her like this, knowing what happened next, was a bit like being kicked repeatedly in the gut.

He gritted his teeth. Seeing someone who had been a close friend – a very close friend, even if it had been for a short period of time – walking to her death wasn't something he ever wanted to go through again. When he'd first transferred here, they'd hooked up, but hadn't been an item long enough to go public. They'd remained good friends, though. They both worked unsocial hours, had had a few late-night drinks.

Matt interrupted his thoughts. 'When she gets into the car, she sits there for a few minutes before she starts the engine. It looks like she's typing a text, but there's nothing that corresponds on her phone log, so perhaps she changed her mind about sending it.'

Peering at the darkened image, Jack nodded slowly. Matt was right. But who bothered to spend that much time composing a text, and then not send it?

Matt spoke again and Jack returned to the present situation. 'Then, as you know, she drives out of the car park, and swings out right into the main street.'

Matt pointed at a different screen, changing to one of the traffic cams, the clarity and colour so good they could see straight into the car as it pulled up at the pedestrian crossing outside the post office. The street was deserted, although there was a queue in the takeaway, and Jack knew it would be busier when the pubs closed.

Jules looked as if she was singing to something on the radio.

Matt sighed. 'She seems pretty happy there.' He drew the words out and Jack felt for him. He wasn't long out of Templemore, the Garda Training Academy, but he'd fitted right in when he'd been stationed in Coyne's Cross, had joined the local GAA, and now coached the under-16s. He pretty much knew everyone. This was his first major case. The phrase 'close to home' couldn't have been more accurate. Danielle's son Ben was on the team, and the Coyne Arms was its main sponsor.

'Where do you pick her up next?' Jack tried to keep his voice level. Seeing Jules so clearly as she waited at the lights in her car was harder to deal with than the blurry image of her walking across the car park.

'We've got her going straight up the main street, then right again towards Coyne House. But this is where it gets interesting. I only spotted it just now.' He flicked to another screen immediately to his left, tapping the edge of the monitor as he checked the keyboard. 'The 137 bus catches her about five minutes later. You can see her car on the internal camera as she passes. But then we lose her after Turner's Gap. She doesn't go through the gates of the Coyne Estate until about 12.30. There's a camera covering the entrance. So we've got an hour and a half unaccounted for.' Matt moved his mouse and another screen came to life. 'Here we've got the 49 bus on the Kilkeel road five minutes after the 137, and there is no sign of a parked car or anything. It doesn't come across her at all.'

Jack looked hard at the screen. 'So where did she go?'

Matt raised his eyebrows. 'My guess is she pulled off the road somewhere. There are a couple of houses she could have called into, or the Coffee Dock car park, perhaps. I mean, it was all closed up by then, but maybe she went to meet someone there – maybe that's who she was texting as she left work?'

'But if she didn't send the text?'

Matt shrugged in response. 'Perhaps she was texting to cancel and changed her mind. I'm guessing, but ...' He shrugged again.

'This is good work, Matt. Danielle's emailing me her CCTV this evening for you to—'

Before he could finish, there was a sharp rap on the door and Donna stuck her head in, her face pale against her dark hair.

'Sorry, Jack. DI needs you. There's another one.'

Chapter 35

IT WAS PAST eight o'clock by the time Grace came out to rejoin Carla on the deck.

'You know, this place really is glorious. We do need to come back when things are quieter.' Grace moved the citronella candle closer to herself. They'd lit new ones, the flames dancing in the evening air, still heavy with the heat of the day.

'You mean when there are no dead bodies turning up? That would be good. Do you mind going up early tomorrow? Sorry about having to be back for the TV news thing. We have to take every opportunity.'

'You're desperate to get to the lab, aren't you?' Grace looked across at her, half-amused. 'You never switch totally off, you know that? You need to learn to.'

Carla sighed. 'I just want to get started on this new skull. Now I've been here, I need to find out what her story was.'

'Her?'

Carla shrugged. 'I could be wrong, but I really feel like it's a her. That's something else that's nagging at me. I know the

217

case files we went through threw up a couple of lads, but I'm sure it's a girl. Which narrows it down to two possibilities.'

Her mind already in the lab, Carla played with the looped ends of the spaghetti straps on her dress as she spoke. It was like a tent, but despite its looseness, she was still warm.

'Not necessarily,' Grace pointed out. 'She – even if it is a she – could have come from anywhere. Statistically it might be more likely she's one of the two local girls who are missing, but you know there's a possibility she's from outside the area. She could have been dumped here and be missing from a completely different part of the country.'

'I know, but at least when I have her face built, I can compare her to them. It's somewhere to start, if only to eliminate them.'

'What were their names again?'

'One is Kellie Murphy. She's the most recent, she disappeared in 2018. She was nineteen, and working at a car dealership in Kilkeel, I think it said.' Carla paused, thinking about what she'd read. 'The other one is Gemma Langan—'

Grace interrupted her. 'She's the one there was a prosecution for?'

'Yes. Seventeen, from Coyne's Cross.'

Grace picked up her glass and opened her mouth to comment, but before she could speak, the peace of the evening was shattered by the sound of a siren. She turned

218

in her chair, trying to work out where it was coming from. Carla did the same, straining her ears. There was no wind. The vehicle had to be on their side of the lough. A moment later it was joined by another one. And another.

Carla glanced at Grace across the table, her glass of wine now frozen in mid-air. 'Something's happening.'

Grace raised her eyebrows. 'Something big. Where's your phone?'

'Charging in the kitchen. Give me two minutes.'

The cottage was cool and dark inside. Picking up her phone, Carla looked to see if there was anything from Jack.

Had they identified a suspect and gone in to arrest him?

The phone only had a whisper of reception. As she lifted it to check if there were any missed calls, it suddenly picked up a signal and several texts came in together – all from Jack.

Out on the deck, the sound of sirens was still loud. Frowning, Carla opened the first text.

'Damn, this was sent half an hour ago from Jack. "Might be tied up in the morning, gap in Jules's last movements. Call before you leave?"'

Carla glanced up at Grace as she rolled her hands expectantly. 'Anything that explains the pile-on?'

Carla scrolled down. 'This came in ten minutes ago … Whoa. "999 call from Coyne House. Body found. Will update."'

She looked at Grace, her eyes wide, shock coursing through her like electricity, images of Jules hanging in the trees shooting into her mind.

Grace's brow furrowed as she took the news on board. 'A body isn't good. But it might not be another murder.' She paused for a moment before she continued. 'I do hope Melissa hasn't done anything to herself.'

'Did she seem the type to you?'

Grace shrugged. 'I'm not sure there's a "type". And she's just lost her sister, horrifically. Something like that could push you over the edge.' She hesitated. 'I know we've only met her for a few minutes, but she struck me as what my mother calls "highly strung".'

Carla sat down. 'Will I text him back? How are we going to find out what's happening?'

Grace looked at her, one eyebrow raised. 'I think he might be a bit busy.'

As if Jack had heard her, Carla's phone pipped with another message. She almost jumped at the sound.

'Jeepers, that scared me.' She looked at the screen, reading the text twice. 'This isn't good.'

'What does it say?'

'"Melissa found in boathouse at CH. Copycat injuries."'

'Oh.' Grace put her glass down fractionally too hard. The sound of the base hitting the china tile fragments on the tabletop rang out across the lough. 'Didn't Jack say they were keeping the details out of the press?' Carla could see Grace's professional mind was already ticking over.

Carla looked at her phone again, willing it to update. 'Yes. No one except a very tight circle knows about the mutilation.'

'That's not good. Someone has a specific grievance against those sisters. Very specific. But ...' Grace looked thoughtful for a moment as she picked up her glass again and took another sip. 'It does make it look like it's a family thing, rather than a random stranger killing. Which is sort of good.' She paused. 'Well, it's not good at all, but you know what I mean.'

Carla grimaced. 'Good that Coyne's Cross doesn't have a crazed serial killer picking off women at random?' She tapped her phone on her teeth. 'Will I text him quickly? He won't answer if he's busy.'

'Go for it.' Grace smiled. 'You'll burn up with curiosity if you don't. Spontaneous human combustion is a real thing, you know.'

Carla threw her a withering look, her thumbs flying over her keypad. Seconds later a text came in.

SOCO on site, will drop over soon as poss. Have pics for Grace.

Chapter 36

CARLA OPENED THE front door as soon as she heard Jack's car on the gravel. It was almost eleven o'clock. They'd been keeping an eye on social media and the local radio news, but there hadn't been anything about an incident at Coyne House.

Jack looked pale as he got out of what looked, from the dust and scratches, like a detective unit car. Carla could imagine what it was like inside.

'You look like you need a drink.'

Carla held the door to the cottage open wide. She'd pulled on a hoodie over her dress, but her feet were bare, the tiled floor cool after the warm boards of the deck.

He grimaced. 'I'd kill for one, but it'll have to be coffee. I'm back to the station after this.'

'I'll bring it out. Grace is on the deck – go on through. There's antipasti, and more cheese that needs eating up, too.'

He smiled at her gratefully and went through the living room onto the deck, while Carla put a pod in the coffee machine. He'd drunk cappuccino the last time they'd been at the Coffee Dock, and it only took a few minutes for the machine to warm up. Putting the mugs on a tray, she carried them outside.

'Here you go. Rocket fuel. So what's the story?'

Jack was leaning on the rail that surrounded the deck as if he couldn't sit down. His whole body was full of tension, the muscles in his tanned forearm taut where he was gripping the smooth wood. Grace was looking at the scene photos on his phone, her forehead creased in concentration.

Jack shook his head as he met Carla's eye. 'Not good. It was Melissa.' He faltered, turning away from her and clearing his throat. 'Exactly the same. Only this time she was strung up over a beam in the boathouse. And no flies … Well, not many, anyhow.'

'Who found her?' Sitting down, Carla winced at his description. She didn't need a reminder about the flies.

'Her husband, Sean. He went into town this afternoon to do some shopping. Maybe they both just needed a bit of space. When he got back, she wasn't in the house. He thought she'd gone for a walk, but then it started getting late and she wasn't answering her phone. He went over to Julia's house to see if she was there. We've still got the place sealed and the officer on duty alerted the station. Sean went back to the house to see if she'd left a note, then later decided to check the cottages – that was when he saw the boathouse had been broken into.'

'Christ, that must have been a shock. Did she have the same injuries as Julia?'

Jack nodded. 'Looks like he took his time, though, and from the amount of blood, the Tech Bureau reckon he did it in the boathouse.'

Grace put Jack's phone down and tapped her fingernails on the stem of her glass, obviously deep in thought. 'He's taking a bit of a risk, doing it on her own property. That boathouse is close to the holiday cottages, isn't it?'

'Yep, right beside them. It's kept locked so children staying in the cottages can't get in, but the padlock was broken. That's what alerted Sean first.'

Carla thought of the map of the estate and lough that they'd looked at earlier. 'Do they have security cameras?'

Jack frowned. 'There's a camera at the main gate, which is left open at this time of year, but there's nothing at the house. Sean said there were privacy concerns over the people staying in the cottages, or something. We're talking to all of them, obviously. Some of them were planning on staying for the week, but are getting ready to leave now.'

Grace picked up her glass. 'Did they see anything?'

Jack let out a big sigh, like a valve releasing steam. Moving off the rail, he pulled out one of the spare chairs. 'Apparently not. But there's a side entrance as well as the double doors on the side facing the cottages. And Sean doesn't know what time she vanished – he went out about three and was back by six thirty. She wasn't at home then, apparently.'

Carla pushed the crackers and butter towards Jack. 'Eat, you need your strength. Three hours seems a long time to be wandering around the town. What was he doing – the weekly shop?'

'Nope, he got the paper and some groceries, and then went over to the Adventure Centre to see Ruairi Brennan. Said he was there about an hour and a half, and then went home.'

Grace leaned forwards. 'So Ruairi is Sean's alibi?'

'He is.' Jack nodded slowly. 'The CCTV from the Adventure Centre will confirm the times, though. Danielle sent over the links to the digital recordings this evening. Matt will have a look at them as soon as he can.' A look of annoyance passed across Jack's face. 'Only having one body trained up on CCTV is a nightmare. And Kilkeel's guy is on holiday.'

Grace put her head on one side. 'Being devil's advocate, what does Sean have to gain from both sisters being murdered?'

Jack let out a sharp breath and raised his eyebrows before he answered. 'Assuming he's not in the picture for it … a huge estate, house, business. Quite a lot, I'd imagine. Anything Melissa would have left to Julia would go directly to him now. Jules doesn't have a partner and neither of them had children. We'd need to look at Melissa's will to be sure.'

Carla played with her skull ring, rotating it around her finger, watching the eyes light up in the glow from the candles. 'It's a bit … well, messy, though. I mean, there are much easier ways to dispose of your wife, surely?'

Jack clicked his tongue off the top of his mouth. 'I'm sure there are. But if you needed to kill both sisters in close succession, there aren't too many ways you could do it without instantly arousing suspicion. A boating accident or something, maybe, but that could be complicated to stage. A random ritualistic serial killer is one way of diverting attention, I suppose.'

Carla pulled a face. 'It's actually horrific.'

'And pretty dramatic.' Grace looked at them both. 'It's almost like a piece of theatre. I feel like the killer's making a point. But whoever did this definitely knows the lie of the land. I'm sure they have local knowledge.'

Carla could see the tension in Jack's face as he spoke. 'I'm keeping this absolutely under wraps until the morning. I don't want anyone local knowing that we know. We might be able to buy ourselves some time. I've pulled everyone in.' There was steel in his tone. 'We'll take a close look at Sean, and his business. See if there are any financial reasons why he might need to kill his wife. One thing is for sure – there has to be a motive for these killings, and if we can work that out, we'll be one step closer to finding out who was involved.'

Chapter 37

DANIELLE SHIVERED AS she unlocked the doors to the Coffee Dock, the hoodie she'd thrown on over her vest top not quite enough to keep out the chill of the early morning shadows. The day promised to be another hot one, but the mist was still hanging on the water, and it was nippy out of the sun. It was almost seven, far too early for any sane person to be up on a bank holiday Monday, although she was sure there were probably fishermen out on the lough somewhere. She'd crept out of the house, leaving Ruairi fast asleep. He'd come home late again, disturbing her as he got into bed.

Inside, punching her code into the Coffee Dock's alarm panel, she locked the main door behind her and crossed the silent cafe to the counter. Dipping down behind the till, she threw her handbag onto the shelf below it, before taking a minute to look out over the lough, the early morning mist swirling in an elaborate dance on the surface.

She'd always been an early riser – was often up at five, getting Ben's lunch ready, doing the laundry and getting the house straight before she left for work. That way, when she came home, the evening was hers. Nine times out of ten, she brought dinner home with her, so she just had to help with Ben's homework and then she could relax, the chores out of the way. But evenings seemed to be the time that Ruairi got things done. To start with, she'd taken it in her stride that he worked late at night, but as the Adventure Centre had become more successful, she couldn't understand why he didn't let the manager do more, or expand the staff. If the business could afford a fleet of 4 × 4s, surely there was room for more day-to-day help.

Danielle wasn't entirely sure why it was only now, after nine years of marriage, that she was seeing that they were polar opposites.

Leaning on the stainless steel counter, she closed her eyes for a moment, relishing the early morning solitude, the peace. She really needed it. Thoughts of Jules kept crowding in when she least expected it, winding her every time.

Danielle turned around, her back to the water, and looked at the counter behind the servery, gathering herself. She knew people thought she was mad, working this week – Ruairi did, too – but she needed to keep busy or she'd be constantly breaking down in tears, and that wasn't good for anyone.

At least getting in at this time meant that she could have everything prepped before the girls arrived, could get ahead of the day by making a pile of their speciality sandwiches and baking some fresh scones. It would be crazy mad. She took a shaky breath, tears pricking at her eyes.

Danielle bit her lip hard and looked around her. Jules had almost become part of the place when they were getting set up. That was before she'd taken the job at the Coyne Arms, and she'd been so excited, sharing their plans. She'd trained in hospitality, had helped order the fridges and worked on the menus. Sometimes Danielle marvelled at what they'd created.

Danielle had had a vision for the Coffee Dock that had been much bigger than Ruairi had even thought possible. What had started with a coffee machine in the corner of the reception area of the Adventure Centre had steadily grown in her mind until she'd suggested taking over this space, originally a boat repair shed, refurbishing it and putting in panoramic windows.

Jules had been so supportive when Danielle had explained the idea. Ruairi had objected at first – had thought coffee was a waste of time, that people wanted to get out on the water, not sit and look at it – but she'd persuaded him to take on more staff to free her up. Opening the Coffee Dock had doubled the hire trade, people coming from all over to make a day of their trip. It had become the starting point for walkers, a meeting point for the locals at the weekends. And it gave her focus.

It meant long hours and more work, but it was worth it. And hiring a good manager for the Adventure Centre, rather than relying on her to do the staff rosters and the accounts, meant Ruairi had time to focus on building the search and rescue team, to train them. He loved being in charge, being the boss of such a successful business, coming and going when it suited him.

Danielle slipped off her hoodie, balling it up beside her bag. It was warm inside, the cumulative heat from the week trapped despite them opening every available window and door. Danielle flipped on the switches under the till, looking up at the ceiling as the fans began to turn.

Behind her the coffee machine clunked and whirred, lights flashing on as it burst into life. She needed a coffee before she went into the tiny space that was her office. The staff rosters needed doing, and the VAT for her accountant, neither of which she enjoyed.

While she waited for the machine to warm up, Danielle bent down to check the contents of the fridges underneath the counter. The girls had neatly cling-filmed all the salads in their Tupperware containers last night. She smiled; she had them well trained, but she could see she'd need to chop more tomatoes and cucumber, and they needed more peppers diced.

Danielle reached for a purple apron hanging on the inside of the open servery door, pulling it on. She'd get the few bits done here, have her coffee, and then take a look at the stuff on her desk when the girls arrived.

Danielle headed for the huge walk-in fridge on the other side of her office, where the salad vegetables were all stored with the cakes. A thump to her right made her jump as she passed the staff kitchen, the door still open as she'd left it the night before. She glanced inside. The window was ajar, gently bumping on the frame as a breath of wind caught it. Puzzled, Danielle went over to close it properly. She'd definitely closed it before she left.

Leaning over the small sink, she reached for the catch, realising as she did so that it was loose, the normally stiff handle pivoting uselessly. Something else she'd have to get fixed. The last thing they needed was a bunch of kids breaking in and trashing the place.

Opening the window wide and pinning the arm to stop it blowing open and breaking, she stepped back. A mug lay on its side in the sink. She was sure that had been on the draining board the previous night. She looked around. Nothing else was out of place.

Had a cat got in and knocked it off? Surely it would have set off the alarm?

Danielle shivered. She didn't like the thought of people or animals in here when the place was empty.

Especially now.

Had someone broken into Julia's cottage, and been waiting for her when she got home?

Feeling her chest tightening, Danielle pushed the thought away. She couldn't deal with that now. She only had so much headspace.

Leaving the kitchen, she opened the fridge door, immediately hit with a refreshing wave of cold air. It helped her tear her mind away from what might have happened – the doctor with the streak in her hair had said she needed to avoid speculating; it would only drive her mad. She was right: Danielle needed to focus on the day's jobs and give her grief time to settle. The Gardaí would find out what happened; her imagination running away wasn't going to make anything better.

Quickly filling the big plastic container they used to carry vegetables to the counter, Danielle could feel goose pimples forming on her arms.

Behind the servery, she put the box down beside the sink and reached for her favourite heavy prep knife.

But it wasn't in its usual place in the centre of the wooden block.

The girls were always using that knife for cutting sandwiches – had they left it out by accident? Danielle checked the servery sink. The stainless steel gleamed back at her from last night's clean-up.

Puzzled, Danielle turned to check the chill cabinet. By the time they opened up, it would be full of freshly made sandwiches, cakes displayed on the glass shelves above it. But right now it was empty. Not there either.

Bobbing down, Danielle checked the fridges, and then between the industrial-sized boxes of cling film that lived on the counter. Had it fallen behind them? Nothing.

Danielle put her hands on her hips and looked around the servery. There really wasn't anywhere else it could be. The girls had their own cutlery in the staff kitchen, and the knife was so big it didn't fit in the drawer. She would have noticed if they'd left it in the sink in there. Frowning, she looked at the knife block. All the smaller knives were in place. But the big one from the middle was definitely missing.

Chapter 38

'ARE YOU READY? Grace? I've put the bags in the boot.' Carla came in through the front door. She'd only been outside a few minutes, had left Grace in the kitchen wiping down the surfaces, but she'd obviously found something else to do before they left the cottage.

'Out here. I'm just having another coffee.'

Carla rolled her eyes. Now she'd got it into her head, she wanted to get back to Dublin, wanted to spend some time in the office to prepare before the TV crew arrived.

Pulling her phone out of her jeans, she looked at the time: 7.15. They really did have lots of time, and she'd already washed her hair this morning, loving the super soft water in the huge walk-in shower at the end of their bedroom. She just had to get home and change, and then head to the Phoenix Park ahead of the interview. In theory, the roads would be clear this early on a bank holiday, so they should make good time. As long as they left by nine at the latest, they'd be fine.

Carla reached for a coffee pod and popped it in the machine, slipping a mug under the nozzle. A minute later, her mug full of a frothy latte, she went outside to join Grace.

She was sitting on the deck with her face up to the sunshine, a navy cardigan slung around her shoulders over a sundress sprigged with yellow flowers.

'Do you think we could buy this place? I mean, with everything happening, Melissa's husband might be open to an offer.'

'Grace!' Carla sat down beside her, shaking her head, trying not to laugh. 'You're incorrigible. I really don't think we should be asking right now, do you? He'll be so deep in shock I don't think he'll be able for questions.'

Without turning her head, Grace smiled to herself. 'True, but hold that thought. Jack can tell us how the land lies in due course. It would be nice to see him occasionally.'

Carla shook her head again. 'You're *so* bold.'

'I know, but don't you love me for it?'

Carla snorted her response and took a sip of her coffee, looking out over the lake, the surface of the water mirror-like. Grace really did have a point – this place would make the perfect weekend bolt-hole.

'I was thinking ...' Grace turned in her chair to look at Carla and picked up her coffee. 'There's an intensity to these murders happening so close together. Normally a serial killer would take time between killings. The joy is in the planning, the anticipation. I'm not seeing that here.'

Carla didn't pick her up on the 'normally' – was anything normal about a serial killer? – but she did have a point.

'Tell me what you're thinking.'

Grace screwed up her nose. 'Clearly he's planned them. The whole MO is significant.'

'Taking out someone's heart isn't easy. The sternum's there to protect it, and there's a lot of cartilage where it joins the ribs. Given that he must have done it reasonably quickly, particularly in Melissa's case, the window of opportunity is really quite narrow. He had to have had some practice.' Carla sipped her coffee.

'So he could be a medic?' Grace looked across at her.

'Or a butcher. Or …' Carla paused. 'Jack said they'd found some wounded deer on the estate. Melissa's husband was going out at night looking for poachers. If you were going for a dry run, a deer would be about the right size and weight. Anything smaller wouldn't present the same challenges as a person.'

Grace looked at Carla, nodding slowly. 'Or perhaps he's got a degree in anatomy, like you?'

Carla shrugged. 'I think he has to have some experience. I'll say it to Jack to check the deer. If they have been mutilated, then it suggests he isn't just here for the weekend.'

'Very true. I'm thinking – why now? What's sparked

this? He's targeted the sisters. It's almost like he's fixated with them for some reason. I've no evidence for that, obviously, but the ritualistic method – cutting out their hearts, and displaying them – suggests there *is* symbolism at play here.'

Carla sighed. Sometimes being with Grace was like being in the office 24–7, especially when she went into analytical mode. Knowing she wasn't about to stop, Carla rolled her hand, encouraging her to continue.

Grace shifted on the cushioned metal chair, making herself more comfortable. 'He wants them to be found. He's making a statement. About them, and about himself. Was he in love with one or both of them, and they spurned him? Is it *his* heart they've broken?'

'Do we need to tell Jack to check out stalkers? Anyone bothering them?'

Grace glanced across the table at her. 'I'm sure he's already looking at that. It could be someone who was a regular in Julia's bar, or someone who has stayed in one of the cottages, perhaps a repeat visitor.'

Her eyes fixed on the distant mountains, Carla took another sip of her coffee. 'But the boathouse isn't that public, is it? You said he was displaying them, wanted them to be found. Melissa could have been there for days before anyone looked inside. Didn't Jack say it's normally kept locked?'

Grace nodded slowly. 'I think it must have special

significance for him. The whole estate does, maybe, given that Julia was found here, too.'

'So it's someone who has a connection to the family, knows the area. Likely a similar age? That puts the spotlight on Sean or Ruairi Brennan a bit, doesn't it? Almost ninety per cent of women are killed by people they know.' Carla stopped for a moment, thinking. 'But perhaps Danielle will be able to think of someone who had a connection to both of them.' She sighed. 'I wonder if she knows yet? Jack said Sean wasn't able to talk to anyone last night, but she'll be devastated when she finds out. From talking to her, she seemed very close to them.'

'She will be. No easy way around it. But both Julia and Melissa were fit, and the post-mortems should show whether they tried to fight him off. Let's hope there's some DNA caught somewhere.'

Carla pushed her hair behind her ear. 'I'm pretty sure Melissa's nails were gels. They'd take a lump out of you. Although Jack said there was a puncture mark in Julia's shoulder. It'll be interesting if they find one on Melissa's body somewhere.'

'It seems likely he drugged them to disable them. When toxicology comes back, it should tell us more about what with.' Grace took a sip of her coffee.

Carla sighed. 'So someone who has knowledge of sedative drugs.'

'He might not need that much knowledge. GHB is easy enough to get hold of.'

'True. Are you finished?' Carla stood up. 'I hope Danielle's OK. I meant to give her my card yesterday. Can we fly past the cafe on the way to the Dublin road?'

'She's not going to be open.'

'Obviously. I'll leave her a note and stick it under the door. I can text Jack about the deer on the way.'

Grace looked at the time on her phone. 'Let's have breakfast before we go, will we? It'll be baking in Dublin and it's blissful here.'

Carla looked at her reproachfully. 'I've got a press interview to do.'

'Just another half an hour, then? I'll make you another coffee. Breathe in that clean air. You'll be glad of it when we get back.'

Chapter 39

ITTING IN THE empty cafe, the whir of the ceiling fans the only sound, Danielle looked across at Jack and Donna, her brain paralysed with shock. It had to be some sort of huge mistake.

How could Melissa be dead? How was she only finding out now? Had he not told her because he thought she had something to do with it?

Waves of shock reverberated around her head.

'Are you sure? I mean, it could be someone staying in one of the cottages?' Her voice wasn't much more than a whisper.

'I'm afraid we're sure. I'm sorry to ask now, but where were you yesterday afternoon?'

'At home. I came in yesterday morning. Staring at those four walls imagining what ... There's no time to think here. Especially ... It's so busy. But then ...' Danielle put her hand to her face. 'I couldn't. Your doctor colleague gave me a lift home. The one with the streak in her hair.' Danielle

240

couldn't think of her name. 'I *spoke* to Melissa yesterday, in the afternoon. She said she was going out for a walk.'

'What time was that?'

Danielle shrugged. 'Before three, I think. I texted her later but she didn't reply.'

'And who was with you yesterday?'

Danielle stared at him. It still didn't seem real – none of this felt real. She realised he was waiting for her to answer.

'I was on my own at home. Becky and Niamh were here all day. I came in later to send you those recordings.'

Across the table, Jack smiled encouragingly. She was starting to hate this table. He seemed to choose it every time he came in. When he'd gone, she'd get the girls to move it, to push it up against another one and make an eight on the other side of the counter. It'd be useful for groups. And she'd never have to sit here again.

'And Ruairi?'

She barely heard him. Beside him, Donna reached across the table and patted her arm.

Danielle looked at her hands, realising she'd been spinning the thin gold band of her wedding ring constantly since Jack had started speaking. She looked back at him. 'What? Sorry?'

'Ruairi?' His prompt was gentle.

Danielle shrugged. 'I don't know where he was. He came home late. I went to bed early with a bottle of wine, so I don't know what time.' Her lip trembled. 'I'm sorry, I can't …' She drew in a breath. 'Why didn't you tell us yesterday? How could you wait …?'

Jack cleared his throat, had the decency to look sorry. 'We needed to, I'm afraid – operational reasons.'

Operational reasons? What did that mean?

A rap on the glass door made them all spin around.

Danielle looked over Jack's shoulder, confused. 'We're closed …'

Through the glass she could see the doctor … Carla – that was it. She'd been so nice. Her friend had died. It was coming back now. *Didn't she know they were closed?*

Jack stood up, pushing his chair into place. 'That's Dr Steele. She's on her way back up to Dublin. Can I let her in?'

As Danielle nodded slowly, he got up and crossed the wooden floor to the door. The keys were still in it.

Danielle stood up as Carla came in.

'I'm sorry to intrude. We were passing. I wanted to leave you my card and then I saw the lights on.'

Suddenly Danielle could feel emotion welling up inside her like the swirling waters of the lake, threatening to overwhelm her. She stood up. 'Can you take me home? I need to go home.'

Danielle felt herself sway, but Donna was around the table in a second, a steadying arm around her.

'I just need my bag …'

As Danielle turned towards the servery there was a bang from the corridor. She started, the sound echoing in her head like a gunshot.

'What was that?' Donna craned to see through the open servery door into the rear corridor.

'The window, I think. In the staff kitchen.' Danielle's hands started to shake. She put her hand over her mouth. 'The girls are coming in at ten … The keys …'

'I think you could close for one day. People would understand.' Still by the front door, Danielle could feel Jack watching her.

'No, we need to open. The bills. The girls should be all right, it's just the keys—'

Carla cut in. 'How about Donna and Jack lock up? They can make sure the girls get the keys. I'll take you home in your car. Grace can follow in hers and then we'll head back to Dublin. How does that sound?'

Chapter 40

THE NEWS INTERVIEW could definitely have gone better.

Sitting in her office, her eyes closed, Carla rubbed her face with her hands. What a day. Danielle Brennan had been in complete shock this morning. It was just as well Carla knew where her house was; she hadn't been capable of giving directions, and driving her 4 × 4 had been like driving a tank. Carla had considered buying a Pathfinder when she'd bought her own Fiat 500X, thinking it would be useful in the mountains, and considering how much climbing gear she could get in the rear. She was very glad she'd gone for the smaller vehicle now.

Grace had followed them, and then insisted they call Danielle's doctor before they left. The poor woman was practically catatonic; she hadn't wanted them to come in. Which Carla totally got – her husband had been reeking of booze when he'd come to the door to see what was keeping her, his eyes bloodshot. He'd taken one look at them and headed inside as if this was their fault.

Thank goodness the roads hadn't been too bad on the way to Dublin and they'd got home in plenty of time, Nigel alternating between being thrilled to see them and meowing accusingly, huffy that they'd left him to be fed by next door. She'd found a suit that looked good and she wouldn't completely melt in, and then she'd driven to the Phoenix Park in twenty minutes. Raph had left the files on her desk, and everything had been going great until she'd walked into the press room and sensed tension in the air, the RTÉ crime correspondent being unusually saccharine.

Carla chided herself. There were times when she could be a total idiot – for a minute she'd believed that the press were actually interested in the FACE lab work. It was boiling, and it was a bank holiday Monday, but she realised as she pushed open the swing doors to the briefing room that they'd brought a full crew with them.

Arc lights and three cameramen for a simple piece to camera?

Carla normally handled the press well – granted, whatever you said could be chopped up and turned into something you didn't say at all – but the interview had very quickly turned into an interrogation session.

Opening her eyes, Carla glanced at the clock on her monitor screen.

How long had she been sitting here, going over it all in her head?

At times like this, all her failures revisited her – Lizzie, Girl X …

Would the Coyne's Cross skull, now waiting patiently in the lab, be another one?

Sighing, Carla moved her mouse to look at Girl X, but she was only half concentrating.

She should have seen it coming, really.

She'd gone into the briefing to talk about Train Ticket Man – *Rocky Mehan*, she corrected herself – and Welsh Woman, now identified as a Jo Griffiths. Instead, she'd been questioned relentlessly about what she'd been doing in Coyne's Cross and the ongoing case unfolding there.

Melissa's murder had been all over the news by mid-morning, and of course Carla had been photographed talking to Jack in the Coffee Dock on Sunday, the white streak in her hair making her unmistakable, even through the glass. They'd also spotted Grace, and assumed that a task force from Garda Headquarters had been deployed in the hunt for a serial killer, that the skull belonged to another victim.

Despite Carla deflecting their questions about Julia and Melissa, the journalist had grilled her.

Her elbows on her desk, Carla ran her hands through her hair, her head starting to ache thinking about it. The questions had come like machine-gunfire, from obvious conjecture to the utterly ridiculous, at which point she'd managed to extricate herself, saying she had a meeting scheduled and reminding her interviewer that they were there to focus on Rocky Mehan's last movements.

Carla took a sharp breath, her irritation building. If she'd thought for one second it was going to turn into a circus of clickbait-inspired cross-examination, she'd have stayed in Coyne's Cross, enjoying the sunshine.

Although 'enjoying' was probably the wrong word, given the situation. And Grace was right. She really did want to get started on the Coyne's Cross skull. The resin casts would be set by the morning, and Grace was due at Mountjoy Prison all of the following day, so Carla wouldn't be disturbed as she started work on it.

Carla looked back at Girl X, her image filling the desktop screen, thinking about her story. Even if they still didn't have a name for her, at least the work they did at FACE gave victims a literal face, a voice, a chance to be heard.

Would Lizzie ever get that chance? They knew exactly who she was, but her case was the polar opposite of Girl X – they had no body.

Three cases, all different – Lizzie, Girl X, and whoever had gone into Lough Coyne. Carla rubbed the tattoo on her forearm. *Like her three little birds. They might be flying with brave wings, but it was her job to bring them home.*

Chapter 41

CARLA TURNED HER car radio up to full as she drove into work on Tuesday morning. She knew better than to switch the news on. Jessie J was much more her thing right now. 'Bang Bang' made her want to dance whenever she heard it – which meant she was getting some amused looks from the other drivers at the lights, and a thumbs up from a workman in the passenger seat of a white van that drew up beside her.

At least music put her in a good mood. It lifted her, whatever the problem. And if she kept away from the papers, she could put the press conference down to experience – she was sure she wouldn't have to wait long for another crisis to knock Coyne's Cross off the front pages.

As she pulled into the Phoenix Park, a WhatsApp voice message came through from Grace:

Looking verrrrrry sexy on the front page of the Daily Mail hun. Snapper caught us at the Coffee Dock.

Holy God, that was all she needed.

After the success of her true crime TV series, Grace was used to being spread across the papers, but it was definitely something Carla could live without.

Flashing her pass and pulling under the barrier into the forecourt of Garda Headquarters, Carla drove slowly off to her right and had to go almost to the rear of the huge Victorian barracks to find a space. At least she didn't have to double-park. Squeezing out, she left her keys in her ignition in case anyone needed to move her car and, keeping her head down, she walked towards the building. No doubt everyone had seen the papers.

The third floor was humming when she got there. The joy of working flexitime meant that a lot of the techs came in early, and were halfway through the day by 9 a.m., when the rest of the world was only starting to get going.

In her office, Carla threw her backpack under her desk and grabbed her lab coat off the back of the door.

Raph had got into the lab ahead of her, already had the resin casts waiting for her on their tubular steel stands, ready to work on. On the bench beside them he'd left the alginate mould he'd made, taken from the original skull.

Cupping the cast in her hands, Carla looked at it closely, recalling the photographs of the mispers she'd seen in the files Jack had given her. She'd found a better photo of Gemma Langan in a press report online, but hadn't read the article – she didn't want to be led by the journalist's interpretation, or misinterpretation, of the facts. As soon as she'd made a start, she intended to look up the case on PULSE and read the statements.

Coupled with the dental development, the spacing between the sutures of the cranium on the original skull suggested a young person to her. Small zygomatics on either side of the face, and the small brow ridge, all pointed to this being a female of European origin.

The cast Raph had made was a perfect replica, enabling Carla to work freely without fear of damaging the skull's delicate bones. She studied it carefully. If only it could speak.

Turning to the bench behind her, Carla pulled open a drawer and began to assemble her equipment. Unwrapping her clay working tools from the embossed soft leather roll Grace had given her, she laid them on the bench alongside the rest of her apparatus: rulers and a micrometer that measured millimetres; a spirit level, so she could gauge the Frankfurt Plane – the line between the lower margins of the orbits and the upper margins of the ear canal – giving her the correct angle the skull would rest at, if the subject were standing normally.

Next came the tissue depth markers that would help her rebuild the missing flesh, and a handful of pins to hold them in the correct places.

Working deftly, Carla used a ruler to draw a line with a chalk pencil along the Frankfurt Plane, passing through the inferior margin of the left orbit and the upper margin of the auditory canal, giving her a midline to check with her spirit level.

Raph had left the clay ready for her, wrapped in cling film so it didn't dry out too quickly. She pressed a wedge of it into the hole Raph had drilled in the base of the replica skull to secure it to the stand. The curved plate with its rubber-tipped grippers had been removed, replaced with a dowel that fitted into the top of the pipe.

The osteometric markers were next – plastic pegs positioned in sixteen crucial locations across the face. When she'd first learned these techniques at university in Dundee, she been amazed that the same measurements developed by three researchers working in the late 1800s were still the basis of what was used today. The values of each of these points, defined and agreed way back then, allowed researchers to make comparative measurements of the skull – and the rest of the skeleton – in a clear manner. The values had been determined by a wide-ranging study of tissue morphology in living and deceased men and women from a range of ancestral groups. The data acted as a baseline to work from; it had been added to over the years, as more research papers were published, but was a vital first step.

When they had more information about the deceased, even if it was just a part of the body to work with, they could see how lifestyle factors might have impacted the subject's face. She'd had cases before where facial ageing had been accelerated by smoking, sun damage or weight loss; others where it had been essential to reflect significant weight gain in the facial development.

Her long hair tied out of her way, Carla hummed as she worked, the soundtrack she'd played on the way into town still fresh in her mind. Once the tissue markers were in place, she would begin to build the facial muscles, and then the skin.

But first Carla gave the skull back its eyesight.

Opening another drawer, she selected a pair of artificial eyes from the rows that looked up at her: blue for this one. They could change the eye colour in the 3-D renders she would create on the computer later, but if this subject was Irish, there was a strong chance they had had blue eyes.

Laying them beside her on the bench, Carla bit her lip as she etched the midpoints in the eye socket with her chalk pencil and then deftly built it out with clay, giving the concave plastic eyes a bed to rest in. Completely absorbed in her work, she pressed the first eye into the clay, using her ruler to double-check the midpoint was aligned with the pupil and the orbit was neatly aligned with the bones of the face. It was protruding slightly so, taking it out, she used a tool to hollow out a little more clay, then replaced it, repeating her checks to make sure it was centred correctly.

This moment always gave her a weird tingling sensation, as if the subject might begin to speak to her – to tell her their story. She wished they would. Taking a step away from the bench, Carla looked hard at her work so far. She was still a long way off, but more and more about this skull was telling her it was female.

Next she built out the muscle groups, rolling balls of clay between her hands and smoothing them into place. The more she worked, the more she became familiar with the subject. The size and shape of the nasal spine, the position of the nasal pyramid, and the pure form aperture at the base of the nose all told her about the subject's nose shape and position. The shape of the jaw spoke to her about how this subject had looked in life. She'd done hundreds of reconstructions over the years, and some features – the lips, eyelids and ears – required a degree of artistic interpretation to get right, but once the eyes were in, it felt like a significant step. As Grace was always saying, accurate facial reconstruction was a combination of science, artistry and just a little magic.

Chapter 42

IN THE BASEMENT of Coyne's Cross Garda Station, Jack sat beside Matt Curran and reached for his takeaway coffee. Jack had bought them both chicken fillet rolls on his way from Coyne House.

'I don't know how you stay awake in here.'

Going through CCTV footage a frame at a time was unbelievably tedious in Jack's book. Thank God Matt seemed to thrive on it. It took forever, though.

Matt looked at Jack over his shoulder, his eyebrows raised. 'It could be the thing that catches this bastard. And it keeps me clear of the grief. This job is shit when it's someone you know.'

'That's for sure.' *And didn't he know it.*

Jack cleared his throat. 'Ruairi Brennan was in bits when I called over yesterday morning. I never for a minute thought Danielle would have gone to work, but I suppose it kept her mind off Jules.' He sighed. 'She almost collapsed when she heard about Melissa. Carla – Dr Steele – said they had to call her GP when they dropped her home.'

Matt took a bite of his roll and flicked his mouse, opening a shot of the main street from what appeared to be a street camera. 'Not surprised. Wasn't far off myself.' He rolled his cursor on the screen. 'OK, so this is where I got to on Sunday. I've tracked Julia's movements on Friday via the CCTV in the town. When she left work she drove out onto the main street, heading this way, but then we lose her for the best part of two hours before she appears on the camera at the Coyne Estate gates.' He scowled. 'No one reported any cars parked up on the main road on Friday or Saturday. You know yourself, it's narrow and there are no verges, so if she stopped on the way home to make a call or something, any traffic would have had to pull around her.'

Matt flicked the mouse again, switching to another set of cameras. 'When I got in this morning, I started to go through the CCTV Danielle Brennan sent.'

'Go on.' Jack could tell he was working up to something.

'It turns out that Julia pulled into the car park beside the Adventure Centre and called into the office.'

'But that must have been after eleven o'clock? Isn't that when the bar manager said she left work?'

Matt glanced at him. 'Sure is. And it looks like she was meeting someone there. Watch – you'll see.'

The screen was divided into small rectangles, each one a different camera at a different angle. Matt pointed at the lower corner of the screen, where a fisheye lens gave a view of the car park. Jack watched as Julia's car pulled in close to the door to reception. As she got out of the car, Matt flicked to a different camera that gave a wide shot of the reception itself.

'There's an intercom on the reception door. She's buzzed in and she stays there about an hour and a half.' Matt pointed to the fisheye camera again and moved the time on with his mouse. 'Here she is, coming out and heading back to her car. Ten minutes later Ruairi Brennan appears, turns off the lights and locks up.'

Jack lifted his eyebrows. 'He told us he was at the centre all evening. Got home around 12.45 a.m. Danielle confirmed he was late. She went to bed about 10.30 and heard him come in, but didn't know what time. He said he was catching up on paperwork.'

'I doubt it was paperwork that they were doing at that time of night.' Matt's tone said exactly what was going through Jack's head.

'We need to bring him in for a chat. But first I want to know if Jules visited on any previous occasions, and I want to know exactly where he was on Sunday night. Can you do that?'

'No problem. How far do you want me to go back?'

Jack kept his eyes on the screen for a moment. 'A month? Will that be enough?'

'I reckon so. It's going to take a good bit of tomorrow, though. I should have clips for you by tomorrow evening. I'll go through the on-street cameras as well, and the Coyne Arms, in case they met anywhere else.'

'That would be great. Let's get all our ducks in a row and bring him in on Thursday morning. He's got some explaining to do.'

Chapter 43

DANIELLE CROSSED HER arms tightly while she waited for the kettle to boil and closed her eyes. It was almost dinner time, but she had no appetite and no idea what was in the fridge. She could hear Ruairi and Sean talking in the sitting room, their voices low, washed out, like old T-shirts where all the colours had faded to a shadow.

She'd only got through Monday because the doctor had given her something to calm her down. She felt as if everything was some sort of blur.

Was that only yesterday? It was as if her life had slowed down; every minute felt like an hour, every hour like a day. Part of her brain still couldn't believe what had happened. Perhaps it was the shock, but really she hadn't been able to take it in.

When she'd got home with Carla, Ruairi had looked like she felt. But then he'd barely been sober since Saturday; his hangover had bleached his tan under his russet beard.

He'd stood in the kitchen doorway as she'd closed the front door behind her, leaning on the frame, trying to steady herself. He was still wearing his T-shirt and pyjama bottoms, rubbing his cropped hair hard with both hands as if the action would massage away the pain. He looked as if he was going to throw up.

Thanks God Ben was with his dad. Thank God it was the summer holidays and he could stay there for the week.

Beside her in the kitchen, the kettle boiled, the sound of it clicking off making Danielle jump.

The day before, she'd gone straight upstairs without speaking to Ruairi, closed all the curtains and curled up in bed, waiting for the doctor to come. They'd barely said a word since then. When she'd thought about it, between her early mornings and his late nights, they'd actually hardly had a proper conversation in about six months. He was working on some sort of development project, he'd said; he'd reveal all when he was closer to finishing it. And she'd been so busy in the cafe with the good weather, she'd hardly noticed that their days off hadn't coincided since she didn't know when.

At least Sean was here now. It was good for both of them, and for him to get out of the house.

Having someone else around made it easier – reduced the tension that was ramping between them. When she'd finally surfaced from whatever tablets the doctor had brought with him, it had been mid-afternoon. Ruairi had already gone to Coyne House to see how Sean was. He'd left a note, at least, so she didn't have to guess whether he'd gone to the pub or the Adventure Centre, or was lying injured in A & E after crashing his jeep.

She'd known she should go, too, but she couldn't face the thought of leaving home, let alone returning to Coyne House.

When he'd arrived on the doorstep this morning, Sean had said the whole place was crawling with Gardaí, that he'd needed to get away.

Danielle ran her hands over her face.

Where the hell had the guards been when Melissa left the house? She'd said she needed to get some air, but surely there had been someone there?

Sean had told them everything again when he'd arrived. It was as if he couldn't stop talking about it, his face in his hands. Ruairi had put his arm around him and they'd rocked each other, their eyes wet with tears.

How were they supposed to go on from here? How could Sean run the holiday cottages and do his own job?

Danielle didn't know. There were just so many questions. And she knew she was avoiding the biggest one.

Who the fuck had done this, and why? And had he finished? Could he come after her, or maybe one of the girls from the town next?

Everyone was scared. But not nearly as scared as she was. Danielle looked at her hand. It was still shaking. *Scared* didn't come close to how terrified she felt.

How was she going to cope going into the cafe? What if whoever had done this was a customer? She couldn't stop people coming in, or hide out the back all day. And she could almost hear the talk – the ghoulish murder tourists and nosy locals who had forgotten Mel and Jules were her cousins, speculating about how this had happened. Victim blaming. That was always everyone's first thought: what had they done to bring this on themselves?

A volley of gunfire echoed around the house and Danielle froze. It took her a moment to realise Ruairi and Sean had put on a video game, the volume turned up full. They'd be sitting there now like a pair of teenagers, mesmerised. Christ, she wished she had a way to get out of this reality and into an alternative one. One where there were no dead people, no bodies lying waiting to be found.

Splashing the hot water into the teapot, Danielle focused on what she was doing.

What was she doing? Would Sean and Ruairi really want tea?

She'd come in and put the kettle on without thinking about it, but they both probably needed something stronger. She turned on the coffee machine and reached for the bottle of whiskey instead.

Chapter 44

THE AROMA OF barbecues was drifting across the nearby gardens when Carla got home from the lab, the air still, heavy with the heat of the day. Grace was out on the patio, sitting astride the lounger, her sunglasses on the top of her head, a glass of wine in her hand. She had her iPad in front of her and was scrolling through the crime scene photos of Coyne's Cross that Jack had sent her.

At the end of the lounger Nigel was crouching, looking at her intently, his tail flicking every time she swiped the screen. As Carla stepped out of the patio doors, Grace jumped.

'Oh God, I didn't hear you. I was concentrating.'

Carla walked over and kissed her. 'Don't worry, babes. Just look at Nigel, he's concentrating, too. He's mesmerised by you.'

Grace threw an evil glare at the huge ginger cat and, looking up at Carla, pouted, waiting for another kiss. Carla smiled, bending down to kiss her again. 'I keep telling you – he loves you.'

Grace turned to look at Nigel with disdain. 'We've got a deal, haven't we, Nige? If you puke in my shoes again, I'm going to turn you into a fur hat.'

She said it in a playful, sing-song voice, but it was as if Nigel understood every word. He continued to study her as if she was his next meal.

Grace stuck out her tongue at him. 'If I'm ever found dead in this house, you'll know I've been murdered by a cat.'

'Funny. Let me top up that glass. I need one, too. Long day. How was yours? What have you been up to?'

'Mountjoy most of the day, then hanging out with Nige here. Be quick with that wine, I've missed you.'

Carla was in the kitchen, piling up the cheeseboard, when her phone rang.

It was Jack.

'Good evening, Sergeant Maguire. How are things down there?'

'Could ask you the same thing. Saw you on the news.'

Carla pulled a face. 'The less said about that, the better. How many ways can you deflect a question without saying no comment, repeatedly?'

'Who's that?' Grace appeared behind her and pulled a grape off the bunch spilling off the heavy board.

'Jack, on a video call. Say hello.' She passed Grace the phone, leaning in to the camera before she let it go. 'We're just going out to the garden, Jack. Give us two minutes.'

Carla grabbed the cheeseboard and the glasses, while Grace followed her out with the bottle of wine, showing Jack the kitchen and garden on the way.

Sitting down at the patio table, Carla propped the phone up against the wine bottle. 'Can you see us both? What's the news?'

Jack looked as if he was in the incident room, sitting at the end of the conference table. Behind him they could see the chairs set out in front of the boards. He quickly brought them up to date on the CCTV discoveries.

Beside Carla, Grace was frowning as he finished speaking. 'So Julia called into the Adventure Centre, did she? Popping in to see her cousin's husband? Very naughty.' She paused. 'But you saw her go back to her car, so she was alive when she left.'

'We did, and then she left the car park and turned right towards Coyne House. Ruairi left shortly after her.'

Grace narrowed her eyes, obviously thinking. 'If they were having a liaison, it certainly pushes him up the suspect list. But if Julia was killed Friday night, would he have had time to follow her to the cottage, take her into the woods and get back home for 12.45 – assuming he's accurate on the time?'

Carla leaned forwards and rested her chin on her hand. 'If Danielle didn't look at the clock, we've only got his word for what time he arrived home.'

On the phone screen, Jack nodded. 'True. He isn't the most reliable witness, but I think he would have been very tight for time Friday night.'

'And where was Ruairi on Saturday morning?' Carla reached for a cracker as Jack replied.

'Definitely at the centre from about eight o'clock – there all day. About a hundred people saw him.' Jack sounded tired as he continued. 'Matt Curran's looking at all the security camera video we can get hold of, and he's going through the recordings from Coyne House to see if their camera might have picked Brennan up Friday night or very early Saturday. The problem is that Ruairi and Danielle's house is right out of the town, inland from the lough, and there are no cameras anywhere along the road once you've gone past Coyne House. And that camera is focused on the gates, not on the road. So we've nothing to confirm his story for Friday night.'

Grace took a sip of her wine. She'd been listening intently. 'He knows the area. If he killed Julia Friday night, he would have known exactly where to leave her body. It would have been dark, even darker under the trees, so he could have been there for ages without anyone seeing him. He knows Danielle is usually asleep when he gets home. He could have got in at four o'clock and nobody would be any the wiser.'

Jack nodded his agreement. 'And he would know where the cameras were on the estate – and potentially how to avoid them. He must have been in and out of there a hundred times over the years.'

Carla hooked her dark hair behind her ear. 'But wouldn't someone have seen her sooner if he'd left her there on Friday night? I mean, you said you thought she was just about visible from the avenue, Jack?'

'Indeed, but that does depend which direction you're going in and assume that you're looking into that patch of woods in the first place. It's possible she was there but wasn't spotted. Like Grace says, it's pitch dark under those trees at night. She could have been killed when she got home and been there all Friday night. Although the flies suggest it was the early hours.'

'But they aren't active at night, are they? The flies, I mean. They need polarised light to guide them visually, and the drop in temperature makes them sluggish.' Carla paused. 'And why kill Julia like that? It's just so drastic.'

She started to reach for another grape and changed her mind, the memories of finding Julia Hardiman still fresh. Beyond the gentle conversation rising from the gardens around them, punctuated by the laughter of children, the sound of the sea breaking on the beach would have been soothing if they'd been having any other conversation.

Never squeamish, Grace broke off a corner of a cracker and popped it into her mouth thoughtfully. 'Perhaps Julia wanted him to leave Danielle? Was threatening to tell her.

The significance of her heart being cut out ties in with that. Perhaps he felt she was cutting out his heart in making him choose?'

Carla glanced from Grace to her phone. 'That theory would make sense if Melissa *hadn't* been killed in the same manner,' she said, 'but perhaps Danielle found out about the affair and killed them both. The symbolism works both ways.'

On the screen, Jack shrugged. 'Perhaps Melissa knew. They were all very close, after all. Perhaps Melissa threatened to expose the affair?'

Carla played with her ring thoughtfully. 'But you said Sean was with Ruairi on Sunday – before he found Melissa, I mean. So he couldn't have killed Melissa unless he did it much earlier in the afternoon, and somehow scooted back without anyone missing him. The Adventure Centre was busy all day on Sunday, too. The whole place had to be heaving, between the weather and the news.'

Jack nodded. 'True. Sean was with Ruairi from about 4.30 all right – that's confirmed by their CCTV. But Sean left the house at three o'clock, don't forget. If Ruairi had arranged to meet Melissa earlier – at, say, 3.15 – he could have killed her and been back at his office by the time Sean called over. Coyne House is a twenty-minute drive from the middle of town, but it's only ten minutes from the Adventure Centre.'

Carla screwed up her face. 'The same applies to Sean. He could have killed Melissa before he arrived. If he didn't kill Julia, he could have overheard someone on the team talking about her injuries and decided to copy them.' Carla looked at him. 'I mean, if it was Ruairi, someone would have seen his car leaving the car park, surely? And you'd have seen it on the Adventure Centre security video, unless he managed to doctor the tape or avoid the camera or something.' She took a sip of her wine as Grace added,

'I just think that the location Melissa was killed in has to be significant. With all the cottages fully let, there's a real risk of the killer being seen. He chose that location for a reason.'

'I thought the same. That's why we're taking our time double-checking everything before we bring Brennan in for a chat.' On the phone screen, Jack looked grim. 'The thing is, if he arrived at the boathouse by water, I don't think anyone would have seen him. And there are no cameras on the lough.'

Chapter 45

STANDING ON THE rough wood of the sun-bleached jetty at Coyne House, Jack put his hands in his pockets and looked out across the water. Behind him, he could hear the Technical Bureau team getting ready to leave the scene. They'd be returning to Dublin shortly, their vans packed with samples for processing.

A fish plopped into the water to his right, drawing his attention. It was probably catching the midges that hung in dark seething clouds above the water. They looked a bit like the inside of his head felt right now – a mass of moving pieces of information that constantly reshaped itself whenever he looked at it from a different angle.

The surface of the water rippled outwards from where the fish had broken the surface tension, concentric circles increasing in size as they spread. He watched them thoughtfully. That's what an investigation was like – the violent event at its centre disturbing the universe in every direction, washing over everyone it touched. They all felt it.

And that first call always kicked off a sick feeling that evil had manifested itself.

But you could only do this job if you learned how to manage that. You still had to eat, to laugh, to live, even when you were digging into the stinking underbelly of society, dealing with horrific acts that preyed on your waking thoughts.

That's why cops hung out with cops – they got it. It was as if they were all in a special club that no one else could understand. Jack pushed his hands deeper into the pockets of his chinos.

What the hell had happened to bring this evil to Coyne's Cross?

He'd thought Limerick had been bad, but it was so beautiful here. The mountains and the expanse of the lough held a mysterious inner strength. It was probably what had attracted the monks all those centuries ago. Across the water, he could see the silhouette of the round tower reaching for the sky, pointing to … He wasn't sure what.

Hearing a door bang behind him, Jack glanced over his shoulder, the sun hot on the back of his neck. Terry Walsh, the Coyne Estate handyman, looked as if he was testing the front door of the cottage he'd just pulled closed. He had a tin of something and a paintbrush in one hand. The cottages were all empty now; the guests had left as soon as they'd been interviewed.

'Afternoon, Terry.'

Terry turned to him and nodded. He stood back to look at the cottage again, as if he was checking the windows were all secure, and then ambled over to Jack. His hair grizzled grey and in need of a cut, he was wearing navy trousers and a navy cotton sweater over a shirt – obviously his working clothes, paint-spattered and torn, the sweater unravelling at the cuffs and hem.

'Sergeant Maguire. How's it going? Terrible business. Terrible business.'

Jack nodded slowly. Terry Walsh was old-school, the type to doff his cap if he'd been wearing one.

'It is. Have you seen Sean? How's he doing?'

'Not today, but I think he's up at the house. I haven't seen his car leave. I'd say he wants a bit of peace and quiet, it's a lot to happen. That nice young lassie of yours was up here earlier. I think she was checking in on him.'

'Donna? Yes, she's great. Did she take your statement?'

Terry sighed sadly. 'She did indeed – lovely way about her. I just wish I could be more helpful.' He shook his head again. 'Terrible business.'

'Were you painting?' Jack indicated the tin in Terry's hand.

'Varnish. Just running a bit of sandpaper over a table inside while the place is empty. The smell's very strong.' He glanced towards Coyne House. 'And now I'm off to do the garden furniture.' He paused as if he was trying to find the words. 'It was the last thing Mrs Hardiman asked me to do, she loved eating outside. Feel I need to get it done. Tie up the ends, you know.'

'I do, Terry, I do.'

'It's important, to tie stuff up, to get it finished, isn't it?'

Terry glanced at the boathouse, and then, as if he didn't know what else to say, nodded to Jack and plodded slowly towards the house, his head down.

Jack stuck his hands in his pockets again as he watched the older man go. They'd all got caught in the ripples of whatever had happened here.

Chapter 46

IT WAS LATE Wednesday afternoon by the time Carla had finished the clay work on the Coyne's Cross skull and had a good likeness. Taking a step away from the workbench, she let out a sigh and rubbed the small of her back, stiff from bending. She'd been concentrating so hard on putting in the last details that it was only now she realised how tense her muscles had become.

But it was done now. The skull, once lost in the depths of the freezing water of the lough, had a face.

And she'd been right – as she'd worked on it, it had become clear that it was a girl's face. One that bore a striking resemblance to some of the photographs she'd looked at.

Now they would make more scans so they could create full-colour renders on the computer, and make another cast so Carla could work up skin tones and colourise the finished model, adding hair and eyebrows. Whatever you did with a computer image, a three-dimensional physical likeness jolted memories far better when it was sitting in front of people on the table at a press conference.

Carla flexed her back again and, pulling a stool over, sat down in front of the clay head. The face was pretty, her nose upturned, her eyes and mouth well proportioned, ears neat. High cheekbones emphasised her eyes; they seemed to stare at Carla, as if trying to communicate an unspoken message, to tell her story.

What had happened to her? Had she drowned? Or had she already been dead when she went into the water?

Carla tapped the long, slim clay-working tool on her knee as she thought; the apron she was wearing over her black jeans and T-shirt was smeared with grey where she'd wiped the tool as she worked. Its wooden handle was smooth from use, the metal tip angled to form a cutting edge on one side, a curved smoothing edge on the other. At the other end, a loop of metal enabled her to pull away clay that was too thick. Sighing, Carla shifted on the stool, bringing the looped end of the tool up to her face and tapping the end of her nose with it.

A significant number of water-related deaths every year were attributed to accidental drowning, while a smaller number represented suicidal or homicidal drowning. Assuming the investigative team in Coyne's Cross found the rest of the skeleton, would they be able to determine cause of death? If she *had* drowned, there was the possibility that diatoms in the water could have passed into her bloodstream and might be found in the marrow of her bones. It wasn't conclusive, but could form part of a bigger pathological picture.

In all the cases that Carla dealt with, it was the accumulation of evidence – the facial reconstruction being part of it – that opened up leads. Drowning as a cause of death was a diagnosis based on the *exclusion* of other potential causes. Statistically, she was unlikely to have been a suicide, but the team would look at everything – when they got a chance; this cold case had suddenly shot to the bottom of the priority list.

But now they had a location and a face, which should bring them halfway to an identification, and, Carla hoped, shed some light on the reasons this girl might have ended up in the lough in the first place.

As Carla sat in the silence of the lab, she swapped the tool into her left hand and reached out to gently smooth the still soft clay, running her thumb over the girl's cheekbone.

Sometimes this was the hardest part of her job – the joy she felt in reclaiming a likeness was tempered with sadness. Often her work extinguished any remaining hope a family had that their lost one was still alive.

But Carla was a positive thinker: closure was vital for everyone.

And so was justice.

Hopping off her stool, Carla pushed the model further into the middle of the workbench, away from the edge, and picked up her heavy silver skull ring, pushing it on to her finger. She always took it off to work with clay. It hampered her dexterity, and if she left it on, she'd end up spending ages trying to get particles out of the finely cast silver features.

She had work to do in her office. When Raph came in, he would take photographs and scan the cast, but she wanted to check the PULSE system for the details of the two missing girls' cases.

With the clay model complete, Carla could rule out the other missing persons' cases she'd reviewed in the Coyne's Cross case files, all of whom had been male, but she wanted to find out more detail on the circumstances of Gemma's and Kellie's disappearances.

Carla looked closely at the face she'd built, inspecting her work. Reaching out, she smoothed the clay under the girl's chin, and as she did so, the overhead lights caught the tattoo on her arm: WITH BRAVE WINGS SHE FLIES.

It was time to let this bird free.

Chapter 47

IN HER OFFICE, it only took Carla a few minutes to log her ID into the PULSE system. The paper records for the Murphy and Langan cases were all in storage and could be pulled if she requested them, but the original reports, and details of the witnesses, would be recorded here. And, more importantly, the girls' photographs.

The system took another few minutes to throw up the cases. Kellie Murphy first.

She'd vanished on 25 November 2018, after a night out at a nightclub in Kilkeel. Carla looked at the date – was that enough time for complete decomposition in the lough? Raph was right that the process slowed down hugely in cold water, and the lough was tidal, fed by the waters of the North Atlantic Drift – not glacial, by any means, but moving constantly. Carla tapped the shank of her ring on her desk as she considered the information. The skull had been found in a particularly deep part of the lough, but if the body had started off somewhere shallower, decomposition could have been more rapid. As on land, there were factors that could drastically impact the rate of decay. She'd read research from Canada that indicated that oxygen levels in water had a direct impact on the activity of the bacteria and marine life that fed on submerged bodies, and therefore the speed of skeletonisation.

Frowning, Carla looked again at Kellie Murphy's photograph. On balance, taking into account the environmental conditions, her disappearance was within the parameters of possibility.

But the image in front of Carla didn't jump out at her as being a match to the face she'd just built. There were definite similarities, but in the photo on the screen Kellie Murphy was very heavily made up, false eyelashes and heavy contouring changing the shape of her face for the camera. Carla scrolled down, looking for another image, scanning the case history as she went.

On the night she disappeared, Kellie was last seen waiting for a taxi because she'd missed the last bus to Stoney Pass. Memories of Lizzie pushed their way into Carla's mind as she continued reading. Lizzie had been heading for the bus stop and, like Kellie, had vanished into thin air.

Unlike Lizzie, Kellie had had a huge row with her boyfriend, Gary, that night. They both worked at a car dealership in Kilkeel – Ken Cahill 4 × 4 – and had been dating for about a year.

Why did that name ring a bell?

Carla tapped the shank of her ring on the desk again, trying to think for a moment before scrolling on. Witnesses had seen Kellie throw her drink in her boyfriend's face. They'd been arguing the week before, too, and apparently tension had been high at work. The boyfriend was detailed as being a 'body repair specialist'.

Huh, Carla thought, *that describes my job rather neatly.*

Gary was aged twenty-four, with no previous convictions.

Extensive interviews had been conducted with her friends and family; Kellie had spoken to her mother or her sisters every day. It was completely out of character for her to vanish without calling home. *Completely out of character.* The phrase jarred with Carla. It had been completely out of character for Lizzie to disappear. And she'd been nineteen, too.

Ken Cahill 4 x 4.

She'd definitely seen that recently, and in connection with something else in this file. Carla leaned in her chair, stretching her back, and looked at the screen, trying to work it out.

Then she had it.

Danielle's Pathfinder.

The spare wheel cover at the rear had 'Ken Cahill 4 x 4' printed across it in gold. The jeep had been parked with its boot facing the lake; Carla had noticed as she'd walked around it to get in when she'd taken Danielle home. Ruairi's car was identical, and had a spare wheel cover, too. She'd pulled in beside it outside Danielle's house. That's what had lodged it in her mind – matching SUVs. And both were gleaming and in fantastic condition, without a scratch on them – which, if the ones owned by her caving and climbing buddies were anything to go by, was pretty rare for rural vehicles. Particularly ones that were a few years old.

They were both 2018 registrations – the same as her own Fiat SUV – and from the second half of the year. Their plates both began with the digits 182, the 2 indicating that the Pathfinders had been registered between July and December.

Had they bought them before or after Kellie Murphy had disappeared?

Was that a coincidence, or was Ken Cahill's the only place near Coyne's Cross where you could buy a high-end 4 × 4?

They were common cars in the country – in south County Dublin, too, where it was more about wealth than their off-road capabilities. But it seemed likely if you lived in Coyne's Cross, you'd go to Kilkeel for anything major. She could imagine Ken Cahill did very good business – in the winter you'd need a 4 × 4 to get anywhere.

Scrolling on, Carla found another photo, from when Kellie Murphy had been in school. She was still wearing make-up, but a lot less of it.

Carla sighed as disappointment flowered inside her. The skull in the lab wasn't Kellie – she was sure of it. She'd enlarge the photo and check all the measurements to be sure, but she knew it wasn't.

Which meant Kellie Murphy was still out there somewhere, with a story to tell.

Chapter 48

'ITOLD YOU, I can't get near it, there are guards everywhere.' Ruairi's voice was low, angry.

Danielle froze in the hall, her runners in her hand. She'd changed into a pale pink vest top and jeans and come down the stairs barefoot, to grab a pair of socks from the laundry basket in the kitchen. The basket that had been there since she'd brought in the washing on Friday morning. When life had been normal.

She strained her ears, listening hard. The kitchen door was ajar.

Who was he talking to in that tone? And what was 'it'?

Her eyes darting around the hall as if she might find some explanation, she waited for him to speak again.

'I'm not moving it. No, I told you. Give it a few days, and they'll be gone.'

The kitchen door creaked, pushed fractionally by a gentle breeze coming through the open back door. It was enough for him to end the call.

'I'll see what's happening. Talk to you later.'

Panic rose for a second – she couldn't walk in now; he would know she'd heard him.

Tiptoeing backwards, she went to the bottom of the stairs, backing up the lower few, keeping to the very edge, careful to avoid the middle of the third stair that creaked when you stepped on it. Danielle could feel her heart beating hard, echoing in her ears. If she waited long enough … She heard his chair scrape in the kitchen.

Rounding the banister as loudly as she could, knocking her runners off the end just for good measure, she let out the breath she realised she'd been holding. Walking down the hall, she pushed the kitchen door open, looking at her runners as if there was something wrong with them.

'You aren't going in to work? Seriously?'

She looked up at her husband as if she hadn't quite heard him. Ruairi shook his head and opened the fridge. He was still in his pyjama bottoms and a T-shirt, despite the time, his phone lying on the kitchen table.

Who had he been talking to?

'What's the point of going in this late in the afternoon? You've been out of it the last two days. It takes a while for those tablets to get out of your system, you know?'

'I know.' She sighed. 'I need to get back some time, though, and the longer I leave it, the harder it will be.' She went over to the laundry basket, still on the end of the table, and started to look for her socks. Her back to him, it bought her a few minutes to calm down.

Was she overreacting? She didn't think so. Why would he be talking into the phone like that? *And like he didn't want anyone to overhear?*

He was right about the tablets the doctor had given her; they'd made the last two days a blur. When she'd woken up late today and reached for them, she'd hesitated. She didn't want to live removed from everything; she needed to be involved, to find out what was happening. Not that she'd thought for one minute that it might be happening in her kitchen. She could still feel the edge of the tablets – she wasn't quite on full power – but she was sharp enough to know something wasn't right.

She'd flushed the rest of the prescription down the toilet so there was absolutely no danger of Ben finding them. He'd be home from his dad's in a few days, and she needed to get with the programme to deal with that – to deal with all of this. She missed him terribly. He'd been texting almost every day, but since Sunday those texts had got harder to answer. He'd been close to Jules and Mel, was devastated at the news. His dad had been very careful to keep him away from the TV, but that couldn't last for ever. When he got home, back to school …

Danielle's thoughts started to run and she cut them off abruptly; she couldn't deal with that now. She could only deal with one problem at a time, and when she'd finally got up, she'd thought getting to work was her immediate issue, coping with the looks and the questions that she was sure were on the tips of people's tongues.

Now she wasn't so sure.

'We both have to get back to work.' She cleared her throat, looking over her shoulder at Ruairi, taking in the phone as she turned. It was lying screen up, but had gone to sleep.

His phone didn't seem to have stopped ringing over the past few days. Danielle had only really registered it this morning, realising at the same time that this was probably the longest they'd both spent in the same place for years. Perhaps it always rang like that, and she just didn't know.

'I need to go back in. I need to be busy or I'm going to go mad.'

'But the girls can run the place fine, it'll be deadly quiet after the weekend.' The fridge door still open, Ruairi stopped abruptly, realising what he'd said.

Pretending she hadn't noticed, Danielle picked up a pair of socks and sat down at the table to pull them on. 'Why don't you go over to Sean's? Are the police still there?'

She kept her tone innocent, her eyes on her feet as she pulled the second sock on.

In her peripheral vision, Ruairi rubbed his hand over his face. 'They seem to be everywhere.'

As he spoke, his phone rang again. He froze, turning to look at it. Danielle could see it was a landline number starting 666. The Garda station. Every station in the country had the same three digits at the start. She'd had to ring them often enough over the years.

'Aren't you going to answer it?' She picked up the phone and handed it to him. 'It could be important.'

It took him a second to react, the ringtone filling the room and her head. She started to put on her runners, as if the phone wasn't the most important thing on her mind right now.

'Hello, Ruairi Brennan.' He paused. 'Yes, hello, Jack. No, I'm at home ...'

Danielle pulled her laces tight and started to tie them.

'Yes, I can come down tomorrow. About ten be OK? Grand so, see you then.'

Ruairi ended the call and let out a sharp breath. 'Jack Maguire wants me to go down to the station. Some questions have come up about the Adventure Centre – who has access to the building and equipment.'

In the middle of pulling on the second shoe, Danielle looked up at him. 'Who has access? What's that got to do with anything?'

Ruairi shrugged. 'No idea. Have to wait and see.'

Chapter 49

SITTING AT HER desk in Garda Headquarters, Carla opened the next file on the PULSE system: Gemma Langan.

Was this her missing girl?

The photocopy of her picture in the file had been black and white, the ink faded. She hoped the one on the system was clearer.

Carla tapped her mouse. Part of her didn't want to look at the girl's photograph.

What if it wasn't her? What if they had to start from scratch, and the skull in her lab ended up being another Girl X?

Biting her lip, Carla scrolled down. And caught her breath.

The photograph of the girl who looked back at her, so much clearer than the images she'd seen in the file, bore a striking resemblance to the model Carla had just finished in the lab. She could feel her heart rate increasing as she scanned the page, looking for a second image to make sure she was right.

She knew well that a likeness wasn't an identification, but now further tests could be ordered. They would start by going straight to Langan's dentist to check her records. DNA was a long shot with only the skull recovered, and would take a few weeks, but if they had something to match to, it was worth a try. Carla wondered why her dental records hadn't come up in the previous search, but with a prosecution and the case closed, perhaps the investigating officers at Coyne's Cross hadn't thought to check. Or perhaps the dentist had retired.

There were all sorts of reasons why a match might not have been found. Raph regularly told anyone who was prepared to listen that if there was a state database for dental records like there was for DNA, it would make their jobs so much easier. It might have the civil liberties crowd in uproar, but teeth were his thing.

Carla clicked down, recognising the names of some of the investigating officers from those she'd heard mentioned when she'd been in Coyne's Cross. She scanned the primary report. Gemma Langan had been seventeen, last seen in late June 2009, at an end of Leaving Cert party. Reported missing by her mother, she was an only child, and had attended the local secondary school. Carla winced inwardly, imagining the pain her mother must have been through. Knowing what had happened was terrible, but that period of not knowing was worse – the wondering, the glimmer of hope that always remained that your loved one may reappear.

Carla had been there.

She was still there, if she was truthful with herself.

Those moments when you thought you could see them ahead of you in a crowded street, or caught their likeness in an audience on TV. Each one was like another twist of the knife. And then the hurt that they might have left voluntarily, the questioning why, and what happened – and if that was the case, questioning why they didn't get in touch. The self-recriminations, the looking for blame. Carla had seen Lizzie's mum go through it all, her perfect world shattered in just a few hours.

Carla's mind went back to that first day in Trinity, wandering the corridors, totally lost and looking for the accommodation office. Lizzie had been doing the same thing, walking in the opposite direction, poring over a map, had bumped straight into her. Those first days in college felt so long ago, but Lizzie's disappearance felt so recent. It was as if time kaleidoscoped, memories mixing, some fading, some vivid. Like the night they'd said goodnight and Lizzie had turned and waved on O'Connell Bridge, heading for her bus stop.

Tapping the heavy shank of her ring on her desk, Carla forced her mind back to the case in front of her, trying to recall being seventeen, remembering the party her year had had when they'd finished the Leaving Cert. Studying for eight subjects – three sciences, art, the mandatory English, Irish and maths, plus a second language – had been the most stressful two years of her life. If she hadn't been brought up speaking Spanish, she didn't know how she'd have got through.

She almost hadn't, in fact – had infuriatingly just missed the points she needed for medicine and had ended up doing anatomical science instead. The undergraduate BSc had been a stopgap that would give her a credit to start in year two of medicine.

But that had never happened.

When Lizzie disappeared it had all gone – to use one of Grace's expressions – 'tits up'. Carla had scraped through her finals and dropped out of Trinity. But being at home, dwelling on that night, thinking too much, had driven her as close to the edge as she'd ever been. She'd applied to do art and sculpture in Dun Laoghaire in a desperate attempt to keep her mind occupied, to keep herself sane.

It wasn't all bad – that was how she'd ended up here, after all. But no exam she'd ever taken, including her PhD, with its peer review and viva, had ever been as difficult as the Leaving Cert. The steam kids let off as soon as the exams were finished was very real.

Carla clicked through the file to the findings of the court case. Peter Drew had been convicted of Gemma's murder,

The fact that her mobile phone had been discovered in his van, and he had no explanation for its presence, had been a deciding factor. He'd pleaded not guilty but the jury hadn't agreed. The judge had given him twenty years, with the possibility of parole after sixteen.

Jack had mentioned that Drew was well known around the place, as he did all the odd jobs, and was considered to be a bit simple. Carla narrowed her eyes as she checked his arrest notes. He'd worked at the church, tending the graves – which was, let's face it, a much more logical place to get rid of a body than the lough. But perhaps sense had gone out of the window in the few moments that had ended Gemma's life.

Carla scrolled on. It had been a unanimous verdict, the case only lasting for two weeks. Open and shut.

Opening her desk drawer, Carla pulled out her notebook, writing down Drew's barrister's name. She flicked to Gemma Langan's photograph again; the likeness to her reconstruction was striking. The elements she hadn't accounted for – a peppering of acne and Gemma's thick curly auburn hair – didn't take away from the similarity.

Part of her wasn't surprised. Recreating a face accurately was what she was trained to do, after all. What did surprise her was a guilty verdict reached so quickly without a body. From the overview she could see on her screen, the evidence seemed to hinge on testimony that Drew had been hanging around Gemma in the weeks preceding her disappearance, the implication that he had been stalking her coming through loud and clear.

Had he become obsessed with her?

He was twenty-two at the time of her death, single, living at home with his mother.

Carla clicked on to look at the names of the prosecution witnesses, and for a moment her hand froze on her mouse.

Of the sixty teenagers present at the party, three had presented witness testimony at Drew's trial – Julia and Melissa Hardiman, and their cousin Danielle. And the end of year party had been held at Coyne House, in the barn that had since been converted into holiday cottages.

Immediately adjacent to the boathouse. Where Melissa's body had been found.

Chapter 50

DANIELLE WAVED TO Becky and Niamh as they headed out of the door of the Coffee Dock and off towards the car park. Niamh's dad waved back, the evening sun slanting across the water behind him. They'd been so good the last few days; Becky had done all the ordering for the week, as well as cashing up yesterday, and had been all set to do today's, too.

Danielle had thought she couldn't face coming in. But as she'd sat up in bed, realising it was almost midday, reading the same line on Facebook over and over again, she'd known that if she didn't get back to some sort of normal, she may never be able to.

So she'd texted Becky to say that she'd be in later, and she'd cash up. And then, eventually, she'd struggled out of bed and into the shower.

Ruairi's voice echoed in Danielle's head as she slid the bolt on the Coffee Dock's glass front door.

When she got there, she'd realised just how much she needed the distraction of sorting out the orders and cleaning the coffee machine. And the relief on the girls' faces when she'd appeared at the door had been almost palpable. The bank holiday rush was over, but they were both exhausted. It was just as well that the day had been much quieter.

Crossing the empty cafe, Danielle returned to the desk in her tiny office. She'd counted the cash and had it all bagged, had put tomorrow's float in the cash drawer on the floor beside the desk. It would only take her another ten minutes to finish, and she could lock up. She just hoped Ruairi had gone over to Sean's. She needed to sort things out in her head.

Sitting down, Danielle fanned her face with an envelope.

Boy, it was hot in this place.

If this global warming thing continued, she was going to have to look at getting air conditioning, or at least another fan.

Behind her, she'd propped the office and servery doors open to try and get some airflow. As she filled in the cash totals in the ledger, she heard the Visa machine on the counter splutter and bleep as it ran out of paper.

Feck it anyway.

Pushing her chair back, she returned to the counter and pulled out a new roll from the Tupperware box under the till, flipped open the machine and replaced it, pulling the end through and clipping the cover in place. She pressed the keypad to repeat the printout.

Watching it to check that it was working, Danielle pushed her curls behind her ears. The machine would be another few minutes and then she could finalise the day's takings, and get ready for tomorrow, and then …

Now she was here, she didn't really want to go home. The tension and the silence had been bad even before she'd heard Ruairi on the phone. But as she looked around the empty cafe, she knew she really didn't want to be on her own either. Danielle crossed her arms and rubbed the tops of them, subconsciously trying to massage away the blanket of fear that felt as if it was slung around her shoulders. Had been since the skull had been found, if she was honest with herself.

As the Visa machine churned out its reconciliation, purple ink on the narrow paper strip, Danielle looked out of the huge windows at the lough. It was always so peaceful out there in the evening. In the distance she could see someone kayaking, could imagine the plop of their oar as it slipped into the calm water.

Maybe she should try and get out on the water again. A shiver ran through her at the thought. She kept fit with weight training at the gym, but in previous summers, Ben had persuaded her to go out with him on her day off, taking a picnic up to Monastery Island at the top of the lough.

This year he'd wanted to compete in online gaming tournaments and build worlds, rather than hang out with her. But then, getting him out of his room at all had been a whole challenge in itself – she'd had to drag him to GAA practice.

Boy, she missed him.

But he'd be home from his dad's soon, and perhaps they could do something together when he got back. She'd spoken to him the previous night and he'd been full of questions about the news.

The Visa machine pipped to tell her it had completed its tot. Pausing to look at it before she tore off the long receipt it had printed out, Danielle didn't hear the sound of footsteps behind her, but she did feel the intense pain of a needle in her shoulder. Falling forwards, she hit the steel edge of the counter, reaching for the panic button beneath the till as she slipped into unconsciousness, the sound of the cafe alarm ripping through the calm of the evening.

Chapter 51

STUNNED, CARLA READ over the Langan case file again, working hard to stop her mind from leaping about. She needed to be logical about this – scientific. And she needed to see the full file and read the court transcript before she could form any conclusions.

Her phone was on the desk beside her, and she reached for it to call Jack. Scrolling through, she found his number, tapping her ring on the desk as she waited for him to pick up. Raph had left CT scans of the Coyne's Cross skull on her desk that morning. Before she'd gone through to the lab, she'd pulled out a piece of heavy grade tracing paper and a pencil and started sketching. Listening to the phone ring, waiting for it to go to his voicemail, Carla picked up a pencil, adding Gemma Langan's thick hair to her likeness with a few deft lines.

The phone continued to ring. Sticking her pencil behind her ear, her eyes on the image she'd created, Carla waited another moment and then ended the call. Perhaps he was interviewing and had it on silent. She texted him instead.

Call me ASAP. Possible ID on your skull.

Feeling anxiety building in her stomach, Carla rested the phone hesitantly on the desk.

Should she call the station? Leave a message there?

Before she could make a decision, a stiff breeze blew in through her open window, whipping around the office and lifting the printouts on her noticeboard. Carla looked up sharply as one dropped to the floor.

Previously hidden underneath the images of Train Ticket Man and Welsh Woman, it was an A4 print of an iconic photo that Grace had given her.

Leaving her phone on the desk, Carla pushed her chair back and went to pick it up. The wind had torn the corners of the thick photographic paper, leaving holes where it had been pinned to the board, and now it lay face up on the blue-grey carpet tiles. Scooping it up, Carla found two pins buried underneath the layers on the noticeboard and pinned it firmly into the top corner.

It had been taken at the start of Covid, at a rally against the abortion ban in Poland. A masked woman in a hooded black leather jacket was holding up a homemade sign. 'WE ARE THE GRANDDAUGHTERS OF THE WITCHES YOU COULDN'T BURN' was painted in confident white capital letters across a huge piece of black card that she held with both hands over her head, the night sky behind the woman a stunning sapphire blue. It was such a striking photo, taken by a woman photographer, Marlena Kuczko. Carla had loved it from the moment she'd seen it – had, when she'd first shown it to Grace, thought of getting the quote tattooed on her arm.

The next day, Grace had appeared with it, printed in full colour ready to be framed. Carla had brought it to work with her, intending to drop it in to a framer on her way home, but somehow she'd got too busy, and she loved having it on her noticeboard. The number of men who had come into her office and had given it a double take – when it wasn't buried under a pile of papers – always made her smile.

Now Carla took a step away and, pulling her pencil out from behind her ear, tapped it on her teeth. There hadn't been a screed of wind today. She'd opened the office windows in the hope of catching a breath of the evening air – or at least exchanging the stale hot air inside the office for slightly fresher hot air from outside. And this was the only piece that had fallen from a noticeboard that was at least three sheets deep in most places.

Carla reached up and began to remove the out-of-date notices. She didn't even know what half of them were. Internal memos and staff socials, a list of useful phone numbers. Taking them all down, she tidied up the board, only half concentrating on what she was doing, anxiety nipping at the edges of her mind.

She looked at the photograph again.

Was someone trying to tell her something? Something about the past?

'We are the granddaughters …' It was adapted from a quote in a book – the original read, 'We are the daughters of the witches you could not burn.' Women who would not be silenced.

What had happened to Gemma Langan that night? If the skull in the lab proved to be hers, what light did that shine on the conviction of Peter Drew? More importantly, did it have anything to do with what had happened in Coyne's Cross in the past week?

Carla took another look at the photograph on her board; the woman's placard carried such a clear message. Carla started as another flurry of wind lifted the pages in front of her.

She needed to talk to Jack, and the sooner the better.

Chapter 52

'DID YOU CALL Jack again?'

Grace looked at Carla from the kitchen counter, the knife she was chopping asparagus with poised above the sturdy pine board. She had changed from her work suit into a flowing cerise pink dress, and had pinned up her hair. Her feet were bare; Carla could see the gold ankle chain she'd given Grace on Valentine's Day peeking out under the hem of the skirt. She looked cool and relaxed.

Carla came into the kitchen and dumped her bag on the kitchen table. It was bulging with files and her laptop, which she'd shoved in the top. She'd left late and the traffic home had been horrendous. She felt sticky and very bad-tempered. She turned to glare at Grace.

'Of course I did, and I left messages at the station. I got that Seamus guy. He said Jack was tied up and would get back to me as soon as possible.'

Grace rolled the knife, her eyes wide with expectation. 'Tied up with what? A break in the case? A suspect?'

Carla looked at her witheringly. 'Now why would he share that with me? I'm only the world-leading expert they brought in to help them with a case that's been plastered all over the media.'

'Sergeant Seamus Twomey doesn't like women.' Grace emphasised her words with a wave of the knife. 'Not ones that have their own lives, anyway. It's insecurity ...'

Carla could see Grace was about to launch into the psychological explanations for misogyny, but she really didn't have the energy. No matter how objective she was, this part of the reconstruction process was emotionally draining. Revealing a face for the first time since the victim died always took it out of her.

'It's because he's short,' Carla sighed. 'And old. And feels threatened. I'll fecking threaten him when I get hold of Jack. I wish I'd taken Donna's mobile number. I've called four times, and Seamus Twomey seems to be the only one manning the phones.' She sighed. 'I need a gin.'

Reaching down, she tickled Nigel, who had appeared at the sound of her voice and was curling himself around her legs.

Grace put the knife down and opened a cupboard above her head, reaching for a glass.

'Do you think the cases are connected?'

'Don't you?'

Stuck in traffic on the way home from the Phoenix Park, Carla had called Grace from the car to update her.

Filling the glass and reaching into the American-style fridge-freezer beside her for a slice of frozen lime, Grace presented Carla with her drink. 'It seems highly possible. But let's face it, Drew can't have killed Julia Hardiman or Melissa if he's inside. So let's take a deep breath and approach this rationally.'

Carla scowled and took a large slug from her glass.

'That's better, you need to unwind. Sit down, I only need five minutes to put this salad together and I'm all yours. I've marinated chicken to put on the barbecue.'

Carla pulled out a chair from under the kitchen table. Grace had pushed open the concertina doors leading to the slate patio – a seamless continuation of the kitchen floor, so it felt as if the kitchen table was in the garden. They only had to move the table a few feet and technically it would be. It was one of the things Carla loved about this house; it had been one of Lizzie's many brilliant interior ideas when her dad had been renovating it. She felt a deep pang, tears pricking at her eyes. At times like this, when she was exhausted and low, she missed Lizzie more than ever. It weakened the defences she had created to manage day-to-day existence in the face of her loss.

Carla closed her eyes and tried to roll the stiffness out of her neck. Grace had put on some moody jazz, but over it, Carla could hear children's laughter coming across from the neighbouring gardens. It felt as far removed from the scenes they'd left in Coyne's Cross as was humanly possible. There was no question that Jack was busy – she knew that – but his not calling or texting was so frustrating.

Finishing up at the counter, Grace poured herself a large glass of white wine from the fridge and came to join Carla at the table.

'Talk me through what you've found again.'

Grace listened as Carla ran through what she'd learned so far about Peter Drew's trial.

Grace tapped her nails on her glass when Carla finished explaining. 'So he was convicted on the witness testimony, despite the absence of a body?'

Carla took another sip of her gin. It was Bombay Sapphire, perfectly measured, and it was hitting the spot even more perfectly.

'Essentially, but the forensic evidence really made the difference. Her fingerprints were all over the passenger seat of his van, and her phone was hidden under a tarpaulin in the back. Her blood was found in the edges of the casing, and the screen was broken.'

'Oh, OK. And he had no explanation?'

Carla leaned back in her chair and pulled her hair away from her face. 'He claimed he'd given her a lift in the van a few times, and he had no idea how the phone had got there.'

'As you would. Giving her a few lifts sort of plays into the stalking theory a bit, too.' Grace toyed with her glass, her face creased in thought.

'Maybe. Would she have accepted a lift if she felt stalked?'

Grace shrugged. 'Perhaps it was lashing rain and she'd missed the bus. Or perhaps the conversation they had when he picked her up gave him all the wrong cues, and he became fixated afterwards. Fingerprints can't be dated. They could have been there for months if he hadn't cleaned his van and no one else had been in it.'

Carla sighed. 'True. How many tradesmen do you know who clean the insides of their vans? I only clean out my car when I have to.'

'Indeed.' Grace took a sip of her wine. 'It does seem a coincidence that your girl's skull turns up and two women connected to the original trial are murdered in the same week.'

Carla pulled an 'I told you so' face.

Grace stood up and went to pick up her phone from the charger point on the kitchen counter. Her eyes on the screen, she powered it up and entered her passcode as she walked to the kitchen table.

'I only had a moment to look, but according to Google, the font of all wisdom, Peter Drew was committed to Mountjoy.' Sitting down, she looked across at Carla. 'Which is where I'm going again tomorrow. Will I make some enquiries? I might even be able to have a chat to him.'

Chapter 53

JACK MAGUIRE BRACED both hands on the edge of one of the tables in the deck area outside the Coffee Dock, his white crime scene suit crinkling as he moved. He looked out over the lough. It was past eleven; the moon was hanging in the cleft of the mountains, almost lighting the sky, its glow reflected on the water. Clouds meandered across it, dark in the middle, the edges illuminated in a halo.

Jack closed his eyes for a moment. He was dog-tired, as much from stress as from the hours he'd been putting in. Behind him, he could hear the murmur of voices as the scenes of crime team worked in the cafe. They were processing every single square inch of the place, from the walk-in fridge to Danielle's tiny cupboard of an office.

This time the week before, he'd been on the phone arranging with Brian that he'd be up to Dublin for the weekend to mind Scarlett, Ollie and Leo – and obviously Buster – on Friday night. And then he was planning to take them to the park on Saturday morning, to wear them all out so Orla could have a lie-in.

Christ, how fast could life change.

He'd had one cold case then. Now he had two brutal murders on his hands, and what was beginning to look as if it could be a third. Jack ran his hand over his chin, already prickly with stubble.

And he'd thought Coyne's Cross would be quiet.

Unzipping his scene suit, he pulled out his phone from the deep pocket of his chinos. It had been vibrating madly all evening – the battery was low – but now was the first time he'd got to look at it. He knew anyone who really needed him could get him via the station. From the moment he'd got the first call, his focus had been entirely on what had led up to the intruder alarm being triggered at the Coffee Dock.

He glanced at the screen, seeing a pile of missed calls from Carla. Realisation hit him like a blow to the jaw.

Christ, he should have picked at least one of them up – she was working on the skull today.

He could see she'd texted, too. As he was about to open the text, a voice behind him made him turn around. The soft light of the night was replaced by the glaring arc lights set up inside the cafe. From outside, it looked like a film set, filled with white-suited technicians like a swarm of huge insects, each intent on gathering fibres and fingerprints, bent in concentration.

'Jack, you got a minute?'

It was one of the scenes of crime team from Kilkeel – Alan, Jack thought his name was. It was hard to tell who anyone was with their hoods up and masks in place.

'We've a nice clear set of prints on the coffee cup on Danielle's desk,' the SOCO continued. 'Young Becky said she had a favourite coffee mug, and that's it, so we've got a control. We'll be able to separate her prints from the girls', and find any that shouldn't be behind the counter. We've also got a very clear print on the panic button under the till. The roll is still in the credit card machine, so it looks like she came out to collect it and was interrupted.'

'Any sign of a robbery?'

A part of Jack was still hoping there was a simple explanation for this: that Danielle had run off after a bunch of kids who had broken in, and maybe tripped and fallen on one of the trails.

The SOCO who might be called Alan shook his head emphatically. There was that theory blown straight out of the water.

'The cash on the desk hasn't been touched. It's all neatly bagged, and the notes are rolled up. The cash drawer is on the floor beside her chair. It would have been very easy for him to stick any of it in his pocket. There's almost a grand there.'

Jack's eyebrows shot up. 'I'm in the wrong job. Point of entry?'

The SOCO shrugged. 'Looking like the back door. Becky apparently said that it's kept locked at all times. We found it open.'

Jack nodded. Donna had gone over to Becky Mulligan's to get an idea of Danielle's movements as soon as they'd realised what they were dealing with. Becky was a bright kid; she couldn't remember seeing anyone strange hanging about. They'd been busy, but Danielle had trained them both to keep an eye out for anything out of the ordinary – as a cash business, she didn't let the girls take any risks.

Jack glanced over the SOCO's shoulder at the activity inside, trying to focus. Every time he looked away, he kept seeing Jules's body hanging, swarming with flies. He didn't want to find Danielle like that, too.

At least they seemed to have time on their side. Young Matt Curran had taken the alarm call. He and Donna had headed straight over in the Coyne's Cross car the moment central station had alerted them that the alarm had been triggered from the panic button under the till. They'd arrived to find the place deserted.

But not the sort of deserted it would have been if Danielle had packed up and gone home.

From the car park they'd been able to see that all the lights were on.

Advancing from the front of the premises, it had looked empty. Leaving Donna at the front, Matt had gone around the building and discovered the rear door open. The cash had still been on the desk, Danielle's handbag and hoodie stashed under the till.

'Anything else?'

'You know Becky said Danielle thought there was a knife missing? We've looked everywhere, and I think she was right. Danielle noticed it had gone on Monday morning, but then you arrived so she didn't mention it until this evening. They say they were sure it was here Saturday. Niamh remembers cutting cakes with it. She wasn't supposed to use that knife, but she said they were really busy and they had a run on chocolate cake or something. They missed it on Sunday, but didn't think too much about it.'

Jack nodded slowly. He'd been at Coyne House earlier this evening, talking to Melissa's husband Sean as the pieces of information had filtered back to him from Matt and Donna, and he hadn't liked one single bit of the picture that had started to form.

He liked it even less now.

Chapter 54

CARLA OPENED ONE eye at the sound of her alarm going off. It was only 6.30, but she wanted to get to the gym before work. She reached for her phone to quieten the birdsong ringing out so she didn't wake Grace. Swiping the alarm off woke the screen, and Carla immediately saw a message from Jack that had come in overnight.

Danielle has disappeared. May have been taken.
Talk tomorrow.

Without thinking, Carla sat straight up in bed, hauling the duvet off Grace, who yelped and opened one eye.

'What's up?'

'Text from Jack. Something's happened to Danielle, that's why he didn't answer. He says they think she's been "taken". Does that mean abducted?' Carla swiped to change screens and scrolled through her phone. 'Let me check the news reports.'

Grace rubbed her eyes. 'I don't imagine it will have been released to the media yet.' Blinking, obviously trying to

311

wake up properly, Grace levered herself up on one elbow. 'But, Christ, that's not good …' For once, she seemed to be lost for words.

Carla closed her eyes and focused on breathing slowly. She could feel panic building inside her.

Danielle had been taken?

For a moment, Carla was back in the Coffee Dock, reaching across the table to hold Danielle's hand, then seeing her to her front door. This was Lizzie all over again, but almost worse, because she'd seen what had happened to Julia and Melissa. Carla's stomach churned as Grace flipped into practical mode.

'What time did he text?'

Carla looked down at the phone. 'Two o'clock this morning.'

Grace turned to look over at the illuminated face of the digital clock on her bedside table, half-buried under a pile of books.

'There's no point texting him back now – he has to be asleep.'

Carla let out a sharp breath, trying to focus her thoughts. 'I'm going to go over there, G. I can't—'

'Don't be ridiculous. You've things to do here and Jack's going to be up to his oxters. He doesn't want you blundering in. Email him all you've got and text him to say you've sent it. Then he can call when he gets a chance. *Having* the information is crucial here, not how it's delivered.'

Carla turned to look at her. She was feeling really sick now – was starting to feel shaky, as if she needed sugar. She tried to sound calm. 'Grace, Danielle's been abducted. Very likely by the guy who killed Julia and Melissa. The information I've got could be vital to—'

'My point exactly. That's why sending it electronically is a much better idea than driving over. Honestly, Carla Steele, you've got a PhD – start acting like someone intelligent.'

Grace fell back on the pillow, screwing up her face. Early mornings really weren't her thing.

Carla opened her mouth to respond, but Grace had a point. Not about acting intelligent – *God, she could be a grumpy cow before she'd had her coffee* – but about the best use of her time. They had to be frantic over in Coyne's Cross.

'This has to be connected, Grace. It's like someone is bumping off the witnesses to Gemma's disappearance.'

'You don't say?' Grace's voice was heavy with sarcasm. 'That seems very likely. But let's take that forwards one step and think about the timing. To me, it suggests that this person doesn't want Drew's conviction re-examined in the light of the discovery of the skull. They know something about Gemma's death, perhaps were involved in it, and by getting rid of the key witnesses, they think their secret will stay buried.'

'But that's mad. Of course that won't make any difference. All the statements were taken at the time. And they are committing more crimes to cover up an old one?' Carla looked across at her incredulously.

Grace sat up and plumped her pillow so that she could lean comfortably against the headboard.

'*You* know that, and *I* know that, but, honestly, when you get to the stage that killing people is your only solution to a problem, you have to question the perpetrator's logic.'

Looking at her phone again, Carla knew Grace was right. Killers weren't always logical people. That was one thing Grace was an expert in. Her work was recognised worldwide; she'd published more academic papers than anyone else in this field in the country.

But whatever Grace thought, Carla knew she needed to contact Jack straight away. This couldn't wait. She opened her email on her phone. She'd taken photos of the reconstructed image before she'd left the lab the day before. She'd email them, along with the information she had about the Langan case.

As if Grace could read her mind, she tapped Carla on the elbow. 'Don't blather, make it really clear in your email. Bullet points. He's going to be stressed and knackered. Keep it simple.'

Carla threw a disparaging look at Grace. There were times when she behaved as if Carla was one of her students. And they all thought she was a total cow.

'Thanks for that. I'd never have worked it out. What time are you in Mountjoy?'

'Ten. I can have a preliminary chat with Drew, if Jack thinks it's a good idea and the governor agrees. Jack won't be able to get up here if it's all going off down in Coyne's Cross.'

Carla pressed her forehead with the heel of her hand. The pressure didn't help the pain that was building there. 'Who could it be? Who could have been involved in Gemma Langan's killing and still be around?'

Carla caught Grace's grimace in her peripheral vision. 'It could be any one of a number of people, but my money's on someone else who was at that party.' Grace started to push the duvet off, as if she was about to get up. 'You can be sure drink, and maybe drugs, were rife. And don't forget … Just because Drew was found guilty, he may not have been working alone. Perhaps he took the rap for someone because he was too frightened to come clean. With no body there was no DNA evidence. She could have been attacked by two men. It's not unheard of. And it's pretty tricky to hoof a body into and out of a boat if you're on your own.'

Chapter 55

THE GRAVEL UNDER Danielle's cheek was cutting into her skin as she gradually surfaced. Her head felt heavy with sleep, weighted somehow. She was cold, her limbs cramped. She turned her head, blinking, although wherever she was, was dark, or dimly lit at least. She felt a breeze stir, making her shiver, became aware of the sound of water lapping at a shore not far from her. She could hear the rustle of trees. And the smell: damp, rotten, organic. And something else?

She tried to move, realising at the same moment that her hands were bound behind her back and her ankles tied tightly together – she wasn't sure what with. The gravel that had been sticking into her chin was also sticking into her bare arm, the ground cold. Something was stuck to her mouth, pulling her skin.

Still groggy, she tried to turn, to get more comfortable, to work out where she was. The movement brought what she thought was a patch of sky into view high above her. She was outside, somewhere damp, out of the sun, somewhere where the ground was hard. So not the woods, but she could hear that the trees were close. Were there walls around her? She moved her head, trying to see. The light was greenish; she could make out the shape of rough stones. Was she in some sort of ruin?

What had happened? She remembered the counter, the pain in her shoulder, falling. And then nothing.

Were people looking for her? They must be. The alarm ... She was sure she'd activated the panic alarm, and Ruairi would be wondering where she was. She had no idea what time it was, but something about the nip in the air, the birdsong, told her it was early morning. *Had she been here all night? Unconscious?*

Fear gripped her stomach, dark like the shadows around her. Was it the same person who had killed Jules and Mel? Panic began to rise like bile. Danielle closed her eyes tight, tried to regulate her breathing, to keep calm. She couldn't panic. She needed to work out where she was. Shimmying like a dying fish on the quay, she tried to wriggle around. The movement brought a searing pain to her cramped limbs and she cried out, the sound muffled by the tape across her mouth.

Why was she here? Who had taken her, and where even *was* here? Questions bubbled through her still sluggish mind, like methane in stagnant water.

Someone would be looking for her. They'd know she'd been taken. They'd know they had to hurry. But how would they find her? She moved another fraction and became aware of a stone wall behind her, close to her head. She was sure it was a ruin. She listened hard. She could hear birds. She could hear the water.

And it made her want to pee.

Chapter 56

I T WAS MID-MORNING when Carla finally got to talk to Jack.

She'd gone into the office early, had called Kilkeel station, and Coyne's Cross a few more times, leaving urgent messages everywhere. Had paced around her office and then gone back over every single note in the PULSE report on Gemma Langan's case.

Raph had already started the casts of the clay face when she finally felt able to speak to someone without yelling, and stalked up to the lab. He was in the middle of a debate with Tina about which of them was more available to respond to a call that had come in from Wicklow district headquarters in Bray, that seemed to involve a pig farm. They both looked up, surprised, when she appeared at the door, catching the end of their conversation.

'You only need to go up there and see what's happening.' Carla stood beside the bench, gripping the edge, her whole body rigid with tension. 'The weather's gorgeous, it'll be ...'

She stopped herself saying 'fun'; instead went for 'picturesque'.

Like Coyne's Cross was picturesque. The thought went through her head like tracer fire. Just because a place was beautiful didn't mean horrible things couldn't happen there. *What the hell had happened to Danielle?*

'You OK? You've gone pale.' Raph looked at her over the top of his glasses, his dark eyes filled with concern.

Carla pursed her lips, about to lie. Then changed her mind. 'No. Actually I'm really not. I think I know who our girl is – I need to get her dental records for you to look at, Raph, so we can confirm.'

'Well, that's good news.' Raph paused. 'Is it worth taking the time to finish up these casts and do the colour work if we've got a possible ID?'

Carla looked pensive for a moment. 'I think so. I think her disappearance could be tied in to the double murder they've got down there. She might have her TV debut yet.'

That was the moment her phone had rung and, scrabbling for her pocket, she'd hauled it out. Glancing at the screen, she'd seen Jack's name and, throwing an apologetic look at Raph, had flung open the lab door to sprint down the corridor to her office, the phone stuck to her ear.

'Yes, exactly. That's exactly what I think.' Reaching her office, she pulled open the door and fell against it as it closed behind her. 'It has to be linked to the Langan case, the timing is just too coincidental.'

Grace had been right about sending that email.

Jack ran back over it with her, making sure he had the details right. He sounded as if he was in the station; there was a hubbub of noise around him. He also sounded exhausted.

'So I need to get Gemma Langan's dental records sent to you?'

'If you could. Raph is a forensic dentist, I'll get him to do the comparison. Do you want me to speak to her relatives if it confirms? I saw a note on the file saying her mother had moved to Dublin.'

'That would be great. It's manic here.'

Carla could hear it in his voice. No one in Coyne's Cross was ready for a serial killer on their patch, even if the crimes were years apart.

'I've requested a copy of the file to be sent to my office from the Kilkeel archives. I can go through it here and see if anything jumps out. You're not going to have time and ...' She was about to say that he couldn't trust a junior, which wasn't very generous to the incredibly sparky, enthusiastic and dedicated team members she'd met in Coyne's Cross, but a part of her needed to do this herself. If Jack had the manpower they could double up, but as she'd guessed correctly, he didn't. She could hear the relief in his voice.

'That would be great.'

'Is there any news?' She hardly dared ask. Listening carefully as he updated her, Carla found herself nodding.

'If there's no forensic lead by this evening, we're going to call a press conference for the morning.' His voice had taken on a different tone – more focused, determined. 'We've more interviews to do. Matt and Donna are going to pick up Ruairi Brennan later to be sure he gets there. He's next.'

Carla drew in a sharp breath. 'Do you think he could be involved?'

She heard Jack move from wherever he was standing. The noise in the background receded and she heard a door open and close. He was obviously looking for somewhere more private to talk.

'He's got a bit of explaining to do about exactly what was going on between him and Jules. And why he didn't mention he'd seen her the night before she was killed. And that's before we even get to Danielle.'

'But both of them … Could he have killed Melissa, too?'

'Sean's his alibi.' Jack's voice was flat. Carla knew what he was thinking: in the vast percentage of cases, killers are well known to their victims. 'And Sean only arrived at Ruairi's office a few hours before he found Melissa. There's a gap of about an hour and a half when Sean was in town that Ruairi was on his own.' She heard movement, as if Jack was shaking his head. 'Perhaps Ruairi was having an affair with Melissa, too, and one of the sisters was threatening to tell Danielle? God knows. I did some checking, and the Adventure Centre and the Coffee Dock are wholly owned by one parent company. They've a fifty per cent share each, Danielle's the other director.'

'And what? He was worried that Danielle had guessed somehow, about the affair? That's why she's been abducted?'

'Perhaps. Whoever did this got in cleanly and knew exactly where the cameras were. There's a blind spot at the back of the cafe, and apparently Ruairi wouldn't pay for cameras inside, so we've no footage at all of anything untoward happening last night. And there was no sign of a struggle.' He paused. 'I don't know what the feck's going on. I'm terrified that we're going to find her hanging from a tree, or the round tower or somewhere.' He took a breath. 'We've teams out looking. I keep thinking, perhaps it's just an accident of timing that the skull was found. Maybe things were coming to a head in Ruairi's private life.'

Carla looked over at her noticeboard, at the photo of the girl with the placard.

Had Julia given him an ultimatum and threatened to tell Danielle? Perhaps Melissa knew, and had threatened to expose him.

Whoever had killed Julia and Melissa had cut their hearts out; it had to be significant. Carla shivered. She didn't even want to think about what could have happened to Danielle.

'I can get the colour work done on this reconstruction today if we speed-dry the casts. Raph already has them under way. If I drive down with it tonight, I can join you in the morning at the press conference, if you need me?'

She could almost hear Jack thinking. 'Good plan. Get those files sent here instead of to your office. It'll be quicker if you're coming down anyway. Bringing the cast with you could make all the difference.'

'I'll call Kilkeel now. If Gemma's disappearance has nothing to do with the case, someone might think you're looking in completely the wrong place, and relax enough to let something slip.'

'Or think we are on to something, and get twitchy. Let's try it. There's no one in the cottage. I'm sure Sean would be happy for you to take it again if you need to stay tomorrow night. I'd guess he hasn't even thought of changing the sheets since you left.'

Chapter 57

'YES, LOOK AT that filling, the MOD amalgam – that's a complex restoration. And this one. And the wisdom teeth are still high in her gum.'

Leaning with one hand on the desk beside Carla, his white lab coat open over a bright red Hollister T-shirt, Raph pointed to the image on Carla's monitor screen with the lid of his gold fountain pen. The X-rays he'd taken of the Coyne's Cross skull before Carla had started the reconstruction, and the X-rays Gemma Langan's dentist had emailed, were side by side, the black and white images ghostly in the bright office.

'This is our girl. We can try for a DNA match but, honestly, the teeth are more reliable. I can do an enamel rod pattern print but …' Raph shook his head. 'Doesn't seem worth it. You've got what you need here.'

Carla sighed, smiling up at him. 'Thanks, Raph. What would we do without your dentistry skills? You could be earning a fortune in private practice, you know.'

Raph looked at her over his glasses. 'But then I'd have to talk to people, put up with all the drama the minute they get in the chair. I had quite enough of that in college. I prefer my patients quiet. Dead is ideal.'

Carla couldn't resist a grin. He was a devil, but a highly qualified and quite brilliant devil.

'I'll call Jack. According to the file, Gemma Langan's mother moved to Dublin after Gemma's death. She was an only child. And reading between the lines, it didn't sound like there was a Mr Langan in the picture at that stage.'

Raph winced. 'They must have been very close.'

Carla looked at the screen again, thinking about the lost girls in her system. They all had mothers. All had people grieving for them somewhere.

Raph put his pen into his top pocket. 'At least we have her now and she can be laid to rest, even if she's not quite complete.'

Carla took a deep breath. He was right. This was one more mystery solved – in part, at least.

'Let's get her finished. Now we know who she is, I've photographs to work to. I'd like to take her to the press conference tomorrow. It's looking like this case really could have a bearing on what's happening over there.'

Raph gave her a mock salute. 'No problem, boss, your wish is my command. I should be ready for you in an hour, then I'm going to get over to Wicklow.'

'Perfect – and thanks, Raph.'

Carla spent the next hour tracking down Mary Langan, Gemma's mother. She'd moved in with her sister to a house opposite Fairview Park. There was no mention of a Mr Langan, but perhaps they'd separated. Losing a child put the worst strain on a relationship. The sisters now ran a B & B, from what Carla could discover online.

And they weren't interested in talking to the Gardaí.

'Why do you want to come here? Can't you tell me on the phone?' Mary Langan's voice was somehow gravelly and shrill at the same time. Carla wasn't sure what she'd expected, but Mary sounded much older – and was considerably more abrupt – than Carla was quite prepared for. 'It's a long time, you know, fourteen bloody years. She'd have come home if she could.'

Carla had mentally scheduled in an hour to get to Fairview before she went home to collect an overnight bag and broke the news to Grace that she was heading to Coyne's Cross again. But it looked as if she wouldn't be needing it.

'I know it's a long time, Mary, but we don't like talking about this sort of thing over the phone. Could I drop in this evening?'

'She's dead, isn't she? Just say it. As if I haven't known all these years. Was it her they found in the lough, then? I knew it as soon as I heard. You'd have thought that old fool Seamus would have called me, wouldn't you? He's some awful gombeen.'

Carla opened her mouth to speak, but didn't get a chance.

'Violet said it to me. She took one look at him, with his fancy cap and his radio and his tunic with the shiny buttons, and she said he was a fool. He couldn't drive a bus and end up in the right place.' Mary drew in a raspy breath, but it wasn't to let Carla reply. 'From the minute they arrested that poor boy Peter, I knew we were all lost. They were never going to find her if they thought he'd done something to her. He wouldn't say boo to a goose, that lad. My Gemma would have run rings around him if he'd tried anything on.' She sniffed loudly. 'They didn't look properly, you know – didn't talk to half the young ones at that party. Didn't even talk properly to her boyfriend. A disgrace it was. A disgrace.'

Carla winced inwardly. She hadn't intended to have any of this conversation on the phone.

As if it had suddenly flared and now her fire was dying, Mary's voice became less sharp. 'She's gone now. That's what you're calling for, and didn't I know it? Thanks for letting me know, love. I can see from the news that they've got a lot on their plates down there now. I remember those Hardiman girls – snooty bitches, the pair of them. That Melissa was the worst. Their cousin was nicer. She was local, but easily led.' It was as if the floodgates of her memory had been opened as Mary sighed. 'I suppose they all were, back then. The Hardimans had money …' She trailed off. 'I've not been back and I'll not be going. We moved there with her dad for the work, and the

328

fresh air and somewhere safer than the city to bring Gemma up, and look what happened. I never liked the place. I was always a blow-in, we never quite fitted.'

'It must have been devastating, Mary. We don't need you to go back. I just wanted to let you know. You might want to arrange a mass.'

'A funeral, like? Have you found the rest of her, then?'

In her office, Carla ran her hand into her hair, pulling at the roots. She'd walked right into that one.

'There are still people out looking. We'll do our absolute best.'

'I'm sure you will, love. Look, I have to go. Thanks for telling me.'

'If you've any questions, Mary, anything I can help with, please call. I'll give you my number. Have you got a pen?'

She heard Mary scrabbling around at the other end. 'Fire away.'

Carla gave her office line and her mobile. 'As soon as we can release Gemma's remains, I'll call you myself. I promise. I want to resolve this, too.'

'I'm sure you do, love.'

Carla could tell Mary was about to hang up; she said quickly, 'And, Mary, we've created a facial reconstruction – of Gemma, I mean. We didn't have enough for a positive ID without it. I just wanted to warn you that you might see it on the TV, or in the papers.'

There was silence at the end of the phone that made Carla curl up inside. The whole point of what she did was to bring victims home, to bring the lost back to their loved ones, but it could be a shock. Carla knew how she'd feel if someone suddenly showed her Lizzie's face. Mary's voice was almost a whisper when she replied.

'Thanks, love, I know you mean well. Thanks for looking after her.'

Chapter 58

IN THE INTERVIEW room in Coyne's Cross Garda Station, Ruairi Brennan ran one hand over his close-cropped hair and stared, wide-eyed, at the cardboard coffee cup on the table in front of him. He looked pale under his tan, and his eyes were bloodshot. Jack wasn't completely sure if that was lack of sleep, or alcohol, or a combination of both. There was a definite whiff off him when the lads had called over to his house.

Jack ticked himself off – he had to stop calling everyone 'the lads'. He'd seen Grace Franciosi's face when he'd said it in the station. She had a point. Donna wasn't any more laddish than Jules.

What had made him think of that?

Jules was dead. Jack took a slow, steady breath. Whenever he thought of Jules now, he wanted to punch something. Hard.

Straightening the manila file in front of him, he looked at his grazed and bruised knuckles. His kitchen door had come off almost as badly, and it hadn't made anything better.

Ruairi had come in easily enough, his face bewildered when Matt said they needed a chat. Sean, Melissa's husband, had pulled into the drive just as Ruairi was being shown the rear of the patrol car. He'd gone, as Matt had put it so aptly, as white as a fecking sheet.

Beside him, Jack could feel Matt's knee starting to bounce under the laminate table with its metal legs screwed firmly to the floor. You didn't get many major murder investigations in your career unless you transferred up to Dublin – Jack had brought Matt in to the interview to give him the experience. DI Rainsford was watching the show from upstairs.

Jack had been like Matt once – young and dynamic and eager. Returning to Coyne's Cross, he'd been starting to feel as if he was getting back on his feet, and then …

'What's this about, Jack? Why aren't you out looking for Dani? I mean …' Interrupting Jack's thoughts, Ruairi threw up his hands in a questioning gesture, shaking his head, as if he couldn't believe what was happening and they were all stupid.

Jack understood. He'd been itching to get out in the car and go and physically look for Danielle himself, but he knew that wasn't the most efficient use of his time. Not when there was even the slimmest possibility that the man in front of them might have the answer. This interview had been delayed long enough.

Jack smiled across at him, using his matey 'we're all in this together' smile that his sister-in-law Orla said made him look as if he was a football coach. It was usually reserved for the terrible trio – for the moments when Scarlett, Ollie and/or little Leo wanted something they couldn't have. It was well practised.

'We're out there, Ruairi, don't worry. We've got the detective unit in from Kilkeel, the whole team here. We've had some top people down from Dublin. We are looking at *every single* detail.' He said it slowly, drawing out the words. 'And we're hoping you can help us with some of that detail. There might be something that's happened that you didn't even notice, but that could give us a lead. We want to go through everything again, on tape if you don't mind, so we don't miss anything.'

Ruairi shrugged and, leaning his elbows on the table, put his face in his hands. 'Fire away. I don't know what I can tell you, but if it'll help …'

Jack pressed the button on the tower system beside him, activating the video and audio to record. A long electronic beep made Ruairi start.

'Do we really need that? Are you arresting me or something?'

'If you're happy to talk to us, we don't need to arrest you.' Jack said it half-jokingly. Beside him, Matt's knee-jiggling increased in speed.

'So, Ruairi, take me back to last Friday night if you can. You were working late?'

Across the table, Ruairi ran his hand over his head as if he was trying to smooth away anxious thoughts. 'The whole skull thing took up so much time last week I never got near my paperwork. I had the VAT to sort out and …' He tapped the tabletop with his fingertips. 'I'm sure you don't want to know all that.'

Jack smiled encouragingly. 'No detail is too small, trust me.' He opened the file in front of him. 'And you got home around 12.45 a.m., you think? That was a late night.'

Ruairi nodded. 'I wasn't really looking at the time, to be honest. Dani goes to bed early – she's always been an early bird, she gets up with the larks – so I knew she'd be out cold when I got back.'

'And you were on your own all evening? Or did anyone drop in?'

Ruairi shrugged. 'On my own. It's quiet at night, easier to concentrate.'

Beside him, Jack could feel Matt tense. 'You sure about that? On your own all evening?'

Ruairi nodded, frowning, as if he'd said it, so it must be so. Jack kept his voice friendly, nonchalant. 'Nobody called in at around eleven o'clock?'

The frown deepened. Ruairi shook his head. 'I don't think so …'

Jack straightened the file in front of him. 'Perhaps you can refresh Ruairi's mind, Matt?'

Matt cleared his throat, played a biro through his substantial hands as he spoke. 'We've got security tape that shows Julia Hardiman pulling into the car park at the Adventure Centre at 11.11 p.m. The camera then picks her up leaving her car and going to the front entrance, where she buzzes and the reception door is opened.'

Matt looked across at Ruairi expectantly. He looked confused, then screwed up his face as if he was trying to remember.

'Did she? I'm sorry, I must have forgotten.'

'You forgot that Julia Hardiman visited you the night before she was murdered?' Jack injected just the right amount of incredulity into the statement.

Ruairi let out a sharp breath. 'You've got to find Dani. I can't—'

'We will, Ruairi, don't worry. Now, can you tell me why Jules called in?'

Ruairi paused for a moment, as if he was deciding what to tell them. 'We were talking about Dani's birthday, I wanted to organise a party, but Jules knows more about that sort of thing.'

'And when's Danielle's birthday?' Jack raised his eyebrows.

'Erm ... October.'

'Nice and early planning, then?' Jack turned over the next page in the file before Ruairi could answer. 'Takes an hour and a half in the middle of the night to talk about a party that's happening in four months' time?'

'Well, you know, I wanted to get it right.'

'And how did Jules know you'd be there at that time of night?' As Jack said it, something he'd seen previously suddenly began to make sense in his head.

'I don't know – perhaps she saw the lights on?' The look of total disbelief on Jack's face pulled Ruairi up. 'Sorry, I don't know ...' He trailed off.

'Did she perhaps text you, to make sure you were there?' Jack's tone was sharp.

'She must have done. I'm sorry, I really can't remember. So much has happened, and honestly I can't think about anything else except Dani right now ...'

Jack went for an understanding look. 'So you won't mind if we look at your phone records, then?'

'Erm ...' Ruairi looked stunned. Jack felt Matt shift in the chair beside him.

'We think Jules may have had a spare mobile phone. We have the records from her smartphone and there is no sign of any texts sent that evening. We do, however, have a strong suspicion that she did in fact text someone, and you seem to be the most likely recipient, from where I'm looking. My point is, Ruairi, that if she had another phone, she could have arranged to meet someone else that night – someone who subsequently did her serious harm.'

Chapter 59

WHEN CARLA GOT home, Grace had the kitchen doors wide open and was sitting at an angle to the table, her feet up on a second chair, nursing a tall glass of wine. Pulling out the carver at the head of the pine table – and quickly checking to make sure Nigel wasn't curled up on it – Carla dumped her bag on the seat. She pulled out another one opposite Grace and collapsed into it.

'What's up? What's the news? Any update on Danielle?'

Carla shook her head sadly, unable to meet Grace's eye.

She wasn't sure if she could string together the right words to describe how utterly shit her day had been. The news about Danielle had been preying on her mind since the morning, and then there had been … well, everything else.

Grace's sigh was loud, summed up how she was feeling. 'Damn. I'm sorry I couldn't call at lunchtime, I've been flat out. Back-to-back one-to-one sessions.'

Grace stood up and padded around the table in her bare feet, her ankle chain just visible under the hem of her blue denim shirt dress. She looked very together, as always – the exact opposite of how Carla was feeling.

Opening the fridge, Grace looked at Carla over her shoulder. 'So, come on – spill. Tell me what's happening.'

Carla sighed and put her head in her hands, massaging her temples. 'I spoke to Gemma Langan's mother.'

'How did that go?'

Carla glanced at her. 'About as well as you'd expect. Jack couldn't come up, and he's thinking of using the reconstruction at a press conference in the morning. We couldn't spring that on her.'

'That's for damn sure.'

Grace put ice into a tall glass she'd retrieved from the cupboard and poured a generous amount of white wine into it. Bringing it to the table, she put it down in front of Carla and pulled her to her in a hug. Putting her arms around Grace's middle, Carla let herself be held for a moment. This was exactly what she needed. Hugs made everything better – a bit, at least.

Gently Grace eased back, kissing the top of Carla's head. 'So tell me?'

Carla reached for her glass. 'She knew. I mean, she guessed the skull was Gemma's. She said Seamus was a gombeen who couldn't drive a bus into town, and that the whole investigation was a disaster. Well, not quite in those words, but that's what I heard.'

Grace sighed. She pulled out the chair beside Carla and sat down as she continued, 'How do people like him end up in the guards? I mean, really?'

Grace grimaced in response. There was bad in every job, but there wasn't much room for incompetence in the Gardaí; the ramifications were just too huge to contemplate.

'I'd guess things were different when he joined.'

Carla nodded slowly, taking a sip of her wine. She needed this. And after the conversation with Mary, and then spending the afternoon with Gemma's likeness, she wasn't able to face the drive to Coyne's Cross this evening.

'What else did her mother say?'

Carla smiled to herself at Grace's tone. She was slipping into professional mode again. She did it unconsciously, but when she did, there was something about the way she asked questions that made you want to reply. She sort of dipped her head and looked at you seriously, all her body language signalling that she really wanted to know the answer and it was important. That you were important.

'She thought Drew was innocent, that he wouldn't hurt a fly, that "Gemma would have run rings around him". Her words.'

Grace took it in, her face thoughtful.

Before she could say anything, Carla decided to move the subject on. There was only so much she could talk about right now without the enormity of the situation swallowing her whole. Grace was always telling her that she had PTSD from Lizzie's disappearance, that she needed to sort it out, and at times like this, she recognised the signs. Carla cleared her throat.

'How did you get on at Mountjoy? Did you get to see Drew?'

It took Grace a moment to answer. 'I talked to the governor about him. It's rather interesting, actually.' She glanced at Carla. 'Apparently he died about two years ago.'

Carla looked at her in disbelief and let out a heavy breath. 'What is it with people connected to Coyne's Cross dying? What happened? He was only … what? Mid-thirties?'

'Thirty-six. And that's the thing. He committed suicide.'

'Oh, shit.' Carla let out a groan. Anything they were likely to learn from Peter Drew was now gone. 'What happened?'

'He hanged himself in his cell.' Grace reached across the table for her own glass and took a sip.

'Seriously? After he'd been inside for almost fourteen years? With remission, he must have only had a few more to go.'

'The governor was a bit cagey about that. He thought it rooted back to a change in cellmate or something.'

Carla pulled a face. 'Like he couldn't live with whoever they'd moved in on him, and that was the only alternative? That says a lot for the system. God, he'd been inside almost half his life, and then that?'

'I know. And if Gemma Langan's mother was right, and he was innocent, then that makes this all a damn sight worse.'

Carla ran her hand into her hair. 'I know. I've brought Gemma home with me to bring to the press conference. Seeing her might throw up something new.' She sighed. 'But I can't face the drive over tonight. I'll go early in the morning. The roads will be clear. If I leave here at six, I can be there by nine.'

Grace reached out and rubbed her arm. 'I'll come with you. I've only one appointment tomorrow, I can reschedule. I need to write up my notes from today and I can do that anywhere.'

Carla leaned over and kissed her. 'Thank you. That means a lot. We can come up again tomorrow evening if you need to be back.' She hesitated, saying what she knew they were both thinking. 'If it wasn't Peter Drew, then there had to be someone else involved in Gemma's death.' Carla screwed up her face, thinking. 'Why wasn't his death on the file, though? Did I miss it? There would have been an investigation in the prison, and presumably Coyne's Cross would have been notified. PULSE would have been updated.'

Grace shrugged. 'Perhaps PULSE wasn't updated, or the update wasn't saved or something. We've all done that.' She hesitated. ' And who knows if the message was communicated properly in Coyne's Cross.' She looked pointedly at Carla.

Carla knew exactly what she was thinking. Seamus Twomey had already proven that his ability to convey messages left a lot to be desired. Had he managed to 'forget' to update the records at the station, too?

Chapter 60

DANIELLE WASN'T SURE how long she'd slept. The previous day, it had taken her ages to fully surface from whatever had knocked her out, and then she'd gone through waves of panic, the cramp in her limbs almost unbearable. She hadn't been able to stop herself from peeing – had, for a second, enjoyed the warmth of urine running down her legs – but then she'd started shivering again, her jeans rapidly cooling, the fabric rubbing her skin.

As the minutes had ticked past, each one stretching interminably, she'd resorted to meditation to try and keep calm, to take her mind out of her body and shut down the panic. Counting the waves on the shore, focusing on the sound of the wind, she'd lifted herself – momentarily, at least – out of the chill, squalid hole she was lying in by focusing on Ben's face, on the memory of his laughter. She couldn't die here – she couldn't give up. How would he cope? They were so close – best friends.

She'd managed to sit up then, to hump around to get her blood moving into her arms and legs, to try and get more comfortable, to try and get warm. Wriggling around, she'd got into a patch of sunlight, the warmth like an elixir, restoring her mind, helping her think.

And then she'd finally made sense of the breeze, of the sounds she could hear. And the ruin.

It had been obvious, when she'd eventually pieced it all together.

She had to be on the island at the mouth of the lough. Which meant the building she was in was the ruin of St Columcille's Church. Not that he could help her.

But knowing where she was had given her hope. She'd wriggled about, trying to find a stone she could rub her hands against to tear the duct tape binding her. And then slowly working away at it … It had helped her focus. If she could get her hands free …

Then the night had come again. So cold. She'd slept fitfully, exhaustion rolling over her in waves.

Why had whoever had brought her here not come back for her?

She didn't know what was more terrifying – being alone, or him coming back. She was sure it was a *him* now, someone who hadn't wanted her to see his face. She had a vague memory, as she'd slipped into unconsciousness, of being lifted. So whoever it was had to be strong.

But she'd been here for so long now – two nights and one whole day without water. And she could feel herself weakening. Above her, she could see dawn breaking, which would make it about four in the morning.

Would he come back today?

Sitting up again, she stretched as best she could and started to work again on the tape binding her hands.

People would be looking for her.

She needed to hold on. It wouldn't be much longer.

Chapter 61

THE JOURNEY DOWN to Coyne's Cross was even quicker than they had expected with Grace driving the Mercedes.

Despite the hour, Carla spent most of the time texting Raph. He had got to the burial site in Wicklow the previous evening, and discovered that the place was humming. There were bits of bodies turning up all over the farm, with a strong suggestion that the pigs themselves may have ingested a few.

Like a plane crash, but worse because we've no IDs.
Farmer denying everything.

Carla had read his texts out loud to Grace. 'There's a press embargo until they work out what the feck's been going on.'

'Does he usually start work this early?'

'Who – Raph?' Carla smiled. 'He likes a challenge. That's why he was so perfect for the department. There aren't too many forensic dentists in Europe with the level of experience he got working in Canada. We're blessed to have him.'

'It sounds like a complex case.'

Carla glanced across at Grace. 'Nine skulls so far, and counting. We're going to be busy.'

'But surely they'll check DNA first?'

'Where they can, but you know the quality depends on how long the body's been in situ. And they need to have something to compare it to, to get a match.'

'If they are missing, these people will be on a database, though?' Grace reached to adjust the air conditioning.

'You'd hope so, but they could be historic. We've no information at the moment. And look at Girl X. We're no closer to finding out who she is, and she was my first case.'

'Very true. Look, here we are.'

Grace passed a cheerful carved stone sign, surrounded by flowers, indicating that they'd arrived at the edge of the town demesne. It wasn't quite nine o'clock, and Coyne's Cross was just waking up, brightly coloured awnings being rolled out over the pavements.

'Have we got time to stop for coffee? Look, that bakery has just opened.'

Carla smiled to herself. One thing she loved about Grace was how she didn't let a major investigation ever get in the way of her stomach.

* * *

The community hall was in the centre of the town, a modern glass building located beside the library. The car park was already filling up when Grace pulled in. Slipping out of the car, Carla put her sunglasses on. Not that the white streak in her hair and her nose ring didn't betray her identity, but sometimes she felt the need to hide where the press were concerned.

She didn't need any more hideous photos of herself splashed across the national press.

Grace had made her clip her hair up in a twist at the back, and wear a white silk shirt, long black pencil skirt, and heels. Carla looked significantly more professional than she usually did in her black jeans and Docs. Grace had a point that while dead people didn't care, the public and the press made all sorts of assumptions based on your choice of clothes. And not always good ones.

Reaching into the rear seat, Grace pulled her jacket off a hanger and shouldered it on while Carla waited for the boot of the car to open magically. She'd wanted to belt Gemma in on the rear seat, but Grace had persuaded her that the boot was just fine, and she was nestled in between their overnight bags – just in case.

Carla picked up the box as Grace blipped everything closed and they went up the broad concrete steps. The doors whooshed open automatically at the top, and they immediately saw young Matt hovering beside the reception area. Recognising them, he nodded a greeting and opened one of the double doors behind him.

'Jack's inside.'

The press conference was considerably more succinct than Carla expected.

The hall was packed, Grace sitting in the front row, her bright red hair like a beacon of sense. Sitting beside Jack at a trestle table covered by a white cloth with the gold An Garda Síochána logo in the middle, Carla had unpacked Gemma and positioned the bust just in front of her.

Joined by a tearful Ruairi, Jack opened with an appeal for information on Danielle's disappearance. The Coffee Dock was a bit outside town, but it was a small town, and people were often out there – walking dogs, teenagers hanging out, locals and tourists on the move all the time. It was just bad luck that there were no dog walkers in the car park the evening Danielle had disappeared.

'We are open to the possibility that recent events in Coyne's Cross could be linked to the discovery of human remains in Lough Coyne at the start of last week.' Jack's voice rang out steady and clear, the room silent, hanging on his every word. 'Those remains have been identified as belonging to Gemma Langan, who was seventeen years old when she was killed. Many of you will be familiar with her case. She disappeared in 2009 after a party at the edge of the lough. It seems her body ended up in the water.'

A hand rose in the audience, and he took a question from the back. 'But there was a conviction in that case. What sort of link are you seeing?'

'There was indeed. Peter Drew was given a life sentence for the murder of Gemma Langan. We don't know what the connection might be, but we haven't had a murder in Coyne's Cross for fourteen years and now we've had two in a week, and another woman missing. We need to take every possibility into account. We're appealing to the public for any information at all that may be related to the recent spate of attacks. You might not think that something you've seen or heard is important, or indeed related, but let us be the judge of that. You can use the anonymous Crimestoppers line. And again, I would reiterate, that line is completely anonymous. Or you can call a member of Coyne's Cross Gardaí. All contact will be treated in the strictest confidence.'

The press had lots of questions for Carla then, about rebuilding Gemma's face and why it had been necessary, but Jack glanced at his phone and brought proceedings to a swift close, shutting down any further questions, assuring the press they'd be kept informed.

He was right – they could go on all day answering increasingly probing queries. There were better things he could be doing.

Standing up, he glanced at his phone again and, turning to Carla, leaned down to whisper in her ear. 'You OK here? I have to get back.'

'Go, we'll catch up. The Langan case files should arrive this morning. Grace wants to go through everything. We'll sort ourselves out.'

Nodding curtly, clearly distracted, Jack headed swiftly out of the rear door of the hall.

Chapter 62

AS THE DOOR swung shut on Jack and the conference room began to empty, Grace mouthed to Carla from the front row. 'That was great, well done.'

Throwing her a smile, Carla stood up and lifted the strong cardboard box she'd brought with her onto the table. About to lift the cast head into it, Carla realised a woman had come forwards from the back of the room and was hovering around the end of the table. Heavily built, wearing a flowered cotton dress, she looked to be in her early seventies, her short hair tightly curled and peppered with grey. She was plucking anxiously at a crucifix on a slim gold chain.

'Can I help you?' Carla caught her eye as she slipped the bust inside the box and flipped the lid over.

'You're with the guards?'

Carla nodded, realising that a sheen of sweat had broken out on the woman's upper lip.

'Dr Steele.' Carla held out her hand.

The woman didn't seem too sure what to do, but took it limply. Her grip tightened as she stepped forwards.

'He didn't do it.' The woman's voice was low. Carla could barely hear her. In her peripheral vision, she could see that Grace had stopped checking her messages, was instead watching them.

'I'm sorry – who are we talking about?'

The woman still hadn't let go of Carla's hand. Her eyes were damp and her face flushed. 'My Peter. He didn't do it. They all said he did, but he didn't. I know him.'

'You're Mrs Drew?' Carla reached forwards and put her free hand on the back of the woman's; she was still clutching Carla's hand as if it was some sort of lifeline. 'Why don't you come and sit down with me for a minute?'

Carla looked around the room. It had emptied now, the chairs, previously in tidy rows, in slight disarray. Only Grace remained. Her eyes had returned to her phone, but Carla could tell her full attention was on the woman beside her.

'I can't. I need to be off. Nobody stood up for him except me. Nobody believed him.' She sniffed loudly. 'Everyone thought he did it – even the kids in the school. I heard them chanting in the playground, "Watch out or Peter Drew will get you."' She looked away from Carla as she continued. 'I kept his funeral quiet, we didn't need the press or locals catcalling.' She took in a breath, obviously struggling with the memories. 'The only person there apart from me was the gravedigger. They all decided he was guilty. Family, too. But *I* know he couldn't do anything like that. He couldn't have hurt a fly.'

Squeezing Carla's hand even more tightly, she gave it a shake and turned to leave. Then, as if suddenly thinking of something, she turned back.

'It won't help Peter, but I hope you find out who did all this. I hope you find them and they roast in Hell.'

Chapter 63

CARLA TOOK A few moments to collect herself as the door fell closed on Peter Drew's mother. She glanced over at Grace. She was still sitting in the front row, tapping the edge of her phone on her knee, her eyes narrowed. It was her thinking face.

Returning to the table, Carla picked up the box. There were so many questions jumping about in her head – questions she wanted to ask Mrs Drew. Questions that she hoped would be answered by the statements in the files that would be coming from Kilkeel.

The woman had been almost rigid with anger. It was obvious that Peter Drew's mother, of all people, would think he was innocent, but it had been the way that she'd said it.

Coyne's Cross was a small town. It was always easier to suspect the man who didn't quite fit. From what she'd heard so far, it sounded to Carla as if Drew was a loner, a misfit, someone whose learning difficulties separated him from his peers.

And hadn't Jack said something about Seamus, that infuriating sergeant, maintaining that the skull couldn't be Gemma's because Drew was terrified of water? If that was true, how did her missing body factor in the explanation the jury were given? Had it featured at all in his defence? And what impact did it have on his conviction?

Was his mother right? Should there be a question mark over a verdict based on entirely circumstantial evidence? That was something that had been bugging Carla since she'd read the case overview in the original file.

Jack had said that the experts they had consulted had looked at the currents. They'd been able to calculate from the skull's location that Gemma's body had to have been dropped in from a boat; that it would have wound up in a very different place if her body been pushed in from the shore.

Would someone terrified of water have gone out in a boat? Would they have the experience, the confidence? Grace was right that it was hard to manoeuvre a dead body, to lift it into and out of a boat. She'd also thought that a burial attempt, whether in the water or not, would suggest care for the victim, and perhaps even remorse. Unless he'd thrown her into the lake, discarded like a piece of rubbish. But everyone who lived near the sea knew that currents could bring bodies back to shore – you'd have to have some knowledge of the tides to be confident the body wouldn't be washed up again. And that took a bit of planning, a keen mind.

'You know ...' Carla jumped at the sound of Grace's voice beside her. She'd been so absorbed in her thoughts, she hadn't realised Grace had moved from her chair. 'I think there's a reason why Danielle hasn't been found yet. I think she's still alive. This abduction is different from the others. He's made his statement with the first two murders, but he was quick, the kills both designed for maximum impact and executed very swiftly. I think he's sending us a different message now, and he's keeping Danielle alive for a reason.'

She looked at the box in Carla's hand.

'The one thing that connects these women – apart from the fact that they are all related – is that they were all witnesses in a trial. I think we need to go through the court records and see exactly what happened that night. The answer to who is behind all this has to be in there somewhere.'

'Jack had to go back to the station, but I'm expecting the files to arrive this morning. We'll need to go through those witness statements. Gemma's mum said something about no one talking properly to her boyfriend.' Carla glanced back to where she'd been sitting beside Jack on the other side of the table, making sure she hadn't forgotten anything.

'Really? You'd think he'd be the first person on the interview list.' Grace pursed her lips. 'Let's get over to the station. We can hole up in a corner and go through everything. I've just got a sense that Danielle is different from the others, but I don't know how much time we've got.'

Chapter 64

B Y THE TIME Carla and Grace got back to the station, the case conference was well under way. Seamus was manning the front desk. He didn't blink when he saw them come in, his previous obstruction in not connecting Carla to Jack obviously forgotten. Unlocking the door to the front hall, he showed them into the main office.

'DI Rainsford said there are a load of files for you in the Detective Unit office. Upstairs, last door opposite the conference room. Everyone's in the incident room. He said for you to get started.'

Leaving them standing in the office, he returned to the front desk. Carla shifted the large box containing Gemma's reconstructed head to her hip and, glancing at Grace, raised her eyebrows.

'We'll just go on up so, Seamus.' Carla said it loudly and headed for the stairs.

She wasn't sure if it was just her he had a problem with, or women generally, but his curtness was beyond rude.

Upstairs, they could hear the low rumble of voices coming from the conference room. At the end of the wide corridor, the Detective Unit office door stood open, a pile of sturdy file boxes waiting for them under the window beside it. Carla went inside and, looking for a clear desk, put her own box down, before returning to find Grace checking the notations on the sides of the archive boxes.

'Here we go. This looks like the first lot of statements – and this one…' bending down, Grace slid several boxes around, checking their labels, 'is the court transcripts.'

They grabbed one each, taking them through into the empty office. Packed full of documents, they were heavy.

'I think you're right, G. There has to be something in here that will give us a lead on the killer's identity. There has to be.'

Carla dumped her box on a desk and pulled off the lid. Beside her, Grace did the same, and they worked silently for a few minutes, checking the contents.

'I just hope it doesn't take us six months to find it.'

Carla lined up the bulging manila files on the desk, spinning them around so she could see them clearly when she sat down. There were pages and pages. Carla glanced at Grace, but she'd already started to read, sitting on the edge of the desk, her brow furrowed.

'We should have brought coffee.' Carla could tell that Grace barely heard her.

'I've got the statements taken on the night of the party here. It looks like the whole year group was there – there have to be at least sixty teenagers. Some of them didn't see Gemma at all, but several of them refer to her boyfriend, Sean.'

Carla looked at her sharply. 'Not Melissa's Sean, surely?'

'I'm looking for a surname.' Grace riffled through the pages in the file in front of her and then went on to the next one. 'Ah, here we are – yes, Sean Twomey. I wonder if he's the relative of —'

'Melissa's husband was Gemma Langan's boyfriend at the time she disappeared?' Interrupting her, Carla did a double take. 'Don't you think that's a bit odd?'

Grace shrugged again, her eyes on the page in front of her. 'Small town. The pool must be pretty limited, and Sean's a good-looking guy.' She turned back to the file and searched for a document. 'Let's see what he had to say for himself.'

Carla turned around. 'You've got his statement?'

'I have indeed.' Grace read on, silently, flipping over the pages as she went.

Carla could barely contain herself.

It couldn't be Melissa's Sean. Surely he would have said something?

But when would he have had a chance? They'd only just announced the identity of the skull, and he was grieving his murdered wife.

Grace cleared her throat. 'So, it sounds like Sean and Melissa started dating before the previous Christmas – the Hardimans normally went skiing, but that year they went in January. She was at boarding school, but they texted and FaceTimed.'

'Long-distance love. Cute.'

'Obviously that wasn't enough for him if he was seeing Gemma on the sly.' Grace read on, summarising as she went. 'Melissa came home regularly for weekends. Sean says he didn't want to go to the party, was quite anti, reading between the lines. Hardly surprising if he knew Gemma was going too, Melissa insisted.' Grace continued scanning the page. 'He says he had too much to drink. He had an argument with Gemma and he didn't see her again. He says he thought she'd gone home.' She flipped the page. 'He didn't find out she'd disappeared until the next day.'

'He thought she'd gone home – he didn't know? That was very chivalric of him.' Carla crossed her arms. 'You'd have thought, even if they'd had a row, that he'd make sure she got home OK.'

Grace pulled a face. 'Have you got the prosecution summation there?'

Carla turned around and checked over the files she'd unpacked.

'I sure have.' Opening the file, she read over it quickly. 'The prosecution suggested that when Gemma left the party, she thumbed a lift or was picked up by Drew on the way back into town.'

'It's a long way to walk to town from Coyne House. That driveway alone is about a mile long.' Grace rested the file she was reading on her knee.

Carla nodded. 'So she might have been happy to take a lift if it was offered by the time she hit the main road.'

Grace stared at the clock on the wall above a noticeboard, which seemed to be filled with memos and fliers for nights out, plus discount vouchers for local cafes.

'Maybe. That's assuming she got to the main road in the first place. I think someone needs to ask Sean about this. See what he can remember, and find out what that argument was about. No one seems to have thought to ask him at the time. Efficient.' Grace's tone dripped sarcasm.

'Do you think they're finished inside? Let's see what Jack thinks.'

Chapter 65

IN THE INCIDENT room, DI Rainsford finished the briefing. He looked like Jack felt. Usually sharply dressed, his grey hair cropped with military precision, he had discarded his suit jacket to reveal a crumpled pink short-sleeved shirt.

As Rainsford finished updating the team, Jack automatically checked his phone.

As if the killer was going to text him an update.

The only unread text he had was from Carla. She'd messaged him to say she was across the hall, going through the Langan documents.

Perhaps she'd find a lead? Christ, he hoped so.

He wasn't ready to find Danielle hanging from a tree as well.

The meeting broke up and Jack headed across the landing, just as Carla appeared at the door to the office. As each of them opened their mouths to speak, a sudden commotion downstairs made them look over the banisters.

Matt was on his way up, taking the stairs two at a time, an open laptop in his hand.

'I've got something. Julia Hardiman's phone has been moved.'

Belting up the last few stairs, a laptop under his arm, Matt careered around the banister and barrelled into the incident room, almost crashing into the inspector.

Glancing at each other, Jack and Carla followed him as he put the laptop on the conference room table and caught his breath.

'Julia Hardiman's phone has been switched on – and it's changed location.' Matt pointed at the map on his screen. 'It last pinged near her house at midnight on Friday. The Tech Bureau looked but couldn't find it. I logged in with her Apple ID and I've been keeping an eye on it. About five minutes ago, it was switched on again, but over here. The tracker pinged and then it vanished. I think it was switched off again.'

'Could someone have been checking the battery?' Carla leaned forwards to look properly.

'Maybe, and I'd guess whoever it was did it really fast because they don't want to give away their location.'

'That's still on the Coyne Estate.' Jack frowned, his thoughts flying. 'There's a lane running down there beside the water that leads to a landing stage, just above Dead Man's Gully. I used to swim there as a kid, I know it well. It's the main access to Monastery Island.'

Grace came in behind them. 'That island is the perfect place to hide someone.'

Rainsford turned and nodded a greeting to her. 'My thoughts exactly. Given how hard we've looked for it, it seems extremely likely that whoever murdered Julia has that phone, and they have also abducted Danielle. It's definitely the best lead we've got at the moment.' He stared hard at the laptop screen. 'We need surveillance in there to be sure of what we're dealing with, and we need to go in quietly, but fast.' He looked at this watch. 'If Danielle Brennan *is* being held there, we've a potential hostage situation with immediate threat to life. I'm not taking any chances. In the first instance, we'll establish an outer cordon at the edge of the estate and an inner cordon where that lane meets the avenue.'

Jack turned to Rainsford. 'If I take the unmarked car, I can be there in twenty minutes, get in close and report back. I know the area. There's a tunnel that leads from close to the landing stage through the caves to the island.'

Rainsford glanced at Jack and turned to the screen again. 'We can get eyes in from Kilkeel with long lenses.'

'They're going to take at least forty-five minutes to get here, and they'll need a drone to see properly.' Jack tapped the map, indicating the dark shape of Monastery Island. 'Grace is right. If I'd kidnapped someone and I wanted to hide them somewhere where there was a very low chance

366

of anyone turning up, that's where I'd take them. It's too far up the lough for most kayakers, and the tours stopped years ago when it became a bird sanctuary. You have to go right around Coyne House and across their land to get to that point.'

The inspector paused, obviously considering his options. Jack was pretty sure a surveillance drone was going to be hard to find at short notice, and he could tell by Rainsford's face that he was thinking something similar.

'Wear a vest. We'll have armed support right behind you.'

Carla cleared her throat. 'I'm a vertical cave and mine leader. If that tunnel leads into caves, it would be madness to go on your own. I can go with you.'

Rainsford looked at her hard. 'We don't send civilians on live operations.'

'I know. I train the army caver and mountain rescue squads. Caves are dangerous, even without a hostage situation.' Seeing the inspector's surprise, she continued. 'I've been on hundreds of training ops, with live ammunition. I know what I'm doing. Jack isn't a caver, he needs trained support. If Danielle's on that island, she could just as likely be in the caves as in the ruins.'

Rainsford nodded slowly. 'You can't go dressed like that. Have you got appropriate clothing?'

'I've spare gear in the car. I'll go and change now, while you work out the details.'

'I need to call the superintendent. There are protocols in place – we don't want this to go pear-shaped. If you two get the slightest sniff of anything, there will be a negotiator, tactical and technical support right behind you – they could just take a while to get here.' Rainsford paused. 'We'll establish a command post within the inner cordon. I don't want anyone blundering in.' He cleared his throat. 'No heroics. Both of you in body armour. It might be called Dead Man's Gully, but I want everyone out alive.'

Chapter 66

CHANGING AS QUICKLY as she could, Carla arrived in the back office just as Jack appeared downstairs, clipping his own navy blue ballistics vest on, another in his hand. She could see he'd added an extra holster to his heavy black belt, his Sig Sauer on one hip, a Taser on the other. She'd changed into a T-shirt, army fatigues and her climbing boots, and had pulled her hair into a ponytail. She'd thrown her climbing gear in at the last minute when they'd come down the first time, and had forgotten to take it out of Grace's boot. She didn't have her caving helmet with her, but she'd manage. The heavy rubber-covered torch Grace kept in her car was waterproof.

Hurrying into the office, Jack passed her the body protection vest, and grabbed a chunky blue light with a thick lead running from it from the top of the filing cabinets.

Wordlessly, she followed him down the corridor to the car, clipping the heavy vest on, the word GARDA clearly marked across the front and back.

Outside, the heat hit Carla as they climbed into the Detective Unit's dusty Mondeo and buzzed down the window. Jack gunned the engine, clamping the magnetic blue light onto the roof and plugging it into the lighter socket.

'That looks like it was issued with the Ark.'

Jack glanced across at her as he reversed out of the space. 'Not everyone expects a heap of shite like this to be a Garda vehicle, even with blue lights in the headlights, and I don't want to use the siren.'

The blue light got them down the main street and out to the Coyne Estate in minutes, the Friday afternoon traffic clearing a path. The sweat was already pouring down Carla's back as they pulled through the eagle-topped gates. Carla felt her mouth dry. She hadn't been here since they'd found Julia's body, and now they were about to drive past that exact location.

His eyes focused on the lane, Jack interrupted her thoughts. 'It's years since I've been down here. The landing stage was the place we hung out every summer.'

Aware of crime scene tape still fluttering between the trees to their right, Carla gripped the door, steadying herself as the car sped along the avenue. She focused on what Jack was saying.

'How old were you when you moved?'

'I was twelve and Brian was fourteen. It was perfect timing for me. Took him longer to settle, but it was a good move, I think. My dad was a lawyer, he got a partnership in a practice in Dublin. My mum was happy to go back and be nearer her family.'

Ahead of them, Carla could see a narrow lane branching off to the left. Jack swung down it, the car bucking as it hit the uneven road surface.

'Did you say you were in Limerick before here?'

'Yep, in the inner city for years.' His arms tense on the steering wheel, he glanced in the rear-view mirror. 'Tough gig. Couldn't be more different to here – well, until this week anyway.'

Carla could tell from his voice that there was something he wasn't telling her about moving back, but this wasn't the time to ask. Instead, she kept her eyes trained on the road ahead.

'You're right about the tree where we found Julia only being visible from certain angles. It looks like it was carefully chosen.' As she spoke, Carla inclined her head to the way they had come.

Jack's face was grim. 'Whoever this is, they know this place.'

Reaching the end of the lane, breaking out of the woodland into the sunshine, Jack slowed and turned down a farm track that ran, Carla guessed, around the rear of the house and its walled gardens.

He reached out the window to pull the light in off the roof before resting his elbow on the window ledge, slowing the car right down.

'From here, we need to proceed with caution.'

Carla glanced across at him, her heart beating hard. 'Why do you think the phone's suddenly been reactivated?'

'Christ knows, but I have a horrible feeling we're about to find out.'

Chapter 67

DANIELLE WAS DOZING when she heard the scrape of a wooden hull on stones.

Waking, confused, she could feel her head pounding, her throat and mouth so dry she knew she was getting dehydrated. Much as she craved the heat from the sun, staying in the shade prevented her from sweating.

She tried to clear her mind, to focus on what had woken her, but everything was getting muddled. She knew she couldn't last many days without water. Food was a different thing. When Ruairi and Ben had their big survival discussions, they'd said you could survive without food for weeks. But not without water. And with her mouth taped, Danielle couldn't even lick the dew from the plants around her. She could feel her energy literally ebbing away with each passing hour, the effects of whatever he had given her making her senses dull.

Now awake, her body rigid with fear, she listened hard. Having woken at dawn, she'd slipped in and out of a fitful sleep; she had no idea what time it was, but it didn't feel late. The sun wasn't too high in the sky. She heard the scraping sound again. She'd know the sound of a boat being hauled up shingle anywhere. Someone had come on to the island.

The crunch of footsteps on the gravel set her teeth on edge.

Who was it?

A moment later, a dark shadow loomed over her and she turned away, her eyes tight shut.

If she didn't know who it was, surely they wouldn't kill her? They could let her go.

She heard another step and sensed someone leaning over her. They grabbed her shoulder and turned her over. At the same time, thick fingers scrabbled at the tape on her mouth and ripped it off.

She'd never felt pain like it, almost passed out with the shock. Then she felt water dribbling over her parched lips; they were bleeding where the tape had taken off the skin. She opened her mouth and gulped, her eyes opening automatically and she yelped, trying to slither away from the man above her.

Unshaven, his grey hair unkempt, he was wearing a navy fisherman's jumper and navy trousers, a sheen of dirt visible even in the dim light of the ruin.

As recognition dawned, his smile was slow, as if he was enjoying her fear.

Terry Walsh.

Melissa's handyman.

What the actual hell?

Chapter 68

BUMPING ALONG THE unmetalled road, winding between wild whitethorn trees, skirting the fields that must have once been filled with the dairy herd, Carla began to realise how big the Coyne Estate was. The fields were overgrown, tall grasses undulating in the slight breeze coming off the water as if they were beckoning them forwards. She shifted in her seat, the ballistics vest hot and unfamiliar.

Ahead of them, Carla could see the lane disappearing along the edge of the lough towards the landing stage, the dark shape of the island looming beyond the trees. She only caught glimpses of the water, shimmering through the dense wall of gorse and brambles that bordered the lane. It looked wild and undisturbed, but she could see that the long grass growing up the centre of the track had been flattened. Carla glanced at Jack, his face taut with concentration, eyes moving from side to side, taking everything in. He glanced in the rear-view mirror and then pulled up.

'Someone has driven down here recently. We're going to need to do the rest on foot. We don't want them to hear the engine, and we can't assume they're working on their own.'

As if she hadn't already been on high alert, Carla could feel a surge of adrenaline pounding through her. Just like when she was climbing and they reached a patch of loose rock, or when she was underground, clambering through a narrow crevice, not knowing what could be on the other side.

'Do you think he's armed?'

'We have to assume so.' Jack pulled over. 'We're about five minutes from the landing stage. Let's get moving, I don't feel like we've got time to arse about here.'

Thoughts of what could be happening to Danielle shot through Carla's head as she pushed her door open. Jack gently closed his own door and glanced at her before turning down the track. In the sunshine, she could imagine that this spot, so far from the main house and any watchful eyes, had been the perfect venue for energetic teenage boys to swim from.

Scanning the trees, keeping pace with him, Carla glanced over at Jack. He was obviously listening hard as he walked, trying to keep his own approach as silent as possible. The sun was high overhead and it was getting hotter by the minute – she could feel it on the back of her neck.

Then she saw a car. Ahead of them, the lane swung down towards the water, and from her side she could see further than Jack could. She stopped, raising her hand, gesturing for him to come closer to her, and pointed ahead.

An old Honda was pulled over at the side of the lane. Jack kept his voice low, lifting his phone to take a photo, deftly texting it to the station.

It only took him a second, and Jack silently indicated that she should come over to his side of the lane. He dropped down, creeping forwards, using the undergrowth on the water side for cover. She fell in behind him. Had he recognised the car? Carla could feel her heart thumping, her mouth dry. She didn't dare ask.

Jack pointed to the bushes beside them. There was a natural opening. Squeezing through behind him, Carla could see a weather-beaten wooden landing stage to her left, and across the water, the island. It rose out of the swirling waves, a rocky outcrop much larger than Carla had expected. She could imagine that as the ice had flowed through here thousands of years before, creating the lough, that it had found a gully, separating the rocks from the land to form the island.

The beach they were looking at was tiny, with jagged cliffs rising on either side. A rowing boat had been pulled up out of the water onto the pebbles. Above it, steps had been hewn into the rock face, leading up to what she guessed must be a path to the church she could see higher up. Grace had mentioned that, in the fifth century, the island had become a hermitage, a place of silent contemplation where monks came to commune with she didn't know what. It looked charming in the sunshine, but Carla could imagine it was bleak and inhospitable in the winter. Was Danielle being held inside, or in the cave system below?

Before she could consider the thought, Jack's phone vibrated with a message. Pulling it out, he showed her the screen.

Car registered to Terry Walsh, Coyne Lodge.

Where had she heard that name before?

Then she had it. Melissa's maintenance man. They were supposed to contact him if they had any problems with the cottage. Carla's stomach flipped.

Thank God everything had been working.

Jack nudged her as, on the island, a dark figure emerged from around the corner of the ruined, overgrown church. Carla reached forwards to grab his arm.

Was this their killer?

Chapter 69

DANIELLE CLOSED HER eyes when Walsh disappeared out of the doorway to her left. She'd barely noticed it before, but remembered it from when she'd come here with Ben. All the kids had messed about here when she was young; jumping off the landing stage and swimming over to the island had been a sort of rite of passage. Her mum would have killed her if she'd had any idea. The island was supposed to be haunted by the souls lost in Dead Man's Gully, a myth supported by the mysterious lights that had started appearing at night and were regularly spotted from the shore.

The church had lost its roof years before, and as she looked at it, the doorway appeared incongruous in the tumbledown wall, its lintel stone holding strong. She still couldn't believe she was here. Her mum had always said she'd die if she swam out to the island; that if the currents created by the caves that had been hollowed into the rock didn't get her, the ghosts or the bogeyman would.

And here she was.

And her mum had been right. The bogeyman was going to get her.

She looked back at the doorway, at the squareness and strength of the lintel stone, paler than the hewn rocks that had been used to build the walls around it. It had withstood the weather for thousands of years.

Could she withstand this? All she could do was hope.

What was he doing now?

She heard the crunch of feet on pebbles, and then in the distance, the sound of a boat being pulled higher up the stone beach. The tide must be coming in if he was moving it. Danielle could feel the fear growing, threatening to overwhelm her.

Had Terry Walsh killed Jules and Melissa?

He'd cut out their hearts and strung them up. Was that what he was planning to do to her?

Then the realisation hit her – the banging window at the cafe inexplicably left open, the house alarm going off … the duct tape on the counter …

Had he been disturbed looking for an opportunity to grab her?

Feeling everything starting to spin, she closed her eyes and she could feel herself slipping away, fear and darkness overwhelming her.

Was this how her life was going to end?

Then she heard his voice again, this time close to her ear. She reacted, pulling away from him, his breath, stinking of tobacco, hot on her neck.

'How are you feeling now, Danielle? Why don't you sit up here and talk to me?'

Walsh reached down and grabbed her by her hair, hauling her upright and towards him. The pain made her cry out, her scalp burning. His fingers twisted into her curls, he dragged her up against the wall. Danielle scrabbled frantically with her feet, trying to get some purchase on the loose stones, trying to lift herself to reduce the pain. She'd had a headache before he'd arrived; now it was blinding, beating behind her eyes.

Or perhaps it was fear.

Walsh released her and she hit the wall hard, the cold stones rough and clammy through her thin vest top. Instinctively, she pulled her knees up, trying to make herself small.

He was pulling something out of his pocket. A smartphone. It took him a minute to unlock it, his grey eyebrows knitted as he concentrated. She could see his hands, his fingers thick, nicked and scratched, calloused from outdoor working.

What was he doing?

'I think that's recording. Why don't you smile for the camera? For your husband, Danielle?' She lifted her head. 'Now you're going to tell me a story. And I'm going to tell you one.'

Chapter 70

IN THE DETECTIVE office in Coyne's Cross Garda Station, Grace turned over another page of the witness statements she was studying, trying to focus. From the moment Carla had volunteered to go with Jack, her stomach had been churning. It was just like Carla to jump in on something like this. As if climbing mountains and caving in her spare time wasn't dangerous enough. One day Grace was going to have to tell her about *her* nightmares – about Carla falling down the side of a cliff or getting trapped underground. But for now, that was going to have to wait.

Grace glanced at her watch. Carla hadn't been gone long. She was keeping out of the way, filling in time while the station mobilised its armed team. DI Rainsford would come for her when he was ready.

Grace drew in a breath. She was always saying worrying never did anyone any good – there was no point fretting about what you couldn't control. Now it was time to take her own advice.

Rainsford was liaising with the superintendent in Kilkeel, to ensure that if Jack sent up the balloon, they had the right team to respond on the ground. Grace had been involved in a whole force training programme for on-site commanders after several barricade situations similar to this had gone badly. She knew they would perform a dynamic risk assessment, prioritising the safety of everyone involved, placing hostages in the top priority position, followed by innocent civilians, followed by police officers, and finally considering the safety of the hostage taker.

Flipping through the files in front of her, Grace tried to focus on the statements surrounding Drew's arrest. There was a box of videos still out on the landing – copies of the tapes made in the interview suite – but there wasn't time to be bothering people looking for a video machine, or to watch them today. She wanted to review Drew's manner in the interview, but the paperwork would do her just fine for now.

She turned the pages, noting the times and dates. As she was looking for Drew's signed statement, another page suddenly caught her eye.

He'd originally been picked up for a parking violation.

Pushing her glasses up her nose, Grace scanned the page. Drew's van had been parked on the yellow lines outside the church – the lines that stopped the whole place getting blocked up when there was a big wedding or a funeral. But on – she checked the top of the page – a Tuesday afternoon at 3.15 p.m., when the area outside was clear of other vehicles, Drew had got a ticket.

Not only that ... When he'd come out from the graveyard, carrying his spade, he'd apparently been abusive to the arresting officer. Grace could feel herself scowling. She'd be pretty abusive, too, under those circumstances.

She read on. The typed pages were already beginning to fade, and she angled them towards the light to make them easier to scan.

According to the officer's statement, Drew had opened the side of his van and had brandished the spade in a threatening manner. The officer was on his own in the patrol car, and had reacted quickly, cuffing Drew.

Grace put her finger under the words and, trying to fight the feeling of incredulity that was bubbling inside her, read them again. The whole scene didn't make sense to her.

Sitting up, she turned over more pages, looking for Drew's statement. Finding it, she pulled it out and laid it beside the arresting officer's statement.

I always park on the yellow lines when I've got the beds beside the front porch to do ... I saw the guard and went back to the van to ask him what he was doing. I was carrying my spade and I pulled back the sliding door at the side of the van to throw my spade inside.

Grace supposed lifting a spade to throw it into the rear of the van could be interpreted as 'brandishing', but ... Puzzled, she went back to the officer's statement.

> I restrained Peter Drew with handcuffs and placed him under arrest for threatening behaviour. He was abusive and struggling. I called for assistance and he began to calm down. He calmed down enough for me to transport him to the back of the patrol car. On locking him into the car, I returned to the van to pull the door closed. At that point I saw what looked like a mobile phone in the back of his van. Thinking it was Drew's phone, I picked it up. On doing so, I realised the screen was broken and there looked to be traces of blood in the casing. It was the same model that had been reported missing with Gemma Langan the previous weekend. I was immediately suspicious, and replaced it for technical examination.

Grace clicked her tongue and looked for the Scenes of Crime Officer's report on the van and the phone. Gemma's fingerprints had been found on the phone, together with her boyfriend Sean's and the arresting officer's.

No sign of Peter Drew's fingerprints.

Gemma's fingerprints had also been found on the dashboard of the van. So there was no question that it was her phone, and she'd been in his van – at some point.

Grace flicked back to the arresting officer's report and

checked out his name. His signature was a flourish at the end of the document: Sergeant Seamus Twomey. Grace shook her head. If anyone was likely to arrest someone for a bit of lip and parking 'illegally' somewhere where it wasn't bothering anyone, it would be Sergeant Twomey.

She looked at the SOCO report again. There had been a tarpaulin and tools in the rear of the van, but no other indication that Gemma might have been held there. Perhaps she hadn't. *Perhaps Drew had picked her up and she'd never left the cab of his van. Perhaps her phone had fallen out of her pocket during a struggle and, seeing it later, he'd thrown it into the back, meaning to get rid of it.*

But that didn't explain why his fingerprints weren't on it.

Grace checked the file again. A pair of rubber gardening gloves was also listed in the inventory of items removed from the van.

Had Drew been wearing gloves when he'd handled her phone, and then murdered Gemma and taken her out to the middle of the lake?

Chapter 71

DANIELLE COWERED AGAINST the wall, but Terry Walsh didn't come closer to her; only his shadow touched her. Taking a step backwards, he squatted down and trained the phone on her.

Why on earth was this happening?

Was he filming her? What ...?

'Tell me who you are.'

Danielle looked at him, confused. He knew who she was.

'Say your name. Quickly, I don't have much patience.'

'Danielle ... Danielle Brennan.' It came out as a rasp.

'Speak up.'

She tried again, louder this time, her voice cracking.

'And tell me who your cousins are.'

Danielle felt her stomach clench. 'Melissa and Julia Hardiman.'

'And tell me who Gemma Langan was.'

Danielle felt something dark open up inside her, cold and deep, like the shaft of a well, rancid water still at the bottom. Still until now.

Was that what this was about? What did he know?

'She was a girl who ...' Danielle coughed, her voice barely audible.

'Say it!'

'She was a girl who disappeared. She was killed by—'

He cut her off. 'Who was she killed by, Danielle? Tell me who.'

'By Peter Drew. He picked her up in his van after a party. She left early and he picked her up.'

'Did he, Danielle? Are you sure about that? Tell me the truth now.'

Danielle looked at him. He was fully focused on the phone, his face rigid with concentration. Keeping it level, he shifted slightly, taking the pressure off his knee.

'The truth, Danielle.'

'What? That is the truth, that's—'

He interrupted her. 'That's what you told the court, I know. But I don't think it's the truth, is it? Peter was a gentle soul, wasn't he? He liked Gemma because she helped him with the rabbits in the graveyard. The priest wanted them all gone, didn't he, but Gemma helped him?'

Danielle shook her head. *What was he talking about? Rabbits? He was mad, he had to be.*

'He killed her, Drew killed her. They found him guilty in court.'

'But did he kill her, Danielle? We don't have a lot of time

here. I need you to tell me what really happened that night. About Gemma going into the boathouse with Melissa.'

Danielle could feel her energy draining, weakness coming in waves of despair. She shook her head. 'No, no – Peter did it.'

'Did he, Danielle? Or did Melissa have a row with Gemma, and hit her perhaps? Did Melissa knock Gemma Langan unconscious and then panic? You'd all been drinking, hadn't you? I bet you all thought Melissa had killed her, didn't you? But instead of calling an ambulance, what did you do, Danielle?'

His voice had hardened. Danielle could feel the tears flowing down her face. She could see that night so clearly in her mind's eye. It had been so warm, a glorious summer. They'd all spent ages getting ready for the party, doing one another's hair. She'd gone into Top Shop in Kilkeel to buy a denim miniskirt to wear with her strappy sandals.

Then Melissa, drunk, stroppy, calling Gemma down to the boathouse for a little chat, claiming what was hers.

Jules had said they ought to go and check to see if Mel was OK, so they'd left the barn where the party was and gone down to the boathouse. When they'd got there, Gemma had been lying on the concrete, and Melissa had been throwing up into the water. Her face had been streaked with tears.

'She tried to attack me. I only pushed her. It was self-defence. You'll have to help me now, you're here, too.'

Danielle had backed away.

'This is your fault, Dani, you've been here in Coyne's Cross the whole time. Why didn't you tell her I was going out with Sean?'

Was it her fault?

Danielle didn't know any more. Melissa's voice rang in her head. 'Don't you go anywhere, Dani. You and Jules, help me get her into the boat. Dad's always saying to be careful swimming here because of the shelf. It creates currents, it's the deepest part. Quickly – help me.'

And they'd got her into the rowing boat tied up inside, opening the boathouse doors just enough to get it out. Then they'd rowed out into the middle of the lough, and Melissa had wrapped a rope around Gemma's feet and tied the spare anchor that had been in the boat to her ankles. It wasn't the proper anchor for the rowing boat, it was much bigger. And then Julia and Melissa had rolled her into the water. And Danielle had retched over the side.

'You thought you'd got away with it, didn't you?' Walsh's voice cut into her memories, and Danielle could feel that same nausea rising. She was going to vomit. There had been blood coming out of Gemma's ear …

'Peter was watching, you know? He saw you. He was terrified. He knew he should have gone to the guards, but he knew he shouldn't have been watching. He saw them go into the boathouse. And the next thing, he sees you and

Julia go in there, and then a boat heads into the middle of the lough, and he can see shapes moving. Sound travels on water you know, caught a bit of what Melissa was saying – enough.' He paused. 'It was a full moon that night. Do you remember? And then he heard a splash. What could he do? He didn't sleep that night, you know? He was sick with fear. How long did it take you to come up with the story? To slip her phone into his van? He never worked out how you did that.'

'I … We …' Danielle stumbled.

It had been Melissa's idea – to say Gemma had said that Drew creeped her out, that he'd been following her. They had to stick to their stories, as if they were coming up with them independently – how they'd all seen him hanging about her. Danielle shook her head. She had no idea what had happened with the phone or how it had got there; she hadn't even seen it that night. It had all happened so fast and been so terrifying that she'd locked everything away in a part of her head where she now couldn't retrieve the details. All she could remember clearly was the boat. And the blood.

'When they brought him in, he hadn't been sleeping. He couldn't think. They questioned him for hours, but he couldn't say he'd been watching, he knew they'd have called him a pervert. And once he'd denied it, it was too late, wasn't it?'

'They told me I had to say I'd seen him talking to her, that she'd mentioned feeling creepy around him.' Danielle shook her head, trying to clear her vision. Everything felt blurry.

'That he was stalking her?'

'Yes, yes,' Danielle sobbed.

How had this happened?

She'd known as soon as Ruairi told her about the skull that it was Gemma's. Melissa had just shrugged it off, saying Drew was convicted, they had nothing to worry about. But she'd *known*.

'Do you know what happened to Peter, Danielle?'

Looking up at him, Danielle shook her head, fear washing over her like a wave. She did know – it had been in the paper – but she wasn't going to say it.

'He died, Danielle. He couldn't cope with prison on his own once I left. We were friends, special friends. So do you know what he did? He hanged himself. He couldn't do another two years, so he killed himself. You framed him, and look what happened.'

Chapter 72

'**H**OW LONG WILL the rest of the team take to get here?'

Carla ducked out from under the bushes to see if there was movement on the island. As she did so, Jack's phone vibrated with a message. He pulled it out of his pocket and opened it.

'Oh, holy shit.'

'What?'

Jack shook his head, turning the screen towards Carla so she could see the video of Danielle, bound and sobbing. They watched it to the end.

As Danielle recounted the story, Carla could feel anger building inside her. She could imagine it: teenage girls, all dressed up at a party; the cocktails being mixed from God only knew what; the row, over God only knew what, that had led to Gemma losing her life. If they'd called an ambulance, she might have been OK.

Had she been alive when she'd gone into the water?

Jack interrupted her thoughts. 'Danielle's definitely on the island – look at the wall behind her. She's inside the church.'

'This has come from Julia's phone?' It was more of a statement than a question, but Jack nodded. 'I think he's WhatsApped this to everyone in Julia's contacts.'

'It won't take long to end up on social media.' Carla glanced over to the island. 'How long will he keep her alive now he's sent this?'

Jack didn't answer for a moment as he forwarded the message on to Rainsford and Matt Curran.

'I don't know. He drugged the others first. If he sticks to the same MO, he's going to need to wait a few minutes for it to kick in.'

'What did the post-mortem say he'd used?'

'Ketamine.'

'That's a fast-acting anaesthetic. We might not have much time.' Carla looked out to the island, trying to clear her head of the video, then she turned to Jack. 'He's made his move, he must know Julia's phone is being tracked. And we can assume he has a weapon. He knows you're coming for him. This could end up being a murder-suicide if we wait.'

Jack nodded, moving a branch to look over at the island. There was no further sign of movement. 'I think we're going to have to move now. Preservation of life is our first duty.'

* * *

The entrance to the tunnel that ran to the island was hidden by brambles and down a steep flight of stone steps cut from the rock, worn in the centre with age. The tendrils of blackberry and briar moved surprisingly easily as Jack pulled them away. Looking closely, Carla could see that the stems had been wired together to create a curtain.

'Someone's been using this entrance.'

'Kids, probably.' Jack looked at her. 'Are you sure you want to come down here? The tunnel leads into the caves under the island, it's—'

'Dangerous? So's crossing the road. I told you, this is what I do for fun. Get moving.'

Carla threw him an impatient look and he trotted down the steps, using the mossy sides of the narrow cutting to steady himself. At the bottom was a rusty iron gate, a thick layer of black paint peeling from the bars. It ran from the ground to the curved roof of the tunnel and looked more like a cell door than a gate.

Jack stopped. From behind him, Carla couldn't see what he was looking at until he turned around to her.

'There's a new padlock on here.' His voice was level, but his eyes full of concern.

'Give it a kick. I bet the hinges are pretty weak. Iron corrodes this close to salt water. Whoever put the padlock on might not have thought to strengthen the rest of it.'

Carla backed up the steps to let Jack get better access. Raising his leg, he aimed a kick at the lower hinge. The flat sole of his boot sent a shudder through the metal, the sound reverberating through the tunnel.

It took another few kicks before the hinges came free from the stone. Jack glanced at her. Carla grinned encouragingly, hiding the wave of trepidation that was building inside her.

She had nightmares about tunnels. Not caving tunnels – they were different – but man-made tunnels, dark and wet and narrow, just like this one, the sound of water dripping through her sleeping mind like torture. In her dreams she felt compelled to go into the tunnel – that somehow Lizzie was at the other end; that the answers she needed were in there. But this was something bigger, something terrifying that left her paralysed and unable to breathe, waking crying out.

Grace had told her so many times that she needed therapy, that it was PTSD, but the idea of talking to someone about her fears was almost as terrifying as the dream itself. That was why she'd started caving in the first place – to prove to herself that she wasn't afraid, that it was only a dream. It had been a challenge at first, but some of the underground caverns she'd seen had taken her breath away in the same way that the uninterrupted view from the mountains she'd climbed had. And caving had increased her stamina and overall strength, especially in her arms, which had benefited her climbing. It had taught her a lot: when she was leading a team of army recruits, the last thing she was going to show them was any level of fear.

But now here she was, literally living her worst nightmare. Only this time it wasn't Lizzie at the other end – it was Danielle, and they were racing the clock to get to her before she was murdered.

Stepping forwards, Jack pushed and lifted the gate to one side, giving them just enough room to squeeze through. Now she was just going to have to get over herself and face her fears.

Chapter 73

IN THE DETECTIVE Unit office, Grace closed her eyes and tried to focus on slowing her heartbeat. She had more files open in front of her, but all she could see was the video that had been shared with all Julia Hardiman's contacts, forwarded to her by the inspector. It had created shock waves around the whole station. And then the phones had started ringing.

Grace tapped her fingernails on the file in front of her, trying not to think about Carla out by the lough with a brutal killer. DI Rainsford had been right not to let Jack go on his own; anything could have happened. But did it have to be Carla with him? They were going to have to have a chat about her need to jump into life-threatening situations when they got home.

But at least they knew who they were dealing with now.

And Grace knew his name had rung a bell; it had just taken her a few minutes to work out why.

The only thing she could do right now was keep out of the way, and wait for the call she'd put in to Mountjoy Gaol, to confirm her suspicions, to be returned. Perhaps she was totally wrong, but she was 99 per cent sure she wasn't.

When Jack had texted through the photo of the car abandoned beside the lough, it had only taken minutes for a name to appear. And then they'd heard his voice on the video.

Terry Walsh. The handyman who looked after Coyne House and tended the graveyard.

And it was clear from his conversation with Danielle that he'd spoken to Peter Drew at length; he was obviously someone Drew had trusted enough to tell his story to.

Grace should have twigged sooner, but she really hadn't taken the name of the maintenance man at the cottage on board. Why would she, unless they needed him?

She jumped as her phone began to ring. Mountjoy. She grabbed it.

The incident room was like a scene from a movie when she hurried in. One of those disaster movies, where everyone is waiting for news of when the world was going to end. Matt was sitting at the conference table with his laptop, his fingers flying across the keys. In the rear half of the room, DI Rainsford was on the phone.

'Fantastic, thanks, I'm on my way,' he said. 'The cordons are secure and the super's already on site. Sergeant Maguire is approaching the island via a tunnel. It's years since it's been used. It may not be passable.' He paused. 'Yes, that's great.'

Grace caught his eye as he clicked off the phone. 'I only need two seconds.'

Pulling on his jacket, Rainsford followed her out onto the landing.

Grace kept her voice low. 'I've just had a call from Mountjoy. It appears Terry Walsh was Peter Drew's cellmate for the last five years of Walsh's sentence. Armed robbery. They were very close. He was released two and a half years ago, and six months later Drew committed suicide. That seems to be around the time Walsh turned up looking for work in Coyne's Cross.'

Rainsford stopped checking his pockets and looked at her properly. 'You serious? So he's been planning this since then?' He scowled. 'Why wait until now to act?'

'I'd guess the discovery of the skull set him off. Once an identification was made, it would bring the story up again. He had some scores to settle first.' Grace raised her eyebrows. 'Reading between the lines, I would suspect that Walsh and Drew had a relationship in prison. Perhaps Walsh had promised to wait for Drew, but Drew's mental health apparently spiralled after Walsh was released.' Grace's voice was hard. 'Walsh wanted revenge – for himself and for Drew. He came here to establish himself and give himself access. Working in the community, taking on Drew's old job at the graveyard and working for Melissa, he'd get to know everyone Drew had told him about, and their weak points. It would also explain the symbolism of him cutting out their hearts. I'd guess he feels his heart had been cut out when Drew died.'

'Interesting.'

Rainsford was about to move when Grace stopped him. 'Tell me, is Sean Twomey related to your Sergeant Seamus Twomey, by any chance?'

Rainsford looked at her, his face puzzled. 'Nephew. Why do you ask?'

'It seems he was dating Gemma Langan at the time of her disappearance, but that doesn't appear to have been taken into account in the witness statements. He was interviewed, but not to the extent he should have been. He wasn't asked about a relationship, and there's nothing in his statement to suggest that Gemma was being stalked by Drew. Nobody seems to have asked him about it, and he didn't volunteer the information.'

Rainsford pursed his lips. 'Really? That doesn't sound good.'

Chapter 74

CARLA DIDN'T GIVE herself time to think about anything other than moving forwards as Jack ventured into the tunnel. Its walls were rough and moss-covered, the low roof arched, only just tall enough to allow them to stand up. Ahead of her, he'd switched on the torch on his phone, creating a bright halo around his feet, but plunging what lay ahead of them into ominous darkness. She switched on Grace's torch.

Walking briskly along behind him, Carla focused on the floor, playing the beam in front of them, avoiding the loose stones that lay along the way. The tunnel walls undulated where, Carla guessed, those cutting into the rock had changed shifts or tools. The tourist guide Grace had read had said something about the tunnel being created by the monks so they could reach the island in bad weather. It had allowed them to keep whoever was living there supplied with food and fresh water, but it had been decommissioned years before. The caves the tunnel led into were tidal, had been used primarily for storage by the same monks, and formed a honeycomb under the island.

'Now what's *this*?'

Jack's exclamation jerked her out of focusing on the history, the only way she could think of to push from her mind the creeping fear of what might be at the other end. He'd stopped ahead of her. He turned to check she was keeping up and shone the light on a pile of brick-like packages, bound in grey plastic, stacked against the side of the tunnel.

'What on earth . . ?' Coming up behind him, Carla could see an old-style Nokia mobile phone was resting on the top.

'Educated guess? Drugs. And a good supply.'

'And a burner phone? You wouldn't get much reception down here.'

'I would say yes and yes. But we need to get moving, we're almost there. The troops can come and check all this out. One problem at a time.'

They pushed on. The sound of water hitting rock grew louder as they neared the end of the tunnel. It was even darker here. As Carla came up behind Jack, he swung the beam from his phone around. She could see the tunnel opened into a complex cave system, the stone shelving down to water, which swirled angrily below them.

Jack glanced at her. 'I think it's this way.'

'We need to link up. Let me hold the back of your vest. Do you want to swap that phone for my torch, save the battery?'

He shook his head. 'Fully charged.'

Nodding, Carla switched off her own torch and stashed it in one of the pockets in her cargo pants, grabbing the back of his body protection.

Glancing at her, Jack edged along a path worn into a ledge, playing the intense light beam in front of him. The smell of seaweed was almost overpowering. Focusing on exactly where she put her boots, Carla held on to his bulky vest. It was a new one, the Kevlar lining protecting against bullets and stab wounds, but not ideal for narrow spaces. Every now and again she felt cool drops of salt water hit her face as a stronger wave broke below them, spitting up under the sides of the rock.

The shelf they were walking along broadened out as they entered another cavern, the air even more chill than the last one. Carla had carried the afternoon heat with her down the best part of the tunnel, but now she was starting to shiver. She wasn't sure if it was actually the cold, or if the adrenaline she could feel pumping through her body was making her hypersensitive. Either way, she was glad of the weight of her body armour.

'Almost there.'

The constant hum of the sea echoed as waves passed through the caverns around them, more of a constant growl than a roar as the incoming tide churned through Dead Man's Gully before it surged through the caves.

Its movement had looked calmer from the shore than it sounded now, its energy dissipating across the expanse of water, but the strong currents below the surface would be deadly for an inexperienced swimmer or boatman.

Ahead of her, she felt Jack slow and she looked up. Over his shoulder she could see light filtered from somewhere above; a warm greenish glow reached towards them, illuminating steep steps hewn in the stone.

Jack turned to her. 'This opening is on the seaward side of the church. Above us there's a small ruin that is supposed to be the hermit's lodge or something, and then the main church. It's not very big – about twenty feet by ten, with two entrances. One's at the far end, facing the round tower across the water. The other is on this side – it used to open into a side chapel that's only a pile of stones now. Only the footprint is really left.'

'You think Danielle's in the main building?'

'I'm sure that's where she is. The guys should be in place now, over beyond on the shore. As soon as we surface, I'll let them know we're here and see if they can organise some sort of distraction to give us a chance to see into the church and work out how to get Danielle out.' Jack glanced at her.

'Surely he'll be watching the end of the tunnel, though?'

'I'd guess he's hoping we've forgotten about it, or assumed the padlock was secure. Even with the currents, a boat's a safer option for getting to the island than these caves. Sean and Melissa have been maintaining that the tunnel has been blocked off for years, in case the holidaymakers in the cottages decide they want to visit and someone ends up having an accident.'

'Someone knows it's here, though. Do you think the drugs are Walsh's?'

'Honestly, if I was going to kidnap and murder someone, I'd move my stash first. It looks like someone has been running a full-scale operation from here. That's a young man's game. I'm not seeing Terry Walsh for it.' He paused. 'Ready for these steps? Careful – they are pretty slippy.'

Jack switched off the torch and stuck his phone into his trouser pocket, so he had both hands free. Their eyes quickly adjusted to the darkness.

Glancing behind him again to check she was following, he started up the steps, then disappeared at the top. Right behind him, Carla realised the entrance to the cave on the surface was bigger than she'd expected. Like the start of the tunnel, it had been cut from the stone of the cliff, the walls uneven where the monks had changed tools and workmen. The floor was covered in fine sand and small pebbles that had drifted up against the outcrops at the base of the walls. Like the tunnel, it was only just tall enough for them to stand in, but this cave smelled of bats, rotting guano and ammonia amplified by the summer heat.

Carla looked around. Jack pulled out his phone and checked its signal, his thumbs flying over the keyboard.

'I'm letting base know we're here.' He stopped and looked at the screen for a few moments. His phone vibrated with an incoming message. 'They're in position. If they can see him, I've asked them to give us a signal. Right, let's move. Follow me. We come out beside the hermitage at the top of the church. We should be able to keep out of sight.'

Jack turned to push aside the brambles, and Carla immediately felt the heat of the day seeping into the cave. She could hear a man's voice echoing across the water.

'This is Colm Hayes, I'm part of the Garda Síochána Crisis Unit. I'm here to listen to you and make sure everyone stays safe. Can you indicate you can hear me?'

His tone was firm but calm. And the distraction was exactly what they needed. She knew the negotiator's first priority was to make contact.

Silently, the brambles tearing at his body armour as he pushed through them, Jack crept out of the mouth of the tunnel. Carla followed him, holding her breath, her heart thumping in her ears. Just as he'd described, she could see the tumbled down walls of what he'd called the hermitage and beyond it, the sheer windowless wall of the church. On the seaward side, where they were, the stone was bleached and weathered.

The voice came again from the shore. '*We have supplies of food and water. Can you tell me if anyone requires medical assistance?*'

Jack indicated with his head for Carla to follow him. They were in the shadow of the high church wall in seconds, standing with their backs against the sharp stones.

And they could hear voices. At least one – a man's voice.

Carla closed her eyes for a second, praying to anyone who was listening that Danielle was still alive. Straining her ears, she listened hard. She was sure she could hear someone crying.

Keeping his back pressed against the rough wall, Jack edged along. The man's voice was getting louder; it sounded as if it was bouncing off the walls of the church as he became more agitated.

'They know now, Danielle. They know what Melissa did. They're here for you.'

Before Jack heard a response, the negotiator's voice rang out again.

'*Can you signal that you have heard me and that everyone there is safe? We can send in water and medical supplies if you need them. Please signal so we know you can hear us.*'

There was a scuffling noise inside and Jack slid further down the wall to the narrow doorway he'd described, peeping inside. Gesturing to Carla to stay out of sight, he unclipped his Taser from his belt.

'*Can you signal to me how many people are on the island?*' The negotiator's voice rang out across the water again. '*My name is Colm Hayes. Are you injured?*'

Carla pressed herself against the wall of the church as Jack darted in through the opening.

'Armed Gardaí! Put your weapon down!'

His voice almost lifted Carla off her feet.

'Put your weapon *down*!'

Moving to the doorway, she could see Terry Walsh, frozen as if he'd just spun around, his face a snarl. The blade of a large carving knife in his hand caught the light. He was only about three metres from Jack – probably less – but a lot closer to Danielle.

Walsh lunged towards Danielle, and Carla heard the electronic buzzing of Jack's Taser being deployed. Walsh fell, thrown backwards by the force of the charge, the knife flying out of his hand. Then Jack was standing over him, rolling him over to secure his hands behind his back, pulling a pair of steel handcuffs from a pouch on his belt.

'He's out cold.'

Jack turned his head to look at Danielle, but Carla was already beside her, taking her in her arms. Lying against a pile of big loose stones, she was almost unconscious, a red weal across her face where her mouth had been taped up. The knife lay on the ground between them.

Carla pulled a flask from the pocket in her fatigues and opened it quickly. The water inside it might be warm, but she'd topped it up when she'd got changed earlier, so at least it was fresh. She poured a little on Danielle's lips. The liquid revived her, her eyes flying open. At the sight of Carla she closed them again, her body sagging.

'You're going to be fine now, I promise. Have a little water.'

Carla dribbled more water into Danielle's mouth. Behind her, she heard Jack on the phone. What felt like only seconds later, she heard the powerful roar of an outboard engine.

Chapter 75

B Y THE TIME they got to the Garda station, Carla was starting to feel as if she'd drunk way too much coffee and was heading for some sort of crash. More adrenaline had surged into her already saturated bloodstream as she'd jumped into the waiting RIB and then been escorted to the command post. It had made her feel almost giddy.

Climbing ashore from the powerful inflatable, she'd found the empty lane they'd left had turned into what looked like a military base.

Around the bend, out of sight from the island, two Garda vans were parked side by side, their rear doors open to reveal interiors heavily kitted out with screens. Uniformed personnel sat in front of them, headphones on. Behind them, two ambulances had pulled up. A group of heavily armed officers, who had been deployed in the undergrowth along the bank of the lough, were standing down as paramedics attended to Walsh. He had been brought across from the island on a stretcher in another RIB, escorted by more armed officers.

Carla had been to all sorts of crime scenes during her career, but inevitably she was looking for remains and things were relatively calm. This was an active operation and had a completely different feel to it, the air highly charged with a sense of anticipation and urgency.

But Danielle was safe.

Thank God Danielle was safe.

Carla wasn't sure how she would have coped if they'd been too late. The thought hadn't entered her head until she'd watched Danielle being wrapped in a silver blanket by a paramedic. Another paramedic had appeared beside Carla with a bottle of water. Thanking him, Carla had realised she was parched. As she drank it, the cold water like wine, it was as if her brain suddenly caught up with itself, and with the true enormity of what had just happened.

After Lizzie had gone, she'd read up a lot on the effect of trauma on the brain – how, during a catastrophic event, different personality types reacted in different ways. Carla had the sort of mind that homed in on the problem, blocking out everything else. In life-threatening situations she was able to think ultra-clearly and rationally, and to process information rapidly. It was a skill that had proved useful several times out on the rock face, whether above or below ground. There had been moments when she'd been on training operations when panic would have meant certain death. In theory, experience kicked in, and you worked a way out of the problem, but that didn't happen to everyone. She'd heard stories where inexperienced climbers or cavers fell more through their own action – or inaction – than through equipment failure.

Carla had learned that it was only afterwards, when it was safe, that the shock could set in. Not always – it depended on the circumstances – but she wanted to get her statement down before she forgot any details. Like the bundles and the phone in the tunnel.

As they approached the Garda station in the dusty Mondeo, Carla ran her fingers into her hair and closed her eyes for a moment.

'You OK?' Beside her, Jack buzzed down his window to put his code into the station yard barrier. He glanced across at her as it slowly rose. Carla opened her eyes and looked at him, a half-smile on her face. She didn't even know where to start to answer that one.

He grinned. 'Sorry – stupid question. None of that was in the handbook.'

'That's for sure.' She opened her eyes wide. 'I'm good, though. I just hope Danielle's OK.'

'They'll sort her out in hospital, and Donna's going debrief her when they give us the nod. They've known each other years. At least she's a friendly face.'

'And Walsh?'

Jack's face hardened. 'Hopefully we'll get an update as soon as we get inside. The phone that was in the tunnel's being examined for prints. If it did belong to Walsh, it might reveal if there was anyone else involved in Melissa's and Julia's killings. We can't assume this is done and dusted. There seem to be a lot of trailing ends around Gemma Langan's death and Drew's conviction.'

Jack pulled into a space behind the station and pushed his door open.

There were still so many questions in Carla's head.

Who had witnessed Gemma's death? If Peter Drew had been watching, did anyone else know what had happened that night, but had chosen to remain silent?

Perhaps they'd never have the answer to that, but the one that was bothering her the most was why three girls would take a fourth out to the middle of the lake and push her into the water, instead of calling an ambulance and claiming it was all an accident.

Three of them.

She could understand one of them needing to cover her trail – Melissa, perhaps, given what she'd seen of her in their brief meetings. But she must have been very manipulative, to persuade her sister and cousin to lie for her – and to put an innocent man away. The only logical reason Carla could think of was that the fight between two drunken teenage girls had been a vicious one, and Gemma had scratched Melissa. Was she frightened her DNA would be found under Gemma's fingernails, and had gone to these lengths to be sure her body was never found?

But wouldn't it have been simpler just to push Gemma into the water beside the slip inside the boathouse and then, when her body was discovered, suggest that she'd fallen in? They'd all been drinking, after all. Carla was sure, had there been the opportunity, that toxicology would have found Gemma's blood alcohol levels to be significant. To say nothing of the fact that the chances of recovering DNA from a body that had been submerged for any period of time was slim.

Why had it been so important that her body was never found?

Chapter 76

'THE HOSPITAL CALLED – Walsh is in intensive care. Weak heart, apparently, couldn't take the Taser.'

Just back from giving her statement, standing in the doorway to the incident room, Carla took a moment to absorb the information. As if reading her thoughts, Jack grimaced from the other side of the conference table.

'Danielle's been sedated, so Donna's on her way back for the moment.' He paused. 'The island's sealed off until the Technical Bureau can get there, but there was a full hypodermic syringe loaded with a lethal dose of potassium chloride beside his body. Between that and the knife, it seems clear he was getting ready to kill Danielle. The guys found a second vial as well, so I think he was planning to kill himself, too.'

Carla sensed, rather than heard, Grace behind her. She'd followed her into the ladies' loo earlier and they'd had a brief hug, but hadn't had a chance to catch up properly. Grace had briefly filled her in on what she'd discovered about Walsh's connection to Peter Drew. Carla's mind was still reeling from the video. She had felt as if everything was moving fast when they'd been at the lough, but it didn't feel as if it was going to slow down even now they were in the security of the station.

As if he was reading her mind, Jack continued. 'They've also confirmed those bundles in the tunnel were controlled drugs – cocaine and ecstasy. Now we need to find out what's on that phone.'

Downstairs in the tech room, his hands encased in blue latex gloves, Matt extracted the Nokia phone from a specialist evidence bag and plugged in the cable that connected it to a secure laptop.

'Now, let's see what this baby can tell us.' He glanced over his shoulder at Jack and Carla. He was enjoying his moment, but Carla just wanted him to get on with it; she was too keyed up for theatre.

Leaning on the plain magnolia wall of the tech room, Grace had her arms crossed, watching Matt work. Carla could tell she was thinking, processing all the information they had so far, drawing on her considerable experience to get behind the crimes, into the mindset of those involved.

Matt laid the phone down beside the computer and his fingers flew over the keys. 'This type of evidence bag is called a Faraday bag – it stops any signals reaching the unit. If this mobile belongs to any sort of organised crime group, they could have set up a kill message that's sent to it if they think it's compromised. That message would delete all the data. The bag stops that. I don't love being down here in the basement, but this room is also sealed to prevent any sort of signal getting through that could interfere with the equipment. The Tech Bureau will have fingerprinted it under the same conditions. Now ...' He paused. 'I'm duplicating the data on the phone, so we can get a look at it without compromising it. Anything that's been deleted, we should be able to get from the service provider.'

As he spoke, the computer screen began to fill with information – numbers, and what looked like text messages scrolling upwards.

'That looks like it's working.'

Reaching for the mouse, Matt picked a random section of the screen and slowed it down so they could see it. He glanced at Jack.

'It's pretty clear what's going on here. This is Julia Hardiman's missing second phone. I'm guessing from this conversation that Rupert Bear is Ruairi Brennan and Hot Stuff is Julia Hardiman?'

'"Bar quiet, leaving early" sounds like it could be a message from her, doesn't it?' Jack clearly wasn't expecting an answer as he scanned the screen. 'They seem to be in a fairly steamy relationship. Can you get me dates, Matt? See if you can tell from this when it started. And I want to see their conversation from last Friday night or Saturday morning.'

Carla clicked her tongue on the roof of her mouth. 'Do you think he gave her a burner phone so if Danielle saw the number or found the messages, she wouldn't guess it was her cousin?'

Jack looked at her, his eyebrows raised as he nodded. 'I think that's a distinct possibility.' He turned to look at the screen again. 'When you go through Friday night, Matt, I think you're going to find the message we saw her composing in her car. Let's see if we can tie the timing into the time clock on the video.'

'Will do. Why do you reckon it was hidden in the tunnel with the drugs?' Matt straightened up, glancing at Jack as he spoke. 'You'd think it would be safer just to drop it into the middle of the lough.'

Grace moved off the wall to join them, looking over Matt's shoulder. Before any of them could answer, there was a sharp knock on the door that made Carla start. She put her hand to her chest.

'Sorry, I'm a bit jumpy.'

She felt Grace rub her shoulder. 'Understandable after today, I think.'

The scenes of crime officer at Coyne's Cross stuck his head around the door. Carla had been introduced to him at some point, but his name had gone clean out of her head.

In his fifties and balding, he had a bushy moustache and intelligent sparkling eyes that reminded Carla of a curious bird.

Coming inside, he put a pile of printouts down on the table triumphantly.

'Terry Walsh's, Julia Hardiman's *and* Ruairi Brennan's fingerprints are on that phone, Jack. It's a pay as you go. We're tracing the SIM as far as we can. Looks like it was bought in Kilkeel.' The sergeant paused. 'And we've found smudges of what look a lot like Brennan's prints on some of the packages you found. We've lots of glove prints, too, but perhaps he got sloppy.'

Carla looked at Jack. 'Does that mean that Walsh and Brennan were working together for some reason?'

Jack shrugged. 'Time will tell. Thanks, Paddy, that's very interesting. I think we need a chat with Ruairi Brennan. Let's bring Sean Twomey in while we're at it, and ask him about what happened on the night of the party. I'm surprised the pair of them aren't hammering on the door. They must both have been sent it, too.'

Carla shrugged. 'Perhaps they haven't seen it yet.'

Jack didn't look convinced as he turned to Grace.

'The DI passed on your thoughts to me on the Langan investigation and the missing interview information. Donna will update us on what Danielle has to say about that night as soon as she's fit enough to talk, but both Brennan and Sean Twomey were at that party, too.' Jack raised an eyebrow. 'Do you ladies want to observe? There's a video link down to these screens from the interview room. And let's put Gemma Langan's facial reconstruction in the interview room with them, will we, and see how they react?'

The scenes of crime sergeant grinned. 'That will be my pleasure. The pair of them get my goat – too cocky by half. I'll organise to get them picked up and brought in for a chat.'

'I'd love to watch.' Grace looked at the screen, the messages continuing to scroll as they were copied from the phone. 'Putting Gemma's likeness in the room is an excellent idea.' Her tone hardened. 'But I think someone held on to this phone because there's a conversation on it somewhere that they need to keep. Perhaps you can see if there's anything relating to Gemma Langan's murder on there, Matt?'

Chapter 77

IN INTERVIEW ROOM 3, Ruairi Brennan was looking distinctly unwell. Wearing a faded T-shirt that looked as if it had been resurrected from the bedroom floor, and jeans with flip-flops, he rubbed his hand over his face, the dark circles under his eyes highlighted by the harsh fluorescent lighting. Sitting at a wood-effect Formica table, a takeaway coffee in front of him, he kept glancing at the bust of Gemma Langan that had been placed on another table at the back of the room. Carla had sourced a red wig that was cut in an almost identical style to the way Gemma had worn her thick wavy hair. The resemblance was striking.

And from the way Ruairi Brennan was behaving, Carla wasn't the only one who thought so.

Carla and Grace had both grabbed coffees and sandwiches while Brennan was being collected. They sat with Matt in the tech room, the largest screen above them switched to the interview room live feed. Grace had a notepad beside her, a pen in one hand and her coffee in the other. They'd collected a sandwich and coffee for Matt, too, and he glanced up from the phone messages to check the screen, taking a bite of his roll at the same time.

Carla glanced at Grace anxiously while they waited. She had a feeling they were finally inching closer to the truth.

Sean Twomey had been at Brennan's house when the patrol unit had pulled up, his BMW parked in the drive beside Brennan's Pathfinder. The curtains had been closed, but through a crack where they hadn't quite been pulled completely, the patrol had seen that the TV in the living room was switched to a video game, the colours from the screen leaping over the walls, the sound drowning out their knocking for some time.

Which perhaps *also* explained why Twomey hadn't noticed that an armed Garda operation had just occurred on his land, the outer cordon sealing off the property for several hours. Indeed, it seemed that he had no clue what had been going on so close to his own home that day.

In the tech room, Carla jumped slightly as Jack appeared on the screen. He walked through the interview room door, followed by Donna Sullivan, cool in a cream silk blouse, her glossy hair slicked into a ponytail. They sat opposite Brennan.

Grace reached over and squeezed Carla's arm. 'You'll be fine after a bath and a good night's sleep. Your nerves are just a bit strung out.'

Carla smiled. 'That sounds very technical. Thank you, Doctor.'

Grace punched her playfully on the arm as Matt reached over to turn up the sound. On the screen, Jack pushed a button on a grey metal box on the wall beside him.

'This is an audio and video recording unit, and this interview is being recorded. I'm Detective Sergeant Jack Maguire, and I'm here with Detective Garda Donna Sullivan and Ruairi Brennan of the Coyne's Cross Adventure Centre and Ard na Gréine on the Ballybeg Road. Thank you for coming in, Ruairi, and agreeing to answer our questions voluntarily. We do appreciate it. We know this is a difficult time and you've been under huge pressure.'

Ruairi bit his lip. 'The hospital said Dani couldn't have any visitors.' He shrugged. 'I wanted to go straight there, but they said she's going to be fine.'

Carla watched as Jack looked understanding. He really should play poker; his face wasn't giving away anything that he might be thinking – about what Brennan's involvement had been at that Leaving Cert party seventeen years earlier, or his decision to play video games when his wife had been kidnapped by a killer. He'd changed after their scramble through the tunnel, now wore a crisp lemon short-sleeved shirt and beige chinos. She glanced at Grace, who was scowling.

'She's badly dehydrated and exhausted, and I'm quite sure she will need some counselling, but she's a strong woman. You'll be able to see her soon.'

Ruairi nodded, picking up his coffee cup, taking a sip.

As if Jack had given her a signal, Donna smiled across at Ruairi, her tone friendly.

'What can you tell us about your relationship with Julia Hardiman, Ruairi?'

Ruairi put the cup down slowly – too slowly – and proceeded to turn it so the logo printed on the outside was at exact right angles to the edge of the table. Then he shrugged, looking from Jack to Donna.

'She's Dani's cousin, we're friends. We all are, Sean and Mel and Jules, and me and Dani.'

His eyes suddenly filled with tears; he rubbed them away with the palm of his hand.

'And you told us previously that she was helping you plan Danielle's birthday party?' Donna's tone was encouraging.

Ruairi sniffed loudly. 'Yes, she came to see me on Friday night … before …' He stopped speaking abruptly. 'Do we have to talk about Jules? I thought this was about Dani.' His shoulders slumped; he rubbed his nose and chin, his normally neatly groomed designer stubble looking as if it needed work.

Jack cut in. 'I think it's about both of them, Ruairi – and Terry Walsh, as it turns out. How well do you know him?'

Ruairi shook his head emphatically. 'I don't know him at all. He worked for Sean and Mel. Do you think he killed Jules?'

Jack opened the manila file in front of him. 'We are investigating that possibility, and that he may have been involved in Melissa's death, too. We do know that he was holding Danielle on Monastery Island. It appears that she had been there since she was abducted from the Coffee Dock.'

His shoulders slumping further, Ruairi shook his head as if admonishing himself. 'I should have thought of that. Nobody goes there any more.'

Jack picked up the biro lying beside his notepad. 'Don't they? How do you know that? Have you been there recently?'

Ruairi shrugged. 'I train out there sometimes. I haven't been there for a while.'

Jack made a note. 'I see.' He looked up. 'Tell me about the tunnel, Ruairi.'

Even from where she was sitting, Carla could see Ruairi pale and his shoulders go rigid. She glanced over at Grace, who lifted her eyebrows, acknowledging that she'd spotted his reaction.

'The tunnel? In what context?'

Jack sat back from the desk and, playing the biro through his fingers, shrugged. 'Do you use it often?'

'Me? No. Not at all, haven't been there for years. We all used to swim off the landing stage. But no, haven't been inside it for yonks.'

'Are you *quite* sure about that?' Jack gave him a moment to respond, but Ruairi just shook his head as if he didn't know what Jack was talking about. Carla could see Donna studying Ruairi as Jack continued. 'In the process of getting Danielle to safety, myself and a colleague discovered there was a new padlock on the gate of the tunnel.' Ruairi shrugged again as Jack went on. 'There's a scenes of crime team checking it out now.'

'Why?' Ruairi looked confused. 'Did Walsh use it? I bet he did. He worked on the estate, he's probably been planning on using the island for years. He's probably the only person who's been near it.'

Jack raised an eyebrow. 'Maybe so. So do you think we should be asking Walsh about the bundles of drugs we found wrapped in polythene and stacked halfway down the tunnel? Enough cocaine and ecstasy to indicate a serious level of criminal activity. And the tech boys tell me that from the traces they've found further down the tunnel, it's been in use for several years.'

'I don't know. I'm not the cop here, Jack, isn't that your job?'

'It is indeed. Which is why I was wondering why there was a mobile phone on the bales I mentioned, with your fingerprints all over it. And not only yours, but Julia Hardiman's and Terry Walsh's as well.'

Obviously annoyed, Ruairi sat back in his chair. 'I don't fucking know. Ask Walsh, he must have given it to Jules before …' He trailed off, suddenly realising what he was saying.

'That's a possibility we've considered, but it doesn't explain how your fingerprints got onto it, does it? You see, we have a video of Julia sending a text message on Friday night, but we know it wasn't sent from her smartphone, which we have now recovered. After your last chat with us, we secured your phone records, and what we believe to have been that text appears to have been sent to your personal phone from the phone we found in the tunnel.' Jack paused. 'When we picked you up this afternoon, your phone battery was dead, so I'm guessing you haven't had a chance to look at your WhatsApp messages yet. We've been trying to reach you to tell you about Danielle.'

Jack's voice was hard. Brennan shook his head, his face confused, his tone defensive.

'I didn't realise it was flat. It happens, you know.'

How could Ruairi Brennan let his phone go flat when his wife had disappeared?

Carla was starting to really dislike him. And he'd been playing video games all afternoon. You'd think he'd be out searching, unless he really didn't care about Danielle at all.

Something Jack had said echoed in her head – *Danielle owned half his company.*

Did that have a bearing on what was going on here?

Carla had no idea.

'Allow me to illuminate you on the video message that was sent this afternoon.' Jack pulled his mobile phone out of his pocket and scrolled through his WhatsApp messages. He turned up the volume and hit *play*.

In the tech room, Carla shivered as she heard Danielle's voice again.

In the interview room, Ruairi looked as if he'd frozen to his seat, his eyes fixed on the screen. From behind Jack and Donna, Gemma's inanimate face looked on, as if she was studying his reaction.

'I've got it. I've fucking got it.' Beside Carla, Matt slapped the desk and she almost lifted out of the chair. 'The skull. When those divers found the skull, Julia texted him. It's all there. They both thought it was Gemma, which means …' He looked at Carla triumphantly. 'They both knew she was in the lough.'

Chapter 78

MATT FLEW OUT of the tech room with the printout of the texts he'd found on Julia's phone, the door slamming behind him. On the screen, Jack was watching Ruairi closely. It seemed to Carla that he had paled even more after watching the video of Danielle's confession.

Which she could well understand – it was a harrowing video.

Now a sharp rap on the interview room door indicated Matt's arrival on the ground floor. Jack smiled at Ruairi as Donna got up to open it.

A moment later she returned to her seat, and passed the pages to Jack.

'For the benefit of the record, Garda Matt Curran has just passed Donna Sullivan a transcript of the text messages downloaded from the Nokia phone that was found in the tunnel that connects the Coyne Estate with Monastery Island. This phone, we believe, belonged to Julia Hardiman. These messages were sent to Ruairi Brennan's mobile phone.'

Carla watched as Jack scanned the pages, then looked up. His face was blank, but his tone hard.

'Ruairi Brennan, we have evidence here that suggests you have knowledge surrounding the death of Gemma Langan that you have not previously shared. I must now caution you that you are not obliged to say anything unless you wish to do so, but whatever you say will be taken down in writing and may be given in evidence.'

As Jack finished speaking, Ruairi's posture changed. Shaking his head vigorously, he put both hands on the wood-effect tabletop as if he was bracing himself.

'That was nothing to do with me. You can see from the texts. Jules was worried sick the skull was Gemma's because she knew where it was. I had no idea. Do you think I would have gone searching for the rest of the body if I'd been involved in her death?'

In the video room, Grace tapped Carla on the arm.

'I knew it. *That's* why he kept the phone. There's a message on there that he thinks he can use as an alibi for Gemma's murder.' Carla glanced at her as Jack continued.

'You were at the party that night, with the others?'

'Yes, obviously. We all were. It was in the big barn – Melissa has turned it into cottages now, but it used to be just this big old stone barn. Her parents were away and it was the start of the holidays – we'd all just finished the Leaving Cert. It was really hot.'

Jack rested his forearms on the table, his fingers interlocked. He looked deliberately casual as Donna took over.

'And who saw you there, Ruairi? How do we know that you didn't instigate the argument that Julia is referring to here, and hit Gemma Langan yourself?'

Ruairi licked his lips and glanced to the rear of the white-painted room, to Gemma's face looking at him, her stare fixed.

'You can ask the DJ Melissa hired in. I was standing beside him all night. Like, *all* night. I didn't move – I couldn't. I had some tabs, I was practically under siege. People had to keep getting me drinks because I couldn't get to the bar.'

Jack's eyebrows met. 'Tabs? You mean you were selling tablets, Ecstasy or similar, to the partygoers?'

'Yes, yes, I was dealing all right? I never left the mixing desk all night.'

Carla watched, transfixed by Ruairi's game play. Getting nicked for selling banned substances wasn't great, but it was better than being arrested for murder.

Jack cleared his throat. 'And this is a business you're still in, is it, Ruairi? But you've upscaled a bit over the years.'

'Look, that stuff you found in the tunnel is nothing to do with me. I got a text saying someone needed a safe place to stash some gear. I've no idea how it got there or what it is.'

'You expect me to believe that? You're going to tell me Terry Walsh left the phone there next, are you?'

Ruairi put his head in his hands. 'Look, I hid the phone all right? Jules and I had this thing going and Dani couldn't find out. That night, she left the phone in my office – I couldn't think of anywhere I could safely get rid of it. I didn't want to destroy it because I knew what she'd said …'

Donna's voice was clear as she clarified what he was saying for the tape. 'You preserved the phone because you knew there would be an investigation into the skull, and you were concerned that it could become an investigation into the murder of Gemma Langan?'

'Yes, yes, of course. But I honestly had no idea it was Gemma to start with. It was only when Dani started acting weird when the skull was found that I realised. They all did – Jules, too.'

Jack raised his eyebrows as he scanned the printout Donna had given him.

'You couldn't get rid of the phone when Jules was murdered, because it gave you an alibi for Gemma Langan's murder?' He flipped over the page. 'You texted her. "It was so busy I never got away from the DJ, do you remember? The tabs were flying. Everyone was stoned."' He looked hard at Ruairi from across the table before he continued. 'And Julia responded, "You were always more interested in making money than in teen drama. You creamed it that night."'

In the tech room, Carla turned to Grace. 'I bet that's why no one else saw the boat go out – they were all off their heads.'

Grace pursed her lips. 'And if they did see something, they probably thought they were hallucinating.'

Carla watched the screen as Jack wrinkled his nose, as if he was thinking.

'It's not exactly conclusive, is it? But it's good to see that you were more worried about saving your own skin than helping us find who murdered your girlfriend.'

'No one else had that number. Just me and her. It's one of my old handsets, I got a new SIM for it.'

'Clever.' As Carla watched Jack, she could tell that he was fighting to keep the sarcasm out of his voice. 'Frankly, these questions you asked Jules by text about the party feel leading to me – like you were trying to establish an alibi. I feel a court might agree.'

'No, no, you don't understand. I had nothing to do with Gemma getting killed. Talk to Sean. He was going out with her. Ask him what happened that night.'

Chapter 79

IN THE TECH room, Carla suddenly felt chill. She rubbed the tops of her arms with both hands. It wasn't cold down here – the absolute opposite, in fact. The room was so well insulated, there was no damp or draughts. This was something deeper. She scowled at the screen.

'Gemma didn't exactly have the most marvellous friendship group, did she?'

Beside her, Grace stood up, turning to lean on the desk, stretching her back.

'Not if Ruairi Brennan is anything to go by. Having an affair with his wife's cousin and covering it up when she's murdered? Nice.'

'And don't forget the drugs. That Adventure Centre is the perfect cover – lots of people coming and going, easy access to the water, and lots of cash going through the till. He's not stupid.' Carla let out a sharp breath. 'And I wonder if Julia was in on it – if she was turning a blind eye to deals in the hotel bar, or the car park. Jack said their CCTV was woeful. Perhaps there was another reason for that, apart from trying to do it on the cheap?'

Grace tapped the pen in her hand on the desk. 'Given their close relationship, it's a distinct possibility. Perhaps that's why Ruairi lives so far out of town, too. Nobody to see any comings and goings. Between the Coffee Dock and her lad – Ben, is it? – it sounds like Danielle is busy enough not to notice too much.'

Carla frowned as something fell into place in her head. 'You're right about the comings and goings.' Things suddenly began to connect in her head. 'I need to talk to Jack.'

Grace looked at her over the top of her reading glasses. 'I think he's a bit tied up at the moment, don't you?'

'He needs to get a warrant to search Ruairi's 4 × 4 – and Danielle's, while he's at it.'

Grace took her glasses off and rolled them in the air. 'I need more, babes. Spit it out.'

Carla stood up and began to pace across the small room, her arms folded.

'Ruairi's and Danielle's Pathfinders were supplied by Ken Cahill 4 × 4 – it's a dealership in Kilkeel. They bought them late in 2018. They are 182 registrations.' Carla paused. 'In November 2018, the other girl who we thought could be a match for the skull disappeared – Kellie Murphy. When I went through the file, it said she was the receptionist at Ken Cahill 4 × 4.'

'You think Ruairi had something to do with her disappearance?'

'I don't know, but clearly he's up to his eyes in illegal activity. If the drugs were being stored in the tunnel, they had to be transported from there to the end user somehow. You wouldn't store them in the tunnel if you were using a boat, you'd store them on the island, or at the island end of the tunnel, at any rate.'

Grace narrowed her eyes as she looked at Carla. 'I'd imagine the Tech Bureau will be examining his jeep and his office.' Grace folded up her glasses decisively. 'But why don't we have a chat with DI Rainsford about your thoughts on Kellie Murphy? In fact, if Ruairi was using his jeep, it might account for the state-of-the-art security system at the Adventure Centre, too. Jack said he didn't do his CCTV on the cheap. Apparently the pictures are crystal clear.'

Carla nodded. She was still thinking about Kellie Murphy. 'I don't know what the car dealership has got to do with this, but it seems strange that two women Ruairi Brennan has potentially been in contact with have disappeared. Did you find a statement from him in the Gemma Langan files?'

Grace shook her head. 'Not yet, but I'll get there. I can't imagine he was very truthful, so whatever he said we can take with a pinch of salt.' She looked thoughtful for a moment, as if she was processing the information. 'Do you want to watch the rest of the interview or go up to the DI now?' She paused. 'And where do you think Matt's gone? I thought he'd be back to see his handiwork land.'

As she spoke, the door opened and Matt appeared. He was carrying a tray of coffees, but he seemed to have lost his bounce somewhere on the other side of the door.

'Here we go, ladies. The DI thought you might like some coffee. He suggested you stayed here until the interviews are over.'

Slipping the cardboard carrier onto the table, Matt produced several packets of sugar from his pocket.

Grace glanced at Carla, who had picked up on Matt's tone, too.

'The DI said ... What's up, Matt? You look like ...' Carla was about to say 'someone died' and thought better of it. '... the world's about to end.'

Matt avoided her eye. 'Erm ... nothing. Everything's good.'

Grace reached for a cup. 'You're a terrible liar, Garda Curran, but if you can't say, we won't ask.'

Matt shifted from one foot to the other. 'I don't know, honestly. Something's happening out there. Paddy asked if I'd seen Seamus, and then shot out the back door. That's when I met the DI. He didn't look happy.'

Carla glanced over to Grace. 'I feel some of your observations about the way the Langan investigation was conducted may have been substantiated.'

Grace took the lid off her coffee. '"Tip" and "iceberg" spring to mind.'

Carla picked up a cup and handed it to Matt. 'Have your coffee. We need to talk to the DI, but it'll hold for half an hour. Jack's going to have a chat to Sean Twomey next. I have a feeling he might be able to bring us even closer to the truth of what actually happened to Gemma Langan.'

Chapter 80

WATCHING ON THE screen, Carla was shocked at Sean's appearance as he was escorted into the interview room, where Jack was waiting for him. And she wasn't the only one. Sitting beside her, Matt looked up from his study of Julia Hardiman's phone log and let out a low 'Oof.' He turned to look at her and Grace. 'He looks shook.'

Grace bent forwards to speak around Carla. 'Everyone keeps saying they are the Hollywood couple. I'm guessing he doesn't usually look like he's homeless?'

Matt shook his head. 'Nope. He's the one with the tan and the designer threads, never a hair out of place. Every girl in Coyne's Cross goes gaga when he appears.'

Carla shifted in the hard seat. She was itching to go and talk to DI Rainsford about her 4 × 4 theory, but that's all it was at this stage – just a theory. A lot of work would need to be done to substantiate it, some of which, she hoped, would be in process as Grace had suggested. They were getting closer to finding answers on what exactly had happened to Gemma

Langan; that was the priority. And Rainsford's suggestion, relayed through Matt, that they stay in the viewing room had sounded more like an order than a request.

Something was happening that involved Seamus Twomey, but whatever it was, it wasn't about to interfere with Jack's questioning. Carla guessed Jack was anxious to get on with it, before Sean or Ruairi had an opportunity to come up with a fantasy explanation for the events described in the video Walsh had sent.

Carla took a sip of the coffee that Matt had brought them, then answered Grace's comment about Sean's appearance. 'G, his wife has just been brutally murdered. How do you think he's going to look? Honestly?'

Grace shrugged. 'I know. But there's something going on with these two. You'd expect them to look rough, but … Well, let's see, shall we?'

Warming her hands on her cup, Carla took another sip, running everything through her head. Ruairi Brennan had been taken to the cells while the forensics examination continued on the drugs they'd found in the tunnel. It sounded as if he'd been Coyne's Cross's main dealer since he was a teenager. Which might explain how he'd funded opening and developing the Adventure Centre. From what she'd seen, all of the equipment was top quality.

But it also raised the question: in a small town, why hadn't he come to the attention of the Gardaí sooner?

They watched the screen as Sean slumped into the seat, both elbows on the table. Dressed in black jeans and a black T-shirt that looked as if he'd been wearing it for a few days, he needed a shave.

Jack glanced at Donna as he sat forwards in his seat, the movement causing Sean to look up and spot the bust of Gemma Langan looking straight at him over Jack's shoulder. He froze, his mouth opening as if he was about to speak, his eyes wide with shock.

'Amazing, isn't it?' Jack said. 'Dr Steele's created an incredible likeness. Understandable, really, given that they were working with Gemma's skull, but it's still quite remarkable.'

Sean drew in a ragged breath and put his face in his hands, his shoulders shaking.

'You're very good to come in and talk to us, I know this is a very tough time. I'm going to record our conversation.' Jack pressed the button on the tower unit as he continued. 'For the benefit of the recording, I'm DS Jack Maguire with Detective Garda Donna Sullivan and it's ...' He flipped his watch around to check, and gave the time and date. 'With us is Sean Twomey of Coyne House, husband of the late Melissa Hardiman.'

Carla found herself holding her breath as Jack delivered the caution, just as he had to Ruairi. Beside him, Donna kept her eyes on Sean, her face relaxed.

443

Jack took the lead again. 'I believe you were at Ruairi Brennan's house from early this morning, and unaware of the operation that was unfolding on your land?'

There was a slight nod. Sean wiped his face with his hands, clearing his throat, trying to compose himself.

'I can't stay at home. There's too much in my head … the games help. They stop me thinking.'

'You weren't aware of a WhatsApp message that was sent to all of Julia Hardiman's contacts earlier today?' Jack's voice was calm, practical. Carla had no idea how he was maintaining this level of focus after the day they'd had. Interviewing suspects looked easy on TV, but it was often a delicate dance – one that required full concentration, reading the suspect's every twitch.

By way of an answer, Sean shook his head. 'Not until your guys called. I only checked my phone when I got here to the station, while I was waiting for you. Jesus.' He looked at the ceiling and bit his lip, sniffing loudly.

'You have been made aware that Danielle Brennan is now safe, and currently in hospital under assessment?' Donna's tone was friendly.

Sean kept his eyes on the ceiling for a moment before looking directly at Jack, as if he hadn't heard Donna. 'He killed Mel and Jules, didn't he? Walsh? He was going to kill Dani, too?'

'We believe that's a strong possibility. And also that Terry Walsh was intending to end his own life on the island. The Technical Bureau are currently examining Julia Hardiman's phone, as well as Walsh's car and home for forensic evidence—'

Sean interrupted him. 'And he did it because of Drew?'

'So it would appear from his statement on the video. We believe he was Drew's cellmate, and that they had a close relationship for many years. He believed Drew to be innocent of the crime he was convicted of.'

Jack paused significantly, giving Donna an opening. 'Drew committed suicide in prison approximately six months after Walsh was released.'

Sean shook his head, his eyes on the ceiling again. 'Mel had no idea. I thought she'd checked his references, but she was so desperate to get someone to work on the place ...' He trailed off.

Donna picked up her biro. 'It's possible Walsh supplied false references. We believe that he came to Coyne's Cross deliberately, and that the discovery of Gemma Langan's skull prompted him to act.'

There was a moment's silence. Carla glanced at Grace, who, sitting beside her, was staring intently at the screen. Carla opened her mouth, but Grace raised her hand to stop her. It was as if Sean was unconsciously waiting for the signal from her. He suddenly broke down, putting his arms on the desk, burying his head in them. His sobs were almost animal – cries of pain.

Jack took a moment before he spoke. 'Would you like to take a break? I know this is very difficult for you.'

Sean lifted his head, shaking it hard.

'No. No, it's time now.'

Chapter 81

CARLA, GRACE AND Matt stared intently at the scene unfolding in the interview room, as Donna picked up where Jack had left off.

'What did Melissa tell you about that night, Sean? What happened during the party? Drew apparently told Walsh that he saw Melissa, her sister Julia and Danielle Brennan in a rowing boat, heading out into the lough.'

Sean shook his head, his voice little more than a whisper. 'She did it because of me. She was protecting me.'

Carla could tell that Jack was working hard to keep his face straight. Beside him, Donna sat up in her chair.

Jack waited another moment before speaking. 'Perhaps you could roll back there a bit and tell us what happened that night?'

Sean drew in a shaky breath. Carla found herself tensing up. Perhaps one of her three little birds was about to have its story finally told. Without thinking, she rubbed the tattoo on her wrist: WITH BRAVE WINGS SHE FLIES.

What had really happened that night?

'I didn't want to go. I knew it would be a disaster. Jesus.' He played with what looked like an expensive heavy gold watch, rolling it around his wrist for a moment, apparently searching for the right words. 'It was the start of the summer break. We'd all done the Leaving Cert and Mel and Jules came back from school to Coyne House. They were both in boarding school. I …' He stumbled. 'I'd been dating Melissa since the half term before Christmas. She came home for weekends and the holidays, but then the whole family went skiing. It was New Year, and … Well, I sort of hooked up with Gemma.'

Donna cleared her throat. 'Did Melissa know?'

Sean shook his head, his tone sarcastic. 'I didn't feel it was something I really wanted to share at that point. And it was a casual thing. Gemma knew I was dating Mel.'

Jack's tone was calm, his voice low. 'And Gemma was happy about that?'

Sean shrugged. 'Not very. She …' He squirmed in the seat. 'I might have told her that things weren't great between us, that we weren't really together.'

Jack raised his eyebrows fractionally. 'So what happened the next time you saw Melissa?'

'It should have been the February half term, but their school did this language trip. And then Easter, but their parents made them stay at school to do grinds, so they were really ready for their exams. She wasn't even allowed home at weekends. So it was just before the party that she came back.'

'And she found out about you and Gemma?'

Sean winced. 'I split up with Gemma before she got back. I mean, it had been very low-key, we weren't like an item in public or anything. People thought we were just friends.' He cleared his throat. 'I wanted to make it work with Mel, but Gemma must have thought ...' He shook his head, muttering, 'Anyway, I didn't want to go to that party.'

Beside Carla, Grace made a grunting noise, and shook her head. 'Here we go.'

But Carla's attention was fixed on the screen.

Jack was nodding slowly. 'So tell us exactly what happened that night.'

Sean sniffed loudly. 'Apparently ...' He drew out the word. 'Mel wanted to talk to Gemma in private, so they went down to the boathouse. Honestly, I was so pissed ... Someone told me they'd seen them walking down there. I didn't ... I couldn't ... Anyway. So I followed them. I reckoned Gemma was going to tell Melissa that we'd had a thing.' He ran his hand over his face. 'Melissa was away, but she thought we were solid ...' He cleared his throat. 'So ... Anyway, I don't know what was said, but when I got there Gemma was laying into Melissa. She'd been drinking, too, and just, like, attacked her. She didn't know what to do. They were actually physically fighting. Gemma had Mel up against the wall of the boathouse, her hands in her hair. Mel was screaming, so I grabbed Gemma off her, and pulled them apart, but …' He faltered.

'Go on.' Jack's voice was low, encouraging.

'Like I said, Gemma was pissed, too, and she was wearing these high-heeled sandals. She fell backwards and hit her head on one of the iron rings sunk into the concrete slip. My boat was tied up to it. We'd been out the day before – me and Mel – over to the island.' He sighed deeply.

Donna's voice was gentle. 'And what happened next?'

'I helped Mel up, but when we turned around there was this big pool of blood under Gemma's head. Her eyes were open and her arm sort of twisted.' His eyes glazed, as if he was looking at the scene in his head. He ran his fingers down either side of his mouth. 'We just stood there, I don't know how long for. And I went over to check her and I saw her phone had fallen out of her hand or her pocket. The screen had smashed. I picked it up and tried to move her into the recovery position, but it was too late. She was just staring at me.'

'You didn't think of calling an ambulance?' Donna shifted beside Jack, her head on one side.

Sean shook his head. 'Mel kept saying, "She's dead, leave her, she's dead." I didn't know what to do. I mean …' He looked helpless. 'Then Mel told me to go. She said to go back to the party and she'd look after it.'

'So you did?'

Sean shrugged. 'I couldn't go back. I mean, I was starting to sober up by then, but I just felt so sick. I started to walk down the drive, I had to get away.'

'Then what happened?'

Sean's face was full of tension, his jaw taut. 'I don't know. There had been a complaint about the noise. I was walking down the drive and I met my uncle driving the other way in the patrol car. He picked me up and … Well, he took me home.'

Carla grabbed Grace's arm. 'Sean had her phone. That's how it got into Drew's van. Seamus Twomey must have put it there.'

Grace nodded slowly, her eyebrows raised. 'He certainly has some explaining to do.'

On the screen, Jack continued. 'So you didn't see what happened to Gemma?'

Sean shook his head. 'Mel told me afterwards. She said Jules and Dani came down to find her, to see if she was OK. They knew Gemma wanted to talk to her in the boathouse.'

'What happened then?'

'They put her in my boat and rowed her out.'

'And I believe Ruairi Brennan was doing a brisk trade while all this was going on?' Jack made the comment sound offhand, but Sean's eyebrows shot up.

'I don't know what he was doing, I didn't see him. Like I said, I left early.'

'What exactly did Melissa tell you about what happened to Gemma?'

'The three of them put her into my boat and took her out to the deep part of the lough, where it shelves. And they pushed her in.'

Donna sounded puzzled as she asked, 'How did they know she'd stay down?'

'There was an old anchor in the boat – a big one, for if me and Ruairi went fishing down by Dead Man's Gully. The current's really strong there. Mel tied that around Gemma's ankles.'

Carla watched Jack's face closely as he tapped his pen on the notepad in front of him. 'You sure it was just fishing you and Ruairi were doing off Dead Man's Gully? That's remarkably close to the island and the tunnel that connects it with your land.'

Sean shrugged and looked blank. 'Obviously – what else would we be doing?'

Was he deliberately ignoring the suggestion that he might be involved in Ruairi Brennan's illegal enterprise?

Carla glanced at Grace, but she was making detailed notes on the pad in front of her.

Carla's mind was racing.

Did Ruairi know what had happened? Had he been dating Danielle at the time? The two divers who had gone to recover underwater camera equipment had found the skull originally, but it had been Ruairi's team who had searched for the rest of the body. Had he deliberately not found it because he knew it was tethered to his best friend's anchor?

Those two were so close – did Sean know that Ruairi was having an affair with Melissa's sister? And had Sean enabled the transfer of drugs from incoming vessels to his property?

Everything felt so tangled. Carla had a feeling that Sean Twomey knew a lot more about his friend Ruairi Brennan than he was letting on.

Donna's voice was hard as she asked the next question. 'And what happened to the boat, Sean? It was your boat, you said?'

'Mel scuppered it. The next day, before anyone realised Gemma was missing, she went out and sank it in the lough, and then swam back.'

'And nobody noticed it was missing?'

Carla could tell Jack meant the Gardaí. A boat vanishing at the same time as a local girl could hardly be ignored. Unless you had a reason to ignore it, of course.

How much had Seamus Twomey interfered in this investigation to protect his nephew? The nephew who went on to marry into the Big House?

Sean shrugged. 'It was my boat. I didn't report that it had gone.'

Chapter 82

'**S**O WHAT HAPPENS now?'

Upstairs, the incident room was surprisingly empty. Carla wasn't sure where everyone was, but as she'd sat down in one of the plastic chairs still lined up in front of the hessian boards covered in maps and crime scene photos, she'd tried not to look at them. She really didn't need to see any photos of Julia and Melissa's bodies ever again.

Jack's voice brought her back to the room, the late evening sun streaming in the front windows behind him, throwing him into shadow.

'We need to do some more work, but I reckon we'll be charging Ruairi Brennan with possession with intent to supply controlled drugs, and Sean Twomey with manslaughter. He's essentially confessed.'

The door opened and Jack looked over as Grace appeared, her lipstick freshly applied, her hair brushed into the silver clip she wore to hold it up. Her suit still crisp, despite the heat, she looked so much better than Carla felt; it was almost as if they were in different stories.

Catching the end of what Jack had said, Grace pulled a face as she came into the room and slid a chair around to sit opposite him. He was standing with his back to the window, his arms crossed.

Grace tapped the the edge of the table with the palm of her hand. 'With the majority of the witnesses deceased, a clever lawyer could tear his statement apart, you know – claim he was "protecting the memory of his wife".' Grace drew the words out, making rabbit ears with her fingers to emphasise the point.

Jack nodded. 'They could, for sure, and if Sean's uncle Seamus had backed him up, saying he was under huge psychological pressure and had fabricated it all ... If Seamus had denied that he'd met Sean walking out of the estate that night ... D'you know, I think that's exactly how it could have played out.'

Squinting into the sun, Carla put her hand up to shield her eyes, trying to see the look on Jack's face. 'I can feel a "but" coming here. What's happened?'

Jack shifted his weight to the other leg. Realising Carla couldn't see him properly with the sun behind him, he moved into the main part of the incident room and pulled a chair up, spinning it around to sit on it backwards. Carla could see that the intensity of the day was starting to hit him, too.

'There's a *big* "but". Apparently, after that video circulated, Seamus heard Sean was being brought in. He tried to get to speak to him before I did. When he couldn't, he found a reason to nip out of the station.' Jack let out a breath. 'He got hold of a service weapon and drove up to the lough. He knew exactly what would happen when all of this started to come out.' Jack paused. 'I have a feeling what we know now may only be the start. And it might not just be this case.'

Carla let out a sigh. 'That's something we need to speak to you about.'

Jack nodded. 'The DI filled me in—'

As if Grace hadn't heard him, she cut in. 'I'm sure Carla's right, and he planted that phone in Drew's van. Sean admitted he'd picked it up that night. He could easily have dropped it in the patrol car and not realised until the next day.'

Carla pursed her lips for a moment, thinking. 'Or perhaps Sean told Seamus about it and gave it to him. I wonder if Sean told the others and they conspired to set Drew up, or if Melissa and Julia just fell in with it when Drew was arrested? Everyone wanted to protect Sean Twomey, apparently.'

'We'll know more from the dates of the statements, who took them, and what order they were taken in. Seamus may have taken them himself, of course, which could put a whole different perspective on things. I'm going to need to check back. With a bit of luck, we'll have a clearer picture when we look at the paper trail.' Jack shifted slightly in the chair. 'We might know more when the DI gets back. He's up at the lough now with the rest of the team. Seamus may have left a note.' Jack cleared his throat. 'I've also just heard the Technical Bureau have found a file full of newspaper clippings about Drew's trial in Walsh's cottage – and they've found the other knives, the ones Walsh used on Julia and Melissa.' His brow furrowed. 'They were left next to the file, as if he wanted someone to find them and connect them. And it appears he had … let's say some "specimens" in jars.' Jack winced as he said it. 'He kept their hearts.' He cleared his throat. 'You were right about the deer, Carla. There were carcasses in the undergrowth near the cottage. Looks like he was perfecting his technique.'

Grace looked up at him, interested. 'Really? I think he'd become obsessed with Drew. They had a relationship in prison, and when Drew killed himself, Walsh blamed the people Drew said had landed him in there. *That's* why Julia and Melissa were hanged – because Drew hanged himself.' She shook her head, and then screwed up her face, thinking. 'Everything comes back to that night. And I'm sure that's why they stayed here – Melissa and Julia, I mean – to be near the lough. They needed to keep an eye on things, to know if Gemma was ever found.' She turned to Jack. 'When we first arrived, everyone kept saying how successful they both could have been, but they both chose to come back here. I mean, I know it's not exactly Hicksville, but it's not the centre of the universe either.'

Carla glanced at her. 'You're right. My God, could you imagine living your whole life chained to a place, to an event …?'

She tailed off, sighing, and for a moment focused on her ring, on the silver skull, its diamanté eyes catching the light.

One silly argument had resulted in how many deaths? Gemma, Peter Drew, Melissa, Julia, almost Danielle, and now Seamus Twomey – to say nothing of Terry Walsh, who was only just hanging on in the ICU. If only Melissa had called an ambulance, they could have claimed it was all a terrible accident and none of this would have happened.

Carla closed her eyes. It never ceased to amaze her how a split-second decision could change a life – lives – so dramatically; how the ripples created by one action radiated so far.

It was just like Lizzie.

Had she decided to turn left instead of right and gone to her death, or crossed the road, or changed her mind about the bus and decided to get the DART instead?

Carla had no idea. She just prayed that, as with Gemma Langan's story, she could get to the truth one day.

Chapter 83

ER ARMS FULL of manila files, as Carla pushed her front door closed with her bum, Nigel appeared and tried to wind himself around her legs. She leaned on the door for a minute, exhausted, the cool darkness of the hallway a welcome relief from the day. In the distance she could hear the chiming of the Angelus bell. Six o'clock. She'd left work early and had got caught in the mother of all traffic jams. It was Friday, and obviously everyone was doing the same thing. She should have known.

But it had been that sort of day.

Carla closed her eyes. Everything had felt like a gruelling climb from the moment she'd woken up. It had been a crazy week, but to top it off, today was Lizzie's birthday.

Under the files, she rubbed the tattoo on her wrist – her three little birds – Carla, Grace and Lizzie, three inseparable friends hanging out at university. But like a flight of swallows weaving on the currents of life, the three little birds had dipped and dived, the flock changing to become the missing girls: Lizzie, Girl X, the Coyne's Cross girl; then Girl X, Kellie Murphy and Gemma Langan. Lizzie was always there in the background, like Grace – part of Carla's flock.

This time the previous week, she'd been in Coyne's Cross …

Carla opened her eyes quickly as Nigel reached up and put his claws in her thigh.

'God, Nige, did you have to do that?' He looked at her mournfully. Grace had been working from home; he probably just needed a cuddle.

Looking down at him, Carla realised there was a holdall she didn't recognise in the hall.

Had Grace been shopping again? It looked full. Or was she going away, and Carla had forgotten?

That was all she needed – a hellish day, and she was going to be stuck on her own all weekend. Her relief at getting to Friday was washed away by a wave of disappointment. She struggled upright from the door as she heard Grace's voice.

'Babes, is that you? Come through. I've got Pimm's and steak and …'

Carla reached the kitchen door to find Grace standing in the middle of the floor with a glass in her hand, wearing a slinky navy-blue wrap dress that was very low-cut. She had her hair pinned up in a gold clip. She looked gorgeous.

'New dress. What do you think?'

'Are you going somewhere? Did I forget?' Carla tried to keep the irritation out of her voice. They'd been over every weekend of the summer trying to synchronise their diaries, fitting in Carla's climbing and caving trips with Grace's love of European capital cities.

What had she missed?

Grace handed her the glass. 'We're not going anywhere.' She raised her eyebrows. 'We're celebrating – sort of. Have you seen the news?'

The glass in one hand, the files in the other, Carla shook her head, sighing.

'I dropped my phone in the lab. It's history, or at least the screen is. I've been working on those Wicklow skulls all day. We all have. There are nine of them, G. *Nine*. Day. From. Hell.'

'So you haven't spoken to Jack?'

Carla shook her head, taking a very welcome sip of her Pimm's.

God, she needed this.

She looked around for somewhere to put the files down. 'Have you heard how Danielle is? I just keep thinking how devastated she's going to be when she finds out about Ruairi and Julia.'

Taking the files from her, Grace went across to the counter to park them and, picking up the jug, refilled her own glass.

'Come and sit down, you're exhausted. As far as I know, Danielle's fine – well, as fine as she can be. And you're right, but that does assume lover boy actually tells her about his

461

extracurriculars. Perhaps he hasn't realised it's all going to come out at the trial, unless he pleads guilty to drug trafficking.'

Carla grimaced. 'If that stuff in the tunnel is conclusively linked to him, he'll be going away for a very long time.'

Grace grinned and opened her eyes wide.

'What?' Carla looked at her suspiciously.

She caught Carla's hand. 'We've got a guest.'

Carla narrowed her eyes, about to ask who. She really didn't have the energy for any of Grace's super bright academic friends. They were lovely, but they could be very hard to keep up with. As if Grace could read her mind, she smiled mysteriously.

'Come and see.'

As Carla stepped out of the patio doors, she could see why Grace was being so coy. Jack Maguire was sitting with his feet up on Grace's lounger, a glass in his hand.

Carla smiled, relaxing immediately. 'You devils. Why didn't you tell me?'

'We tried. I rang the lab when I couldn't get you on the mobile, but Raph said you were busy and in, I quote, "A Very Bad Mood".' She made air quotes with her fingers. 'He said he was hiding.'

'Raph? He did not.' Carla threw a mock scowl at Grace.

'He actually did. But it's all fine, because Jack's here and he's got lots of news to make your day much better.'

'Are you good with smashed phones, too, Jack?' Carla sat down heavily on one of the garden chairs Grace had pulled up to the patio.

Jack grinned at her. 'Good to see you, too, Dr Steele.'

Carla raised her eyebrow. 'So …?'

Behind them, the doorbell chimed and Grace turned to answer it.

'That's dinner. I ordered in. Jack apparently does a mean steak, so he's in charge of the meat, when we get the barbecue lit.' Grace grinned. 'The salads are gorgeous – Butler's Pantry. *And* there's cheesecake. I'll be back in a second. I'll leave you two to chat.'

Carla took another sip of her Pimm's. The evening was definitely improving. 'So you were just passing, were you?'

Jack laughed, nodding. 'Absolutely, thought I'd pop in.' He looked across at her. 'You were right – about the Cahills and the 4 × 4 garage. It turned out the Kilkeel drugs squad have had them under surveillance for some time. For some reason, no one connected Kellie Murphy's disappearance with the activity they were monitoring at the garage itself. Different division, time … I don't know, but when they did …' He grinned. 'It was like a house of cards.'

'How on earth?'

'It was the missing piece that set everything in motion. It all hinged on her boyfriend. He was interviewed at the time, has been working there for years.'

'Gary, the body repair specialist?' Carla wasn't sure how she'd remembered his name, but it sprang straight into her head.

'That's him.'

She could tell from Jack's face that he was still holding the ace in the pack.

'Go on …'

'When we looked at Ruairi's 4 × 4, we realised it had been modified. Nissan stopped putting the spare wheel on the back of the Pathfinder before 2018 – his had been moved, and a whole load of extra storage space had been built into the boot where it would have been kept. You couldn't tell from the outside, but the floor had been raised as well. All this was Gary's handiwork. That's how Ruairi was moving the drugs. Not always to the Cahills' garage – we reckon they were being picked up at the Adventure Centre, too – but every time his or Danielle's vehicle went in for a service or needed something looking at, we reckon it was being unloaded.'

'Both of them were spotless, not even a scratch. That's what made me notice them. They were probably in and out of the body shop like yoyos.'

Carla took another sip as Jack continued. 'Exactly. When the drugs team from Kilkeel started asking young Gary about the modifications to Ruairi Brennan's vehicle, and then about Kellie, he fell apart. Turns out she'd sussed what was going on and thought she could get a pay rise out of Cahill's son Laurence, if she kept quiet.'

'But she didn't get it?'

Jack shook his head ruefully. 'We haven't quite got all the pieces yet, but we think Laurence Cahill panicked over something she said in the row with Gary – Cahill was in the club that night. We reckon he saw her storm off and then picked her up near the taxi rank. We knew there were no taxis and she'd walked down the road a bit, but she disappeared off the city centre cameras.'

Carla nodded; she'd read that in the file. Jack took a sip of his drink and reached down to tickle Nigel, who had wandered out onto the patio.

'About a week after she disappeared, the Cahills started resurfacing their car park. It looked like routine maintenance. We found her today, under the new tarmac. Well, we found a body we suspect is her. Let's hope it is.'

One more of her little birds was home.

Carla smiled, but it was a sad smile. It was a resolution, but finding Kellie alive would have been the ideal outcome.

'Let's hope it is her, then at least her family will have closure.'

It was the not knowing that was the worst.

Carla felt tears prick her eyes and, putting down her glass, rubbed her face. 'Sorry. It is good news, it's just been a long day.'

At that moment, Grace reappeared. Carla looked around at her and tried to smile. Immediately reading her, Grace went over and squeezed her shoulder, pulling her into a hug,

'Don't cry, babes. They wouldn't have connected her disappearance with the modifications to the vehicles and the drug seizure if it hadn't been for you spotting the registration date on Ruairi's and Danielle's jeeps. You did good, girl. I'm so proud of you.' Before Carla could say anything, Grace continued. 'Did Jack tell you he's staying? He's helping to set up a new unit up at the Park. He might be working with you.'

Carla raised her eyebrows as Jack smiled sheepishly. 'It's because of the Langan and Murphy cases. It's all your work, so they must be desperate to ask me, but, well … There's talk of forming a cold case squad up here in Dublin. I've come up to meet the chief super – you might know him, Dawson O'Rourke? I worked with him in Limerick. After … Well, I could do with a change of scene.'

'So you're actually staying? Ah, the bag in the hall.'

The new dress. She didn't say that bit.

'Just for a few days, while we see what the story is. Grace insisted.'

'Cold cases? Seriously?' Realising what he'd said, Carla stared at him.

Cases like Lizzie's. Carla looked up to Grace, her eyes full of tears now. This was happening today – of all days? *Lizzie's birthday.*

Grace knew what she was thinking. She leaned over and kissed her.

'Maybe you'll be able to team up. One day you'll find her.' She reached down to run her finger over the words on Carla's wrist: WITH BRAVE WINGS SHE FLIES. 'You'll keep flying until you find her. Your wings are brave, my love.'

Acknowledgements

This book owes its genesis to two random and unrelated elements, the first of which was a character writing prompt for my online coaching and mentoring group Writers Ink. Maria McHale, business coach and journalist and my amazing Writers Ink partner, posted a photo of a woman leaning on a pub bar for our wonderful online writing group. She had a white streak in her hair, a tattoo and a nose ring, and that photo lit a lightbulb in my head. Carla Steele was born. Thank you, Maria, that prompt has made a whole book!

The second element was a course that I stumbled on while confined to home during the pandemic. Run by the University of Sheffield, it was an online course in forensic facial reconstruction, something that I've been fascinated by for a long time. It gave me the tools of Carla's trade and immediately she made her presence known on the page. Then Jack showed up in her office and Nigel vomited on Grace's shoes and we had a story...

No book is possible without an army of people behind it, particularly one like this that rests squarely on the experience of experts in the field – I needed a bit more than an online course to ensure I had the details correct. If there are any mistakes, they are entirely my own.

Hugest thanks to Dr Brid McBride, Director of Science and Development at Forensic Science Ireland who was so incredibly helpful and provided invaluable detail to make Carla's working environment true to life. We were introduced by Gerard Lovett (ex Special Branch) whose book on the history of the Special Branch is excellent – thanks so much Gerry. Brid was one of the first people I spoke to when I started writing and one of the most important. I've taken some liberties with the geography of Forensic Science Ireland's offices, but I hope you won't notice unless you work in Garda HQ.

When you're writing a book like this, it's the small details that can trip you up and Professor Jim Fraser, Forensic Investigator and author of *Murder Under the Microscope*, is wonderfully generous with his time in answering my questions – he has over 40 years' experience as an expert witness, case reviewer, senior police manager, independent consultant, policy adviser and researcher, and has dealt with thousands of criminal cases. He's the man you want on speed dial when you write crime – thank you so much Jim!

In this book there's rather more pathological detail than there has been in others, and that gives me an opportunity to thank ex Irish state pathologist Professor Marie Cassidy for all her help and support over the years. She read my first terrible attempt at fiction many years ago and lent me a pile of her own books, including the brilliant *Bernard Spilsbury: His Life and Cases* (which I now have my own copy of), to help me get a better grasp on the dead. I was thrilled when Marie agreed to launch my debut novel *Little Bones*, and now her own writing career has taken off spectacularly with *Beyond the Tape* and her first fiction *The Body of Truth* (do order both, you'll love them!).

This book owes a lot, too, to Kyle O'Connell, Director of Irish Film and Television Services, who I've worked with many times on live-streaming projects, but who, in his spare time, works with Coastguard search and rescue. His experience has appeared in more than one book! Massive thanks Kyle, getting the detail right is key (in everything!).

In *Three Little Birds*, Grace owes much to author and psychoanalytic psychotherapist Maxine Mei-Fung Chung (order her books *The Eighth Girl* and *What Women Want*, they are excellent). I absolutely love her company and she's quite brilliant, just like Grace, although their specialities are a little different.

The team at Atlantic books have been amazing – Sarah Hodgson my editor, Hanna Kenne on editing too (thank goodness for your patience, Hanna!). Felice McKeown is a genius on marketing and Dave Woodhouse the sort of support on the sales front that every author wants (and needs!). Thank you all so much for your time and expertise in bringing Sam Blake to the shelf. And thank you Dave's dad for reading and loving Sam Blake!

Simon Hess, Declan Heeney and Helen McKean at Gill Hess are the marketing team in Ireland and understand me so well – they are amazing and like the third wheel – you would never have heard of me if it wasn't for them.

On the subject of wheels, Mairéad Hearne, my PA, is the one who truly keeps all the wheels on and spinning in the same direction. She's an absolute joy to work with and holds everything together – I can't thank you enough Mairéad! If I manage to turn up in the right place at the right time, it's down to Mairéad.

Most importantly, you're reading this because of the unwavering support, patience and wisdom of my incredible agent Simon Trewin, who this book is dedicated to. A creative sounding board and the voice of sense, he is entirely responsible for Sam Blake being in print. This is book ten; I can never thank him enough.

And last but by no means least, thank you to you, my reader, for getting to this last page. Without you I wouldn't have this wonderful career and be able to spend so much time with the characters in my head. The reviews and emails I get from all of you are amazing and I am thankful each and every day. Leaving a review on Amazon or Goodreads means going the extra mile and makes an enormous difference to a book – I'm indebted to every reader who leaves their thoughts, thank you.

For those of you who want to find out more about my writing process, what I'm reading and what I'm watching, and get advance news of the next book, I'd love you to join my Readers' Club at www.samblakebooks.com. As a thank you, all members can download the eBook of *High Pressure*, my digital and audio exclusive standalone thriller, for free. It's a bridging book between the Cat Connolly series and my psychological thrillers and features Anna Lockharte from *No Turning Back* and Brioni O'Brien from *Remember My Name*. All my books are set in the same world and regular readers will spot connections – Easter eggs – hidden in the text. *High Pressure* is gripping and fast paced and one of my best reviewed books – I hope you enjoy it!

For more gripping thrillers, join the

SAM BLAKE
READERS' CLUB

Get exclusive writing and an insight into bestselling author Sam Blake's books delivered straight to your inbox.

Members are the first to hear all the latest book news, find out when new books are published and have the chance to win books and other prizes in regular competitions.

Plus you'll get a FREE THRILLER by Sam Blake as soon as you join.

Scan the QR code
to join or visit:
www.samblakebooks.com

THE ESTATE

www.penguin.co.uk

By Denzil Meyrick

The DCI Daley Thrillers
Whisky from Small Glasses
The Last Witness
Dark Suits and Sad Songs
The Rat Stone Serenade
Well of the Winds
The Relentless Tide
A Breath on Dying Embers
Jeremiah's Bell
For Any Other Truth
The Death of Remembrance
No Sweet Sorrow

Kinloch Novellas
A Large Measure of Snow
A Toast to the Old Stones
Ghosts in the Gloaming

Short-Story Collections
One Last Dram Before Midnight

Standalones
Terms of Restitution

The Frank Grasby Novels
Murder at Holly House

THE ESTATE

DENZIL MEYRICK

bantam

TRANSWORLD PUBLISHERS
Penguin Random House, One Embassy Gardens,
8 Viaduct Gardens, London SW11 7BW
www.penguin.co.uk

Transworld is part of the Penguin Random House group of companies
whose addresses can be found at global.penguinrandomhouse.com

First published in Great Britain in 2024 by Bantam
an imprint of Transworld Publishers

A CIP catalogue record for this book
is available from the British Library.

ISBN 9781787637191

Typeset in 12.75/16pt Minion Pro by Jouve (UK), Milton Keynes
Printed and bound in Great Britain by Clays Ltd, Elcograf S.p.A.

The authorized representative in the EEA is Penguin Random House Ireland,
Morrison Chambers, 32 Nassau Street, Dublin D02 YH68.

Penguin Random House is committed to a sustainable
future for our business, our readers and our planet. This book
is made from Forest Stewardship Council® certified paper.

For my old friend Stephen Mcfadzean,
who left us far, far too soon.

PROLOGUE

Jemima Gore, much sought after television presenter, turns in her swivel chair to face the large screen. The show's logo disappears and is replaced by the face of a man; well-groomed white hair and strangely contrasting dark eyebrows garland a long, tanned face. His brown eyes should be soft, but instead they spark with intelligence and focus. He is framed by a backdrop of snow-capped mountains and the straggle of an Alpine village. High-gabled roofs are blanketed in white, making this world look gentle and forgiving, at odds with the hard-edged, calculating nature of the annual Davos summit taking place amidst this glorious winter scene.

Gore speaks as she swings into position, removing her glasses and sitting back, confident that this guest won't hesitate or need much, if anything, in the way of prompting or encouragement. You'd be amazed the deleterious effect live TV can have on the uninitiated, but he is a consummate professional, his voice and opinion sought and respected across the financial world.

'We're joined by Sebastian Pallander from hedge fund Pallander Glossop. Good morning, Sebastian.' She smiles at the screen.

'Good morning, Jemima,' Pallander says, running a gloved finger rather awkwardly under the collar of his white shirt.

'We've been discussing the growing fiscal gap between industrialized Asia and its less developed regions. You invest widely in that part of the world, what's your take?'

Pallander smiles wanly. 'Yes, the GDP variance in countries sharing borders is often remarkable.' The voice is received English with an undertone of the continental – maybe French, German, Dutch. It's hard to tell.

Gore looks up from her notes. She's wondering why Pallander hasn't expanded on the subject. Normally, you give him a start and away he goes. *Normally*, the only problem is stopping him. She puts the brevity of his reply down to the cold. She's been to Davos many times, and can still feel the sharp, freezing air hit her lungs. 'There is a discussion planned for this afternoon on this subject. Can you tell us what form that is likely to take, and your views on the Indian prime minister's seeming reluctance to give smaller nations in that part of the world a hand up?'

Hugely magnified on the massive screen, he coughs, excusing himself.

'I can tell it's very cold there, Seb.'

'Bitter,' he replies, then splutters again. 'To answer your question, I feel that if India and other countries like it commit to regional support, we potentially have the most financially buoyant area on the planet. After all, we've seen what China has done. And though that's a one-nation policy, it can be adapted to work across borders.'

'Dynamic enough to challenge China in terms of production? As you say, their success is unparalleled.'

'Well, yes.' Pallander swallows hard. 'The population disparity can be almost nullified if we have a united Asian sector prepared and equipped with the necessary finance with which to compete. For instance,' he hesitates. 'For instance . . .'

Gore leans forward in her chair as Pallander coughs again and brings a handkerchief to his nose. He makes a strangled noise; it comes from deep in his throat. Suddenly, he clutches his collar and tears at his silk tie. His dark brown eyes flash with panic. One last, desperate glance before he drops from view, falling in front of the camera. Quickly, the screen goes blank.

Gore stares. The voice in her ear prompts her into action. She swings to face her audience. 'Well,' she clears her throat. 'There seems to be a problem across in Davos.'

'Go to Dillon's piece – now!'

The voice in her ear is insistent.

Jemima Gore gathers herself. 'Sebastian Pallander's suffering from a frog in the throat. Easily done in a place as cold as that.' She grins reassuringly, aware that some viewers will have been unsettled by the financier's apparent distress. 'Now, for a lighter look at the Davos summit, of course it's none other than Dillon Searle. He's managed to find a nice, warm restaurant – imagine that!'

She smiles until the red light vanishes and she's counted out.

'Off air.'

'What the fuck was that?' Gore shouts to her producer.

'You saw the same thing I did, Jem.'

'Pallander's been enjoying the hospitality too much, that's obvious. It's just sheer excess over there. Booze, drugs. You name it.'

'I can imagine. Three minutes twenty, then on to Tony Wiltshire down the line. OK?' The reply is curt.

'What the fuck happened to conversation?' Gore mutters as she checks her script.

She listens to the countdown as Dillon Searle's piece comes to a merciful conclusion. Now it's an interview with an unimaginative minister for agriculture via the internet. He's clearly sitting in his lounge, on a couch with blue cushions that match his political inclinations.

The remaining twelve minutes go by in the usual blur.

'*Three, two, one – and we're out!*'

Jemima Gore sighs. Another *Money Morning* show done. Ten more until she's finished and moves to the more obvious prestige of *Newsnight*.

The assistant producer approaches with a large Styrofoam cup of coffee.

'Durga, you're a star. Mind you, I'd prefer a large gin.' She likes Durga, they've enjoyed many drinks together. She's clever – a Cambridge graduate, going places. Gore hopes to take her to *Newsnight*, eventually.

The younger woman looks at her sadly.

'What is it, what's wrong?'

'I have bad news, Jem.'

'Has Roy fucked off with that runner at last?' When Durga doesn't smile at this sliver of gossip they've been enjoying and speculating over for more than a week, Gore knows it's serious. 'Well, spill the beans, come on.' She takes the coffee and sips at it tentatively.

'It's Sebastian Pallander.'

'Fuck him! He made me look like a real twat earlier. The morning after the night before. They're all there for a jolly, you know. That's why they have it in a place like Davos. The cold is the only thing that's keeping them awake.'

'He's dead, Jem. He collapsed just as we lost picture. Massive heart attack, they're saying. But I was thinking, surely it's too early to be certain of the cause?'

'What?' Gore's mouth is gaping. 'This better not be a wind-up?' She tests Durga with a look.

'Of course not. I wouldn't joke about a thing like this.'

'Fuck. Seb Pallander, dead. It's the end of an era.'

'I'm sorry. Did you know him well?'

'Just professionally.' Gore is lying and is conscious that her expression shouldn't give her away. She was seduced – she seduced – Seb almost ten years ago. Maybe it was a mutual thing, she can't remember. He was in his sixties then but had the body of a thirty-year-old. Work done, yes. Though it was the hard hours in the gym that made him a most energetic lover, not the cosmetic surgery. She remembered he still had streaks of dark hair back then.

'I'm sorry to be the bearer of bad news.'

Gore ignores this and shades her eyes against the glare of the studio lights as she shouts blindly to the control room.

'Roy! Are you there? Make sure I'm on the roster for News. I knew Seb Pallander. And as the last person to interview him, I should be on *The Ten*, surely to fuck?'

Durga observed the presenter with a neutral expression, yet again wondering if broadcasting is for her.

1

Three Months Later

Cara Salt looked out of her office window in some dismay. The cool April morning was about to turn into a warm spring afternoon. Though, whatever the weather, she'd rather have been anywhere but at work in the crumbling old tenement building in Glasgow's Hope Street. It was a relic, spanning three police forces over fifty years. It seemed everyone – including Police Scotland, the latest occupier – simply forgot to shut the place down.

Salt had convinced herself that its survival was due only to the fact that hardly anyone knew it existed. Occupying two floors of a tenement, just above a newsagent's, the offices of the Succession, Inheritance and Executory Department (SIE) were where old, sometimes unwanted, often deliberately ignored records were kept.

This outpost of policing dealt mainly with those who refused to adhere to the lawful terms of the wills and wishes of the departed. It had once been located in the Strathclyde Police's HQ at Pitt Street in the city, but that building was gone, so this new home had been found.

SIE was the intersection between civil and criminal law;

where the terms of inheritance were ignored, and possession became criminal theft.

Thirty years ago, the department hit the headlines when
its then officers secured the return of two eighteenth-
century duelling pistols to the son for whom they were
intended. This backfired spectacularly when said son
turned the pistols on the brother who had unlawfully
taken possession of them. But that was long before Cara
Salt's time. And nowadays the department operated in
almost complete obscurity.

As her mind wandered, almost inevitably Salt's thoughts
drifted back four years to her appointment as a detective
inspector in the Serious Crime Squad. Her time there
ended almost as quickly as the shot she'd fired.

The *regrettable shot*, as she'd come to think of it.

In truth, Cara Salt had lost much more than a coveted
position that day. Though she tried to avoid it, fighting
hard to keep the man's smiling face from her mind – there
it was. This struggle had become an internal daily mantra:
why had she done this? Why hadn't she done that? It took
genuine physical effort to subdue these thoughts. It was a
nagging worry that kept springing up. Most people wondered if they'd switched off the cooker or locked the front
door. For Cara Salt, it was this slow torture – a harrowing
daily mantra.

Salt tore her gaze away from the sunshine, traffic and
pedestrians of Hope Street and sat back in her chair, her
hands cradling her head. She gazed along a crack in the
high ceiling that ambled its way on the diagonal from one
part of the ornate, but woefully outmoded, cornicing to
another.

As each month went by, the crack edged a little further
along. She supposed she should report it to Buildings and

Infrastructure. But something in Salt liked the ceiling the way it was. Part of her wondered what would happen when the crack spanned its entire length. Perhaps the roof would cave in, and she along with the rest of the office would land on the Turkish couple who owned the franchise for the newsagent's below. This was one of the many distractions Cara Salt deployed to maintain her own sanity.

Salt sighed and reopened the screen she'd been toiling over on the computer. The case involved the rights of ownership to a cafe in rural Aberdeenshire. An elderly man who had run and maintained the place for four decades now faced eviction by a nephew who'd been left the cafe in a will. The case had remained firmly in civil jurisdiction until the occupier decided to barricade himself inside, made an improvised flamethrower out of an aerosol and threatened to assault anyone who came to remove him. Though local officers had dealt with the matter in the first instance, Salt had been asked to tie up the case. To that end, she'd sent the redoubtable DC Ewan Walker to make the necessary enquiries.

Ewan was another misfit. Now in his early fifties, he held the view that policing of the 'old school' was the only approach. He had little respect for senior officers in general – even less if they happened to be female – but he and Salt had managed to strike up a decent enough working relationship. Salt knew she could trust him, which was something, at least.

The last member of the team was Emma McKay. She wasn't a police officer, her job title being Administration Assistant. While there was little doubting her impressive typing speed, any other task placed before her proved enormously difficult. She was the daughter of an ACC's best friend and, as such, invulnerable. Salt tasked her only with jobs she was sure McKay could achieve. This was another *fait accompli* that came with the job; pointless to push back against it.

Cara Salt read a few paragraphs on the Aberdeenshire coffee shop case and shut the computer down. Anxious to enjoy at least part of the day and unwilling to sample another of McKay's beverage-making disasters, she decided that a coffee of her own was in order. It was time to take a short break at the little place across the road.

Though officially a small restaurant, the owners had set up a few tables out on the pavement. As long as the weather was decent, it was a good space to clear her head of SIE's stultifying boredom.

Salt made her way through the general office. McKay's desk was at the door, an impromptu reception – not that anyone ever visited the department.

'Emma, you've got the mobile number if you need me, OK?'

'Aye, no bother,' said Emma, still eyeing her desktop screen. 'Aw, this is a pain in the arse,' she said, grabbing the screen with both hands and propelling it back and forth on her desk.

For a moment, Salt considered asking her what was wrong, but then decided that she wasn't interested and walked past. She pressed the security button on the door jamb and stepped out into the dark, dank stairwell, pulling the heavy door firmly behind her.

As she checked her handbag for her purse, a voice echoed up the close stairs.

'Are you DI Salt, by any chance?'

The detective inspector took a step back. The man looked respectable enough, advanced middle age, overweight but neat and tidy with a jacket and tie. But every police officer of her vintage had built up any number of former adversaries more than ready to do real harm.

'Who are you?' she said, positioning her leg ready to kick this interloper down the stairs.

The man looked up at her with a mystified expression. 'You didn't get the memo, then?'

'What memo?'

'I'm Abernethy Blackstock – your new DS. Well, sort of, if you know what I mean.'

Salt had been advised of an elusive detective sergeant the day she'd been transferred to the department. In all honesty, she'd lost any hope of the position being filled. But here he was.

'Right. I see. I'm about to go for a coffee. Will you join me?'

Abernethy Blackstock blinked at her for a moment, unsure. 'Yes, I suppose so.' He hesitated. 'Do you think they'll have green tea?'

2

Glaister Comyn Murray, one of Scotland's premier lawyers and notaries public, had their chambers just off Edinburgh's Royal Mile. The building was wrought of solid granite, seemingly as permanent as the occupants themselves. The firm had an unbroken hundred and fifty years of heritage to prove this.

Sebastian Pallander, in life, had been one of their richest and most prestigious clients. In death, nothing had changed. They were tasked with managing a fortune that could number in the billions. It was a privilege, an honour; and as per the detailed instructions they had been left by their deceased client, the firm intended to deal with it quietly and determinedly. Pallander had dictated every little detail: from the distribution and investment of money and assets, to where in the wood-panelled room beneficiaries of his largesse were to sit.

Tom Bristow, full partner and executor of the Pallander Estate, had been sitting at the desk on the little dais for nearly an hour, preparing to make the great man's last wishes known. It had been an unseasonably warm April and, his preparations complete, the lawyer stared through a dance of dust motes illuminated by shafts of bright morning sunshine into the room before him. One by one, he took in the neatly laid out wooden chairs, picturing the individuals who were to occupy them.

In fact, not all of the chairs were intended for actual beneficiaries. Pallander had left instruction for two random members of staff, completely unknown to those attending, to sit in the midst of the gathering. These junior members of staff had absolutely no legal function in proceedings but were tasked with merely 'sitting attentively, absolutely not engaging with anyone present. They are to take casual notes as to their impressions of those around them, and their reactions to my last will and testament.'

Though Bristow thought such a practice bizarre, he was untroubled by such specific instruction. During the course of his thirty years at law he'd experienced many stranger directions. And he had known Pallander well enough to recognize that the late billionaire could be eccentric when not in the public gaze. He'd also had a heightened mischievous streak. The executor reckoned that this was being done purely to unsettle those interested only in discovering how sizeable a slice of pie they were about to receive. He specialized in this part of the law and had seen everything from tears to fistfights at such events. And though he hoped for none of the latter, he was painfully aware that he knew very little about those about to receive. However, two burly security guards were sitting in an anteroom watching proceedings via discreet cameras placed around the room, ready to intervene if things became less than dignified.

Bristow checked the time on his Patek Philippe Calatrava. The beneficiaries were to be shown into the room in five minutes. He picked up his mobile phone and made the call, as per instruction. There was a slight pause before a conspicuously foreign ringtone sounded in his ear.

'Yes, are you ready?' The voice on the other end was terse. Not, he thought, from the UK.

'Yes, ready, and all in order.'

'Good. Please be precise in every detail. I will be watching.' The call ended as abruptly as it had begun, replaced by a long, dull tone.

He was, of course, fully aware of the cameras, but had been under the impression that they were for security only and could be used in evidence if the need presented itself. He had had no idea that he was to be scrutinized in the course of his work. This didn't make him nervous, rather irritated. It was as though he had to be monitored, checked up on. Bristow took a deep breath, discarded the knowledge he was being observed remotely, and composed himself. In many ways his job was a performance. He always performed well.

Elizabeth Pallander, the grieving widow, was first to enter the room. She did so on the arm of her elder brother, Charles Stuart-Henderson. Dressed in a plain black frock, she smiled weakly at the lawyer on the dais. Her bobbed grey hair was tinted blonde, which, alongside a fine complexion, dusted by the lightest cosmetic touch and unsullied by plastic surgery, made her look much younger than her actual years. Without doubt she was a beautiful woman still, with a tall, noble bearing. Though her time at the side of a restless, wilful husband had taken its toll, this was only visible in the sadness in her blue eyes. Maybe it was grief. Then again, maybe not.

Stuart-Henderson, on the other hand, was big and rumbustious. His frame, once sleek and athletic, had long-since gone the way of a man in his late sixties, when muscle turns to flab. So much so, the expensive suit he was wearing looked fit to burst at the seams. In common with most tall men, though, he carried his excess weight well. What made him look powerful would have rendered a less vertically favoured individual plainly fat. Despite being a notable Edinburgh banker, the loss of his family's land and titles many years before still bore down heavily upon him. And though the red hair of his youth had faded, his notorious temper had not.

The pair looked along the well-spaced chairs, each of which bore a name tag on its rear.

'Why are we not at the front, Tommy?' Stuart-Henderson addressed the executor in a friendly enough manner, though his irritation was palpable.

'Following instruction, Charlie. To the letter, as you'd expect.' The exchange echoed the familiarity between the two men. Edinburgh's high society was as small as its air was rarefied.

'Don't tell me – did he detail the seating arrangement?'

'He did indeed.'

Bristow attended to his papers, avoiding further discourse with the man now swearing under his breath.

'It doesn't matter where we sit, Charlie. I just want to get this over and done with.'

Elizabeth Pallander was once more an arbiter of peace between her husband and brother, even though one of them was now deceased. As the widow took her allotted seat near the middle of the room, she reasoned that this was likely to continue until the other passed away.

'It's just typical of the man, Ellie.' Her brother used the nickname he'd given her when they were children. He was the only person who did so. 'This whole thing will be a bloody charade. You mark my words.'

'It will be what it will be,' she said wearily.

The heavy door burst open. Alicia Pallander, always known as Alice by the family, appeared in a fluster of gratitude to whomever had shown her to the right room. She wore her own style – dyed bright-red curls bursting out from under a bucket hat, a denim jacket over a colourful pair of dungarees – and cared nothing for the conventions of such occasions. As the third child of the Pallander family, little in the way of expectation had been placed on her shoulders, and she had duly obliged. She was an artist; and though hardly any of her output had sold or even been admired, other than among her father's friends, coerced into purchase, she muddled along with regular handouts from her mother.

It was to her mother she made a beeline, kissing her on the cheek.

'Hi, Uncle Charlie. Why are you two not sitting at the front?'

'Oh, don't set him off again, darling,' said Elizabeth.

'It's a slight, plain and simple.' His feelings articulated, Stuart-Henderson folded his arms determinedly, further endangering the stitching on the sleeves of his well-cut suit jacket.

Alicia looked for her seat over the top of her round, wire-framed spectacles.

'The names are on the backs of the chairs, dear,' said Elizabeth.

'Oh, the front, how lovely! I better grab it before Tabby bullies me off the bloody thing.' Alicia sat down on one of three chairs placed just before the dais. She hefted her large canvas shoulder bag on to her lap and produced from it a hand mirror, into which she gazed, prodding and poking at her unruly curls.

A slight man of nearly middle age was next through the

door. He was a grey man in a grey suit – utterly bland and unmemorable. Silas Pallander had his mother's build and complexion, though there was little left of his fair hair, now shaved at the sides so as not to draw attention to his balding crown. Finding his name on a chair, he sat down with a sigh, removed a mobile phone from his pocket and proceeded to scroll through it.

'Good morning, Silas,' his mother greeted him, put out that he hadn't acknowledged her.

'Is it? Anything but, I'd say. You know what I think of this nonsense. It's a waste of time, Mother.'

'Hear him!' said Stuart-Henderson. 'First thing he's had right in a while.'

Silas returned his attention to the mobile phone, but no lip-reading skills were required to decipher the plain expletive on his lips.

The entrance of second child Tabitha Pallander was akin to the sudden arrival of a squall at sea. The door banged open, and in stepped a striking woman, tall, dressed in the dark purple of an exclusive business suit, jacket and trousers, cut to fit her lean frame. A tumble of lustrous brown hair flowed down her back, held in place by a pair of Persol sunglasses. She sighed, quickly catching her name on the back of a chair. Front and centre, a placing not lost on her elder brother as she swept past, stopping only to kiss her mother on the cheek.

'Chin up, Mummy. A day to be endured then forgotten, I'd say.'

'Yes, dear.' Elizabeth Pallander was sad that Tabitha ignored her uncle, despite sharing much of his blustering personality and temper. They had barely spoken in years. As her father's favourite, the young woman with the stellar results from Oxford had become the *chosen one*. Tabitha had been his deputy and was now in *temporary* charge of the company from which the family derived much of its wealth.

'Now then, Tommy. Let's get this going as quickly as we can, eh? I have to be in Frankfurt by four this afternoon.' Tabitha addressed the executor with the same casual authority her father would have used.

'I'll do my best,' said Bristow.

From behind the closed door of the meeting room, raised voices could be heard. Elizabeth Pallander turned in her seat. The last thing she wanted was unrest and arguments. As her eldest daughter had eloquently put it, this was a day to be endured then forgotten, with, she hoped, as little fuss as possible. But it was a rare event indeed to have her children gathered together under the same roof. And despite the solemn nature of the occasion, unlikely to proceed without let or hindrance. She gritted her teeth and waited for the door to open.

When it did, two men were framed in the doorway. Jean-Luc, one of the Pallander twins, was shouting at a younger man in a suit. As they moved into the room, Jean-Luc appealed to his elder sister for assistance.

'Who the bloody hell is this, Tabby?'

'How should I know? You didn't think it was just going to be happy families, did you? I'm surprised we don't need a bigger room – like the Usher Hall, for instance.' She looked at Bristow. 'Is all in order here, Tommy?'

'Indeed it is, Ms Pallander. The quicker everyone is seated, the sooner we can proceed.'

'Come in and sit down, Jean-Luc. Whoever this gentleman is, he doesn't need you in his face.'

'Wow, my sister the peacemaker,' said Silas, dragging his attention away from his phone.

'My brother, the twat,' Tabitha replied.

Jean-Luc, a head shorter than the interloper, took a seat at the back of the room, as per his seat allocation. Like his sister Alicia, he had an unruly head of curly hair, his face tanned from much time spent surfing when he wasn't trying to save the planet. The stranger walked to the front and sat beside Tabitha. The name on the back of his chair read *J. M. Walker*.

'You're not Johnnie, by any chance?' said Charles Stuart-Henderson, and laughed at his own joke.

Elizabeth Pallander stood. 'I do wish you'd all behave like adults. If you have no respect for yourselves, please have some for me.' Sitting back down, she stared into space, the strain of it all showing on her face.

'Sorry, Mum,' said Tabitha.

'It's always the same, darling. I've been dreading this for weeks. It's worse than the funeral.'

'Mummy,' the voice came from behind Elizabeth Pallander. 'Don't get so worked up.' Audrey, the other half of the Pallander twins, came into the room and hugged her mother fondly. 'Look, I'm beside you. Good morning, Uncle Charlie.' She had a bright, pretty face like her mother's, set off by a similar bobbed haircut. 'Hi, everyone – Mr Bristow.'

'At least your father had the good sense to sit you beside us.' Stuart-Henderson turned in his chair and addressed the room. 'Some decorum, please, everyone.'

Elizabeth Pallander grabbed her daughter's hand and smiled. 'It's so good to see you, dear. I'm looking forward to you visiting with the children. I've missed you all.'

'Yes, it'll be fun. Just get this beastly stuff over and done with first, eh? I know Daddy was what he was. But I can't get him out of my head. Those pictures from the news.' Audrey wiped away a tear.

As she spoke, all eyes drifted to a woman in a flowery dress, who sat at the back of the room. She smiled at the enquiring faces before turning her attention to the dais and Bristow.

'Who's that, Ellie?' said Stuart-Henderson.

'I've no idea. Please don't gawp at the poor woman. If she's here, she has every right. Otherwise, they'd never have let her in the building.'

Executor Bristow surveyed the scene. Everyone was here.

'Ladies and gentlemen, may I say how nice it is to see you all. In order that the wishes of the late Sebastian Pallander may be expressed as he wished, please let me proceed. I am not permitted to answer any questions now. But if you are unsure of any part of this last will and testament, a copy will be provided to each of you. If anything else remains unclear, or any of you have objections to what is detailed in Mr Pallander's will, please make this known in writing to the executory panel for consideration. That in mind, I must point out that everything contained within is in accordance with the legal advice and laws of this jurisdiction. Thank you.'

Bristow took his time to catch the eye of each person gathered in the room. Then he drew a deep breath and began reading the last will and testament of Sebastian Pallander.

3

The little cafe was busy but, given the blue sky, the detectives were able to remove themselves and enjoy their drinks out in the seated area on the street. Glasgow rarely enjoyed the weather for such al fresco activities. DI Cara Salt raised her head, letting the sun bathe her face in warmth.

While she had ordered a full choca mocha, Abernethy Blackstock was content with his green tea, which he sipped at primly, holding the little cup between two stubby fingers, his pinkie raised like a belted earl. She studied him carefully, noting his round face topped by thinning grey curls, cut neatly into his head. His nails were well manicured, though his fingers were stubby. His white shirt was well pressed without a crease, set off by a dark blue bow, the like of which she'd not seen since her father – an ex-cop – died the previous year. Blackstock's round glasses gave him the studious look of a much younger man who had been spending some time in the last century.

'Not bad.' He took another sip. 'You know, I never get a decent cup of green tea in any of those coffee chains. I'm quite impressed.' He smacked his lips as though proving the point. 'Do you spend a lot of time here?' he said, taking in his environs, a hint of disapproval in the question.

'The coffee machine in the office doesn't work, and neither does the secretary.' Salt shrugged. 'It's not as though we're waiting for an urgent call to arms up there.'

'Not overly pushed?'

'Plenty to do, but it's mostly time-sensitive box-ticking exercises.'

'Easy to become complacent.'

'Not with me on your back. The job might be shit, but we'll do it well. At least we can retain some pride, eh?'

'A commendable attitude, ma'am.'

She cocked her head to one side, brushing a dark strand of hair from her eyes. 'What do people call you? I mean, apart from Abernethy, that is.'

'Mr Blackstock.' The reply was swift, its message leaving no room for interpretation.

Nonetheless, Salt thought she'd give it a try. 'No nickname at all?'

'No, ma'am.'

'Right. You can dispense with the ma'am, by the way. And before you say it, I hate gaffer or boss. Plain Cara will do nicely, thanks.'

Blackstock raised one eyebrow. 'I see. If you don't mind, I'll stick to ma'am. Then we all know where we are.'

'The DC calls me Cara, it'll sound odd if you don't.'

Blackstock took time to consider this. He narrowed his eyes and held his head to the side as though listening to something intensely.

'What's up?'

'I could have sworn I heard a tree pipit. How strange.'

'What's a tree pipit?'

'It's a type of bird. I've never heard them in Edinburgh at this time of year.'

'A west coast thing?'

'Maybe Argyll, further west. I didn't expect to hear one in Glasgow.'

'So you're a twitcher?'

'No, I wouldn't say that. More a bird fancier.'

'You and the rest of the male population.'

His expression grew serious. 'I don't approve of the kind of behaviour you may have encountered from some of our colleagues. I'm sure you know what I mean. You'll have no sexual harassment or innuendo from me.'

Salt hadn't meant anything by the remark, though she'd had her fair share of unwanted advances from male colleagues in her sixteen years in the job. 'I'm glad to hear it. Nothing worse than a randy DS under you.' She smiled.

Blackstock swallowed hard at his sip of green tea, his face reddening. 'I can assure you I'm no such thing. I'm not even sure if I can call myself a detective sergeant any more.'

'You've been busted back to constable? Maybe I should have read the memo.' Salt was suddenly engaged.

'No, nothing like that. I'm retired – well, I have been retired. They've never been good enough to inform me of my rank. I say "detective sergeant" out of habit. But who knows what I really am.'

'You're on that clawback scheme, then?'

'Is that what they call it?'

'Something like that. I have to say, though, the minute I can retire that's what I'll do. A JCB won't be able to claw me back.'

'You say that now. Once you've spent nearly seven months with bugger all to do apart from stroke the cat, you'll soon change your mind.'

Stifling a laugh, Salt nodded. 'Aye, hard to know how to pass the time, I'm sure.' She listened for the tree pipit, but all she could hear was traffic and the yapping chatter coming from those inside the cafe. 'So, tell me about yourself.'

'Thirty years as an Edinburgh bobby, what more is there to say?'

'Edinburgh?'

'Yes. I hope that's not a problem. This is the brave new world of Police Scotland, remember. And SIE is a national operational squad, isn't it?'

Salt took in his earnest expression. In all honesty, even she wasn't sure just what SIE was. But it would be good to have another pair of hands to share the load. She wondered how much Blackstock knew about her department. They spent more time knee-deep in paperwork than practical policing. That said, taking into account his neat, ordered demeanour, she assumed that paperwork might just be his thing. And she'd never worked with an ornithologist before – or at least she didn't think she had. Plentiful arse-holes, yes. But never a man with such a hobby.

They went on to discuss aspects of SIE's work. Blackstock seemed engaged and interested by what she had to say.

'You'll commute every day, will you? Have to be honest, I wouldn't fancy that,' said Salt.

'I am commuting, but it's not as bad as you think. Maybe forty minutes. Though we all know about the roads these days.'

'Forty minutes from Edinburgh? You in a jet?'

Blackstock looked puzzled for a moment. 'No, not Edinburgh. Gosh, I'd never attempt that. I have a little cottage on the bonnie banks.'

'Loch Lomond?'

'Yes, just outside a small village.'

'I'm guessing you chose it because of the birds?'

'I did. It was my retirement gift to myself.'

Salt frowned. 'I never thought of a house as being a retirement present – unless it's in the Algarve, that is.'

'I can see what you're driving at.' Blackstock fiddled with his tie and squinted into the distance. 'You see, my wife and I are estranged.'

'Oh, I'm sorry to hear that. Not unusual in this job, mind.'

'Sadly, she left me when I retired. So I can't blame my job for the state of my marriage. I suppose I just got under her feet, cramped her style – lunches with friends, and the like.'

'You mean you bought the house on Loch Lomond as a little place to watch birds and now you're living there?'

'Something like that. We'd agreed to buy a holiday home when I handed in my cards. I thought it would be a nice surprise. But while I was keen on spending time with bar-tailed godwits, she rather fancied Tuscany.' He shrugged miserably.

You poor sod, thought Cara. A career spent catching the worst scum imaginable, and you retire to a broken marriage. Strangely – for she was not a particularly empathetic person – her heart went out to him. His plight reminded her a bit of her own life. Always the right intentions, rarely the right choice. That neatly summed up her experiences with the opposite sex. And even though Salt was only in her mid thirties, she'd already missed out on the right guy – *the one*. Ever since then, she'd lost her enthusiasm for trawling through endless dates with men who invariably ended up irritating her. Ultimately, their only crime being they weren't him. A heavy dose of police-acquired cynicism didn't help. She reckoned, however, that she was content enough alone. Too old to change, too old to absorb someone else's peccadilloes. A life spent mourning what might have been.

'We better get back. I'll show you more of what we do across the road, Abernethy.' Salt stopped. 'Can I call you something else? I mean, it is quite a mouthful.'

'My wife calls me Abby. I can't say I've ever liked it. Though I never objected.'

'No, that won't do. It'll bring back memories every time I open my mouth. How about Abs?'

Blackstock sighed. 'If you want. I've certainly been called worse.'

'OK, Abs. Let's get up there and make absolutely no difference at all in the fight against crime. Well, our kind of crime, at least.'

The pair crossed the busy street and made their way to the offices above the newsagent's, the preserve of SIE.

4

June

Jean-Luc Pallander strode up the steep hillside as though he was stepping into a car. A life spent outdoors gave him a fresh, healthy look. Though he and his twin sister shared the same curls, his were bleached blond by sun and sea.

The fight for the environment never ceased. It was something he could be proud of. Plus, it took his mind off the unexpectedly poor financial fare offered up by his father's estate. Rather than being beneficiaries of large sums of money and property, it appeared that Sebastian Pallander's children were to earn it, in a way yet to be specified.

Since the death of his father, he'd felt strangely rudderless. That was, to the extent he'd ever had much in the way of direction. He was way down in the family pecking order. While Tabitha and Silas fought it out to be the chosen one, he and his other two sisters were left to find something to fill their lives. This they'd done independently of their father, though, to be fair to him, if they'd ever needed his help, he had been forthcoming, in his own austere way.

Now he was gone, Jean-Luc felt an unexpected void.

He'd spent weeks on end in the small sailing yacht his father had bought him. First in the safety of the Thames estuary, then touring up the west coast, settling on a small island in the Hebrides. There he spent weeks thinking, exploring his real feelings for his father.

As the days passed, he found that he couldn't remember when he'd last had a shower, never mind what day it was.

The loss of Sebastian Pallander had hit him much harder than he'd ever thought possible. This was as much of a shock as the loss itself.

For most people – in terms of compensation – having a million pounds paid into your bank account would have been more than acceptable. But for the Pallander children, it simply wasn't enough. After all, their father was a multi-billionaire; they had all expected greater riches.

But when he thought about it, he'd come off lightly. JL had never been interested in 'the company', as his father's work was invariably termed. He had no head for figures and lacked Sebastian's cold ruthlessness. They argued a lot; and latterly, Jean-Luc had steered clear of anything fiscal – and therefore his father – as often as he could.

He pictured his eldest sister Tabitha's face as the lawyer read out the terms of the will in the stuffy room. On reflection, no wonder she was angry. She'd worked at her father's side for almost fifteen years. Her reward – apart from the million pounds left to each sibling – was a demotion to mere executive at Pallander Glossop, with little real power or influence. Fired from her previous eminence as CFO when she'd widely been expected to take over as boss. It was a slap in the face for their father's favourite child. Jean-Luc had also watched Silas, his elder brother, snigger – until he discovered his own fate: removed from the company altogether, and left to manage the farms, lands and small businesses in Scotland, their actual ownership having been left in its entirety to his mother.

Silas had stormed from the room, Tabitha not far behind. And though Jean-Luc had laughed at the time, he felt guilty about it, if only for his mother's sake. She'd tried to call them back, her expression one of embarrassment crossed with weary resignation at the inevitability of it all.

Uncle Charlie had also been administered a hard kick in the teeth. He'd been responsible for the lands surrounding what had been the Stuart-Henderson family pile at Meikle House: the place Charlie should have inherited had it not been for a feckless father, and sheer bad luck. With that duty now casually passed on to his nephew, Jean-Luc feared the old man, as they knew him, was about to explode, his ruddy face deepening a few shades of red.

Alice had clearly wanted more to help fund her art. And Jean-Luc thought her comment to the executor had been most apposite.

'This is all we get for being Sebastian Pallander's children? Do you know what a mouldering pile of shit that was – is?'

All the same, they'd pocketed the 'cool million', as he'd heard his uncle Charlie call it.

Though, what was a million these days? What did it buy? There was a time you could have invested it safely and lived out the rest of your life comfortably on the interest. But nobody could do that now. Certainly not a Pallander child, used to the best of the best.

And as for the legend *until you can live up to expectations*. What on earth did that even mean? Though he'd questioned Bristow as to the process by which they were all to be judged, Jean-Luc was still none the wiser. As their father had kept his family hanging on to will-o'-the-wisp promises in life, so he did in death. As far as they all were concerned, apart from the million pounds gifted to each of the beneficiaries – five children, their mother, Uncle Charlie, and the lands of the estate in Scotland bequeathed to their remaining parent – everything else was to be consumed by the organization that had dominated their lives: Pallander Glossop – the company.

Jean-Luc thought again of his twin sister, Audrey. She alone had shrugged her shoulders and sighed, as if she would give away every penny to have her father back. It was a cliché, almost expected of her. But the rest of the family all knew her comments to be sincere, typical of the person who'd helped them all, at one time or other.

As he neared the summit of the hill, Jean-Luc turned to look out over the Firth of Clyde. A blue river wound under a bluer sky. Just below, Dumbarton Rock and its castle stood sentinel over the place, a guardian for the ages. Ancient Britons, Romans, Scots, English, Vikings and Frenchmen had taken in their world from that very spot. Possessing what they thought to be eternal, only for their own eternity to cast them down to dust, as epochs turned.

Who will come after me? he wondered. The world of fervid battles with axe and sword, the wooden wheel on a mud track, lives of squalor and the simple things, were so very far away in time. The planet had come further in these last two centuries than it had done in millennia. What would the next two hundred years bring? Perhaps the earth would make its catastrophic last stand, and all that came before would be as nothing. This potential oblivion was becoming more real by the day.

Jean-Luc Pallander had not inherited much of his father's great wealth. He most certainly wasn't as academically clever as his older sister, Tabitha; or as kind as Audrey, lacking almost all her noble attributes. Thankfully, nor did he possess the fermenting loathing and jealousy of his older brother, Silas. But he could still make a difference. He could help save the planet.

As Jean-Luc crested the hill, the great swish of the wind turbine blades seemed almost elemental. They were pulled back out of sight of most folk who passed by on the road far below or ploughed the ancient waterway of the Clyde. But there they were, great towers. And as they had many blades, many sides, so were their purposes manyfold. This new 'green' route to clean energy scarred the landscape, destroyed the habitat of birds, animals, fish and insects alike, and robbed the hills of their soul. They were the refuge of politicians. *Look, we're doing the right thing. Vote for us!*

Jean-Luc saw the truth behind the perfidy. He intended to put an end to the lies. The charlatans knew full well that the only way to save the planet was for its human population to disappear. But in the pyre of humanity's own making, everything would die with them.

He was here to end the current myth of sustainability. As he approached the towering blades swinging in the sky, he removed the box from his rucksack. It was a biscuit tin, like the one they used to joke their father collected pennies inside to give to their mother. But it was packed with enough explosives to make a point, to draw the world's attention to the images of a falling tower as it crashed to the ground. A symbol, the harbinger of honesty, and an intimation of what was to come.

Jean-Luc readied himself to strike a blow against the dissemblers that would echo not only along the Clyde Valley, but across the globe. He removed a mirrorless camera from his bag. With it, and his improvised bomb, he didn't look back as he made his way under the flashing blades to the base of the great tower. Only for a second did he pause to consider if he'd have gone this far when his father was alive.

The plain answer in his head was no.

He pulled the switch to arm the explosives.

5

Cara Salt awoke to a dull ache in her head and a dry mouth as an accompaniment. She'd had a restless night filled with bad dreams, all of which seemed very real.

At one point, she found herself the only person who could save the lives of millions from some deadly but unspecified threat. She failed, looking on in horror as terrified people died, seas boiled, and fire scourged the earth. One man rose from the tumult to point his finger at her.

'You've failed!' The voice was so loud it woke her up.

But Salt had experienced this dream so many times in various forms it had become routine. The scene changed; the challenge was always slightly different. But her father always arrived in time to accuse her of inadequacy. It stemmed from as far back as primary school, when she failed to win the prize for best student in her year. Her father had been a senior police officer, with limitless ambition for his daughter. When she applied to join the police, he'd been appalled, and did all he could to stop her. But despite his eminence, he couldn't.

She experienced this dream at least once a week. And on each occasion, when she awoke to that familiar feeling of worthlessness and self-loathing, she pictured her father on his deathbed. Even though they'd barely spoken for years, and he had all but lost the ability to converse, he spent his last few breaths in a stinging rebuke.

You should have gone to university – been something special.

These words echoed in her head day after day.

Salt padded into the kitchen of her small flat and made some strong coffee. Pushing down the plunger for her was akin to an act of devotion, the same routine every morning – or sometimes afternoon, if she wasn't working. Still blinking away sleep, she yawned her way into the lounge and switched on the big TV bracketed to the wall. It was her only self-indulgence. She didn't buy expensive clothes, had no time for jewellery, hated holidays and posh houses, so the purchase of a high-end television could easily be excused. After all, it was rapidly becoming her only friend. Marriage had claimed just about everyone with whom she'd been close – or so it seemed. The preoccupations of children and the hamster wheel of existence meant her old pals had little quality time for her. She wondered if they ever thought of the friend they'd left behind as they embarked on their new lives. She doubted it.

Almost as soon as she flicked to the morning news, she wished she hadn't. It was the usual spiralling tale of strikes, wars, disease, tragedy and unrest. All fuelled by the weasel words of politicians of every stripe.

She took a large gulp of coffee and laid her head back on the couch. The prospect of another day at SIE was doing nothing to fire her enthusiasm. She considered her detective sergeant for a moment. Abernethy Blackstock seemed like a decent enough person. She remembered her surprise at the sadness she'd felt when he described the split from his wife, later rationalizing that it was an echo of her own life, filled with abandonment and disappointment. In any

34

case, he was proving to be efficient and uncomplaining. And his wit, dry as it was wry, had helped buoy her along as she toiled away at SIE.

'With some breaking news, it's over to our reporter at the Kilpatrick Hills in West Dunbartonshire.'

Suddenly the television had her full attention. Salt squinted at the screen.

'Kenny McNeil, you've just arrived at the scene. Reports of an explosion at a wind farm there. What can you tell us?'

'Hello, John. Details still a bit sketchy here. We're being kept well back from the incident. What I can tell you is that, from where I'm standing here on the Kilpatrick Hills, just above the town of Dumbarton, I can see a large plume of black smoke rising above a wind turbine farm. We're told locals heard what can best be described as a loud pop, just after six thirty this morning. Many worried it was an explosion and called local police. There's little doubt that there has been an incident at the wind farm, but as to what it is, we'll have to await developments. I'll bring you more as I have it.'

Salt took in the scene and wondered what could have happened. She'd never associated wind turbines with any kind of instability. After all, they were at the forefront of green policy. These days, though, who really knew?

She shook her head at the pointlessness of it all – of everything. Salt drained what was left of her coffee, idly took in a piece on a woman whose cat could impersonate the late Bruce Forsyth, and decided it was time to get moving. She was soon under a really hot shower, readying herself for another day of boredom and drudgery.

When Salt arrived at her tenement offices, she was pleased to find her deputy already in place. In fact, he was staring out of the dirt-smeared window down on to Hope Street with no little fascination.

'Good morning, Abs,' she said, wondering what he was looking at.

'Good morning, ma'am,' he said absently, eyes still fixed to the window.

'What is it?'

'I wish I had my binoculars.'

'Let me see.' Salt made her way to the window.

'Just over there on the building opposite.'

'Yes, a bird. I see it.'

'A great tit. Unusual at this time of year and in a city centre location. Quite the find.'

'You think?' said Salt.

'Oh yes. These birds are normally busy with fledglings at this time of year. It highlights just how the seasons are shifting.'

'Usually Edinburgh tits, are they?'

'We're not still going down the Glasgow hatred of Edinburgh police officers route, are we?'

'When in Glasgow, tell jokes about the Edinburgh polis. It's what we do.'

'I know. I worked with a cop who'd transferred to us from Glasgow once. Got married to a local girl or some such. Called Lothian and Borders officers "social workers in uniform", if I remember correctly.'

'That sounds about right. Anyway, we're all one big happy family now, eh?'

Blackstock looked at her doubtfully.

'OK, I know what you mean. But you're one of us now. Make the most of an exceptional policing opportunity.'

'Rather late in the day, wouldn't you say?'

'Never too late, Abs.'

An unusual tone emanated from Blackstock's phone. He picked it up, pressed the screen and raised a brow.

'What's up?'

'Take a look, ma'am. I'm not sure if you've heard about the incident at the wind turbine farm at Dumbarton?'

'I saw it on the news. Why?'

Blackstock handed Salt his mobile phone.

One dead in wind turbine explosion. Nothing conclusive, but foul play suspected.

'Another bloody idiot protestor,' said Salt. 'Looks as though they copped it in the act.'

As Salt was about to head into her office, leaving Blackstock to the reams of paperwork she'd offloaded on him yesterday, she heard the phone ring at reception.

'It's OK, Emma. I'll get it!' Salt pressed the outside line extension. 'Police Scotland, SIE. DI Salt, can I help you?'

'Salt, Cara Salt?' The voice on the other end was frightfully posh.

'Yes, may I ask who's calling?'

'ACC Dixon – Frank Dixon. Do you have a moment?'

'Yes, sir – of course.' Salt tapped her shoulder, the universal signal that a senior officer was on the other end of the phone. Blackstock took the hint and disappeared into the main office to give her some privacy.

'You'll have seen the news?'

'You mean the wind turbine thing, sir? Yes, I have.'

'Good, very good. I would like you to take a look over there.'

Salt was bewildered. 'Me? With the greatest respect, sir, you may be on to the wrong department. This is SIE.'

'Young woman, I know which department I've called! Not quite senile yet, you know.'

Salt held the phone away from her ear, but still couldn't

fathom why she was being asked to attend an active incident.

'You'll have heard the name Sebastian Pallander?'

'The guy who died on TV a few months ago. Money man. Yes, I have.'

'Between us, because it hasn't been made public yet, his son was caught up in the explosion this morning.'

'Explosion, sir? So, it's foul play. I just assumed it was some idiot messing about trying to make a point.'

'Assume nothing, DI Salt. I'm surprised your father didn't instil that into you.'

'You knew my father, sir?' Cara Salt could feel her heart sink.

'I worked with him for many years. His junior, of course. The man should have been the chief constable – commissioner of the Met, even. Why he was passed over, I can't imagine. Too much of a straight talker, I'd say.'

'He was certainly that,' said Salt with conviction.

'Always kept a close eye on your career before he passed. I used to keep him up to speed, you know.'

'*Really?*' Salt realized that this sounded too incredulous so changed tack. 'I mean, gosh, I'd no idea.'

'Anyhow, haven't time to rattle the old gums. Get over there and have a look. You're expected, so don't worry about clearance with the MIT.'

Sensing he was about to end the call, Salt rushed a question. 'Can I ask what involvement will this department have, sir? It doesn't sound like our purview at all, if you don't mind me saying.'

'I thought you'd be up to speed with the Pallander situation. Sebastian Pallander's will was read recently. Kids are in receipt of bugger all. Predictably, they are making a fuss – raised a joint legal action against their father's last wishes. They include our unlucky turbine man, Jean-Luc Pallander. He was placed at the scene by his co-conspirators. Out of the woodwork like a shot when their nonsense becomes too real. Go, have a look, then come to Gartcosh and tell me what you think.'

'Yes, I will, sir. Right away.'

'Oh, and be sure to take Abernethy with you.' The call clicked off abruptly.

Salt placed the phone back on the cradle and thought for a moment or two. She was aware of the Pallander death. After all, it had been all over the news for days earlier in the year. She kicked herself for not being aware of the controversy surrounding his last wishes, though. And she'd noted how the assistant chief constable had referred to 'Abernethy', rather than DS Blackstock.

As she got ready to make for the Kilpatrick Hills, Cara Salt thought about her father.

6

DCI Alex Peel was fretting over a computer screen. Though the day was warm enough, up on the hills a chill wind blew. Dressed only in an inexpensive suit, he felt rather unprepared.

'You can see here, sir,' said a white-suited SOCO officer. 'The drone shot clearly shows the distribution of human *material*.'

Peel, in his late forties and feeling it, hated the use of euphemisms to disguise anything. 'Call it what it is, Sergeant: body parts! Bloody *material*. This poor Pallander chap has had his bollocks blown to kingdom come.' He took a breath. 'I presume we are talking about only one individual?'

The sergeant looked peeved. 'Nothing we can be sure of right now, sir. Even the identity of our dead man. Though I know witnesses have placed him here.'

'Don't say that! I've already informed the ACC. Anyway, we found his car on the access road. And the remains of a credit card with his name on it. What more do you need? In any case, everyone knows who these Pallanders are. Where there's money, there's shite – and shite always heads in our direction. Do what you have to, but make it quick. This place will be crawling with braid any time soon.'

He watched the SOCO officer hurry away with the laptop under his arm.

'Bloody bosses,' he mumbled to himself.

He pulled a cigarette packet from his trouser pocket and, despite the wind, cupped the flame of his lighter sufficiently to ignite a smoke. Taking his first draw, he sighed, and spotted another two figures heading in his direction. One a plumpish man in a fluorescent police incident coat, the other a lean woman wearing a leather jacket and black jeans.

'Fuck, Joan Jett meets Christopher Biggins.' This thought given voice was carried away on the stiff breeze.

'Are you DCI Peel?' said the woman as they came within a few feet of him.

'I am. Who are you, and why have you been allowed to pass through the cordon?'

'I'm DI Salt, this is DS Blackstock. We're here from SIE on the orders of ACC Dixon, sir.'

'What?' Peel screwed his face up at this statement.

'He's from Gartcosh, sir,' said Salt.

'I know who Dixon is! What department did you say you were from?'

'Succession Inheritance and Executory,' said Salt wearily. She couldn't count how many times she'd been asked to explain the initialism. It always added to her suspicion that nobody knew anything about the department of which she was head.

'You're a bit premature. Our dead man's family aren't ready for his will yet.'

'It could be a part of a larger case, sir. The ACC said you were expecting us.'

'Oh, aye, I do remember him saying something. I was

busy at the time, as you can see.' DCI Peel was answering Salt but staring at Blackstock, who had his head cocked as though he was listening for something, his eyes tight shut. 'What are you doing, Sergeant?'

'Oh, just taking in the surroundings, sir. Getting one's bearings – that kind of thing.'

Peel shook his head. 'OK, do your own thing, why don't you.' He massaged his temple with the thumb and finger of one hand. 'Listen, what can I do for you both? I need a coffee, so make it quick.'

'Just wondering what you've found out so far?' said Salt.

'Yet to be confirmed, but it looks like one dead man, who appears to be Jean-Luc Pallander. And before you say it, yes, I know who he is. His car was found on the access road.'

'Yes, we passed it on the way up,' said Blackstock.

'I wondered why he parked it there, until it was pointed out to me that the approach to the turbines is covered by CCTV. He was obviously keen not to be identified. Now he's a bloody jigsaw puzzle.'

'Do you think he'd come to blow up a turbine?' said Salt.

'Why else would he trudge up here with a box full of explosives?' Peel was already tiring of this interrogation. 'He's one of these damned eco warriors. My guess is the device went off early, leaving him – well, leaving him all over the place.' He gestured airily with one arm.

'Odd, isn't it?' said Blackstock.

'It's not something I'd attempt myself,' replied Peel. 'But I've taken a look at him online. He's into this big time. Didn't need to work, so spent his time on civil unrest. Though how gluing yourself to the roof of a train is helping the environment, I'm not sure.'

'You don't mind if we have a word with SOCO, do you, sir?' said Salt.

'Get suited and booted and you can do what you like. Just don't get in the way.' Peel flicked his cigarette on to the grass, extinguishing it with the toe of his left shoe. 'Right, I'm off to get a caffeine hit. You're welcome to join me. I'm desperate to know just what it is you actually do.'

For Salt, his broad grin said it all. Yet another smart-arse ready to take the piss out of her department. But this was her job. 'We'll take that poke about, if you don't mind. I'd like to get a sense of what happened here. The ACC clearly thinks this is important work, even if you don't – *sir*.'

'Knock yourselves out.' Peel's mind was already on coffee and a warm car. He ambled away with no further comment.

'What a twat.'

'Sorry, ma'am?'

Salt raised her brows. 'Get your mind off the birds and back on your work, Abs. I know what you were listening for.'

7

Following a long chat with SOCO, Cara Salt was at a loss as to what else she could achieve on the hills above Dumbarton. In fact, she wasn't sure why she'd been sent in the first place. Even if this case did eventually come under her remit, there was nothing she couldn't have picked up from subsequent forensic and crime reports.

Not that it wasn't gruesome enough. Jean-Luc Pallander's head had been neatly cut in two, as though by way of a sharp axe, not an explosion. SOCO officers had shown them the bottom half, his lower set of teeth – miraculously intact – and chin, complete with straggling beard, its blond hair singed near the bottom lip. The spinal cortex was poking clear of the rest of the grisly remains, looking unnervingly like white asparagus sprouting from a field of blood and gore.

Though they offered to show her the other half of the head, she declined. SOCO officers were still at the grim business of collecting and cataloguing Pallander's remains, spread over a very large area. Everything down to the last chip of bone would have to be collected before they were finished.

The son of the man who'd died on live TV had chosen an even more spectacular way to leave this mortal coil.

She and Blackstock left the SOCO team to their unenviable task, and made for Salt's Mini Cooper S, parked back up on the access road. The scene below had turned from being a bright, sunny – if windy – morning into a sullen afternoon. The Clyde, winding its way out to sea, had lost its earlier sparkle, replaced by a dull grey matching the sky above. Rain was on its way, and Salt didn't want to be caught in it.

'Jump in, Abs,' she said to Blackstock. Though what followed, as the detective twisted and turned his way into the Mini, bore little resemblance to any kind of jump.

Puffing heavily, his face red, Blackstock inserted his right hand down the side of the passenger seat in an effort to secure his belt.

'What's up?' said Salt, taking in the look of revulsion on his face.

'I knew this car had an unfortunate odour. I put it down to some air-conditioning malfunction.' Blackstock pulled his hand out from the side of the seat. 'But now I've found this.' He produced the mouldy green remains of what had once been a sandwich.

'I wondered where that had gone,' said Salt, with the air of someone who had genuinely misplaced her lunch – by the look of things some days, if not weeks, ago. 'It was tuna, onion and mayonnaise. I really enjoyed the first half of it. I couldn't work out where the other half had gone.'

'Mystery solved, then,' said Blackstock. 'Do you have a plastic bag, ma'am?'

'Are you going to be sick? I haven't started the car yet.'

'No, for this.'

'Och, just pitch it out the window. Biodegradable, right?'

'Indeed I will not. I'm not in the habit of *pitching things* out of the window. In any case, there are journalists hanging about. How will it look if they see police officers littering?'

'You're probably right. We'd be on the front page of the *Daily Record*. Not for the first time, in my case.'

Blackstock's expression was enough to give Salt the distinct impression that if he were to appear on the front page of a newspaper, it would be a quality broadsheet, not a Scottish tabloid. It was all she could do not to laugh, as her deputy held the offending sandwich as far away from his face as humanly possible.

'We'll stop at the first bin, Abs. Don't worry.'

Blackstock craned his head round to the back seat of the car, where detritus had literally piled up. There were empty soft drink cans, crushed cigarette and crisp packets, old newspapers. The back of the Mini looked like a skip. 'Will we have time to empty the rest of this rubbish while we're at it?' he sighed.

'Hey, don't sweat it. I like my cars *lived in*. I suppose yours is cleaner than the day it left the dealership.' Salt laughed.

'In fact, it probably is. They left sheets of mucky paper in the footwells. Though I've had her a while, I like to keep her neat and tidy.'

Salt took off down the access road until they eventually reached the dual carriageway.

'Bugger, I haven't set the satnav for Gartcosh. Doesn't matter how many times I go there, I always get lost.'

'Don't worry, I know the way,' said Blackstock confidently.

As it turned out, DS Blackstock was just like having a large satnav sitting in the passenger seat. Once she'd stopped at the first available garage and looked on as her deputy disposed of the mouldy sandwich, as well as the majority of items littering the back seat, he proved to have a marvellous sense of direction. It was all 'right here', 'left there', 'slow down'. In fact, after a while, Salt became almost mesmerized by his regular clear and precise directions. It was like a chanted mantra, sending her toward salvation – or in this case, Police Scotland's Scottish Crime Campus. Their journey took just under forty minutes, Salt's interpretation of various speed limits being rather liberal.

From the outside, Salt had always felt the building looked austere. Where once men had forged steel, police officers now solved the very worst crimes, in what looked like a Soviet-era block of flats.

Once inside, though, light spilled down the large atriums. Leafy plants were so ubiquitous the place looked like the Botanic Gardens. The symmetrical design and square-paned windows had more than a hint of Charles Rennie Mackintosh, though what the great architect would have made of this palace of policing was open to interpretation. The Scottish Crime Campus seemed to be populated by a particularly handsome set of officers and clerical staff. It was as though the mean streets of Glasgow had been left far behind and everyone floated in a futuristic Valhalla. Salt, however, knew better. This was a place to be avoided at all costs, just as its predecessor at Pitt Street in Glasgow city centre had been. Best to stay as far away as possible from policing's own 'great architects', in DI Salt's opinion.

As they passed through security, Salt asked where ACC Dixon might be found. But before the officer could get the words out, Blackstock piped up to say he knew the way, so not to worry. His talent for directions, it seemed, was not limited to highways and byways. After a tramp down a corridor, the swish of an upmarket lift then a short flight of stairs, they found themselves in an area of more plants. Amongst the exotic foliage bloomed another good-looking member of the clerical staff.

'Can I help you?' he said in dulcet, calming tones.

'DI Salt and DS Blackstock here to see ACC Dixon.'

'Of course, ma'am. I'll just see if he's available. And nice to see you again, DS Blackstock.'

As the young clerk attended to the business of checking the availability of the ACC, Salt eyed Blackstock suspiciously. 'No stranger in these parts, Abs. Don't they say that in the Westerns?'

Blackstock sniffed. 'I've never been very fond of that genre. Let's face it, once you've seen one, you've seen them all.'

Before Salt could enquire further as to her colleague's overfamiliarity with the Scottish Crime Campus, the clerk put down the phone.

'The ACC will see you both now.'

The pair were shown through a set of fire doors and along a corridor. Dixon's office was at the very end: *Assistant Chief Constable F. D. Dixon* engraved on a brass nameplate.

'Impressive,' said Blackstock. 'You know you've made it when your door is the last, facing up the corridor.'

'Same with lavatories, isn't it?' said Salt, serially unimpressed by offices in general.

The door was pushed open by the clerk, and he showed both detectives in. The office itself was just as impressive as the door. At one side sat a trophy cabinet, mainly featuring tiny figures atop a variety of silver cups. At first, Salt thought they were football related, but soon spotted that each figure was wielding a golf club. ACC Dixon appeared through another door behind a large desk. He'd eschewed a uniform – unusual in Salt's experience of senior officers – and was wearing an expensively cut dark-blue suit.

'Thank you, Andrew,' said Dixon pleasantly. 'It'll be green tea for you, Abernethy. What about you, DI Salt?'

'Oh, a cup of coffee would be nice,' she said.

The clerk went to fetch their drinks and Dixon ushered them through into the inner office, which was, in effect, a lounge, complete with couch, easy chairs, a large TV screen on the wall, and a drinks cabinet.

As Salt contrasted this magnificence with her own work-space, Dixon urged them both to take a seat.

'Well, Abernethy, how is life on the loch? I must say, I envy you from an ornithological point of view.'

Blackstock beamed at the ACC. They were very similar in build. Both of medium height, carrying perhaps a little too much weight. But while Blackstock was definitely Marks & Spencer, his superior appeared to be a Savile Row man.

'The opportunities are indeed abundant, sir. And with the lighter nights, I have so much more time to enjoy it all. Do you know, I had a European green woodpecker at the weekend?'

'My goodness! Very early. Good spot. I must come out for another visit.'

During this discourse, it became more than obvious to Salt that Dixon and Blackstock weren't only acquainted, they were friends. She wondered how a senior officer from Glasgow who had worked his way up the greasy pole and a former Lothian and Borders detective had become so friendly. But on rapid analysis, she realized that there were many wheels with wheels, both in the job and socially, where relationships like this could be considered inevitable.

'Now, don't feel left out, DI Salt.' Dixon stood and

reached into the inside pocket of his jacket. 'I found this. Thought you might like to have it.'

Salt thanked him and looked at the photograph. A little girl in a white dress and bunches. No more than four years old. She was holding her father's hand. As usual he looked tall and commanding, while beside him stood a younger version of Dixon, a broad grin on his face.

'That was taken at Lochinch – you know, the police social club. I'd just been promoted to detective sergeant. In no small part down to your father, I must say. He was a fine man.'

Salt felt a mixture of sadness and resentment every time she saw her father. And though she had absolutely no recollection of the photograph being taken, she remembered the frilly white dress well. It was odd knowing what an influential and respected figure her father had been in the police. He was a dyed-in-the-wool Glasgow man, unhappy when the city force was merged into the new Strathclyde service. He'd passed away under Police Scotland, an organization of which he took a cuttingly dim view. 'Policing and politics don't mix' became a mantra in his last few years.

'Thank you. It's nice that you remember him with such great fondness.' She saw Dixon search her face, seemingly reading her feelings.

'Not easy being a father in this job, you know. I don't need to tell you the sights we see. The last thing you want is for your children to take the wrong path.' He smiled.

'Yes, I'm sure,' said Salt.

'Now,' said Dixon. 'To business.'

He reached for an iPad mini on the table at his side. The television screen burst into life, filled with an image of Sebastian Pallander. Salt recognized him from the footage of his death, captured live on TV.

'Sebastian Pallander,' said Dixon. 'Hedge fund manager,

financier, erstwhile banker, financial genius – and, we sus-pect, potential criminal on a massive scale.'

Salt, while taken aback by this revelation, was equally surprised as she noticed Blackstock nod his head sagely, as though he had known this for some time. 'I had no idea, sir,' she said. Her gaze returned to Blackstock, who was staring at Pallander's image on the large screen.

'The fact you know nothing of Pallander's business undertakings is no surprise, DI Salt. In fact, had it not been for his sensational death, few would recognize him at all. Let's face it, unless you're interested in all things finan-cial, these people are on the edge of consciousness. Despite their influence on just about every part of society, includ-ing princes, presidents and even nations.'

'We should come clean, at this point I think, sir,' said Blackstock.

'Yes, you're right, Abernethy.'

Salt stared between them.

Dixon sighed. 'We, in conjunction with some of our col-leagues at the Met, were very close to bringing Pallander to justice just before he died. Another few months and we'd have had what we needed. We were betrayed at the last minute.' He nodded in the direction of Blackstock. 'Much of the dangerous work, collecting evidence and the like, was carried out covertly by Abernethy here. I won't trouble you with the ins and outs at the moment. But it's fair to say that we owe him a great debt of gratitude. You can read everything in the files I'll make available to you after this meeting.'

It took Salt a few moments to process this information. 'So, Abs here worked for you undercover on this case?'

'Abs?' Dixon chuckled. 'I think I'll start calling you that, Abernethy. It's fair to say that much of his work was done in that manner, yes. You'll know that DS Blackstock is a qualified accountant – a forensic one, at that.'

'No,' said Salt, looking at Blackstock with new eyes. But to be fair, she thought, he did look more like an accountant than a police officer.

'In another lifetime,' said Blackstock in his own defence.

'Absolutely. It'll take you time to absorb everything, DI Salt. And there's a great deal to absorb,' said Dixon.

At this point, Andrew appeared with refreshments. Once they all had a mug, and some of Police Scotland's best biscuits, they were ready to resume. This short interlude had given Salt the chance to think.

'Can I ask something, sir?'

'Of course.'

'I take it that we're dealing with the executor. I mean, you suspect that funds of doubtful provenance have been distributed as per Sebastian Pallander's wishes, and it's our job to find out where they've gone and to whom?'

Dixon shot Blackstock a furtive glance.

'Obviously, it's no coincidence that DS Blackstock has been posted to SIE. I'm sure you understand. I had intended to introduce your investigation into Pallander gradually. But events have rather dictated the pace, I'm afraid.'

Dixon stood, arms behind his back in true police style. He paced over to where Salt was sitting. 'Listen, I know that since – well, since the *incident*, you've found yourself rather underused at SIE. It's a backwater, much more suited to someone on the road to retirement. To be quite honest, I don't know what future the department has. It's something of a relic, as you know.'

'Yes, I'm well aware of that, sir. Police Scotland's version of being sent to Siberia.'

'The main reason SIE still exists is that it's been conveni-ent. Convenient to people like me who want to do things rather under the radar, so to speak.'

'I don't understand, sir.'

'It's no coincidence that Abernethy finds himself in your department. But it's also useful to note that your presence is of the same nature.'

'You mean I was placed at Hope Street on purpose – not as a punishment?'

'Yes, by me personally. It wasn't just some throwaway rebuke.' Dixon stood over Salt. 'You've been in this job long enough to know that there are factions dotted here and there in this new force.'

He paced round the room a bit more. 'Any investigation requires funding. And any special request for money must go before the Audit Committee. And once it's been there – again, I'm sure you know what I mean – the request is open to scrutiny, not just from those on the committee itself, but just about every Tom, Dick and Harry who takes an interest.'

'But you want to keep this quiet, yes?'

Dixon nodded. 'First of all, your department is fully funded. Granted, most of that funding is never accessed due to the mundane nature of the majority of your cases. But it's there, nonetheless.'

'You'll pardon me when I say I wasn't aware of that, sir.'

'No reason you should be, DI Salt. Your role is oper-ational, not managerial.' The answer seemed terse. But after all, Dixon was a very senior officer; being curt came with the rank.

'And you intend to utilize these extra funds so that everything is under the radar.'

'Absolutely.' Dixon paused. 'I'm sad to say it, but no organization is free from certain elements who are anxious to look to their own advantage rather than the public good.'

'Corrupt officers,' said Salt flatly.

'Right again. We know that Pallander had police officers on his payroll. We don't know who they are.'

'Police officers?' Salt thought for a moment. 'Surely they'd have to be at a very elevated level to make any difference to Pallander's world? We're not suggesting that, are we?'

Dixon retook his seat. Brushed creases from his trousers with both hands. 'I greatly regret it, Cara, but it's not just the beat bobby or struggling detective who are open to temptation. When the likes of Pallander want things done, they'll move heaven, earth and senior officers to enable it.'

Salt was genuinely shocked. Yes, she'd come up against bent cops before. On one occasion with devastating consequences. But she'd never imagined the men and women who ran the national police force to be anything but incorruptible.

'We were betrayed by someone *very* high up when we nearly had Pallander, ma'am,' said Blackstock.

'Do we know who?' Salt glanced from Blackstock to Dixon.

'I think it would be fair to say that we *suspect*.' Dixon delved into the inside pocket of his suit jacket again, producing a small, bright-red flash drive. 'I want you to take this home and hold on to it. If anything happens to me or Abernethy, look at it. But most definitely not on a Police Scotland device. Once that's done, destroy it. I repeat, this is only to be done if anything happens to either DS Blackstock, myself or both. Is that clear, DI Salt?'

She took possession of the little flash drive, examining it between her thumb and forefinger. She cleared her throat nervously. All of this was a shock – every bit of it. 'Yes, sir, of course. But what happens if I take a look at the content of the flash drive when you and DS Blackstock are still hale and hearty?'

Dixon glanced at Blackstock. 'I find everything is better in context. If you read what's on that little device now, it won't make any difference to my or Abernethy's lives. But it may do something else to yours.'

'I don't get it.' Salt looked between them.

'It's the old adage: sometimes it's better not to know. Anything else?'

'Yes. Do I have any choice as to my involvement in this case?' Cara realized that she wasn't describing her feelings properly. 'I mean, you know how close I came to not being here during the Charfield case, sir. I have a feeling in my gut that this might be even more dangerous.'

Dixon drew in a deep breath. 'I cannot force you to become involved in this. But knowing what you now know, and being the current head of SIE, it would be very awkward. Taking into account the unfortunate events of the Charfield case . . . Well, it may be rather difficult to find a niche for you, if you know what I mean.'

'You mean other officers don't want to work with me? Be honest, sir. I can take it.'

Dixon nodded slowly. 'Yes, you're absolutely correct. Of course, they don't know what I know. If they did, they'd carry you shoulder high. Life is unfair, Cara – in your case, really unfair. But this is a chance to rectify all that.'

Salt sighed and gazed at her right hand. She'd never been able to grow her fingernails like her friends could. While theirs were long, sleek and painted to suit some outfit or other, hers were bitten to the quick. It was maybe nervousness, or perhaps a childhood habit she couldn't break. The very thought of putting herself in harm's way again made her shake and feel sick to her stomach. Though SIE seemed boring and pointless, it had been like spending her days wrapped in an extremely tedious ball of cotton wool. Little satisfaction was to be gained from the job, but at least she knew she'd get home safe and sound at the end of the day.

'And for what it's worth,' said Dixon, 'you'd be doing work of national importance. Suffice it to say, Mr Pallander was involved in financial dealings with people he shouldn't have been anywhere near.'

'Criminals, gangsters?' asked Salt.

'Yes, in some respects. But on a much greater scale. Since the Ukraine conflict, Russia has been rightly ostracized in terms of international trade.'

'But Pallander wasn't interested in any embargoes?'

'We think not. But this is what we must prove. Or what *you* must prove, DI Salt.'

8

The two local constables had been kind, if rather over-awed by the grandeur of the big house. They were young and inexperienced, though they had performed their duty with great sympathy and understating. So much so, Elizabeth Pallander almost reached for her purse to tip them. It was an automatic gesture.

Their message had been a devastating one. And as she sat alone in the lounge, surrounded by old paintings and even older ornaments and knick-knacks, she struggled for breath, her chest tight as a drum at the news of her son's death.

The door swung open. Charles Stuart-Henderson stood in the doorway, shuffling from foot to foot.

'I'm so sorry, Ellie,' he said. 'I came as soon as I heard. Sullivan sent for me.'

'It's very kind of you to take the time,' she said in a whisper.

Stuart-Henderson studied his sister. She'd always been slender. Her height and long limbs adding a gracefulness he could never hope to match. Now, however, she looked pale and drawn, the soft skin on her still youthful face too spare, stretched over her skull like a mask. He supposed that it was just that – a carapace. He was one of the very few who knew his sister's real feelings. How she'd struggled for years at her late husband's side. But now he'd seen how Sebastian's death had hit her hard. She reminded him of a tattered flag in the wind, being blown in almost every direction at once, flailing. Though he hadn't liked his brother-in-law, Stuart-Henderson had to admit that his were large shoes to fill.

'Seb always told him that the green obsession would get him into trouble.'

Elizabeth looked at her brother in bewilderment. 'What on earth was he trying to do?'

'Make a bloody nuisance of himself, that's what. Well, he's paid a heavy price for it – we all have.'

This comment seemed to pull Elizabeth back into something approaching reality. 'You mean the price of grief?'

'Aye, that too. But it'll mean all kinds of problems, mark my words.'

'I'm sorry, you've lost me, Charlie.'

She stood and walked to the big bay window that looked over the grounds of Meikle House, down on to the river below. The great baronial mansion was built amid the remains of a much older castle that had once housed her forebears. Its grounds ended with a long, narrow, private road that had been built in the reign of James VI of Scotland. Though she possessed no title, Elizabeth Pallander could trace her ancestry back to that Stuart king. That descent had formed the backbone of the family for generations, until her father had wasted a small fortune and Meikle House ended up in the possession of the late Sebastian Pallander.

The spring sunshine, washed by heavy showers, lent the dark sky an almost ethereal quality. Her attention was caught by a golden eagle as it flew just above the Douglas firs on the ridge above the house.

'What are you watching?' said Stuart-Henderson.

'The eagle's back. It's the first time I've seen him in an age.'

Stuart-Henderson shook his head and groaned as he took a seat on the red couch. 'I really am sorry, Ellie. It's just too hard. Nobody should have to bury their child.'

Elizabeth's only reply was to swallow back the tears she'd been brought up to subdue. 'What are the problems you're talking about?'

'Ellie, your husband died only a few months ago. We've had a very public distribution of his wealth – all according to his last wishes. The whole nature of the thing was bizarre. JL's death will set tongues wagging. You know what people are like.'

'My son lost his life. It's a tragedy. What else is there to say?'

'It's a soap opera for the terminally stupid.'

'Do you think he did it on purpose? Took his own life?' Elizabeth turned to face her brother.

'I've just spoken to McWilliams, the chief superintendent. The police don't know for certain yet, but they're working on the theory that he was about to blow up a wind turbine. Something went wrong with the explosives.'

Elizabeth scanned the sky, to find the golden eagle again, but it had gone with the sunshine. Great spots of rain were now thudding against the window. They quickly transformed into a thoroughgoing downpour.

'You should come with me to the lodge. The reporters will descend on this place like flies. I'm surprised they're not here already.'

'They won't get inside the house, and I'm certainly not going out. I've had the gamekeepers block the road. If they come, they'll have to do so over the hills and on foot.' She shut the curtains to emphasize the point. 'I'm safe here.'

'Don't put it past them. I'm not talking about Menzies from the *Courier*. The tabloid chaps will be here, you mark my words.'

'Where is he now?'

'Menzies?'

'No, Jean-Luc!' Her eyes flashed with irritation.

Charles Stuart-Henderson wasn't keen on sugar-coating what had to be said. He wanted to tell his grieving sister that her son was spread across a large part of West Dunbartonshire. But given the circumstances, he relented. 'His remains are with the police, Ellie. Do the rest of the children know?'

'I have no idea.'

'I'll call them.' Stuart-Henderson removed a mobile phone from his jacket pocket.

'No!'

'Sorry?'

'They'll know, trust me. And if you call them, they'll want to talk to me. And quite frankly I don't have the strength to go through this over and over again. I'm going to lie down.'

With all the dignity and poise she could muster, she then raised her chin and left the room.

'Do you want me to organize the staff? Tell them what's happened?' her brother shouted as the door shut behind her.

No response. He decided to do it anyway. He would go in search of Sullivan, the housekeeper.

9

Salt and Blackstock were back in Hope Street, the former now utterly confused by the morning's events. It wasn't every day that you discovered the job you thought you were doing wasn't really *your* job at all. And to make matters worse, you were part of something that sounded not only dangerous but verging on the illegal. Most certainly off the books as far as Police Scotland was concerned.

'You should have told me,' said Salt, addressing the man sitting opposite her.

'Orders, ma'am. I'm sure you understand.'

'No, not really. I feel as though I've fallen down the rabbit hole. Aye, and you're not the hapless twitcher I took you for.'

'Hapless?' Blackstock looked put out.

'No, you're shifty rather than hapless, to be honest.'

'That's me told. I shall try to remain as un-shifty as possible, ma'am.'

'Good.'

'We better get going. There's no time like the present, ma'am.'

'Go where?'

'I'd start with the mother, if I were you. But it's your call.'

She had more respect for Blackstock following the

conversation with Dixon. Salt was still annoyed at the way he'd been able to pull the wool over her eyes, but this was an opportunity to rescue her own career – however risky. Do this right and she'd have a chance to progress in the police, despite her father's predictions and her mishap. But what was the point of proving a dead man wrong? And judging by what the ACC said, she wasn't sure she'd judged her late parent properly anyway. Perhaps he wasn't a remote, uncaring man who was obsessed with her success or perceived failure.

'Tell me more about them – the Pallander family, I mean. I assume you are intimately acquainted with them,' said Salt.

'Pretty easy to summarize, ma'am. You know about our deceased patriarch, Sebastian. His wife is from an old Scottish family. It may have been a love match when they were young, but one thinks that rather died on the vine. People say she was coerced into the marriage in order to save Meikle House. Whatever the truth, she has always proved to be a good foil for her husband's perceived excess.'

'And what about the children?'

'I think they were set against each other to see who would emerge as a suitable heir. Silas and Tabitha are the oldest. She's a smart cookie – very like her father. Silas is the oldest child, but distinctly number two in the pecking order. A bit of a wimp, from what I hear. Desperately jealous of his sister, certainly. Must be hard to be born to the top job then mess it up.'

'And the other three?'

'The spares, I think one would call them. Alicia – Alice to the family – is an "artist".'

'Why say it in that way, Abs?'

'Well, it's like me wanting to be a rock star. The aspiration just isn't enough. She can paint a passable landscape.

62

But if it wasn't for Mummy's handouts, she'd have to find a proper job.'

'OK. And Jean-Luc has a twin sister?'

'Audrey. The exception that proves the rule. Neither avaricious, bombastic nor grasping. Lives a quiet life in Oxfordshire with her husband and children. Kind soul, they say. Good can come from even the worst families.'

'And let me guess: Jean-Luc was the wild child, the rebel?'

'I think so. As much as he was allowed to be. Not easy within the Pallander family dynamic, I'd say. I heard his father sent men to pull him off an anti-oil protest when he was a teenager. Didn't go easy on him either.'

'Makes me glad of my dysfunctional upbringing,' said Salt, deep in thought.

'You and me both, ma'am.'

Salt bit her lip for a moment or two. 'OK, we go to Perthshire. We'll take your car. I don't want mine getting muddy on these bloody country roads.'

'I'm surprised you're bothered, given the state it's in inside. But if I'm to drive, I'll take the main road, not some farm tracks, ma'am. We should stay relatively mud-free.'

As Silas Pallander still had the company jet at his disposal for a short time longer, he decided to use it. Heavy rain spilled from a leaden sky as his chauffeur-driven Mercedes pulled up beside the Bombardier Global 6000 on the runway at London City Airport.

He flicked through his iPhone as his PA braved the weather to make sure the plane was ready to board. After a few moments reading about politics, football and general gossip the door clicked back open and Anna Marchand sat beside him, brushing rain off the shoulders of her coat.

'Give them five minutes, Mr Pallander. It's a new pilot and he's just familiarizing himself with the controls, apparently.'

'Are you fucking serious?'

'Yes, of course I am.'

Silas cast his eyes along the length of the sleek private jet. Though he'd been flying all his life, he still couldn't muster huge confidence in the process. But the journey between London and the small private airport near Meikle House would be less than an hour.

'Where are the usual guys?'

'Sorry, who?' Anna was fiddling with a MacBook.

'The usual pilots – the ones we've had for years. I don't think I've ever flown in this plane without one of them at the controls.'

'I have no idea. Shall we begin our deep breathing, Mr Pallander?'

A smatter of heavy rain slashed against the window.

'Yes, that would help. Thanks, Anna.'

She placed the laptop in the footwell at her feet and turned to Silas. 'OK, you know the score. Sit up straight, close your eyes and breathe in through your nose with me.'

He did as he was told. He heard Anna do the same.

'That's it. Problems in – problems out. Problems in – problems out.' Anna opened one eye to check on her boss's progress. He was breathing as instructed, his eyes tight shut. In many ways, he was like a little boy. But most men were, in her experience. 'You're doing well. Just feel the anxiety drift away like melting snow,' said Anna in her slow, low, French-accented voice. 'That's it.'

'This is doing the trick.'

'Don't speak!' Anna put a long finger to his lips, as she ran her other hand through her mane of wet red hair. 'Keep going.'

Fred the chauffeur turned round in his seat and looked at them through the unengaged privacy glass. Anna stuck her tongue out at him, and he turned back with a grin.

'OK, sir. We should be feeling a little more relaxed now. A couple more times.'

Silas Pallander finished his last supervised breath and opened his eyes. Though he did feel calmer, the thought that he'd never see his younger brother again made him infinitely sad; a cold, hopeless emptiness that shocked him. 'I might just pop one of these tranquilizers. After all, it's going to be bloody hard back at the house. It was bad enough when my father died – and hardly anybody liked him.'

'Mr Pallander! You shouldn't say such things.' Anna nodded towards the chauffeur to alert her boss that he would be listening. 'Your father was a wonderful man – truly brilliant. People like him never win popularity contests because everyone is jealous of their success. He was a treasure. You don't need pills and potions. It's mind over matter.' She bent forward to retrieve the laptop, furtively wiping away a tear as she did.

'Right, we're being waved aboard. Have you got an umbrella?'

She glared at him, her coat still damp, hair hanging down in straggles. 'What do you think, Mr Pallander?'

'Well, we can make a bolt for it. Come on.' Silas pushed open his side door, just before the chauffeur could get to it.

'You go,' said Anna, 'I'll follow. I have a few things here to get together.'

'OK – don't be long.'

Pallander left the car and scurried towards the jet, his jacket pulled up over his head. Anna looked on as a smart air attendant rushed towards him with an umbrella.

'He's putty in your hands, girl,' said Fred, now back in the car.

'I don't know what you mean, Freddie. He's my boss.'

'Not for long, he ain't.'

'Like you, Freddie, I exist only to serve.' Anna winked at the driver then placed the laptop and a mobile phone in her handbag.

'Have a safe journey, girl,' said Fred as she exited the car. He watched her cross the tarmac towards the jet. No scurrying for her. She walked straight-backed on to the jet, rain or no rain.

'That's the spirit,' he muttered to himself, before starting the engine and pulling away.

On board, Silas was sitting on one of the executive flight chairs. No risk of deep vein thrombosis here. Though the aircraft could be reconfigured, there were currently only eight such seats, plus a bedroom and bathroom. It was luxury in the extreme. It had been Sebastian Pallander's second home, prior to his death. Now it would be used by the fat executive Baucher, who would replace Tabitha as boss of the company.

The attendant showed Anna to her seat and handed her a towel to dry her hair.

The pilot made his way to where they were sitting. His white shirt and black trousers were neatly ironed into sharp creases, while his epaulettes bore four gold bands.

'Mr Pallander, I'm Captain Ashiri. It is an honour to pilot this aircraft for you today.' He smiled broadly, holding his hand out for Silas to shake.

'Thank you. Your work is much appreciated.' Silas glanced out of the window. 'This rain is still heavy. Will we be able to take off?

'Yes, sir. We shall leave in approximately five minutes.

And please, don't worry about the conditions. They are to improve shortly. I hope you have a good flight. Please ask an attendant if you wish to know anything from me.'

'Thank you, Captain Ashiri.' Pallander watched the pilot head back to the cockpit. 'Where's he from, Anna?'

She ignored the question. 'He's very efficient, I think.' She was brushing her damp hair back off her face now.

'You think?'

'Sounds that way to me.' She shrugged.

Silas bit his lip. 'Excuse me!' He called to one of the flight attendants. 'Can I have some water, please? I have to take a tablet.'

'Of course, sir. Right away.'

Anna looked on as her boss closed his eyes and began his deep breathing. The dismissive shake of her head was barely perceptible.

10

The first thing that struck Salt when she stepped into Blackstock's electric Nissan was the spotlessness of it all. He'd said it was perfect, and it was. Despite having a registration proving it was around two years old. There was no detritus in the car at all; no overflowing ashtray, discarded crisp packets, muddy footwells – nothing.

'I don't think I've ever been in a car as tidy as this,' said Salt.

'I don't understand why people want to drive about in mobile skips. If I went to your home and found all sorts lying about on the floor, I'd be shocked. How is a car any different?'

'Prepare yourself for a shock if you pay me a visit.'

Blackstock programmed the satnav for as close to Meikle House as the device would recognize.

'I thought you knew the way?' said Salt.

'I do. But I don't know if there have been accidents, roadworks or the like. This way I'm prepared.'

Though this made absolute sense to Salt, it wasn't something she'd ever considered. If she was driving to a place she knew, she just drove. Normally to the accompaniment of the grunge bands she'd loved as a teenager. 'Will this thing get us there? I mean, does it have the juice?'

'I make sure it's fully charged every day, ma'am. We'll get there with charge to spare.'

'Fabulous, I'm sure. But what happens when we get to deepest, darkest Perthshire and discover there are no charging points, eh?'

'There are,' said Blackstock abruptly. The detective sergeant checked his mirrors and started the car by means of a button on the steering column.

And so, their journey began. They joined the motorway, and soon the hubbub of Glasgow was far behind. Little towns and villages swept by to the eerie whine of the electric engine. And despite Salt's request, Blackstock refused to 'give it heft' by putting his foot to the floor. For her, being in an electric vehicle was a novelty, and Salt wanted to examine every aspect of the experience.

Their conversation began to peter out once Blackstock stopped droning on about this place and that as they passed by. He appeared to know every aspect of history and landscape. In truth, she was left with a nagging feeling of inadequacy, quietly wishing that she could muster the same knowledge on a subject – any subject.

But like her father before her, Cara Salt engaged in little else but her job. She'd lost hope of ever snagging a husband – wasn't sure if she even wanted one since *he'd* gone. She liked a drink, but the abuse of alcohol could hardly be marked down as a hobby. She enjoyed reading, or at least the thought of it. But more often than not she found herself giving up on books well before they reached their conclusion. This was either because she couldn't relate to the characters, or the plots were so mind-numbingly dull that she barely cared what happened next. The last book she'd picked up was about a young female journalist who seemed impossibly heroic. It looked interesting but soon began to drag and she lost interest. She'd googled the author only to find he was a man in late middle age who, by the look of his picture, suffered terrible constipation.

Her friends – before they were consumed by marriage and children – had tried hard to interest her in various life-improving activities. There was skiing, the opera, wild camping, sailing, golf, amateur dramatics; the list went on and on. None of them appealed, and it wasn't because she found no merit in the activities. Cara Salt had spent an entire childhood being directed by her father. She had done – exclusively – what he wanted to do, no questions asked. And now the endless list of diversions that had been laid out before her amounted to little more than one of the joyless to-do lists her father had so favoured. These days, apart from a quick coffee or a rushed lunch, her friends were gone, and she settled for the TV and the odd long walk.

As the countryside flashed by, Salt reasoned that, at last, she had a case in which to lose herself.

'Penny for them,' said Blackstock.

'Just musing on the pointlessness of existence, that's all,' Salt replied.

'Ah, that old chestnut. I must admit to having considered that myself since – well, since I've been on my own.'

'You've got your birds.'

'Yes, endlessly fascinating. But they don't tend to be very good conversationalists.'

'Parrots?'

'Indeed. But few and far between on Loch Lomond.' He paused to listen to an instruction from the satnav. 'Though a widowed lady from the village has taken a great interest in me.'

'Tell all, Abs.'

'She has her own bungalow. Well-heeled, by all accounts.'

'A looker?'

'In her day, I should say so.'

'And when was her day?'

'As she's eighty-three, I'd say at least sixty years ago.'

Salt laughed. 'Oh well, you're at least doing better than me. Though the window cleaner winked at me last week. And before you say it, he has no teeth, so it's a no-go.'

'I see. Unfortunate.'

'How long do we have to go?' For Salt, the countryside had become more pleasing; the hills had a greater roll, the vistas where more appealing. It was the Perthshire she remembered as a child on endless cold, wet camping trips.

'About half an hour, I'd say,' said Blackstock.

'What do we call ourselves when we get there?'

'I'd rather hoped you'd got that covered, ma'am.'

'Well, we can't say we're from SIE, that you're under-cover and I don't know what I am, can we?'

'No, not the best solution, ma'am.'

DI Salt thought hard. She reasoned that although any family would have been visited by police officers already regarding the death of a family member, it was doubtful they'd have spoken to officers who had actually visited the scene. 'We're liaison from Glasgow, Abs. We were at the turbines, so we can tell the mother what we saw. What's her name again?'

'Elizabeth Pallander, ma'am. But I would tread warily when it comes to being too descriptive.' Blackstock took in his passenger with a doubtful expression.

'I'm not going to tell her we found his bollocks three hundred yards away from his arse, am I? We need an *in*. Liaison is the very thing.'

'In my experience – undercover, I mean – being as unspecific as possible is the best policy.'

'Oh, aye. So, we just blunder round the houses as we tell a grieving wife and mother that we really don't know anything. No, that won't do. Leave this to me, Abs.'

The drive thereafter was – despite Blackstock's prediction – made along muddy country lanes. Once they'd passed Kinloch Rannoch, they turned on to a narrow, single-track road. Three men in Barbour jackets emerged, two of them with shotguns cracked over their arms. When Blackstock produced his warrant card, they were permitted to go on their way, up a road that wound up a hill and into a veritable forest of deciduous trees at odds with their more numerous coniferous counterparts.

'That can't be legal,' said Salt. 'If they're gamekeepers, they should be wrangling poachers, not directing traffic with menaces.'

'In places like this gamekeeping covers a multitude of sins, ma'am.'

Blackstock halted the car when they reached a set of tall, ornate gates.

'This is us, ma'am. Meikle House,' said Blackstock.

'Go on, then,' said Salt, nodding her head in the general direction of an intercom unit on a post supporting the gates.

'I'm not sure that I'll be completely anonymous, you know.'

'Meaning?'

'Though I mainly shadowed Sebastian Pallander in office settings, I can't be sure we won't encounter people from that world, if you like.'

'The children, you mean? What's left of them,' said Salt.

'No, I never met them – purposely. But you never know. I'd like to assess that when we get in, if you don't mind.'

Salt sighed as she exited Blackstock's car. Here was where

the deception would begin. She walked to the intercom, noting a CCTV camera higher up on the post, trained in her direction. She pressed the buzzer.

'Can I help you?' The reply was curt.

'Police. I'm DI Salt. We'd like to speak with Mrs Pallander, please.' Salt was equally businesslike.

There was hesitation before she received an answer.

'Are you aware that Chief Superintendent McWilliams is in the house already?'

'No, why should I be? We're from the Liaison Department in Glasgow. I'm sure I don't have to tell you why we're here.'

'I see. We'll buzz you through. But you'll have to pass security at the main door.'

Salt bridled instantly. 'We are police officers on an investigation, not a laundry company. Open these gates. I'll expect to see Mrs Pallander at her earliest convenience.'

As she walked away, she heard a buzz, and the big gates slowly swung open.

11

Silas Pallander was happier now they were flying high above the clouds. In fact, the sky was so blue, the sun so bright, he had to remove his Persol sunglasses from the inside pocket of his jacket and put them on to protect his eyes from the glare.

He gazed at Anna for a few moments. She was typing feverishly on a MacBook, the keys providing a percussive element to their journey, sounding just above the low rush of the jet engines.

He thought of his brother. Unlike most of his siblings, he and JL had rubbed along pretty well. Apart from the usual big-brother-little-brother badinage, their relationship had been one of the least turbulent dynamics within the family. Though their father's last wishes had punctured his children in different ways, Jean-Luc seemed least affected. His earlier attempts to create an efficient renewables company had failed. Their father had shown little interest, and it had wound up a job for the liquidators.

It was then that Silas realized just how different they were in character. The elder Pallander son would have died to have such a business failure on his conscience. Jean-Luc didn't seem to care; and in any event, his focus had long been on environmental activism. His dabbling in business had been yet another manifestation of what was expected of a Pallander child. The notion was that each of them should be a mini version of their father, perfect in every possible way.

'What are you so busy with, Anna?' said Pallander.

'Just a report.'

Silas bit his lip. 'I haven't given you anything for weeks.'

'It isn't for you, Mr Pallander.'

'It's for Baucher, isn't it?'

Anna sighed, looking at him for the first time in the conversation. 'Yes, it's for *Mr* Baucher.'

'I'm sorry, Anna. This thing with my brother isn't helping my manners. I know you had no choice but to work for the man who's taking my father's place.'

Anna gazed out of the window at the white clouds passing just underneath the aircraft. 'I did.'

'Did what?'

'Have a choice. You said I had no choice, but that's not true.'

Silas furrowed his brow. 'You mean they offered you another position?'

'Yes, they did.'

'Are you being purposely coy? We've always been able to talk. What did they offer you?'

'You won't like it.'

Now he was bemused. 'Listen, I'm more concerned with what's happening to me and my family than your travails. But we've known each other for a long time. I like you, and it matters to me what happens to you, OK?'

She stared at him, her big blue eyes wide and guileless. 'They asked me if I wanted to come and work with you in your new job on the estate.' Anna held his gaze for a moment before recommencing her typing.

'A joke, right?' Though Silas was smiling, it was a thin, nervous expression.

'No, I don't joke, you know that. When have I ever joked with you?'

'Fuck. Why didn't you say something before now?'

'There was no reason. I decided not to take it. I wanted a different boss – a promotion.' Anna's shrug was of the Gallic variety.

'OK, so after being my PA for years, you just decide to jump ship. How nice.'

'It's nothing to do with *jumping ship*. It's a career choice. I'm not tied to you with chains!'

Silas sighed and checked his phone. His PA continued typing. The hiatus lasted for almost two minutes.

'I didn't ask to be in charge of the estate, you know. I get that you didn't want to be stuck in Scotland. It's a shame, though. You must remember how beautiful it is? I don't know how much you've really seen of the wider estate since . . . well, before.'

Anna closed the lid of her laptop. 'When your father took me in as an orphan, you mean? I don't want to have this conversation, Mr Pallander. I made my decision, and that's the end of it.'

'I thought we were friends, Anna.'

'We work together. Maybe for too long, yes?'

'Really? I mean, haven't you been happy?'

Again, the shrug.

'At least say something, for fuck's sake!' Silas banged his fist on the arm of his flight chair out of frustration.

'You're under stress, I don't want to add to that.'

'You're – not – making – any – sense.' He said the words in isolation, an arrogant staccato. 'I didn't think for one moment you would abandon me like this.'

'You should have found yourself a wife.'

'That's none of your damned business!'

'It is when all you want to do is treat me like one.'

'That's nonsense.'

'Is it? You've been making passes at me for years. Asking advice on clothes, your home – everything.' Anna leaned forward in her seat. 'Look at this very morning, for example. The breathing. You're like a child, a child-man. Getting you ready to step on a plane isn't part of my job. A wife should help in such matters.'

It was Silas Pallander's turn to lean forward. He lowered his voice so none of the flight crew could hear. 'So, a couple of years ago – in the Shard – that was just you being my PA?'

She shook her head; a strand of red hair fell over her face. 'I was drunk. I felt sorry for you. One of the biggest mistakes of my life. It was like a two-minute *entr'acte*.' In her anger, Anna had reverted to her native French.

'A bloody intermission! You cheeky bitch!'

Silas shook his head in genuine disbelief. He'd always assumed that Anna held a candle for him. And apart from their little *indiscretion* after an office party, they had, in a mutually unspoken way, decided to keep their burning desire for each other quiet, their relationship business-like. But that fantasy was now at an end.

'Suck it up, you sad little boy,' said Anna. She got to her feet and walked to the back of the jet, where the toilet and bedroom were located.

Despite his anger, Silas Pallander felt genuine shock. His was the genuine pain of loss and dread of parting, as though the woman he'd coveted for so long had genuinely been his spouse. His heart, broken following the death of his father and brother and even more by his demotion, was now becoming a weight in his chest, too heavy to bear.

77

The fact he was trapped on a private jet amidst so much misery made the situation even worse. He couldn't seek solace in the bedroom because she was in there, and he desperately didn't want to inflame the situation further. He hoped her mood would pass. After all, who knew what his fiery redheaded assistant might do or say in the heat of the moment?

Then he remembered the new pilot had told him just to ask if he wanted to know something. He'd spend as much time in the cockpit as he could – the rest of the flight, if need be. But just as Silas Pallander got to his feet, the plane seemed to plummet in the air. He was flung forward, catching his chin on the chair on which Anna had been sitting, knocking off his sunglasses. He was roused from momentary unconsciousness by a scream. A flight attendant flew headlong towards him down the aisle between the chairs. She lay still on the floor. A pool of blood was forming on the thick beige carpet underneath his head.

When he first felt a gentle touch on his brow, he flinched, expecting it was the precursor to a blow, a blow that might be the last thing he'd ever experience. But as he lifted his head, he saw Anna. Her alabaster face paler still, eyes wide with shock.

'Quick, get to your feet. Come with me!' She dragged Silas off the carpet, helped her stumbling boss to the bedroom at the back of the plane and closed the door.

Anna struggled with the lock, eventually managing to secure it. As she tried to catch her breath, the aircraft veered to the right, knocking her off her feet. She landed with a thud, her face only inches from Silas's.

'Anna, what's happening?' he squealed.

'I don't know, honestly, I don't know.' Anna pushed

herself into a sitting position and cradled Silas's bloodied head in her lap.

'I just want you to know I love you, Anna. I always will.'

Silas's eyes closed as he drifted into unconsciousness. And then there was an urgent knock on the bedroom door.

12

Cara Salt wasn't sure what to make of Meikle House. That the place was huge and beautifully situated on the banks of a river in a small – she assumed private – valley, there was no doubt. But despite expensive paintings, opulent furniture and ornaments, she was surprised to note that some things were less than pristine. For instance, the room in which they'd been asked to wait had a tartan carpet that had seen better days, the pile worn flat to the warp and weft in places. The couch they sat upon was sprouting straw from one arm. Generally, there was an air of damp and decay about the room. It reminded her of a flat on the Royal Mile in Edinburgh where an old boy-friend had lived when he was a student. It had fading grandeur.

'This isn't what I expected,' whispered Salt under her breath.

Blackstock looked at her blankly. 'I don't know what you mean.'

'Well, I thought it would be rugged on the outside, and all *Vogue* magazine indoors.'

'I've never seen *Vogue* magazine, ma'am.'

'You don't have to have read it to notice holes in the carpet and half a cornfield bursting out the sofa.'

'Remember, this is a very old house.'

It was clear to Salt that this impressed Blackstock. But she could detect something else. Whereas her detective sergeant looked awkward in most situations, here, and in Dixon's office at Gartcosh, he seemed at home. 'She comes from Heilan' gentry, then?'

'Much grander than that. The family descend from the Stuart kings. The family name is Stuart-Henderson, after all.'

'That makes things worse, surely? You expect your aristocrats to pay a little more attention when it comes to curating our nation's history.'

'Precisely the opposite, I'd say,' said Blackstock.

'And you know this how?'

'Because I'm one of them, ma'am.'

'Aye, right,' was Salt's initial response. But as she looked for a witty riposte from Blackstock, she noticed that none was forthcoming. 'You're serious, aren't you?'

'Yes, sadly I am. I was brought up in a place not unlike this. Not quite as big, but equally grand.'

'You'll be telling me your ancestors were kings next.' Salt laughed.

'Yes, as a matter of fact they were.'

She was about to interrogate Blackstock further on the matter when the door was flung open. Standing in the uniform of a chief superintendent, complete with braided cap, fancy epaulettes and brown gloves, appeared a man of average height. Salt hadn't seen a uniform like it for years and was surprised they still existed.

'Who the devil are you two?' said the senior officer, a distinct Highland sibilance in his voice.

'I'm DI Salt and this is DS Blackstock. We're here on family liaison from Glasgow. We visited the crime scene this morning. Not a pretty sight, sir.'

It was abundantly clear that Chief Superintendent McWilliams wasn't interested in anything she had to say. He was staring, almost open-mouthed, at Blackstock.

'Abernethy – I mean, sir. Is that you?'

'Yes, sir, I rather think it is.'

'Please don't call me "sir", *sir*.' The chief superintendent removed his cap and held it out in front of him like a shield, passing it through two hands nervously. 'My goodness, I've not seen you since we were at Fettes.'

'True enough, Innes. It's good to see you again after all this time.'

Salt looked between the two men as though she was witnessing something new to mankind. Had it not been for the fact her father had drummed into her as a child that gaping wouldn't be tolerated, her mouth would have been hanging open in amazement. She whispered to Blackstock, 'You and I have to talk, Abs.'

Ignoring his boss, Blackstock continued to address the chief superintendent. 'I think it's important that we try to convey at least something of what happened earlier today, Innes. If it were my son – well, I'd like to know how he died. Wouldn't you?'

'Of course. And I know you'll be able to couch it just so. No doubt about that.'

Salt observed the two men further. There was clear subservience on the part of the senior officer, while Abernethy appeared to find nothing unusual in a chief superintendent fawning over a retired detective sergeant. In her whole career, she'd never seen anything like it. Blackstock suddenly had the air of someone utterly at home in his skin. Her instinct had been right – Blackstock was very comfortable here. The connection between her second-in-command

and the assistant chief constable now became obvious, where hitherto it had been unclear.

'I'll show you through to speak to Mrs Pallander. I wonder, does she know you at all, Abernethy?'

'I met her when I was a child. Too many years ago to remember, I'm sure. Though she knows my family passingly well.'

'Yes, just so,' said McWilliams. 'Will you come with me, please, Abernethy?' He made to leave the room but checked himself when he saw Salt rise to her feet. 'DI Salt, I think it best that Mrs Pallander be bothered as little as possible. One officer will be able to relate the circumstances behind her son's death. We don't want to overwhelm the poor woman.'

Salt opened her mouth to speak but was beaten to it by Blackstock.

'If that's true, Innes, then DI Salt must be the one to speak to her. After all, she is my superior.'

'Very well. If you feel DI Salt should be in the room, who am I to argue?'

McWilliams said this with a confused look on his face. He waved Salt forward into the corridor. Soon, all three of them were making their way along musty passageways to meet the widow of the late Sebastian Pallander.

13

Tabitha Pallander had heard the news of her younger brother's death when walking in the woods near her home on the outskirts of Oxford. Her uncle Charlie had been the harbinger of this particular doom, his name showing in bold letters across the screen of her iPhone. She was quickly learning to dread a call or message from him. It had all happened so quickly. First her father, now her brother.

On her own, accompanied only by her two lurchers, Tabitha wound her way back home in an almost dream-like state. She played out images of Jean-Luc. A young boy on a beach in the south of France; a smart young man playing violin so beautifully at a recital in the Wigmore Hall; driving a red Ferrari by Lake Como; bringing his girlfriend, Tiz, to meet the family for the first time, just before they married. She recalled that her father disapproved. But then, as she knew best of all, finding her father's approval had been an almost impossible task.

Tiz, she thought. How would she cope? Tabitha resolved to find out when she made it home. Though she wasn't sure how close she and Jean-Luc had been in the last year or so. Tiz wasn't happy at Jean-Luc's ever more radical views on how to address the climate issue. He'd paid a heavy price for his beliefs, it seemed.

Tabitha Pallander loved these woods in every season. But now, with everything blooming, the force of life pulsing through the mulchy ground under the great canopy of the trees, she felt the promise of renewal. In effect unemployed, this place in summer should have been the perfect analogy for her life. Time for a new beginning.

But everything had changed. Her father had gone, leaving her with nothing. And now her brother. Tabitha's heart ached.

Tears. She hated anyone seeing her cry, so she stopped and leaned against an old oak. It was a sight that would have surprised some members of her family and shocked others. This strong woman, the second voice of the Pallander clan, cut down by the sheer force of emotion. She surprised herself when her body convulsed in sobs. But the dam had burst, the forces too strong for it to resist.

The whole thing reminded her of the flutter in her chest during the desperate race to be number one in her father's eyes. It had been there since early childhood. The circumstances were very different, but she felt that anxiety back now as though she was going through it all over again. She'd always known she was cleverer, quicker, braver and stronger than her brother Silas. But the sheer effort it took – every day – to maintain this in front of her father was almost crushing. And it had all been in vain. For Tabitha, what hurt wasn't the loss of an expected fortune. No. She lamented her ebbing power. That was the real prize she'd struggled for.

She felt crushed. The bright flame in the family; its one genuinely free spirit.

'You stupid little bastard!' she wailed at the top of her voice. The trees made no comment, only shifting, leaves rustling in the light breeze under the bright blue sky. The sun twinkled through foliage and branches, making the world magical, despite the great emptiness in her heart.

'Are you all right?'

The voice came from behind. Tabitha swung round to face it, as her dogs thudded back to her side from their rooting around on the woodland floor. They barked, keeping the stranger with the red rucksack at bay.

'Jake, Langtry, be quiet!' Tabitha chided her pets. Dutifully, the dogs' barking lowered to a menacing growl.

'I'm sorry, I heard you shouting. I assumed you were in some distress – silly of me, really.' The man shifted his weight from foot to foot, clearly embarrassed.

'No need to be sorry. It was me who was roaring to absolutely nobody. Thank you for checking up on me. Very kind.' Tabitha held out a hand. 'I'm Tabitha Pallander, by the way.'

'Thomas – Tom Durling, pleased to meet you. I say, are you sure you're feeling OK?' he said, noting her red-rimmed eyes and a tear on her cheek.

'I've just had some rather bad news. My younger brother died in an accident this morning. I'm afraid to say it caught me rather by surprise.'

'Damn, no wonder.' He looked about helplessly. 'Is there anything I can do for you at all?'

'No, nothing, thanks. I'm only about half a mile from home. I'll pour myself a stiff whisky when I get back, that should do the trick. My uncle swears a good dram will cure all ills. But thanks again.' Tabitha smiled at Durling.

'Well, I hope to see you again. We've just moved here, and I do so love walking in these woods.'

'Oh, where did you move from?'

'Cornwall – just near Bude. But I have a new job, and as much as we loved our old home, it was completely impractical. I'm not quite at the helicopter level of salary yet.' He laughed thinly.

'I'm sure you'll love it here.'

'Well, I'll leave you to this beautiful day. Nice to have met you, Tabitha. And please accept my sincere condolences. What a terrible thing to have happened.'

She thanked him and watched as he strode back to the path on the other side of the oaks. No matter how dark the world, there was still light somewhere, she thought. Tabitha set off for home.

Durling stopped when he'd gone far enough to be out of sight of the woman he'd just met. He listened quietly, hearing her make her way through the woods before he removed a mobile phone from the right side-pocket of his rucksack.

He waited until the call was answered. 'I've made contact. As you predicted, she's walking through the woods. There aren't many people about right now.'

He paid close attention to the voice on the other end of the call before ending it without ceremony, shrugging off his rucksack and placing the phone back in the side pocket. He listened with his eyes closed. The man who called himself Durling unzipped the rucksack and checked its contents: a small Primus stove, three freeze-dried food sachets, some peanuts, a small tarp and a Mac-11 compact machine gun. It wasn't the most modern – not even the most efficient. But he'd been using it for almost three decades. And with any luck, it would always be by his side.

He secured the rucksack again and thrust it over his shoulder. Wandering off the track, he looked around for a reasonably well cleared piece of ground that wasn't abutted by widow-makers: trees that were in immediate danger of collapse or likely to shed high, heavy branches. Finding himself a spot quite quickly, Durling removed the tarp from the bag, set it up with some cordage and lit the little stove. He unstrapped a large bottle of water from the side of his bag and poured it into a stainless-steel mug. After all, everything stopped for tea. And right now, he'd nothing to do but wait.

14

A big, rather florid man of late middle age opened the door, to find Chief Superintendent McWilliams, DI Salt and DS Blackstock standing there. He frowned at McWilliams then looked the other two police officers up and down as though they'd sprung fully formed from another planet.

'What's this?'

'Sir,' said the chief superintendent, fawning in much the same way he had to Blackstock. 'This is DS Blackstock and DI . . .' He hesitated.

'DI Salt, sir,' she said for him, irritated that her detective sergeant had seemingly overtaken her in the pecking order.

'What do you want? My sister is grieving the loss of her son. It's a terrible tragedy. That, on top of the trauma of suffering her husband's untimely death. We've spoken to the chief superintendent, why on earth should we want to speak to you?' But then it was Charles Stuart-Henderson's turn to hesitate. He cocked his head and stared at the detective sergeant. 'Blackstock, you say. No relation to Torquil Blackstock, I suppose? You have look of him.'

'My elder brother, sir. I'm Abernethy.'

Stuart-Henderson's expression changed almost instantly. 'You mean wee Abernethy? Good gracious, you were a toddler when I last saw you. What a thing! Come in, come in. How is Tor these days? I haven't seen him in – well, must be ten years, at least.'

'He's well, sir,' said Blackstock. 'Spends most of his time in South Africa.'

'Yes, that's right. Your family owns half of the Transvaal. I'd forgotten. Well, please tell him I'm asking for him.' He shook his head and smiled. 'I can still hardly credit it's you. My, how time flies. *Tempus fugit*, indeed!' He showed the police officers into a space he described as an anteroom. 'You must forgive Elizabeth, she's been through so much. Please, what is it you wish to relate to her?'

Blackstock opened his mouth to speak, but before the words would come Salt provided the answer.

'We visited the scene of Mr Pallander's death this morning. I thought maybe his mother would like to hear what happened. Properly, I mean.'

'A dreadful accident. I'm sad to say it, but Jean-Luc sometimes sacrificed his own safety for these hobbyhorse notions. He thought himself a daredevil. I thought him rather reckless, not to say foolish. I take no pride in knowing I was correct in this assessment. So much life wasted.'

'If you don't mind me saying, sir, I'm not entirely sure his death was down to *any daredevil antics*. Though we can't confirm anything yet, the strong feeling is that Mr Pallander's death may have been foul play. It's an ongoing investigation, of course. This is what I mean about Mrs Pallander being in full possession of the facts,' said Salt.

At this news, the blood drained from Stuart-Henderson's face. He stepped back and sat heavily in an armchair. His head bowed, chest rising and falling as he breathed deeply. 'This is the worst news – the *very* worst,' he muttered to himself before looking at Chief Superintendent McWilliams with narrowed eyes. 'Why didn't you mention this, Innes? I told you, not a varnished story. I may be in a castle but it's not a fairy-tale one!'

'I'm so sorry, sir.' McWilliams glared at Cara Salt. 'This is the first I've heard of it. Glasgow operates like another country when it comes to information sharing – still.'

Stuart-Henderson stroked his chin. 'My sister will want to know, of course, however hard. She's no shrinking violet, DI Salt. But perhaps it's best you relate these events to me in detail, and I'll break the news to Elizabeth.'

'I think it would be better if we spoke to her,' said Blackstock. 'There are certain things we need to know, Charlie. I suspect only she can tell us.'

'On your head, Abernethy, on your head. But go easy, will you? I'm sure you understand. I shall place my faith in you, young man.'

Though none of this mutual backslapping appealed to Salt, she recognized that her colleague's antecedence had undoubtedly opened doors. And opening doors was half the battle for any police officer. 'I think it would be for the best, sir,' she said. 'After all, the media will make the connection before long. I'm sure that's not how you want your sister to learn about things.'

'No, indeed. Please give me a moment to prepare her for the shock.'

Charles Stuart-Henderson got to his feet and disappeared through a set of double doors into the main reception room.

Before the doors closed, Salt caught a glimpse of a woman standing by a window. Then she turned back to face her colleagues. 'What a nice little club, eh?' She looked between McWilliams and Blackstock. 'It's a shame you have to be an aristocrat or a senior police officer to be a member.'

While the chief superintendent raised his chin defiantly, DS Blackstock looked uncomfortable.

'That name, it rings a bell,' said McWilliams.

'What name?' the other two asked in unison.

'Salt. It's unusual enough in Scotland. I recall there was a Glasgow detective that everyone in the city worshipped. I never quite understood why. His name was Salt.'

'My father,' she replied. 'And if you don't understand why, *sir*, I suggest you take a look at his career. He brought some of this country's most dangerous criminals to justice. Of course, not the same opportunities up here in the sticks, I wouldn't imagine.' Salt had issues with her domineering father, yes. But she was damned if she'd hear anyone take him down – certainly not for what he'd achieved as a police officer.

McWilliams narrowed his eyes at this comment. 'We deal with serious crime. It may differ in nature to the city, but there are some ruthless criminals in this area. Poachers, for one.'

'That reminds me of a story my father told me. He cracked the biggest case of poaching in the country.'

'Absurd,' said McWilliams.

'Not in the slightest. Happened in West Nile Street, if I remember correctly. The poor animals were carcasses in the back of a van by that time. But my father collared the perpetrators.' She smiled.

Before her superior could reply, the double doors to the reception room swung open again. Stuart-Henderson ushered them inside. The room was large and bright. Light poured in from the triple-aspect windows; views down a bank to a fast-flowing river, and across farmland and woods to hills that were fading blue in the hazy distance, now the rain had cleared. Salt wondered how much of it belonged to the Pallanders.

Elizabeth Pallander took a seat in a winged-back chair. She was dressed casually in a jumper and slacks. And though she looked reasonably composed, Salt could see the strain in her tight expression.

'Good evening,' she said in a small voice, a contrast to her brother's booming baritone.

'I think we'll let the Glasgow officers take it from here,' said Stuart-Henderson. He looked on as McWilliams backed out of the room, as though he was bidding farewell to a dowager empress. Stuart-Henderson introduced Salt and Blackstock, not failing to mention the latter's family.

'Gosh, such a small world,' said Elizabeth. 'I remember your brother, of course. He was quite the catch, in his day. Those blond curls.'

To Salt, her smile seemed warm and genuine.

Blackstock nodded. 'Curls are the only thing my brother and I have in common, ma'am. He bagged the good looks, I'm sad to say.'

'And the title,' said Stuart-Henderson.

'Yes, that too,' said Blackstock, a hint of regret in his voice.

'Please, take a seat, both of you. Can you arrange some tea, please, Charlie?'

'I will.' He stalked off in search of one of the staff.

'Now, please tell me everything. And don't feel you have to spare me.'

Salt went on to describe the scene on the hill they'd witnessed early that morning. Despite the verity Elizabeth Pallander sought, Salt was careful not to include some of the more gruesome information.

'I see. Charlie tells me that you're not entirely sure this was an accident. Is this true?'

'It is, ma'am. Though we don't have any direct evidence to communicate to you, as yet. But you can rest assured that nothing will be left to chance, and the investigation will be most thorough in nature.' As she said this, Salt remembered the shabby DCI Peel they'd encountered on the hillside above Dumbarton that very morning, as he recklessly discarded his cigarette end into the grass. The investigation would be thorough, though. The ACC would make sure of that.

Elizabeth sighed, and her eyes brimmed with tears. 'We all take risks in our lives, I suppose,' she said, dabbing the corner of one eye with a handkerchief. 'Unfortunately, my son Jean-Luc had that devil-may-care attitude even as a child. I've been warning him all his life. I'm not naive enough to imagine he wouldn't cross people with his protesting at this and that. I wonder, if this isn't the *accident* we thought it to be, would it have happened if my husband had still been alive?' She bowed her head for a few moments.

Salt reckoned that she would have been unable to cope with news like this in such a dignified manner. Even though she had no children, the detective inspector could empathize with the visceral feeling of pain and loss. It was all she could do to stop herself from weeping. Loss was loss. It crept up on you when you least expected it – seeped into your bones, your soul.

'I must ask you a question, Mrs Pallander,' said Blackstock.

'Please, I know you have a job to do. Ask me anything.'

'We would be grateful for a copy of your late husband's will. I know that's a big ask. But if Jean-Luc's death was murder, we need to cover any angle, ma'am.'

'That damned will!' Elizabeth Pallander stood and walked

over to the window overlooking the river. Golden light now filled the room, from the sun beyond the tree-framed hills. 'It's nothing like we agreed. I had a bigger shock than anyone when it was read.'

'I apologize for asking this, Mrs Pallander. But were you expecting more?' said Salt, earning a disapproving look from Blackstock.

'I suppose that's a very clever question. I've never thought of it like that before now.' She composed herself. 'I think I became very accustomed to not worrying about money or property. My husband dealt with all that, and he was exceedingly good at what he did. He left me this house and more than enough money to last the rest of my life. That was as we'd agreed. But our children – I'll never understand why he did what he did. Each and every one of them suffered for their father's success. I thought he knew that. Now, I'm not so sure. Of course, you shall have a copy of the will. I'll arrange it immediately. Our lawyer is in Edinburgh. He can courier a copy over.' She looked at her watch. 'A bit late in the day to catch him now, mark you.'

Salt looked at Blackstock. 'We can stay around tonight – in the hotel at Kinloch Rannoch. We'll be able to pick it up in person tomorrow.'

'You'd be welcome to spend the night here, DI Salt. But my family are coming back home – what's left of them. Trust me, though they are my own flesh and blood, you'll be more comfortable in a hotel. There's going to be a lot of emotion about.' Elizabeth's face bore an infinitely sad, almost hopeless expression. 'God forgive me, but they are so wounded by all of this. Goodness knows how they'll cope with losing a sibling. Privilege isn't always what it appears, Inspector.'

Suddenly the big double doors burst open, and Stuart-Henderson appeared. He looked distracted – panicked, almost.

'What on earth is wrong now?' said Elizabeth.

Stuart-Henderson glanced at the police officers, as though he didn't want to converse with her in their presence.

'Just tell me what's going on, Charles. I can see it in your face.'

Her brother swallowed hard. 'It's Silas. He was on his way here in one of the company jets. All contact with the aircraft was lost somewhere over the Midlands. They've disappeared into thin air!'

15

Tabitha Pallander could see her phone lighting up on the table in front of her. But her strength had been sapped. She couldn't face any more messages from her remaining parent or siblings. It was just too hard, too soon.

In any case, she knew what would happen. There'd be hysteria, the search for blame and recrimination; all of which would culminate in them accusing each other of some shortcoming or failure, while their mother desperately tried to keep the peace. It was a ritual that had played out for as long as she could remember. Even though, now, the players were diminished in number.

These fleeting thoughts brought memories of family holidays in France to mind. Her father – as out of character as it seemed – had always been keen that his family spend what he called *real* time with each other. By this he meant retreating to a remote gîte somewhere in the French countryside, short on amenities and methods of communication. It was character building, a glimpse of how things were for everyone else, though they all knew that their father kept in touch with his many business interests by means of a satellite phone that travelled everywhere with them. On at least two occasions she could remember, a helicopter had descended on their rural retreat to whisk him off to deal with one crisis or another.

The image of Jean-Luc, barely more than a toddler, crossed her mind. Somehow, he'd managed to climb on to the roof of the glorified shack that was the family's temporary home. She remembered how her father oh-so-gently coaxed him back to safety, before setting about his son with an old slipper, by way of punishment. It was his favoured method, though Tabitha recognized she'd been fortunate to miss out on some of his greater excesses.

Those trips were miserable. She remembered missing her friends, her horse – her life. And no lessons in humility were learned. The only outcome was the underlining of how much the Pallander children didn't want to be poor and disadvantaged. They looked down on their impoverished peers even more as a result. She was more than aware that this had never changed. Like it or loathe it, she recoiled at the thought of the poor and disadvantaged. Tabitha knew this was an enormous character flaw. But it came as naturally as breathing.

'What a bunch of brats we are,' she mumbled to herself as the phone buzzed again, moving itself across the table in its urgency to attract her attention. 'Fuck off, will you?' It was guilt versus sorrow. Guilt was winning, and she hated herself for it.

She looked at her watch: just leaving half past six. Her husband John would be home soon. She'd given the cook the night off, their intention being to order food in from the excellent Chinese restaurant in the village. It was her attempt at being like everyone else, she reasoned. One of her very few nods to leading a normal life.

Tabitha took another swig of whisky. The spirit warmed her throat and eased her mind. On reflection, she worried that she drank too much. But this was a problem for future Tabitha. She consigned her concern to the chest of drawers in her head that contained every problem in her world. It was an exercise in self-delusion, she reckoned. Her father would have thought it nothing more than survival by any means.

Distantly, Tabitha heard the dogs barking in the kennel. It was unusual, as the animals normally settled quietly after a long walk.

The phone buzzed again.

'Oh, leave me alone, will you? There's nothing I can do for him now. I don't want to join your collective bleating and wringing of hands!'

Calling her feelings out made Tabitha feel better.

Another noise. A door? It would be John.

Like most married couples, they had settled into a routine that suited them both. They were together and apart at the same time. Busy lives dictated the manner of their relationship. In reality, they had very little in common. John had jumped at the chance of being married to the future boss of the fabulously rich Pallander family. John's family had money that, as an only child, he would one day inherit. He was good-looking enough – entertaining in his own, quiet way. But nothing more than an insurance policy for Tabitha in case the Pallander family failed, and she was cast asunder with nothing. That far off possibility now seemed much closer than she could have ever imagined.

It was a mutually assured relationship. Another term she'd heard her father use, picked up from the theory of nuclear weapons making the world safer rather than leading it to the brink.

'John, what do you want from Mr Chow's?' Tabitha stretched and yawned. It had been a conspicuously bad day, but life – her life, their lives – had to go on. She was aware that this sangfroid also came from her father. What was done was done.

As she turned to go and find her husband, strong hands clasped round her throat. At first, Tabitha thought John was playing an unwelcome prank. But as a cloth was forced over her face, its pungency making her choke, the truth hit her like a wave of icy water.

As Tabitha Pallander felt sheer panic in her heart, an irresistible tiredness enveloped her. The smell was overpowering now, and through her fading consciousness, she tried to struggle.

In seconds her legs buckled, and everything went black.

'Use the parcel tape to bind her legs!' The whisper was a loud and urgent one.

As though in a dream, Tabitha was helpless as two men dressed in black balaclavas, showing only their eyes, worked to bind her arms and legs. This they did in an efficient, practised manner.

One of the men tugged at the bonds, then wrapped a cloth blindfold round her eyes and taped her mouth shut.

'We haven't got long.' The attacker's voice was rough and commanding. 'Take her legs.'

Between them they hefted the unconscious, bound figure of Tabitha Pallander from the floor, one man at her shoulders, the other her feet. They marched quickly through the house, carefully, as though they knew the layout off by heart.

'Posh, isn't it?' said the man holding her legs.

'You never mind what the fuck it is. Just keep moving.'

Soon, they hurried through the open front door and over the gravel drive to the dark Mercedes van. Then their burden began to stir.

'You never gave her enough!'

'What's she going to do, raise the alarm? Lean her against me and open them doors, you prick.' He grabbed Tabitha's full weight as his accomplice pulled open the back doors of the van.

Tabitha Pallander was thrust, none too gently, inside. One man locked the doors and both made their way to the front of the van.

They were about to jump in when a strangled noise came from the shrubbery beside the driveway.

'What's that?' said one.

'How should I—' He yelped as a stone hit him on the head.

Both dark-clad men made their way to the bushes, each holding a pistol before him. As they approached, a man stepped out of the shrubbery.

'Time's up, gentlemen.' Before they could react, multiple bullets from an automatic weapon were emptied into their bodies, and they danced the dance of death. Both men were soon slumped, stone dead in flooding pools of their own blood.

The gunman walked to the body of the first man and removed a set of keys from his pocket. He went to the van and inserted a key into the lock on the back door handles.

Tabitha was now semi-conscious. She saw light fill her vision as the blindfold was removed from her eyes. Desperately, her befuddled brain tried to make sense of what was happening.

The man pushed his head before hers.

'Hello, again. Remember me?'

Tabitha stared at the man she'd met in the woods, wide-eyed.

16

Chaos ensued at Meikle House when it became clear that Silas was missing.

Salt and Blackstock made their excuses, promising to do whatever was in their power to try and find out what was going on.

The pair managed to find the hotel and booked two rooms. The village was almost the picture-perfect notion of what anyone who thought they knew Scotland assumed it should look like. Neat stone houses huddled round a square, amongst hills and pines. In the ruggedness was beauty; in the beauty was a beating heart of bold determination that had marked out this country for centuries. The *Brigadoon* town square looked as though it had been wrought for a film set, as far away from the poverty and crime of some of Scotland's sprawling city schemes as it was possible to be.

They booked in, left the few possessions they'd taken with them and found a little pub that looked quiet and friendly. Salt called the ACC when she was outside, drawing deeply on a cigarette. Such was the length of the conversation, she had time to smoke two as he filled her in on the latest on the death of Jean-Luc Pallander and the disappearance of the plane carrying his brother.

Salt returned to the bar to find Blackstock twirling an empty glass at their corner table.

'How did you get on, ma'am?'

'This ma'am business. I've told you, it's Cara.'

Blackstock sighed in an expression of resignation. 'Sorry, Cara.'

'Anyway, I should be calling *you* sir, shouldn't I? I feel as though I'm working with royalty.'

'Oh, no royalty, Cara. Scottish nobility. Into the bargain, most of us are impoverished. Living in draughty old piles that are falling apart at the seams. We're not all the Pallanders, you know.'

'Yes, I sort of guessed that. It doesn't stop people fawning over you, does it? Look at McWilliams. I thought he was going to ask you out.'

'That's why I don't make much of it. It's dogged me all my life. And don't listen to this tosh about my brother owning most of the Transvaal. He lives there to escape tax. And while we used to own a lot of land in South Africa, that was sold long ago to pay bills and keep the estate in Scotland going. It's why I'm here. I had to find a job.'

Salt didn't know how she felt about this. Though her late father had been no socialist, he reserved a particular dislike for the 'blue bloods', as he termed them. She wondered what he would think of his daughter working with one.

Blackstock knocked these idle thoughts from her mind. 'What was the ACC saying?'

'Jean-Luc Pallander was nowhere near close enough to the wind turbines to damage them when the device went off. He'd never displayed any signs of feeling suicidal, despite some newspaper stories. They were peddling the old just-lost-his-father, deep-depression stuff. But we may never be able to definitively say whether it was an accident, suicide or something darker. They're working on it.'

'But taken in tandem with the missing aircraft, it's hard to believe that it's all just down to bad luck.'

Salt nodded. 'I can't help feeling sorry for the mother. She's brave, but when she was told about the plane, I saw the spirit drain from her.'

'Yes, so did I,' said Blackstock. 'But what I've heard consistently since I've been investigating Pallander senior is that she is used to having a great deal to worry about. For a start, not only did Sebastian sail close to the wind financially, he wasn't exactly the monogamy poster-boy either.'

'Makes sense. It's your classic upper-class philanderer. Self-centred bastard who thinks wealth gives him the right to use people any way he likes. Prick!' The last word was spat out with no little vitriol.

'We've all been hurt, Cara.'

'You've managed to keep going. You deserve credit. But let me tell you, when you're abandoned – well, it shifts your faith in humanity. Certainly faith in men – present company excepted, of course.'

'Men in general or one man in particular?'

'One man in particular.' Salt heard herself sigh and damned her own lack of self-control.

'What went wrong, if you don't mind me asking?'

'I shot him.' Cara gazed into Blackstock's eyes unflinchingly.

'Well, that's bound to end most relationships, I'd venture.'

Cara smiled wanly. She was impressed that Blackstock had refrained from pressing her on the matter. After all, it wasn't a run-of-the-mill end to a relationship.

'Shall we get something to eat and discuss what we do next? I'm famished,' said Blackstock.

'We don't have much to plan. We go back to Meikle House tomorrow. There's nothing we can do about the private jet. So, we wait.'

'Simple but sensible, I suppose.'

'We work it out – study everyone and everything. The force legal team want to see Pallander's will when we have it.' She blew out her cheeks. 'I reckon most of the family are on the way home. If this is something – and we don't know yet, Abs – but if we get the sense that it's all rotten, we go for it. Your pal Innes isn't going to do anything, is he?'

'Men like Innes have spent lifetimes making little fiefdoms for themselves in the countryside. They don't amount to much. In the case of the Pallanders, we already suspect our dead patriarch was in receipt of large sums of money from the Russians. And there may be more. I think we must try and find out how much the rest of the family knows. Particularly Tabitha, Silas and the mother. They were the only family members involved with the company directly, I think.' He got to his feet. 'I need another drink. Can I get you something?'

'A large glass of red, please,' said Salt.

'You know what serves as red wine in places like this. It'll be like vinegar.'

'I don't care. I just want a drink. I know I'm mixing in exalted circles, but I'm not at the stage of swilling the stuff round in my glass and nosing it.'

As Blackstock strode to the bar, she did think that he had a rather aristocratic bearing. He was straight as a guardsman, charming in his own way. But underneath it all was the hint of superiority. Not in a swaggering, arrogant way. But a natural ability to command respect. Cara

Salt could never believe in the class system; her father would never have allowed it. She supposed that the apple hadn't rolled far from the tree after all.

'I took a quick sniff. My goodness, nearly seven quid for that,' said Blackstock. 'It's disgusting.'

Salt grabbed the glass and took a couple of glugs. 'Tastes fine to me.'

Blackstock placed his glass of whisky on the table and eased himself on to his chair with a groan.

'Sore?'

'Old age. Serves me right for lying in the long grass for hours on end waiting for some bird or other. Trust me, once you get to fifty, it's all over.'

'Don't even need to be that old if you're a Pallander.'

Blackstock leaned forward in his seat. 'I know this has all been very sudden for you. And it must seem somewhat strange. But the people we are investigating – or about to investigate, at any rate – mix in dangerous circles. There may be people here who'll give nothing for your life or mine.'

'What aren't you telling me?'

'Just about everything, ma'am. And before you protest, don't. I say ma'am on purpose. We're in something big – I just know it.'

'I'm going to have more wine, Your Lordship.'

They sat in silence for a while. Though she joked about it, from the minute Salt had been told about this case, she knew in her heart that there was something else to it. Call it intuition, the instincts of a police officer, but the notion was very real. Money brought power, and power corrupted. They were only here because of their autonomous budget. It was all behind-the-hand stuff. And while she felt a certain thrill at being an off-the-books renegade, their vulnerability wasn't lost on her.

Salt drained her glass of red wine and stood. 'You ready for another?' Blackstock nodded. She went to the bar, reassuring herself that only Pallanders seemed to be in danger. The homemade bomb could have been an accident. But add a missing private jet and . . . well, evidence was piling up.

17

Tabitha Pallander woke to the bustle of central London far below her room in one of the city's many fine hotels. They'd arrived in the middle of the night, using the names Mark and Judith Keating. Nobody knew where they were, not even the staff of their home back in Oxfordshire. Durling's message was emphatic. *No police, nobody from the company.* He was more evasive as to his role in saving her from abduction.

Time would tell.

John wasn't singing this morning. The hotel room in which they'd spent half the night was unremarkable – nice enough – but not one of the opulent suites in which they'd stayed around the world. John soon appeared with a towel around his waist, drying his hair with another.

'I still can't believe this,' he said, sitting on a chair beside a small table. 'This isn't my wheelhouse.' His face was pale, bewildered. As always, he would have to endure his wife's calculating authority in a crisis. It was infuriating. But she was so much better than he was under stressful circumstances.

'It's your wheelhouse now, darling,' said Tabitha. 'You work in a merchant bank, for fuck's sake. It's not as though you aren't used to a hairy moment or two. Shit, you and your pals nearly took down the world's economy not that long ago.'

She was aware of her prickliness, short temper. Her whole frame ached from the attack she'd suffered during the attempted abduction, and the ruined bodies of her would-be kidnappers were plastered across her mind's eye, dominating her thoughts. She'd witnessed many a boardroom massacre, as her father ate up company after company, ruthlessly destroying people's careers and incomes. Seeing real bullets, gore, the stuff of suffering and death on her own doorstep, was something very different.

'How can we trust this Durling, eh? We don't know who the fuck he is!' John was busy pulling on a sock. His socks were always the first items of clothing he donned every morning. Tabitha often wondered why.

'Let me see, John. There was me trussed up, about to be dragged away in a van, until he saved me. It's enough to engender trust as far as I'm concerned.'

She shook her head and reached for her mobile phone that wasn't there. Strange, she thought, how empty she felt without it. After all, even she was old enough to remember her father carrying a great brick of a phone when nobody else had such a thing. In her lifetime, humanity had become reliant on gadgets that they'd done so well without.

Tabitha found herself having to pull out of the thought. The sedative she'd inhaled during the attack was still muddling her mind. She couldn't focus – certainly not in the way she'd become accustomed.

'What do we do now?' said John. 'I mean, are we just supposed to sit here and await instructions from a man none of us know? It doesn't make sense.'

'Listen, it's not that long since my father died. Yesterday my brother was blown to pieces on some bloody hillside in

Scotland. And someone tried to kidnap me. Does any of this make sense? Because I just don't think so.'

'We should call the police. Now, not a minute to lose.'

Tabitha Pallander regarded her husband as he stood, his towel discarded, grey socks pulled halfway up his calves his only nod to decency. 'Yes, let's get the police. What a bloody good idea! I mean, it's not as though you and I wouldn't be languishing in jail if the police weren't utterly corrupt, is it? All the corners we've cut in our lives. Us, along with half the country's politicians. That's right, isn't it? You're only free to stand there with your cock out because the entire system is rotten to the core. Yet you're the man who wants to call the police. "We can trust them, it'll be fine." Don't be so fucking naive!'

'What about your mother, the rest of your family? She's just lost her husband, a son, now we've disappeared off the face of the earth. How do you think she'll feel?'

Tabitha remembered the day her father had died. Her mother, this woman who'd always been so quiet, strong and dignified amid the controlled chaos of Sebastian Pallander's life, had broken down utterly. She seemed, for a few weeks at least, to shrivel before their eyes; no longer the one safe haven in the storm of life. How she'd managed to find herself again, Tabitha didn't know.

Her own dual role in the business and family had been a difficult one. Tabitha, supposedly being groomed to take over the business when her father retired, accompanied him everywhere. She couldn't help noticing the illicit liaisons, his betrayal of her mother again and again. But she was a grown-up, a woman of business, a woman of the world. She had to divorce her loyalty to her mother from her career. The lines were narrow, walking a tightrope, but she'd never lost her balance. Though residual guilt nagged at her every time her family were together. She could never work out how Sebastian Pallander, her own father, perpetrated the deceit with such ease. She supposed it could only have been achieved with the tacit acceptance of her mother.

'You're not answering. We have to tell our families. If you don't, I will.'

Tabitha fixed him with a stare, then in a flash was out of the bed, across the floor and pinning him against the wall, one hand round her husband's throat, the other squeezing his exposed testicles.

'You'll do what Durling says, you miserable bastard. For fuck's sake, have some real balls. We'll do what we're told!'

John squealed in pain and slid down the wall, sobbing.

'I wish I'd run a thousand miles away from you when we first met. You're just a psycho like your father. I should never have married you,' he hissed through his tears.

'Aw, poor John. Stuck with the evil Pallanders.' She laughed, her head back. 'You were a failing student when I met you, remember? Mummy and Daddy were so proud of their little boy being at Durham University. But what they didn't know was that their pride and joy was up to his eyeballs in debt because of the amount of coke he was sticking up his nose. You'd half of Colombia up there. And you couldn't ask Mummy and Daddy for a loan, because they already suspected you were up to no good. And you haven't forgotten that, had it not been for me, and my father paying your debts, you'd be six feet under by now.'

John was about to say something pitiful in his own defence when a loud knock sounded at the door. He and Tabitha looked at each other.

'What should we do?' whispered John.

'Go into the bathroom out of the way. And get some

bloody clothes on!' hissed Tabitha. She stood back from the door, grabbed a complimentary dressing gown and tied it round herself. 'Hello, who's there?'

'Room service, madam.' The accent was foreign. But that wasn't unusual for a London hotel.

'We haven't ordered any room service,' she replied.

'No, I understand. I have a package from Tom. He said you would want it.'

Feeling only slightly relieved, Tabitha made her way to the door, released the latch and opened it a crack, while still holding the handle tightly. A small Asian man in the white jacket, black trousers and red bow tie that served as the hotel's uniform was standing in the corridor, a silver tray held out in front of him in one hand.

'Madam?' he said. 'This package is for you, from Tom.' He smiled broadly.

Throwing caution to the wind, as was her wont, Tabitha Pallander opened the door a little further. 'Is there a note, any message?'

'Only that you would know who Tom was and to take possession of the package.'

'I see. Hand it to me, please. I'm not dressed yet, I'm afraid.'

'Of course, madam.' The waiter handed her the package through the partially open door, inclining his head slightly as he did.

Tabitha held the item in her hand as though it was a hot coal. She heard him cough and realized that he was waiting for a tip.

'Oh, I'm so sorry. We arrived very late last night. I haven't any cash. But as soon as I do, I'll be able to give you something for your good work.'

The man gave her a shallow bow, though the broad smile

on his face had disappeared. Tabitha shut the door and examined the parcel. She was going to shake it but thought better of it, remembering how her brother had died the previous day.

'What's that?' said John, emerging from the bathroom, he too now wearing a hotel towelling robe.

'How should I know? I don't have x-ray eyes. Here, make yourself useful and open the damned thing.' She tried to hand the parcel to her husband, but he raised his hands in the air in a gesture of surrender.

'Whatever is happening to us is your fault, not mine. You open the damned thing.'

With that he stepped back into the bathroom and slammed the door shut.

As Tabitha heard the bolt slide into place, she cursed him under her breath. It was something she found herself doing more often in their strained marriage. She eased herself back on to the bed and examined the new delivery cautiously. Then she removed a nail file from her handbag and sliced at the brown paper packaging. To her relief, as she did so, the familiar iPhone branding revealed itself. She pulled the box open, and sure enough, there was a phone, its black screen reflecting her anxious face.

Just as she went to pick up the device, it burst into life, with a ringtone that sounded like an old-fashioned telephone box.

Tabitha's heart pounded in her chest, and her hands shook so much she couldn't prise the mobile from the box. Instead, she poured the device out on to the bed, and went about the business of answering the call.

'You still asleep?' Durling's voice, for the little time she'd known him, was familiar and comforting.

'Why all the cloak and dagger? I thought this was a

bloody bomb. Couldn't you just have come to our room?'
She looked up to see her husband edging his way out of the
bathroom, relatively confident now that the parcel wasn't
going to spontaneously combust. She glared at him with
disdain.

'Listen, you don't think our excitement last night went
unnoticed, do you?'

'What do you mean?'

'I had to break my cover. They'll have had eyes-on somewhere. They'll find me and tail me.'

Remembering the roundabout route they'd taken to the
hotel during the night, and the change of cars, Tabitha
understood. 'What now, then?'

'In the box you'll find a small charger. The Apple Pay is
linked to two credit cards, one Amex, the other Visa, in
your assumed names. They're both clean and can't be traced.
Use them for whatever you need, but stay in the room as
much as you can – for obvious reasons, yeah?'

'Yes, we can get room service. But how long can we keep
ourselves holed up here? I mean, we have no cash or anything. I can't even tip the staff.'

She heard him laugh on the other end of the line.

'I know you're used to carrying about great wads of cash
to impress people, but the world's moved on. Cash isn't an
option right now, OK?'

'OK.'

'We might need to move you at short notice, so be ready.
And don't forget to use your new names.'

'I won't. But how are we supposed to contact you? No
number came up when you called.'

'That's the way we want it. I'll call you every couple of
hours. If you don't hear from me, something is wrong.

There's one mobile number in your contacts. In an emergency, and I mean *emergency*, call it. But not for any other reason.'

'What about my mother? She's been through enough.'

'We'll get word to your mother, don't worry about her. And we're watching the hotel. I'll call you again at eleven. Get some breakfast, act as normally as you can.'

'But don't leave the room. How normal is that?'

'It's a dirty weekend with your lover. Make the most of it. And keep the phone on and charged.'

Tabitha looked across at her husband in the robe. She shook her head.

'What?' John whispered with a shrug.

'Tom, who are you, and why are you helping us?'

But the line was dead.

18

Cara Salt was smoking outside their hotel. In a way, she felt guilty sullying the clean, fresh air with her cigarette smoke. Birdsong was carried on the light breeze, and the sun was already warm in the blue sky.

'Why do I live in Glasgow?' she asked herself in a quiet voice. It didn't take long for her to reason that with her work and her friends – such as they were – being in the city made sense. She longed for a place to get away from it all, though. The good thing about being single, without a social life, was that she'd built up a creditable reserve of cash. What about a holiday home? she wondered.

She said hello to a sad-looking man of late middle age wrestling with a seemingly ferocious dog on a lead. The animal was straining to get to her, teeth bared as it barked incessantly.

'I must apologize,' shouted the man above his pet's aggressive protestations. 'He's a lovely dog, really.'

'I'll take your word for it,' Salt returned.

'If you're on holiday, there's a smashing coffee shop on the square. I go there a lot – with friends, you understand. I do enjoy a coffee and good company.' The dog, having lost interest in Salt, was now hauling its owner down the street. 'Maybe see you there – for coffee, of course.'

Salt smiled by way of a reply. Though, as the man and his dog made their chaotic way into the centre of the village, she wondered if their passing of the time of day had, in fact, been an invitation.

'He must be twice your age,' said Blackstock, suddenly appearing at her side.

'Weirdo,' Salt replied. 'I thought only women "enjoy a coffee with friends".'

'Rather a sweeping statement, if you don't mind me saying. And it's not every day a passing dog walker asks you out.'

'Don't worry, you'll get used to it. I'm like a magnet to these oddballs – always have been. A retired sergeant stalked me for about three months until I kicked him firmly in the balls. It's the only way, Abs.'

'Yes, retired sergeants can be tricky,' replied Blackstock.

'Ha! Too early for subtleties. I don't wake up until I've had coffee.'

'I had some about two hours ago.' Blackstock checked his watch. 'Yes, just before six.'

'Six?'

'Didn't want to miss the opportunity of catching the morning birdsong. And we can't reasonably go to Meikle House before ten, it would be impolite.'

'It would?'

'I think so. People need time to get going in the morning.'

'You don't.'

'Unfortunately, I've always been a restless soul. Sleep doesn't come easily. The hours of darkness are normally a battle between my busy head and sleepfulness. The former usually wins.'

'Shit, I sleep like a log.'

'You are very fortunate, I assure you.'

Salt felt a vibration in her pocket. She pulled out her mobile phone, a puzzled look on her face. The screen informed her that no number was available. 'Hello, who is this?'

Blackstock studied her.

'Cara Salt, yes?'

'Yes. But I want to know who you are.'

'That doesn't matter. I have information for you regarding the Pallanders.'

Quickly, Salt had to weigh up the fact that she had no idea who she was speaking to, against receiving information that may or may not be helpful to her and Blackstock. She chose the latter. 'What information?'

'An attempt was made to abduct Tabitha Pallander last night.'

'What?' The caller now had Salt's full attention.

'Her attackers, two men, were killed. She escaped and is now safely in hiding. I want you to pass on some information to Elizabeth Pallander. And I also want you to take a call from Tabitha. It's important. I have to take a step back.'

'OK, hold on, buddy. I need to know a few things first. How did you get this number? How do you know who I am? And what is your connection to Tabitha Pallander?'

There was a crackle and a thud on the other end of the line. 'I don't have time for this. Just do as I ask. I'm aware of the, let's say, special status of your department. And it's safe to say I am a friend of the family.'

There was hesitancy there; she could hear it. 'Not good enough, pal. I need to—'

Salt heard a loud crash, followed by shouting and muffled voices.

'Hello, what's happening?' There was no reply. Three rapid tones followed, then the line was dead.

'What's going on?' said Blackstock, as Salt worked away on the phone, desperately trying to find the caller's number.

'Shit, that's what's going on. We need to get up to Meikle House. Something's wrong – very wrong. I'll brief you on the way up. And we'll need to tell the ACC.'

'Who was that?'

'They called my personal phone, not my police issue one.' Salt produced another phone from her pocket. 'Only my friends and what few relatives I have left know this number. And the man on the end of that call was neither.'

'Something to do with the Pallanders?'

'Yeah. I'm getting the distinct impression that this thing is getting too big for us to handle.'

'Our little department, you mean?'

'No. Police Scotland,' said Salt, eyeing her deputy with a mixture of concern and genuine fear.

19

Tabitha Pallander had showered and changed into the clothes she'd been given the previous evening. The sweatshirt and jeans fitted passingly well, but they were a million miles from her normal mode of dress. She hated trainers too, had done all her life. But now she was wearing a pair, complete with a thick, spongy sole.

Whoever it was who'd picked out these clothes had been kinder to her husband. He was dressed in a reasonably neat pair of chinos, a white t-shirt and a blue sports jacket. He'd been given shoes, pale brogues, superficially not unlike a pair she'd gifted him the previous year, but clearly minus the outrageous price tag.

'These things are half a size too small,' said John, wincing as he laced up the shoes.

'How do you think I feel? Looks as though I live in a trailer park.' She hesitated. 'But you know what? I'm lucky to be alive, so I don't really care, to be honest.'

'What time is it? I don't have a watch.'

'Aw, poor little Johnnie. Can't live without his JLC. Such a shame.'

'Cut the shit, Tabby. You've got the phone. What bloody time is it?'

'Calm down, will you? It's just before nine. We have to hang tight until we hear from Tom.'

'What would we do without, Tom, eh?'

'I don't know about you, but I'd be busy being dead, probably.'

The room was suddenly engulfed by a very loud modulating whine. John dived off his chair and did his best to push his thin frame under the bed. 'Fuck, fuck, what's that?' he screamed, his nerves completely shot.

'It's the fire alarm,' shouted Tabitha above the wailing. 'We stay put, got it?'

John continued to cower on the floor, trying his best to block his ears from the alarm that was so loud and high-pitched it was almost painful.

Tabitha did her best to stay calm. Time was, she'd have been spared the fire drill in a hotel, a senior member of staff warning them that it was about to happen. But now she heard voices and the sound of distant knocking.

In seconds, someone hammered on their door. 'Quick, we must evacuate hotel! No drill, no drill!' The English may have been broken but the message was clear. They had to move.

'I can't take any more of this!' said John, holding his head in both hands to banish the screeching alarm.

Outside the door, they could hear rushed footsteps and animated, panicked chatter as other guests rushed past.

Tabitha pushed the phone into the pocket of her tight jeans, grabbed the box it had arrived in and thrust it into the handbag she'd been given. She rolled off the bed and grabbed her husband by the collar, all in one quick motion.

'Quick, we have to get out.'

'But Tom told us to—'

'He didn't tell us to burn to death. Move your sorry arse!' She pulled at the much bigger man, hauling him to his feet and towards the door.

The hotel corridor was in chaos, thronged with anxious people, crying children and hectoring staff. Nobody seemed to know which way to go, until a stout man with a suit and a hotel name tag beckoned them to follow him.

Tabitha and John did just that, his hand firmly grasped in hers. She could smell burning and hear people coughing. As they turned a corner where the stairs and lifts were located, a cloud of acrid smoke poured from one of the lift shafts.

'Here, the steps,' said Tabitha, pushing open a fire door on to the landing. Mercifully, though the stench of burning was still strong, the stairwell was free of smoke.

'Why this way? We should be taking the lift,' said John, hurrying behind her.

'The fire seems to be in one of the lift shafts! How long until it's in the others?'

'Shit!' John pounded past her on the stairs.

'Last of the great gentlemen,' she said.

The further they progressed, the more crowded the stairwell became. Men, women and children, all in a state of panic, thudded down the steps. The effect was that Tabitha and John were being carried along in the throng, like a crowd leaving a football match. Even if they'd wanted to stop, it would have been impossible. Tabitha felt the handbag being torn from her shoulder in the crush, but the phone was deep in her pocket. At least they were making steady, if somewhat chaotic, progress. Still, the feeling of being enveloped in a mass of frightened people wasn't a pleasant one.

Tabitha was now well behind John, whose head she

could see bobbing above the snaking line of people. A landing door opened below, and an elderly man and woman appeared, the latter crouched over a walking stick. As nobody could stop in the headlong rush downward, the man found himself taken up in the throng, while his wife was knocked underfoot and disappeared.

Tabitha caught a glimpse of her between many legs and feet, and though everyone was doing their best to step round or over her recumbent body, she was taking blow after blow, all unintended.

When Tabitha was almost alongside the woman, she held out her hand. 'Hold on!'

The elderly woman looked up, her frail parchment face already bruised, and held out a bony hand for Tabitha to catch. They were within inches of each other – almost touching – when a large boy, his eyes wide in terror, barged past the old lady, knocking her hand away and flinging her back to the floor.

'You bastard!' Tabitha shouted at the top of her voice. But it was barely audible in the general press of screaming children and frightened, shouting adults.

As they progressed, she passed the old man, his whip-thin body pressed up against a small recess in the stairwell, looking back, waiting for the crowd to part so he could go back to save his wife. Tabitha felt a stab to her heart, knowing that his efforts would likely be in vain, that his wife may not survive. She tried to look back over her shoulder to see what had happened. But the throng of people pressed her forward.

Yet more doors were opening from corridors leading on to landings, more people surging through. Those behind them were waiting until a space opened up, so they too could escape. Tabitha had lost count of what floor they were on, though she realized that the lower they were, the more fetid the air with smoke and fumes.

Tabitha could feel herself tiring, her calves aching, on the verge of cramp. She willed herself forward through the gathering smoke, gritting her teeth, trying to breathe. Out of nowhere, as though from another soul, she heard gasps and grunts turn into a full-throated howl. A few moments passed before she realized that this had issued from her own throat, in the desperate push for survival.

Just as Tabitha Pallander felt she could no longer keep herself upright, the stairwell filled with light. She was propelled through a set of fire doors out into the broad atrium she recognized from their hurried arrival the previous night. It was strange, though, as eerie orange sunlight diffused by billowing black smoke filtered through the glass roof. The horde surged across a shadowy hell, where ghosts of people dashed about in the unnatural gloom. Soon screams were replaced by coughing, as the crowd from the stairwell fractured in every direction, each man, woman and child looking for a means of escape.

Tabitha was momentarily bewildered, an island in the shifting panic that seemed to wash past her, as though in a waking nightmare. A little girl clutching a teddy bear stood motionless in the crowd, bawling fit to burst. Tabitha was too far away to help her. A tanned man was being sick in a huge plant pot, no doubt struggling with panic and smoke inhalation. Then she felt her throat contract further in the acrid air, her eyes streaming, turning her surroundings into an amorphous blur of people and objects. She'd been exposed to smoke and fumes on the way down the stairwell. It was beginning to take its toll.

Tabitha's heart pounded in her chest, pumping as much blood as it could round her system. But between her watering eyes and the thickening smoke blocking out the sunlight, another feeling began to overtake her. She felt suddenly exhausted, almost unable to move. Her brain was preparing to soothe her to an almost inevitable end, the last service it would ever perform. Her reactions slowed; even her panic began to subside.

She had a sharp intake of breath as a strong hand grabbed her shoulder, propelling her forward by sheer force.

'John, you made it!' she called out. But when Tabitha turned her head, the figure hauling her to safety was a fireman wearing fluorescent yellow clothing and breathing apparatus.

Soon, she was out in the relatively cool, clear air of a London street. The fireman pulled off his breathing mask and helped her along the pavement and away from danger.

'You OK?' he shouted as he lowered her to the ground, her back against a wall.

'Yes, thank you,' she gasped. 'My husband – I don't know where he is.'

'Don't worry, we're doing our best to get everybody out. Just stay there, the paramedics will be with you soon.' With that, he rushed off, back on his selfless mission to save lives.

Tabitha Pallander thought how odd it was, sitting in the morning sunshine in the middle of London, moments after fighting for her life. Thoughts of her dead father, her mother and siblings paraded before her. For the first time, she realized that if she was in real danger, so were they.

Sirens sounded. The emergency services were dashing about. Pedestrians, confined to the other side of the road, cast her curious glances; cars, vans and taxis, held up by the fire, sounded their horns, contributing to the cacophony of noise. The day-in-the-life bustle of one of the largest cities on earth. How many times had she passed by a terrible accident, with irritation at the inconvenience the only thought in her head.

The pavement was cold, the wall straight and hard against her back. Tabitha wanted to get up but couldn't. She heard her breath rasp in her throat, the bitter taste of smoke, burning and death making the bile rise.

She looked up to see a man looming over her. He wore a mask over his face and the green uniform of a paramedic.

'Just sit still, please. What's your name?'

'Tabitha – Tabby,' she muttered.

'OK, my name is Ravi. I'm going to give you an injection and some oxygen to combat what you've been inhaling. First, are you allergic to anything at all that you know of?'

She wanted to say John, her husband, until a wave of guilt swept over her, in the realization that she still didn't know where he was. 'No, I'm not allergic.'

'Do you suffer from any chronic disease? Heart problems, asthma, diabetes, kidney problems, cancer?'

'No, nothing like that.'

'OK, here we go.'

The paramedic placed an oxygen mask over her mouth and nose. The impact was immediate. It was like drinking a glass of chilled mountain water. Suddenly she felt her senses return, the beat of her heart slow.

The paramedic pushed up the sleeve of her sweatshirt, found a vein and thrust a hypodermic needle into her arm. That done, he placed a small clip over Tabitha's thumb, then listened to her chest with a stethoscope. 'You seem to be in not too bad shape. You're suffering from smoke inhalation, obviously. Keep the mask on, please.'

'Am I going to be OK?' said Tabitha, pulling the oxygen mask from her face to do so.

'You'll be fine. We'll take you to hospital – just as a pre-caution.' He looked round. 'It'll be a while, but we'll get to you. Here, wear this.' He draped a silver Mylar blanket over her shoulders.

He was tucking the blanket behind her back, when, over his shoulder, Tabitha saw two men across the street. Both dressed in black, they were staring directly at her, each with a searching, intent gaze.

As realization dawned, Tabitha pushed the paramedic back, using his body to lever herself off the pavement, her eyes still fixed on the dark-clad men. They were on their toes now, jostling to find gaps in the traffic.

'Wait! You need to go to hospital!' shouted the paramedic.

But Tabitha pushed him away and took off round the corner and down a lane. She didn't stop until she'd reached another main road. As usual, traffic was moving at a snail's pace. She scanned the vehicles. Just ahead was a double-decker bus. Tabitha rushed forward, crouched between two cars and made it on to the bus just before it moved away, all the time trying to stem the constant need to cough up soot from the fire.

Though it had been many years since she'd been on public transport, she knew what to do. She was grateful to find the iPhone in her pocket. Quickly, ducking as she did so, which earned a puzzled stare from the driver, she waved the phone over the pay-point. The machine blinked and bleeped, the driver nodded, and she was off, straight up the stairs.

Thankfully, the only person on the upper deck was sitting near the front. Tabitha slouched along the passageway, one hand shading her face, until she found a seat near the back and elected to sit on the floor in front of it.

The bus was moving now, though not very quickly.

Tabitha pictured the men in dark clothes. She'd calculated that the first place they would look for her would be the many taxis on the street. After all, who escaped on a bus?

Tabitha Pallander made herself as small as possible, and hoped she was right.

20

The news was out, and the press had turned up in force at the Pallander estate to find out more. Two harassed police constables were holding them off at the end of the long, narrow road that led to Meikle House.

Blackstock's car pushed through the media scrum of cameras, microphones and jostling journalists, both officers flourishing their IDs. They were allowed to pass and made their way to the house on the hill in the striking valley.

They parked at the side of the building, in a space hidden by tall hedges. Where there had only been a few vehicles the previous evening, there was now a throng of all manner of cars, vans and even a couple of motorbikes.

'Half the world's here,' said Blackstock, as he slotted his electric Nissan into one of the few available spaces.

Cara Salt was deep in thought, playing the mystery call over and over again in her mind. Though the caller had been calm enough, the urgency in his voice and the abrupt end to their conversation shouted to her that he was in danger. She too felt the panic.

They gained access to Meikle House after a short wait at the front door. The detectives were shown into a small sitting room with a TV. Salt reckoned that it was the pre-serve of the staff, with none of the ornamentation or grandeur of the family quarters upstairs.

A woman in a tweed trouser suit brought them a tray of coffee and biscuits. She was of middle age, with dyed blonde hair and a kind face that bore an expression of sheer stress.

'I'm Maggie Sullivan,' she said. 'I kind of manage the house – but just about manage everything, if truth be told.'

'Kind of?' said Salt.

Sullivan raised her eyes to the heavens. 'It's complicated. As you can see, there are lots of colonels and not many soldiers in this place. Of course, it's madness right now. But I can't help worrying – well, you know what I mean. I'm hearing so many stories.'

Salt asked to speak to the family as soon as she could. She'd been unable to glean any more on the whereabouts of Silas Pallander, and she wanted to be able to pass on Tabitha's plight to Elizabeth in person. It wasn't a task she relished, but then that was the lot of the police officer, often the first with bad news.

'Mrs Pallander is with our security people at the moment,' said Sullivan.

'Your security people?'

'They're based in Zurich. I don't know, they protect wealthy families like the Pallanders.' Sullivan shrugged.

'Not very well, by the looks of things,' said Blackstock.

'I don't think anyone expected this, Sergeant,' said the harassed housekeeper.

'What are they like to work for? The Pallanders, I mean,' said Salt.

Sullivan looked unsure. 'I've managed a few big houses, and they're all much the same in terms of what's required day-to-day. But this family expect their privacy, and it's my job to make sure they get it. Of course, that's all gone by the board now. But they're good employers, and I'm well rewarded for what I do.'

Salt had always been able to judge the difference between what people said and what they actually meant. It was clear that Sullivan was holding something back. Admirable, in terms of loyalty, but unhelpful for police officers trying to get to the bottom of what seemed like an all-out assault on the family.

'I'm heading for a puff while I can.' Sullivan brandished a packet of cigarettes.

'I'll join you,' said Salt.

The pair left Blackstock and walked down the corridor for a few yards then through a door marked *Exit*, leading on to a little grassy space surrounded by high walls.

'This is my wee hiding place,' said Sullivan. 'Here, would you like one of mine?' She thrust the packet out towards the detective with a trembling hand.

Though Salt preferred her own cigarettes, she took one to be sociable. The housekeeper could prove a handy person to know. 'Cheers,' she said. Salt produced her lighter and soon the pair were puffing their cigarettes into life.

'This must be a nightmare for you – all this fuss, I mean,' said Salt.

'You can say that again. My job is almost impossible as it is. This makes it so much worse.' Sullivan took a deep draw, her eyes flicking about the little courtyard. It was as though she was being a naughty schoolgirl grabbing a fleeting illicit pleasure.

'Do you really like your bosses?'

'Och, a wee bit of that. Decent enough folk, but my goodness they're demanding.' Sullivan looked Salt straight in the eye for a moment, her mouth half open as though she was about to say something.

'What's up?'

Sullivan shook her head and took another puff. 'I'm only here to put my lad through university. His father buggered off and left us high and dry. But I'll not let it ruin Sam's chance of having a better life than me.'

Salt shrugged. 'Everybody's got to serve somebody. Is that not what Bob Dylan said?'

'Aye, true. But maybe not people as demanding as the Pallanders.' Sullivan's voice was almost a whisper. 'But the pay's good. I couldn't get anything like as much elsewhere.'

Salt gave a nod in agreement. 'Most of us are stuck in jobs that we can't stand.'

'You don't like being in the police, then?'

'More often than not. But we all have to do something.'

Sullivan cast her eyes to the grass at her feet. 'I'll admit it. I'm scared. I wish I knew what was going on.'

'Me too.'

'Don't say that! If you don't know how to protect us, who does?'

Salt nodded. 'Listen, whatever is happening, it's concerning the family, not you. There's no need to worry.' Though Salt spoke the words with confidence, she was far from sure herself.

'Nothing against you, but I'm not convinced.' Sullivan took one last draw, let the cigarette fall on to the grass and stubbed it out with her toe. 'Here, you do the same. I'll pick them up and get back to work. We can't have cigarette ends on the grass.'

Salt followed suit and extinguished her cigarette as instructed. She left Sullivan picking up the butts and dropping them into a bag she produced from her pocket.

The detective pondered on their chat as she made her way back to Blackstock.

'You're back,' said Abernethy.

'I am. And none the wiser. It's clear Mrs Sullivan is scared, but I don't know why. At least they have their own security here.'

'I wonder who this private company is?' said Blackstock.

'We'll need to find out. As you say, they're not doing very well, are they? Stick on the news, will you?'

Blackstock grabbed the remote control and soon managed to find the BBC news channel. The feed was from a drone or a helicopter above central London. A pall of black smoke was pouring from a building not far from Whitehall, the centre of UK government.

'That looks bad,' said Salt. 'Turn up the sound.'

The police officers listened as a reporter near the scene described a hotel fire.

'*You see behind me the Sire Hotel, belonging to the Home Hotels Group. Smoke from this fire can be seen across the city and beyond. For those of you who don't know it, this is the kind of place you might stay if you were visiting the capital on a budget. Given the time of year, there will be a lot of families in residence from all over the world. I've just spoken to Superintendent Ali Palloo. She tells me that the operation to extinguish the fire and rescue staff and guests is going well. But no word of potential casualties, as yet. As to the cause of the blaze, we'll have to wait. It's early days here in central London. More as soon as I have it. Back to the studio.*'

The screen flashed to a grim-faced host who announced that, although the emergency services were at the scene quickly, the scale of the fire meant that there were likely to be numerous fatalities.

'That means there *are* numerous fatalities,' said Blackstock.

Salt nodded sadly. As in her conversation with housekeeper Sullivan, it paid to try to read between the lines. Too few people had learned the art.

'I don't know what we're supposed to do here,' said Blackstock. 'Yes, we can investigate, but what? There's so much going on.'

'OK, I think we concentrate on each family member. So far we know that Jean-Luc is dead, Silas is missing and Tabitha is in hiding. We have to find the remaining children.'

'One would imagine that their own people have secured the remaining children, no?' said Blackstock.

'You'd think. But we better be sure. We'll check with Dixon about what's happening once we've spoken to Elizabeth.'

Though Salt was addressing her colleague, her eyes were firmly on the television screen. Black smoke continued to billow from the Sire Hotel. From above, via live newsfeed, she could see tiny figures spilling out on to the street amid the parade of police, fire and ambulance vehicles, their blue lights flashing in the chaos.

'It's awful,' said Blackstock. 'Go on holiday and that's how things end up. You know, I've never been able to get my head round the exigencies of fate, have you?'

'Shit happens,' said Salt dispassionately.

'Rather callous, don't you think?'

'Yes, but fate is rather callous. You're a man in your fifties. How likely is it you could drop dead of something that's been working away on you that you've had no idea about? Take cancer, for example.'

Blackstock stared at his boss. 'That's how your father died, wasn't it?'

'It was. But it can happen to anyone. I love the way people cruise through their lives every day without a care. As if death doesn't exist. While all the time there it is stalking each and every one of us. And what's really shit is – and it marks us out from all the other creatures on the planet – we know for sure what's going to happen, that we're going to die. The only point of conjecture is why the fuck are we here at all?'

'Goodness, philosophy at this time of the day. You're a woman of great contradictions, ma'am. If you don't mind me saying.'

'Why contradictions?'

Blackstock thought for a moment. 'It's a rather gloomy outlook. A touch of Nietzsche about it.'

'If you say so, Your Lordship.'

Blackstock ignored the barb. 'The contradiction is that it comes from someone who obviously cares for the fortunes of others. Also, as you deprecate those who cruise through life as though death doesn't exist, from my sure and certain knowledge of your police career you've put your neck on the line many times to save these very individuals.'

'Do you know, there's only one thing worse than a smart-arse.'

'Which is?'

'A social worker – that was our motto for your old force, wasn't it?'

Blackstock mimicked a yawn.

The phone in Salt's pocket buzzed. She grabbed it and checked the screen. Though the number was displayed, it wasn't one of her contacts.

'DI Salt, who's calling?'

Silence, the indistinct noise of an engine.

'Hello?'

'Tom Durling said you could help me.' The voice was strained, panicked.

'Who is this?'

'Tabitha. Tabitha Pallander. Who the fuck are you?'

Though the eldest daughter of the Pallander family found herself *in extremis*, there was no hint that she'd lost any sense of self.

'I'm DI Cara Salt. I'm investigating what's happening to your family, Tabitha.'

'Right, well, I can tell you exactly what's happening to me at this very moment.'

'You're supposed to be in hiding at an undisclosed address. I got a call earlier.'

'That address is currently burning to the ground.'

'You were in the Sire Hotel?'

'I was. And the man who rescued me isn't calling. To add to this, I'm being pursued by two men. Not to mention the fact I've lost my husband.'

'Is he dead?' asked Salt.

'I have no idea. When I say I lost him, I mean I *lost* him. We were separated when trying to escape the hotel.'

'Where are you now?'

'I'm on the top deck of a bus.'

'Where?'

'You heard. But I can't stay here for ever. Should I just get off and make myself known to the police?'

Salt felt a sudden chill. 'No, don't do that. Definitely not!' That she was even thinking this way came as a shock. But for Salt it was a gut reaction. She'd learned to trust those.

'You mean the Met's in on this too? I was told not to call them. But surely they're not all on the take?'

'We can't be sure.'

'I think I lost the men who are looking for me. But I'm

buggered if I'm going to go round the route of the fifty-seven bus, or whatever it is, until I die. And though he's a useless bastard, I'd like to know where my husband is, thank you. I suppose I could go to the office, yes?'

'No, just let me think for a moment.' Salt thought about Dixon. He felt their own force couldn't be trusted. If that was so, what about the Met? She needed space. She needed to place Tabitha somewhere she knew to be absolutely safe.

'Hello, are you still there?'

'Yes. I'm thinking.'

'Oh, just take your time. I'm in no rush,' said Tabitha, sarcasm palpable on the line.

'Go to this place. Tolland's Computer Supplies. It's on Fossie Street. Get a taxi but make sure you're not being followed. Do you have money?'

'I've got Apple Pay, if that's the same thing. Who on earth is at this . . . shop?'

'Ask for Sorley. I'll make sure he's expecting you.'

'OK. I'll spin around on this a bit more and wait for a quiet street. What do you think?'

'Yes, try that. But find a cab as quickly as you can. The less time you're on the street the better.'

'I've got to go. Please don't leave me in the lurch the way Durling did.'

'I won't. Call if you have problems.'

'I will, you can rely on that.'

The call ended.

'So you don't trust the Met? I agree,' said Blackstock. 'But who is Sorley?'

Salt shook her head and sighed. 'I used to work with him.'

'A cop?'

'An ex-cop.'

'Oh, that's interesting.' He searched Salt's eyes. 'And what else?'

'He's my ex. Well, he's one of them. But he's the one who got away, if you know what I mean.'

'The one you shot, by any chance?' asked Blackstock.

'Yes, I'm afraid so,' said Salt, biting her lip.

21

Silas Pallander awoke in a small, dark space. His first instinct was to call out for help, as his brain desperately tried to piece together why he was there. He remembered Anna Marchand holding him close, her warmth, her perfume. But after that, darkness. His head was thumping, and he was struggling for breath in this musty place.

'Anna!' he cried, searching in the darkness for the one person who could help him make sense of it all. 'Anna!'

Silence. He felt tears welling in his eyes, the familiar ache of fear and sorrow tightening his throat, tugging at his stomach.

Silas reverted to type, curling himself into a ball on the floor, rocking backwards and forwards as he'd done as a child – as he'd done in the office in Toronto when he discovered his father had died. Though he knew it was weak, pathetic, everyone had to deal with what was in front of them in the best way they could. This was his coping mechanism.

As he rocked to and fro, he began to piece together the last moments he could remember. They were on one of the company jets. He'd fallen, hurt his head. Yes, it was still throbbing. He remembered Anna locking them in the bedroom, holding him, comforting him.

Anna. Even her name was a salve. She'd been his rock for so many years. Their relationship was like a marriage without sex. Well, apart from that one time. Of course, he'd longed for her for years. It wasn't just because of her beauty. No, that was too simple. She knew how to do everything, how to help him. He relied on her steadiness, her calm authority.

Though he had many faults, Silas had no high opinion of his own self-worth. His father had seen to that with great enthusiasm. When a child is reminded of their perceived shortcomings again and again, it becomes the mantra of their lives, a rebuke designed to last until the grave.

You're useless. You'll never amount to anything. *Why do you walk that way? Why can't you do this? Are you stupid?*

He wanted to banish the voice in his head, but it was impossible. It had been there for so long.

In the breathless darkness, he remembered visiting one of his friends as a boy. He must have been all of eleven years old, and it was one of the few times he'd managed to escape the cultches of his family, if only for one night.

The house was so much smaller than theirs. Yes, it was in the countryside, but they had no servants, apart from the woman from the village who came to light the fire and clean.

Piers did chores. He had to muck out the stable, polish his father's car, tidy his own room, wash dishes. The list had seemed endless to the young Silas Pallander. He did none of these things. And though he supposed that all of this must go on in the many homes his family possessed, it all happened far away from his gaze.

At first, he'd felt bad for Piers, one of the few boys at the

Oxfordshire prep school who didn't taunt him, who didn't make a fool of his accent. Having spent his young life at Meikle House, Silas had acquired the hint of a Scottish accent. It was something that seemed endlessly amusing to his peers. He lost it as quickly as he could, practising soft vowels at the mirror every night until the Caledonian burr was gone. But they soon found something else with which to taunt him.

Piers was a shy, intelligent boy, who hated games and loved books. Being much the same in nature, Silas became his friend. And when they could, the pair used to talk about their favourite writers, and the places they'd conjured up between the pages of countless books.

Any pity at the tasks Piers was forced to perform on a daily basis soon subsided. They'd been asked to make a small pot out of clay in art class that afternoon. And though Silas felt his efforts at pottery were better, he was almost taken aback by how Mr Anderton, a smiling man who smoked pungent cigars, praised his son for his work.

That's a work of art, my boy. It's special. Do you know, I'm going to take that to the office, put it on my desk. Well done, you!

Silas was still rocking as he remembered what had happened when he took his pot back home. He'd been desperate to see what his father's reaction would be to something he'd made with his own hands, his imagination. Silas knocked on the door of his father's study and waited for the inevitable 'Come!'

He'd held the little pot out to his father, telling him how he'd made it himself in school. A broad smile had spread across his father's face as he flung his head back and began to laugh. But the laughter hadn't lasted long.

Never bring shit like this to me again. You want to be a

potter, be a potter. But you leave this house and you never come back!

His father had taken his work and smashed it on the floor, grinding the pieces under the heel of his shoe.

That's what I think of your little pot, idiot.

After that, Silas Pallander no longer felt sorry for Piers Anderton and his chores. He envied the boy so much their friendship ended. And he was once more alone.

Silas didn't know where this memory had come from. But as he sat curled up in the dark, he supposed it was just another recollection of the misery of his childhood. If that misery had ended there, things wouldn't have been so bad. But as he grew, his father had never behaved any differently towards him. He'd taken great pleasure in promoting his younger sister to one of the most important roles within the company, while Silas was there only to make up the numbers.

'Anna,' he whispered, as warm tears spilled down his face.

Suddenly, there was light. Harsh, bright light that made him shade his eyes after so long in the dark. A door opened and a figure was pushed into the little room. It was her, Anna. He managed to stand and catch her before she fell. She looked up at him. Her face was red, tear-stained, mascara smudged around her beautiful blue eyes. There was a livid bruise on her cheek. He raised one shaking hand and touched it gently, like a lover.

'Don't, it hurts,' said Anna, leaning her head into his chest.

'Who did this? Why did they hurt you?'

'I don't know. I was tied to a chair. A man . . .' She began to sob. 'A man came into the room and hit me.'

Anna held on to Silas, her long nails digging into his arms, her breath hot against his chest.

142

'What's happening? Why are we here? This is a nightmare!'

'They drugged us. I – I tried to stop them hurting you, but there was nothing I could do.' She looked back up into his face. 'I'm sorry.'

Silas's heart soared at her touch, her closeness. He pulled her to him, feeling her every sob through his own body.

'At least we are together now.'

'No, no, we aren't.' She pushed him away. 'I'm just here to tell you something.'

'What?' Silas could feel his heart sink.

'They want you to answer their questions.'

'Questions? I don't know what you mean.'

'They're going to hurt me if you don't,' she wailed.

'They've hurt you already.' He searched her face.

Anna leaned into him again, her breath hot on his neck. She whispered in his ear. 'Don't tell them anything. Don't worry about me. They want to hurt your family, to know things about the business. Don't tell them. What happens to me isn't important. Promise me.'

Again, without warning, the door burst open. A large man, dressed in black from head to toe, wearing a black plastic mask that gave him a blank expression, grabbed Anna's arm and pulled her from Silas's grasp. When she yelled in pain, Silas tried to fend the man off but was sent spinning by a punch to the gut. He collapsed against some old boxes, gasping for breath. The door slammed shut and the room was once again plunged into darkness.

Distantly, he could hear Anna scream, a wild, untrammelled roar of pain.

'Fuck,' he said to himself as he curled back into a ball on the floor, his body quaking, tears spilling down his face.

22

Sullivan arrived back in the little sitting room to let the police officers know that Elizabeth Pallander would see them soon, and that she sent her apologies for keeping them waiting.

'You feeling any better, Mrs Sullivan?' asked Salt.

'Yes, I am. Sorry for moaning at you outside. I suppose everyone gets fed up now and again.'

'You don't have to tell me that.'

Salt smiled at Sullivan, who left to go about her business.

'What's her problem?' asked Blackstock.

'I think she finds working with the Pallanders rather stressful. I mean, can you see yourself working for this lot?'

Blackstock raised his eyes. 'Typical staff, if you ask me. Nothing's ever good enough. You'd think she'd be grateful for the job.'

Salt bridled, for the first time seeing the dismissive aristocrat in her colleague. 'She's a single parent, trying to pay her son's way through university. You made enough about having to get a job because of your brother. You don't think she has a right to be pissed off?'

Doing her best to cool her temper, she sought a corner of the room away from Blackstock. She grabbed her mobile from her pocket and searched the contact list. For a moment, she feared she'd deleted his number. In her heart, though, she knew that would never happen. For her, real love was a strange, elusive thing. So elusive, in fact, that when she encountered it for the first time the fear of being hurt overcame the chance to change her life, and she'd ruined everything. She played the whole thing out in her mind again and again.

What if. . .?

Salt cleared her throat as the dial tone sounded in her ear. For reasons she lamented, her heart was beating faster, and her throat was dry.

'Hello.' The voice was both familiar and unfamiliar at the same time. 'Cara, is that you?'

'Yeah, hi, Sorley. How are you?' As she said the words, she remembered their last meeting. Tears, accusations, ill-feeling – self destruction, as far as she was concerned. A final parting, or so she thought.

'Surprised, that's how I am.'

'I know, it's been a while, right?'

'It's been three years, Cara.'

'As long as that? Wow, how time flies, eh?'

'Any more platitudes?'

'Please don't be like that.'

'You mean pissed off you've called? It's the truth, no matter how little you like it.'

'Oh, for fuck's sake! Grow up! It's been years. Can't we just have an adult conversation for once?'

'We had too many *adult* conversations, if you remember.' He hesitated. 'After what happened, when I was recovering in hospital and you shagged my mate, remember?'

'That's not how it was, and you know it.'

'Right, I see. Well, sorry if it seemed like that to me at the time. Maybe it was all the morphine they were using on me to try and quell the agonizing pain. Why are you calling?'

'I need a favour.' Salt's words came out in a rush. She screwed up her eyes ahead of the response.

'No way. Whatever it is, the answer is a most definite *no*!'

'Steady on, you nearly burst my eardrum.'

'Good, I'm bloody glad.'

Salt could hear the lilt of Benbecula in his voice. His accent had always made her heart melt.

'Right, I'm off. Things to do, you know. Things to do without you.'

'Wait! When I said I wanted to ask you a favour – well, that's not completely true.'

'Eh?'

'I've already asked you, and you said yes, actually.'

'Are you pissed, Cara?'

'No. But are you at work?'

'How do you know about my work?'

'I'm a fucking detective, Sorley.'

'Oh, yeah. I used to be one of them too, remember?'

'Listen, I don't have much time.'

'That's sad. I'll light a candle for you.'

'You'll have heard of the Pallander family, yes?'

'The guy who popped his clogs on the telly? Who doesn't know about that.'

'Well, his daughter is on her way to your shop.' Again, Salt was aware that her words had come out in a rush.

'She's what?'

'Listen, it's a long story. She's being pursued. We can't trust the Met – well, I don't think so. I need somewhere for her to lie low. You know, off-grid.'

'I own a shop in the centre of London. It's hardly

off-grid. And in any case, I've had enough of you to last me at least three lifetimes. Send your escapee somewhere else.'

'I can't, Sorley. There isn't time. It's all I could think of. They're going to kill her.' Again, Salt screwed up her eyes and waited.

'That's just fantastic. This woman's fleeing for her life, for some reason, and you decide that sending to her to a shop on the high street is a good idea. It's no wonder you never reached chief inspector.'

'There's the hut.'

'What hut?'

'The place you go to paint. The one on the marshes.'

'You know about that too? Have you turned into some kind of super-stalker? I shouldn't be surprised. You've always been mad as a box of frogs.'

'Please, I wouldn't have asked if I wasn't desperate.' Salt heard a noise in the background – a slamming door, she thought.

'Is this Pallander woman about five eight, with dark hair and a shit dress sense?'

'I'm sorry, I have no idea.' Salt bit her lip.

'I am going to strangle you, Cara Salt,' said Sorley in a whisper.

The phone went dead. DI Salt grimaced and put the mobile back in her pocket.

'Everything OK?' said Blackstock.

'No, not really, but it's the way it is.'

'Isn't it always?' he muttered.

As Salt stood biting her nails, Sullivan put her head round the door. 'Mrs Pallander would like to see you both now.'

The detectives were shown into the same sunny room

they'd been in the previous day. There was no sign of Charles Stuart-Henderson, but four new people were present. On a sofa a man and woman sat together holding hands. Though the woman bore an uncanny resemblance to a much younger Elizabeth Pallander, Salt thought she was less refined, dowdy somehow. The man at her side looked slightly ill at ease, as he gazed at the police officers. A woman in a floral-patterned dress sat on the floor near Elizabeth Pallander. She looked demure enough, apart from the curly, postbox-red hair, black lip-gloss and a pair of purple Doc Marten boots. Beside her, on a wooden chair, sat another woman. She was dressed in jeans and a t-shirt and looked pale and drawn.

'Good morning, officers,' said the lady of the house.

Salt could feel the charge of emotion in the air. It hung like veiled sorrow, ready to burst through.

'I must introduce you to two of my children, Alicia – Alice,' she said, pointing to the woman sitting on the floor. 'And Audrey. Audrey is – was – Jean-Luc's twin.' Elizabeth gulped back her tears.

'I'll always be his twin, Mummy.' Audrey cried her mother's tears for her.

'Alan is Audrey's husband, and Claire is Alice's – well, Alice's companion.' Elizabeth cleared her throat. 'Everyone, this is DI Cara Salt and Sergeant Abernethy Blackstock. We know his family, lovely people.' Elizabeth beamed at Blackstock, making Salt feel rather excluded.

Introductions over, Salt asked if she could speak with Elizabeth privately.

'This is my family, Inspector. There have been too many secrets between us in the past. Please tell us what you know. Chief Superintendent McWilliams has already visited. There is still no trace of Silas or the plane, I'm sad to say.'

'Yes, I was aware,' said Salt. 'I'm sorry. I know every attempt is being made to locate him.'

'I'm really concerned about my daughter, Tabitha. We all tried to contact her last night without success. But Charlie had a call late on to say she was safe and well. Lying low, it appears. I can't blame her – not the way things are going.'

'I can tell you that she is safe. But we've had to place her in hiding, off-grid, so to speak, Mrs Pallander.' Salt looked round the worried faces in the room. 'Under the circumstances, and having taken advice from our assistant chief constable, we have been detailed to fetch her back here from London.'

'Why? Can't the police in London bring her home?' said Audrey. Her pale face harboured eyes red-rimmed by the flood of tears she'd cried since arriving home to be at her mother's side.

'I must tell you that attempts were made to abduct your sister last night. These attempts were thwarted, but we feel it will be best, as far as this case is concerned, if the whole thing remains as . . . well, as discreet as possible.'

'Meaning you don't trust your colleagues in London?' said Audrey, addressing Salt then looking at her husband for reassurance.

'No, not at all. It's just procedure.' Salt was aware of the blatant lie. She had also failed to tell what remained of the Pallander family that Tabitha had escaped a hotel fire and another potential attempted abduction that very morning. But she reasoned that people could only take so much. In any case, Tabitha was safe now, as far as she could tell.

'You must take the helicopter,' said Elizabeth Pallander. 'We have one here. It'll be available in no time.'

'Oh, I hadn't thought. We were about to catch a flight. A

scheduled one.' Salt looked at Blackstock, who seemed very serious. 'How many people can travel in it?'

'Four, excluding the pilot. He's a local man we've used for many years. My husband used to refer to him as a solid chap. Let me assure you, this was high praise indeed from Sebastian. I just want Tabby home, Inspector. Please let me help with this. I must feel as though I'm doing something to save my own children!'

'I just don't know, ma'am. It would appear there are coordinated efforts against your family. It's hard to tell who's behind them. But given the nature of this business, my boss thinks it's best the whole thing is kept pretty quiet, if you know what I mean.'

'I was in the army, you know,' said Alan. 'It sounds to me as though you have no idea from where the threat is coming. You're keeping it quiet because you suspect that the police have been compromised. That's it, isn't it?'

'That's a question that's well above my pay grade, Mr – sorry, I didn't catch your surname.'

'Glossop, Alan Glossop,' he said, a hint of defiance in his raised chin.

'As in Pallander Glossop?' asked Salt.

'My late father was Sebastian Pallander's business partner. I have no connection to the business – never had, as it goes.'

'I see.' Salt could hear the attempt to hide his regret. She addressed the room. 'The ACC is coming to speak to you all today. I'm sure he'll be able to answer the many questions you must have. I know he wants to talk to your personal security people.'

'Worse than useless,' said Glossop.

Elizabeth Pallander interjected. 'I think what Alan means is that the company that deal with our security are rather out of their depth. They are used to securing the business and here, sometimes. You know, events, functions and the like. I don't think anyone expected this to happen – not in our wildest imaginings.'

'And you all got here without a problem?' Salt looked round the room at the other Pallander children.

'We met in Brighton early this morning. Andy brought us up in the helicopter,' said Alicia.

'We only knew about Jean-Luc,' said Audrey. 'Mummy waited to tell us about Silas. Now all this with Tabitha. It's just unbearable.' She laid her head on her husband's shoulder and sobbed quietly.

'How safe are we here?' said Glossop. 'I mean, you two aren't going to stop an attack, are you?'

'There's an armed unit on its way from Aberdeen. They'll look after you until we can work this out. And there will be local officers too. Chief Superintendent McWilliams has personally vouched for them.'

'He's a sound chap. Damned good with a pitching wedge into the bargain,' said Glossop.

Ignoring him, Cara Salt carried on. 'The ACC will fill you in.' She checked her watch. 'He should be here within the hour. And if you wouldn't mind giving him a copy of Mr Pallander senior's will, please.'

Elizabeth nodded wearily.

'Why are the armed officers coming from Aberdeen?' Alicia asked. 'Would Glasgow not make more sense? You are from Glasgow, yes?'

Salt shrugged and again made her apologies. Her boss would be able to answer all their questions. Though she too wondered how they could maintain the safety of the Pallander family without Special Branch and resources from Glasgow.

Salt and Blackstock excused themselves, saying they had to speak to the ACC. They walked down the corridor side by side.

'It makes sense, Abs.'

'What does?'

'Taking the helicopter.'

'Didn't go well for Silas, did it?'

'That was a company jet. This is piloted by a local man.'

'I don't think it's safe.'

'You're scared of helicopters, aren't you?'

'Yes,' said Blackstock without preamble.

Salt's mobile rang.

'Yes, Tabitha?'

'This man is insufferable! He wants to take me to some bloody marshes on a motorbike.'

DI Salt sighed and asked to speak to Sorley.

23

Tabitha Pallander was far from mollified following her call with Salt. If anything, she felt even less safe.

She looked around the shop, a muddle of old laptops, monitors, plugs, pins, cables and tiny spare parts she didn't recognize. It was, in short, a veritable junk shop – modern, no old pots and pans here, but a junk shop nonetheless.

She could hear the proprietor's raised voice as he argued with the detective. It was clear he was unhappy at having to perform any kind of service for a woman he'd never met. Even so, there was something intimate about their conversation, no matter what passed between them. And though Tabitha could hear only one side of the discourse, she thought it sounded much like what might pass between a bickering husband and wife.

'Shit!'

She looked on as her host threw his mobile phone across a counter.

'Temper, temper,' said Tabitha in a mocking tone.

'No wonder. The reason I came down here was to rid myself of all this crap. I hated doing bollocks like this when I was getting paid for it. It's even worse now I'm doing it as a favour,' said Sorley.

'So, you make a habit of rescuing damsels in distress?'

'No, I was a police officer.'

The look on his face said *don't ask me anything else.* Tabitha chose to comply and left him to his own devices for a while.

Sorley fidgeted with a computer keyboard for a couple of minutes before casting it aside. He looked at his new guest. 'How did you end up in my shop?'

She sighed. 'Long story.'

He waited.

'OK. Last night people tried to abduct me – there were two of them. A man I'd met in the woods about four hours earlier shot and killed them both, before taking my husband and me to a hotel under an assumed name.'

'Don't tell me, the hotel that's currently ablaze?'

'The very one.'

'So, you escape the fire, then what?'

'I was being treated on the pavement. I spotted two guys staring at me. When they rushed to cross the road, I took off. Now I'm here.'

'What happened to the guy who rescued you last night?'

'Who knows? He told me that if he didn't call for any reason, I should get in touch with your DI Salt.'

'Mine? You've got that wrong.'

Tabitha was suddenly dog-tired. She spotted a plastic chair by a pile of laptops and made for it. 'I feel as though I haven't sat down for a month.'

'Can I get you a coffee?'

'That would be most welcome. Milk, no sugar, please.'

Sorley disappeared into a back room, returning a few minutes later with two mugs. 'It won't be what you're used to, but it's wet.'

'Thank you.' She took a sip. The brew was bitter and

astringent. She shuddered but decided not to say anything. 'So, what do we do now?'

'Like Cara said. I have a little fishing hut out on the Essex marshes. We head there and lie low until the cavalry arrives.'

'How long to get there?'

'Well, two hours at this time of day – even with a motorbike.'

'Motorbike? I've never been on one before,' said Tabitha.

'You're kidding.'

'No, never. My father thought them dangerous. I agree.'

'My father thought going to the mainland was a reckless thing to do, and that nothing good would come of it. But I stopped listening to him when I was about fourteen. Just grab on to my waist and go with the flow.'

'That doesn't sound too technical, at least.' Tabitha gathered her courage and took another sip of coffee.

'It isn't difficult. Finish up and we'll go.' Sorley slurped at his mug.

'Can I ask you something?' said Tabitha.

'If you must.'

'What is it with you and this Cara?'

'We're old colleagues.'

'You were in the police?'

'Yes, in Glasgow.'

'Why did you leave?'

Sorley raised his eyes. He pulled at the neck of his t-shirt, revealing a large, puckered mark on his left shoulder.

'Is that a gunshot wound?'

'It sure is.'

'Nasty. Who shot you? Some low-life bastard, I bet.'

'Cara Salt. You know, the inspector you've been taking advice from. She shot me.' He smiled.

Tabitha took a couple of minutes to process this information. But on consideration she decided to make no further comment on the matter. She had plentiful problems of her own to cope with. Like the handbag she'd been given being torn from her shoulder in a burning hotel.

'Can I ask you a favour?'

'Another one? Aye, you might as well,' said Sorley.

'Do you have such a thing as a charger for an iPhone?'

'You kidding?'

'No.' Tabitha looked puzzled.

Sorley gestured airily with one hand around the electrical repair shop. 'You've come to the right place.'

He's a smart-arse as well as being common and rude, Tabitha thought.

When they arrived back in the little room with the TV, Salt was surprised to find ACC Dixon there, idly watching a business programme on a news channel. She took the opportunity to tell him about the offer of a helicopter, and the developments with Tabitha Pallander.

He drew a deep breath and massaged his temples with both index fingers. 'Highly irregular, of course.'

'But this isn't exactly a *regular* case, is it, sir?'

They spoke for a few minutes, until the senior officer decided that, under the circumstances, they should take Elizabeth Pallander up on the offer. The only alternative now was waiting for a police helicopter. Not only would that take time, but it would also lead to the inevitable leaking of what was happening to the family to the wider Police Scotland. On balance, it was decided that covert haste was more important than the rules.

'Get Tabitha Pallander back here as quickly as you can. Our choices are limited, as you know.'

'Yes, sir.'

'And before you go, I have more information.'

'Sir?'

'We found other remains on the hill at Dumbarton. DNA evidence. Two ruined corpses – almost as one, I'm told.'

Salt glanced at Blackstock in surprise. 'Meaning Jean-Luc was possibly forced into setting off the device?'

'It's possible, yes. Though whoever did that coaxing got more than they bargained for. Just gets more sinister by the minute.'

Salt considered this.

'Too early for any DNA matches?' said Blackstock.

'Yes, but I'll keep you informed.'

'Sir,' said Salt, 'I was just wondering how secure Meikle House is? I mean, I know we'll have armed officers here, but given the nature of things . . . Well, just a thought.'

'And a sound one. I have two armed units, one from Inverness, the other from Aberdeen. As far as they're concerned, there has been a threat to the house from a criminal gang targeting fine antiques. That's the line and we stick to it. Things are pretty secure.'

'Do you expect problems – here, I mean?'

'My dear, I expect problems everywhere. The press is still gathering back down at the end of the road. All we need.' He sighed. 'Now, go and find this pilot chap, and get going. I'll be gone by the time you're back, but the men we have around the place are sound, so don't worry.'

'Not from Glasgow, you mean?' said Blackstock.

'Correct.' Dixon hesitated. 'The armoured unit has something for you both.' He eyed Salt. 'I'll understand if you decline, Cara. But I'd counsel otherwise. We know our adversaries are a ruthless bunch. Don't want to be found wanting, eh?'

'I don't have a firearms certificate,' said Salt. 'Not any more.'

'No matter. I've managed to get past that. Take it or leave it, the choice is yours.'

Salt gulped, her throat suddenly dry. Her mind flashed back to the moment she'd pulled the trigger. In slow motion she saw Sorley's shoulder explode into a shower of blood and bone. 'If you're willing to trust me, I'll take it, sir.'

'Good, Now, I must get upstairs and tell this poor woman that we can find neither her son, nor his plane. Keep in touch.'

And with that, Dixon departed with yet more bad news for the Pallander family.

24

The little yard behind Sorley's shop was tumbledown. A rusting mountain bike sat beside an old fridge, its door removed to reveal a cracked plastic interior. Various crates, boxes and other detritus wrestled for space with a red motorbike. Judging by the gleaming fairing with no trace of even the tiniest spot of mud, the latter at least was well looked after – cherished.

'I didn't know you dealt in scrap as well as computers,' said Tabitha, eyeing it all with distaste. It reminded her of the hellholes her father used to take them to on holiday in France and Switzerland.

'You'd be amazed what people bring to me – that fridge, for example. An old lady had me pick it up to keep my milk in. Of course, the damned thing is broken beyond repair.'

'Has it ever crossed your mind that people are just taking advantage of you? You're like a waste disposal service.'

Sorley smiled. 'Yes, it has. But I like to help, if I can. There's more to life than money.'

'There is?'

'Yes, you should try it.' He handed Tabitha a crash helmet. 'I haven't met many rich people – one or two, really. I know you're very well-off.'

'How?'

'I googled you on my phone when I was making coffee – simples.'

'So, you've met a rich person.' She shrugged.

'In my experience, the rich spend so much time acquiring their wealth, they forget how to use it. The whole thing defeats its purpose. Come on, we need to get you appropriately dressed.' Sorley nodded to a rotting shed in the corner of the yard.

'What as, a scullion?'

'I always thought they were wee onions.'

'Oh dear. In that case, I won't enlighten you. Lead the way.' She followed him towards the shed.

'This place used to be a pub, hence the yard,' said Sorley.

'How intriguing.' Tabitha curled her lip.

He opened the tiny padlock that secured the shed door. Again, more stuff, old tools, boxes of what Tabitha considered to be rubbish.

'You're not worried about being broken into, are you?'

'I hide things in plain sight. What self-respecting burglars are going to want to break into the shed when they see the mess of the yard?'

'Point taken.' Tabitha stepped into the shed gingerly, sniffing at the odour of engine oil and something musty she couldn't identify.

Sorley was working away at a large box under a bench. 'Here it is,' he said with a note of triumph. He pulled the box out on to the floor and removed an old black leather jacket with red and white stripes at the shoulders. 'This'll do the job nicely.' He held the jacket out.

'Hey, I'm not wearing *that*.'

'Yes, you are. You need some armoured clothing. And this is it. Belonged to an old flame of mine, as it goes.' He brushed dust and cobwebs from the jacket.

'Not this Salt woman?'

'No, not her.' The reply was curt. 'Here we are – the trousers.'

'Was your girlfriend a stick? How do you expect me to fit into those?'

'I'd have said you're about the same size, to be honest.'

'In that case, there's something seriously wrong with your eyesight!'

'Just get changed. You're fleeing for your life, remember? I'll go and get my leathers on, then we'll be ready to rock, as they say on Harris.'

'The island'

'Well, it's part of one. Och, never mind.'

Sorley strode off, leaving Tabitha to consider her new attire. There was something refreshing about Sorley, in a way. She wasn't used to men like him. Though he appeared to live and work in utter squalor. And she was sure she'd detected the taint of body odour on his person. Something that could have ruined a career on the board, where she came from. However, he'd managed to take her mind off the current reality of her life, fleeing from strangers who meant her harm.

Tabitha was suddenly seized by guilt that she hadn't tried to find out if her husband had escaped from the burning hotel. She'd known for a very long time that she didn't love him – if she ever had. It amazed her that it had taken this turmoil to focus her mind on her failing marriage. But by the same token, she didn't wish him harm. 'Poor bastard,' she whispered to herself.

Her mind flashed back to the jostle to escape, the smoke, the screams, panic – the relief of getting out the street. Tabitha never thought she'd be relieved about central London's fresh air.

Then something struck her. It surely couldn't be a co-incidence that the hotel in which she sought sanctuary went up in flames at the very moment when she was a resident. She could see the features of the men dressed in black over the shoulder of the paramedic. It was their grim-faced intent that had given them away.

People had died. Of that there was no doubt. They'd died because of her.

To try and banish this thought, Tabitha took off her jeans and pulled on the leather biker trousers. As she expected, though she managed to hoist them up, there was no way they would fasten round her waist. As much as she tugged and squeezed, they were at least an inch too small.

Quite exhausted by it all, she pushed herself up on the workbench and sat with her head in her hands.

'You not ready yet?' Sorley was resplendent in smart black leathers and biker boots.

'I told you they were too small.' Tabitha took to her feet and pulled at the leather trousers she'd been given. 'You see? Rubbish.'

'No problem. That's why I brought these.' Sorley held out his hand, displaying a selection of safety pins. 'As my mother always says, you can't go wrong with safety pins.'

'Can I ask you something?' said Tabitha, taking the largest safety pin on offer.

'Aye, on you go.'

'They set a fire at the hotel to flush me out, didn't they?'

'You've just thought of that? First thing that crossed my mind when I was told about you.'

His gaze shifted as though he was recalling something distasteful. His ex-girlfriend, Tabitha surmised. But she was still angry at herself for not connecting the hotel fire with her attempted escape.

'I've been pretty stupid, I know.'

'You're still in shock. Trust me, I've been there, it'll take a while. But once you find out how your other half is, things will get easier – hopefully.'

'How am I going to find out?'

'A friend of mine is having a look now. He's a PI – a good one.'

'You're full of surprises, Mr – whatever your name is.'

'Aye, full o' tricks, me. And it's MacLeod, by the way. Let's hope my resources are sufficient to get you out of here safe and sound.'

Tabitha squeezed into the leather jacket. It was tight, but at least she managed to pull up the zip. 'You aren't filling me with confidence,' she told him.

'Put it like this: neither of us have a choice. You can thank Cara Salt for that.' He placed a crash helmet over her head. 'There. If anyone recognizes you, they deserve to abduct you.'

Tabitha swore at her rescuer, but the expletive was lost in the depths of the helmet as he dragged at her leather trousers and temporarily secured them with another large safety pin.

'I could have done that perfectly well myself, thank you,' said Tabitha.

'Aye, but how long would it have taken you, eh?'

When she glared at him, Sorley flipped down the black visor, obscuring her eyes.

'Perfect. Time to go!'

25

Salt and Blackstock had to walk down a path into an area of pine trees to get to the helicopter pad. The air was fragrant, the ground neither wet nor dry. It had an unusual bounce, created by a considerable depth of dead pine needles piled on top of each other. For Salt, the headiness of it all felt like taking a shower using some exclusive gel or shampoo. She was suddenly revived, reinvigorated.

With them came a young police officer carrying an automatic weapon strapped over his shoulder by a webbing belt. Though it rather spoiled the ambiance, Salt felt reassured by his presence.

Birds sang, making Blackstock gaze into the trees in an attempt to spot the source. In moments, the scent of damp earth and plants became tainted with a hint of something else: aircraft fuel. Salt plodded on, the firearm holstered under her left arm weighing her down far more than the reality of its heft. Thoughts of the last time she carried a weapon crowded in on her.

Before Salt gave in to the desperate urge to cry out at the pain of memory, the sheltering trees opened out into a large clearing. A blue passenger helicopter sat in the middle of a landing pad. A large, cylindrical fuel tank stood a hundred yards or so away from a hangar. Nearby was a temporary building Salt thought must be an office, from which a man in dirty overalls stepped out to meet them. He was wiping his oily hands on a rag as he approached.

'Hello, there, I'm Andy Wootton, pilot to the gentry.' He smiled. He was indeed a local man, with a distinct Perth-shire accent. His face – once handsome – was now deeply lined. He had a small scar above his upper lip. It wasn't hard to see he'd had a life and lived every moment of it.

'I'm DI Salt, this is DS Blackstock.' They shook hands.

Salt eyed the aircraft. 'Will this get us to London and back without stopping? Sorry, I have no idea about these things.'

'Aye, she should – no bother. It's not as though I haven't done that before.' Wootton glanced at the armed constable. 'Who's your friend?'

'Don't worry about him, Mr Wootton.' Salt turned to their escort. 'Get yourself back to the house, Fraser. And thank you.'

'Yes, ma'am.' The young constable turned on his heel and was soon lost in the curtain of pines.

'A lot of fuss about the place. Nobody's said a word to me,' said Wootton. 'But I've a rough idea what's been going on – especially with all that about poor Jean-Luc plastered all over the news.'

Blackstock, avoiding the subject, took in the helicopter. 'Is she in good working order? I mean, is the aircraft safe?'

Wootton laughed. 'A nervous one, eh?'

'Yes. I must confess, I'm not entirely at home in the air,' said Blackstock.

'No need to worry. Safe as houses in this thing. Man, I can only think of five or six major accidents this model of helicopter has had over the years. I'll take the risk if you will, right?'

'Seriously?' Blackstock's face was pale.

'I'm only pulling your leg, my man. I used to be in the army. You should see some o' the things they made us go up in back then. Death traps, every one of them.'

'How long have you been retired?' Salt asked.

'I wouldna say *retired*, to be honest. But at any rate, I left. Did some oil rig work and other bits and pieces. Mr Pallander hired me as personal pilot to the family six years ago. I've never looked back.'

'Why did you leave the army, Mr Wootton?' asked Salt.

'Well, I could ramble on about all sorts and tell you how unfair it all was. But, in all honesty, it was the drink. Simple as that.'

'Drink?' Blackstock's face was a vision of disbelief.

'Aye. I was too fond of whisky for a while. But flying and Famous Grouse don't mix. Unless you're flying low, that is.' The pilot laughed at his own joke.

'Very funny.'

'Do you know where we're going?' said Salt, ready with her phone.

'Flight plan sorted. You gave the destination details to Mrs Sullivan. She's very efficient, right enough. A nice lassie. Though I don't fancy her job, trying to keep that place running. Anyway, the route is in the navigation system and cleared with air traffic control. No changes, I take it?'

'No, still on track. When can we leave?' Salt was in a hurry. The less time Tabitha Pallander was out in the open the better. 'Did you give air traffic control a reason for the flight?'

'Usual family business. Listen, they're not interested what you're doing, just that you're doing it safely and within the rules.'

'Good.'

'We're all fuelled up. Just give me a couple of minutes to change out of these and we're away.' He strode back into the makeshift building.

Blackstock was under one of the rotor blades, squinting up at the mechanism, one hand shading his eyes from the sun.

'Do you know anything about helicopters, Abs?' Salt asked.

'No, not a thing. But it doesn't take an expert to spot something hanging off, does it?'

'As long as *we're* not hanging off, there's no problem, is there?'

Blackstock made a face.

In a few minutes Wootton appeared again, this time in a uniform, of sorts. In fact, he looked like a rather dishevelled airline pilot, his shirt badly in need of the services of an iron, trousers rather too long, bunching up on top of a pair of black slip-ons. He was carrying a small satchel and had a pair of sunglasses balanced on his thatch of salt-and-pepper hair.

'Time to go.' He swung open a wide door and pulled out a little ladder that had been neatly concealed within the fuselage. 'Roll up, roll up,' he said, inviting them to board.

'You go first, Abs,' said Salt. 'I want to see how hard it is.'

'The four steps on to this thing are the easy part, trust me.'

Blackstock eschewed the offer of a hand up from the pilot and stepped into the aircraft without difficulty, Salt following on behind.

Once aboard, she noted two sets of double seats – plush leather, like an expensive car – so there was plenty of room for Tabitha when they found her. Andy Wootton slammed the door behind them and soon appeared in the pilot's seat. Once he was belted in, he removed an iPad mini from his holdall and slotted it on to part of the dashboard, a maze of little dials, LCD screens, buttons and levers. The pilot then turned round to face them and began his list of pre-flight checks.

'Right, people, this is where it gets serious. Put your belts on, then the headphones provided. Make sure you get the ears correct – left and right – OK? You'd be amazed the folk that don't do that properly.'

The detectives did as they were told. Soon, Wootton's voice rasped in their ears.

'Right, tell me who has anything offensive in their possession.'

The police officers looked at each other. Salt was first to speak.

'We're both carrying side-arms, if that's what you mean.'

'I knew that. It's OK, as long as you keep them where they are with the safety catches on. I mean little aerosols, deodorant, perfume, you know.'

Salt shook her head. 'No, nothing like that. I have some lippy, if that counts?'

'That's not going to blow up in your handbag, is it? Good, we're ready to go.' Wootton turned back in his seat, ready to address the controls and begin the flight.

'Actually, I have a small aerosol, now you mention it,' said Blackstock.

'You do?' The pilot turned back again, looking non-plussed.

'It's this.' Blackstock delved into a trouser pocket and, following some seat squirming, produced a tiny container, no larger than a lipstick. 'Breath spray. I do find so few restaurants provide after-dinner mints these days. Helps freshen one's palate after a meal.'

'Really? Well, that's a good idea, Sergeant,' said Wootton. 'Give it here.'

Salt observed her number two, who – somewhat defiantly – took the opportunity to spray his mouth a couple of times before he handed the tiny can over to the pilot.

'If we crashed, the investigators would definitely remark how sweet the smell was from your detached bonce, eh?' He took the aerosol, opened his door a crack and pitched it out of the aircraft.

'Hang on! That's bloody expensive – forty quid a bottle,' stuttered Blackstock.

'More fool you. Have you not heard of chewing gum?'

Salt shook her head, almost laughing at Blackstock. Why she hadn't noticed this on their first meeting was a mystery to her. His manner was most certainly *different*.

For Blackstock's part, he raised his head and turned to look out the window, as though suddenly aloof from the proceedings.

'OK. Some little house rules. Don't move about. And if you want to speak to each other, go ahead. I'll leave the cans open, but if I start speaking, you pay attention, right?'

The police officers in the back nodded in unison. Then there was a sudden ping from Blackstock's phone. He pulled it out of his jacket to see the message, which he regarded with one raised eyebrow.

'Oh, and another thing: switch off your bloody phones.'

As the passengers attended to this, Wootton brought the aircraft to life. From her window, Salt could see the great rotor blades whirl slowly round, their angle rising as they increased in speed.

'Here we go,' said the man in charge.

The rise of the aircraft was, at first, barely perceptible. However, when Salt looked out of the window at her side, they were climbing parallel to the tall trees around the small landing pad. The pines soon disappeared, to reveal a panorama of their surroundings.

Meikle House itself – more sprawling than Salt had imagined – began to look like a doll's house. She noticed how the place had been cleverly constructed amidst the ruins of a castle. Part of one old tower still clung to a steep slope above the river. She could spot the little blots that were the armed officers from Aberdeen and Inverness guarding the building's perimeter. Her eyes followed the long, single-track road leading into the valley that seemed to be the Pallanders' isolated fiefdom. A mountain rose at her side, tall with a sharp peak – the way a mountain should be, she thought. As the aircraft banked, Salt could see the silver of rivers and streams far below, little lochans and the tiny spots that were cattle and sheep dotted around fields that appeared to hold back the sprawling pine forests.

As they banked further, altering direction, she felt the cold steel of the firearm pinned under her arm in a webbing shoulder holster.

'Who was your message from?' she asked Blackstock, trying to move on from squeamish thoughts.

'Oh, just my wife,' said Blackstock awkwardly.

Wootton, who had been speaking to air traffic control, his conversation only obvious because of the movement of his lips, now chose to rejoin them.

'Your wife has no need to worry, Sergeant Blackstock. We'll have you back in her arms in no time, mate.'

Blackstock considered this. 'If you can do that *and* fly a helicopter,' he said, 'then you are indeed a most talented man.' Even via the tinny headphones, Blackstock's sarcasm was palpable.

'Well, lady and gentleman, just sit back and enjoy. We'll

be going into cloud cover soon for about twenty minutes. But after that, please feel free to take in the views on the way down to the big smoke and beyond. Over and out.'

He was right. In a few moments the helicopter cockpit darkened as they headed into the clouds. This coincided with the shadow that passed over Salt's heart. Despite her plan to rescue Tabitha going well so far, Cara Salt suddenly felt cold, and heavy, and she couldn't explain why. The sensation was visceral, a physical manifestation of her doubts and fears.

Amid the gloom, she tried not to think about it.

26

The road out of London was the usual stop-start. Long lines of steel, glass and rubber, threading along the arteries of a city as indifferent to their presence as any man or woman was to the bacteria that occupied their guts.

Tabitha had been pleased that her headset was connected to Sorley's wirelessly, so at least they could talk during the journey. Though, for her, the main topic quickly became asking whether or not anyone was following them. Being a motorcycle novice, she didn't dare turn round in her seat to look for herself.

Tabitha had seen many pillion passengers on such vehicles casually hanging on to little side handles, or in some cases with folded arms – especially in the city. And though their passage east from the teeming centre had never reached speeds in excess of twenty-five miles per hour, she clung steadfastly to Sorley's torso, trying her very best to sway as he swayed, lean back as he leaned. So far, Tabitha thought she was doing rather well.

'Try and relax. You're squashing me,' said Sorley, his voice buzzing in her helmet. 'And don't worry, I can only see half of London following us.'

'What?'

Even through the helmet, he could hear the panic in her voice.

'I mean, nothing looks any different to any other day I spend trying to get through this shit.'

They rode on, street after street, road after road, until buildings began to thin out, and grass and trees weren't parts of parks or boulevards but existed in their own space, as nature had always intended.

'Which way are you going?' Tabitha asked, her vice-like grip of Sorley's waist now gentler, her movements more natural.

'Down the A13 would be too obvious, but I'll do my best to mirror it. Luckily, all the days the bloody main road has been closed has forced me to find alternative routes, so we should be OK.'

'Where is this "hut"?' Tabitha asked.

'Not far from Benfleet. If you've heard of that?'

'Of course I've heard of it.'

'Nice place, don't you think? I sometimes go painting there.'

'I've never been.' Again, the expression in Tabitha's voice was hard to misinterpret.

'I guess you don't paint, then?'

'My father used to – years ago, when we were young.'

'But not in Benfleet.'

'No, the French Riviera, usually. He used to try and find the same places Churchill painted.'

'Aye, that makes sense,' said Sorley sarcastically.

Now, they were in the heart of the commuter belt, where the further you travelled out of London, the more opulent homes became. Terraced streets transformed into semi-detached residences, which in turn grew gardens and outbuildings. These dwellings expanded until they became mansions. Some were old or in a classic, admirable style, while others loomed like gaudy eyesores, monuments to their owners' lack of taste and surfeit of money, testimony in many cases to the inverse relationship of earning power to common sense. So Sorley had always reckoned, anyway.

'You OK? You've been quiet the last few miles,' Sorley said.

'Just thinking of John, my husband.'

'Don't worry, I'm wired to the phone here. If my mate calls, I'll let you know.'

Tabitha felt a strange disconnection to reality the further they travelled. It was like living in a dream, being part of something without real involvement – like a movie. The helmet, though not as claustrophobic as she had initially feared, blocked out any sense of the outside world, muffling sound and deadening the senses. Tabitha had always thought being on a motorbike must be akin to being on a bicycle. But she'd been wrong. She'd often condemned those who campaigned to be able to choose whether or not to wear a crash helmet as being imbecilic. Now, regardless of the danger, she could see the appeal of feeling her hair blown by the wind, part of the environment through which they travelled.

Suddenly, Sorley swerved round a corner and on to a country road.

'Fuck, you didn't give me much warning there,' said Tabitha, tightening her grip round Sorley's waist. When he didn't reply, she felt a flutter of fear in her chest. 'Is someone following us?'

'No. No, I don't think so.' But Sorley's gentle Hebridean lilt now had an edge, a clipped quality that betrayed his own thoughts. 'Just a van tailing us for a mile or so. Looked suspicious, but I'm sure it's OK.' The words were reassuring, but his head swung from one rear-view mirror to the other and back.

Sorley, more gently this time, turned another corner. They passed a large roadside pub, where people were enjoying the fine weather at tables in the beer garden, while their offspring played in a little swing park.

Tabitha looked on with envy as the tableau passed by. It was odd how individuals occupying the same space could be experiencing something so different. Families eating chicken curry and drinking beer, their children playing happily all around. But the world had always been an odd place; Tabitha had seen enough of it to know that.

'Tabitha, hold on to me tight, do you understand? And whatever you do, don't let go!'

Sorley's voice was urgent in her ears. She felt the bike roar beneath her as he gunned the engine. The world began to pass by much more quickly. Trees, cars, fences, walls and buildings became a blur, her fear increasing with their speed.

'Sorley, what's happening?' she called out desperately.

'Be ready to brace yourself when I shout.'

'Brace for what?'

'Just do it when I say. And, whatever happens, don't fall off!' He was shouting now, the noise of the engine louder and louder.

Had Tabitha possessed the courage, she'd have turned to face whatever Sorley was fleeing. Instead, she huddled low into the small of his back, clinging on for dear life.

'Now!' Sorley shouted.

In moments their progress slowed dramatically. Tabitha screamed, thinking they were about to hit something. But before she could react, the bike tilted, the tarmac road coming alarmingly close to her face. Her first instinct was to hold her hand out to try to push the road. But even with no experience on a motorbike, Tabitha knew that would just knock her off.

Sorley slammed on the brakes, and the world swung before them. Tabitha saw his leg thrust out on to the road, sparks coming from the steel pads on the soles of his biker boots. In a split second they turned to face the direction from which they'd just come. The bike swayed alarmingly from side to side as Sorley fought to maintain control.

Mercifully, they returned to an upright position just in time for Tabitha to spot a white Transit van flash past, travelling in the opposite direction.

'What the fuck?' she yelled, as their speed once more increased.

'The van, it's following us!' Sorley looked into the vibrating mirror beside his throttle and could make out enough to see the vehicle was now executing a three-point-turn in the road behind them. 'No doubt about it. How the fuck can that happen?'

'I don't know!' Tabitha wailed into her helmet.

'We have to hide, there might be more of them.' Sorley was desperately searching for a place to take the bike off-road, mentally picturing what was in front of them based on previous journeys along this same route. But his mind was cluttered, fear sending his thoughts in all directions. He'd only just managed to keep the motorbike from slipping from under them as he'd executed the emergency U-turn. His mouth was dry, hands shaking as adrenaline pumped through his body. The only clear thought he had was his hatred of Cara Salt. Here he was, his life in danger once more, and all because of her. He cursed the day he met her.

It was just as he was thinking of her that something came to mind. His alternative route wasn't as familiar. But there was a farm track ahead on the right, he was sure of it – well, nearly sure. He could picture the scene: a broken-down gate, a track running through a field into trees.

'OK, I have a plan. I just hope the place I'm thinking of is still the same.'

'Me too,' Tabitha replied with a whimper.

To his left, Sorley could see a clump of trees at the end of a long field that looked vaguely familiar. He was sure they were close. Some cows grazed contentedly. One turned its head at the shrill sound of the bike's engine.

Though he now lived the city life, Sorley was a country boy to his bootstraps. There wasn't much in the way of cattle in Benbecula, and what there were roamed free on the island's spartan pasture. But he knew enough about farming to know that where there were cattle in places like this, there were closed gates.

Sorley realized he didn't have time to scope out alternative places to hide. He had to make the calculation. Were they far enough ahead of their pursuers to be able to stop and open the gate?

He didn't know who was following them, but he'd seen enough to know that they were professionals. They'd been tailing the bike for about twenty minutes before he was forced into evasive action. They'd sat back, disappeared from view for a few minutes, made themselves less visible. It was only his instincts that had told him to run.

Before he had time to make the decision, the gate appeared in view. And he was right: no broken-down affair this time but a modern tubular steel construction, closed tight to keep livestock in. On the bright side, the little track was still there, marked out on the dry ground in two stripes, no doubt the work of robust tractor tyres.

'Can you open a gate?'

'What?'

'Open a farm gate? Och, never mind. We're soon going to find out, one way or the other.'

Sorley slowed the motorbike and brought it to a halt at the gate. 'Quick, open it and I'll drive through, then you close it, right?'

Tabitha Pallander's legs were like jelly when she hoisted herself off the bike and ran to the gate. The helmet felt very different off the bike, heavy, blocking her vision. She was no stranger to farm gates, as it happened, but this one was new, and the sprung handle was stiff.

'Hurry up!' Sorley shouted. He was trying to calculate how much distance he'd been able to put between them and the white van. Given the time it would have taken them to turn, plus his increased speed, they might just about make it.

Tabitha forced the handle up on the spring, shifting the heavy gate just enough to make room for the motorbike to pass through the opening.

'Right, close it. Come on!'

Tabitha pushed the gate back into position and again forced the handle up against the thick metal spring. At first, the closing mechanism appeared to stick, but with a shove she managed to secure it. She dashed back to the bike, revving a few yards away, and soon they were speeding across the field, tyres slipping on the gritty track.

In moments they reached the trees. Thankfully, the farm track continued on under the thick canopy of leaves. Sorley throttled the bike forward, slower now, keen to avoid any incident on the much slicker path through the woods.

He spotted an old wooden building, partially collapsed – too small to be a barn, too big to be a shed. It was set in undergrowth, tall grass and weeds.

'Help me get the bike behind here.' He slowed to a stop, then he and Tabitha dismounted and pushed the bike through rough ground and undergrowth behind the building.

'It stinks,' said Tabitha.

'Chicken shit,' Sorley replied.

'No, it does! Oh, sorry.' Tabitha realized he'd meant real chicken shit as opposed to misgivings about her opinion of the smell. She collapsed into the long grass and took off her crash helmet.

'Stay there.' Sorley too had divested himself of his helmet.

'Where are you going?'

'Back to check the road. Don't move.'

Sorley took off, stopping at the treeline on the edge of the field. Sweat poured down his face. He wiped it away as he stared across the field to the road. There was no sign of the white Transit van.

He was about to turn and head back to Tabitha when he heard a distant engine.

To his dismay, the white van slowed as it reached the farm gate and then stopped.

27

Silas Pallander knew it was daytime. High above him was a little skylight that had been painted over. Some of this paint had chipped off. So, by looking up, he could mark the passage of day and night, light and dark.

All was quiet. He hadn't heard Anna's screams or pleas for mercy in hours. He was beginning to think he'd never hear her again. He still couldn't work out why they'd tortured her. He was the son of the multi-billionaire, after all.

Silas was not a man who lied to himself about his own limitations, though he knew many who did. They were targeting Anna so that he would do as they asked. He wasn't sure if they knew of his devotion to his PA or whether they just thought this would be a faster route to getting what they wanted. That breaking a woman's resolve would be an easier job than dismantling his. Clearly, they didn't know the personalities involved.

If they'd tried to put him through what he'd heard Anna endure, he'd have done anything they'd wanted within minutes.

You're a coward. Too stupid to play rugby. Too scared to play with your friends.

He was a child again, standing in his father's study at the family's Kensington town house.

His father's taunts never ended.

You don't grow. I should pour water and shit on you every night, so you'll get bigger.

In the early part of his life, Silas had been devastated by his father's put-downs. But as he grew, he began to realize that his father's spiteful vitriol was intended to push his son on, toughen him up. That Sebastian Pallander was from a poor background was well known. It was clear he wanted nothing but the best for his children and would do anything to stop them coming to harm. In that way, he'd been a caring father. It was just hard to tell where care stopped and bullying began.

Tabitha had never suffered in that way.

Your father can see himself in her, his mother used to say. In the end, he supposed, he was always fighting a losing battle for his father's affections, his confidence.

He was on the floor again, his back against the cold, whitewashed wall. He drew his knees up to his chin and clasped his hands under them. If he gave these people what they wanted, he would die. Of this, he was reasonably sure. But what could they want? He now had neither money nor influence within his father's company. His career was over. His father's last will and testament had ensured that.

Ultimately, though, what was death but an end to suffering? It was an escape valve, placed carefully for those who could endure no more. A blessed release.

This was how he'd always felt. Throughout the torment of his childhood, death had been his friend. No matter what his father flung at him, regardless of the cruelty of his schoolmates and teachers, he could rely on death.

Silas Pallander decided he would disempower everyone; his captors, his dead father, his detractors, all those who whispered behind his back, opining how far away the son was from being the father.

Yes, with death's help, he would defeat them all. People would talk about it, admire him.

He had the courage to fight back. They couldn't break him. He was brave.

Silas was buoyed by these thoughts, reinvigorated by the perverse promise of his own demise.

Then he heard voices.

'Please, let me sleep! Where are you taking me now?'

Anna's voice was plain. He heard one slap, then another. He flinched; eyes tight shut as she groaned in agony.

'Tell me what it is you want!' Silas shouted, his voice a pleading whine.

The door swung open. Anna was flung bodily inside. He hurried over to her. Her face was even more bruised and battered than the last time he'd seen her. She was kneeling on the floor, sobbing.

'I don't know what to do. Honestly, I don't know how I can make them stop!' She muttered something in French that he didn't understand.

'What do you mean?' asked Silas.

He cradled her in his arms. Anna looked up. His first instinct was to wipe away her tears, but she pushed him away.

'No, don't touch my . . . the pain.'

Silas could see clots of dark blood in her red hair. Anna grabbed his hand. Her voice was barely a whisper. 'I know what they want. They told me.'

'What? I'll do anything. I don't care, as long as they stop this.'

'They need your signature.'

'What?'

'Please don't make me say everything twice. They need your signature on a document. I don't know what it is – it could be anything.'

'Yes, yes, I'll do it!' he shouted without further thought. 'What have I got to lose, apart from a career as a backwoods estate manager? Fuck it!'

He laid Anna carefully against the wall. Once more, her tears flowed freely. Silas walked to the door and banged it with his fist.

'I'll do it,' he shouted. 'I'll sign. Let's just get this over with, please!'

Apart from Anna's quiet sobbing, he heard nothing by way of a response.

'Are you listening to me? I'll do it. Come on!'

This time, he battered both hands against the door, tears of exasperation flowing down his cheeks. Silas hammered and screamed at the top of his voice, determined that someone – anyone – would listen.

Because of this loud protest, he didn't hear the footsteps on the other side of the door. But the metallic sound of a key in the lock made him step back. Two giant men dressed in the kind of white overalls he'd seen in TV police dramas stood before him. Hoods were pulled up over their heads, their features obscured by identical white masks, featureless like porcelain dolls. As one, they reached out and caught him by each shoulder. Silas Pallander called out in pain.

'Please don't hurt him!' shouted Anna.

Silas was dragged along a corridor like a child between the two faceless men. The toecaps of his highly polished Tricker's Oxford shoes scraped against the floor. As he tried to regain his footing, he received a sharp punch to the side of the face.

They stopped at another door. He was led into a small, dark room. Overhead a strip-light flickered into life with a sharp ping. It bathed everything in a cold, unnatural light that made him blink after the relative dim of his cell.

Facing him was a scuffed table and a simple wooden chair. He was thrust roughly on to the latter.

'Sit down and shut the fuck up.'

The accent wasn't English but the sentiment behind the request was. Silas leaned on both elbows, head in hands.

'Are you going to kill me?'

Another blow, this time to the back of the head. The men who'd dragged him here were now standing behind his chair. 'What did I say?'

Silas felt as though he was living one of the nightmares he'd suffered as a child. He felt detached, as if he were observing himself from afar. The man who was sitting behind the rough desk was him in a dream; not real, not corporeal. The porcelain features of his captors were real, no mere flight of fancy.

The door opened again. A woman entered. She was wearing a dark business suit and red stiletto-heeled shoes. No attempt had been made to hide her oval, olive-skinned face. Her hair was pulled back into a bun, stretching her sculpted eyebrows and giving her eyes a feline quality. She had a black leather attaché case under one arm.

'I am going to give you three documents to sign. You won't read them. Just sign, and your woman will live. Not just that, your family will survive. For make no mistake, we will kill them all, as we did your brother.'

Silas desperately didn't want to ask the question but couldn't help himself. 'What about me?'

'You sign.'

She pulled some documents from the attaché case, then

put a blank sheet of paper on the table in front of him. Under this, she placed a printed sheet. All that was left for him to see was the space for his signature, his name printed underneath in bold type. She handed him a Montblanc pen.

'You sign now.'

Silas held the pen in his trembling hand. As demanded, he signed, his signature a spider-scrawl across the page, but still recognizable.

As she repeated the process, Silas caught her scent. It was expensive, but he couldn't place it.

'And again,' she commanded, the papers placed in front of him in exactly the same fashion as before.

Silas signed again, and then they went through the motions a third time.

He watched her neatly and efficiently place everything back in the attaché case.

'What now?' he asked.

The woman in the red shoes didn't reply, just turned on her heel and left the room.

Silas Pallander half turned in his chair. But before he could speak, a heavy blow landed on the back of his head, propelling him into darkness.

28

The skies began to clear and, as predicted, the helicopter was once again bathed in sunlight. Salt glanced from her window to see a small town hugging two sides of a river. Roads in and out of the place twisted like branches of a tree. Now and again, sunlight would flash from a vehicle far below. The police officer in Salt wondered what everyone was up to, how they fitted into the world, what they were doing. As she gazed down, she realized that was her lot in life, to observe others.

'OK, the rest of the journey should be in bright sunlight, folks.' Wootton's voice crackled in their headphones.

But something was nagging at Cara Salt. Without warning, she had again the fluttering feeling in her chest that regularly presaged a problem. She had no idea from where these feelings came, but during the course of her life – especially the time she'd spent as a police officer – they had become more frequent.

'Penny for them,' said Blackstock.

Salt drew the headphone mic closer to her mouth, as though trying to keep her comments private. 'I'm not sure. Just a feeling.'

'I'm sure everything is going to plan. This MacLeod sounds like a solid enough chap. And Ms Pallander is nothing if not resourceful. Though, from what I've heard, someone's in for a tongue-lashing if this plan does actually work. Tabitha Pallander does not suffer fools gladly. Your friend may have bitten off more than he can chew.'

'I hope she'd be grateful he's trying to save her life.'

'She should be. But this is the anointed one, remember? Well, up until the will was read. Rather a handful, I think.'

Salt continued mulling everything over, hoping that logic would quell her negative feelings. It didn't work. Now she had to worry about the dynamic between Sorley and Tabitha. When she closed her eyes, the vision of his shooting leached into her mind. Quickly, she opened her eyes again.

'Mr Wootton, can I ask a question, please?'

The pilot turned to face her. 'Yes, ask away.'

'Will this thing crash if I check my phone?'

He smiled. 'No, of course it won't. But it's rules and regs – you know what I mean.'

'Funny. I know we've only just met, but I didn't have you down as a strict observer of the rules.'

Wootton considered this for a moment. 'Well, if you'll take responsibility for the crash when your signal inter-feres with the electronics – go for it!'

'Ma'am, I must confess to thinking this may be a bad idea. We'll be there soon. How long, Mr Wootton?'

'An hour, maybe a bit less.'

'You see? I'd hang on, if I were you.'

Salt bit her lip. She could see beneath Wootton's sarcasm that he wasn't really bothered by her use of the mobile phone. And the fluttering in her chest had not abated. 'Sorry, Abs.' She grabbed her phone, switched it on, and waited.

'Can't guarantee you'll get signal.'

'We'll see.'

'I may as well check in with the ACC, in that case,' said Blackstock.

'You've changed your tune!'

'Who knows, he may be able to help. If there's a problem, that is.' Blackstock shrugged.

Just when Salt was about to give up hope, a bar of signal appeared on her screen. The device flashed with notifications. Quickly, she went to her text messages. Her heart pounded when she discovered there was one.

'Anything?' Blackstock asked.

'Hang on.'

Salt opened the message. Her window cleaner was being forced to put his prices up, and he was very sorry. She sighed, then opened her calls app. There it was, one missed call from Sorley. Her instincts had been right. She dialled up voice messages, pressing the phone to her ear. There was the usual preamble of time and date of the call, then she could hear snatches of Sorley's voice. She wasn't sure whether the original message was corrupted or whether the fault was with her line in the helicopter, but she could only make out a few words.

Big trouble . . . they're on to us . . . pick up the phone!

'Mr Wootton, can anything be done to boost the phone signal?' Salt asked breathlessly.

'No, sorry. She's an old bird. Mr Pallander intended to update the electronics but never got round to it. I think he enjoyed the peace, to be honest. He didn't get much of that, sadly.'

'Shit.' Salt looked at Blackstock, who was busy typing on his phone. 'What are you saying to the ACC?'

'Just keeping him up to speed.'

'OK. Probably best.'

'What is happening – with Sorley, I mean?'

'I can't really hear. Keeps cutting out. He doesn't sound happy.'

'Thought as much from your expression.' Blackstock typed a few more words then trousered his mobile.

Salt gazed back out the window. They were flying over hills and little lakes now, the landscape spread out below them like a map. How could they know? she asked herself. The only possible answer was that Tabitha must have been followed to Sorley's shop.

If you try to shoot me, you'll kill him.

Salt tried to exorcise the memory from her brain but, as ever, it was persistent.

Or you better hit me with your best shot. Because if you don't, he's dead meat, and so are you.

She could hear the sharp report of the side-arm, the pistol recoiling in her outstretched hands. Then she saw a crimson splatter, and Sorley's eyes went back in his head. He sank to his knees, his face pale – grey, almost.

She fired again.

DI Cara Salt had endured this memory before – often. This, though, was a new experience, a visceral one. She could smell the cordite in the air, see the flecks of spittle on Sorley's hair as his captor yelled.

'Are you quite all right, ma'am?'

The tap on the shoulder brought Salt back to the here and now.

'Yes, I'm OK. But we have to get down there as quickly as we can. I owe it to my friend.'

They were running now, the motorbike abandoned behind the chicken shed. Though both Tabitha and Sorley had ditched their crash helmets, they still wore the bike leathers and boots.

The woods became thicker the further they went. Tabitha tripped over a tree root and fell, yelping with pain.

Sorley pulled her to her feet, and they carried on their mad dash.

'Where are we going?' said Tabitha, as she was dragged along by the hand.

'Where it's darkest, and we have a chance.'

They carried on, over tree stumps, down little paths, even climbing a fence. The soft ground underfoot was treacherous and energy-sapping. Miraculously they kept their feet, but their biker boots and leathers weren't designed to aid fast passage.

To his right, Sorley spotted a tiny path that led up a hill and through oak trees. 'This way!'

Tabitha grunted and panted as she gained the rise. Was it only last night she'd been flung into this nightmare? 'I need to rest,' she said breathlessly. 'I can't go any further.'

'On your own head be it.'

They halted beside two great oaks. Sorley leaned on his knees, gasping for air. He tried to work out how far they'd come from the chicken shed. Maybe quarter of a mile, perhaps a little more.

Tabitha was sitting, her back against an oak. 'I've always wanted to do this,' she said.

'What, run from a crew of murderous bastards with a boy from Benbecula for company? Got to say, my bucket list is rather more expansive.'

'No, sit on a forest floor beside a tree.'

'You've never done that?'

'Maybe as a child, but I can't remember. Certainly not as an adult – I've never had the time.'

She was about to expand on this when Sorley put one finger to his mouth, hushing her. Sure enough, in the distance, they could hear voices. At first they were lost on the breeze, but they became louder with each passing second – or so it seemed.

'What are we going to do?' Tabitha held her head in her hands, all thoughts of escape now receding.

Sorley MacLeod's mind was working overtime. He was weighing up their options, and they weren't good. He looked on as a leaf floated to earth from the canopy high above. 'OK, I have an idea.'

'What, make ourselves invisible?'

'Yes, that's the idea. But we'll have to be quick. Here, push yourself up.'

Sorley interlaced the fingers of both hands, turning them into an impromptu step, as though he was helping a rider on to a horse.

'You mean?'

'Unless you think you can vault up to it, yes.'

'I can't climb – I get vertigo. Heights, can't cope with them.' Tabitha looked more terrified now than ever.

'Listen, it's easy. We don't even need to go that high. The canopy of leaves is pretty low. Look, you can almost reach up and touch them.' He stood on tiptoes to demonstrate, his outstretched fingers still several feet from the foliage. 'It's our only chance, Tabitha.'

As she looked up into the tree, voices broke out again. They were closer – much closer. Had they been speaking English, she could have understood. But the language was Slavic.

'It worked for Charles the Second,' whispered Sorley.

'Funny, I'm getting more of a Charles the First vibe here.' She took a deep breath. 'Come on, I'll give it a go.'

Sorley cupped his hands again. This time Tabitha stepped on to them with one filthy boot. 'Grab a branch and I'll do my best to push you up,' he said, already straining as he took her weight.

Tabitha stretched as far she could. Still no branch was within reach. 'I need to be higher,' she groaned.

With one last heave, Sorley pushed her further up the tree, his cheeks puffed out, face red with the effort.

Tabitha managed to hook the fingers of her right hand round a sturdy branch. At the same time, looking down tentatively, she spotted a knot on the tree that she felt would be wide enough to take a foot. As Tabitha pulled with her right hand, she sought out the knot with her left foot.

'That's it,' said Sorley breathlessly.

Tabitha's first attempt failed. Her foot slipped on the knot, the sole of her biker boot slick with the detritus from the woodland floor. With a gargantuan effort, Sorley managed to keep her upright.

'One more time,' he whispered with the last of his breath.

Tabitha repeated the process, and although she felt awkward, vulnerable, she managed to find purchase on the knot. She pushed hard, pivoting in the air, and grabbed the branch above with her left hand too.

'That's it. Just pull yourself up on to that thick branch.'

Sorley wrung out his hands, trying to loosen them off after propelling Tabitha into the oak tree. He looked on as, like a gymnast, she swung herself up and managed – not without a slip or two and a desperate grasp – to access the stouter branch above that protruded from the great tree.

With ease, and despite the pain in his hands, Sorley flung himself at a branch, caught it and pulled himself up, his feet slipping and sliding as he scaled the gnarled tree trunk. In moments, they were sitting together in the crook of the thick branch and the tree.

'You did well,' said Sorley. 'I wish you'd told me you were a gymnast.'

'Nearly twenty years ago – and we didn't climb trees.'

Sorley held up his hand. The voices were getting close now – very close.

29

Had Silas Pallander not woken up with a splitting headache, he'd have thought he was dreaming. For he was lying in Anna Marchand's arms, as she gently stroked his hair.

He tried to piece together what had happened. He remembered signing three documents, the details of which had been kept from him.

'Anna,' he said, his voice cracking.

'Take this – only very little.' She held a bottle of water to his mouth. He did as he was told, sipping at it.

'They made you sign?'

'Yes,' said Silas, feeling warmer and more cared for than he had been in years. He looked up into Anna's face. Despite the bumps and bruising, the clumps of dried blood in her hair, she was still so beautiful.

'What?' she said, turning her head away, as though ashamed of her injuries.

'No, please. Just let me look at you.' Silas drank her in. He could feel the rise of her chest as she breathed. 'I love you, Anna. I always have,' he said, searching her face.

She hushed him. 'Now is not the time, Mr Pallander. Later, maybe we can talk.'

'If there is a *later*, you mean.'

'I thought they would kill you.' A fat tear meandered down Anna's face, over the shadow of a bruise and the hint of the freckles that made her look so young in the summer.

'They can do what they want, if they just leave me here for a while longer. Have you seen them again?'

She shook her head. 'No, not since they left you back in here. I haven't heard anything either.'

'It's like that in here. You can't hear them. Not unless they're almost outside the door. The walls are thick.' He wanted to add *unless they're torturing you* but thought the better of it.

'We can't just stay here. You've done what you had to do. Either they kill us or let us go.' Anna's battered face took on a determined expression.

'How can they let us go?' Silas sighed.

Anna pulled away gently, helping him up into a seated position. 'Keep taking sips of the water.'

'Where are you going?'

She stared at him, her blue eyes wide. 'I can't stand this. If they kill us, then so be it. If not – *c'est fini.*'

'Anna, don't!' Silas tried to get to his feet, but his head felt as if it was about to burst. 'Please stay with me for a while.'

She turned and smiled at him. 'I must know,' she said. 'I'm sorry.'

Silas had to give credit where credit was due. She was brave. But in this case foolish too, he felt. Being here with her reminded him of the last day of a beautiful holiday. The kind where you would tarry on the terrace, breathing the air, feeling the sunshine on your face until it was time to leave, to go back to the humdrum reality of life, with all its cares and woes.

'Hello!' Anna was calling out, battering the door with her fists.

Silas screwed up his eyes, waiting for the door to be flung open once more, for their captors to punish her, abuse her again.

'I want to fucking speak to you! Come on!' Her French accent was strong now.

Despite it all, Silas smiled. The way she swore sounded so strange – funny, if things hadn't been as they were. It always amused him when she swore. If only they were back in the office with their little flirtations.

He waited for her to call out again, but all was silence. 'Anna?'

Just as his heart was about to burst with sadness, she appeared round the stack of shelves between him and the door. Her expression was one of confusion.

'What's wrong?' Silas asked. For a minute, he imagined she'd been shot or stabbed, and was about to stagger forward and die beside him on the floor.

'The door is open,' Anna said. 'There is no one to be seen or heard.' A broad smile broke out across her face.

'No, no, that can't be true.' Silas stared at her.

'It is true.' She held out her hand. 'Come with me.'

She pulled him to his feet gently, taking time to look into his face to make sure he wasn't going to pass out. Anna planted a kiss on his cheek and, still holding his hand, pulled him towards the door.

Silas was surprised to see it ajar. The door he'd hammered on to try to stop them hurting her, to stop her screams. But still, he was cautious.

'Come on, they are gone,' she implored.

'They're just playing with us.'

'Always the pessimism. Come, take my hand again.'

Reluctantly, Silas Pallander followed his personal assistant through the door and into a dank corridor. It stank of neglect.

'Careful,' he said, as they reached another door. Undaunted, Anna turned the battered brass handle.

'Look,' she said, pointing to a stairwell bathed in a shaft of sunlight from above.

Silas stared into the light. Where were they? Where had their captors gone? The questions still tormented him.

'I saw her face.'

'Whose face did you see?' Anna looked puzzled.

'The woman who made me sign the documents. I saw her face. I can identify her.'

Anna narrowed her eyes. 'Do you see her now? *Allez!*' She took the concrete steps two at a time.

Silas was powerless to move. The whole thing seemed so bizarre. He waited at the bottom of the stairs for a scream, the rattle of bullets. But nothing happened.

Anna reached the top of the stairs, her smile stretching from ear to ear. 'We're free! They have disappeared. Come quickly, Silas.'

She'd called him Silas the night they made love after the party in the Shard. He felt as though his heart would burst with joy as he ran up the steps to join her.

She stood in what remained of an office. The small panes of what had once been a window had been smashed. A big desk was turned over, sheets of paper littering the floor. On the wall, a painting of an aircraft had been slashed and now jostled for space with bold graffiti in red and black spray paint.

Anna picked up an old-fashioned phonebook from the bare concrete floor. She looked up and smiled. 'We're in Belgium, Mr Pallander.'

They walked out of the broken front door. Facing them was an overgrown runway, clumps of grass and weeds poking through the concrete right down its length. In the distance, a handful of cows grazed on green pasture before some scattered trees. The air was warm and the sound of traffic from an unseen road could be heard in the distance.

Silas Pallander and Anna Marchand's eyes met. She rushed into his arms, sought his lips with hers and kissed him passionately.

30

Sorley MacLeod and Tabitha Pallander were frozen still with fear. Some of the men from the white van were visible through the leaves. Tabitha could see the balding top of a man's head, the great ring of white flesh making him look like a monk. Sorley looked into her eyes, silently imploring her with a shake of his head not to move or make a sound.

The men were arguing. They talked quickly in their own language. The tone of their voices gave away the meaning, as surely as though they were speaking English. The balding man was pointing at one of his companions, prodding his finger again and again in the direction of an unseen individual. He rattled out a few words, until suddenly he stopped, hushing the rest of them, a hand cupped to one ear.

Tabitha stared into Sorley's blue eyes. She wasn't sure she'd ever seen bluer. He worked in what could best be described as a dump. But there was something attractive about his brio, the confidence he instilled within her even in this perilous situation. She tried to picture her husband John like this, up a tree, fleeing for his life. Then she felt guilty because she still didn't know his fate.

The balding man held up his hand to maintain the silence.

Sorley wanted to sneeze. He suffered from hay fever. Being stuck up a tree in the middle of a field at this time of year was his idea of hell.

The man broke the silence, speaking under his breath. He turned to the tree in which they were hiding, and ran his hand up the rough oak, as though admiring a fine piece of furniture. His eyes followed his hand as it went higher up the bark.

Tabitha tasted bile in her throat. She narrowed her eyes and prayed silently. She could picture the dead men on the driveway of her house. Closing her eyes tightly, she tried to banish the memory. Instead, she saw herself sitting down in London, staring over the shoulder of the paramedic at the dead-eyed men across the street.

The balding man shouted, making both Tabitha and Sorley start.

He was walking away now, calling out orders left and right. As soon as he was out of sight, and just as quickly as they'd arrived, their tormentors disappeared.

'What now?' whispered Tabitha.

Sorley put a finger to his lips.

The men's voices were becoming fainter, being absorbed by the trees and foliage.

'OK, very quietly,' said Sorley, 'can you get back down?'

'I think so,' Tabitha replied, already edging off the sturdy branch. 'But where are we going?'

'Back the way we came. We pick up the bike from behind the shed and we try to get to the rendezvous with Cara.'

'Will they wait? Because we won't be on time.'

'They'll wait,' said Sorley, with much more confidence than he felt.

Tabitha grabbed another branch and managed to swing down on to the woodland floor. She bent her knees to cushion her landing. Sorley was slower and less graceful. He half shinned, half climbed down the trunk, jumping the last four feet or so.

The pair took off, Sorley in front, Tabitha following, dreading the tough run back to the chicken shed.

But her protector was sure-footed, and mercifully in possession of a fine sense of direction. They stopped every now and then to listen. There were no sounds of danger, as far as they could hear.

Tabitha was surprised when she saw the tumbledown shed up ahead. The journey back seemed infinitely shorter than in the other direction. She supposed that not being chased this time had much to do with it.

'I'll grab the bike,' said Sorley. 'You have a look and see if the coast is clear. Remember to stay back from the treeline.'

Doing as she was bid, Tabitha edged her way towards the field they'd crossed to find cover. She knelt down, suddenly fearful that the safety pin holding up her trousers might let her down at any minute.

At first, all she could see was the white Transit, sitting in the field at an angle, not far from the gate. She peered into the bright sunlight, trying to discern whether or not there was anyone inside the vehicle. She sighed with relief when, having moved along the trees, she managed to find a decent view of the cab. It was empty.

Tabitha was about to turn back towards Sorley when movement caught her eye. On the edge of the field was the figure of a man, meandering across the grass. He was fifty yards or so away from the van, seemingly untroubled, smoke rising from a cigarette at which he puffed now and again.

She hurried back to the shed, where Sorley was already astride the motorbike.

'Coast clear?'

'No,' Tabitha replied breathlessly.

'Eh?'

'There's a man not far from the van.'

'Shit.'

'What now?'

'We have to go for it.'

Tabitha tried to picture the relative distances. They were much further away, but the man in the distance didn't have a bike.

'Right, get on,' said Sorley. 'We push the bike to the tree-line, then make a break for it, OK?'

Tabitha's head swam as Sorley took the handlebars and she pushed at the back seat of the bike. She felt the sense of unreality sometimes brought on by flu or a heavy cold, somehow removed from what was going on before her eyes. Everything seemed still – no birdsong on the air, no traffic on the road. The whole world, she felt, was holding its breath, ready for the next bad thing to happen in her life. The sensation was as bizarre as it was terrifying.

Nearing the field, Sorley turned to her. He put on his helmet, and she followed suit. He nodded and they clambered on board. Sorley clicked the ignition to the first position, turning on the helmet radio.

'Right, I'll count to three then I'll turn her over.'

'What about the guy in the field?'

'If he gets in the way, I'll drive the bike at him. Just hang on tight. This is our last chance.'

She grabbed his waist, praying for the first time in years.

'OK. One, two, three . . .' Sorley stood, and with one quick push of his right leg he fired the bike into life. Thankfully, it was well maintained, and the engine throttled with a noisy growl.

Tabitha was glad to be hanging on to Sorley's waist so tightly, as the bike almost tipped up into a wheelie. Sorley wrestled it under control. She looked to her left through the helmet's shaded visor. Sure enough, the man she'd last spotted quietly puffing at his cigarette was now running full pelt towards the white Transit. She could see he had a phone to his ear, his stride lengthening with every step.

Sorley could see him too. And like Tabitha, he was calculating relative distances. Though he was sure they'd make it past the van first, there was the added complication of the road. From the corner of his eye, he spotted movement to his right and saw a large red tractor trundling along the road. Now he had something else to fit into his calculations.

Tabitha tried to keep sight of the man. It was difficult, as they were travelling at speed over rough ground, turning the world into a churning, vibrating series of snatched images.

'It's going to be close!'

Again, she could hear the tension in Sorley's voice via the helmet radio. Tabitha felt helpless. All she could do was hang on for dear life.

They were closing in on the van now, but so was their tormentor. Sorley edged the bike to the right, making sure the van was between him and the man. It was easy to push a motorcyclist off a bike if one was determined enough. And, for the first time, Sorley wondered if the man was carrying a weapon or had left it in the van. There was no doubt that the rest of his party was armed – he'd seen the weapons.

Sorley pushed his head down over the front of the bike. He felt Tabitha tuck in. For a novice rider, she was no slouch.

The man was within yards of the van. But in seconds

they would be through the gate and out on to the road. The tractor was slow, but having a much shorter distance to travel it was nearing the gate. Sorley gunned the throttle.

As they sped past, he caught a glimpse of the man. He'd stopped and was fumbling something into his hands.

'A gun!' Sorley yelled. It was now or never. Certainly, he didn't have time to wait until the tractor was safely past the gate.

As he exited the field and skidded left on to the road, Sorley MacLeod fully expected the world to turn upside down and the tractor to hit his bike. And though he'd slowed somewhat to take the turn, black smoke billowed from the tyres as the bike keeled over to the left against the momentum, on to the hard tarmac of the roadway.

For a sickening moment, Sorley thought he'd lost control, and they were destined to skid across the road and, at this speed, into oblivion. But with all his strength he heaved the machine back on to the perpendicular, his arms aching. In his mirror, the tractor flashed its lights and sounded a loud blast on its horn.

They swayed a bit on the road, but they'd made it.

Sorley was about to congratulate Tabitha, when he heard her gasp into the mic.

'What it is?'

Her voice was quiet. She sounded confused.

'I think I've been shot.'

'Can you hang on?'

'Yeah, I – I think so.'

Sorley felt her body press into his back, her grip even tighter around his waist.

He knew he had to put as much distance as he could between them and their pursuers. He could picture them flooding out of the woods and back into the Transit van.

'Hang on, Tabitha. Please hang on!'

But even as he said the words, Sorley knew he'd have to pull the bike to a halt the second he felt her grip loosen. He gritted his teeth and took the open road as fast as he could.

31

DI Salt knew they were close to the landing place Sorley had described. From the map, they'd transposed the exact coordinates for the aircraft to follow. But still she doubted herself.

'Our destination makes sense, doesn't it, Mr Wootton?'

'Don't fret. I checked it carefully.' The pilot's voice crackled in her headphones. 'Put it like this, we land on the wrong place on these marshes, and it'll be "Abandon ship!", not "Happy landings!".'

The very thought made Salt's stomach churn. But in her brief experience of the man, Wootton exuded confidence – in a relaxed, devil-may-care way, but confidence just the same.

'You OK, Abs?' Salt turned to her detective sergeant.

'Just dandy,' he replied, in the offhanded fashion to which she had become accustomed.

'Like that, is it?'

'One might say I often approach these occasions with no little trepidation. Once you spend time undercover, you'll know what I mean. And of course, flying never helps.'

'We should be over the rendezvous point in a minute or so,' said Wootton, scanning the horizon through his Ray-Bans.

Though Salt had never been to Sorley's little fishing hideaway in person, she had managed to bring it up on Google Earth. This made her feel slightly sleazy, but looking down from the helicopter, the unusual landscape was at least kind of familiar. Tiny islands were dotted about here and there in a monotone paisley pattern. Yachts and other small boats were anchored near the coast. The place felt ancient, timeless.

As they flew, she saw other, more solid-looking parts of the marshes with less standing water. In her mind she could see the image she'd looked up: Sorley's fishing hut on a piece of land like this, within the marshes proper, but not of them. It was typical of the man, a halfway house. Like their relationship, neither one thing nor the other. When she thought about it, that was her whole life.

'Here we are,' said Wootton.

Salt dragged her mind away from metaphors and lost love, and stared down at what could have passed for an island in a lonely sea. While she knew the surrounding waters weren't deep, the impression of isolation was there. It was then she spotted a little wooden construction on the edge of this islet, at the end of a straight, narrow road. She instantly recognized the place. The small causeway facilitated access through the marshes, but the little hut was so isolated. She scanned the island and the thin strip of road as Wootton circled the helicopter. Her heart sank when she realized there was no sign of a motorbike.

Then she remembered the snatch of a message she'd heard on her phone.

'By my calculations,' said Blackstock, 'they should have been waiting for us.'

'Nobody about,' added Wootton.

Salt wondered why men always felt the need to back

each other up, even when the answer was obvious to every-one. 'I can see that,' she said, rather sharply.

'Do you want me to land, Inspector?' said Wootton.

'What do you think we should do? Look for them, maybe?'

'We could, but what would that achieve? Can't be sure of places to land in terrain like this. Reminds me of the Falk-land Islands – parts of it, at least. And we have to keep an eye on fuel. We need enough to get back to Meikle House – with as little fuss as possible, you said.'

There it was: *you said*. Salt couldn't count the number of times she'd heard the expression. Her father, belligerent colleagues, her more irritating friends, Sorley . . . Sorley. The thought of him made her heart sink again. *You said* was his favourite expression.

'OK, just land, if you think that's the best thing to do.'

'Landing now.'

The helicopter swooped low on the tiny island, describ-ing a circle over the water and land. Wootton studied it all with a practised eye, judging the very best place to put down. Having decided, he hovered over the chosen spot, lowering the helicopter slowly until it kissed the ground.

'Thank goodness,' said Blackstock, the tension in his face that had been present throughout the flight from Scotland disappearing.

Wootton waited for the rotor blades to come to a rest before suggesting they take a poke about.

Removing her headphones in the now silent helicopter and hearing voices unfiltered by the communication system was something of a shock for Salt. It was odd how quickly the human mind adapted. Wootton opened the door by her side and helped her down the few steps on to the island.

'Are you going to call him again?' said Blackstock, appearing at her side as his boss gazed across the archipelago of marshes.

'I'll try.' She pulled the mobile from her pocket and checked the screen. No signal. 'Fuck!' Salt swore at the top of her voice.

'They might have been delayed somehow. You don't know,' said Blackstock.

'Yeah, that message really sounded as though they were just in a traffic jam, didn't it? Do you have any signal, Abs?'

He shook his head, as did Wootton, mobile in hand.

Salt huddled into her leather jacket. Though the sun was warm enough, there was a stiff breeze coming off the marshes and the open sea beyond. Dark clouds were gathering out there, black, ominous skies. She walked to the little causeway, shading her eyes against the glare. The single-track road was narrow, an almost straight line over hummocks of land and patches of rippling water. The place smelled of the land and sea, of earth and water – a strange, ethereal mix. As she gazed, Salt saw no motorbike, heard nothing of the telltale roar of an engine.

'Where are you, Sorley?' she whispered under her breath, into the thick collar of her jacket.

32

As they sped along, Sorley still felt Tabitha's tight grip round his waist. By his reckoning, although this wasn't his accustomed route to his fishing hut, they were about ten minutes out. Checking his mirrors, he couldn't see the white Transit at any point along the straight they'd just traversed.

'Tabitha, how are you doing?'

No reply.

'Tabitha!'

Still nothing.

Up ahead, Sorley spotted a tree-covered lane, one of many in this part of the world. He could already smell the tang of the sea and see the landscape changing rapidly. He slowed the bike, turned on to the lane and stopped a hundred yards or so down it, under the overhanging branches of a willow tree.

Sorley eased himself off the bike. Tabitha slumped forward, mumbling something, one hand still trying to grip his waist.

He placed the bike on its stand, took off his helmet and examined his passenger. Lifting her visor, he saw her half-closed eyes, her lolling head. He checked her leathers. There was no sign of any damage. But then, as her head flopped forward again, he saw it. On the far side of the white crash helmet was a long, dark gash that ended in a point. Though the Kevlar outer skin had not been entirely breached, the force of the impact was obvious. It might have been a loose stone churned up by the motion of the bike, but the more he examined it, the more he was sure that only the glancing blow of a bullet could have wrought that kind of damage. He quickly calculated that the angle of the shot and the tough Kevlar were all that had saved Tabitha's life. If it had been any more direct, the bullet would have penetrated the helmet instead of being sent spinning off. That said, it was no wonder she was groggy.

'Tabitha, I'm going to take your helmet off and check you over, OK?'

She mumbled a reply.

Carefully, Sorley slipped the helmet off her head. He searched her hair where he reckoned the bullet may have struck. There was no blood, no bone, though she groaned when his fingers passed over part of her skull.

He knelt over her, gently holding her head between his hands. 'Listen, you were right. You were hit by something, but it's OK. You're just a bit dopey. Apart from that, you're fine, yes?'

She looked back at him, eyes swirling. 'Not as bloody dopey as you,' she replied in a slurred whisper.

He smiled and reached down into a narrow pannier on the fairing of the bike, removing something with his right hand. 'I'm sorry about this. But unless I manage to rouse you a bit, they won't miss the next time.' Sorley removed the lid from a bottle of spring water and poured it liberally over Tabitha's head.

Following a few deep breaths, her eyes opened wide with shock. 'You bastard!'

'Hey, take it easy. You might have concussion or something.'

'You'll have bloody concussion if you do that again.' Tabitha was, as ever, indignant.

Sorley flourished her crash helmet, complete with its damaged Kevlar. 'You've been lucky. But it's not over. We have about ten minutes or so to go. I need you to stay alert and hold on.'

Tabitha pushed wet hair off her face with one hand. 'Let's just get going.'

'Are you sure you can go on? I mean, we could try to hide out. But that's not going to be easy. These guys are pros.'

'I'm OK, apart from being wet and having a splitting headache. Let's just go!'

Sorley helped her on with her helmet and remounted the bike. Soon, he was edging out of the lane, back on to the main road.

'Just shout if you have a problem.'

'I have a problem,' Tabitha replied. 'People are trying to kill me.'

Thankful that there was again no sign of the Transit van, Sorley revved the bike on to the road and sped off in the direction of the marshes and rescue. Though he knew they were late, he was sure that Cara Salt would wait for him. Estranged they may be, but he still recognized her as his soulmate.

Salt was fretting now. She'd had Wootton contact Meikle House via the helicopter's radio to ask the ACC to try to raise Sorley on his mobile. The phone was off. Now she feared the worst. It wasn't as though they could mobilize the local police to try to find her ex-boyfriend. The position was hopeless.

'We'll give it as long as you need,' said Blackstock at her elbow.

'No point us just hanging about here. They haven't made it. I just know it.' Salt blinked back a tear. Her heart was sore and her throat ached. She'd nearly killed Sorley once before. Now she'd finished the job. 'Maybe we could scout about and look for them? Do we have enough fuel, Mr Wootton?'

'I could follow the road for ten minutes or so – but no longer. Just let me know what you decide,' said Wootton. He turned on his heel and headed back to the helicopter.

The dark clouds were overhead now. Salt felt little spits of rain on her cheek. They hid her tears.

'All is not lost, ma'am,' said Blackstock. 'We're not beaten yet.'

'Platitudes, Abs. Nothing but platitudes.' She shook her head. 'I'm sorry, none of this is your fault. But this case is impossible. We have so few resources, and we're clearly facing determined professionals. How could they know Tabitha was with Sorley? There could be an army of these bastards out there.'

Blackstock scraped at the ground with the toe of his shoe but didn't reply.

'How many people have lost their lives just because of greed? Millions, I reckon. So many lives wasted for money. It stinks. We should be ashamed of ourselves as a species. I fucking hate people!' Salt yelled the last sentence at the top of her voice.

Blackstock lifted his head, as though sniffing the air. 'Do you hear that?'

Still lost in the misery of her thoughts, Salt looked at him. 'Hear what?'

'It's a motorbike. I'd bet my life on it.'

Salt inclined her head, standing on tiptoes, looking down the causeway. 'I can't hear a thing apart from gulls. Hey, and my ears have twenty years on yours.'

'But you haven't been listening for birds all your life. Yes, a motorbike engine. Look, I can see them.' Blackstock pointed along the straight causeway.

Sure enough, Salt could see a speck of red against the darkening sky, flying along in the distance between little patches of land and water. 'Quick, go tell Wootton to get ready.'

Blackstock hurried off as Salt squinted into the distance. But her joy at seeing them was stopped in its tracks when, not far behind the motorbike, a white van loomed, travelling at speed. She called out to Blackstock. 'They've got company!'

Blackstock hurried back from the helicopter. 'What is it?'

She pointed. The DS gazed along the causeway.

'I don't suppose it's a friendly escort.'

Salt was breathing heavily now. Of course, the bike would make it to the helicopter before the van. But they all had to get in the aircraft and take off. Judging by Tabitha Pallander's experiences alone, these people were ruthless enough to shoot a helicopter out of the air. It quickly dawned on Salt that all their lives were now in danger.

'Draw your firearm.' Salt spat out the words to her detective sergeant.

'Ma'am, are you sure? We have no idea what we're facing.'

'Just do it.' Salt was already wrestling the pistol from the shoulder holster under her arm.

Crimson blood exploding in slow motion.

Salt took a breath, banishing the memory of the last time she'd fired a weapon in anger.

His eyes rolling into the back of his head. Falling, slowly, like a felled tree. Sorley!

'Bastard!' Salt cried out, hoping this heartfelt cry would stop her mind working overtime. She could see both vehicles clearly now. From behind, she heard the rotor blades of the helicopter beginning to turn. Wootton had been a soldier, and he'd calculated the danger just as she had. They were going to have to leave quickly – if they managed to leave at all.

Though the causeway appeared to be dead straight, it had a curve. Imperceptible when staring down its length alone but very noticeable as the bike now faced her head-on, the white van not far behind. She could see flashes coming from its passenger window. They were firing on the bike.

Salt rushed to the causeway, almost tripping on some loose rocks.

'What are you doing?' Blackstock shouted.

Salt ignored him and took up a firing position on one knee, just at the point where the causeway joined the islet.

'Don't be stupid, ma'am – Cara. They won't hesitate to—'

Blackstock's words were lost in the thud of the helicopter rotors. Salt pushed him away, again noticing a flash of gunfire from the van.

She took deep breaths. All she could hear was the thud of her own heart in her ears. The motorbike was near enough for her to see Sorley bent over the handlebars, his pillion passenger hanging on for dear life. In seconds they would be past her. She prayed none of the gunfire from the van would hit them.

One, two, three. They were past, the high buzz of the motorcycle engine like a harrying insect. Salt held her weapon before her with both hands. The firearm felt strange, it had been so long. But she felt sheer hatred for the people who were trying to kill the only person that had ever meant anything to her – Sorley.

She took aim and fired. The first shot missed. So did the second. She saw a flash of flame from the passenger window and instantly felt the rush of a bullet passing her cheek.

Salt pulled back the trigger once more. The scene played out before her in slow motion. The van's windscreen shattered, and the vehicle slewed across the roadway. It hit a small embankment and reared up, twisting in the air and crashing back down in a huge splash of water, as though an enormous boulder had fallen from height into the marsh. Now lying on its side, the water was only deep enough to cover half of its height. Smoke rose from the hot engine, sullying the sky.

Salt gazed at the vehicle, motionless. Still in the kneeling firing position, almost in a trance. She felt strong arms grab her and she was pulled towards the helicopter. Half-dragged inside, she was thrust into a seat and strapped in. A pair of headphones was clamped over her ears.

The helicopter rose smoothly off the ground. She heard Wootton call out for everyone to get down. Instinctively, Salt thrust her head forward against the seat in front.

They were rising quickly now, much faster than she remembered their ascent from the woods at Meikle House.

As the helicopter banked away from the marshes, Salt had her first clear view of the scene below. Standing beside the wreckage of the van stood a balding man, an automatic weapon held loose by his side. He just gazed at the aircraft, making no attempt to fire on it. Somehow, as she stared at him, his inaction chilled Salt to the bone.

'Everyone OK?' Salt recognized Wootton's voice in the headphones.

She turned in her chair. Instead of Blackstock, Sorley MacLeod was strapped in beside her. Tabitha had instantly fallen asleep, exhausted by her ordeal. Blackstock stared out of the window, his expression impassive.

'Sorley.' She held her hand against his mud-spattered face.

'Cara, what a surprise.' He smiled at her broadly.

'I thought you were dead.' The tears began to flow now.

He pulled her to him, as much as the seat belts would allow. 'So did I. Especially when I saw you with that gun in your hand.' Sorley MacLeod laughed heartily.

She rested her head on his shoulder and soon drifted off to sleep.

They pulled up beside a warehouse on the Southside of Glasgow. The operation hadn't gone to plan, but now she knew for sure they had one of the city's most notorious criminals trapped. Five marked cars and a personnel carrier arrived in her wake; lights flashing but no sirens, as she'd ordered.

She looked across to the man in the passenger seat. 'You good to go?'

'Aye, I'm just awaiting your every command, ma'am.'

'Don't be like this, Sorley – not now. I got the job and you didn't, so what?'

'It's not about that.'

'Yes, it is. You're going to split us up with this jealousy, trust me.'

'My daddy was a crofter, not an ACC.'

'Fuck off!'

'Are we going in there or what, ma'am?'

She saw the expression on his face. It was cold, distant – like talking to a stranger.

'DI Salt to all units. Go, go, go!'

Police officers streamed from vehicles into the sprawling warehouse. She followed them, DS Sorley MacLeod in her wake.

The police team spread out, connected to each other and to Salt, the OIC, by radio earpieces.

'You go that way,' she said to her DS.

There were two sets of stairs leading to offices at the very top of the building. One left, one right. Salt took them two steps at a time. She stopped by a half-open door before kicking it in, firearm outstretched before her. Nothing. Same in the next two rooms.

'DS MacLeod to DI Salt, over.'

His voice sounded stilted, as though he was reading from a piece of paper.

'Go ahead,' she replied.

'Requiring assistance on the other side of the landing, over. Room twelve.'

Salt raced out of the empty room, pelting across a metal walkway with a dizzying drop to the warehouse floor below.

The door to room twelve was ajar.

She hesitated on the right-hand side of the door, weapon held above her head. 'Sorley, are you in there?'

'Come in, Inspector. Not like you to be shy.'

Salt swung into the room, her firearm again in front of her. She wanted to scream when she saw Sorley on his knees, a stout arm round his throat, gun at his head, his radio smashed on the floor in front of him. It was a trap.

The gangster's eyes flashed with hatred. 'Put your gun down or—'

Her instinct kicked in. It took a split second to calculate that if she surrendered her weapon, they'd both be dead. He was the worst kind of psychopath.

She didn't wait to hear what this madman had to say. Cara Salt fired two shots.

The gangster fell back, as Sorley's shoulder exploded.

DI Cara Salt screamed.

'Don't tell me . . . It's the dream again,' said Sorley.

Salt was disoriented. But she quickly gathered her thoughts and remembered she was in the helicopter. 'Yes, the dream. Sorry.'

'One day you'll miss me and only hit him.'

'Yeah, one day.' She stared out of the window at patchy low clouds beneath them; glimpses of a silver river as it meandered past fields and villages.

'What are you thinking about?' Sorley asked.

'Back there – when we were taking off.'

'What about it?'

'The guy from the van. Why didn't he fire on us? He had a gun, I saw it.'

'Maybe he just didn't want a helicopter crashing on his head. Reasonable, I'd say.'

'Oh, yeah? I'm not convinced.'

'What other reason is there? Maybe the gun wasn't working after the crash. Maybe his head was all over the place – maybe he wanted Tabitha alive. I'm just glad he didn't bother.'

Salt nodded and closed her eyes again. But sleep was not her intention. Her instincts were calling to her again – and Cara Salt needed to listen.

33

It had taken Silas and Anna time to decide what to do with their new-found freedom. While he wanted to run to the nearest police station and summon help, she was more cautious. Who knew where their erstwhile captors were? Maybe this was just another one of their mind games.

She reasoned that they didn't know why they had been incarcerated, or – in her case – tortured. That it couldn't all be for his signature. Anna persuaded her boss that the best thing to do was to lie low until darkness then find a taxi willing to take them to the nearest big town. To their amazement, Silas still had his company credit card in his shirt pocket. With that, she said, they could go anywhere they wanted. Even though they would have to be cunning about it.

As always, Silas agreed with her. They crossed a field and found a gulley overgrown by trees with a stream running through it. Though they had no food, they now had shelter and water. The chances of anyone finding them were remote. They would wait until darkness, or at least dusk. If anyone was searching for them, it would be much more difficult to do so at night.

'Can't we just find a public phone box? Call the cavalry?' said Silas.

'There are no such things in this country. It's a backward place, not like France.'

Silas raised his brows at her obvious bias for her home nation.

'You must try and remember what they made you sign, Silas.'

'I told you – they wouldn't let me see. But I would bet my life it was some kind of contract.'

'I can't think what it could be. I mean, you are no longer part of the company.' Anna made a bewildered face.

'Thanks for reminding me.'

'You will be happy in Scotland. But you know it's not for me.'

'You'd rather stay in the company and betray me.'

'I need the money!' Anna's eyes flashed with anger under the bruises and cuts inflicted on her by their former captors. 'You are rich, no matter your father's will. You have no idea what the world is like for ordinary people like me.'

'My family took you in when your parents died. We did right by you.'

Anna Marchand stared into space. Then she turned to Silas, her voice quiet, almost a whisper. 'It was kind. But I was only in the way – a cuckoo in the nest. And anyway, your father couldn't wait to send me off to boarding school. I have never been part of your family.'

Silas thought back to the day she had arrived at Meikle House. The shock of red hair, the freckles, her huge blue eyes. Anna was younger than him, but from the first day he saw her, thoughts of every other woman disappeared. But his father had laid down hard and fast rules around the French teenager, the orphaned child of old friends. She stayed at the house for one glorious summer before being sent to school in Switzerland, and thereafter drafted into

Pallander Glossop to be trained as an executive personal assistant.

'Your father was kind to me. I would have been left with nothing, destitute. But there was no sense of belonging – of being loved. I thought my parents had money, but it was gone. They'd made bad choices. I was one of them.'

'You can't say that. You mean so much to me – and the others.' He reached out to touch her, but she shied away. 'I'm sorry.'

'Don't be sorry. You were always good to me. Not like Tabitha.'

Silas raised an eyebrow.

'She would do anything to be her father's favourite. She must be devastated at the way things have gone for her.'

Silas didn't want to go back over all that had happened since his father's death. After the initial shock, he'd reconciled himself to the fact that his father had never respected or valued him as a colleague or a son. Even when they were growing up, it had been Tabitha all along who was being groomed to take over. It had taken him too long to realize it. The whole thing was odd, bizarre. As though the collective future of the Pallander children, mapped out from birth, was cast asunder. First, by Tabitha usurping his position as the next in line, the rightful heir, then by all the siblings being marginalized and left with scraps.

The bright sunlight that had flitted between the leaves and played on the rippling river was now a shade of red gold. The early summer day had seemed endless. But dusk was beginning to shroud the glade.

'We go soon, yes?'

She hadn't spoken in a while. They'd both dozed off, relieved to be free, glad to be going home.

'What's the plan?' said Silas.

'There's must be a road nearby. We get a lift to the nearest village. From there, we can organize a taxi.'

'It's a company card, Anna. They'll be able to see what we're doing.'

'What else can we do?' Her eyes blazed again. 'We have to take a chance, or we'll be stuck by this river for the rest of our lives. Is that what you want? Please trust me.'

'I'm sorry, Anna. But what if nobody stops for us?'

'They'll stop.' Deftly, she unbuttoned her blouse, revealing the cleft in her breasts. 'We were in a car crash a few kilometres up the road. We must find help.'

'Good cover story.'

'It will do.'

They waited for another half an hour until darkness fell. A gibbous moon helped them find their way to a road, where they waited for passing vehicles heading in the right direction of Asser sur Live, the nearest place of any consequence. The night air was cool, with a light breeze wafting the scent of honeysuckle all around. The darting shapes of pipistrelle bats could be seen against the velvet blue of the darkening sky.

On the road, a sports car flashed past, sounding its horn in derision. Then a lorry, the driver holding up his hands as though to say *Sorry, I can't take passengers*.

'Maybe you were wrong about the lift,' said Silas.

A few minutes passed before more headlights arced across the trees, followed by the distant rattling of an old car.

'You think?' said Anna.

She went and stood at the side of the road, waving her arms. An old man driving an equally venerable Citroën pulled to a halt beside her. Anna leaned into the passenger window, explaining their imaginary situation in rapid French.

'Come on, he can take us!' she shouted.

Silas and Anna squeezed into the back seat of the car, and they rolled slowly away. The driver kept up a perpetual chat. Now and again, Anna broke into his diatribe, and though Silas understood little of the language, her voice sounded suitably distressed.

A straggle of lights, no more than five miles down the road, heralded their arrival at Asser sur Live. The old man, amidst a paroxysm of coughing, slowed the car to a stop beside a red-brick cottage.

'He wants us to go into his house while we organize a garage.' She winked. 'It would be good to be out of sight and in the warmth, I think.'

'What garage?' whispered Silas.

'You know what I mean.' Anna scolded him with her wide eyes.

The man – Gaston, Silas gleaned – led them into his home via a narrow stone hallway. They were shown into a kitchen, where a small fire brooded in the grate in front of a rudimentary table and some chairs. Gaston produced a bottle of homemade wine and some chipped tumblers. He poured an equal measure into each glass and handed one to them both.

'*Salut!*'

Gaston lit a Gitanes, coughing at his first draw as blue smoke drifted to the nicotine-stained ceiling. The room smelled of roasted tobacco mixed with the sweet wine and an all-pervasive odour of garlic. With this, and the heat of the fire, Silas Pallander began to feel his eyelids grow heavy.

Anna and Gaston were chatting away in French. And it was obvious to Silas that he was imparting directions to her. He waved his arm one way then another, described a turn with the flick of the wrist then, '*Voilà!*'

Silas noted absently that the old man didn't speak with the free-flowing, almost poetic tongue of Anna Marchand. His accent was rougher, his words almost guttural.

Anna leaned in. 'The taxi service isn't far away. I asked about it and a garage – just in case. Give me the credit card and I'll get things organized. The owner is in his bed, apparently – a notorious early riser. I'll wake him and we can get out of here. Bruges is only forty kilometres away.'

'Can't you phone him?'

'With what? We have no phone and neither does Gaston.'

'Then I'll go,' said Silas, putting his glass down on the table, an action Gaston assumed was intended to garner more wine, which he attended to liberally.

'You don't speak French, remember?' said Anna.

'I'll come with you, then.'

'No, stay here. Don't be rude. It will only take a few minutes. Gaston tells me that the taxi owner is very friendly and helpful. I will make him an offer to take us to Brussels instead of Bruges, without using the card until we get there. That way, they'll be off our scent. Even better, perhaps I can persuade him to take us to the Channel. I don't know.'

Reluctantly, Silas Pallander handed over the credit card. Anna spoke to Gaston, and the old man struggled to his feet to show her to the door.

'I won't be long,' she said over her shoulder, as she disappeared back down the narrow corridor.

Silas sat back in his chair. The fire was warm, and the wine palatable and potent, if a little sweet. He took another gulp, laid the glass on the hearth and very soon nodded off.

Silas wasn't sure how long he'd been asleep. But dawn was breaking through gaps in the shutters on Gaston's kitchen window when he awoke. The old man was curled up on the rustic sofa across the room, snoring quietly, a half-empty bottle of wine on the floor beside him.

For that split second on waking, before the world and all its problems permeated his mind, Silas stretched. Then he realized there was no sign of Anna.

Maybe she was in one of the bedrooms, the taxi driver she was trying to cajole having been unavailable? He hoped so.

Silas went over to the old man. He shook him awake more roughly than he'd intended. Gaston started then opened his eyes with an oath, his old, callused hands bunched into fists, ready to punch the person responsible for this rude awakening.

'*Ou est Anna?*' Silas said in his best French.

Gaston rubbed his eyes, blinked and shrugged. '*Comment devrais-je savoir?*'

Though Silas couldn't understand the words, their meaning was obvious. The old man didn't know. His instant reaction was to go through the cottage, checking each room. First was a less than welcoming bathroom, complete with an ancient iron bath and accompanying layer of scum, then a bedroom barely big enough to house the double bed. Another tiny room with a sofa and one easy chair, that must have served as Gaston's lounge, was also empty.

Silas stood in the hall and rubbed his hair until it stood on end, a habit since childhood when he was overwrought. Gaston appeared, talking incessantly in rapid, incomprehensible French.

Silas grabbed him by the arm. 'Take me to the taxi!' he shouted, each word slow and deliberate. Gaston muttered something else unintelligible. '*Le taxi!*' said Silas, pointing desperately to the front door.

The old man pulled on a weather-beaten flat cap and waved Silas towards the door.

They left the little cottage and were soon out on to a village square. A cafe was in the process of being set up by its owner, a spare, middle-aged woman who hallooed at Gaston as they walked past. The air was fresh, the smell of flowers hanging from pots on almost every building adding to the feeling of summer and all that it promised.

Silas Pallander's mood, however, was dark and cold. He berated himself for not going with Anna to help cajole the taxi company owner. Why had he succumbed to the sweet homemade wine? Why had he fallen asleep in front of the warm fire? In a lifetime of poor choices, these were just the latest, he reckoned. His heart was thudding in his chest as Gaston led him down an alley off the square. In front of him sat a white villa, with three taxicabs parked at the door.

'You talk him,' said Gaston haltingly, pointing.

Silas strode up the front steps. He lifted an ornamental knocker and hammered it three times. Eventually, a bleary-eyed man in his forties appeared in the doorway. He was dressed in a vest and trousers, hanging loose from a pair of red braces. He rubbed his eyes, squinting at his visitors.

'*Qui est-ce?*' he said to Gaston.

'Andre, *il est Anglais. Tu as parlé à sa femme hier soir.*'

Andre regarded Silas with puzzlement. 'The old man, he has finally lost his mind, no?' he said in heavily accented English.

Silas was relieved that Andre spoke English at all. 'I'm looking for my friend. She came to speak to you last night about hiring a taxi.' He pointed to the cars in the small yard, as though the very concept of a taxi might be foreign to the man who owned them.

Andre wagged his finger in Silas's face. 'No, you are wrong. No woman came here last night. I was in this house all night, I promise you.'

Silas held his hand to his forehead in a gesture resembling a salute. 'About this height, with red hair – very beautiful. You must remember her.'

'Why would I lie to you? Of course I would remember such a woman. But she was not here.' He made a face.

Silas pushed his hand through his hair once more.

Then he shouted 'Shit!' at the top of his voice.

34

Meikle House had been astir since Tabitha's arrival. The armed police guard was still present, though Dixon had gone back to Glasgow. As Salt learned, he was treading a fine line in his attempts to keep the Pallander situation quiet and the baying press from finding out the truth. Something she'd worried about, realizing the enormous task at hand. When a high-profile person disappeared or died, everyone wondered what was happening.

She was standing at the front of the house, having a cigarette and watching two armed cops pass the time of day. Tabitha and Sorley were yet to rise. They had all spent the night in Meikle House. Elizabeth Pallander was keen for that to continue, though Charles Stuart-Henderson was more reserved about the whole thing. But Elizabeth was chatelaine in her own home, and his muted protests had fallen on deaf ears. Salt and Blackstock would move out of the hotel, and rooms in Meikle House would be found for them. Salt knew that the gesture wasn't purely altruistic. Elizabeth would have realized that having the detectives on hand would lend an extra layer of security. But for the inspector, being on the spot had its own advantages.

Salt was looking for Abernethy Blackstock. According to the staff, he'd left at dawn to go birdwatching. She was amazed that he could be so relaxed after what had happened on the Essex marshes. But it took all sorts.

She was surprised to hear her name called. When she turned round, Sorley was striding towards her across the big lawn.

'How are you, Cara?' he said breezily.

'Not as good as you, by the look of it. Shit, anything could have happened to you yesterday, and you look as though you don't have a care in the world.'

'Everyone has a different approach. In any case, I've been meditating.'

Salt looked at Sorley, half a smile spreading across her face. 'Aye, right. And I'm just about to get some Tai Chi in.'

'You'd be amazed how good life is when you're not dealing with shit every day. Best thing I ever did was leaving the job. You should try it. Aye, and I do enjoy some meditation. We've all got to find our place in all this.' He took a deep breath, drawing at the warm scented air. 'And anyway, each day is a bonus. When I saw you kneeling with that gun, you can imagine the thoughts that were going through my head.'

'I've missed you,' said Salt.

Sorley sniffed.

'What?' She screwed up her face.

'Missed me. You didn't the last time.'

'For fuck's sake. No, I *missed* you. All this time. Ach, don't worry about it.'

She made to walk away but Sorley MacLeod stood in her path. 'I know what you meant. But we can't do that to each other again, can we?'

230

'I only said I missed you. It wasn't a declaration of undying love. Don't flatter yourself.'

'Wow, there's gratitude. I mean, don't worry that I risked my life to save your bacon.'

'My bacon?'

'If I remember rightly, it was you who called me yesterday – got me rolled up in all this – right?'

'I didn't have a choice.' Salt folded her arms.

'And neither did I, as it turned out.'

'You can leave any time you want.'

Sorley rubbed the fingers of his right hand together. 'Not without compensation. My bike – fuck knows what's happened to that. Not to mention the bloody trauma of it all. I want some dosh.'

'You'll need to speak to the ACC.'

'No, no. My days of pleading in front of senior officers are over. You got me into this, you get me out with suitable financial reward. I know how this all works, remember.'

'You'll never change. It's always about you.'

Silence reigned for a moment.

'Your new DS – what do you think of him?'

'Abs? He's a good guy. A little old-fashioned, but he's a solid cop. Why?' Salt eyed her ex-colleague suspiciously.

'Just wondering.' Sorley's face bore an unreadable expression.

Salt was about to ask what was up when she heard her name called for the second time that morning.

'Inspector, can I have a word? It's good news.'

Charles Stuart-Henderson was standing on the edge of the lawn.

'There you go, more good news. I appear, and all is well,' said Sorley.

'Huh, for a price,' said Salt, walking away. 'A gun for hire.'

'We'll leave the guns to you, Caz.' Sorley smiled as he watched her walk away.

Salt was led back to the reception room where Elizabeth Pallander conducted her business. She smiled broadly at the inspector.

'My son, Silas. We know where he is.'

'That's fabulous. Where?' said Salt.

'Belgium.'

'That's where they took him?' Salt looked confused.

'I don't have many details. But he was with Anna March-and, his PA. Rather a friend of the family. She's still missing, apparently.' Elizabeth wrung her hands. 'Lovely girl – French, you know.'

'OK, let's concentrate on what we can do to get Silas back,' said Salt.

'That's taken care of.' Charles Stuart-Henderson eyed her down the bridge of his nose. 'We're keeping this in-house.'

'I don't know what you mean.'

He went on to explain to the police officer how they'd hired a French security company used by Pallander Glossop for dealings in that country. They were happy to make a foray into Belgium, it appeared. The security firm were to uplift Silas and bring him back to Meikle House.

'And you can trust them?' Salt asked.

'I would say that it all sounds very well organized. Compared to, say, the danger my niece was placed in during her *extraction*. I have one hundred per cent faith in them.'

It was all Salt could do to hold her tongue. Though her expression must have spoken volumes, as the lady of the house intervened.

'That's enough, Charles. This woman and her team saved

my daughter's life. I'm grateful and you should be too. We've lost Jean-Luc, but there's nothing to be done about that. My other children are now safe here. With Silas on his way back, we can ride this – whatever it is – out.'

Salt ignored the altercation. She was too busy considering recent events. *If* the French security company managed to extract Silas Pallander from Belgium and get him safely home, the whole family were sitting ducks in Meikle House. Yes, they were under police protection, but with the ACC having to answer awkward questions about the operation, the future was uncertain. So far, they'd managed to mitigate whatever danger had been placed in front of them. But the root cause of the attacks on the Pallander family remained a mystery.

There was a knock at the door. Stuart-Henderson dealt with the interruption by way of a perfunctory 'Come!'

A man in the style of clothes worn by the staff of Meikle House stood in the doorway. 'Ma'am. Sir.' He acknowledged Salt with a curt nod.

'Yes, Chalmers, what is it? We're damned busy here, you know.'

'Sir, Mrs Sullivan. We can't find her. I thought, under the circumstances, I should let you know.'

'Since when?' said Salt, beating Stuart-Henderson to his reply.

'Early this morning. She was supposed to brief the staff at six thirty. When she didn't appear we thought that she must be involved with – well, you know – what's been going on. But it's now almost nine and there's no sign of her.' Chalmers looked perplexed.

'Have you checked her quarters?' asked Elizabeth.

'Yes, ma'am. When there was no reply, Mr Thomson used his pass key. There was nobody there.'

'You should have said something earlier,' said Stuart-Henderson.

'Come with me, Mr Chalmers. I would like a word, if that's OK?' said Salt, looking at Elizabeth Pallander.

'Yes, please go ahead, Inspector. Surely, nothing else can go wrong?'

Salt left with Chalmers. She asked him to take her to Mrs Sullivan's rooms. It turned out that the manager of Meikle House lived in an annex of the building. Her quarters, a small kitchen, lounge, bedroom and bathroom, were neat and tidy, nothing out of place.

'You know her, Mr Chalmers. Is this unusual? Disappearing, I mean? I know some people are flexible with their hours.'

'I've been here for two years, ma'am. I've never known her be late for anything. In fact, I wonder if she ever sleeps.'

Salt took another look around Sullivan's quarters. She spotted a gardening magazine on the coffee table, picked it up and held it up to the light. There was the indentation of handwriting, as though it had been used to lean on while either Sullivan or someone else wrote a note.

'Can you find me a thin piece of paper and a pencil, please?'

'Yes, I have a notepad, will that do?'

Salt thanked Chalmers and went about her business, placing the paper on top of the magazine and lightly tracing what had been pressed into its front page. Before long, the job was done.

Meet S. 6 am

Salt checked that what she'd managed to lift from the cover was all that it contained. It was. She looked at the note again.

Meet S. 6 am

'Do you have any idea who "S" might be, Mr Chalmers?'

He bit his lip. 'No, not offhand. We have a kitchen porter called Sean. But I can't imagine why he'd be meeting with Mrs Sullivan that early in the morning.'

'Thank you, Mr Chalmers.' Salt thought for a moment. 'Can you please make sure this room is secured and nobody else enters?'

'Yes, certainly. Do you have any idea what could have happened to her, Inspector? It's so odd – some of the staff are worried. It's unusual, you know.'

'Try not to worry. I'd like to speak to the staff – those who are here today. Where's the best place?'

'In the Great Hall. That's where Mrs Sullivan usually briefs us, if none of the family are using it. But I'm sure that's not the case today.'

'OK. In about an hour. Can you round everyone up?'

Chalmers assured her that it wouldn't be a problem then left to organize the meeting.

Salt fished her mobile from a trouser pocket and dialled. 'DS Blackstock, where are you?' The question was sharp.

'Yes, hello. I'm just going to have a quick shower, ma'am. I'm afraid I got rather muddy down by the river. I had a good morning, relaxing – after yesterday, you know.'

'Wow, that's just fabulous. I'm so pleased for you.' Salt's tone was mocking.

'Ma'am?'

'Get your shower and meet me in the Great Hall. I'm sure you'll be able to find it. It's great and it's a hall. Next time you want to go birdwatching, you ask me, right?'

Salt ended the call and then fumed quietly for a few moments. She wandered back outside Meikle House. Despite its size, the place was making her feel distinctly claustrophobic. Her head ached. Nothing seemed right, nothing at all.

She found a bench in the sun, held her head back and breathed deeply at the scented air of the Perthshire countryside.

'Told you you'd be meditating before long.'

Salt opened her eyes. Sorley was silhouetted before her.

'Bugger off, Sorley. I'm thinking.'

'Then we're all in trouble.'

'Ever wish you hadn't wished for something?'

He grinned at her. 'Not recently.'

As always, Sorley MacLeod managed to irritate and reassure her at the same time. She smiled back.

35

The morning sun shone brightly over London. Today, there was no pall of smoke hanging over the city centre to the west. The hotel fire had been extinguished. Five people had lost their lives, and many others were seriously injured. The news had spread round the world.

Across the city at the Shard, all was – as intended – a hive of activity. People thronged the entrance foyer: businessmen and women, in casual but luxurious attire, denoting their status more subtly than the brolly and bowler hat of old, thronged busily like flocks of birds. A high-end Swiss watch here, a Prada handbag there. It was all akin to a secret society, these brands that had become the passport to exclusivity, the clandestine mark of rank and success. Seen by all, noted by few.

Pallander Glossop prided itself on being an investment company for the purist. Like a Tricker's shoe or a Huntsman suit, this was a company of quiet reliability. Not trendy or in-your-face, but a dignified indication that if you were accepted as a client then you knew you'd made it. It was silent power; the way most things worked in this old country. If the UK could be taken apart and assessed from within, companies like this were found at the heart of everything, simply going about their business.

It was fine to have a nice address – and they didn't come much more prestigious than the Shard – but not one of the higher floors. No, leave that to super-luxury hotels, galleries and less sophisticated businesses. The eleventh floor was where the company did its business. And business had been good for so many years. They had similarly located offices in the great cities of the world; quiet, restrained but the very epitome of class and reliability.

The floor itself resembled a hive, with a wooden-panelled, private world at its centre, positioned at the huge window while other, open-plan stations fanned out all around. But the queen – or king – bee was no longer in residence. In fact, within the hub of the central office and its corridor of power leading to the view over the Thames, only shadows dwelt. These were the men and women that kept the business running while the vacuum at the top ate away at confidence in an oh-so-quiet way.

Pallander Glossop had been wrought in the image of its founding partner, Sebastian Pallander. Even the office layout was a glimpse into the mind of a man who thought himself at the epicentre of everything he touched. Whether it was family or business, London or Seoul, in person or not, his spirit inhabited the organization totally and utterly.

But that spirit was on the wane, indeed almost gone.

Many thought even death wouldn't end his dominion. After all, the apple, in the shape of Tabitha Pallander, had not fallen far from the tree. But now she too was gone.

If 'flux' was a word within the Pallander Glossop lexicon, then it was whispered only by those who felt themselves in good, safe company, not those who thrived on idle gossip. As for the rest, the worker bees huddling around the core that gave them life, it was business as usual. There was no need to worry because SP, as he was known to the wider staff, would have made provisions, would keep them safe even from beyond the grave.

There is a curious phenomenon in groups of people who worship nothing but flesh and blood, bone and sinew. And it's reciprocal. The more someone considers themselves divine, the more their acolytes confirm the notion. But every army needs a flesh-and-blood, corporeal, live-and-kicking general, each nation a head of state in similar fettle. And no matter how strong its infrastructure, panic was beginning to take hold within the top rank on the eleventh floor of the Shard, spreading out likes ripples of water on a pebbled pond, even to senior staff in satellite offices across the globe.

Ulrich Baucher couldn't bear to take his late boss's chair. Even though he was now designated CEO of Pallander Glossop, as per the strictures of Sebastian Pallander's will, he remained firmly ensconced in the office of Chief Operations Officer, his old job. This wasn't about respect. No, he was paralysed by fear.

He scrolled through the endless parade of figures, funds under management, open-ended or otherwise. He noted something not quite right here, something else disappointing there. It was second nature for the sixty-two-year-old who'd been staring at figures for more than fifty years, beginning with his father's wholesale meat business in Frankfurt. He had a natural aptitude for this, able to extract the truth behind numbers, as a conductor derives emotion from a musical score. He'd asked for a complete review of assets under management and the fiscal health of the company. Now he was waiting for this report most impatiently.

He pushed his chair away from the computer and gazed at his own image on the wall. Painted from life, he and Sebastian Pallander were drinking sundowners in Singapore, his square, solid frame across a card table from the elegant, long-limbed Pallander.

'You left us all in the shit, Seb,' he whispered. 'How could you do this, to us and your family? What were you thinking?'

Baucher mulled it all over in his mind. History told him how the fortunes of nations were often at the mercy of their kings, and that sons might not be the men their fathers were. But in Tabitha Pallander he knew they would have been in good, if somewhat truculent, hands. Why Sebastian had decided to demote her in his will, he couldn't think. She'd been groomed for the job for years. Always at her father's side while the lamentable eldest child hoped beyond hope she'd slip up. She never did.

She should be sitting here with this stress, this panic. He, Baucher, should be sunning himself on some warm, distant beach, his long road to retirement mapped out; there to be anticipated and enjoyed.

Baucher didn't like London. His little part of Pallander Glossop had been the office in Zurich, over which he ruled like a client king. He supposed he felt a portion of guilt when it came to the capital. After all, his father had been part of something evil that had rained bombs down on this place. But if the Bauchers were anything, it was resilient. His father escaped execution at Nuremberg, going on to create a successful business and father many children.

But could guilt pass from father to son? Yes, it could. And he felt it every day.

Baucher stared at four little images on the desktop screen in front of him. It was an arrangement set up by Pallander himself. The great man liked to make sure those closest to him were going about their business assiduously.

In one window, the Operations Director was staring at

his own computer, his head cradled in his hands as he leaned back in his chair. The other three windows showed people busy looking busy at their desks. A smile at a Zoom call here, the furtive finger up the nose there.

'Are you all comfortable?' said Baucher. Since he'd become the boss, he'd been amazed at the time these people wasted. They dozed, played games on their phones, made calls to secret lovers, disappeared – often abroad – on the flimsiest excuses.

But he didn't have the strength to batter them back into shape, not now. He was becoming an old man, with a weak heart and draining energy. If he'd had any inclination that he'd be left to protect their pensions, payoffs and a myriad of other little perks, Baucher would have run a million miles. But now his future depended on keeping the place afloat.

The buzzer on his desk did its thing, indicating an internal call, most likely from his Swiss PA, Sylvester Andersen.

'May I come through for a word, sir?' His tones were as precise as the best watches from his homeland.

'Yes, please do, Sylvester.'

Andersen was normally unflappable, but as soon as he appeared in Baucher's office it was apparent that there was something very wrong.

'What now?' Baucher said wearily. 'You are rapidly becoming a pariah in this place. More bad news every time I see you.'

'Sir, we have had a message from Mr Pallander's law firm in Edinburgh. It's about a letter of credit.'

'A letter of credit? My word, is this the nineteen-eighties? I thought they were a thing of the past.'

'No, sir. It would appear that is not the case. Here is a copy of the original document. I have summarized the contents.' Andersen handed his boss sheets of paper. 'I would have used the company intranet, but as we suspect it to no longer be secure I thought you should see this the old-fashioned way.'

'So, we are moving back in time.' Baucher donned a pair of horn-rimmed reading glasses and examined the documents he'd been handed. By stages, his face grew pale, his jaw dropped and his hands began to shake. 'This is some mistake?'

'No mistake, I think,' said Andersen. 'I have had it checked and rechecked by our financial and legal teams – in the strictest confidence, you understand. It appears absolutely genuine, sir. They are a very venerable and respected firm. They have long dealt with Mr Pallander's interests.'

Taking off his spectacles, Baucher marvelled at his assistant's skill. The man always acted on his own initiative, and he was rarely wrong. 'You have kept this from the four?' He flicked a leg of his glasses towards the monitor bearing the images of the other senior company officers.

'Yes, sir. Everything through you first, as you have stipulated. I didn't want to trouble you until I'd had it verified. I'm sorry, sir.'

Baucher placed both sheets of paper on his desk and stared at them as though awaiting spontaneous combustion. 'All we have worked for – everything – gone in an instant.'

Andersen inclined his head almost imperceptibly. 'So it would appear. The only way we can honour the terms of this letter of credit would be to divert the money from client accounts.'

'Twenty-one billion dollars to be transferred into the Pallander Family Trust account. It's insane!' Baucher wiped his brow with a hanky. 'How long do we have?'

'Forty-eight hours for compliance and verification. But as that's already been done, what else is there to do? We are still awaiting written confirmation from the trust. But no doubt that will come.'

'But he gave his family nothing! I don't understand. And in any case, we are a company, a business, not his personal wealth fund. He had no right. We must be able to challenge this.'

'It is a matured loan, sir. If you go into the small print on the letter of credit, you will see Mr Pallander bailed this organization out to the tune of five billion dollars twelve years ago. The resultant sum, as per the conditions of his loan to the company, is above board. Interest, penalty fees, loan arrangements, facilities, etc.'

'The interest is crippling. And the signatures on this document? I have never seen it.'

'As you know, sir, by the constitution of our agreement with the Pallander Family Trust, only two signatures including Mr Pallander's were required each way. The company document was originally signed by him and Mr Glossop. The trust side by Pallander and his son.'

'Silas? He hated the boy. Look how he was treated in the will.'

'No, sir. Not Silas, Jean-Luc.'

The silence in the room was deafening. Pallander Glossop was to be killed stone dead by the man who had given it life. And the people who had signed the death warrant were themselves deceased.

'The national regulators will never let this pass, never.'

'As I alluded to, only one formality must be observed prior to the credit mandate being actioned, sir. But that's only a matter of time, I would think.'

'What is it?'

'The request must be signed by both Silas Pallander and Miss Tabitha, sir.'

Baucher shook his head, making his heavy jowls follow suit. 'They'll do what's best for them. Maybe this is why they were given bugger all in the will?'

'Quite possible, sir. But the letter of credit was legitimately lodged with both parties. It was signed by our company officers. We have no legal recourse to dispute it.'

'This will mean drawing on client funds – a lot of them! Too much to remain solvent.'

'Yes, sir.'

Baucher thumped the ornate desk before him. 'Bring the four in. Accept no excuses. If we can't stop this, it means our end too. We must find out exactly what funds we have under management and what we can trade off. And then we pray.'

Andersen nodded, turned on his heel and left to do his master's bidding.

Baucher gazed back at the painting on the wall. 'Sebastian. You were my friend. Now I could go to jail!' He threw his mobile phone across the room. It smashed against Pallander's face.

The man with the tanned skin and dark eyebrows stared back with the merest hint of a smile.

36

DI Cara Salt was surprised by the number of staff now gathered in the Great Hall at Meikle House. Apparently it took thirty-two souls to look after the needs of the Pallander family. This included gamekeepers, gardeners and general staff. But still she felt the whole thing excessive in the extreme.

She cast her eyes to the panelled walls, covered in old coats of arms and the hideous trophies of dead animals no doubt killed by the brave Stuart-Hendersons. It all chimed with what she'd learned. Salt had taken a sudden dislike to her hosts.

As the staff gathered, an elderly woman made her way towards the inspector, wringing her hands as though she was nervous.

'Yes, can I help you?' said Salt with a smile.

'I'm so sorry to bother you, officer. I was just wondering what on earth is going on in this house? You know we're hearing all manner of tales. The staff are worried.'

'Don't worry, I'll answer all the questions I can at the meeting.' She smiled.

'You know, I've been here since I was a lassie – my first job. Meikle House belonged to Mrs Pallander's family in those days.'

'Good people to work for, I imagine?'

The woman leaned in. 'No, a sorry bunch o' bastards, they were. Treated us all like shite on their shoes. Let nobody tell you any different. Mr Pallander, God bless him, put an end to all that. We were given better wages, bonuses at Christmas. Aye, and talked to civilly, into the bargain. I cried the day he died. God forgive me, but I've watched that clip over and over again, each time praying he'll recover.'

'The TV clip of him dying, you mean?'

'Aye. Sounds a bit morbid, I dare say. But that's the way I've been feeling ever since he left us, poor man.'

Salt had thought of Pallander as the big businessman, ready to fell all that came before him for his own ends. The revelation that he was a good employer surprised her.

'I'll leave you to your business, lassie. But please do your best to help us feel a bit better about things. Mrs Sullivan disappearing is the last straw, I swear.'

The woman went back to her seat in the hall, shaking her head as she went.

'I think we're ready, Cara,' said Blackstock tentatively, knowing he was still in his superior's bad books.

'Right.' She turned, noticing Sorley MacLeod was standing at the back of the room, his arms folded, leaning on a door jamb. She winked at him, and he winked back.

'Ladies and gentlemen, if I can have your attention, please. I'm Detective Inspector Salt, and this is my colleague Detective Sergeant Blackstock.'

The gathered staff of Meikle House mumbled their collective welcome.

'As you know, Mrs Sullivan didn't turn up for work this morning. First of all, I'm looking for anyone who saw her in the early hours. I'm told she often went about the place, checking up on things at odd times.'

A thickset man with a head of dark curls took to his feet. 'I think that will be me, if you please.'

'You are?'

'Gerald Finney, head gamekeeper, ma'am.' Finney had a strong Dublin accent. 'I was just about to take a wander at about five this morning. I saw her outside the kitchens, speaking on a mobile phone. To be honest, I got the feeling all wasn't well.'

'Why?'

'She seemed agitated. Her voice was raised – that kind of thing.'

'Did you hear what she said?'

Finney held a flat cap, turning it round in both hands before him. He glanced at his fellow members of staff, as though seeking approval before answering the question.

'The more information I have, the quicker we can find out what's happened to Mrs Sullivan,' said Salt, to encourage the gamekeeper.

'She said, "No, not today. I won't do it." I heard her quite plain, so I did.'

'Anything else?'

'Now, it was none of my business, so I went on my way.'

'And you heard nothing more?'

'No, I did not.' He swallowed hard. 'I'm here to tell you that she and I often didn't see eye to eye. I mean, her job was in the house. Mine was all around. She wasn't my boss, nor me hers. Sometimes she was wont to forget that.' Finney donned his cap, then sat down and folded his arms for emphasis.

Salt sighed. She felt like Hercule Poirot, everyone gathered before her in this old mansion. 'I'm trying to piece together Mrs Sullivan's whereabouts prior to her disappearance. Does anyone know if she has a particular friend with a name beginning with the letter "S"?'

Glances were cast at the police officers, and whispers passed from behind hands.

'I'll tell you.' A young woman took to her feet. 'Mrs Sullivan was *friendly* with a member of the family. I don't know about the "S", though it does form part of the name.'

Looking round, Salt saw grimaces, lowered heads, more furtive glances.

'Ach, you all know it fine, yourselves. It's been on the go for ever. So don't look at me as though I'm a Judas. Inspector Salt, the whole house and his wife knows fine that Mrs Sullivan and Mr Stuart-Henderson have been on more than friendly terms for years. Aye, and if you're looking for the "S", there it is in his name.' She took her seat, head held high.

'Can I ask a question?' This from a young man in the formal staff suit.

'Yes, of course,' said Salt.

'My mother was telling me last night that the whole centre of London was closed down yesterday because of Miss Tabitha. She says that half the army was on the streets looking for her.'

Salt heard Sorley chuckle. 'I can tell you that's not true. And I'm here to focus on Mrs Sullivan. If anyone knows any more about her movements late last night or this morning, please speak up.'

A girl – barely out of her teens, Salt thought – took to her feet.

'I'm Diane. I do general work around the house. I live in the staff quarters.'

'Hi, Diane. What did you see?'

'I'm in the habit of taking Mrs Sullivan a cup of tea to her office at around eight in the evening before I finish my shift. I usually work from lunch until then – helping out with meals and the like.'

'Did you take her her tea last night?' said Salt.

'I did. But she wasn't there. I went to her apartment. She was there, right enough. But she only opened the door a crack. Stuck her hand out to take the tea, if you know what I mean.'

'And this was unusual?'

'I don't know. It's never happened like that before.' She bit her lip. 'I just got the feeling she wasn't alone, that's all.'

This brought silence to the hall. The staff at Meikle House seemed to be a loyal enough bunch. But as with the Pallander family themselves, the passage of recent events had left them bewildered and willing to conceive of just about anything.

'I'd like to ask a question.' A middle-aged man got to his feet.

'Yes,' said Salt.

'I live in Kinloch Rannoch. Do you know, it took me nearly an hour to leave last night, and nearly an hour to get back in this morning.'

Many heads nodded and there were mumbles of agreement.

'I didn't come here to be herded about by armed police officers and be cheek by jowl with the press. They're just after scandal. I can't stand them. And who knows what danger we're in, given all the stories. I'd like you to guarantee our safety, please, Inspector.'

Ragged applause broke out. Salt couldn't blame them. The whole situation was bizarre. How could anyone know where they stood, including her? But she had no choice other than to pour oil on troubled waters. 'I know this is a difficult time,' she said. 'But as you can see, we the police are here in large numbers. Everyone is safe. Please don't worry.'

'Tell that to Mrs Sullivan.' This from a disembodied voice.

'I'd like to ask a question.' This time a large woman in an apron took to her feet.

'Please go ahead,' said Salt, now feeling more like an agony aunt than a police officer.

'There was a mistake in my wages last week. Aye, and it's not been rectified this time round. If you ask me, Mrs Sullivan should be back behind her desk, not swanning about with all and sundry.' She nodded to emphasize her point, then sat back down to the approbation of some of her colleagues.

'I'm sad to say that there's not much I can do about that. And I'm sure we'd all like to see Mrs Sullivan back behind her desk.' Salt cleared her throat. 'I'd like to thank you for your time. And if any of you remember something else, please seek me out and let me know.'

As the staff of Meikle House streamed out of the hall and back to work, Salt turned to Blackstock. 'Well, that was enlightening and frustrating, all at the same time.'

Blackstock inclined his head. 'And potentially difficult, I hesitate to venture.'

'Stuart-Henderson, you mean?'

'The very man. Charlie has rather a reputation for being *explosive*, one could say. Confront him with accusations of an affair with the missing Mrs Sullivan, and you will likely find that out for yourself.'

Salt made a face. 'He can be as explosive as he likes. I want to find Sullivan. And I don't care how I do it.'

'That's it, Cara. Give it the full beans, as always.'

Sorley MacLeod had wandered over to join them.

'If you'll excuse us, this is police business,' said Blackstock curtly. 'I've worked with rabble-rousers like you before. I've no time for troublemakers. Especially civilians.'

'Oh, OK – civilians, is it? While you're at it, then, go and find someone to authorize my payment for mutual assistance and nearly getting my fucking head blown off yesterday. Anyway, who died and made *you* boss?' Having made his point, Sorley glared between the two police officers and stomped off.

'Was that really necessary, Abs? We owe the guy, right?'

'The fact remains, *ma'am*. He has no place in operational discussions, ex-job or not.'

'Listen to yourself. What is it between you and him? You barely know each other.'

'Perhaps I'm not as emotionally involved with Mr MacLeod as you are.'

Cara Salt took a deep breath, trying desperately to hold on to her temper. It didn't work. She grabbed the much taller Blackstock by his collar and pulled him down towards her face. 'Don't ever speak to me like that again, on duty or off. I know you think you're something special – an aristocratic James Bond or some bloody thing – but be in no doubt, I'm in charge here, not you. And I'll speak to anyone I see fit. Do you understand?'

She then pushed him away, forcing Blackstock to take a couple of involuntary steps backwards. 'Whatever you say, ma'am.'

Before either of them could say any more, Salt's phone buzzed in her pocket.

'DI Salt.' Her irritation was still plain.

'Good morning, ma'am. I'm sorry to bother you. This is

Sergeant McIntosh from the police station in the village. We were given your number because of all that's been happening up at the house.'

'How can I help you, Sergeant?' For some reason, Salt felt butterflies in her stomach.

'I've had a report of a body in the river – och, about a mile or so from where you are. I know there is a missing person at Meikle House. I thought you might like to come and have a look?'

'It's good of you to think of us, Sergeant. Can you give us directions?'

'I can do better than that. I'll pick you up. We'll need the Land Rover for this one, I'm thinking. I can be with you in the next hour or so. A constable has already secured the area.'

Salt thanked him again and ended the call.

'Trouble?' Blackstock asked.

'I think we might have found Mrs Sullivan. And not in a good way.'

37

The drive, much of it over rough ground, wasn't for the faint-hearted. Though McIntosh, a stout, solid police officer of the kind Salt much admired, proved himself to be rather an expert in off-road driving, the Land Rover the perfect vehicle for the job.

Salt was feeling every jolt and tumble in her back. An old injury from early on in her career; she'd jumped when staying put had been by far the more sensible thing to do. The broken bones and trauma weren't worth it. Now, the pain mixed with a feeling of unreality. Salt had spent so long wishing herself out of that isolated office in Glasgow. She wondered if she'd grown soft, no longer up to the rough and tumble of real policing. But this was beyond rough and tumble; it was like something from a nightmare.

Beside her, his face flickering in the sunlight shifting through the trees, was DS Abernethy Blackstock. Salt felt no regret at their exchange of words. She didn't need to be told that she had feelings for Sorley MacLeod, suppressed rather than hidden. Either way, such matters were none of her sergeant's business. Though quite why he and her former boyfriend were locking horns like rutting stags, she couldn't fathom.

The Land Rover's progress slowed by a riverbank.

Through the trees, Salt could see two officers in fluorescent police jackets standing beside a man dressed in waders and a drab-olive gilet. McIntosh drew up beside the little group, and they all got out.

The sun felt warm on the back of her neck as Salt stepped gingerly through the undergrowth to the edge of the river. As she stared into the water, she saw a body was semi-submerged by the bank, held fast by a tangle of low-hanging tree branches. Long, flaxen hair followed the direction of the river's flow, fanning out from the deceased's head in a rippling display. As always, Salt found these types of circumstances unutterably sad.

'I defer to you, Inspector. It'll be another hour before the forensic team arrive from Perth. If you'd like to take charge, I have no objections.' McIntosh studied her, awaiting an answer.

Salt bit her lip. Though the body was most likely that of Maggie Sullivan, housekeeper of Meikle House, she couldn't be sure until she could see the deceased's face. As it was, the body was lodged face down in the water. It would be bad form to move anything before the SOCO team had a chance to do their bit. But time was of the essence.

Salt was aware that the local officers who'd been first on the scene were in quiet conversation with the angler, who had presumably discovered the body. The man was around six feet tall and reasonably broad. That'll do, she thought. Salt approached him.

'I'm DI Salt. I believe you found the body, sir?'

'Aye, I did. Och, what a terrible thing. It's a fine spot for trout, you know. I've had some great catches at this wee nook. Though I didn't expect what was caught up here this morning.'

'Sergeant McIntosh will take a full statement from you

back at Kinloch Rannoch. But in the meantime, can I ask you a favour?'

'Aye, please do. I'll help you if I can.'

'Can we borrow your waders, please?'

Those gathered eyed Salt sceptically.

'You're welcome to them, aye,' said the man. 'But I think they'll fair drown you, if you don't mind me saying.'

'Abs,' said Salt. 'Stick on these waders. I need you to step into the river and see who this is. Be careful, we don't want to dislodge any potential evidence.'

Blackstock looked at his boss open-mouthed for a moment, before shaking his head. 'This is highly irregular, ma'am. We should wait for SOCO, surely?'

Salt took a step towards him and spoke quietly in his ear. 'Time is of the essence, DS Blackstock. If this is Mrs Sullivan, then we may well have a murder to investigate, along with everything else.'

'Nonsense, they'll send a Major Investigation Team. We'll have nothing to do with it.'

'An MIT? Come on, live in the real world, man. Just do what you're fucking told, for a change.'

Salt stepped back, just as the fisherman finished removing his waders.

'I can't thank you enough, sir,' she said. 'Tell me, how deep is the river at this point? You're the man in the know.'

'It'll be no more than three or four feet at the bank, Inspector. She's high, right enough. But the bank angles down into the deeper part of the river. Your officer will just have to be careful to keep his feet, that's all. In fact, if you don't mind me imparting some advice, I'd have a line tied round his waist, just in case. You've lost one poor soul today already. You'll not be wanting to lose a second.'

'No, indeed not, sound advice. Sergeant McIntosh, can

you please ask your men to find a length of rope and secure it round DS Blackstock's waist before he enters the water.'

'I have just the thing in the back of the Land Rover,' said McIntosh.

'See, there we are, Abs. You'll be safe as houses. Just move her enough to get a look at her face. I needn't tell you your own business.'

Blackstock was about to speak when he was handed the waders, and, almost simultaneously, a bird dropping landed on his head.

'They say it's good luck,' said McIntosh.

'Well, they're wrong,' Blackstock replied testily. 'And another thing, ma'am. Life has – as yet – to be pronounced extinct. This really is a fool's errand.'

'So, you think she's still alive?' Salt eyed her DS unblinkingly.

'Now you're being obtuse.'

'Just get the damned thing done, Abernethy.' Salt hadn't been well disposed to him earlier. Now she felt positively irritated by this posturing minor aristocrat. She'd noticed that he bridled when given the order. No doubt this was a product of working undercover on his own initiative for so long, combined with his own sense of entitlement.

Blackstock secured the waders over his shoulder. They were loose on his slightly thinner frame, but they would do the job. He held his arms up as the two local constables tied an oily tow rope round his waist.

'There we are, no time like the present,' said Salt, knowing it would irritate her deputy.

'Go carefully, mind. It'll be right muddy underfoot,' said McIntosh. 'Hang on to the tall weeds and branches as you go.'

With a deep sigh, and a face like thunder, Abernethy

Blackstock made his way to the water's edge. The constables stood behind him, the rope hanging loose.

Blackstock reached out and grabbed one of the branches of the tree that had ensnared the drowned woman. Gingerly, he padded down the bank, hanging on to a sprouting of reeds here or a clump of rough grass there. Soon, he took his first tentative step into the river.

'Bloody hell! It's freezing,' he shouted.

'Aye, she'll no' warm up until later in the summer. You'd be amazed how much snow and ice is still melting off the hills. It all channels down here,' said the fisherman.

'Fabulous,' said Blackstock under his breath, as he began to make his way down into the river, not far from where the body was bobbing in the now disturbed water.

Salt stood on the bank, remembering what she'd learned of the woman she suspected was lying dead before her. Efficient but living on her nerves, she reasoned. Doing her best to keep her son at university but struggling. A woman in the wrong place at the wrong time, like so many before her. She'd liked Sullivan during their brief acquaintance.

There was little doubt that a positive identification would make Salt's life infinitely more difficult. But she was still alive, breathing warm summer air beside this Perthshire river. It was much more preferable to being dead in it, she reminded herself.

Blackstock was within feet of the corpse now, the water almost up to his waist. His breathing had shortened; Salt could see he was feeling the cold. He almost slipped but managed to grab a branch just in time to stop his fall.

'This is bloody maddening!' he called out, splashing a clenched fist into the river.

'You're nearly there,' said Sergeant McIntosh. 'You keep

a good grip on that rope, boys,' he cautioned his constables.

There was something of a slick surrounding the deceased, an oily residue that made Salt's stomach churn. The closer Blackstock got to the body, the more it bobbed in the water. It was as if new life had been breathed into the corpse, the remains now trying to struggle free of the submerged tree branches.

Salt held her breath as Blackstock reached out to touch the body. As he did, it appeared to move inches from his grasp. He tried again and, to everyone's shock, the corpse began to roll against the disturbance in the water. One arm flailed into the air, and slowly, grotesquely, the body flipped.

'Fuck!' Blackstock swore at the shock of it all, taking an awkward step back from the dead woman. He then missed his footing, thrashed about trying to arrest his fall, but in moments toppled over, his head disappearing below the water.

'Pull, boys!' shouted McIntosh, his voice echoing round the woodland, sending birds protesting into the blue sky.

As if copying her sergeant, Cara Salt took an involuntary step away from the water's edge at the sight of the corpse on its back. Sullivan's face was familiar and unfamiliar at the same time. Yes, she was recognizable to Salt, but her lifeless features looked almost like a waxwork model. One that had been beaten. Salt had witnessed this often. All sense of life, of being, utterly gone, more often than not by means of extreme violence.

She heard Blackstock's frantic roar as he was pulled up the bank on the rope.

Salt forced herself to gaze at the corpse. She could see a corner of her tartan suit – her uniform – and the zip of the blue Barbour jacket she was wearing. It was heartbreaking.

Blackstock was now on the bank, gasping for air. McIntosh had wound a fluorescent police jacket round him in an effort to warm the detective up, but still Blackstock shivered uncontrollably, a product of shock as much as the cold.

Salt felt a pang of guilt as she approached him. 'Are you OK, Abs? I'm sorry, that's not how I expected things to go.'

He looked up at her, his face streaked with mud. 'Please don't speak to me, not at the moment.' He pulled the jacket tighter round himself.

'We better get this one to the cottage hospital,' said Sergeant McIntosh. 'Shock and a good ducking in the cold can be a dangerous combination.'

Salt nodded, barely hearing him. Though she tried to rationalize what had happened over the last few days, nothing made sense. She wanted to catch who had done this terrible thing to Sullivan; she wanted to end the misery of the Pallander family and those trying to protect them. She wanted Sorley MacLeod.

She knew only too well the difference between wanting and getting.

38

Ulrich Baucher felt as though he had opened the lid of Pandora's box, and, true to form, there was no way of closing it. The further he probed, the more irregularities he found. It wasn't quite Madoff, but the hitherto quietly respectable fund management company that was Pallander Glossop would never survive.

Baucher squirmed in his chair in the HM Treasury building on Horse Guards Road, in the heart of Whitehall. Here was power, real power, wrought in Portland Stone and drenched in tradition. This place had been the heartbeat of the British economy for so many years, it was hard to imagine an alternative.

But Baucher wasn't here to celebrate tradition. No, his job was to do everything he could to keep himself out of jail.

He cursed his tailor as he sat in the uncomfortable chair in the corridor outside the minister's office. He'd told the man to cut the waist more amply. As it was, he felt as though his suit trousers were going to cut him in half. He'd been waiting in this very spot for nearly an hour. Only transient politicians would think to treat people of his eminence in the business community in such a way. It infuriated him. What were they, apart from here today, gone tomorrow functionaries? Men and woman who'd managed to shin their way up the greasy pole, now desperately trying to hold on until they saw the opportunity to make a break for the very top.

Down the corridor, a buzzer sounded. A besuited man behind a tiny desk answered the call quickly.

'Mr Butcher, the minister will see you now,' he called.

Baucher got to his feet, wrestling his trousers back into position. 'My name is Baucher,' he said, 'not Butcher.'

'I do beg your pardon, sir.' The man's reply was perfunctory and disingenuous. 'The door directly in front of you.' He returned his attention to a computer screen.

'Piece of shit,' Baucher mumbled under his breath. He rapped the door sharply with his wedding ring, opened it and entered the minister's office.

A woman in a bright-red jacket was behind an enormous desk that dwarfed both her and the office. This wasn't the Chancellor, nor even the Chief Secretary to the Treasury. No, the Right Honourable Marion Palmer was merely part of the machinery of this place – or so he assumed.

'Mr Baucher, please take a seat,' she said. 'Let me just finish this and I'll be with you in a jiffy.'

Jiffy. Baucher mulled the word over as he sat in the low chair that was much more comfortable than the one he'd been forced to endure for so long. It was typical of English onomatopoeia. He'd never liked this notion, ever since he'd learned to speak the language. He toyed with the idea of surreptitiously unbuttoning the waistband of his trousers. Had he been sitting across from a man rather than a woman, he probably would have done it. But, envisioning the calamity of a potential wardrobe malfunction, he was forced to endure the feeling of being slowly eviscerated.

Marion Palmer finished what she was doing by signing

a document with a flourish. She smiled at Baucher as she removed a pair of reading glasses.

'Now, I have been briefed by the Under Secretary, Mr Baucher. This all sounds quite awful. Your company being bled dry by its dead founder. The Chancellor would have met with you himself today, had he not been in India trying to drum up some trade. Nothing we've done there recently seems to have worked out well. Including your own company's initiatives, I think.'

Her voice was clipped. But attained upper-class, rather than the genuine article, Baucher observed. She smiled without warmth.

'That is a great pity,' Baucher replied. 'For I believe if we are to rescue the company and save the funds we manage, it must be achieved by an intervention by government.' He tried to look grim and determined. The former wasn't difficult.

'I think we are some distance from that, Mr Baucher. In fact, it is rather fanciful, to be honest.'

'Why so?'

'The very thought that we should ask taxpayers to stump up to bail out your company when we can barely grant adequate pay rises to nurses and doctors – well, wouldn't go down at all well, would it?'

Baucher was rather taken aback by her candid response. But he wasn't finished. 'When an organization like Pallander Glossop gets into trouble, it can have serious consequences for the entire economy. You must surely acknowledge that?'

Palmer eyed him levelly. 'Mr Baucher, I have a doctorate in economics. I studied at Oxford and Harvard. I founded and ran my own very successful company before I entered politics. I do not need you to tell me the *real* fiscal *politik* of all this. The fact is – and you have been a senior company officer for forty years – the corporate governance of Pallander Glossop has been a joke, almost since the day it sprang into existence. How you managed to keep the ship afloat for so long is beyond me.'

'Mr Pallander was a financial genius.'

'He was certainly adept with the art of smoke and mirrors, Mr Baucher. A real magician, as it turns out. If he wasn't dead, he'd be in court right now. No, this sorry mess is to be investigated by the Department for Business and Trade. I dread to think what they'll uncover. I do have their preliminary assessment, if you'd like to read it? It's fair to say your late boss treated Pallander Glossop like his own personal wealth fund.'

'But the Chancellor ... We are *friends.*' Baucher was clutching at straws. His main objective had been to avoid a DBT investigation. And of course, a bailout would have been fabulous. But all that now seemed fruitless. 'We spent a lot of time together in Bavaria. We share many *interests.*'

Baucher said this in such a way as to drench the last word in innuendo, the hint of something distasteful – something he could perhaps reveal if things went against him. The fact that the Chancellor of the Exchequer had a taste for the young, blonde German women Baucher was happy to supply had been his get-out-of-jail-free card. He trusted that it still might serve him.

'If that's a threat, Mr Baucher, let me tell you this. In the absence of the late Sebastian Pallander, your own finances will come under forensic scrutiny. Now, I know you to be a cautious, if somewhat avaricious, man. But allow me to let you into a little secret.'

Baucher sighed. 'These games will do neither of us any good.'

'You don't know what my little secret is yet.'

Baucher waved his hand in a gesture of surrender.

'Your old boss died at a very opportune moment – for him, that is.'

'I don't like riddles.'

'Let me make it clear for you, Mr Baucher. Mr Pallander was under the protection of the Security Service before he died.'

'What?' Baucher sat up in his chair.

'You're surprised, I see. But I'm not. It isn't something suitable for office gossip, I don't suppose.'

'Protection from whom?'

'That's classified. But I'm sure you can take a guess or two. In times of trouble, sometimes the solutions we seek are worse than the problems they are intended to solve. Yes?'

'You are talking nonsense.'

'Are you aware his family are virtual prisoners on their estate in Scotland?'

Baucher shuddered. Meikle House was a cold, dull place, as far as he was concerned. For once, he pitied Tabitha Pallander. Then something crossed his mind. 'Jean-Luc Pallander. He died recently. They said it was an accident. Is this not true?'

'I don't know, Mr Baucher. But my advice to you is to go back to the Shard and ready yourself for the DBT investigation. I'm sure you'll want to be prepared. To the extent you can be, at least.'

Baucher knew exactly what she meant. *Go back and cover your arse.* At least there was still some honour left between the regulator and regulated. But it was cold comfort.

Baucher took to his feet. 'That is it, then. Short and sweet. There will be many people – rich, influential people – who will be very angry with you. But I thank you for being so candid with me, Mrs Palmer.'

'They won't be angry at me. Nobody knows who I am. Their anger will be reserved for you and your organization. And please don't thank me. Thank your friend, the Chancellor. Right now, I'd hang on to as many friends as you can, Mr Baucher. Good day to you, sir.'

Baucher left the Treasury a wiser, yet more troubled, man. He cursed the day he'd set eyes on Sebastian Pallander. Now it would be a dash to save his career and reputation, a fight to save his liberty. Baucher wasn't frightened of the fray, but in this instance it was a fight he could only lose.

39

Silas Pallander was on the balcony at Meikle House, a large glass of malt whisky in one hand. His face was drawn, bags under his eyes. For those who knew him, it looked as though he'd aged ten years in the last few days.

He leaned on the balustrade and gazed across the family estate. The magic mountain Schiehallion dominated the skyline as the evening light gained sway. It made the great peak look almost blue, otherworldly. As a child, he'd been fascinated by its many legends of fairies and folklore. He'd need more than magic to bring Anna Marchand back, though. Silas pictured her battered and bruised face as she led him to safety in Belgium. But that safety had come at a cost, one he was finding almost impossible to bear.

He heard footsteps behind him on the balcony. Silas recognized the tread – he'd been hearing it for most of his life.

'Help yourself to a drink, Tabby.'

He heard the clink of the decanter on glass, as she accepted his offer.

'It's time for a truce, Sil,' she said, joining him by the balustrade.

His gaze remained on the mountain. 'So, it's time for a truce when you say it is, yeah?'

'For fuck's sake. We're all in this mess, and you still can't behave like an adult. We're all losers in this, you know.'

'They found your husband safe and well.'

'What's that supposed to mean?'

'Well, he's fine, isn't he? I'm sure you can work that out.'

Tabitha thought for a moment as she took a sip of the whisky.

'Oh, I get it. My husband's safe, but Anna isn't. Is that what you mean?'

Silas didn't reply.

'May I remind you that Anna is your PA, not your spouse.'

Silas turned, his face set in a scowl. 'What do you know about it? I mean, really? You think you're all-seeing. But that simply isn't the truth.'

'I know you hung about her like a sad little puppy dog. I know you couldn't take your eyes off her when she first arrived. You were walking about with a perpetual bulge in your trousers until Daddy sent her off to school. Pathetic.'

'A lot's happened between us over the years.'

Tabitha chuckled. 'Let me tell you. Anything that happened, she did for a reason. To further ensnare you – squeeze you even more under the thumb. Trust me, you're not her type.'

'There we go. Tabitha knows everyone's innermost thoughts, wishes and desires. Well, if you're that fucking clever, why don't you find out what happened to poor Mrs Sullivan? Why they blew JL to smithereens? Why I ended up being kidnapped from one of our own company jets? Why they had a go at killing half of London to get to you?'

'Big brother, you really hate me, don't you?'

'I used to. Daddy's little girl. But I'm just indifferent now.

Anyway, what have we got left? A million quid each and this rotting old shithole.'

Tabitha gulped down her whisky and poured herself another. It was good, full-bodied, a Glen Scotia. Not one of these drams that felt like swallowing weak tea and furniture polish.

'At least you got a job out of it,' said Tabitha.

'You did too, but you turned it down. Couldn't stand the thought of not being the boss. I know you thought you were a shoo-in for that.'

'Do you think it was easy? Working for him, I mean?'

'I *know* what it was like working for him. I was there first, remember.'

'That's not what I mean, Sil. There are problems – big ones. We had to borrow money. A lot of money. A few months ago.'

'The two of you hid that well.'

'I had no choice. You know how things were with him. Though I still don't know where he got it. I don't think it ever went through the books at PG. But it was secured by the company in some way. I'd gamble anything on that.'

It was Silas's turn to pour himself another whisky. He sat down at the wrought-iron table and sighed. 'So, where did this money come from? And more to the point, why did we have to borrow?'

'Daddy made some bad choices. Poor decisions.' Tabitha took a seat beside him.

'You don't say.'

'The money came from somewhere. I don't know the full extent. But I think I know what happened recently. The only answer can be Russia.'

Silas swallowed his whisky. 'Fabulous. It's a wonder I'm still alive. Fuck knows who's after us. The FSB, for all I know.'

'I think that's why his estate was the way it was. The lack of money, I mean. Our jobs.'

Silas laughed as he poured another drink. 'So, he cut us off to keep us safe. Is that what you're saying?'

'Maybe.'

'But you didn't get the sack. You were sidelined, exactly the way I was.'

'Huh! You took it – sucked it up like a good boy. He knew I wouldn't. I suppose it made things less obvious.'

'This is classic, just fucking classic. Do you remember the time he took us all to that shack in Switzerland? No running water, a dry toilet . . . fucking rats.'

'How can I forget?'

'It took him two days to bugger off in a helicopter and leave us to it. We were there for half the summer.'

'Anna was there. It was the summer her parents died.'

Silas's face took on a look of indescribable misery. Tears welled in his eyes. 'Yes. I do remember.' He held his head in his hands. 'He's done it again. Left us to face the music. Bastard!'

'He has. But you can't really legislate for dying, can you, Silas?'

'He could *legislate* for anything.'

'I suppose we have to trust Baucher.'

'Shit, we might as well throw ourselves off this balcony right now, if he's our last hope!'

'Yeah, it's not much, I admit.' Tabitha rolled her eyes.

They sat in silence, the brother and sister who – by virtue of the fact of being Sebastian Pallander's eldest children, the repository of his hopes and legacy – had suffered the most.

'Do you think she's dead? Anna, I mean.'

Tabitha stared at her brother. 'You really love her, don't you?'

'I suppose I do.' Tears began to spill down his face. 'She cradled me in her arms. They'd beaten her so badly, but she cradled me.'

Tabitha stared at the lilac sky. 'You know, every time I begin to feel sorry for you, I remember what a prick you are. "She cradled me . . ." Grow a pair, will you? You're going to need them!'

Tabitha slammed her glass on to the table and stormed off.

Silas drained his and sobbed for the woman he loved.

40

Salt sat in the room she'd used for the interviews, reflecting. She had been right. No Major Investigation Team arrived at Meikle House to investigate the murder of Maggie Sullivan. In fact, the message she received from ACC Dixon was as curt as it was unhelpful. She was to cope and 'bring the perpetrator to justice'. How hard could it be, after all? The suspects must surely be confined within the walls of Meikle House.

Salt and Blackstock interviewed everyone present at the time of the murder. This included the Pallander family, staff and the armed police officers in the grounds.

Reactions had been varied. Charles Stuart-Henderson had swallowed hard when Salt imparted the news, a single tear meandering down his cheek. No histrionics, but enough to persuade Salt that he and Sullivan had much more than just an employer–employee relationship.

Audrey – the late Jean-Luc's twin – had become hysterical at the news. Salt discovered that the main reason for this was that her husband refused to join her in the bosom of the family at Meikle House, keener to take his chances away from the stifling embrace of the remote house. Salt could empathize with this line of thinking.

She was beginning to regret her decision to move from the hotel.

The staff, for whom Sullivan had been their boss, were devastated. And yet, for all their lamentation, Salt quickly discovered that none of them had close individual relationships with the dead woman. No nights out in the bright lights of Kinloch Rannoch, no special friends. It all seemed rather distant to Salt, who had spent a career having drinks with colleagues. She had to remind herself that not all workmates had the almost enforced esprit de corps of police officers, who mainly socialized with each other because of the shifts they had to work.

Ultimately, though, nobody seemed to wish Sullivan dead. Everyone's attitude to the housekeeper was one of remote sadness. A collective emotion rolled up in the general air of unease at Meikle House.

When she asked Blackstock if this attitude was common in big houses – he having experience of such things – her DS merely shrugged. It appeared that the staff in the homes of the old aristocracy often mirrored the families for whom they worked. This normally involved a certain distance between colleagues, depending on their job status. It all seemed strange to the Glasgow detective. But then she remembered her relationship with her own father. That she'd loved him, there was no doubt. But despite all the years she'd spent trying to be anything other than him, here she was, in charge of a major case.

Preliminary interviews done, she was no closer to any kind of theory surrounding the housekeeper's death. Perhaps the post mortem in Aberdeen would offer up some clues. On the surface of it, nobody seemed to have tangled with Sullivan enough to bear a grudge. But the proof of that particular pudding would be in the eating. Because, as much as the ACC might wish it, Salt wasn't sure that every-thing could be so neatly contained within the house itself. Anyone could have laid in wait for Sullivan. Indeed, the murder could have been committed by a total stranger; the circumstances in which the Pallander family found them-selves a complete coincidence.

To that end, she asked Blackstock to take two constables from the number guarding Meikle House and go door to door, to ask the locals about anything or anyone seeming suspicious.

By nine o'clock, Salt was ready for bed. Protecting the Pal-lander family had been hard enough. Now she was investigating a murder with barely any resources. And the mental strain made everything worse. The press were pushing for more information. They'd set up a little encampment at the end of the long road to the house. They demanded she come and speak to them several times a day. She refused. At least, she consoled herself, if they knew as little as possible of what was going on, they were limited in what they could put in the newspapers, on tele-vision, radio and the internet.

Salt tried to reconcile the individuals she knew in the house with the possibility that one of them could be a mur-derer. She just didn't see or feel it. It didn't make sense, somehow. It was yet another product of lazy thinking by a senior officer. As far as Salt was concerned, that happened a lot. Throughout the history of policing, how many guilty people had walked free just because the men at the top of the tree required neat, uncomplicated conclusions?

Could there really be such a wide-ranging conspiracy against one family? Thinking back to the abduction, pur-suit and escape of Tabitha Pallander, there certainly were far too many coincidences. Whoever they were up against appeared to have eyes and ears everywhere.

Even Blackstock had nothing to offer. Though he'd been out in the grounds at the time Sullivan disappeared, it turned out his obsession with rare birds had taken him two miles away from Meikle House in the opposite direction to the river where the housekeeper's mutilated body had been found. She was still irritated by her DS, though. OK, perhaps she shouldn't have ordered him to go into the river. The gruesome truth had been uncovered, but the whole episode had negatively affected their working relationship, there was no doubt.

With all this echoing round her mind, Salt decided to approach sleep in the manner she would have done at home. Though her room was basic, in the manner of faded grandeur, she had a bathroom. So, she ran a bath and hoped the warm water would soothe away the stress in her back and neck before bed.

As she lay back in the deep bath, moments from the last few days drifted by like dreams. There was Sorley darting past her with Tabitha Pallander on the motorbike, as she knelt to shoot at their assailants. Sullivan's blank, dead face staring at her, as though she was demanding an answer to why she had died. Then the almost surreal views from the helicopter, as towns slipped by underneath them like living maps, every street, building and car in miniature.

Salt tore herself away from these thoughts, got out of the bath and towelled herself dry. She slipped into a large t-shirt that had once belonged to Sorley. More and more, she began to realize that her affections had never strayed from the sandy-haired son of the Hebrides. All it had taken was a return to proper policing and a series of coincidences to reveal this.

Salt's phone was charging by her bed. She picked it off the nightstand, found her earbuds in the depths of her handbag and began listening to the soothing sounds of her sleep app. First came a quiet, reassuring voice then a series of sounds that could hardly be called music. Nonetheless, they were designed to relax the listener, and it worked. Lazily, Cara Salt reached out to the bedside lamp and turned it off. The curtains in the room were old and thick. Only the merest hint of the long, bright night slipped from their edges.

She tapped the screen of her phone to stop the app. Soon, she was drifting off to sleep, and dreams of rivers, birds and men in oversized waders.

Salt was normally a sound sleeper, habitually waking up to the tinkling alarm on her phone. So, it was with no little surprise that she found herself awake in the darkness of her room. The phone lay beside her on the bed. She reached to read the time on its screen – almost ten past three in the morning.

Putting her wakeful state down to a troubled mind and the unfamiliarity of her surroundings, Salt turned on to her back and closed her eyes. She was still tired, so sleep would come. She desperately didn't want to go through the mantra on her app again.

Just as she felt the fuzzy warmth of tiredness, a floor-board creaked. Salt's eyes snapped open. She held her breath. Toyed with the idea of switching on the bedside light but then reasoned that very old houses like this one creaked and groaned all the time. She settled back down.

The gloved hand that covered her mouth and nose a moment later came as a shock. Salt tried to scream but the sound was muffled. She kicked out at the figure leaning over her in the shadows on the right side of her bed, but her legs were impeded by the heavy old sheets and blankets.

The hand was pressing down so hard that she was finding it hard to breathe. She sensed a face moving closer to hers, the smell of bad breath, the stench of alcohol and sweat.

'You listen to me.' The voice was low, rasping. 'Do whatever it is you have to do but leave this place. You're not wanted here. Do you understand?'

The gloved hand pushed harder, making Salt lash out with her free left arm. Again, it was to no avail. She was merely thrashing about in the darkness.

'Or maybe I shouldn't give you the opportunity to leave, eh? Maybe I'll just finish you off and leave you somewhere for the rats and foxes.'

Salt was panicking now. She felt the desperate need to force herself away from the hand, to run out into the cool night air as far away from Meikle House as she could.

Without warning, her room was suddenly bathed in light. The hand was whipped away from her face and she heard a grunt of pain. Salt forced herself up on the bed. Abernethy Blackstock had wrestled another man to the floor, and he was in the process of kicking her assailant in the side.

'Stop, Sergeant Blackstock!' cried Salt at the top of her voice.

It was enough to bring him to his senses. Blackstock turned the groaning man face down and handcuffed him quickly and efficiently.

'What the fuck?' Salt was out of the bed now, staring down at Blackstock and the man who'd tried to smother

her. Her colleague's expression was hard to gauge; a mix of hatred and anger, she thought.

'Take a look, Cara.'

Blackstock pulled the hair of the man he'd subdued. Charles Stuart-Henderson's eyes stared out of his startled face, his teeth clenched against the pain.

41

Stuart-Henderson was taken to the cells at Kinloch Ranoch. Initially, Sergeant McIntosh raised an eyebrow at the hour and identity of the man in custody. But when he heard the story behind Stuart-Henderson's arrest, he was more sanguine. He called the local doctor to tend to his new prisoner.

Back at Meikle House, Salt decided not to wake Elizabeth Pallander with the news, but rather to arrange a meeting first thing in the morning.

The chatelaine invited Salt to breakfast. The pair sat either end of a long table. Elizabeth appeared to have no knowledge of what had happened, limiting her conversation to what the police officer wanted for breakfast, general observations about the weather, and how pleased she was to have Tabitha and Silas back safely.

Salt exchanged pleasantries for a while before deciding that it was time to address the events of the previous night.

'I have to speak to about your brother, Mrs Pallander.'

'I see.' Elizabeth continued to butter a slice of toast. 'He was drinking rather heavily by the time I went to bed last night. It's Charles's default position, you see. He doesn't show much in the way of emotion. Rather bottles it up.

Been like that since he was boy. This has all been too much for him, I fear.' She took a deliberate bite of toast.

Salt explained how Stuart-Henderson had attacked and threatened her, and that he was now in custody. She had heard of the sangfroid displayed by the aristocracy at times of stress. And though she'd admired the way this woman had coped with the death of a husband and son, plus the travails of two of her other children, she was shocked by her host's reaction.

'Your word against his, then?'

'I beg your pardon?' said Salt.

'Just you and he witnessed the events, therefore it's one person's word against another. A drunken misstep, wouldn't you say? We've all done it.'

'My sergeant forced him off me and arrested him.' Salt was becoming more strident now. 'Your definition of a misstep doesn't match mine, Mrs Pallander. Threatening a police officer is bad enough. But the content of these threats, plus assault, mark this out as something much more serious.'

Elizabeth stared at her unblinkingly. 'My dear, please don't think that this will go any further. My brother has been involved in one scrape or another for most of his life. None of them have touched him. It's the way of things, you see. People in our position are permitted a certain latitude.'

'Not in my world, Mrs Pallander. He won't get away with it.'

'He will. You have my word.'

Cara Salt took a sip of coffee and rose from the table.

'You've hardly touched your breakfast, Inspector. Do eat some more. Goodness knows you need to be properly nourished to cope with the task in hand.'

'I didn't come here for breakfast. I came to tell you about

your brother's actions and their consequences. I have a murder investigation to be getting on with. Or will nothing come of that either?'

'Inspector, you're being rather petty, don't you think? I'm sorry to say that, as a guest in my house, you've shown very little respect for me or my family.'

Salt banged the table with a fist. 'I'm here to *protect* your family. Perhaps you should remember that!'

She turned on her heel and left the room. In the corridor, she met Sorley MacLeod. He had a rucksack slung casually over one shoulder.

'Going somewhere?' said Salt.

'Home, thankfully. Your ACC has finally agreed to pay up. It's not fantastic, but at least it will cover my bike, and the shop being shut, plus a bit more for my trouble.'

Salt wanted to say so much, but only a few words would come. 'Please stay for a while.'

'Eh? Are you kidding? This place is as toxic an environment as I've ever seen. These people are completely out of touch with reality. And the operation to protect them isn't far behind. If you want my advice, get your arse out of here as quickly as you can.'

'I need somebody I rely on – completely, I mean.'

'Those days are gone. Another world.' He shook his head. 'I have a different life now – so do you. There's nothing worse than trying to rake over old bones to rekindle the fire.'

'Wow, the master of the mixed metaphor.'

'See, we can't even have a short conversation before you start pulling me apart.' Sorley hoisted the rucksack higher up his shoulder. 'You take care, OK?' He embraced Salt and planted a kiss on her forehead. 'Keep in touch. You obviously know where I am.'

'I will. Safe journey.'

Salt watched him leave, feeling a strange sense of a premature ending. She'd been happy to end the great majority of her relationships. These men that had filled her life for a while but who had ended up being either self-centred or needy. Sorley was different. But despite the emotions that were churning away within her, she couldn't put her finger on just why she felt it all so strongly now.

Cara Salt stared out of a large window with a view across the wide, ornate steps leading up to the front of the property. She saw Sorley jogging down the steps in his usual fleet-footed manner. She'd always admired his natural fitness. Remembered how hard he'd had to work when recovering from the shooting that could so easily have ended his life.

Then there was her friend's advice when she went to cry on her shoulder.

You shot him, Caz. Be serious, that's going to end any relationship. There are plenty more fish in the sea. Just don't fire a gun at them.

But as Salt gazed down on her departing ex-lover as he chatted amiably to the armed cop on the steps, she couldn't help thinking how spurious this advice had been. There may be plenty of fish in the sea, but it was a vast, cold, empty place. She couldn't swim in it any more.

Sorley glanced up, a look of concern etched across his face. Involuntarily, Salt stepped back from the window, anxious not be perceived as watching him go, like a sad puppy. *Never watch them out of sight.* That was always her grandmother's advice to those witnessing the departure of a loved one.

For Sorley MacLeod, the pain he felt on parting from Cara Salt seemed almost too much to bear. He could still smell her perfume, taste her skin on his lips. But while he knew how he felt about her, he couldn't put himself through the chaos of her life again. Cara didn't recognize it, but she was almost impossible to love. She was locked into a life of emotional withdrawal.

Leaving the cop to his work, Sorley almost bumped into Tabitha in the drive. 'It's yourself. How's the head?'

'Fine. I'll say something for you, you must invest in good crash helmets,' said Tabitha.

'I do. You can't be too careful where the old heid is concerned.'

Tabitha glanced at the bag on his shoulder. 'Off somewhere nice?'

'Aye, back home – to London. Computers don't fix themselves, you know.'

For some reason, Tabitha Pallander found herself without anything to say. She'd been appalled by the state of Sorley's shop and the place he lived in. But he'd most likely saved her life. And the time they spent together had made her reconsider her taste in men. Sorley was rough and ready, but he was real – and charming to boot.

Tabitha caught him by the shoulders and planted a long, lingering kiss on his lips. When she pulled back, she laughed at the expression on his face.

'I know where you live, remember.'

At the window high above, Cara Salt felt her stomach churn. She'd seen the kiss, the mesmerized look on Sorley's face.

She turned on her heel and rushed away.

42

Baucher sat at his desk in the Shard feeling ever more desperate. The Chancellor had been his last hope. He really thought his friendship with the second most powerful man in government might be enough to save Pallander Glossop. Instead, he been greeted by a low-rent Rottweiler, a functionary put in place to save the blushes of her boss.

It was the old story: when you're flying high, everybody wants to be your friend. But friends are hard to come by when life takes a turn for the worse.

Everybody has a problem nobody else wants to hear about. Baucher's father had been a master of such aphorisms.

The big man tried to force himself to think of the many problems in hand. It was a Herculean task, one he was too old and too tired to perform. The simple truth was that nothing could be done to save Sebastian Pallander's most senior company officers. Their fate was inevitable – even though they had done nothing wrong. But nobody would believe that.

He'd had the painting of himself and Pallander removed from the wall. In its place was an empty space, symbolizing – in his mind at least – the meaningless-ness of their relationship.

'Shall I put it in the store or hang it somewhere else?' the building manager had asked.

'Neither. Burn it! I never want to see it again.'

The man looked appalled, as though he was being ordered to destroy an object of veneration. Baucher had shouted him out of the room, the large painting almost too big for him to carry alone.

His desk phone rang with an internal call.

'Baucher, speak.'

It was one of the receptionists. 'Sir, I have a message for you. A rather odd one.'

'Spit it out, man!'

'A woman asked me to pass this mobile number on to you, sir. She refused to give a name, but said that you would most definitely want to speak to her.'

Baucher thought for a few moments. This mystery woman was either some nutjob or a reporter already sniffing the mighty fall of Pallander Glossop.

'Give me the number.'

He needed something to divert his mind. If it was a nosy journalist, at least it would make him feel as though he was still worth something as he shouted them down. He took a deep breath before dialling, then waited in silence for the call to connect.

'Hello, Mr Baucher.'

The woman's voice was slow and low. Not English, he thought.

'Who are you and what do you want?'

'First of all, you will not speak to me like that. You will be respectful.'

'I'm not in the mood, madam. Good day to you!' Baucher almost removed the phone from his ear, but then caught a few words on the other end of the call.

'I know about the letter of credit.'

Baucher waited.

'I know who your company is really in debt to.'

For once in his life, Baucher was lost for words. His response was a non-committal grunt, acknowledging nothing other than the fact he was still listening. After all, he considered, this could just as well be a disgruntled employee clever or cunning enough to have pieced together what was going on. If so, he would play along, ready to ensnare them.

'I want to meet with you, Mr Baucher. There is a way out of all this – the only way.'

'Where, when?'

'A public house in Kensington, the Churchill Arms. It's far enough away from the City so that your presence will not attract attention. Come in the corner door and turn right. I'll be wearing a red jacket and drinking Pimm's.'

'And when is this clandestine meeting to take place?'

'As soon as you can get there.'

Baucher thought some more. 'All right. I don't know how you've come across the information you have, and of course it's complete nonsense. But I want to find out what you're trying to achieve, and a cool beer would be most welcome. But I tell you this. Mess with me and you'll get more from this corporation than you expect.'

'Good. I assure you your trip will be worthwhile. But I too have conditions. You must tell nobody where you are coming and do so alone. Use a public taxi, not your chauffeured car or any other company vehicle. The venue is being watched. Any sign that you have breached these conditions will mean that your opportunity to save your skin is at an end. Do you understand?'

'How do I know I'll be safe?'

'You're in a very public place. You must take your chances. Be there by noon.'

Before Baucher could say more, the line went dead. He looked at his watch. Almost ten thirty. These days in London it would be quite a feat to get to Kensington from the Shard in time.

For reasons he could not explain, he felt galvanized by the call.

Baucher pushed himself up from his chair, feeling every year of his age. Somehow his body had become heavier over the last few days. It was amazing how problems could impact a person in all ways imaginable.

He shrugged on his jacket and entered his private elevator without a word to his PA or any other member of staff. On the ground floor, he had the choice to walk through the concourse or leave by the executive exit. He chose the latter. In minutes, he was out on the streets of South London beside the city's tallest building. He had no problem hailing a black cab; the place was always thronged with taxis, waiting in the expectation of large tips from fat cat financiers.

'Where to, mate?'

'The Churchill Arms in Kensington. And I'm in a hurry. Get there quickly and you'll find me very generous.'

'Received and understood, squire. You'll never have been to Kensington as quick.'

Baucher climbed in and sat heavily on the back seat, bemoaning his tired limbs as the taxi began to wind its way through the busy London streets, his driver taking a side street here, jumping a red light there. Baucher kept his head in his phone, anxious not to engage the man in conversation. And to be fair, after a couple of questions, first about football then politics, the driver got the message.

When they reached the Embankment, the taxi driver reassured him that this was a quick route to their destination, and not to worry. Baucher took him at face value and stared at the Thames, still grey and forbidding even under a glorious blue sky. For some reason he remembered the case of the Vatican banker, Roberto Calvi. Though he'd been a young man at the time, it had always fascinated him. Baucher supposed it was the first time the harsh realities of the world hit him. Since then, he'd had plentiful opportunities to see society as it truly was, not just the shadow marketed to the general public. His latest predicament was only the most recent example, but by no means the least dangerous.

He checked his Vacheron Constantin again. He reckoned they were making good time, already heading for the west of the city. He closed his eyes for a moment, his lids heavy with stress and sheer exhaustion, lulled by the motion of the vehicle.

'Wake up, mate, we're here!' The taxi driver roused Baucher from the unintended sleep into which he'd fallen.

'Yes, yes. You have done very well.' He pulled a bulging gold money clip from his pocket. Baucher always liked to have ready cash about him. The plastic world was all very well, but sometimes only real money you could smell and hold in your hand would do. He counted out two hundred and sixty pounds and passed it through to the driver.

'Thank you, squire, above and beyond, mate.'

Baucher stepped out of the taxi on to Kensington Church

Street. The pub across the road was a blaze of colour, festooned with all manner of flowers sprouting from hanging baskets on just about every portion of the building.

If this was to be where it all ended, it wouldn't be the worst venue, he thought, as he crossed the road and made for the corner entrance. It was like a garlanded tomb.

Stepping inside, his attention was taken by more items hanging from the walls and ceiling. A nondescript catalogue of the absurd, including Victorian chamber pots, a banjo, part of a bicycle frame and an old wartime radio set, not unlike the one he remembered from his father's house when he was a boy. Numerous images of Winston Churchill – or 'the great enemy', as his father had christened him – hung from the walls. There was a pleasant murmur of customers, not raucous or unwelcome. Considering the time of day, he wasn't surprised. Located as it was in one of London's exclusive neighbourhoods, this wasn't the kind of place to have customers falling about at lunchtime.

He glanced to his right. Tables and chairs on each side, leading into a restaurant – Thai, judging by the smell emanating from the place. This part of the pub was empty, save for one middle-aged woman in a red jacket. Bird-like, with sharp features. She smiled at him.

'You made it. Mine's a Pimm's. Make it a long one, will you?'

'Of course.'

Baucher inclined his head and made his way to the bar. A young man with bleached blond hair hanging to his shoulders and a tanned face greeted him warmly in an Australian accent. 'All right, mate. What can I get you?'

Baucher, who felt as though he needed a drink, despite the early hour, ordered a large Scotch, and the Pimm's for his new companion. The transaction over, he took them to the table.

'I hope it's to your taste, madam,' he said as he sat down heavily opposite her.

'It's exactly what I asked for. What could they possibly do wrong?' She lowered her voice. 'And don't call me madam, it makes me sound like an escort.'

Baucher was surprised how English the woman sounded. He supposed he'd been expecting something else after their brief conversation on the phone. He wasn't even sure this was the same person. 'I don't think I can trust you. How do I know this isn't a set-up, and you're some journalist on the make?' he said under his breath.

'I can understand your reticence. But think of it this way. We are just two friends having a lunchtime drink. I know things in this country are regressing at a rapid rate of knots, but surely having a quick snifter during one's lunch break is still just about permissible, eh?'

'Yes. I suppose it is – just about.'

'And you could hardly be in a worse position, no?'

He took a sip. 'I want to know who you represent.'

'By the end of this conversation, Mr Baucher, all will become clear.' She sat back in her chair, eyeing him like a cat would a mouse. 'You're older than I imagined.'

'Just what did you expect?'

'I don't know. Suave, somehow.'

'You're thinking of my dead predecessor. He looked younger than me when I met him almost forty years ago and that remained the same until he died. This, despite being eight years my senior. But I assume you know all this.'

She smiled, regarding him from under her brows. 'I know you're pretending to be busy. But what is there to be done in the circumstances in which your organization finds itself?'

'Increasingly little. Though I find I am developing an inexplicable hatred for my closest colleagues. That aside, I feel the way anyone would, faced with imminent ruin and possible incarceration. Its unsettling, to say the least.'

'Yes, I think I can help you with that.' She leaned down and picked up a leather attaché case from the floor. 'As you know, there is no way out for your company. But for you personally, there is.'

Baucher took a drink and considered this. What did the attaché case contain? Documents, he reasoned. He was at the stage where he'd have signed away his home just to rid himself of the dreadful reality that gathered around him like fog. 'And how might this miracle be achieved?'

'Don't worry about the execution. Mr Pallander was a wily chap. He constructed the organization to ensure you were all at risk if the need arose. Only he could save or ruin you. Clever, I suppose. But not much fun to be on the receiving end. And even though it didn't end up the way he expected, his machinations didn't die with him.'

'Well, let's cut the suspense. What's in the case?'

'Contained within is the guarantee for your absolution from any suggestion of wrongdoing. While Mr Pallander introduced consequences for those whom he trusted and worked with most closely, he was equally assiduous as to the process of redemption. In short, if you do what I ask, I assure you that in no way will you be connected to the debacle going on within your organization.'

'I'd like to know how?'

'Leave that to me, Mr Baucher. You have one simple task to perform.' She laid the attaché case on the table between them. 'In here are three documents. Each must be signed and returned. Then you will quietly resign from your role, walk away, and nobody will be any the wiser as to the way in which Pallander Glossop drained money from almost everyone with whom it came into contact.'

'That's nonsense. We manage all investments with great care.'

'Oh, you do. But most people – even corporations – miss the odd penny added on here and there. You know very well that just a dollar added to every portion makes for a tidy sum. Your company has been doing this for years. Rounding things down.'

'Of this "rounding down", I know nothing,' said Baucher. But this was a lie. He remembered as if it was yesterday the moment when Pallander had told him of his little scheme. At first, he'd been shocked by the simplicity of it all, and that Pallander would consider such a thing. But in the event of discovery, it could be written off as poor accounting. The theft was perpetrated without a pattern. A bright computer specialist had inserted some lines of code into the Pallander Glossop accountancy software. And without any written or verbal evidence, a hundred forensic accountants would never have spotted it. Baucher had taken his share and kept quiet. But clearly the seductive ease of it all had given Sebastian Pallander a taste for deceit.

'To bleed a company dry through personal greed is astonishing. Part of me is glad he died and doesn't have to face the shame of it all. My less charitable side is sad he is not here to take the blame.' Baucher paused, breathless with anger – much of it directed at himself. 'Let's say we go along with your little scheme here – if only as a thought experiment. Who is to sign these papers?'

'Tabitha Pallander.'

For the first time, Baucher looked at the woman in

disbelief. 'I can maybe tell you something about the lady concerned that you don't know.'

'Please do.'

'Tabitha Pallander is the most difficult woman in the world. How am I to persuade her to do something when I have failed at this very task for years? You see, her father could never say no to his precious little girl. That was my job. And it was the hardest job I've ever had to do, let me assure you.'

'You will succeed and walk away with a nice little present, or spend the rest of your life in prison. And you know what happens to wealthy men in jail.'

Baucher removed a handkerchief from his pocket and mopped his brow. London was unbearable at this time of year. And the stress he was feeling made matters worse. 'And if I fail?'

'Is failure really an option?'

'This present, what's it worth?'

'A hundred million dollars.'

'I don't believe you.'

'We thought this might be your response.' The woman produced a mobile phone from an inside pocket of her jacket. 'Here, take this. There will be a call for you directly.'

'What nonsense is this?' But as he took the phone, it began to buzz in his hand. He checked the screen. *Caller's number unavailable.*

'Answer it,' his new companion demanded.

Baucher clicked on the call. As he listened, his mouth gaped open. His pallor became less and less healthy. After a few moments, he spoke. 'Yes, I understand,' he said, just before the call ended. His hand shook as he handed the phone back across the table.

'So, will you do as we ask?'

'Yes.' Baucher's reply was instantaneous, but his expression was distant. For while he was physically still in the London pub, in his mind he was experiencing something else entirely.

43

DI Cara Salt had only been in the room with ACC Dixon for five minutes. But already she had a sinking feeling in her gut, and the out-of-body sensation that so often presaged terrible news coming her way.

The armed officers surrounding Meikle House were to be recalled – at least, all bar two. Police Scotland could no longer justify the expense. As far as the hierarchy was concerned, the Pallander family – what was left of them – were safe at home, the immediate threat over. The detectives present would continue to liaise with the family, as well as investigate Sullivan's murder. The body had been taken to Aberdeen for a post mortem. If any further forensic assistance or extra manpower was required, the request would be considered. But unless something untoward happened, the feeling was that the Pallanders had enough money to ensure their own safety.

Dixon ran his hand through his grey hair.

'All my efforts to keep our hosts safe have backfired, I'm sad to say. You're now like fish in a barrel.'

'Does the chief constable know what's really happening here?' asked Salt. 'What about the Home Secretary – the First Minister?'

'There's more.' Dixon sounded weary.

'There always seems to be more,' Blackstock observed. They were in the small office that had once been the preserve of the murdered Sullivan. Dixon was behind the desk, while Salt and Blackstock sat across from him.

'There have been developments in the Jean-Luc Pallander case.'

'The second DNA markers found at the scene, sir?' said Salt.

'Yes. A woman has come forward.' The ACC checked his notes. 'Amanda Campbell. Her husband Robert was apparently in league with young Pallander – helped him construct the device, no less. He got cold feet, according to his wife. Arrived at the scene to confront Jean-Luc and persuade him not to go ahead with the destruction of the turbine.'

'And that was enough for the boss to write it off,' said Blackstock flatly.

'Indeed. The favourite scenario is of two men wrestling over the explosives. One, intent on using it, the other trying to stop him. The theory being that it was detonated by accident, killing both men instantly.'

'Is this Campbell woman to be trusted, sir?'

'On the face of it, yes. She's been a climate activist for thirty years. Back when we still considered such people as cranks. Her husband too. There is photographic evidence of him and Jean-Luc Pallander together only days before the explosion.' He leaned back in his chair and sighed.

For Salt, this was the straw that broke the camel's back. Initially, when Dixon had told them of the potential threat to the family, she'd agreed to help. But things had changed.

'Sir, if you don't mind, I'd like to know what you've told the chief constable. I mean, does he know about the abduction of Tabitha Pallander, and the nature of her rescue? What happened to Silas, and the outcome?'

The ACC looked at her sternly. 'DI Salt. I have informed my superior of everything he needs to know. Maybe too much.'

'With the greatest respect, sir, we can't go on hiding the truth from the man making the decisions. It's madness!'

Dixon smiled. But Salt recognized a tired resignation behind the expression.

'Take a look at this, Cara. It speaks louder than words.' He slid his laptop across the desk to Salt. 'Just press play.'

Blackstock left his seat to look over Salt's shoulder as she clicked on the video. Two men were sitting on leather chairs, in what could have been an expensive restaurant or club. There was a buzz of conversation in the background, laughter and the clink of glasses. Salt's heart sank as she recognized Sebastian Pallander and Police Scotland chief constable Sir Ryan Banks.

'Do you have everything in place, Ryan?'

The audio was choppy but easy enough to understand. For Salt, it was a shock to see Pallander alive and well. She was surprised how good he looked, given the quality of the footage and its date stamp in the top left-hand corner of the screen. This meeting apparently took place only two days prior to the hedge fund manager's death.

'Everything is in place. North and south of the border. We can give you as much time as you need.'

'Good. It will be worth your while, my friend.'

'And as commissioner of the Met, I can be of so much greater service.'

'My political allies are briefed. The Met is suitably trussed. Sir Anthony will announce his retirement next week.'

Salt felt nothing but revulsion as she watched her chief constable smile sickeningly. 'Oh, to have your money,' he said. 'Wheels within wheels, Sebastian.'

'When I return from Davos, we will put the plan into operation.'

'The Russians won't know what hit them.' Banks took a large gulp of his drink.

'But still, we must take care. They may be down but they're not out. They're still dangerous. Especially when they lose so much money.'

When the screen went blank, Salt stared on, mesmerized by what she had seen.

'So, you see, Cara, nothing is quite how it seems.'

'The bastard!' said Blackstock, with real venom.

'It's only thanks to you we managed to penetrate this, Abernethy.'

Salt frowned. 'So, you knew about this, Abs?'

'Yes, I'm rather ashamed to say I did, ma'am.'

'But under strict orders to say nothing. My orders, DI Salt.'

She shook her head. 'Why on earth didn't you tell me?'

'It's safe to say that Sebastian Pallander intended to take advantage of Russia's . . . well, *new position* in the world. Since their invasion of Ukraine, they have had no legitimate means of investing money or creating new capital – anything.' Dixon retrieved the laptop.

'And Sebastian Pallander was going to help with that?' said Salt.

'Not just *going to*. He'd already pocketed a huge amount of money via Pallander Glossop in Switzerland just before he died. Russian money.'

'From the very top,' said Blackstock.

'But he died. So, what's happened to the cash?' said Salt.

'That's it. None of us know. The presumption is that Tabitha would be well informed. Hence the effort to get her.'

'You think she is? I've got to say, I have never had that impression, sir. If she's hiding information like that, she must be the best actress in the world.'

Abernethy Blackstock spoke up. 'You'll remember Silas was forced to sign some documents, ma'am. Our theory is that whatever he signed involves the transfer of the Russian funds. After all, only he and his sister held executive positions within Pallander Glossop, not Elizabeth or her other children. It seems natural for Sebastian Pallander to have had some contingency plan in place to hand the Russian funds back should everything go awry. It makes sense that he would keep it in the family.'

'But they didn't know about it.' Salt thought she'd found the flaw in their argument.

'You'd be surprised at the sheer number of documents senior executives sign about which they have no clue,' said ACC Dixon. 'In any case, their signatures on the original paperwork could have been obtained by stealth. After all, it appears that Sebastian Pallander's back was against the wall.'

'Really? But he was one of the richest men in the country, sir,' said Salt.

'Yes, you could be forgiven for thinking that. But we believe the company was in trouble. Significant trouble.'

'In what way?'

'I'll leave Abernethy to explain that. It's rather over my head, I'm ashamed to say.'

Not for the first time, Salt felt rather like the piggy in the middle when it came to the ACC and her subordinate. It now appeared Blackstock had been much better informed than she realized. Maybe Sorley had been right not to trust the man.

'Quite simply, ma'am, Pallander Glossop have been stealing their clients' money for years. It's done in a subtle way, but it involves undervaluing their assets by small margins. When you're talking about billions, the sums involved are no longer small. We surmise that some bright spark has spotted this. If it gets out, Pallander Glossop face an existential threat. Even if they tried to pay back what they skimmed off, they'd expose themselves as fraudsters, leaving aside the fact that the astronomical sums involved would be certain to break the company. Meanwhile, the Russians now want their money back.'

'Senior company officers are clearly at risk of imprisonment. In a desperate effort to recoup funds over the last few years, they've invested most unwisely. As the situation's spiralled downwards, Pallander was left with few options.' Dixon sighed. 'But as we can see, he had friends in high places. Most of whom will be busy covering their own backsides, I venture.'

Salt was deep in thought. 'Is this why Silas lost his job and Tabitha was demoted to a position she was never going to take – in her father's will, I mean?'

Dixon smiled. 'Well, it would make sense. Despite his machinations and perilous position, Pallander was loyal to his family. They're out of the immediate firing line. They'll be questioned, but it'll make it much easier for them to hide behind a lack of knowledge as to what was actually going on. Good lawyers will get them off the hook, I'm sure. The wronged family left penniless by a wicked, criminal father. That kind of thing.'

'In any event, whatever company money he left them would be worth nothing when the truth about the fraud came out,' said Blackstock.

'They got the petty cash.'

'Something like that, ma'am,' said Blackstock.

Though it was a lot to take in, at last, for Cara Salt, it made perfect sense. A struggling company about to be crippled by its own wrongdoing. A desperate need to find funds. The under-siege Russian oligarchs were the perfect solution. 'But how on earth are our senior police officers and politicians involved, sir?' Salt asked.

'Hard to say, at the moment.' Dixon's face was grave. 'Could be one of two things. Abernethy?'

'Ma'am, one theory is a lot of very influential people have money tied up in Pallander Glossop. They're the hedge fund managers of choice for princes and presidents across the globe.'

'And the second theory?'

'Well, that's a tad more involved. But it would do no harm for the embattled Russian economy to lose even more wealth. Further destabilization, a threat to those in the corridors of power, et cetera, et cetera. It could be politically motivated.'

Dixon spoke. 'Of course, our body politic couldn't be seen to be involved in such a thing, no matter how noble the cause.'

'And the rest of Pallander Glossop are just collateral damage?'

'DI Salt, we're all collateral damage.'

'Sullivan?'

'A warning from our Russian friends that time is running out, perhaps?' Dixon shrugged. 'I suspect they'll believe that Tabitha is the key. The beating to death of a family retainer might be seen as sufficient motivation to do the right thing. Or maybe she just got in the way.' The ACC opened his hands in a gesture of helplessness. 'Either way, it's unlikely we'll find who killed her. Hence the lack of interest from the chief constable.'

Something still troubled Salt – had done from the start. 'Pallander's death, live in front of the TV cameras. Natural causes?'

'As far as we know,' said Dixon. 'His body was spirited off by the Swiss authorities then cremated at the wishes of Elizabeth Pallander.'

'No PM?'

'I presume not, Cara. But to be honest, if there was one, I doubt if I'll ever see the results.' Dixon looked almost broken. 'We can only rely on the fact that his premature death suited none of the other parties – including the Russians.'

'But is it still possible the Russians got to him? I mean, they've done it before, all over the world, sir.'

'So many questions, and so few answers. But I want to make something clear. Whatever the truth of this matter, both of you can walk away now, if you want. It's above and beyond the call of duty to ask you to stay.' He looked between his officers.

'And what happens to the innocents? Their only crime being born a Pallander, sir?' said Salt.

'That is indeed a good point. I must admit, I'm very nearly at the end of my resources to protect them.'

'They have to be moved. To different locations.'

'Where do you suggest? There's nowhere to go unless the family themselves find a safe haven. It's a conversation I'm about to have with Elizabeth Pallander.'

'OK, but until then we still have a duty to them. I didn't join the police to run away, sir.' Salt's face was set.

'Nor I,' said Blackstock. 'Even though I'm officially retired, of course.'

Salt raised an eyebrow.

'We and the family may be perfectly safe. Only time will tell.'

Dixon gathered his papers. Salt considered the moving parts. To come out of this mess unscathed would take luck. And luck had never really run her way.

'All this was on the flash drive you gave me, I take it, sir?'

'Correct, Cara. Things have moved on a bit since we compiled the information on that, as you know. Now, please wish me luck with Elizabeth Pallander.'

The ACC got to his feet.

44

Ulrich Baucher had never liked Scotland. The moment he landed in Glasgow he felt ill at ease being any-where near the Pallander family's centre of operations. He couldn't count how many times he'd had to sit through stultifying meals or go on long walks through the grounds of Meikle House. He'd always been convinced that Sebas-tian Pallander inflicted such experiences on his senior company officers by way of a test, or even as a punishment. If you didn't show sufficient interest in the Perthshire countryside, laugh at the endless capers of his children or pay sufficient obeisance to the great man himself, you would soon be shown the door.

Under the circumstances, this would be the most diffi-cult visit of all.

As he stepped into the helicopter that was to take him to the house, Baucher held the attaché case tightly under his arm. It contained only a few papers. But they could utterly change his life – save it, even.

The pilot smiled at him as he was ushered on to the aircraft.

'Fine day, sir.'

'That all depends upon one's perspective,' said Baucher, as he huddled his large frame aboard. He made himself comfortable for the relatively short flight. He'd told Elizabeth Pallander he had a few business issues to talk to her about. Hence the visit. His real aim was to corner Tabitha. That wouldn't be easy, though.

'What a way to end your career,' he muttered to himself, as the rotor blades began to turn.

Tabitha Pallander looked down from the balcony as the first van full of armed police officers rolled down the long driveway. She remembered the intruders at her home in England, the panic in the smoke-filled stairwells and atrium of the London hotel from which she'd escaped. Then there was the mad dash to the Essex marshes on Sorley MacLeod's motorbike.

She smiled at the thought of the man who'd saved her life. In her line of work, Tabitha Pallander didn't meet many men like him. It was strange how people – seemingly from nowhere – managed to get under the skin. Here was a match for her. Since his departure, she'd found herself thinking more and more about him.

They say that women are attracted to men who are like their fathers. Maybe that is true. Though they came from very different worlds, Sorley did resemble her late father. The same rock-steady reliability, even under the most trying of circumstances. No privilege in his background or her father's.

She'd also been thinking a lot about her father since her return to Meikle House. The place was a repository of memories and old feelings – both good and bad. She remembered Silas daring her, when she was seven years old, to stand on the balustrade on which she was now leaning. She'd climbed upon the narrow stone structure, with its vertiginous drop, without a thought. When she jumped back down, she'd dared her brother to do likewise; after all, that was the deal. But he'd turned on his heel, only to walk straight into their father, who'd been watching them the whole time.

'Get up there, Silas,' he commanded.

The eleven-year-old shook his head.

'Do – as – I – say.' Their father's words were staccato, on the beat, as if to music.

'I'm scared.'

She recalled with horror how their father had dragged his son across the balcony and forced his head over the long drop to the paved patio below.

'Why are you scared? Why?' he demanded of the trembling, wide-eyed child.

Tabitha remembered Silas wriggling free, running away, tears flowing down his young face. Though she now looked back on the incident with revulsion, she wasn't sure that had been her attitude at the time. The seven-year-old version of herself had felt better than her older brother; braver, stronger; like Sorley.

'You're my clever little girl.' Sebastian Pallander had leaned over his daughter and planted a kiss on her cheek. 'And for that, you shall have a reward.'

Tabitha fingered the locket still around her neck. It was gold, in the shape of a heart. In one half, a faded image of her father, dark-haired, smiling. In the other, the little girl she'd once been, long hair in plaits framing a round face with big blue eyes.

Had that been the day her father had forged his opinion of them both? She the leader, destined to become her father's right hand, her brother weak and disappointing. She doubted it. Knowing him so well, she thought it likely Sebastian Pallander had made up his mind long before this incident that his eldest son was not fit for the task of being his heir.

But where were they now? Hunkered down in a rambling old mansion in what had once been the maternal family castle. Embattled against the world in much the same way her mother's ancestors had been during the various tumults that swept Scotland for generations. These people had been tough, prepared, capable. Tabitha Pallander wasn't sure that applied to the most recent incarnation of the family.

As she watched the police personnel carrier disappear behind some trees, Tabitha heard the distinctive thud of rotor blades. Her mother had told her that Baucher, the man who now occupied the job that should have been hers, was due to arrive. As usual, he was doing so in style. Through the years, she'd found Baucher a frustrating barrier to what she wanted to do. And as Chief Operations Officer, his power within the company had been considerable. Baucher had made a little fiefdom for himself in Switzerland. And though her father had been happy with the situation, she always felt that the irascible German lived too much of the high life to be trusted. Her father, however, had been the shrewdest person she'd ever known, so Baucher must have done something to warrant his position. But she wasn't looking forward to seeing him again.

Fortunately, his business appeared to be with her mother. Loose ends, they'd been told. Tabitha resolved to stay out of his way, just in case. Who knew who was responsible for what had happened to her in the last few terrifying days?

'Is that Bismarck's helicopter I hear?' Charles Stuart-Henderson's appearance on the balcony startled her. He was using his favoured nickname for the German.

'I thought you were in the clink, Uncle Charlie?'

'Just a misunderstanding. Good old Chief Superintendent McWilliams soon had it swept under the carpet. I should bloody well think so too. The amount of money I send to their benevolent fund is ridiculous. Yes, and all the free financial advice I provide for the little shit.'

'You should never have threatened the inspector, Charlie.'

'Well, you know, I had one or two too many. I hate her slinking about everywhere. Bloody police are useless anyway. They've gone now, most of them. Wish they'd all bugger off.'

'She probably saved my life.'

'Well, if you think so, Tabby.'

'I do.'

They looked on as a helicopter thudded its way down through the trees to the landing platform where their own helicopter was situated.

'They'll have to send a bloody palanquin to bring the fat bastard up to the house. He'll never make it under his own steam.'

'Charlie, you're so unkind. Daddy liked him a great deal. And we do have a golf buggy down there, remember.'

'I hate to tell you, Tabby, but *Daddy* wasn't always right about people, you know. He always had his favourites. And a miserable bloody lot they were too.'

'Meaning?'

Stuart-Henderson tapped his nose ostentatiously. 'Never you mind, dear. I know you think he was a bloody saint. He wasn't, let me assure you.'

'The pair of you never got on, Charlie. We all know that. But we wouldn't be standing in this house if he hadn't saved it, would we?'

'Bollocks! Like everything else, he saw an asset he could exploit. Nothing more.'

Tabitha smiled. There was no point arguing.

'Where's the bloody decanter? If I'm to suffer that arse over dinner, I'll need a few stiffeners.'

'Just don't go falling out with the police. We need to keep what's left of them onside. I'm sure they're only here because of what happened to poor Mrs Sullivan.'

'Yes, tragic. She was a fine woman, in her own way,' he said dreamily. 'But be assured, you can never rely on the constabulary to perform any task efficiently. Unless you've had a jar or two and you head for the car. Or you need a pee on a long trip and nip out to the verge. Oh yes, on you like a bloody flash then, eh?'

'Isn't it time you retired and found a hobby?'

'Maybe. I was going to, until certain obligations to your father persuaded me not to.'

'My father? What do you mean?'

Charles Stuart-Henderson sighed. 'I can't really tell you. Shouldn't do, at any rate. Especially after what's transpired over the last few months.'

Tabitha wasn't interested in her uncle's withering opinions on just about every subject or person under the sun. But any link to her dead father was always intriguing. Added to this, Tabitha had always felt as though she was party to her father's innermost thoughts and feelings. 'What on earth are you talking about?' she enquired.

'Something and nothing, really. Though I understand why he wanted me to stand guard over it. Something your mother can't know, that's for damn sure.'

'It's a woman, isn't it? I spent enough time in my father's company to know how fond he was of the opposite sex. He was always as discreet as he could be, but some things are so obvious.'

'And you didn't feel as though you should tell your mother? Pretty rum do, if you ask me. I've felt guilty about this for years. But what can one do?'

'You didn't see fit to tell her either, did you? No wonder you feel guilty.'

Stuart-Henderson took a seat on one of the wrought-iron chairs. 'It was long ago,' he said. 'A misstep. Best forgotten about. You know, you'll find as you get older that some things are best left in the past – where they belong.'

'Look, whatever you think of your sleeping dogs, you can't just leave them lying about everywhere. Come on!'

Stuart-Henderson squinted into the blue sky. 'To be honest, it's been rather preying on my mind. You know, since your father passed.'

'For fuck's sake!'

'Now, now, Tabby. You sound like Sebastian – and we don't require another of those, thank you. I'll tell you, but you must promise never to whisper a word to Elizabeth.'

Tabitha nodded.

'We manage a trust fund at the bank on your father's behalf. Well, it was on his behalf. Now the money belongs to the recipient.'

'Why wasn't it part of his estate?'

'Yes, that's where it gets a bit tricky. It was a discretionary fund – you know, paid out in increments when appropriate. That sort of thing.'

'Yes, I'm well aware what a DTF is, thank you,' said Tabitha.

'Two weeks before your father died, the trust was paid out in full.'

'What? To whom? You must know the identity of the recipient.'

'Her name is Augusta Manella.'

'Who the fuck is that?'

Charles Stuart-Henderson swallowed hard. 'Now, don't go off the deep end, Tabby. This is just as I feared, otherwise I would have been freer with this information before now.'

'Go off the deep end? I'll pitch you over that bloody balcony, if you don't tell me everything!'

'Augusta is his daughter. Lives in Mexico – at least those are the details in the trust.'

It was Tabitha's turn to take a seat. She stared at her uncle blankly.

'I know it's a shock, Tabby. But your father, as I said, was no saint. Women bloody loved him, you know.'

Tabitha took a long moment, then said, 'I was aware of how he conducted his life. The fact that there is a by-product isn't the greatest mental leap of all time.'

'No, I dare say. And maybe I shouldn't have told you. But with your father gone . . . Well, it's water under the bridge, really. We kept the whole thing quiet at the bank. I know we're supposed to be silent arbiters. However, you know how people are.'

'You stayed on at work mainly to protect this?'

'Yes, I did. He had certain leverage over me. I won't go into it.'

'I don't want to hear any more about your drunken indiscretions, thank you.'

'Good, because I'm not going to tell you. Suffice it to say, your father bailed me out on a few occasions when things got a bit choppy.'

'I bet.'

They were interrupted by voices. Tabitha stood up and looked over the balcony. 'The conquering hero cometh,' she said dismissively.

'Baucher?'

'Yes. Fatter than ever.'

'Bratwurst and beer, I shouldn't doubt.'

'And welcome to bigotry corner, where no cultural trope is left unexplored. No, don't try and change the subject. I want to know more about this Augusta, whoever she is.'

'Manella.'

'Whatever. So, two weeks before my father dies, he signs the money over to her. The trust is in effect over, right?'

'Yes.'

'And there's nothing the executors of my father's will can do to get it back?'

'No. They did try. But the money was gone. Nothing illegal about it. Odd timing, perhaps.' He shrugged.

'Indeed. And what did my father deign to give this poor girl? The same buttons we so ungraciously received, I don't doubt.'

'Well, not exactly. But although the bank's side of the agreement has ended, I'm still at the mercy of client privilege and confidentiality. You of all people should understand that.'

Tabitha Pallander set her expression in a half smile, half glare. 'I swear to you, Uncle Charlie. If you don't tell me the sum, I'm going straight to Cara Salt to tell her I think you killed Sullivan.'

'Don't be ridiculous! This is all so unnecessary. Your bloody father's problem, not mine. I'm just the poor sod who had to help him.'

'Just tell me, Charlie!'

'It was a reasonably large sum,' said Stuart-Henderson guardedly.

'What, one mill – two? Just spit it out.'

'I can't give you the precise sum Ms Manella received – you know, exchange rate, fees, et cetera.'

'Don't treat me like a child. I'm warning you.' Tabitha wagged a finger in her uncle's face. He hesitated, and then sighed.

'Around three hundred and twenty million. US dollars, if that's any consolation.'

'OK, I'll do the jokes.'

'No joke. That's roughly the sum that was transferred to Mexico. I know it's a shock. But don't blame me. I was just doing my job.'

'*Just doing your job!*' Tabitha was almost lost for words. 'You've kept this secret for all these years and said nothing, not even to your own sister. You should be ashamed.' She thought for a moment. 'How long had the trust been active?'

'Oh, I'd say twenty-five years or so.'

'Fuck. I don't know what to say.'

'There's nothing you can say, my dear. The job is done and dusted.'

Tabitha sat back in her chair and angled her head to the sky, wondering what other skeletons were set to jump from cupboards.

45

Much against her own best judgement, Cara Salt and Abernethy Blackstock had been persuaded to join the family and their guest for a late dinner, as Elizabeth Pallander had called it. It was very late, nearly ten, by the time they took their seats at the table.

They were sitting in the 'small' dining room that was more than twice the size of her flat. The room was wood-panelled and smelled like her grandmother's old dining-room table, thick with the polish of decades. The walls were adorned with watercolour landscapes, recognizable as the area around the house, all seemingly by the same artist. Though Salt's appreciation of fine art was limited, some of the paintings looked laboured, out of kilter – something to do with the perspective, she thought. She noticed they were painted by Alicia Pallander, the artist in the family. The room was topped off by a mini chandelier, sparkling above the table. It looked pretentious, out of place. If the family were going for close and intimate, they'd failed miserably.

Salt was seated between Blackstock on her right and Audrey Pallander on her left. The latter surprised her with a much more down-to-earth, normal approach to life than she perceived from the rest of the family. The other Pallander children she'd met were either wildly arrogant, hopelessly damaged, or both. The image of Tabitha kissing Sorley squarely on the lips flashed through her mind.

Audrey chatted happily away about the same kind of things Salt and her friends might discuss: clothes, cars, television, music. The detective found it all rather refreshing, especially considering the stress of the last few days and the murder of Mrs Sullivan, which hung over the gathering without being given voice.

'It must be so exciting – being a police officer, I mean,' said Audrey, looking genuinely interested.

'It has its moments,' said Salt. 'Certainly in the last few days.'

Audrey's expression changed. 'I know you're sworn to secrecy, but I can't imagine what my poor brother went through before he died. I suppose we all try to put death to the back of our minds. I'm afraid it rather haunts me. You know, when and how, that kind of thing. Bit morbid, sorry. And my brother . . . well . . .' Her eyes filled with tears.

'Best we don't know, to be honest,' said Salt. But since she'd first stepped into a Glasgow mortuary as part of her training, the inspector had been all but consumed by the mystery of death. It clung to her like a wet jumper, invisible to all but Salt herself. Though she could never acknowledge the obsession. No, that would make it real – like a cancer diagnosis.

She remembered staring at the grey corpse on the pathologist's gurney. The absence of spirit, the loss of dignity – the end of everything was both a horror and a comfort, she felt. She'd seen people ruined by pain and illness slip away with a smile on their faces, the whole process of dying a welcome release from a tortured life. Equally, Salt had witnessed the opposite: fear, terror, horror at the end of existence. This had been her father's end. A big strong man, admired by so many, ending his days screaming for deliverance. He was destroyed by the cancer that took his life. She'd always thought of him as immoveable, a force of nature. But he had succumbed in the end like so many others. Not raging at the dying of the light, more begging it to stay.

The day he'd died, painfully thin and prematurely aged, thoughts of her own mortality began to plague Cara Salt. It was something else she never shared with anyone. However, more and more, it gnawed at her. Death's tolling bell had become ever present in her life. And never so much as in the last few days.

'I suppose it's the natural cycle of life,' said Audrey. 'Bloody sad, though.'

Salt took a sip of wine, accidently catching the eye of Charles Stuart-Henderson, something she'd been trying to avoid since the meal began.

'Are you enjoying the wine, Inspector?' he asked with a sneer.

'Yes, very nice, thank you. Delicious, in fact.' Though she really wanted to jump on the table, run across to him and stick a fork in his eye, Salt felt this course of action may damage her career as a police officer, so decided against it.

'None of your cheap supermarket plonk here, my dear. I don't suppose you'll have tasted much decent wine. Not on your salary, eh?'

'I don't think it matters to some people what they drink, so long as it's wet and gets them drunk. What do you think?' She smiled at the banker, a hint of disapprobation in her eyes.

'Now, Charles. What did I tell you about trying to behave,' said Elizabeth Pallander. 'I do apologize, Inspector.

I often wonder how nice it would be if alcohol had never been invented. I've rarely met anyone who is improved by it.' The glance at her brother was intentional.

'Ignore my uncle. He's been plastered since nineteen sixty-five, from what I gather,' said Audrey, with a giggle. 'I heard about his disgraceful behaviour to you – unforgiveable. I don't suppose he has apologized, has he? Uncle Charlie isn't big on apologies, you know. I suppose we've all been there. You know, waking up with a sore head and remembering what you've done. I know I have.'

Salt decided that she definitely liked Audrey. She had none of the Pallander dismissiveness – the effortless superiority. But she'd seen that a hundred times. Individual members of one family could be as different as chalk and cheese.

'You're very quiet, Abernethy,' said Elizabeth. 'I heard about your terrible experience down at the river, finding poor Mrs Sullivan. I still can't come to terms with it – I don't think any of us can.' She looked around the table, to much mumbled agreement.

Blackstock placed his knife and fork side by side on his plate and took a sip of wine before he spoke. 'It was ghastly, I must admit. But my feelings are immaterial. We must save our sympathy for the deceased.'

Salt was taken by his sincerity, but she couldn't help feeling that he was displaying another emotion, almost hidden, but not quite. Perhaps her aristocratic detective sergeant still bore a grudge against her for placing him in that position.

Ulrich Baucher was sitting beside Elizabeth Pallander. He made her look even more waiflike, his square, solid bulk and large round head almost dominating the table. He'd only spoken briefly to the Pallander matriarch during the meal so far, seemingly more intent on his trout than conversation.

Salt watched him gaze at Abernethy Blackstock.

'Your name is Abernethy, yes?' said Baucher.

'Abernethy *Blackstock*,' the police officer replied, with a weak smile.

'An unusual name, no?'

This time Blackstock's response was rather terse. 'Maybe these days,' he said. 'But there are still a few of us dotted about Scotland.'

'Started out as smugglers and sheep stealers, eh, Abernethy?' said Stuart-Henderson. 'Though it appears the poacher has turned gamekeeper.' He laughed heartily at his own joke.

Baucher was still staring at the police officer. 'You know, I have a very good memory for faces. I've been trying to work out where I've seen you before. I think the answer is Bern. Am I right?'

Salt felt her stomach tense. But Blackstock adopted a confused expression.

'I wish. It's a place I've always wanted to go. Anywhere in Switzerland would do. A friend of mine bagged a lesser white-fronted goose there recently. Very rare – I was most envious.'

'He shot it?' Baucher asked.

'Took a photograph, actually. I'm rather against shooting birds, I'm afraid.'

'Ha! You can't eat a photograph.' Baucher began to chortle, turning his round face red.

'You won't want the next course, then. It's pheasant,' said Stuart-Henderson. 'Bad luck, old boy.' He joined Baucher in a hearty laugh.

Tabitha slammed her wine glass on to the table.

'What on earth's the matter, darling?' said Elizabeth.

'It's not that long since my father died. My brother – well, no time at all since he was blown to pieces. I've had armed men chasing me halfway across the country, and then Silas's kidnap. Not to mention poor Mrs Sullivan. Yet here we are acting as though nothing's happened, laughing and joking. It's bloody pathetic!'

'Now, darling. We're just trying to take our minds off it all for an hour or two. What's wrong with that?'

'I'll tell you what's wrong with that. We're like sitting ducks. Whoever is out there can just pick us off one by one. We don't even have a police guard any more. And there's so much more . . .'

Tabitha glanced at her uncle, who shook his head, almost imperceptibly.

'I can't imagine what you mean, Tabby. If someone was going to "pick us off", as you put it, surely they'd have been here long ago? I know the last few days have a been a struggle, but let's not make things worse.'

'I agree with Tabby,' said Silas. 'You've no idea what we've been through. It's as though none of it has happened. And nobody cares about Anna. She could be dead, for all we know.' He jutted out his chin and took a gulp of whisky; something he'd been doing a lot since he arrived back at Meikle House.

'Gosh,' said Alicia. 'I don't think I've ever heard you two agree on anything. It's a landmark day!' She giggled on the shoulder of her companion, her curly, bright-red hair dancing in time with her shoulders.

'Can't you go and murder a painting or something?' said Silas. 'The only reason you survived is because Mummy gave you so much money to fritter away on a career for which you have no aptitude. What are you going to do now we're all on the bones of our arse, eh?'

'And don't say sell paintings,' said Tabitha. 'You must realize that Daddy gave money to people to buy them?'

Alicia looked at her mother. 'Are you going to allow this, Mummy?'

'No, I am not!' Elizabeth Pallander banged her fist on the table, almost upsetting her wine glass. 'Now, please, in memory of Jean-Luc, if nothing else, let's try to have a quiet family meal with our guests.'

The children settled, sulkily. Baucher continued staring at Blackstock, who in turn was pretending not to notice. Then, as though the family argument was of no consequence, the big German spoke.

'I definitely know your face, Mr Blackstock. Tell me, have you always gone by that name?'

Blackstock opened his mouth to speak, but the arrival of a waiter ended the exchange.

'Excuse me, ma'am. I have a message for the inspector. I'm told it can't wait.'

Elizabeth nodded her assent with a sigh, and the waiter leaned in to impart his message.

Salt dabbed her mouth with her napkin. 'I'm so sorry, please excuse me. I have police business to attend to.'

'Really? Can't it wait until we finish our meal?' said Elizabeth Pallander. She was seemingly oblivious to the fact her children were glaring at each other, Stuart-Henderson was helping himself to too much wine, and Baucher was still taking in Blackstock from under furrowed brows, deep in thought. 'We were having such a nice evening.'

'Please accept my apologies, Mrs Pallander. But I really have to go.'

Salt got up from the table. But before she could leave

Meikle House's small dining room, Blackstock caught her sleeve.

'Do you want me to come with you?'

Salt forced a smile. 'No, enjoy the rest of your meal, Abernethy. I can handle this.'

She followed the waiter from the room.

46

Salt was taken down a maze of corridors to a small room just off the kitchen. She found Sergeant McIntosh across a table from a thin, ferret-faced man she didn't know. Both were tucking in to bowls of soup, the policeman slurping loudly.

'It's yourself, ma'am,' said McIntosh, wiping his mouth with the back of his hand.

'And what can I do for you, Sergeant McIntosh?'

'I'm sorry to have dragged you away from the dinner. People tell me they keep a fine table. Though I must admit, I've never had the pleasure.'

Salt glanced at the other man. 'And your friend is?'

'Morris, Inspector,' the man replied. 'Alec Morris. I'm from the village.'

'Mr Morris is a wildlife photographer, ma'am. He does well, don't you, Mo?'

'Not too badly. It keeps the wolf from the door. And, och, well – I couldn't see myself in an office pushing a pen. As a way of earning money, there's not much to beat nature and the great outdoors. It began as a hobby, you know.'

'There's nothing more soul-destroying than pushing a pen for a living,' agreed Salt. 'I've tried it. Now, what can I do for you, Mr Morris?'

'It's more what he can do for you, ma'am,' said McIntosh. 'Show her your computer, Mo.'

Alec Morris leaned over and picked up a leather satchel from beside his feet. He removed a laptop, opened it and switched it on.

'It would maybe help if you could take a seat beside our man, please, Inspector.'

Salt took the seat beside the photographer and watched as he sifted through hundreds of tiny thumbnail images on the screen.

'You see, I set night cameras – mostly tied to trees, some on to rocks. That way, you can catch animals and birds that are wary of being around folk. Behaving naturally too. I leave them up for a day or so. They ran out of battery, so I went back to collect them sooner than usual this time.'

For some reason – instinct probably – Salt could feel her pulse quicken. 'Where do you place these cameras, Mr Morris?'

Morris's tongue was poking out from between his teeth as he trawled through the thumbnails. 'All over. Well, where I get permission, that is. Despite the laws about free roaming in this country, you'd be surprised how many landowners and their gamekeepers take exception to me filming. I lost a good few cameras when I first started doing it – I quickly learned to ask permission. Mrs Pallander and her brother have always been really kind to me that way. I give her a present of a few framed images every Christmas – by way of a thank-you, you understand.'

'So, these cameras were recording within the last few days?' said Salt.

'Aye.' He paused. 'Ah, here we are.'

McIntosh was now standing behind the pair of them.

'I'm sure you'll find this of interest, ma'am. I did, that's for sure.'

Salt looked on as Morris brought up a video. The image was in monochrome. 'No colour?'

'These are night-vision cameras, Inspector. But when it gets light, they revert to black and white. Still, they have good resolution. Now, here we are. You can see the time and date stamp in the top right-hand corner.' Morris pressed play and the video sprung into life.

For a few moments, Salt saw nothing, just the rustling branches of a tree opposite the camera. Then, out of the blue, something passed the lens. A figure – man or woman, she couldn't tell. 'That was a bit quick. Can you slow it down, please?'

'The first thing I did. Here, take a look.'

As Salt looked on, watching the footage frame by frame, a female in wellington boots and a Barbour-style jacket stepped into view in a slow tread. For a split second, the woman turned her head to one side. Sullivan's profile was unmistakable.

'You see, ma'am. It's most definitely her. On the morning she disappeared, too,' said McIntosh.

Salt sat back from the screen. 'Wow.' She turned to McIntosh. 'I suppose this is on the way to the river, Sergeant?'

'Aye, it is that. But there's more.'

Salt's mouth was dry as she turned her attention back to the computer screen.

'This is about twenty minutes later,' said Morris. He played the clip at normal speed. In the left-hand corner of the screen, something moved, flashing past the camera, a mere glimpse. 'I'll slow it down again.'

Salt sat forward, squinting at the image. In the first two frames, nothing was clear, just a blurred image. But on the third frame, Morris paused the footage. 'You see? The back of another individual, I'd say. Taller, definitely. You can tell when the images are placed side by side.'

Sure enough, Salt could see the shape of a back, perhaps an ear, and, below, the toe of a boot. 'Yes, I see it,' she said.

'It's a pity, right enough. Just out of shot. But there nonetheless.'

Salt leaned back in her chair again. 'I'll need a copy of the footage, please. I hope you don't mind?'

'There's more, ma'am,' said McIntosh.

'Aye. We didn't get lucky the first time. But we got a better look on the way back,' said Morris, hitting fast-forward.

'What do you mean?' Salt watched as the images sped by.

'Here we go.' He slowed the video just as another figure stepped into view.

Involuntarily, Salt shot to her feet, nearly knocking Sergeant McIntosh over. Her gasp almost turned to a scream, but she managed to halt it in her throat. 'This footage, Mr Morris. The date stamp is correct, yes? It was captured round about the same time?'

'Yes, Inspector. Just over an hour after we saw the toe of that boot.'

Salt looked at McIntosh. 'Can I have a word with you? In private?'

'Surely, ma'am.' McIntosh turned to the photographer. 'Just you finish your soup, Mo. I'll be back shortly.'

The police officers left the room and moved away from the plate-rattling bustle of the main kitchen. They found a recess down a quiet corridor.

'How many men do you have at your disposal, Sergeant McIntosh?'

The portly policeman rubbed his chin. 'Six, if you count the rural men and those off-shift. Mind you, young Angus Deans is away on holiday with his new wife – a late honeymoon. And my senior constable John MacAndrew has Covid. So, we're pretty stretched, if you know what I mean.'

Salt, who had never worked in a rural area, sighed. 'And you'll have access to firearms, yes?'

'Once upon a time, yes. But not since the arrival of Police Scotland, I'm afraid. We'd have to go to Perth and get permission in triplicate from a chief inspector, or above. Things are getting worse, and no mistake. I'll be glad when I retire next year.'

'I see.' Salt rubbed her forehead, desperately wondering what to do. 'I want you to make sure that Mr Morris doesn't talk about what we've just seen, OK?'

'He's an honest, decent man. I shouldn't think that will present a problem, ma'am. But I have to say, I'm a wee bit confused. I thought you'd be pleased at what we turned up. I mean, isn't it a potential witness? Likely never knew how close he came to the whole thing.'

'I fear it's anything but, Sergeant. Please keep all this close to your chest. I have to try and work out what to do.'

McIntosh looked surprised, shocked even. 'I see. Then we do have a problem, ma'am. I understand your dilemma.'

Salt stared into his open face. 'Whatever happens, I think it will happen soon.'

'Aye, sounds about right. Everyone's here in the house. If I'm thinking along the same lines you are. My goodness, such wickedness.'

'I want you to speak to the men at the door and the gate.

Get them to come back to the house. But please, Sergeant, do it quietly.'

'You have my word. I'll get who I can from the village too.'

'Can I have your mobile number?' said Salt.

'You can.' He grabbed his phone from his pocket and worked on the screen. 'I'll send it to you.'

That done, Salt bit her lip. 'Bring the men into the house but keep them quiet. Leave one of the armed constables at the front entrance.'

'Nobody at the gate?'

'Whoever is coming won't go through the gate, Sergeant.'

'Right, I understand. I'll get down to business, then, ma'am.'

As he walked off, Salt admired the policeman's uncomplicated approach. He hadn't questioned her about what was going on, but rather had come to his own conclusions. A proper, old-fashioned cop, her father would have said. They were few and far between these days, she reckoned.

Salt found a quiet room with a couch and a few chairs round a coffee table. She took out her phone, hovering over one name. Though she desperately wanted to hear his voice, talk to him, she knew that Sorley would be back in London. Back to his own life. She wasn't part of that. That much was clear from their last meeting.

Nonetheless, she called him.

The number you have dialled is unavailable. Please try later or leave a message.

'Typical,' she whispered to herself. Where could he be in London, to have no signal? Or maybe he did but he was with someone. If Tabitha Pallander hadn't been right upstairs in Meikle House, she'd have suspected her.

She shook these bizarre thoughts from her head. On

many occasions in her life, Salt had felt alone, isolated. But never as much as she did now. She got to her feet and wandered over to the big standard lamp that illuminated the room. She switched it off and sat for a while in splendid isolation.

Cara Salt had to think.

47

Tabitha Pallander was in her room watching a movie when she heard a soft knock on her door. A few days ago, she'd have jumped up and answered it without a thought. But now she decided that caution was by far the best policy.

Looking round the room, she picked up one of the stout brass candlesticks on the mantelshelf over the fire. She hefted it in her right hand and tiptoed to the door.

'Who is it?' she said boldly.

'Baucher. I need to talk with you. It's urgent.'

'Fuck off. I knew you weren't here just to run things past Mummy. It didn't make sense. You could have done that over a Zoom – on a phone call, come to that. I have absolutely nothing to say to you.'

'You will have plenty to say when I tell you what's happening. You must trust me, Tabitha.'

She hesitated for a moment, then, reluctantly intrigued by what Baucher had said, she turned the heavy key in the mortice lock and opened the door.

Baucher was bathed in the light from the corridor. The sun was at last sinking into the summer sky beyond Meikle House. His fat face was bloated and puffy, sweat running down his forehead.

'Can I come in?'

'If you think you'll make it. You look in worse shape than normal.'

'I had too much to eat this evening. It's a failing, you know.'

'You don't say.' She stood aside and allowed Baucher entrance into her room. 'Sit there,' she said, pointing to a chair beside a chest of drawers.

Baucher did as he was told, moving slowly and awkwardly. Once he was seated, he pulled out a handkerchief and mopped his brow. 'I hate the summer in this country. It's so humid, it's hard to breathe. Your room is so far away from mine.'

'Try losing ten stone and you might feel better.' Tabitha noticed the little attaché case that Baucher had placed on his knees.

'Regardless of the circumstances, you can always be relied upon to be rude, Tabitha. Don't you ever tire of it?'

'Not where you're concerned. Just say what you've come to say. Then I never have to see you again.'

Baucher sighed. 'Like your father. Everything must be a war. But have it your own way.' He raised his chins. 'I made a discovery in the office a few days ago.'

'Which office? Your little kingdom in Switzerland or the real office in London?'

'In London. I'm sad to say that my new job requires my presence there most of the time.'

'My job, you mean.'

'Not my choice, I assure you.' Baucher gestured airily with his hands. 'In any case, when I tell you the hopelessness of it all, you will realize that you are welcome to my job any time you want it.'

Tabitha sat on the bed and laid the candlestick at her side. She still mistrusted the new boss of Pallander Glossop, but in his physical condition he could be of little danger to her. 'Well, do go on. Tell me your tale of woe. You know I won't believe it.'

'That is up to you, Tabitha. But I promise you, it is no lie.'

'That'll be a new departure for you.'

Baucher shook his head. 'The company is insolvent. It's as simple as that.'

'Wow! I knew you'd ruin everything, but this is fast work, especially where you're concerned. The last time I looked we were in rude health. Billions under management, huge profits.'

'Those were ghost accounts. The truth is that your father had been losing money for years. I've checked – bad investments in Asia, poor decisions in the tech sector. An infrastructure project in the USA that is haemorrhaging cash. That's just the tip of the iceberg. It's like death by a thousand cuts. Big ones.'

Tabitha remembered arguing with her father over the massive investment into green energy infrastructure across America. She'd always felt that the political will to complete the project was lacking at the very highest levels. Clearly, she'd been right. But what worried her more was that Baucher's tale of fiscal implosion might hold water. She remembered her father's obsession with Asian stocks; the notion that India and its neighbours would one day overtake the Chinese colossus to the east. She'd never been confident that would be the case, yet Sebastian Pallander continued to plough billions into the Asian market.

'It gets worse,' said Baucher.

'Go on.'

'A few months before your father died, things became so bad that the problems could no longer be covered up.

Sebastian knew that if Pallander Glossop was to stay afloat he needed a massive injection of cash.'

'Wait, I was there – there beside him through all this. He was raising cash, yes. But in preparation to fund the take-over of a chain of companies in Brazil. Coal mines, steel works, power companies. It had tremendous potential, despite the price.'

'It was a lie, Tabitha. He was raising money to keep us trading.'

'OK. But if what you're saying is true, who has that wealth to invest? Especially nowadays. It's brutal out there. When American banks start failing – no matter how insignificant they are – the whole world holds its breath and keeps its money close. You know that.'

Baucher mopped his brow again. 'The Russians.' He shrugged. 'Who else?'

Quickly, Tabitha Pallander walked it all through in her mind. Yes . . . Of course. The Russian state, the oligarchs – almost one and the same – needed somewhere to place their assets. After all, following the invasion of Ukraine they were financial pariahs across the globe. 'Don't tell me. They want their money back?'

'They do. That's why I'm here.'

'Working for the Russians against the company you run. You must be so proud.'

'To be honest, I don't really know who I'm working for. Though it seems that has been the case for a long time now.' He gave her a long look, then said, 'There is a way out. For you, for your family. Me, also.'

'Fuck. Less of a double agent, more a double-chinned agent, then?'

'How childish.'

'Tell me, how this can be turned round? Nobody messes with Russia, even now.'

'The Pallander Family Trust. Your father set it up – remember? You are a signatory, after all.'

Suddenly the scales fell from Tabitha's eyes. Yes, her father had placed various safety valves deep within Pallander Glossop. Mechanisms designed to protect the family from unforeseen circumstances. 'But you'd be transferring live funds to the trust. The money belongs to investors – the Russians – not us.'

'The family is a creditor like any other. It's the way your father constructed it.'

'A silent debt. Just sitting there to be actioned whenever appropriate.'

'You always were a smart girl, Tabitha. Once this is over, you can build your own hedge fund.'

Tabitha jumped up from the bed. 'Signatures. Does it require two family signatures to put into operation?'

'It does. You will be killing off Pallander Glossop. But with the cash you can save your family. Your father may be dead, yes. But his family still lives. And trust me, they will come after you.'

'I think they already did.' Tabitha's face was pale now. At last, it all made sense.

'You will remember there were three of you who could action this letter of credit. But your father is of course no longer with us.' Baucher coughed, making his face even redder.

'Leaving just me and Silas. And given that he signed something when he was kidnapped, that leaves me.'

Baucher shifted uncomfortably on the small wooden chair. 'You are correct, of course. But missing the major point, I think.'

'You know, I'm getting tired of these little games. Just tell me!'

'We know our friends in Russia want their money. That's a given. The drive to put the family claim via your father's financial instrument is being managed by that law firm in Edinburgh of whom he was so fond. The question is, who is pushing the buttons?'

He stared at Tabitha Pallander.

'You think it's *me*?' Tabitha flung back her head and laughed. 'Remember, I didn't know this instrument *existed*. How can I be involved?'

Baucher took in the young woman he'd always known would one day stand in his way. Things hadn't worked out as he'd anticipated, but nonetheless, here he was, desperately seeking her help. He wanted to trust her, but still wasn't sure if he could. 'You think it's Silas?' he asked.

'Oh, come on. My brother? Do me a favour. What was his last job at Pallander Glossop? Managing the car parks, I'm sure.'

'But he signed very quickly. The tale of his kidnap. Elizabeth told me all about it. It all sounds unlikely, no?'

'Our jet went missing!'

'Yes, it did. No sign of it. But that's easy to arrange when your name is Pallander.'

'But that is predicated upon having the brains to think it up.' Tabitha ran a hand through her hair. 'No, given it's not me, and it can't be him, who else? Somebody within the company?'

'Nobody knows. It came out of the blue when we were contacted by the family lawyer.'

'They won't say who's instructing them?'

Baucher shrugged. 'No. But then I suppose it doesn't really matter.' He laughed mirthlessly. 'Either way, you are in a predicament from which it will be hard to extricate yourself – or the family – without access to these funds. This is your chance.'

'And what will happen to you?'

'Sadly, for me, the war is over.' Baucher mopped his brow once more. 'With a little luck I will manage to extricate myself from this mess. Who knows? But my advice is to sign these papers.' He held up the attaché case. 'It will make no difference to the company. It's already gone – finished. But you alone can save the Pallander family.'

Tabitha stared at the attaché case and bit her lip.

48

In the darkness, Salt had taken time to work through many things. She supposed that she'd spent much of her life as a renegade, an outlier. But this time, things were different. The images she'd seen on Morris's footage had changed everything. They were all – everyone in Meikle House – part of some elaborate plot of which she could barely conceive.

When you can't trust anyone, trust yourself. It'll happen in your career, you can rely on that.

As always, her father's words had been prophetic. The more the last few days had unfolded, with all their attendant horror, the more she'd thought the endless advice he'd imparted to her had been intended for this very moment. That the resolve she must now find could be provided by the very man she blamed for her own failings as a person.

But who really succeeded in life? Those who made billions, like the Pallanders? She didn't think so. They were as dysfunctional as any family she'd encountered. Mostly unhappy, theirs was a perfect example of money not bringing contentment.

Salt stepped out of the darkness of her curtained room into the relative brightness of the corridor. Little sconce lights placed along its length were an echo of the flaming torches that would have once illuminated the castle on this site.

For a moment, she considered leaving Meikle House; quietly slipping away through the grounds in the darkness, finding a way home and disappearing for a while. When this unusual case had emerged, she had been delighted – thrilled – to be liberated from the drudgery of her life in the office above the newsagent's. Now, she looked at things very differently. Now, she knew her life was at risk.

Salt thought back to the hillside above Dumbarton where Jean-Luc Pallander had lost his life. To ACC Dixon's plush office at Gartcosh, where she had first learned of the trials and tribulations of the Pallanders, and her unlikely part in protecting them.

Was any of that true? She didn't know.

All she could picture now was Sullivan's ruined face as her lifeless body was hauled from the river. Everything seemed to be embodied in her sickening demise. Had it been a warning to them all, or something else? Salt knew she was much closer to the truth. But, as ever, the truth was a difficult place to go.

She was startled when a member of staff exited a door.

'Good evening, ma'am.' The young man was dressed in the same drab suit and white shirt that most of those working at Meikle House wore. 'Can I help you with anything?'

'No, I'm just going out for a quick puff.' Salt held up a packet of cigarettes.

The dark-haired lad – from the village, judging by his accent – looked about him as though he was about to impart a secret. 'Could I tap one off you, please? I've been gasping for a smoke for the last couple of hours.'

'Sure. You can come with me, if you want?'

The pair made their way to a side door and walked to the front of the house, out of the shadows. She handed the young man a cigarette. A blue velvet darkness was descending upon the gardens and beyond. The air was warm and still. In the sky, a full moon was beginning to hold sway over the last remnants of light from the sun, its red, sinking glow becoming a memory. Meikle House was lit up now, light spilling from almost every window along its grand front elevation. The tall Douglas firs beyond the garden were dark silhouettes, standing sentry round the grounds.

'Cheers,' the young man said. 'I forgot to bring mine from the house this morning. Hardly anyone smokes here. Mr Pallander didn't like it. They're all like sheep – the ones that've been here a while, anyhow.'

'I see,' said Salt.

'You spoke to me earlier – you know, in the hall.'

'Yes, I remember now. You've seen plenty of us over the last few days.'

'Aye, just a bit.' He smiled. 'You know everyone's freaking out round here.'

'I don't blame them.'

He took a long draw on his cigarette. 'Folk reckon that something's going to happen. Something bad, like. After poor Mrs Sullivan, you know.' He looked at his feet.

'Yes, that was really horrible. But don't worry, that's why I'm here.'

'Aye, that's what I thought. You know my gaffer reckoned she saw someone slinking about in the woods earlier.'

'Who's she?'

'She works in the kitchens – helps the chef, and that. I'm her assistant.'

'What did she see?'

A crow began to caw in the gardens. Its call echoed from the building, affording it an ethereal, chilling quality.

'Nutjob, if you ask me. Said she saw a man dart into the trees when she was going back from the herb garden.'

'Really?'

'Aye, cuckoo, like.'

'People see all sorts of things, especially when folk they know well pass away. When my dad died, I saw him sitting in my living room. As clear as day, he was. Just for a split second.'

'Fuck, you must have shat yourself. Sorry for swearing.' He laughed nervously.

'It's OK. I'm not going to arrest you. In fact, it was quite comforting. Just the mind playing tricks, trying to make you feel better, that's all.'

'I've only been here for a month. It took them three weeks to get me the right size jacket. The last one had arms nearly down to my feet.'

They both laughed. Salt, despite her problems, found this a welcome relief. She marvelled at how nicotine and a joke could help things along.

'See your pal's away too.'

Salt felt her stomach sink. Yes, Sorley had gone. She wondered if she'd ever see him again. This had probably been their last chance. She wondered, now, if she'd placed him in harm's way for the wrong reasons. If the decision to send Tabitha Pallander to his shop was nothing but a sub-conscious way of bringing him back into her life.

'Yes, he's off back to London.'

'Right. Long drive at this time of night, eh?'

Salt nearly missed the implication of what he'd said, so deep in thought was she. 'Sorry, what did you say?'

'I mean, how long does it take to drive to London from here? Seven, eight hours easy, I'd say.'

Salt was confused. 'No, I think he was taking the train.'

'Eh? No trains at this time of night.'

'You've lost me, I'm sorry. Who are we talking about?'

'Your pal. You know, the other policeman. The one that likes birdwatching. I've seen him out with his binoculars, and that. Watched him put his case in a car a wee while ago. They were having a posh dinner upstairs. He left early, the cook says.'

Cara Salt's eyes widened. 'I'm sorry, you'll have to excuse me.' She stubbed out her cigarette with the toe of her suede boot and rushed back into Meikle House.

The young man watched her go. 'Aye, no' bad for an old bird,' he mumbled to himself, before taking another draw on his cigarette.

49

DI Cara Salt took the stairs two at a time. Mercifully, there were few people about in the part of the house where she and Blackstock had been given rooms. She was muttering to herself as she went. 'You bastard! You complete and utter bastard!'

She reached the floor on which both rooms were located. Striding past her own door, she rushed down the passageway, stopping at Blackstock's room. The door was open – no clothes in the wardrobe, no items on the nightstand.

This presented Salt with another problem. One she couldn't put on the back burner. She'd had a plan, but now it was ruined.

Salt could feel her heart pounding in her chest.

I knew it was coming. Even though I didn't feel it. But I knew I'd be OK.

These were Sorley's words from his hospital bed after he'd been shot. At the time, she hadn't understood what he was trying to say. It was about the affirmation of life. Quite simply, he'd never thought that the bullet she'd fired would kill him. Something in his subconscious told him so. Salt had heard tales of such prescience from others, but now she felt a similar way. Though, rather than being reassured, buoyed by this sense of invulnerability, Salt felt the opposite. It was as though she was about to partake in the final act of her life, the last curtain call.

Salt knew she had to ground herself, rid herself of these extraneous thoughts.

Her first instinct was to call ACC Dixon, to tell him that Blackstock had disappeared – to tell him everything. This only raised the concerns she'd already subconsciously considered. She couldn't be sure who to trust. But she was certain of one thing.

She was roused from her thoughts by a noise – a deep click. Suddenly, everything was black. The room was plunged into darkness.

The rest of the house was the same. Salt pulled one of her mobile phones from her pocket and turned on the torch function. She made her way to the main staircase in the eerie gloom, her phone a pinprick of light to guide her. She'd been right. For some reason, the power at Meikle House had failed. Below, at the end of the great staircase, in the reception hall, she could see tiny lights dancing on the walls where others were also using their mobiles to light their way.

Salt dialled McIntosh. The bright screen of the phone lit up her face. Right now, it seemed as though he was the only person upon whom she could rely. Well, she hoped so, at least.

'Yes, ma'am.' The sound of his voice was immediately reassuring.

'Blackstock's gone. Taken off in his car, Sergeant.'

On the other end of the call, she heard McIntosh hesitate. 'Do you really think it's him, ma'am?'

'I do, but I couldn't be sure. I was working out how to

approach him. Now it's too late. He told me he was at the other side of the estate when she was killed. Now we know he wasn't. Why would he lie, Sergeant McIntosh?'

'Damn me! Sorry, ma'am. But if there's something I can't stand, it's a bent officer – if it was him, that is. How could he do such a thing? She was a lovely woman, just doing the best for her son. I often had a chat with her when she was good enough to make a cup of tea in the passing. I've always kept an eye on this place. Seems not a close enough one, though.'

'Whereabouts are you, Sergeant?'

'I'm driving up from the main road, ma'am. More bad news, I'm afraid to say.'

'Tell me,' said Salt.

'A lorry has turned over just at the Mossie Burn. The bugger went on fire. The boys are still looking for the driver. It's blocking the whole main road. Luckily, I'm on your side of it.'

Salt swallowed hard. Her throat was as dry as a bone. 'This is it, Sergeant.'

'What, ma'am?'

'Whatever is going to happen is going to happen tonight. We've hardly any boots on the ground, the road to Meikle House is blocked, the place is in darkness, and my number two could be a killer.'

'I'll get back to the house as quickly as I can, Inspector.'

'Please do!'

Salt ended the call. Her foreboding hadn't been misplaced. Whatever was in store for the Pallander family – for them all – was at hand. She dashed down the main staircase of Meikle House as quickly as the scant light from her phone would allow.

50

Tabitha Pallander had been deep in thought before the lights went out all around Meikle House. What Baucher had told her had made her uneasy.

The power outage itself wasn't unusual. After all, they were in the heart of the countryside, isolated. Rural electricity supplies were notable for their unpredictability. However, what worried her was that the backup system hadn't fired up as it was designed to. In an outbuilding abutting the main house were four big generators, there to cover a power failure just like this. Her father had them installed after a dinner party attended by an exclusive group of guests had been ruined by a power cut.

Tabitha grabbed a member of staff as he rushed by with a torch. 'Get someone to go to the generator room and power up the generators, will you?'

'I'm just back from there, Miss Tabitha. I can't get them to start. There's a pool of fuel on the floor. I'm worried about a fire.'

'OK, round up some bodies and get the place cleaned up. And please, get the power on as quickly as you can.'

'I'm not sure that will be easy.'

'Why?'

'Och, it looks as though the place has been vandalized.

Someone's been in there messing about with wires and all sorts. The same folk that jettisoned the diesel, I shouldn't wonder.'

Tabitha left the man to go about his business. And though she'd tried not to let it show in front of a member of staff, she was scared. Something about this cast her mind back to the attackers in her home, and the fire in the hotel. This outage could be no coincidence; the interference with the backup system was clearly deliberate.

Tabitha rushed down to the large entrance hall, where she found Alicia and Audrey. Even in this light, her youngest sister looked drab in her plain frock and low-heeled shoes beside their flamboyant, artistic sister, with her curly, bright-red locks and purple wedges.

'Thank heavens for mobile phones, sis,' said Alicia, as she cast the beam of hers in Tabitha's face.

'I thought there were generators,' said Audrey, wringing her hands in the gloom.

Tabitha was about to tell them what she'd found out, but one look at Audrey stopped her. The last thing she wanted was panic. 'Something must be up with them. I've sent one of the staff to go and have a look.' It was a lie but a white one, at least.

Tabitha was relieved when they were joined by Inspector Salt.

'I'm told your generators aren't working,' said Salt. In the torchlight, her face looked drawn, high cheekbones pronounced in the shadows.

Tabitha widened her eyes, an expression that said, *Don't tell them any more.*

Salt took the hint. 'I'm sure they'll get them going.' She smiled at Alicia and Audrey. 'Can I have a quick word, please, Tabitha?'

The pair left the other two Pallander women chatting amongst themselves.

'This isn't good,' said Salt. She went on to tell Tabitha about the burning lorry that was blocking the road, cutting them off from help. Tabitha, in turn, let the detective know that the generator room had been sabotaged.

Salt blew out her cheeks. 'How hard do you think it would be to get the family together?'

'Well, Alice and Audrey are here, as you know. We'd just have to get hold of Mummy and Silas.'

'What about your uncle?'

'Really? If you're thinking what I think you're thinking, will he be in any danger?'

Salt considered this. She was in no rush to renew her acquaintance with the man who'd threatened her in her bed. And given he'd probably be drunk now, he was likely only to hamper what they were going to try to achieve. 'OK, we'll leave your uncle to his own devices.'

'Tell me what you think, Inspector. What you *really* think. I don't want you to sugar-coat this in any way. I know things aren't good. Daddy's left us in a real mess.'

'Your father died owing some really bad people lots of money, Tabitha. They want it back. And I think they'll go to any lengths to get it.'

'I know. It's just been explained to me. There's a letter of credit lodged at Pallander Glossop. My father must have arranged it before he died. It bankrupts the company, but it gives us the money to pay back the Russians. At least that's what he wanted us to do, I think.'

'You don't agree?'

'No, I don't. Daddy was stealing from the company – from our clients. I know that for a fact. And just because he did this without anyone's knowledge, doesn't mean we won't be in the frame for it. I was a senior company officer, as were others. We all share the responsibility. And in any case, he shouldn't have borrowed Russian money. It's illegal!'

'I suppose he was trying to minimize the impact on you all.'

'That's why he left us with nothing and removed Silas and me from our roles in the company. So kind.'

'Tabitha, I don't think you understand. Someone's coming *tonight*. Who do you think it is?'

Tabitha's face drained of colour in the light from Salt's phone. 'The same people that tried to kidnap me?'

'I'd say so.'

'They want me to sign the letter of credit.'

'And then they'll want their money.'

Salt looked round. Alicia and Audrey were still standing not far away. But their conversation had stopped, and they were looking intently at Salt and Tabitha.

'Let's get everyone together,' said Salt. 'Do any of you know where your mother or Silas are?'

'Mummy's out in the garden. I just saw her,' said Audrey.

'Good. Go and get her and wait for me. You too, Tabitha.'

'Wait, if this is all going to happen tonight, how are they going to get here? I mean, the road's blocked, right?'

Salt shook her head. 'They have a plan. For all we know, they might be here already.'

'So, what do we do?'

'First, we get you all out of the house. Then we think.'

'There's something you're not telling, Inspector. I've lived my life trying to judge what other people are think-ing. First my father, then all the many other piranhas in business that were trying to best us. Trust me, I can tell when I'm not getting the full picture.'

346

Cara Salt looked her straight in the eye. 'Honestly, it doesn't feel right. Too many things are happening we can't explain.'

'Yeah, like who was Durling, and why was he helping me, for instance?'

'Yes, exactly. But other things too. I don't know, just an instinct.'

'My father told me always to trust my instincts.'

'Don't worry, I do. Go and join your mother. I'll go and find Silas. Where's his room?'

'Second floor, on the right, at the end of the corridor. You can't miss it.'

Salt looked on as Tabitha rushed off and grabbed her sisters and ushered them out of Meikle House.

Again, Salt took the stairs two at a time. On the second floor she turned right, as Tabitha had directed, and made her way past old paintings and further remains of dead animals hung on the wall. Salt pictured the heads of each of the Pallander family similarly displayed, testament to the triumphs of some as yet unseen foe.

At the end of the corridor, she came to a door emblazoned with a large silver S. Though it no doubt stood for Silas, it was likely the work of his much younger self. Perhaps an affirmation that he did exist within this dysfunctional family.

Salt hammered on the door with her fist. At first, she was sure she heard two voices in the room beyond, but when Silas opened the door, she could see nobody else behind him.

'Do you have company, Mr Pallander?' The room was bathed in the flickering light from two scented candles.

'No, not at all. What made you think that?'

Salt was surprised by his demeanour. Since he'd arrived back from Belgium, he had been moping about the house, drinking too much and lamenting the absence of his assistant, Anna Marchand. The detective had guessed that he was either having an affair with the woman or wanted to. Either way, she found his behaviour immature and embarrassing. Salt would have liked nothing more than to kick him up the backside and tell him to behave like a man. But he looked somehow different now – there was even the shadow of a smile on his thin, careworn face.

'What is it, Inspector? I'm dog-tired.'

'You need to come with me. I think you and the rest of the family are in danger. There's a lot going on you don't know about.'

'Isn't there always.' This statement was flat, delivered with a sigh. 'No, I won't be coming. I've been kidnapped, beaten and used by this family too often. I said after the will that I wanted nothing more to do with the business or my family. I just want to be left alone, OK? Nothing that's happened in the last few days has changed that. Please leave and go about your business, Inspector.'

'I'm not kidding, Mr Pallander. You're in danger!'

He eyed Salt levelly. For the first time she could see something of the steel she'd seen in his sister Tabitha.

'I'm not going anywhere.'

Silas slammed the door in Salt's face. The police officer tarried for a few moments at the door, listening. Yes, there it was again. She was sure she could hear whispers. She bit her lip and tried to think what to do. Salt certainly couldn't force him from his room. And he was hardly likely to move on the strength of her instinct.

'Your choice, you child,' she said under her breath. For

Salt, the rest of the Pallander family now became her priority. She made her way back along the corridor.

'We wait here, OK?' said Tabitha.

The night was cool but not unpleasant, as what remained of the Pallanders huddled under an ornamental balustrade. The huge lawn stretched before them, picked out in the flitting light of a full moon through clouds.

'But, darling, this seems so over the top,' said Elizabeth Pallander. 'Who on earth are we hiding from? And more to the point, where are we to go?'

'Yes, Tabby,' said Alicia, 'I'm getting bloody cold. All this just because the lights have gone out.'

'I say we listen to Tabby and Inspector Salt. Look what's happened over the last few days. We need to be careful.' Audrey was shivering under a throw she'd picked up from one of the couches in the reception hall.

'Wait, what's that?' Tabitha pointed to the lawn, where a dark figure was making its way towards the house in a slow, careful tread. 'Quick, get back in here. Whoever it is, we don't want them to see us.' Tabitha urged her family further back into the recess under the balustrade.

'Nonsense,' said Elizabeth, striding out from her hiding place. 'I'd recognize that gait anywhere. Sergeant McIntosh, over here!' she called.

'Mummy!' shouted Tabitha. But sure enough the figure stopped, then began to walk in their direction. The closer he came, the more obvious it was that it was indeed none other than McIntosh.

'Aye, so you're under here. A wise precaution,' he exclaimed. 'Where's Inspector Salt, do you know, ma'am?' McIntosh addressed Elizabeth Pallander.

'I'm here,' said Cara, newly arrived in the garden. She'd

also spotted McIntosh's progress across the lawn from the front door. When he'd changed direction, she guessed he'd located the Pallander womenfolk.

'Where's Silas?' asked Tabitha.

'He won't come,' said Salt.

'Oh, how bloody typical.'

'I can't say I blame him, Tabitha,' said Elizabeth. 'I'm not entirely sure why I'm here. When the lights went out, I thought I'd go for a stroll. Might catch more of the stars in the darkness. Are you sure this is necessary, Inspector?'

'Yes, I am *very* sure,' said Salt. 'I guess the best place to go would be somewhere in the trees. But we need to get across this lawn as quickly as we can, OK?'

'What about the helipad?' said Tabitha. 'There are outbuildings there. At least we won't be out in the elements. Yes?'

'Good idea. Let's go. As quickly as we can, everybody, please.'

The little group were together now: the Pallander sisters, their mother, Sergeant McIntosh and Salt, the tiny lights on their mobiles darting across the lawn as they ran toward the trees and the path to the helipad.

As they reached it, Salt stopped and held one finger to her mouth. They all stood still, wondering what she was listening to. But in a few moments the modulating thud of a helicopter engine could be heard.

'The police helicopter?' Tabitha asked.

Salt hoped it was. But something told her that no help would come this night.

'Get into the trees,' said the detective as she listened more intently.

'If they're coming here, it's stupid to be down at the helipad, isn't it?' said Tabitha.

A bright shaft of light flashed through the trees above their heads.

'I think they're going to land on the lawn,' said McIntosh.

He was right. The aircraft, using its searchlight to show the way, appeared over the trees then hovered above the great lawn.

'Come on. This is it!' roared Salt as the helicopter slowly lowered through the darkness.

'They'll bloody well ruin the lawn. It took thirty years for that to take properly,' said Elizabeth Pallander wistfully. Her eldest daughter pulled at her arm, as the little band made its way further into the trees.

Salt remembered taking this path with Abernethy Black-stock. So much had happened in such a short time. She shivered in the cool air.

When they arrived, there was no sign of life at the tiny aerodrome. The helipad itself was empty, with no lights showing from within the hangar or the jumble of little out-buildings huddled around it.

'I don't suppose Wootton is about?' said Elizabeth Pallander. 'We could all simply fly off, if this is all so dangerous.'

'You don't expect him to be here day and night, do you?' said Audrey.

'He lives here, darling. That tiny shack is his office and his home.'

'You know how to treat your staff.' Before Salt could stop herself, the words were out.

'His choice, Inspector. He values his privacy – much as I used to.' Elizabeth glared at Salt. 'I do wish somebody would tell me what's going on.'

'Daddy owed money to some bad people, Mummy,' said Tabitha. Everyone apart from Salt stared at her. 'There's a lot you don't know – all of you. When you owe so much – billions – this is what debt collecting looks like.'

'We should get inside,' said Alicia. 'Do you think it's just us they're after? I mean, Claire is back at the house.'

'So is my remaining son – and my brother,' said Elizabeth Pallander, her voice suddenly strained, as though the peril of the situation had only just dawned on her.

'I'm sure your girlfriend will be fine,' said Salt.

'She's my *companion*. How many times!' said Alicia, her eyes flashing with irritation.

'Oh, sorry. I didn't realize.'

'Easy mistake to make, Inspector,' said Tabitha.

'Please stop arguing, girls. It appears to me that it doesn't matter what this family has to face, we'll all still be arguing until the end. It's clearly never going to stop.' Elizabeth looked miserable.

'Why don't we go in? At least we won't be out in the open,' said Audrey. 'We can decide what to do. It's such a pity all those policemen left today.'

'Yeah, what a coincidence,' said Tabitha sarcastically.

'Things are bad,' said Salt. 'I don't know who is in that helicopter or what they're going to do. And no, it's no coincidence that the police officers have gone.'

'So, why were our armed officers removed?' Elizabeth asked.

All Salt could do was shrug her shoulders. There would be a time when all that had happened to the Pallanders would be explained. This wasn't that time.

'The assistant chief constable was such a nice man. Told me how important it was we were all here together at the house,' said Elizabeth.

'Where's your sergeant? I mean DS Blackstock, not Sergeant McIntosh here,' said Tabitha.

Before Salt could answer, Sergeant McIntosh stepped in. 'Ladies,' he said, 'I think at this juncture we should take cover in the trees, not the buildings. This way.' He led on. 'Aye, and best we stop waggling those lights. And be quiet about it.'

As Salt trudged into the trees beside the helipad, she gave silent thanks for the presence of McIntosh and his wealth of knowledge. They might have to run, and she didn't reckon the family would know their own estate as well as the local bobby.

The little group of Pallanders and police officers hid amongst the trees.

51

All was deathly quiet for those gathered – strangely so. Despite the landing of the helicopter, they could hear no raised voices, or any indication of what might be going on at the house.

Tabitha Pallander made her way to DI Salt's side. 'I've been thinking. Maybe I just go and sign anything they want.'

'On the face of it, that sounds sensible. But as long as you're here and you haven't signed, they need you. After that . . .' Salt stared into the other woman's eyes to emphasize her point. 'Listen, Tabitha, please. I know I'm a nothing to you – a functionary. But these people aren't here to make empty gestures. They won't stop at anything to get back what they think is theirs.'

'OK, I get it. And I don't think of you as a mere functionary. You and Sorley saved my life – probably. But how will they get the money from the family once it's been mandated by the company?'

Salt tried to keep her expression neutral but failed. 'I don't know. But this isn't a corporate deal, where the worst you have to fear is financial ruin. They'll do this in steps. First, they'll get the money out of Pallander Glossop. Then they'll get it from the family. I don't think they're going to find that too hard, do you? And remember, we don't know what your brother signed – or promised.'

'Well, that could be anything. He doesn't even know – I asked.'

'You really don't like him, do you?'

Tabitha made a face. 'He disappointed Daddy so much. My grandfather was like him, you know. An itinerant Swiss shopkeeper who could only ever scrape a living because his head was in the clouds. That's Silas all over.' She swallowed hard. 'It's bad, isn't it? I mean, the bloody Russians. Everyone knows what they're like.'

'Well, judging by recent events, I can only agree. You were there on the marshes. Those guys weren't messing about.'

'No. They definitely weren't at my house to sell double-glazing either. I'm still wondering about Durling. I thought he was from the company, but he wasn't. I think they got him in the end.'

'Wait a minute, I hear something,' said Salt. 'Quiet, everybody!' she hissed.

There it was – a distant voice coming from beyond the trees.

'Mother! Tabitha!'

Salt could make it out now.

'It's Silas,' said Tabitha.

'Definitely?'

'Yes, of course. I've been listening to that whining voice all my life.'

'Mother! Tabitha! I need to speak to you. Come out!'

'Could be a trap. He might be under duress,' said Salt.

'If he's under duress, he'll give us all up, trust me.'

Salt told the rest of the party to stay where they were, under the guidance of Sergeant McIntosh. She and Tabitha tiptoed through the trees, anxious to see if Silas was alone. The bright moon cast its pale light across the house and beyond.

'I can't see anything,' said Tabitha.

'This way.' Salt led her across the treeline to get a better view of the whole lawn. 'There he is,' she whispered.

'Typical. He was standing on the only part of the lawn where we couldn't see him. The story of his life, I'm afraid.' Tabitha's expression had hardened. There was clearly little love lost between brother and sister.

'What do you want to do?' said Salt.

'What do you suggest?'

'We're rapidly running out of options here. I'll go and find out what he wants.'

'What if it's a trap?'

Salt shrugged. 'This is the softly, softly approach. They've sent him to pass on what they want.'

'Me – they want me, Inspector.'

'We'll soon find out. And, please, just call me Cara. After all this – if I survive – I doubt I'll even be a constable, never mind an inspector.'

'Wait.' Tabitha grabbed the detective's arm. 'Remember poor Mrs Sullivan.'

'Don't worry, I know who did that.'

'You do?'

'Yes.' Salt was angry, her mouth twisted in disgust. 'This is my job, Tabitha. I have to do as I see fit. If anything happens to me, take your family as far away from this place as you can. Then find help.'

Salt stood up straight and made her way through the trees and on to the lawn. She strode towards Silas Pallander, her chin up, displaying a confidence she didn't feel.

Silas stared at her, a look of suspicion on his face.

'Where are they?'

Salt held out her hands in a gesture of ignorance. 'Your guess is as good as mine. Far away, I hope.'

'I don't believe you.'

'I don't really care what you do or don't believe. Just tell me what you have to say, Mr Pallander.'

Silas's eyes darted towards the trees. He rubbed his chin with one hand before he raised his voice and started to speak.

'Everything is going to be OK. They've sent Anna to speak to us. All they want is their money. Tabitha, I know you're there. Just some signatures – that's all it is. We'll be free of this. They'll be good to us.'

Salt laughed and gave him a slow, ironic clap. 'And the band played "Believe it if you like".'

'I'm telling the truth. This is all so unnecessary.' He raised his voice again. 'But Tabitha already knows that!'

'What do you mean?'

'Do you really think the first my sister knew about this was when somebody came to her house in the middle of the night? Come on, Inspector, I didn't expect you to be so naive.'

It was Salt's turn to raise her voice. 'You're just trying to goad someone who's not there. Give it up, Silas. I'll come with you and see what your PA has been sent to tell your family.'

'They're not interested in you. You're just a *plod*. Be serious, for fuck's sake.'

'You don't have many options, Silas. They're not here.'

A broad smile crossed his face. 'I think you'll find you're wrong.'

Cara Salt spun round. There, in the silver monochrome of the moonlight, one by one, the female members of the Pallander family appeared from the cover of the trees.

'You better not be lying, Silas.' Salt's face was grim.

'Or what?' he sneered.

'Or I'll kill you. I've shot a man before, and I won't hesitate again. I don't care who you are.' Salt knew it was bullshit, but she took great comfort from the wary expression that now crossed Silas Pallander's face.

'Are you all weak at the knees, Silas? Seeing your fantasy shag again?' Tabitha's scorn was unremitting.

'I'm just the messenger. If you've any sense, you'll sign the fucking thing and then we can get on with the rest of our lives.'

'And if I don't?'

'Then things will change.'

Suddenly, Salt snapped her head to the left. There, from the shadows, came a man dressed in black, with a machine gun slung over his shoulder on a strap.

'Abernethy, you bastard!' she said through gritted teeth.

'How delightful to see you again, ma'am.' His smile was sickly and contrived. 'Everyone, back to the house,' he commanded. 'Now!'

Back behind the scatter of small buildings next to the Pallanders' heliport, a man was leaning against a wall, breathing heavily, trying not to be seen. He'd come on foot across country, and the walk had been a tough one.

During the journey he'd had time to think, to plan. Getting hold of the hunting rifle and ammunition had been the easy part. He'd hoped to arrive at Meikle House before anything kicked off. But he was too late. The thud of rotor blades proved that.

He'd seen the Pallander women, the local police sergeant and the Glasgow inspector huddled under the trees. He'd watched them leave, heard them chatting urgently amongst themselves before they decided to break cover.

He had no choice other than to stay hidden. Surprise would be his only ally.

He'd listened with interest to the rumours he'd heard in a nearby hotel. Strangers in the village, the death of the housekeeper. And because he knew something about the predicament in which the Pallander family found itself, he was ready for just about anything.

He bit his lip, thinking on the best – the most sensible – course of action. He could smell the smoke of distant coal fires on the air. It reminded him strangely of Halloween. Though the weather had been quite warm during the long summer day, it was now cool. It made him shiver. But he reasoned that good old-fashioned fear had more to do with that than the temperature.

A voice in his head was yelling at him to run, to go home and leave the Pallander family and those who assisted them to their fate. But that wasn't something he could do. It wasn't in his nature. And in any case, contained within that house was something very important to him.

He had the lay of the land mapped out in his head. Meikle House was cocooned on three sides by tall pine trees, protected by the river on the fourth side. He decided to skirt the great house using the trees as cover. After that? Well, after that he'd have to see how everything unfolded.

Just as he was about to move, the moon broke out from behind a cloud and an owl hooted in the trees to his left. Carefully, he set off.

52

The straggle of Pallander women, Salt and Sergeant McIntosh walked up the steps to the main entrance of Meikle House, urged on by Silas. The gun-toting Abernethy Blackstock brought up the rear.

Soon, they were in the entrance hall, now devoid of people.

'What's the motivation, Abs?' said Salt. 'Did you have too much of the high life when you were undercover? Fancied a little yourself?'

Blackstock said nothing, his expression neutral.

'Lost for words? You know, I wondered how they managed to find Tabitha when she was on the run with Sorley. But that was your little job, wasn't it?'

'Your best policy would be to shut up, Cara. What I did or will do is my affair. And as far as motivation is concerned, you'll find that by the time you get to my age, you'll want rather more than a broken marriage and a pair of good binoculars. Keep moving!'

'Where are the staff?' said Elizabeth Pallander urgently.

'In the Great Hall, I think,' Silas replied. 'But they'll be fine, Mummy. Everything's going to be fine, trust me.' A broad smile spread across his face.

'Like it was fine for Mrs Sullivan, you mean?' said Tabitha.

'Be quiet and follow your brother,' said Blackstock, his voice carrying none of the slightly effete affectations of the rather eccentric police officer Cara Salt had known.

'Yes, all will be revealed. It's going to solve our problems, honestly.' Silas took the stairs two at a time, his family following less than enthusiastically.

It didn't take long for Salt to realize where they were going. This way led to the 'small' dining room, where only a short time ago they'd had that late dinner.

Silas pushed open the door. The place looked so different without electric light. The moon cast its eerie glow through two great un-curtained windows. Three large candles burned in the middle of the table. They cast shifting shadows that flickered around the room, pooling in dark recesses. The candles fluttered as the small party made its way in. Little wisps of smoke straggled from the burning flames. The air was heavy with the scent of wax and the night air, brought in on the clothes of those now gathering.

A shaft of diffused moonlight lit up one side of the face of the person sitting at the head of the table. Anna Marchand was perfectly still, her lips parted, cuts and bruises still visible, despite the shadows.

'Now we know why my brother's smiling,' said Tabitha.

'Do shut up, Tabitha. Anna's here to help us. She's been through a lot for this family.'

Silas went to her side and caressed her face like the lover he wasn't.

Anna looked up at him. 'Please, Silas, take a seat with the others. You all must hear what I have to say.'

'Just get on with it,' said Alicia, shaking her head. 'This is ridiculous. It's a pantomime.'

'Well said.' Tabitha clapped ironically. 'As though a jumped-up secretary can do anything to relieve this predicament. Where did you spring from, anyway?'

Anna began, her accented voice quiet at first. 'Your father had to struggle to keep the company afloat. Things didn't go as he expected.' She took them in one by one with her big blue eyes.

'And how do you know this?' Elizabeth asked. 'I'm sure he wasn't confiding in you, Anna. After all, you were Silas's PA, were you not?'

'Please, I'm just saying what I have been told to say. You're making this so hard.'

Anna held one hand to her forehead, while Silas glared at his family.

'For fuck's sake, can we give her time to speak! It's typical of you all, talking when you should be listening.'

Anna continued. 'Tabitha must sign the letter of credit, extracting funds from the company – please. Otherwise, the company's creditors take everything, and you are left in so much danger.'

'I don't understand,' said Tabitha. 'Baucher is here in the house. He wants the same thing as you. We don't really know who he represents, he isn't saying. So, who's pulling your strings, eh?'

'You should be careful, Tabitha. They'll have Abernethy here do his stuff.' Salt sneered at her turncoat colleague. 'How much are you and the ACC making from this, you bastard?'

'Be quiet.' Though Blackstock said the words to Salt, he didn't look in her direction.

'Yes, we should all *shut up*, because I know what you're prepared to do to get money. I think it's time to spill the beans, Abs, don't you?'

Salt stood as Abernethy Blackstock strode towards her, the machine gun now held out in front of him.

'Please, stop this!' wailed Elizabeth Pallander. 'Abernethy, your mother would be so ashamed of you.'

Her pleas were ignored. Salt stepped back, Blackstock lunged at her with the butt of the automatic weapon. It caught her squarely on the jaw, dropping her to the floor with a yell.

Tabitha and Audrey ran to the detective's aid, as the rest of their family gasped in horror.

'You'll pay for that, my friend,' said Sergeant McIntosh, his hands balled into fists.

Tabitha and Audrey helped Salt back to her seat. Her mouth was pouring with blood.

'She needs a doctor,' said Elizabeth Pallander.

Blackstock swung the weapon round the table, pausing on each of them in turn. 'Sit down and listen or you'll get what she got!'

Salt's head lolled forward as she coughed blood on to the polished wooden table in front of her.

'Tabitha, just sign this damnable thing,' said her mother. 'It'll make no difference to us. We'll survive – just do it. I don't want to see anyone else hurt.'

'It's stealing, Mother. We're taking the funds from the people who trusted us to manage their investments. The people who've given us everything we've had over all these years.'

'The investors will lose their money either way,' said Silas. 'The company's going down whatever happens in this room tonight, and you know it, Tabby.'

'It's perfectly legal!' shouted Anna Marchand. 'Your father did this to keep you all safe. Tabitha *must* sign.'

'So, we end up with nothing once more,' said Alicia. 'And

to make matters worse, we have to suffer the humiliation of being a family whose company robbed its investors of their cash.'

'What is worse, humiliation or death? I know what I would choose.' Anna's eyes flashed at Alicia Pallander.

'It's the only thing that makes sense,' said Silas. 'Surely you all see that? We can't be blamed for what Daddy did. But we can save ourselves!'

'You appear to have been told a lot – and in great detail, Anna. Strange you don't know by whom,' said Tabitha. She folded her arms across her chest. 'I won't sign. I don't care what clever plan Daddy thought up to steal money from people. It stinks.'

'Tabitha! It's wrong to speak ill of the dead. Your father isn't here to defend himself,' said Elizabeth. She'd been watching the to-ing and fro-ing of the conversation like a tennis match, her eyes darting from one person to the other.

'Don't be so naive, Mummy. My father has plenty to answer for. Things you couldn't possibly imagine.'

'Well said,' Salt mumbled through her bloodied mouth.

'But it's not fair for me to be the one to make the decision. We're all here, after all – well, what's left of our family, at least.' Tabitha swallowed back tears. 'Alice, what do you think I should do – sign or not?'

Alicia Pallander ran her hand through her curly, bright-red hair. 'We don't live in the wild west. People can't just come and kill us. This is Great Britain. We should try to pay back the people who invested with us and keep the company going. Otherwise, we have nothing – no future.'

'Audrey?' Tabitha turned her attention to her youngest sister.

Audrey cleared her throat. She fingered a ring her twin

brother Jean-Luc had given her. 'I feel as though I'm speaking for two – both me and JL.' She fought back the tears. 'He would have hated this, and so do I. We've lived a good life on the backs of people who trusted us. We can't just hide away in bankruptcy and watch them drown. Don't sign, Tabby.' She turned her attention to Marchand. 'Go back and tell your masters that we're the Pallander family. And we do the right thing!'

'Mother, what about you? Try to think without emotion, please,' said Tabitha, pleading with the woman who had given her life.

Elizabeth Pallander stared at the table. Unlike Tabitha, she'd been unable to stem the tears. 'I married your father because I loved him. Oh, some people thought I'd been put up to it to save this place – and my family – from ruin. But that simply wasn't true. It never has been.' She raised her head and gazed at Tabitha. 'Do you really think I was blind to the kind of man he was? Really? No man or woman in his position gets there without spilling a little here and there, making enemies – making mistakes. I am fully aware that he was no angel. But I forgave him because I loved him. Still do and always will. But as to this tawdry deal, you're right. I'm proud to have a daughter who knows right from wrong and keeps me right too. I will not steal from anyone. Never.'

'You're very brave, Mummy.' Tabitha turned her attention to her brother Silas. 'We all know what you want: to save your own miserable skin. But you're outvoted before you start. We'll hear you out, though.'

Silas got to his feet and walked back to be beside Anna. 'Well, Tabby, you get what you want, just like you always do. Of course, I think you should sign. I'd be mad to say otherwise. You're just doing this to spite me. And I know it. If I'd realized what they wanted from me, all they had to do was ask. There was no need for kidnapping and what they did to Anna.' He stared down at her. 'Look at her – all of you! But she still had the guts to come here and help us. We get what we deserve, simple as that. God help us all.'

'There we are, then. Not unanimous, but it'll do. What now, Sergeant Blackstock? Do you mow us down with your machine gun?' Tabitha stared at the man with the gun.

For a few moments there was silence, a pause loaded with so much feeling, so much hatred, disapproval and sadness.

Without speaking, Blackstock looked to his right. In the darkness, the door at the other end of the room creaked open.

The candles on the long dining table guttered in the draught, turning the shadows in the room into a looming chaos of shifting shapes on the high walls.

'I've heard enough!'

The disembodied voice came from the gloom at the far end of the room.

As they all stared, the figure of a man emerged into the flickering candlelight. At first, he was unrecognizable. But when the moon appeared from behind a cloud, it sent a shaft of light spilling through the windows, illuminating a ghostly face.

Sebastian Pallander stood before his family, his eyes casting about in defiance.

53

The reaction of those in the room at the sight of the dead man differed. Audrey screamed at the top of her voice, whilst her sisters sat open-mouthed. Elizabeth Pallander grasped the edge of the table and held herself with as much dignity as she could muster. Audrey pushed her chair back, the screech of wood jarring everyone present. She vomited on the floor, the sight of her father returned from the grave too much to take. Silas walked over to his father, his eyes wide in disbelief.

'We . . . we buried you,' he said, and leaned over to touch Sebastian on the arm, as if he didn't believe what he was seeing was real.

'Sit down, Silas,' said Sebastian Pallander dispassionately. 'No, not beside Anna. Back to where you were.'

To underline this, Blackstock levelled the gun at him, gesturing Silas towards the chair.

'You bastard!' Elizabeth Pallander was on her feet. 'How could you do this to your children? To *me*?' Her voice quivered. She was shaking so much she had to steady herself against the table.

Sebastian sighed. 'Sit down, Elizabeth. I've had enough of your histrionics to last a lifetime – and more.' Now he walked behind Anna Marchand's chair. He put his arms on her shoulders. She reached up and held his right hand in hers.

'*What?*' Silas was back on his feet. 'You and her?'

'Do grow up, Silas. You've always been such a sad little shit,' said Sebastian.

Silas rushed at his father. But before Blackstock could intervene, the older man sent his son flying with a vicious right hook.

'You have no idea how much I enjoyed that. God forgive me, for it must be a sin to hate one's own son. But I do.' His dark eyebrows arched over his face, his features almost skeletal in the moonlight. He showed no sign of emotion at being reunited with his family, who'd thought him dead and gone for months.

'What about me?' sobbed Elizabeth. 'All those years of marriage. I was faithful to you. Made a home, held you close, brought up your children. For this!'

'You have this house. It's what you always wanted. I heard you say you loved me. Ha! Our marriage ended years ago, while you played the laird up here. You and your drunken brother are welcome to this mausoleum!'

'And what about us, Daddy? What about Jean-Luc? Who killed him – was it you?' Audrey stared at the man who'd come back from the dead, her breath intermittent little gasps, specks of vomit on her chin.

'I did no such thing! He killed himself with his own wilful stupidity. Do you think I don't mourn him? And why would any of you think I'd kill my own son? But if I could use his passing to help you save yourselves, I hoped it would be enough. You are all so stupid, so spoiled. I should have known you would do anything but the right thing. I wanted to be gone from you all for good. But you left me with no choice. Do you think I'm enjoying any of this!' Sebastian Pallander's roar echoed round the long, high-ceilinged room.

'You just had to carry on this elaborate charade,' said Salt, nursing her bloody jaw. 'You used your son's death to terrify your family into bending the knee.' The detective coughed up more blood, as Audrey Pallander came to her aid.

'And so what? It was either that or see them all dead. I was gone, there was nobody coming for me. You – all of you – were different. I had no choice but to borrow the money. The company was finished. Baucher and my dear Tabitha would never have agreed to do it. I fought to save the company – now I fight to save you.' He kissed Anna Marchand on the top of the head. 'The fight is over. It's time to save ourselves.'

'So, you're Augusta Manella,' Tabitha said to Anna. 'I wondered. My father's "daughter". What a good disguise! You and my father were going to leave it all behind and live off the little nest egg you accumulated.' She laughed. 'You had my stupid uncle absolutely fooled.'

'My daughter – my heir. You are a hypocrite! How often did you watch me bend the rules? You bent them yourself, for that matter. Now you are too proud, too honest, to do the right thing.' He leaned across the table towards his eldest daughter. 'I watched you destroy your pathetic brother for years when you were children, just to get what you wanted. Oh, my dear Tabby, like it or not, you are just as reprehensible as me. Sign, let us go and I'll help you. You won't be harmed, I promise. Don't sign, and I can also promise you I can no longer keep any of you safe.' Pallander looked at each of them in turn.

'Like you helped Tabitha?' said Salt, through the pain. 'That was the Russians who tried to kidnap her. They were going to use her as leverage. But you protected her, didn't you? Or tried to, at least.'

'Never mind who did this or that! It's done. Sign, Tabitha. Do it now!'

Sebastian nodded to Blackstock. The corrupt police officer grabbed Tabitha Pallander by her hair and dragged her over to her father and Anna Marchand.

'Fuck it!' Tabitha said through gritted teeth. 'I just want you out of our lives, Father. Give me the pen.'

Anna produced the documents from her bag and slipped them across the table to Tabitha Pallander.

Audrey shook her head, her eyes shut against the scene before her. 'We're your family – your wife and children. You faked your death, but our grief was real, Daddy. And instead of grieving for Jean-Luc, you saw it as an opportunity.' She slammed the table with both fists. 'I never want to see you again! Do you understand?'

'Don't waste your breath, Audrey,' said Tabitha, as she signed the document in front of her with a flourish. She noticed Silas's signature just above hers. 'It was a ruse, wasn't it? You and my brother?' She was gazing at Anna.

'What do you mean?'

'You and my father arranged Silas's "kidnapping". Let me look at your face!' Tabitha reached across the table and grabbed Anna's chin, rubbing her other hand roughly across her face. The bruises smeared across the Frenchwoman's cheeks, nose and forehead, making her look comically hideous – a circus clown.

'What is this, Anna?' Silas staggered from his chair, where he had been recovering from the blow administered by his father. 'You bitch!' he began to scream.

'Grow up, all of you!' Anna yelled. 'You have privilege and money, and still you moan and cry like little kids. I came here with nothing – no parents even. You all treated me like dirt. Except for you, Silas. No, I was so sick of your doe eyes devouring me every minute of the day. Did you ever think I could be yours? It's why your father sent me away to finishing school. To get away from you, Silas. To get away from you all!'

Tabitha wound her hand back and slapped Anna square in the face. 'That's what a real bruise feels like.' She looked at her father. 'Go, just go! You have what you came for. You didn't try to protect me. Your man was there to extract my signature first and foremost. The Russians got there first, that was all. What little plan did you have to convince me, Daddy?'

Sebastian Pallander shook his head. 'Look at you all. What's left of you, at least. Clever Tabitha, too full of her own importance to see what was before her eyes.'

He turned to Alicia. 'You – the artist. So good at what you do, I had to pay people to buy what you paint.'

Next, his gaze fell on Silas. 'My eldest son. I feel sorry for you. Maybe I shouldn't have tried to push you the way I did. But I feared for you out in the real world. I was right. You have made a mess of your life, and that will continue. One day you will find yourself in the gutter and wonder how it happened.'

He leaned on the table with one hand. 'Audrey, I think you are the only child of which I'm proud. They say the meek shall inherit the earth. Have it, my dear. Maybe it will open your eyes to the horrors that surround us.'

'And you, my dear Elizabeth. So high, so mighty, as you treasure your precious aristocratic blood.' He smiled mirthlessly. 'Well, here it is.' He gestured expansively round the table. 'What do you think of this blood now? And who will pay for your precious estate when I'm gone? I know you always expected to live the life to which you became so accustomed. All of it on my back, my intelligence. Time to think for yourselves! Tabitha has signed both the action of the letter of credit and the release of the funds from the family trust. My job is done.'

Pallander gazed between them all one last time, as he watched Anna place the documents in the attaché case.

'I'd like to say it's been good to see you all. But that would be a real lie to no purpose. Come on, Anna.' He helped her out of the chair. 'Blackstock, let's go. I will do a deal for Anna and me. You can all be happy with what you have. Enjoy the fruits of my labours while they last.'

Without a backwards glance, the resurrected patriarch of the Pallander family rushed from the dining room, Abernethy Blackstock taking up the rear, walking backwards, his gun trained on those left behind. He smiled at Salt.

'Get well soon. You have something there to remember me by.'

Quickly, he turned on his heel and was gone.

54

The exchange had taken only minutes. The lingering shock cast silence over the room.

Salt felt as though she'd been hit by a truck. Her head ached and her vision swam.

'I can't let him go without a fight!'

She got to her feet unsteadily and made for the door. She patted her jacket, expecting to find her service pistol. Then, through the fug of the blow from Blackstock, she remembered that she and McIntosh had been disarmed by him. Still, not even knowing what she would do, Cara Salt carried on.

'Ma'am, you're in no fit shape to do anything,' shouted Sergeant McIntosh. When she ignored him, he disappeared from the room after her.

McIntosh followed DI Salt down flights of stairs, amazed by her agility given the blow she'd suffered. He joined her, searching with their phones for any sign of Blackstock in the gloom.

When they reached the entrance hall, all was quiet. Their footsteps echoed in the dark, empty space. Only the moonlight streaming through the great arched windows afforded any light.

'Ma'am, please. It's over. You can do nothing. We did our

job and protected the family.' McIntosh was at her side. 'They'll be making for that helicopter.'

Without comment, Salt paced forward, being careful not to fall, her head still spinning. Just as she made it to the front door, Blackstock emerged from the darkness of the vestibule, still holding the gun.

'You disappoint me, Cara. Didn't you reason that I was here to protect Mr Pallander until he managed to leave?'

Salt lowered her head. She could hear that thud of rotor blades again, as the helicopter on the lawn prepared for take-off. 'How will you escape, Abs, walk?' She had to shout above the din.

'No, I have our old friend Wootton to take me. He is, at least, still loyal to Mr Pallander. It's called taking your chances, Cara. Something you are peculiarly bad at, I note.' He smiled. 'ACC Dixon is already out of the country, as is the chief. I shall live a life in the manner to which I was born. Far away from Scotland, but hey, never mind.'

'I'm so pleased for you. What an achievement,' sneered Salt.

'But the last thing I need is you and Sergeant Plod here making things difficult. I take no pleasure in killing. But sometimes one has no choice.'

This too was shouted, for at that very moment the helicopter carrying Anna Marchand and Sebastian Pallander rose into the air. Red lights flashing at its nose and tail.

Salt lunged at Blackstock, but he was ready for her attack and moved aside in one fluid movement, like a dancer. Her kick missed the target and she tumbled on to the floor. The aircraft soared and soon disappeared over the tall firs that bordered the lawn of Meikle House.

'You stay where you are too, Sergeant. I bet you wish you were back in your cosy little police station with your feet up and a cup of tea on the go, eh? Sad, really. At least you were part of something much greater than yourself, eh?' Blackstock raised the gun and pointed it straight at the fallen figure of Cara Salt. 'Not much of a life to lose, I don't think, *ma'am*. Sadly, you'll go the same way as that nosy bitch, Sullivan. Just couldn't mind her own business – had to know everything. But this time, it's personal.'

The gunshot rang out on the night air, stark, alien and deadly. As the sound of rotor blades faded, silence fell in the grounds of Meikle House.

McIntosh edged towards the dead police officer. 'What a waste of life,' he said quietly.

'He got what he deserved! He killed Mrs Sullivan and he'd have killed both of you without a thought.'

Out of the shadows stepped Sorley MacLeod, a hunting rifle before him.

'Aye, he did that,' said McIntosh. 'I'm guessing Maggie must've seen something she shouldn't.'

'No doubt. Poor woman,' said Sorley.

'Sorley,' said Salt, still on the tiled floor of the entrance hall, where Blackstock had intended to kill her.

'You saved me once – kind of,' he said to her. Then he gazed at Blackstock's sightless eyes staring back at him. 'I knew he was wrong from the start. I told you, Cara. Instinct.'

'For somebody who refurbishes computers, you're still a good cop.' She held her jaw, the pain of the smile she attempted fading on her lips with the pain.

'Could be again,' said McIntosh.

Their conversation was ended by more thudding helicopter blades.

'That'll be the rest of them, off with Wootton,' said Salt.

'Let them go,' said Sorley. 'Somebody else's problem.'

The last aircraft slid over the trees on the Meikle House estate, and the noise soon subsided.

Sorley knelt down and cradled Cara in his arms.

'What now, gaffer?' he asked, kissing her gently on the forehead.

'I want my DS back. That's what,' said Salt.

55

BBC Newsnight, *two days later*

Jemima Gore stares at the television camera in front of her, making sure the expression on her face is exactly right for the news she is about to impart when the light turns red.

'*Three, two, one – on air!*'

'Good evening. The events surrounding the collapse of the UK's largest hedge fund, Pallander Glossop, read like a novel.'

'*Camera two.*'

Gore swings to face a new angle. 'We have a sorry tale of deceit, dishonesty, greed and betrayal – not to mention a return from the dead.' She fixes the camera with a silent stare for a moment, her face oozing a mix of sincerity and surprise. 'As you may know, I was the last person to interview legendary hedge fund manager Sebastian Pallander before his "death" live on *Money Morning* in January. I wish I'd known then what I know now. To help with that, joining me down the line from Westminster is our International Editor, Martin D'argent. Martin, can you help us understand this breaking news story?'

'Yes, Jem, I'll try.' D'argent is balding, with a round face and ruddy pallor. He blinks before he speaks. Behind him, the Palace of Westminster is picked out in the gloom. 'Pallander Glossop are – *were* – one of the most successful hedge funds in Europe, with billions under management.'

'So, what went wrong?'

'It's emerging that the company has collapsed after a clause invoking a family trust was initiated over the last couple of days. This was effected by none other than Sebastian Pallander, the financier who *died* during your interview with him in January, as you say.'

'It's a good trick if you can pull it off.' Gore laughs. The gag is choreographed. She doesn't want it to appear insincere, so holds a hand to her mouth to hide the perfidy. 'Yes, I know I have the reputation as a tough interrogator, but not that bad.' Another contrived laugh.

Down the line, D'argent throws his head back in a poor imitation of mirth. 'We believe the company makes Madoff look like a pickpocket.' He pretends to compose himself. 'The BBC understands that Pallander appeared before the family on their estate in Scotland, fresh from the grave, as it were, and coerced certain members to sign the document releasing money into the family trust from Pallander Glossop. These funds were then passed on to to his creditors in Russia.'

'In effect bankrupting the company, am I right?'

'That's not all. It's thought that Pallander had been using funds from senior figures in Russia to keep the hedge fund going following disastrous investments in India and the United States. Of course, this is against the sanctions placed against Russia since the illegal invasion of Ukraine. He turned Pallander Glossop into a Ponzi scheme of hitherto unequalled proportions. So many have lost everything here, Jem.'

'What is the government saying, Martin?'

'This is a breaking story, as you know. But we're told by the Treasury that once these funds were released, they were immediately transferred out of the country. Several senior officers at Pallander Glossop have reported to police stations in London. The company is now insolvent and ceased trading as of ten thirty this morning.'

'And what of the ghostly Sebastian Pallander?' Gore's tongue is firmly lodged in her cheek.

'Literally the billion-dollar question.' D'argent consults his notes. 'Government officials tell us he is no longer in the UK, though everything is being done to bring him back to face charges of fraud at the very highest level.'

'And the money. Is there any chance of recovering it?'

'It would be wrong to speculate. But it would come as somewhat of a surprise if it hasn't found its way back to those who propped up Pallander in the first place.'

'The Russians. Is it possible we'll never see him or the money again?'

'It's possible.'

'Martin D'argent at Westminster, thank you.'

Gore eyes the camera once more, one eyebrow raised. 'Well, this sorry tale gets more and more bizarre. We hear members of the police and a private ambulance firm in Switzerland are being investigated for their alleged part in the faked death of Sebastian Pallander in January.'

Jemima Gore sighs, then stares down the camera lens as it pulls in for a tight shot of her face.

'This audacious crime has repercussions that could rattle the UK economy. In a few moments I'll speak to the Chancellor of the Exchequer about that. First, a piece on Pallander Glossop from our very own financial editor, Vivian Parry.'

'And we're out. Back in four minutes thirty.'

The gantry calls the shots. Gore sits back in her chair and requests her make-up be touched up for the next segment. On a monitor, we can see the Chancellor having a lapel mic arranged on his jacket by a technician.

'Polly, thank you.' Gore addresses the make-up lady as she arrives at her side. 'Trust me to get a pimple on my nose with all this going on. Can you keep it hidden, please?'

Polly goes to work on the unsightly spot. She's of early middle age, with the hairstyle of a twenty-year-old. 'It's amazing, isn't it? How the other half live? I don't know.' She flicks powder on Gore's nose with a brush. 'I heard you knew this Pallander quite well. What's he like, then?'

'Whatever gave you that idea? I've interviewed him a few times, that's as far as it goes.'

Though this is a lie, Jemima Gore is happy to tell it. Now, she wants nothing to do with Pallander, past, present or future.

For some reason, she thinks of Durga, her old assistant producer back at *Money Morning*. She was surprised to hear that the young woman had left television and is now working for a humanitarian charity.

Not everyone has what it takes. What an opportunity missed, she thinks.

EPILOGUE

Two months later, Mar-le-Mar Club, Crimea

The couple are seated on matching recliners. The woman is pale. Though her face is taking on some of the sun, it's making her freckles more pronounced and streaking her red hair with shades of gold.

Her companion is older, grey-haired with contrasting dark eyebrows. His body is tanned and wrinkled, legs thinner than they should be.

The weather is baking. But in this part of the world in August it usually is. They are on a terrace in front of their apartment, raised above the breaking waves of the Black Sea. It's idyllic, a paradise. They've both come a long way, done a lot. Though their horizons are limited, Russia is a big country. It's no hardship to stay within its borders, not really.

She turns to him, under the shade of a great umbrella canopy.

'Now we get what we deserve, Seb.'

'Stick with me, kid,' he replies, knowing it's a cliché but not caring. After all, he's just pulled himself out of a massive hole that would have devoured him. His new masters didn't get back every penny they'd invested, but he's Sebastian Pallander. They know he'll make them back ten times what they lost. It's an equitable arrangement. He's done it before, and he can do it again.

'I shouldn't be in the sun for too much longer,' says Anna Marchand. She's pleased with herself too. This is the life she's dreamed of since growing up in the faded grandeur of a Paris apartment gone to seed, the family money all but exhausted.

Finally, they've settled into this little piece of heaven on earth.

A waiter arrives. He's dressed in black trousers, a short white jacket and white gloves. He carefully places the tray with two glasses of champagne on the table between Pallander and Marchand. He removes the first glass and hands it to Anna, the second to Sebastian.

'Thank you, Nikita,' says Pallander.

The waiter nods and walks smartly away.

'He fancies me,' says Anna. 'They can't get enough of red hair here. It's strange.' She hasn't lost her French accent. She never will.

'Go with him, then.'

She laughs. 'You pig.' She takes more than a sip of her Krug Grande Cuvée.

Pallander smiles at her. He's dry, so slakes his thirst with two gulps of champagne. It's no way to appreciate the stuff. But he doesn't care.

'I wonder what Silas is doing?' she says idly.

'His mother's bidding, I'm sure.'

'And chasing after a local girl with red hair.' She giggles and takes another drink.

Sebastian Pallander feels it first. It's as though every muscle is cramping, from his legs up. He yells in pain and tumbles from the recliner, gasping for air.

'Sebastian!' Anna cries, and gets up to go to his aid. But her legs won't hold her. She falls, half-slumped over her chair, with a thud. She tries to breathe. A pathetic wheeze sounds in her throat. Then there is silence.

For minutes, there is only the sound of sweeping waves. Two men appear from nowhere. One, with a suit jacket slung over his shoulder, takes in the scene: the blue sea, the warm sun on his face. The other is wearing jeans and a black t-shirt. He's carrying a good Sony camera.

'Some piece of ass,' says the cameraman, in Russian. 'Can I fuck her?'

'Disgusting! I know you're not joking.' The man in the suit looks at him with genuine distaste. 'Just take the pictures. And make them good. They'll be in every newspaper and website in the world in the next few hours.'

Sebastian Pallander and his paramour are dead. And while the state is poorer, those who entered the deal with the financier are infinitely better off.

It's how things work.

The camera flashes another three times before the men leave.

A wave crashes on the beach below the terrace, then withdraws with a hiss on the sand.

ACKNOWLEDGEMENTS

As always, to my wife Fiona. We've been through a lot and just keep rolling. She is my strength.

To editor Finn Cotton, and copy-editor Lorraine McCann – so important. Editors are the sword and shield of any writer.

To my lovely agent Jo 'fab' Bell. I'd trust her with my life. And how we laugh!

To you, dear readers. Because without you, it means nothing.

And finally, echoing my dedication, to Stephen Mcfadzean, my old pal. A more decent man will be hard to find. We'll all miss you, bud. Heartbreaking.

Denzil Meyrick is from Campbeltown on the Kintyre Peninsula in Argyll. After studying politics, he enjoyed a varied career as a police officer, distillery manager, and director of several companies. He is the No.1 bestselling author of the DCI Daley series, and is now an executive producer of a major TV adaptation of his books.

Denzil lives on Loch Lomondside in Scotland with his wife Fiona and cats. You can find him on X (formerly known as Twitter) @Lochlomonden, Facebook @DenzilMeyrickAuthor, or on his website: www.denzil meyrick.com.

Don't miss Denzil Meyrick's dazzling murder mystery . . .

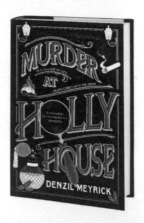

A village of secrets

It's December 1952, and a dead stranger has
been found lodged up the chimney of Holly House
in the remote town of Elderby. Is he a simple thief,
or a would-be killer? Either way, he wasn't on
anyone's Christmas wish list.

A mystery that can't be solved

Inspector Frank Grasby is ordered to investigate.
The victim of some unfortunate misunderstandings,
he hopes this case will help clear his name. But as is
often the way for Grasby, things most certainly
don't go according to plan.

A Christmas to remember

Soon blizzards hit the North York Moors, cutting
off the village from help, and the local doctor's husband is
found murdered. Grasby begins to realise that everyone
in Elderby is hiding something – and if he can't uncover
the truth soon, the whole country will pay
a dreadful price . . .

Out now in Hardback, Ebook and Audio!

If you loved *The Estate*, don't miss Denzil Meyrick's gripping new mystery . . .

A case shrouded in secrets.

It's just before Christmas, 1953. Grasby and Juggers are investigating a puzzling murder in the remote village of Uthley's Bay. A fisherman has been found dead on the beach, with a stocking wound tight round his throat.

A festive mystery for one and all.

Hundreds of pairs of stockings, in neat cellophane bags, soon wash up on the shore. A blizzard cuts off Grasby and Juggers from help, and the local innkeeper is murdered. Any remaining Christmas cheer goes up in smoke as the villagers refuse to talk, leaving the two detectives chasing false leads in the snow.

A winter wonderland with no escape.

To make matters worse, Grasby can't stop thinking about stockings. Why does everyone seem to be enjoying strangely high standards of hosiery, even beneath their oilskins? Who is the sinister bespectacled man snooping around their hotel? And how can they solve the murder when everyone in the village is a suspect?

Order now!